IMPROVED LIES

Brian Kennedy

Durban House

Printed in the United States of America.

For information address:
Durban House Press, Inc.
7502 Greenville Avenue, Suite 500, Dallas, Texas 75231

Library of Congress Cataloging-in-Publication Data
Kennedy, Brian, YEAR -

Improved Lies / Brian Kennedy

Library of Congress Control Number: 2007929258

p. cm.

ISBN: 0-9779863-5-7

First Edition

10 9 8 7 6 5 4 3 2 1

Visit our Web site at
http://www.durbanhouse.com

To my loving wife Shelley,
an inspiration in all things.

Acknowledgments

Deep appreciation to Bob Middlemiss and John Hiner for encouragement and guidance. Many thanks to Shannon, Janice, and Ann for decoding my handwriting. Special thanks to you, esteemed reader, for giving a new author a read.

The ball shall be played as it lies.

Rule 13-1, *USGA Official Rules of Golf.*

Except as otherwise provided in the Rules, a player shall not improve or allow to be improved: the position or lie of his ball.

Rule 13-2.

These rules are intended to the end that the truth may be ascertained and proceedings justly determined.

Michigan Rules of Evidence—Rule 102.

I hadn't been sleeping well since I broke off my twenty-year romance with the girl in the red and white wrapper a week ago. Declaring "You don't own me," I had crumpled a nearly full pack of Marlboros and tossed them into the wastebasket. Except my steady wasn't going quietly. On top of leaving me jumpy, hungry, cranky, and fidgety, the break-up had left me sleep deprived.

On this, the last Friday in April 2000, with a couple of Jack Daniels under my belt, I'd finally fallen into the depths of deep, restorative sleep. So when the phone rang I fought to remain beneath the surface as long as I could. In my dream, I had converted the ringing of the telephone to carnival background noise. I didn't want to leave the fair. When the phone rang my arm had just settled around the shoulders of a statuesque blonde in a white sundress. As we settled into our seats for the Tunnel of Love, she turned her head, her long golden tresses obscuring her face. I was going to be very happy if she was who I thought she was.

But the phone dragged me to the surface a second before recognition. As I felt for the receiver, I could see the luminescent dial of the alarm clock radio. 3:36 a.m. I grunted hello. On the other end of the line was a male voice on the edge of hysteria.

"Ken, help me! My wife's on the floor. There's blood everywhere. It's on my pajamas. It's on the phone. Oh my God! It's on my hands. She's not moving. The police are here. You must come right away!"

I sat up in bed to clear the fog of sleep. The voice sounded vaguely familiar. "Slow down. Slow down. Who is this?"

"It's me, Ted. From the club."

The tumblers were beginning to click, but not quite fast enough. "Ted?"

Frustrated panic on the other end.

"Ted Armbruster! You represented my mother, Marjorie. The malpractice case."

Now clarity. I'd just seen his wife Amanda alive, well and vibrantly beautiful earlier that evening. The image of her in a pool of blood on the floor refused to register. Without thinking I blurted, "Can't be, I just saw her—"

"Listen to me. Listen to me. Somebody has hurt her horribly. She might be dead. I need your help now. You must come now so I can explain to the police." He was frantic.

Now I knew whom I was talking to, but what was he saying? Wife on the floor, blood everywhere, police on the scene, and all this from a client who could pay his bills. Time for me to wake up and get my head into the problem. I pulled the chain on the bedside lamp and shook my head to clear the cobwebs.

"Oh, sorry, Ted. I was fast asleep. We shouldn't talk on the phone. I'll be right there. What's your address?"

"It's 1608 Bonnie Brae—right along the fairway of number 15."

"Okay, okay, I know where it is. It'll take me about twenty minutes to get dressed and get there. I want you just to answer these questions yes or no. Understand?"

"Yes, I understand."

"Did you do it?"

"No," emphatically. "I didn't even know she wasn't in bed until..."

"Ted, just yes or no, is that clear?"

More subdued, "Yes, it's clear."

"What police agency is in your house?"

"I don't know, they're everywhere. The driveway is full. More cars are arriving all the time. My neighbors are standing out in the street.

Some of the police have brown uniforms. Some officers in blue uniforms are just coming in the door. Detective Bliss is standing right here."

That wasn't the best news I'd heard. "Okay, that's the sheriff's homicide detective. The sheriff's deputies are in brown, and that's the state police in blue. Here is what I want you to do. This is important. Don't say anything to them. Don't answer any questions. Be polite. Be pleasant. But most important, be quiet. Tell them that your lawyer told you that you are not allowed to say a word—nothing, or he won't be your lawyer."

His panicked voice came back. "What do you mean you won't be my lawyer? I'm scared to death. Amanda is face down on the floor. I tried to turn her but then all that blood got all over. She's not moving. The police want to talk to me. I told them I would talk to them if they would just let me call you."

"Calm down, Ted. I didn't mean to upset you. It is very important that you listen to what I am saying. You are to say nothing to the police. Do you understand?"

"I understand. Say nothing to the police."

At that, I could hear Sgt. Bliss's booming voice in the background. "All right, Armbruster, you've had your call."

I told Ted I was on my way, repeated my advice on silence and asked him to put Bliss on the phone. I probably could have heard Bliss's voice even without the aid of the phone.

Ted's voice was replaced with a guttural growl. "All right, counselor. Your guy said he would explain if we let him call you. Believe me, he's got some explaining to do. His pretty little wife is lying face down in a pool of blood with one hell of a divot in her skull."

"Divot?"

"Yeah, isn't that what you duffers call taking a chunk out of the ground? Well, there's one hell of a bloody divot in the back of the lady's noggin, and on the floor right next to her is a golf club which your client freely admits to be his. I'm no forensic man, and I'm just guessing here, but I'd be shocked as hell if the blood all over the club and your client's p.j.'s didn't match 100% with wifey's. In case you're wondering, she's dead, stone dead."

I heard Ted cry out in the background. "No! No! Help her. You've got to help her."

Bliss ignored Ted's cries and continued. "When the first officers arrived, your client was sitting at the foot of the stairs not more than a few feet from the golf club and his pretty little wife. So, yeah, he's got some explaining to do."

This was an awful lot of bad news to be getting while still coming awake. "Listen, detective, if it's all the same to you, I'd rather he did his explaining to me first. I'm invoking my client's Fifth Amendment rights to silence. You are not to ask him any questions. Take no statements from him. He is to say nothing. Anything unclear about that?"

Bliss snarled back, "No, all very clear. Standard shyster tactics. Wrap the perp up in the Constitution, to hell with the victim's rights. If your fine, upstanding citizen of a client doesn't want to cooperate, we'll just shag his ass down to the jail; let him see how the other half lives. We got room in the suite with Backdoor Benji. His most recent girlfriend just made bail yesterday."

Just before the phone hit the receiver, I could hear Ted's frantic voice: "No, no, I want to cooperate. Just wait for..." Silence.

Bliss was a throwback. Miranda was just a pothole to detour around. His mission in life was to see that no guilty man go free. Certainly not on his watch. His philosophy, refined over twenty-five years of police work, was that if a couple of innocent fish got caught in the net, that was the price society needed to pay to keep the sharks from feeding.

Confession may be good for the soul, but it's definitely not therapeutic for a criminal defense. Hearing my client's protests about wanting to cooperate and knowing Bliss would give him every opportunity to do so, I pulled on a pair of jeans and a sweatshirt as quickly as I could rummage through the heap of not quite dirty laundry gathered on the bedroom easy chair. I flicked the wall switch for the overhead light.

Even the brighter light and my voice on the phone had elicited only a partial lifting of the head from my bedmate, Max. Max experienced none of my difficulties in getting a good night's sleep. He snored like an overweight lumberjack and slept like Rip Van Winkle on drugs.

"Get off that bed, you bad dog," I yelled, pulling my wallet out of the pocket of the wrinkled slacks at the foot of the bed. He snorted and began a sleepy stretch of his one hundred pound frame. He wasn't moving fast enough to suit me. I grabbed my secret weapon from the nightstand, a fully loaded squirt gun. Once I shook it, sloshing the contents around, and aimed in his direction, he quickly slunk off the king-size bed. He looked back accusingly. Max, a Rhodesian ridgeback-mastiff mix, had taken easily to training since I'd acquired him as a puppy three years ago. But the "no dogs on the bed" lesson went in one big flappy ear and out the other. He was less than enthusiastic as I opened the door to the back yard and shooed him into the crisp air.

"Man, it's really cooled off," I noted. "I'm going to need a coat." I splashed cold water on my face and ran a brush through my hair. The angular face staring back at me from the medicine cabinet mirror looked higher mileage than I remembered. Memo to self: update appearance one of these days. As I brushed my teeth I took stock of what I knew of Ted. Ted was one of the old time insiders at the Lake Pointe Golf and Country Club. He had been friendly and welcoming when I joined the club five years earlier. His cordiality proved to be more the exception than the rule.

One of the justifications I'd used to spring for the $5,000 entrance fee was that membership would provide a fertile source of new legal clients. His mother's malpractice case was by far the biggest dividend on that investment. Over a post-round beer he'd told me of his mom's medical misadventure and, as the statute of limitations was near, asked if he could bring her in to talk it over. A year later the doctor's insurance company wrote Marjorie Armbruster a $250,000 check. The one-third retainer fee more than covered my investment in membership.

Amazingly, I found my car keys in the first place I looked. They were on the kitchen counter next to the pizza box from two nights earlier. I slid the keys in the pocket of my leather bomber jacket and walked into the garage, hitting the opener. As the light from the opener switched on, I could see my pride and joy gleaming. That little '69 280 SL Mercedes had been my vehicular calling card for the twenty years since I'd bought it used. A recent paint job and some leather work had the fire-engine-red metal and deep black leather looking almost new. It was a little like Dick Clark, forever young, as long as you didn't look underneath the floor boards. My six foot frame barely folded into the low slung seat with little room to spare. I slipped the key into the ignition and prayed. Click, click, click. Shit!

"Come on, honey. Don't do this to me now. Please." Nothing. Just the clicking of a dead battery. In a car thirty-years-plus long in the tooth, you expect a few problems. The most recent of which was some kind of intermittent electrical problem that drained the battery. Multiple expensive trips to the shop had yet to cure the ailment.

The driveway from the lakeside cottage I was renting sloped gently to the street. On about half of the earlier occasions when I'd managed to push the car to the slope and jump in to engage the clutch, the motor caught. Not tonight. In fact, I'd failed to jump in on time. So I found myself chasing the car into the street, praying it wouldn't hit the old oak at the corner of the drive. I stood in the middle of the street, my heart pounding, my mind racing, and time wasting. What the hell was I going to do at four a.m.? A wrecker, if I could find one, would take too long. Ditto a taxi, if one of the two in town was working at that hour.

My only recourse was my next door neighbor, Billy. Good old Billy. He, like me, was one of the few year-rounders at the beach. At age forty-five he'd been milking a workman's comp claim for a construction-related back injury for as long as I'd known him. "No sense in working when they'll pay me not to" was his motto. The only medication I'd seen him take was Southern Comfort p.r.n. He'd be cranky if I could rouse him from his pint induced hibernation, but he'd help me.

So after banging my knuckles raw on his door, there we were in the dark, running jumper cables from his Ford F-150 to my little red flivver. After the electrical transfusion, my car was purring like a cat and Billy was standing next to the window in his robe, shivering, wanting to jaw.

"So what's this about murder at the country club?"

I looked up from the bucket seat and saw his whiskered face framed in starlit sky. "Listen, Billy. I've lost almost a half hour because of this frigging car. I'm late, maybe too late. Gotta run. But I owe you a fifth and a full account when I get home. Okay?"

"Only one fifth? Seems kind of stingy for an emergency wrecker at four a.m., wouldn't you say?"

"All right, all right. I'll make it two," I yelled as I maneuvered around his truck and sped off toward the country club. Turning from Beachside Drive onto Old State Road, I let my mind turn back to the thoughts that had left me staring at the ceiling before sleep. With the death of my father five years ago, I had become much more conscious of my own mortality. Now, at thirty-eight, time was ticking and I was getting nowhere fast. The roadmap of my life at what could be fairly called the halfway point was a zig-zag of convenience over ideals and hopes lost in cul-de-sacs.

Yeah, I'd made it through law school, and my practice was paying the bills. In spite of cigarettes and booze, my health was good. I could swim a mile, walk ten, do twenty-five pushups without breathing hard, and hadn't missed a day of work in over ten years. But the dreams I'd had coming out of law school had turned out to be just that: dreams.

I envied my parents' steady devotion to each other. But my marriage to Jackie, my torts study partner, hadn't even survived to graduation. Since then every commitment had ended badly. One-night stands weren't the elixir they'd been in a younger day. My relationships with law partners were equally short lived. The visions of being a crusader for justice that had sustained me through the rigors of night law school at Wayne State had dissolved against the practicalities of keeping the lights on. Whatever justice might be, I knew it wasn't always the same thing as obtaining the best possible result for my client.

I had fallen asleep knowing I was coasting through life. If I didn't soon engage the clutch and take firm hold of the wheel, I'd lose my way entirely. Now, speeding along deserted roads in the predawn, I felt an almost forgotten sense of eagerness and purpose begin to stir. This case could be my salvation. I'm not given to premonition, yet no sooner had the fog of ennui begun to lift than I was washed in a precognition of doom. *This case will prove your undoing.* Hitting the main highway, I weighed the emotions and decided without hesitation: "Better to have loved and lost—." I stepped on the gas and accelerated toward whatever the future held.

2

Driving beneath the branches of trees just starting to leaf out, I took inventory of what I knew about Ted and Amanda. Ted Armbruster must've been getting close to the outskirts of his sixties if he hadn't already entered the city limits. He had taken over the family's tool and die business when his father, Martin, died eight years ago. Under Ted's stewardship, the business was slowly withering. The company, Armbruster Machine, in its glory days had employed 225 workers. Now, with the auto companies' one-sourcing, over one-half of Armbruster Machine was in mothballs. If the work force was still over 100, I'd be surprised.

During my last couple of visits to the country club, I had heard the boys in the men's locker bar saying Ted was in hock up to his ears to Lumberman's State Bank. Like most banks, they had been happy to lavish money on the company for expansion and modernization when times were good. Now that times were tough, they were in the midst of what they called an "agonizing reappraisal." Word in the locker room had it that the bank's workout officer would soon have an office next to Ted's at company HQ. In short, the vultures were circling.

As far as I knew, the company's problems weren't from lack of effort on Ted's part. He went in early and he came home late. I'd had clients who worked in the shop describe him taking off his coat and tie to get in and repair a fault in a locked-out punch press. He'd travel with the salesmen to meet the customer purchasing agents. But with the passage of time, the buyers his father had treated to football games and lap dances at topless bars had retired, moved up or out and were gone.

Ted, although a pleasant man, was not the back-slapping, story-telling good ol' boy his father had been. The box seats at Red Wings, Tigers and Lions games were victims of mandated cost cutting. Business wasn't what it used to be. Nevertheless, Ted had soldiered bravely on. The family business was his father's legacy. The workers now depended on Ted. He had taken it upon himself to meet with each of the employees the company had to lay off. He cried with some of them and promised them all that better times were just around the corner. But that corner just kept getting further away.

I had never met Ted's first wife, Jane. As I had heard it, they'd been childhood sweethearts and married right after graduation from Notre Dame. Jane worked in accounting at the company while waiting to get pregnant. Apparently, the stork didn't have 1608 Bonnie Brae on his route. Numerous visits to fertility specialists had proved unavailing. Then just as they were in the final stage of approval for adoption, a drunk crossed the center line on M13 one misty New Year's Eve. When Ted awoke from a four-day coma at Lake Pointe Medical Center, his mother had to tell him that Jane was gone.

As usual, the drunk had walked away. Actually, he had run away and hid in a car wash one half mile up the road. He then lay low for four days at a Saginaw relative's before the police caught up with him. It was too late then for a blood alcohol test. Ted had no memory of the accident due to the retrograde amnesia associated with a concussion and a massive brain hematoma. Jane was dead. There were no other eyewitnesses to contradict Willard Hackworth's claim that a deer had run in front of him, causing him to lose control. As I remembered, he'd pled to negligent homicide and did six months instead of the ten years he deserved for vehicular manslaughter.

Until he met Amanda, Ted had carried his athletic 6'2" frame in a slouched posture. His luxuriant mane of salt and pepper hair was decidedly more salt than pepper. And he still had a limp in his left leg from right-sided neurologic damage. Nevertheless, he was still a handsome man with an air of dignity. A smile tugged at the corners of his lips rather than filling his face as it once had. But he still took the time to dress well. Whenever I had seen him, he looked dignifiedly stylish. He favored expensive sport coats, wool slacks and a vest. He followed his father's tradition of a boutonniere in his lapel. When he shook your hand, he would grasp it firmly and look you straight in the eye. I didn't know Ted particularly well. What I did know of him, I liked.

He and Amanda were a strange match. She had to be close to twenty-five years his junior. My contact with her was the same as most men's: look up from whatever you were doing to watch her pass. She was a leggy, raven-haired colleen of milky complexion. She carried her 5' 10" height with an athletic grace and a smile that teased: "I know something you don't." Her height didn't stop her from wearing high heels, which showed off her well-turned calves with distinction. Her green eyes bubbled with mischief. She'd been in her sophomore year at Northwood when she married Stanley Drzwiecki, a sheet metal worker at the Chevy plant, who had pursued her since high school. Stan was a great dancer and had apparently swept her off her feet and down the aisle. However, Stan was also a great pool player who spent too many nights a week at Chubby's Tavern and various other felt-tabled Meccas for their marriage to last long. Two years later, the marriage ended in a childless divorce.

After that she'd graced the reception area at Armbruster Tool & Die for four years. She attracted salesmen, junior execs, and other visitors to the waiting room in a pheremonal mating dance without end. They would hover about her desk like hummingbirds to a pollen-laden hibiscus. By all accounts, she had been friendly but professional. She lent a glamorous air to the plebeian surroundings of the company waiting room. She scrimped on her living arrangements, sharing an apartment with her sister and driving a rusty ten-year-old Olds Cutlass. But she did not skimp on her hairdo, makeup or clothing. Not an eye would stay glued to a trade magazine when she bent over a file cabinet or got up to fetch the visitors' coffee. As she bowed to deliver his coffee, many a middle-aged visitor's eyes would lose focus from the high cheekbones of her face in an attempt to catch a glimpse of the crests of the swell beneath her blouse. She was tall. She was slender. She was beautiful. She was classy.

There were those in the secretarial pool at Armbruster who thought Amanda a shameless gold digger who took advantage of poor Mr. Armbruster's loneliness. Her defenders argued that compassion for his loneliness and suffering opened her heart to him. Whichever, those cleaning up after the company's annual softball game and picnic at Memorial Park saw her sitting across from Ted at a picnic table down by the lakeshore long after darkness had settled in. She had her hand on top of his on the picnic table. The two of them spoke in quiet tones until their cars were the last two parked up against the fence of ball diamond number 4. Within six months of the picnic, they'd been married at First Congregational Church and the groom had footed the bill for a $50,000 extravaganza reception at the country club. Doris, her replacement at the front desk, was fat, frumpy and fifty. The hummingbirds went looking for other flowers.

As I neared the Lake Pointe Country Club on Old Parish Road, I couldn't help but remember seeing Amanda less than ten hours earlier, perched on a stool in the club's bar, looking beautiful and very much alive. She and her longtime bridge partner, Jillian Simpson, had teased and flirted with my brother and me for an hour or so the evening before. Knowing I was to look upon Amanda again in a few minutes looking decidedly less lovely sent a shiver up my back. Our paths had crossed only hours ago, and now they were to cross again. But this time the only footprints leading away from the encounter would be mine.

The lights on the stone entrance to the country club were visible ahead of me. Even though it was no warmer than 40 degrees on this late April morning, I had the 280's side windows cracked almost halfway. The car's heater and defrost suffered from chronic pulmonary insufficiency associated with old age. The blower fan rattled and creaked with a tired rale. If I didn't crack the windows, the windshield fogged or frosted faster than I could wipe it with the locker room towel I kept on the console. Maybe soon I would need to store her highness for the winter, only letting her out in the depths of summer. But summer was approaching, and my bank account was near enough empty that the refill light blinked intermittently. A tidy retainer on a murder case should help avoid financial stall.

Lake Pointe C.C. found itself surrounded by farm country in transition. For the first sixty-five years of its existence the country club had consisted of nine holes located in Lake Pointe proper. The original clubhouse was an old utility shed that had been remodeled and expanded to the extent that it crowded the course. Errant shots landed on the patio or occasionally broke windows in the dining room. Hoping it would one day become an eighteen-hole course, and wishing to have a fancier clubhouse, the members moved to the country thirty-five years ago. The farmland they chose ten miles out of town featured uncut woodland, into which the first nine holes had been carved. Over time the original members, like Ted's father, built dignified homes on large wooded lots along the course. The cachet of country club living became a must for the socially conscious with new money in their pockets. Membership soared during the salad days of the auto industry. Ten years later the second nine was added. The old money lived in the sylvan tranquility of the back nine. The new money built half-million dollar and up mansions on the barren cornfields of the recently opened front nine. I glanced over as I passed to see the shadowy hulks of newer homes standing too close to each other on treeless lots and thought, Not for me, even if I had the money.

I drove past the driving range and chipping green and then the parking lot bathed in the spillover of light from the cart barn and a couple of parking lot lamps. The clubhouse was a dark shadow hunched on a rise standing dark sentinel between the old money of the back nine and the newly minted on the front side. I could easily guess the number-one topic of conversation in the grill and dining room over the next few days.

A half mile past the club entrance I turned left through the brick and wrought-iron entrance gate to Bonnie Brae Drive. I headed down the manicured boulevard toward the light show of patrol car flashers midway up the block. The stately homes recoiled and shrank from the garish reflection of red, blue and white revolving in a slow-motion strobe. In the windows, curtains were pulled back. Residents gathered at the ends of their winding tree-lined drives. Small groups of twos and threes convened in the grassy median of the boulevard. They pointed and called out as I passed. My 280 SL was a well-known resident of the club parking lot. But for sharing a mutual affection for golf, I probably would have known few of them. We traveled in different circles.

A uniformed deputy quickly nixed the idea of pulling into the Armbruster driveway. "Where the hell do you think you're going? This is a crime scene." I didn't recognize the deputy.

"Sorry, that's my client in there. I'll park it in the street."

I backed out and just managed to get out of the way as an ambulance careened through the Bonnie Brae entrance gate with full lights and sirens. Had I misunderstood about Amanda's being dead? Was Jillian

Simpson still with her and in need of medical help? As I reversed my way around the patrol cars and found an open spot next to the curb two houses down, the ambulance slewed into the white stone drive at 1608 Bonnie Brae. I killed the ignition, searched around on the console for a pen, and picked up the fresh legal pad I'd tossed on the passenger seat. On my way to Ted's drive I heard Thad Granger, manager at the local S.G. Hayden Securities office, calling to me from his driveway across the boulevard from the Armbrusters'. Thad, as always, was immaculately attired. He jogged over, his customer's-man smile as fresh at 4:30 a.m. as at noon.

His blue silk pajamas with robe to match topped Birkenstock sandaled feet. His reddish-brown coiffure was combed without a hair out of place. Amazingly, considering the hour, he had a beeper clasped to his robe sash and a cell phone peeking out of the pocket of his pajama top. I wondered, even in these times of the unending bull market and after hours trading, who would need to get in touch with him so urgently in the wee hours of the morning.

"Hey, Ken, what's going on? I thought I heard screaming last night when I got up to take a leak. Just had gotten back to sleep and all hell breaks loose with cop cars everywhere. Lorraine Sexton claims she heard a deputy call it murder-suicide." That caused me to pause. If Ted was dead, the big profile case with big retainer was history. But having talked to Ted with the police right there, that didn't seem likely.

"Don't believe every rumor that comes along, Thad. Figured you'd know that in the brokerage business. Nice p.j.s."

"Yeah, yeah. So what did happen then?"

I turned and started up the drive, calling over my shoulder, "That's what I'm here to find out."

As I turned up the red brick drive, I still had almost half the length of a football field of tree-lined darkness before I would reach the house. I could see the first buds of new leaves appearing on the branches. In the cold air I wondered if they were having second thoughts about venturing forth too early. The home was a two-story fieldstone colonial that bowed out into an antebellum portico supported by four massive pillars. A large veranda stretched on both sides away from the main entrance. The veranda was in shadow. I could see the outline of what I guessed to be another couple of deputies swaying slowly back and forth on a glider held by chains from porch beams. Their faces glowed in the staggered cadence of cigarette drags. As I neared the entrance, a voice came from one of the seated smokers.

"Hey, Jimmy, look what the cat dragged in. It's Lake Pointe's own Johnny Cochran."

I didn't recognize the voice. His partner's voice was familiar to me. It was Jim McIntyre, a lifer with the sheriff's department.

"Little early in the morning for ambulance chasing, isn't it, counselor? In fact, you darn near beat the ambulance to the scene. You know, Bill, I don't think I've seen that before."

McIntyre had been a deputy for over twenty years. I had worked with him on cases right out of law school back in my days as a fire-breathing, take-no-prisoners prosecutor. But four years of fire breathing burns you out. You find yourself repeating old jury arguments from rote. Always seeing the bad side of people makes you myopic about human nature. So I took the antidote and crossed over to the defense. That work was no closer to the grail of justice, but at least it was a change. So Jim and I knew each other as friend and foe from the start of our careers. An undersheriff prior to his boss's getting beat in the last election, Jim wasn't particularly political, and so the new sheriff had kept him as part of the furniture when he remodeled the department. Jim was a good cop.

"Gentlemen. Good morning. All the ruckus didn't disturb your nap behind the bus garage?" I retorted.

Lake Pointe was a peaceful town and generally very quiet after the bars closed at two. After the last of the drunk drivers had been pulled over and put to bed in jail by 3:30 a.m., a little siesta for the on-duty cops from 4:00 a.m. to 5:30 a.m. behind the Metro bus garage was not unheard of.

I climbed the three steps onto the porch and toward the massive oak entrance doors, which stood ajar. As I neared the door, McIntyre leapt off the glider, throwing his cigarette into the flower bed. "Whoa, wait a minute, Ken. Where do you think you're going? This is a crime scene. We're out here to prevent gawkers." His partner got up behind him.

"Easy, gentlemen. Ted Armbruster is my client. I beat the ambulance here because he called me, with Detective Bliss's okay."

"You're his lawyer? Bliss is expecting you?" There was a look of surprise and confusion on McIntyre's face, which only made sense to me later.

"Yep. I told Bliss no statement until I got here."

"Okay then. Bliss is inside with what's left of what had to be a real pretty woman. Don't touch anything."

Some things you never forget. Out of the vast kaleidoscope of images the human brain processes every waking minute, only a few remain in short term memory beyond an hour. Even less can be recalled a day or a week later. But an infinitesimal percentage of mental pictures last a lifetime. This striking tableau would be with me forever.

A majestic chandelier hanging from the rafters fully lit the foyer. Amanda lay face down on a black-and-white-checkered marble floor. Her prone form gave the impression that her last movements had been an attempt to crawl. Both arms were bent up at the elbows as if she had been doing push-ups. Her white skirt was hiked up to her hips. Her legs were bare of the garter and gossamer stockings she'd featured earlier that evening and were bent at the knees. She lay not far from the base of the spiral stairway to the second story landing and balcony.

Her head was toward the entrance door. From where I stood upon entering, I could see her magnificent mane of hair desecrated by a gaping wound near the crown of her head. The blood dyed her hair an ochre rust color and was pooled about where her face lay on its right side. Her head was turned so her left profile faced the ceiling. I could see no damage there. She was still beautiful. Her high cheekbones and aquiline nose topped full lips and a rounded chin. She looked to be at rest. Her eyelids covered the green eyes that had been laughing and full of mischief so very recently. The silky green blouse she'd worn that evening at the club was soaked across the shoulders with blood.

All around her, sparkling in the light from the chandelier, were pieces from the large gold-corniced mirror that hung askew on the wall by the stairs. The way the mirror canted forward allowed the pieces of glass still in the frame to reflect the scene on the floor below. At the same time my direct gaze was fixated upon Amanda lying amidst the blood and broken shards of mirror on the floor in jagged images of red, white, and green, my peripheral vision was jolted by the same images distorted in the stairway mirror. The glass on the floor sparkled and reflected the mirror back onto itself. It was an eerie double image of violent death that I have seen both awake and in dreams ever since.

I stepped in the doorway from the vestibule to the octagonal reception room. I stayed close to the wall until I stopped near the entrance doors to the main living room. From there I could more clearly see Amanda's lower body. One white high heel hung half off, half on her left foot. Her right foot was bare. Four feet away the right shoe leaned at an angle against the bottom of a group of three golf bags standing against the curved wall that rose to follow the staircase to the second floor. The juxtaposition of death, a woman's fashion complement, and men's toys was disconcerting.

Nobody noticed me come in. They were busy with the ambulance crew. A deputy and two blue-uniformed state police officers stood and watched while two paramedics kneeled beside the body. A heavyset female with short blonde hair had her fingers on the carotid artery while the male was seeking signs of life at the wrist. The male then moved to place the stethoscope on Amanda's posterior left chest. He was careful to keep his tennis shoes from the pool of blood beneath her head and upper torso. With gloved hands he carefully rolled up her blouse. As he knelt by her hips, I watched him move the band of her green brassiere aside and lean in with the instrument. After a few seconds of silence, he shook his head. He turned to Detective Phillip Weston, who stood nearby, note pad in hand, camera hanging from his neck.

"Nothing, but we'd better do this right and roll her over so I can listen to her chest. You've got your pictures, right?"

"She's a DOA. But we should roll her over and listen for heart sounds on her chest so we can say we did. But she's gone. No pulse, no respiration."

"All right, but do it carefully." These were the first words I'd heard from Phillip Weston, a veteran of the detective bureau who had been taking pictures with the 35 millimeter camera he wore about his neck. He continued addressing the paramedics. "But I'm telling you, I felt for a pulse when I got here a half hour ago. Nothing. The first deputy on the scene was here fifteen minutes before I was. He said she was without vitals then. What took you guys so long to get here?"

The female paramedic looked up from her crouch. "We had a head-on neck injury up by Oscoda. Dispatch said no big hurry on this one on account of we 'would just be acting as a meat wagon.' Looks like dispatch had it right. She's been gone a little while."

Two of the officers bent down to assist. After pulling Amanda's right arm in close to her side, they started to roll. As the EMTs maneuvered her from front to back, her white skirt rode up higher on her thighs. From my vantage point, it was impossible not to notice the lacy red panties covering her buttocks. Not only were the stockings and garters gone, she was no longer wearing panties that matched her bra. Earlier that evening, while still vital and alluring, she had granted me the briefest of glimpses between her knees. Then, her underwear had matched. What had happened on the path from the barstool to the vestibule floor to explain the change?

As Amanda came to rest on her back, her head flopped over so that the right side of her face was now visible. The blood had not covered the right cheekbone, which had been in contact with the floor. Instead it streaked her face like red tears, running from the forehead down. Some dripped over her right cheek and onto the plastic gloved hand of the deputy who was holding her head. The source of the red tears was obvious. She had an angry gaping wound across the forehead that appeared to still ooze as they held her head up. Above the right ear a similar tearing gash appeared to have clotted. The female paramedic crouched to straddle the torso as soon as Amanda had come to rest on her back. She raised the sweater and pushed the green bra cup up on the left side so that the lower half of her breast was now exposed. She put the stethoscope in her ears and placed it above Amanda's heart. After thirty seconds of silence, she shook her head and stood up and away.

"Nothing. Not a whisper. You can wait for the ME to make it official, but she's dead."

Weston answered, "Yeah, Dr. Halprin is on his way. For now let's get her back the way she was."

So far no one had even looked at me, and I had barely taken a breath. So overpowering was the sight of this beautiful woman, so recently full of life, now so obviously dead, I'd forgotten to breathe. But when they tried to roll her back on her stomach, her head hit the floor. I made an audible gasp.

Weston looked over at me, noticing me for the first time. He bellowed toward the front porch, "McIntyre, you idiot. I told you nobody in or out without my say so. This is a murder scene, not a neighborhood barbecue!" He turned back to glare at me.

"Edwards, what the hell do you think you're doing here?"

I could hear the glider creak as McIntyre and his partner got up to answer their superior's summons.

"Well, and a very pleasant good morning to you too, Sergeant," I said as I started to walk around the octagonal foyer, staying close to the wall and away from the group gathered around the body. "I'm here to see my client, Mr. Theodore Armbruster, who called me with Lieutenant Bliss's permission. Is he still here?"

As is often the case with attorneys, the best way to answer a question is with a question. This seemed to dampen Weston's ardor a moment, and he turned away from me and toward the wide double doors giving entry to the center of the house.

"He's in the living room talking to the lieutenant. I'll see if he's receiving any more visitors."

The alarm sounded in my head as I continued toward the door after Weston. I dropped my friendly tone. "Hey, I told Bliss no statement. What the hell is he doing talking to my client when I specifically told him no statement without me present?"

Weston turned at the entrance way. "Counselor, this is a crime scene. As far as I'm concerned, you got no business here. If the lieutenant thinks otherwise, fine. But until he says so, if you move another step, I'll have to arrest you." He said this to me and then over my shoulder he pointed to Deputy McIntyre, who was now standing in the doorway with a hangdog look on his face.

"McIntyre, drag your sorry ass in here and escort our esteemed legal friend outside."

As McIntyre started to move toward me, he spoke contritely to his superior. "I'm sorry, detective, Edwards said Bliss was expecting him. And you told me when I got here that a lawyer was coming. Counselor, are you coming quietly?"

I nodded with resignation. I started toward the deputy but in so doing passed before the double doors to the living room and looked in. What I saw stopped my progress. The back of Ted's head and shoulders was visible over the sofa. Leaning in toward him intently from an arm-chair on the right of the coffee table was Bliss's massive bulk. To the left of the table I could see a plush rocking chair bobbing up and down as if its occupant had just arisen. Before I could step any further toward the living room, Bliss barked, "Get that asshole outta here!"

McIntyre grabbed my left arm and Weston squeezed my right biceps painfully. They turned me toward the front entrance. I yelled over my shoulder at the living room, "Bliss, I told you no statement. What the hell are you doing? Ted, tell him nothing. Not a word."

Ted turned to look over the back of the couch. He looked like a zombie; ashen, slack-jawed, and dazed.

"Little late for that now, hot shot," Bliss crowed as he brandished a yellow legal pad over his head.

My escorts, seeing the pleasure Bliss was taking in taunting me, relaxed their pace to the door long enough for me to fire a return salvo. "Whatever you've got there ain't worth spit, Bliss. My client invoked his right to counsel. I'm here to see my client, and you are having me dragged forcefully from the room. How long do you think that'll stand up in court?"

"Longer than you think, counselor. Longer than you think. You want to talk to your client? Go wait for him at the jail."

He waved the legal pad at the officers in a shooing motion. They were gentle but firm in escorting me to the front door. I glanced over my shoulder at Amanda's death scene. Red pooling on black and white checkerboard marble. Raven hair fanned over a green blouse. White skirt hiked, exposing tanned legs all the way to a derriere covered in red panties. This view was a macabre parody of the sensual glimpse from earlier that evening. Nothing sexy about this perspective, only a strange sense of loss over a woman I hardly knew. And the white pump she'd dangled alluringly from a barstool only hours ago, now leaning askew against her husband's golf bag. I recognized the bag as Ted's from the signature head cover. The Notre Dame Irish leprechaun stitched on his driver's head cover was dancing a madcap jig, a wild grin splitting his face, oblivious to the horror before him.

My senses overwhelmed with grotesque images, I was deposited on the front porch. As I walked back down the driveway to my car, my heart was racing and my head spinning. Why was Bliss so confident? What was on that pad he had so gleefully flourished? If it was a statement, how did he expect he'd ever be able to use it? But most troubling was the strange emphasis he had put on the word client, as in "talk to your client." What the hell had he meant by that? And who had gotten out of the rocking chair too quickly for me to see?

I made my way through the clusters of neighbors with my open hands raised to fend off questions. "Can't discuss it now. Gotta run. Excuse me, please."

The car jumped to life on the first turn of the key. And as I maneuvered around the people and patrol cars, I spoke disdainfully to it. "Great, just great. Where were you when I needed you?"

On the way into town I passed the state police crime lab van heading in the opposite direction. From what I'd seen and heard during my short stay on Bonnie Brae, it didn't look like much forensic sleuthing was going to be needed. I could only guess what Bliss was crowing over on that legal pad, but I was sure I wouldn't like it.

My brain started turning over the prospects of quashing a confession taken over a lawyer's express invocation of the Fifth Amendment. My client had invoked his Sixth Amendment right to counsel, and yet Bliss had brushed me away like a fly. No way could that trampling of constitutional rights pass muster in court. Yet Bliss had looked so smug. Why? Soon find out, I thought. I grimaced remembering the time wasted waking my car, and cursed her roundly:

"Sweetheart, how could you do this to me? I treat you with tenderness. I lavish money on you. I've eaten hot dogs and soup for a week so that robber, Helmut, would heal you when you were sick. And this is how you treat me? Damn it! Your little sit-down strike probably just cost Ted any chance he had."

I realized how foolish I must look, ranting away pounding on the wheel, when the guy next to me at a red light in town beeped at me and rolled down his passenger window.

"Everything okay over there, fella?"

"What? Oh. Great, just great. Thanks for asking."

What really dominated my thinking on the way in to the jail were the relentless images of Amanda alive juxtaposed with Amanda dead. Within the last eight hours I'd seen her at her radiant best and then at her dead worst. The images flashed by like pictures on a computer screen saver. And the ones that kept repeating were the shots of her panties, red as she lay in death, and green during the brief glimpse she'd given me in the bar at the club earlier on Thursday night. When had she changed and why and with whom?

Nearing the jail, I reflected back on my last encounter with Amanda. Thursday, April 27th, was one of those teasers that the weather gives Michiganders. Winter has long overstayed the official arrival of spring in March. Then all of a sudden a strong southwesterly chases the jet stream north and for a day or two it is in the 70s. People go crazy. Women raid closets and drawers for summer wear. Boaters show up at the marina. Tennis players hit the courts. And golfers start rearranging their schedules to get in a round before the icy talons of endless winter take hold again. Hearing the forecast, my brother Matt and I had agreed to meet at the club for our first round of the year.

Matt had come up from St. Clair Shores on Thursday afternoon for an all-expenses-paid tour of the scenic Lake Pointe Country Club. Our agreement of many years standing was that we would take turns being each other's guests at our respective clubs. The guest, having made the three-hour drive, was to be treated by his host to greens fees, dinner, drinks, and since Matt insisted upon it, cart fees. Lectures on how golf was such a better game when played afoot fell on deaf ears with Matt. Me extolling the healthy virtues of a five-mile walk was like Clinton trying to persuade the Moral Majority that he was really a good guy.

Matt's golf bag was a leviathan of size and heft comparable to Rodney Dangerfield's in the movie *Caddyshack*. Caddies would quake at the sight of it even before they attempted to lift it. That Thursday afternoon had been perfect. We teed off at 1 p.m. under sunny skies streaked with high cirrus clouds. The 70-degree temperatures had our windbreakers off by the third hole. The first day of golf season is like spring training in baseball. Anything is possible. Hope rises like the sap in the trees.

Maybe this year I'll knock a few strokes off the handicap. The persistent slice will become a sweet little draw. Concentrate on the short game. Learn to get up and down, and life on the links goes from the outhouse to the penthouse. Over the winter my muscles had forgotten the bad habits from last fall. Very simple swing thoughts were working; smooth turn of the shoulder and finish down the target line. As an 18 handicapper, my score of 89 was cause for hope, and my satisfaction dimmed only slightly in losing twenty bucks to my brother's 85.

We played some gin in the men's locker and headed upstairs for drinks and dinner around 7:30. The club's dining facilities are divided into two parts. The formal dining room requires at least a sport jacket. The banquet booths running along the windows in front of the piano bar allow golf attire. Smoking is permitted in the bar. And since Matt was still a slave to tobacco, we sat there.

"Bother you if I smoke?" Matt inquired three drags into his Marlie, noticing my eyes fixed on the cigarette.

"No more than it bothered me to see you sink that thirty-footer on 18. Go ahead, enjoy."

The golf course and the bar were my two favorite smoking venues. If I was going to kick the habit, getting through the afternoon and evening was a good test. It's just that mentally saying no every thirty seconds was tiresome. The upstairs barman, Eddie, was behind the long upholstered bar across the aisle from us, his eyes glazing over as we gave him much more detail than he wanted to the question "How was it out there, fellas?" Two stiff Jack Daniels were the prelude to a couple of thick medium rare sirloins accompanied with a nice Pinot Noir.

Just as we lifted our glasses to toast each other with the last of the wine, Amanda Armbruster and Jillian Simpson made their entrance from the dining room into the bar in high spirits. Both were dressed for dinner in the formal dining room. To see them was to know that neither lacked the means nor the taste in clothes that showed them off to appealing advantage. In their mid-thirties, they were young for country club wives. Both were without children. Both were habitués of the exercise gym located at the far end of the locker rooms. Both were slim-waisted and had firm figures that bespoke rigorous diet and self-discipline. They walked with a feline grace. Jillian, her blonde hair cut just below the ears, wore a black glittery dress that shimmered as she moved. As they entered, Amanda's left hand, from force of long habit, flipped her thick black hair up from under her collar and down over a green silky blouse. The blouse was tucked into an off-white linen skirt that hugged her hips and covered her silk-stockinged legs to the knees.

Jillian I knew well from our mutual days as aspiring thespians at the Lake Pointe Players. Amanda I knew less well. But she always smiled and said Hi in passing. The ladies smiled and made a mock curtsy as I modified the toast Matt and I were sharing.

"To the flowers of Lake Pointe womanhood."

"Here, here," Matt replied as our glasses clinked. As Amanda bowed, her blouse parted long enough to expose full breasts swelling against a green brassiere. We rose and I introduced my brother and invited the ladies to join our table. But after exchanging questioning glances and surveying the post-dinner wreckage on our table, they declined. "No thanks, fellas." Amanda smiled, her voice a caress to the ears. "Ted and Jim are downstairs finishing up a gin game from this afternoon and promised to be right along. Jillian and I are going to have a brandy and a little girl talk."

I signaled Eddie to put their drinks on my tab and watched the ladies slide onto the barstools directly across from our booth. Occasionally, they would swivel with their brandy snifters in hand to chat with us. They asked Matt where he was from, whether he was a lawyer too, was he married, and if he had beaten me. He answered St. Clair Shores, no, he had found an honorable profession in telecommunications, he was divorced with no children, and yes, he was pleased to say, he had beaten me. Jillian asked me if I had stopped trying out at the Players when I didn't get the part as Clarence Darrow in *Inherit the Wind.*

"No, I've been meaning to. There were a couple of parts I would have liked. But I've just gotten so busy at the office I didn't know where I would find the time. Boy, I would have loved that part as Darrow, but Frank was great in it."

The bar stools were higher than the circular bench around our dinner table. So when the ladies turned to speak with us, their knees were at our eye level. As we would look up to chat with them of necessity, the gaze had to pass from bended knee to head. None of the stopping places in between were low rent. I kept reminding myself to make eye contact and not be too obvious. However, on one of their rotations from bar back to us, Amanda's knees parted for a couple of seconds as she adjusted herself in the seat and recrossed her legs.

With that vista of the stairway to heaven before me, my eye contact resolution went out the window. I peeked. Her ecru silk stockings clung to well-rounded calves. Just as I was trying to force my eyes to her face, the gates opened before me. Surely I couldn't be faulted for seeing that which was before me unbidden. She was wearing a garter belt. This sexy frill has almost become extinct in the era of pantyhose. The pearly straps extended beyond the top of her stockings at mid-thigh into the gathering shadows. Then, like a sunset in the tropics, I got that little flash of green. She was wearing panties to match her bra. Even after she had closed the gates by crossing her knees, I was transfixed. That flash of green was imprinted on my retina. Jillian's voice brought me out of it.

"Ken, Ken, are you with us? I asked you about that adorable dog of yours, Max. That's his name, isn't it?"

"Sorry. I was lost in thought," I managed. "Delicious, oh, I mean, he's fine. Max is great. Thanks for asking."

I looked up and over to Amanda. A little smile played on the corners of her lips and her eyes twinkled. I think she knew what kind of thoughts in which I'd been lost.

"Oh, what kind of dog do you have?"

"He's a hundred-pound mix of three quarters Rhodesian ridgeback, one quarter mastiff. Lovely animal and a great friend."

We laughed and talked for maybe a half hour after the plates had been cleared away. Amanda and Jillian were regular golf partners and were eager to talk golf. So we whiled away the time trading war stories. Matt had an 8 a.m. appointment in downtown Detroit with a prospective big customer. As it was getting late, and he had a three-hour drive back home, he closed the pleasant interlude.

"Ladies, it's not my custom to leave two sweet lovelies alone and unprotected in a bar, but I have an important meeting in the morning and miles to go before I sleep. It's been very pleasant talking with you."

I got up with Matt and offered to go down to the men's locker to check on their husbands' progress. Jillian demurred. "No thanks, Ken. I'm sure they'll be along shortly." She gestured toward the bar man, who was sorting through the guest checks and totaling them on his calculator. "Eddie will make sure we come to no harm, won't you, Eddie?"

He nodded, smiled, and returned to his work. Eddie had baby-sat countless wives of card-playing members over the years. With that, I shook hands with the women, getting close enough to inhale the heady scent of their perfumes, then Matt and I took our leave. As we headed down the bar and through the piano lounge toward the side entrance, I looked back down the bar to wave. Jillian had turned away with her elbows on the bar. But Amanda was facing sideways, her eyes following our departure, white high heel dangling from her left foot. She smiled and raised her hand in farewell.

As I waited for the light three blocks from the jail to go from red to green, it was that little wave that stuck in my mind. She had been so alive and alluring then; so cold and dead now. I couldn't shake the glimpse of her thighs from the bar. As the light went from red to green, I puzzled at how her dainties had gone from green to red. And where had the stockings and garter belt gone? Amanda had taken some kind of walk on the wild side since last I'd seen her. But with whom and where and when? Had that walk led her to the pool of blood? Maybe Ted could answer these questions.

5

The Law Enforcement Center housed the Lake Pointe City Police Department in the front. The county sheriff's office and jail occupied the rest of the three-story building. The crime and punishment industry in Lake County had outgrown the old jail with its iron bars and cells thirty years earlier. Twenty years ago, the county had recognized the need, and ten years later, the new facility had been built. It was supposed to be state of the art and escape-proof. The eleven different prisoners who had gotten into the ceiling ductwork and out to freedom apparently didn't know that. During the eighty-three year life of the old jail, nary a single prisoner had left before his appointed time. Three years of litigation between the county, the architect, and the contractors had resolved the problem and paid the bills of four different law firms. Nothing like conflict. It was the sun and rain that made law practices grow.

The throaty rumble of the 280 SL's exhaust was amplified as it echoed off the walls of the jail. Once I turned the key, I sat in the silence of a city asleep. I realized how tired I was and stretched my neck back on the headrest. I shut my eyes against the yellow-orange glare of the security lights and took stock. A lot had happened in the eight hours since I had been joking and laughing with Amanda. I had seen bodies dead by violence before, in person, while in the prosecutor's office, and on film as a defense attorney. Whatever the number required to get used to it, I hadn't reached it. Never before was it somebody I knew. Never somebody I had touched, talked to, let alone sneaked a peek up her dress hours before. The contrast between the blood-matted, lifeless face on the floor at Bonnie Brae and the animated, vibrant beauty in the bar played in my head like a grotesque before-and-after advertisement: alive, dead, alive, dead. I had to open my eyes to stop the carousel from turning.

My anger at Detective Bliss was an effective antidote. What the hell was he doing? Rather than sit and stew over the problems my balky car had caused, I shook myself and took a look in the mirror. Not good. Thirty-eight years of age shouldn't look this bad. But many of those years had been a study in the ravages of high stress, inadequate sleep, poor eating habits, booze and cigarettes. Super-impose on that long-term foundation the short-term effect of playing golf and partying with my brother, and subtract the shower and grooming I didn't get after Ted's call, and the guy looking back at me looked like his regular visits to the county were as an inmate, not as an attorney. Vowing to add a healthier lifestyle to my no-smoking program, I climbed out of the car and headed for the entry portal. Standing in the glare of the arch light beneath a video camera, I hit the buzzer.

"Good evening, counselor. Bliss said we might be expecting you," came a voice tinnily through the speaker. It was a voice I recognized, Ike Johansen. Ike had been a turnkey for longer than would have been necessary to get off the graveyard shift. But a nagging wife who would've lost a congeniality contest to Xanthippe was all the excuse he needed to sleep through the day.

The buzzer sounded and I walked into the decompression chamber between the outside steel door that snicked shut and the inside door that buzzed open. I walked into the tiled entry room that formed an L shape around the security glass of the CFO's office. The room was brown tile wall and floor lit by caged lights. There were four glass-walled cells with tile bunks behind me and to my left. I could see a high-mileage woman plucking her eyebrows in the reflection from the tempered glass of her cell. Her make-up, teased hair and black body suit made it apparent she was awaiting a morning arraignment on a soliciting charge. The contrast between her tarty looks and Amanda's refined beauty in the club bar was striking.

In the cell next to her, a thirty-five-year-old blonde man with his blue blazer in his lap and his matching power tie askew over a soiled white button-down shirt sat on the corner of his bunk, his face in his hands. Too many drinks after work followed by an erratic drive home was my guess. He looked up at me for a moment as if I might be his salvation. Not recognizing me, and me looking more like the night janitor than his rescuing angel, he resumed his mournful gaze at the floor. The usual bouquet of vomit, urine, antiseptic and despair filled my nostrils. As always, I was thankful to be a visitor and not a guest.

I walked to the control window, which was equipped with a built-in microphone. Ike leaned over the counter and smiled at me. "Hey, Kenny, my man, you look like you should be one of our customers instead of some high-paid shyster come to fetch them out."

I fingered the stubble on my squarish chin. "Nice to see you too, Ike. When the phone rings in the middle of the night, we can't just tell the client to take two aspirin and call me in the morning. As a foot soldier in the army of justice, I must answer the bugle when it blows."

Ike laughed. "Yeah, bullshit, it doesn't hurt when the guy blowing the bugle's got more money than he knows what to do with. I don't see you down here for some poor guy can't afford to pay ."

"Ike, you're too cynical. How's your lovely wife, Mildred?"

Ike's smile evaporated. "She's fine, and how's your hemorrhoid?"

I laughed. "No problem. A little Preparation H and it's gone. Think that would help with Mildred?"

His smile returned. "Oh, man, if only, if only. Listen, Bliss called just before you got here. Said to tell you he was just getting some loose ends cleaned up at the scene. Said you'd know what that means. Anyway, he'll be another twenty minutes. What loose ends is he talking about?"

I thought for a minute. Nothing came to mind. "The only loose end I associate with the good Detective Bliss is that largish bulk attached to his backside below the belt. So what he means, I can only guess."

Ike's eyes wrinkled along his deeply etched laugh lines. "Ah, another member of the 'Bliss is just another word for happiness' club, I see."

Then I remembered. "Hey, that's right, Ike. Bliss made life miserable for you a few years ago, didn't he? As I recall, the jury saw it your way and our mutual friend, the detective, was left sucking wind."

Ike beamed at the memory. "You got it. Got my job back, back pay, and an apology from the sheriff. But that SOB Bliss still treats me like something the cat puked up."

As I remembered the story, Bliss had been the head investigator of a mini-scandal at the jail some years back. The turnkeys were accused of smuggling cigarettes and dirty magazines to the inmates and trustees. Ike had been seen in Devo's Bar with two trustees sharing a beer while off duty. But the squealer who fingered Ike for arranging a non-sanctioned conjugal visit with a girlfriend had been roughed up by his cell mates and couldn't remember the details too well once he got to the witness stand. The outcome of the investigation and trial was that Ike did his time at the jail as a paid employee on the outside of the cell instead of a resident on the inside. He liked Bliss even less than I did.

An idea occurred to me. "Listen Ike, I know you want to stay on the good side of Bliss, but maybe I could ask you a favor. As you can see, I'm not looking my courtroom finest at the moment. As long as I have to wait, can I use the intake shower to try and take a few of the barnacles off?"

Ike thought about it, looked at the clock, checked the video monitors and said, "Hell, if you don't mind, I don't mind. There's probably a rule against it somewhere, but I'll be damned if I know where. Just make it quick and keep your mouth shut. There's soap and shampoo in there, and I've got a disposable razor in my locker you can use. Plus, I'll promise not to look at the monitor. Ol' Gertie up front is probably asleep in the radio room, and if not, she can't see well enough to tell you're not a prisoner."

So I walked to the other side of the room to the intake shower. Ike buzzed the door and I stepped in. There was still some water in the gutters next to the raised square rubber pad beneath the shower. The door clicked locked behind me, which was a little disconcerting. I sat on the bench at the far end of the room and pulled off my socks, feeling like this was just part of the bad dream I'd been having since the phone woke me. When I saw the camera staring at me from over the door, I nearly backed out. But I was this far already, so I slid off my pants, socks and underwear, unbuttoned my shirt and started the water running. I grabbed the liquid disinfectant soap and stepped onto the pad.

Compared to the trickle from the antiquated plumbing at the cottage, the water pressure was amazing. Needles of water stung every part of my body. I sudsed up, washed off and was out from under in less than three minutes. I grabbed the two threadbare towels sitting on the bench labeled L.C.S.D. and dried off. I was dressed and out of there in no time at all. Ike slid me his razor through the prisoner property chute. In five minutes, I felt like a human being again. He even had combs in a sterilized jar. I didn't look good, but I didn't resemble someone facing a vagrancy charge either.

I had no more than handed Ike back the razor and comb when the buzzer sounded again. I looked through the Lexan glass as Ike keyed the intercom. I could see on the black-and-white monitor in the back corner of Ike's office the top of a bald head as it bent to look in the outside door. I heard Ike say, "Can I help you?" when the head turned to look up.

I recognized who it was before he announced himself. It was Lake Pointe's Mr. Silk Stocking, M. Stanton Browne III, Esq. What the hell was he doing here? I couldn't imagine M. Stanton shagging his ass out of bed for the drunk driver in the blue blazer. Maybe the guy was the son of one of M. Stanton's big annual retainer clients. But then M. Stanton would've sent one of his associates.

Then it dawned on me. The empty rocking chair. M. Stanton was Ted's next-door neighbor and probably as such did his corporate legal work. But what would M. Stanton be doing in the middle of a murder case? He knew as much about that as I knew about patent and trademark law. Nothing at all.

M. Stanton was of immaculate style and, as far as I could tell, little substance. His name was a case in point. On appearance in court or first introduction, he articulated his first initial, as in: "M. Stanton Browne for the defense." Or "M. Stanton Browne, pleased to meet you." My colleagues and I, who occupied lower rungs on the legal ladder, had speculated over beers on what his first initial stood for, with "money," "megalomaniac," and "mean" splitting the votes about evenly. An apocryphal tale had circulated since I came to town attesting to Browne's scrupulousness about his name and personal space. The story, without lawyerly embellishment, had it that at the annual Bar Association Christmas party, a new associate with an excess of holiday cheer under his belt committed the affront of placing a friendly arm around the senior partner's shoulder and hoisting his glass to toast "All the best for the holidays, Stan." He was gone by Easter.

A regular regimen of exercise in his firm's on-premises gym kept his six-foot-two-inch frame in athletic trim. His career was everything mine was not. He was rich and successful. He had a pretty wife and a country club home. He served on the hospital board and the Dressler Foundation, Lake Pointe's biggest charity. His law firm was the biggest in town and he was the chief rain-maker. He represented lots of doctors and dentists as they set up their professional corporations and partnerships. He made sure they paid Uncle Sam and their employees as little as possible and himself as much as the traffic would bear. He advised them to own their BMWs and Lincolns in the name of their professional corporations, to attend lots of medical seminars in the Rockies, the Caribbean, and Europe, and to designate a room or two of their homes as deductible offices.

M. Stanton was on a first name and referral fee basis with all the tax shelter vendors. He had his clients owning limited partnerships in California fruit orchards, Orlando apartment complexes, Texas cattle feed lots, and Wyoming oil drilling programs. He'd set up his client's IRAs, Keoghs or profit sharing and pension plans so that their employees would vest as late as possible in as little as possible, while the good doctor vested in the forfeits for those employees who were let go just ahead of vesting date. He advised his clientele to hire lots of part-time employees and few, if any, full-timers, so as to hold down benefit and unemployment costs.

His father had been a former chief of staff at the hospital, and his generous contributions to University of Michigan Law School had helped pave the way for M. Stanton's admission. After law school, he had come home to Lake Pointe and had risen steadily to become the senior partner in Butler, Browne, Steele and Thompson. Butler was long since dead. The firm had four partners and a revolving portfolio of four or five associates who would last one to five years and then move on or be moved on. Outside of one or two associates who had, during their brief tenure, played on the Hammurabi's Bar softball team, I could never keep track of them. It seemed at every bar annual meeting Butler-Browne was introducing some fresh face as the newest member of their firm. They never said much about the ones moving on.

I could hear the tinny squawk of M. Stanton's response over the intercom but could not decipher it through the protective glass. Ike raised his eyebrows and walked from the far corner of the booth where the intercom was back to the window where I was standing.

"You know some guy named Stan Browne? He claims he's a lawyer. Matter of fact, he claims he is Mr. Armbruster's lawyer. What's the deal?"

I tried not to let my shock at this turn of events show. "Actually, his name is M. Stanton. He gets quite upset if you call him Stan. He's a lawyer, all right. But if you saw him inside of a courtroom in the last five years, it was to ask the judge if he was free for golf in the afternoon. He's Armbruster's neighbor."

Ike looked up and over his shoulder at the monitor, and I followed his gaze. Squire Browne was staring up into the camera, shifting impatiently from foot to foot. The light reflected off of his bald pate, which appeared disproportionately large in the camera's eye. Definitely not M. Stanton's most appealing profile. I saw his left hand start to reach for the intercom and smiled to see him jump when Ike hit the electric interlock at the same moment. By the time M. Stanton recovered to grab for the door handle, Ike had taken his thumb off of the release. M. Stanton got it right on the second try, but then Ike put him through the same routine in the vestibule. Ike shrugged as if it was none of his doing.

M. Stanton strode into the reception area, paused to crinkle his nose, and looked the place over with distaste. His eyes found me leaning against a side wall and paused. Over my fifteen years of practice he had mostly ignored me, being no more civil than circumstances required.

That was okay, I didn't much like him either. This time as our eyes met there was no false veneer of amity in his look nor his words.

"See here, Edwards. The detective said I might expect to find you here. You can go on home. Ted's a long-term client. He has asked me to represent him in this tragic matter."

"Since when did you become an expert on criminal cases?" I snapped back. "That wasn't perhaps you in Ted's living room leaping out of your chair at the sound of my voice? What kind of great lawyering caused Bliss to be looking like the cat that ate the canary?"

His face reddened as he pointed at me with his index finger and spoke in an angry lecturing tone. "Listen, I told you. You're off the case, if you were ever on it. So unless you hang around these nether regions like some night feeder looking for prey, you should leave."

"When did you get elected sheriff, asshole?" I felt my blood beginning to boil and stepped toward him. As he stepped in to meet me, the speaker carried Ike's voice loud and clear.

"Knock it off or I'm hitting the security alarm. Mr. Browne, please approach and state your business here. Edwards, back off!"

With that bucket of cold water we both stood down from battle stations, and Browne stepped to the window to address Ike. "I am attorney M. Stanton Browne. Mr. Armbruster is my client. I'm here to await his arrival. By the way, you need to do something about that door system. Quite aggravating."

Ike's face furrowed as if he had just smelled something not quite to his liking. "Sorry about that, Stan. It seems to work fine most of the time. Must be a real shortage of legal work in this town. This Armbruster guy hasn't even arrived in the jail yet and he's got two lawyers fighting over his case. That's assuming you are a lawyer. I know Mr. Edwards is a lawyer, but I've never heard of you. You got some ID?"

Browne looked to see if I'd overheard this exchange. I looked back at him and raised my eyebrows in mock surprise and made a mental note to buy Ike a beer the next time I had a chance. Browne returned his attention to the booth window. "Listen, old fellow. I am M. Stanton Browne the third, senior partner in Butler, Browne, Steele and Thompson. I've been practicing law in this town for twenty-five years."

Ike didn't much care for the old fellow reference, and M. Stanton definitely was not his type of guy. "Look here, Stan. Been senior partner on the night shift for Bond, Sherman, Greeley & Millen, our last four sheriffs, for over twenty-five years, and I'm telling you I've never heard of you. So, do you have ID or don't you?"

M. Stanton gave an exaggerated sigh and reached for his wallet in his inside jacket pocket. While he fumbled I silently mouthed, "Ask about the M." Ike obliged. "Need your full name for my log sheet. What does the initial stand for?"

"I don't use it," he replied stiffly.

"If you are unable to comply with department regulations, then please step outside."

"Milton." I could barely hear the whisper. But Ike resolved all doubt.

"Like in Uncle Milty. My dad loved Milton Berle. You named after him?"

"Certainly not." M. Stanton snorted and continued to dig through his pockets.

Instead of his wallet, he retrieved what appeared to be a super-compact Palm Pilot or digital phone. He patted his back trouser pockets and came up empty. "Actually, in all the confusion, I must have left my wallet at home. I'm a neighbor of Ted Armbruster's on Bonnie Brae. I talked with him and Detective Bliss about fifteen minutes ago. The detective said they would be transporting my client in shortly and asked me to meet him here. He told me I would probably find Mr. Edwards here. Call Detective Bliss if you want to, or Mr. Edwards can vouch for me." He turned to me. "Ken, tell the man who I am."

The full impact of what Browne was saying was dawning on me, and I felt the anger bubbling but kept my response to measured disinterest. "Sorry, sir. The only attorney Browne I know wouldn't know his ass from his elbow in a murder case and wouldn't go near one. So while you look familiar, I can't vouch for you."

I turned to Ike and added: "No state bar card, no wallet, and no driver's license at five o'clock in the morning. I'd be careful here, deputy."

Browne started to sputter as Ike came around from behind the counter. "Sorry, sir. No tickee, no washee. Afraid you'll have to wait outside. Department regulations."

And out the door Browne went, looking balefully back at me. Ike played the lock buzzer game with him on the way out, leaving Browne stuck in the vestibule turning red and muttering threats. As screwed up as things were, I had to laugh at his discomfiture. Ike was loving it, too.

"What's that stuffed shirt doing here?" Ike asked.

"Not too sure, Ike. I can't imagine I'm going to like it."

We contented ourselves for the next few minutes talking about the opening of trout season and watching Browne pace agitatedly around the entrance. Before long there was a loud series of beeps and the garage door behind the control booth began to furl upward. A pair of headlights from a patrol cruiser lit the area and then the car pulled in. I could see Ted in the back seat with his arms behind him. Deputy McIntyre got out of the passenger's side door as the garage motors cranked into action to return the steel door to its closed position. The deputy opened the cruiser door and helped Ted out. Ted was turning his head from side to side, looking lost. I got to my feet, and from where I stood I could see Ted take a couple of uncertain steps with his hands handcuffed behind him. The deputy took his elbow to steady him. Ted's hair was disheveled. He looked frightened.

Bliss walked in through the garage entrance looking supremely pleased. He had been a high school football hero, but apparently not quite good enough for a major college. He ended up at Northwood University on scholarship as a linebacker and graduated with a degree in law enforcement. He was certainly big enough to play linebacker. His playing weight on a 6'2" frame had probably been in the 210 to 225 area. Too many years and too many beers, and now his gut hung over his belt and his collar was open to allow his massive neck room to move. The ruptured capillaries on his nose gave testament to a long-standing relationship with Mr. Bud Weiser. His massive shoulders anchored biceps that looked capable of bench pressing 250 pounds. The arms terminated in hands the size of Easter hams.

Browne buzzed insistently, and Ike let him in without the horseplay. M. Stanton pretended I was already gone. While he complained to Bliss about Ike's treatment, I took a long look at this self-styled avatar of legal success. We were anything but of the same ilk. There stood the tall patrician. Here sat the poor plebeian. M. Stanton was dressed in a blue mohair blazer. Every lawyer owns a blue blazer. But M. Stanton's looked like it sold for a thousand at Sak's. The one in my closet had cost me a tenth of that at Joseph A. Banks. The gold temples of Browne's reading glasses lay outside the breast pocket like jewelry on blue velvet. His oxford shirt had the initials M.S.B. monogrammed on the pocket. The jeweled cufflinks on the sleeves carried the same stylized logo. His tan slacks were wrinkle free down to the Gucci loafers. If clothes made the man, M. Stanton had arrived. Only the flush of anger reaching to the top of his nearly bald pate and the perspiration beading on his forehead ruined the GQ look.

Bliss brushed off Browne's complaints over his greeting at the jail but did exchange a look with Ike that spoke volumes about their history. But nothing was going to bother Bliss at the moment. He was feeling pretty chipper. "Good morning, gentlemen. If you will excuse us, we need to book, fingerprint and photograph Mr. Armbruster."

I tried to keep my cool. I was at sea in a leaky boat without a can to bail. But still, I couldn't keep the anger out of my voice. "Detective Bliss, what were you doing talking to my client after I had invoked his constitutional right to silence?"

Bliss placed his massive paw over his mouth and fingered his cheek as if lost in thought. "Jeez, counselor. I don't remember exactly what you said on the phone. You were none too prompt in arriving. By the time you got there, I understood you weren't Mr. Armbruster's attorney after all. Lawyer Browne consulted with his client. We all talked and decided the best thing would be if Mr. Armbruster cooperated and told us what he knew." He held up a manila file divider. "I've got a signed waiver of Miranda rights here in my folder, witnessed by Attorney Browne. Wanna see it?"

I glanced at Ted, who looked like he was on Thorazine. He was trembling. His eyes were bloodshot and glassy. He swayed on his feet. It looked like he hadn't slept in a week. His voice was a tremulous croak. "Oh, my God, Ken. Amanda is dead. I told Officer Bliss here I didn't hurt her, but I felt it was my fault. Now I'm at the jail. They have me handcuffed. They say I am under arrest. What's going on?"

"We'll talk in a minute, Ted. Let's just be quiet for now."

I turned to M. Stanton, who walked from the counter to stand at Ted's side. Browne put an arm in a fatherly fashion on Ted's shoulder and in response to my look of disbelief, spoke to me in the condescending tone he'd been working a lifetime to cultivate.

"Listen, Edwards. Ted is a neighbor and a long-term client. So when I saw the police cars, I walked over to see if I could help. Detective Bliss was kind enough to admit me to the house. He told me that, based on your instructions not to cooperate, he'd have to arrest Ted on the information he had. I wanted to spare Ted any more suffering, what with the shock of Amanda and all. So I conducted a brief consultation with Ted. He told me he had nothing to hide. I felt it was the best thing to follow the detective's advice and to avoid Ted's being carried off to jail."

My frustration with the evening's events and general contempt for Esquire Browne bubbled up again. "You based that decision, I assume, on your vast experience in criminal law? When's the last time you saw the inside of a courtroom? Seeing that Ted is here in handcuffs, I can only conclude your brilliant strategy to keep him out of jail didn't have the desired effect."

M. Stanton impressed me as the type of guy with blood pressure problems. For the second time in five minutes his face flushed crimson. "I told you, Edwards. You're off the case. Send Mr. Armbruster a bill for your time. Go chase an ambulance or two or whatever it is you do."

At the mention of his name, Ted stirred as if waking. "Wait now. I did call Ken. I asked him to come and help me. I need to talk to him. Detective, you told me I'd be able to. What's happening here?"

I shot a glance at Browne as if to say, "Little hasty trying to push me out the door, eh?" And then I turned to Bliss. "Detective, I'd like a word in private with my client to find out if, in fact, he is my client. You have a problem with that?"

Bliss ran his left hand through his full, thick mane of brylcreemed hair, then examined the grease on his fingers while he thought it over. While he was thinking about it, Ted spoke in a quiet voice. "Please, detective. I've done everything you've asked me to do. I got Ken out of bed in the middle of the night to come and help me. I'd like to explain to him."

This seemed to tip the balance. "It's highly irregular. He hasn't even been processed yet."

Then he smiled and held up the folder with a couple of loose sheets filled with handwriting partially visible at the bottom. "But Mr. Armbruster has been cooperative, very cooperative. And I told him if he cooperated with me, I'd cooperate with him. I'm always as good as my word. I'll give you five minutes. You can use Cell 3 over there. We'll turn the sound off."

He motioned to Ike, twisting his thumb and index finger and pointing at holding cell 3. Ike depressed the button for the electric lock on the glass and steel door, which began to buzz. He held it until I got over and pulled the door open. Before entering, I turned to Bliss and asked, "Do you mind taking the cuffs off now that he is here in jail?"

Bliss nodded and Deputy McIntyre took the keys out of a belt loop to free Ted's hands. As he was doing so, Browne started to walk toward the cell door. I pushed the door almost closed. "You don't think you've caused enough harm already? I want to talk to Ted privately."

Browne kept walking and put his hand on the side of the door to pry it open. "Edwards, are you hard of hearing? I'm his lawyer, not you. And I don't see how his talking to you is going to help him."

Still playing tug of war with the door, I replied, "Let's see. You were okay with him talking to a police detective who has arrested him for murder, but you don't want him talking to me? I hope you've got yourself a rather large malpractice policy with the premium paid in full."

That seemed to work better than the punch in the solar plexus I was entertaining as plan B. He paused as a cloud of uncertainty moved across his face. Before the cloud cleared, Ted spoke up. "Stanton, please wait outside. I dragged Ken into the middle of this in order to help me. I want to talk to him for a few minutes by myself."

Browne considered this, gave one of his audible sighs and said, "Well, I don't advise it." But he released his hand from the holding cell door and stepped away.

Ted and I walked into the cell and sat on the tiled bench as the door clicked shut. Through the glass door I could see Bliss huddled with the deputies and M. Stanton standing a few feet away, fiddling with a cufflink while he stared in at us.

"Ted, are you all right? I'm so sorry about Amanda. Do you need a doctor? You don't look so good. Anybody you want me to call?"

Ted took a deep breath and shuddered. His hands trembled like he had Parkinson's. He spoke in a quiet monotone. "Can you call my mother? She thinks the world of you. Tell her, tell her—I don't know what to tell her. I don't know what happened. I played golf with Jim Simpson. Didn't I see you out there?"

I nodded. Then he recited his recollection as if he were in a dream state. "We were at the club with Jim and Jillian for dinner. Had a few drinks. Too many, really. Jim and I had a gin game going from after golf, and so we went downstairs to finish that. Boy, did I take a beating. The girls said they'd wait for us in the bar. Then they sent Eddie down to say they'd meet us at Heather Hollows. I guess we were taking too long. Anyway, I kept asking for a rematch since Jim had so much of my money. Stupid, really, really stupid. By the time we went upstairs, the club was empty. I drove Jim over to Heather Hollows in our car since the girls had taken his. Then I really made a fool of myself. Amanda was in a booth with Jillian. Some Latin lover type had his arm around her and they were all laughing and acting like I wasn't there. I lost it. I yelled at Amanda and I might have pushed that other fellow. Next thing I know Amanda's crying. The bartender is calling the cops and I'm in my car headed home. That's it. That's everything I know." He slumped forward and stared at the wall across from us.

"I know this is difficult, Ted, but there has got to be more. What happened? How did Amanda get hurt?"

"I don't know. Believe me. If I knew, I'd tell you."

"Okay, what did you do when you got home?"

He looked up in thought, and then went on. "I stormed around for a few minutes feeling like a fool. It was our annual spring golf weekend up north. I had to get up early. So I took a couple of sleeping pills and went to bed. That's it. That's everything."

Was he avoiding mentioning Amanda because it was too painful, or because he had yet to figure out his story? "Can't be everything," I said. "A lot has happened since you went to bed. How did the police get there?"

He shook his head to clear it. "Yes, yes, yes, I know what you are asking. Those pills really knock me out. I was dreaming that Amanda was screaming or arguing or yelling. Then I think I heard the crash of the mirror breaking. But I wasn't sure if I had dreamt it. Then I heard a cry. No, maybe a moan and a door slam. I got up and when I got to the top of the stairs, there she was."

At that he convulsed like he was going to be sick. "Oh, my God. She's dead. She really is dead."

The sobbing left him gasping for air. I saw Browne move toward the door and held my hand up to forestall him.

"Ted, I've got to ask you. Did you hurt Amanda?"

He looked at me as if he hadn't heard properly. "Never. Not last night. Not ever."

This he said looking me straight in the eye with timbre in his voice. As I looked into his face, trying to discern the truth of what he was saying, Bliss had his arm extended in the air making a circular motion with his index finger. Time to wrap up.

"Ken, she was just lying there. She twitched a couple of times when I called her name. She was lying on her face. I started to roll her on her side to put her head in my lap, but she made a noise like I was hurting her. So I just left her as she was and kept calling her name. But she wouldn't answer."

I put my hand on Ted's shoulder and could feel the tremors coursing through his body. "Did you call an ambulance?' I asked.

Ted ran a bloody hand through his thick salt-and-pepper hair, concentrating. "Ken, I don' t know. I think so. I called somebody. I was just there stroking her hair, talking to her, waiting for her to move, and the next thing I heard was somebody pounding at the door. It was the sheriff."

"Ted, do you know who did this?"

He seemed lost in thought for a few seconds and then replied, "Nobody."

"What do you mean, nobody?"

"Nobody would want to hurt Amanda. She was so beautiful, so full of life. Who would do that to her? Maybe she fell on the stairs."

Remembering the carnage in the hall, I didn't want to plan on an accidental death defense. But with Bliss getting antsy, I needed to cut to the chase and find out if planning a defense was to be part of my future. "Ted, what is M. Stanton doing here? You called me and I came as soon as I could . But my damn car wouldn't start. Did you call him?"

He considered the question for a minute. "No," pause, "no. I don't think I did. Maybe. It seemed like he just came. After I called you, the detective took me out of the hallway and sat me down in the living room to wait for you to come. Detective Bliss was very nice to me. He got me a glass of water. He told me everything would be all right. Then Stanton came over. You know he lives one house down from me. We've been friends a long time. He handles my business affairs." It sounded like a litany.

"Yes, but I don't think M. Stanton has much experience with criminal cases."

The mention of the words "criminal case" got his attention. "What do you mean? Are they blaming me? But they told me if I—" His voice faded to nothing.

"I don't know what happened to her, but I do know that the police think it's murder and they have arrested you."

He looked at me in disbelief. "No, no. Stanton and Detective Bliss talked, and they told me that if I cooperated and answered some questions, this would help clear the whole thing up for them and I could go to the hospital with Amanda. Bliss told me that you and he did not get along well and that if I had you as my lawyer, it would interfere with his investigation. He said he'd have to proceed on the information he had, which would include arresting me and bringing me down to the jail. I told Stanton I didn't hurt Amanda. So Stanton told me to go ahead and give him my witness statement, that it would help clear matters up. Didn't I do the right thing?"

I chose my words carefully. I feared Ted was right on the edge. "Well, Ted, it is not what I would have advised. You had your hands behind your back in handcuffs, which is not how they normally treat witnesses. I think they are going to be keeping you for awhile. Detective Bliss sounded like you gave him a handwritten statement, did you do that?"

Ted responded quickly. "Uh, uh, no. He talked to me for a long time and I told him everything I could think of. Then he got out a card and read me that stuff you hear on TV about right to a lawyer and anything you say can be used against you and things like that. I asked him why he was saying that to me. He said it's just a matter of routine, so I signed this sheet of paper saying I would talk to him and give him my witness statement, and he started his tape recorder. But when he was done and went to replay it, the tape had broken. He wanted me to write it out, but I had a hard time even signing my own name. My hands were shaking so bad. So he said he would write it out for me and I could sign it. So I did. He was very nice to me. And Stanton was there. Did I do something wrong?"

I sighed, I couldn't help it. "Well, Ted, it's hard to say right now. It's not what I suggested."

We both sat in silence like a couple of lost souls. I noticed a bobby pin on the floor by my feet. Left over from a prisoner, I assumed. I twisted it in my hands, thinking what a mess things were. It snapped and I looked over at Ted, who was staring fixedly at the broken pieces in my hands. "I know this is not the best time, but Ted, you have to make a decision. Who is your attorney, me or M. Stanton?"

"Can't I have both of you? Both work together?"

I considered the prospect, genuinely tried to think how it could work. There was no way. I figured I'd stick him with the him-or-me approach, and surely Ted would want a lawyer with a good reputation in criminal cases. "Afraid not, Ted. Mr. Browne and I do things much differently. Maybe you noticed, we don't cooperate well. It wouldn't work."

He seemed torn. He looked through the glass at Browne looking fresh from the pages of GQ. When he glanced back to me in my jeans and bomber jacket, he caught me removing the speck of toilet tissue I'd used to staunch the shaving nick from my recent jail makeover. He started to speak a couple of times, but no words came.

Finally, he said, "I'm sorry, Ken. If I have to choose, then it must be Stanton. I've known Stanton for twenty years. He's handled both my business and personal affairs. He's my friend. He's my neighbor. I trust him." I must have reacted because he added, "Not that I don't trust you. I called you. I'm not sure. Maybe I did call Stanton too. It seemed like it was taking you awhile to get there. M. Stanton gets along with the detective and you don't."

"See where his good relationship and advice have you sitting now, Ted?"

"Yes, yes. I know. But Stanton said it'll all be straightened out. I'm sure I'll be home in the morning."

"I hope so," I said, knowing there wasn't a snowball's chance.

Ted reached over and put his left hand on my knee, then pulled it back with a start when he noticed the dried blood on his fingers. He held both of his hands in front of him and stared at them. "Oh dear God, Ken. Amanda's gone. Who could've done such a thing?"

He shuddered and began to sob. Since he was everybody's number one suspect, including mine, I didn't respond. Rather I put my arm around his shoulder and tried to think of something to say that would help him. I drew a complete blank. So we sat like that until the dull thud of somebody knocking on the heavy glass door made me look up to see Bliss looking in at us. The lock clicked and he opened the door.

"Time's up, counselor. We've got the lab boys here who need samples from his clothes and hands. I want him printed and mugged before shift change. Let's go."

I stood and turned to offer my hand to Ted. He sat slumped, trembling slightly, and still trying to catch his breath between sobs. Instead of using my hand as an assist to rise, he shook it weakly and gasped. "I'm sorry, Ken. So sorry."

"Me too, Ted." I tried to withdraw my hand, but he hung on a minute, then let go.

Bliss stepped out of the cell doorway to let me pass and added just loud enough for me to hear as I walked by him: "Gee, I'm sorry too." I felt his massive hands on the nape of my neck and the sharp twinge as he squeezed my neck and then released so that I stumbled sideways. "Ooh, careful there, counselor, don't want you to hurt yourself."

"Fuck off, Bliss. You haven't heard the last of this."

Bliss straightened

"Why, you his lawyer?... No." He relaxed. "Then I expect we've seen the last of you. In fact, I've seen all of you I want to see." He turned to the control booth. "Johansen, unlock. Attorney Edwards' got no client, so he's got no business here. He'll be leaving."

I heard the buzzer and walked toward the door feeling utterly defeated. Before I reached the door Browne walked over, sticking out his hand, but not quite able to contain his glee at seeing me get the bum's rush. "Look, Ken, sorry about the confusion. No hard feelings."

I looked at him like Howard Hughes might've looked upon a handshaking leper, reached for the door instead of his hand, and walked out. What a debacle. Hired and fired on the biggest case of my career, and the sun hadn't come up yet.

I dragged myself over to my office and moped around, growling at Yvonne, the receptionist, and my secretary, Janice, for most of the day. But no surprise to me, I couldn't concentrate on anything. So I left around four in the afternoon. On the way out to the beach I stopped at the liquor store to pick up the Southern Comfort, my road service fee. So I ended the day where I'd started, with my neighbor, Billy Starkweather.

"This stuff tastes like shit," I told him as we sat around my living room with the fire dying in the fireplace, the clock heading toward midnight and the seal just off the second bottle. Max was stretched full length at my feet, snoring steadily as I idly stroked his flanks with my left foot.

"Yeah, but it's good shit," Billy responded as he leaned over to light the Marlboro dangling from my lips. "Damn good shit," he added, sitting back and taking a deep swallow.

6

Losing that case felt like getting dumped by the woman you loved. I'd had experience with that too. I was moody. I was distracted. What with having to quit smoking all over again, I was testy. I couldn't concentrate. In fact, I thought about the case as often as I thought about a cigarette.

Almost all criminals deny guilt. But Ted had seemed so shocked by his wife's death at the jail. Was it just the realization of his own brutality bursting from beneath the surface? Or had he been confronted with his wife's fatal injuries from the top of the stairs, a waking nightmare in which he was still trapped? His denial in the cell had the ring of truth to me. If he were innocent, who was guilty? And if he were innocent, or even if he weren't, and I could get him off, my future would be made. Oh, I'd won some cases, pulled a couple of bunnies out of the hat. But nothing that would register on the legal Richter scale like this one. I ached to have the feeling I'd had for the thirty-minute drive out to Ted's the morning of the murder, resurrected hope for my law school dreams of a valiant legal career.

This is the case defense attorneys dream about. The evidence is overwhelming. The media has convicted already. Every barstool pundit has called for the reinstitution of the death penalty in Michigan. A society murder occupies dinner table and water cooler conversation all over town. Even if you lose, the lawyer gets incredible free ink. You are supposed to lose anyway. And if you could pull it off—Oh, man, if you could pull it off. I had some ideas, things that were worth looking into, motions to make, angles to pursue that might give the defense a fighting chance. What was the story on the Latin lover? Where did Amanda's underclothes get changed? And why?

Just when I'd start to wrap my brain around things that could be done on the case, there would come the realization that I was on the outside looking in. It was depressing. I'd held the brass ring in my hand for just an instant. Then it slipped away. But it continued to haunt me. It glittered in the distance, out of reach, but never far out of mind.

I vowed not to think about the case and get back to the cases I did have. That was an impossible promise to keep. The drumbeat of media stories was inexorable. The media had a great story and they weren't letting go. Every day a new sensational headline or an old detail revisited.

Jealous Hubby Tees Off On Wife

"Country Clubber" Arraigned

Jealous Husband Caught Red Handed

Motive For Murder: Love Or Money?

Slain Angel Of Charity Laid To Rest

I couldn't stay away from the stories beneath the headlines. The murder weapon was, as Bliss had claimed on the phone, a sand wedge. In fact, it was a club recently banned by the PGA for non-compliance with the rules. The Solarz Super Wedge was a club I'd almost bought for myself. I'd seen guys at the club using them last season, pre-banning, to great effect. The club was a loft wedge that popped the ball high in the air and imparted terrific back spin, causing the ball to land and stop on a dime. It was great for hitting a chip shot over a bunker or green side trees. I guess all the ridges and grooves on the club face were what made it work so well on the course, and so poorly before the PGA's rules committee. There was a lot of griping in the locker room when the country club pro, Willie "Sonny" Raines, had the clubs removed from members' bags. He'd also included with the January dues statement a notice that anyone caught with the club during a tournament would be disqualified.

Even before evidence had been introduced at the preliminary exam, *The Lake Pointe Leader*, citing "reliable sources close to the investigation," ran a story under the headline:

Hubby Confesses

The story claimed police were in possession of a signed statement from Ted admitting guilt. That resolved any mystery as to what was on the legal pad Bliss had been waving.

A day or so later WJNT's pert reporter, Jennifer Caldwell, took her news crew out front of the yellow police tape that ran from entrance pillar to entrance pillar, blocking the drive to 1608 Bonnie Brae. Breathlessly she confided, "TV 20 has learned the police have obtained an admission from accused murderer Ted Armbruster that only months before his wife's brutal death, he increased the life insurance policy on Amanda from one hundred thousand to two million dollars. Our investigation reveals that Armbruster Industries was in dire financial straits and in danger of bankruptcy without an injection of cash. The company's cash needs are said to closely match the amount of the policy increase."

Jennifer turned and pointed up the drive to the house.

"Police theorize that Armbruster's finances were a house of cards about to collapse, thereby threatening his country club lifestyle. They speculate that the ugly violence which rocked the halls of this stately home in the early hours of April 28th was part of a plan to cash in on the policy. Our sources believe that only the prompt reaction of trained law enforcement officers short-circuited a cover-up or claim of an intruder, and thus prevented the accused from cashing a multi-million-dollar murder jackpot."

There was little doubt that the police officer leaking his theories was Bliss. Perhaps he thought riling up a good old-fashioned lynch mob would be a refreshing change from drawn-out court proceedings. Each television story slipped in footage of Ted in an orange jumpsuit being assisted from a patrol car and into the courthouse for his arraignment. The ten-second shot showed Ted with his hair blowing every which way in the wind and his arms in front of his face to shield the glare from the camera lights. He sure looked guilty to me, even after a jail shower had washed all the blood from his hands.

Then, because the appetite for the story was inexhaustible, all the media profiled the deceased as Lake Pointe's Mother Teresa. The clip from last year's United Way kick-off breakfast featured Amanda as co-chair exhorting volunteers to give their all for the less fortunate. They even found a photograph of Amanda with a tiny cerebral palsy victim on her lap. Two years earlier *The Leader*'s society page had caught Amanda looking particularly fetching in ball gown and tiara at the Dressler Foundation Charity Ball. It was that picture that accompanied every print story juxtaposed with a mug shot of Ted. In fact, the steady conversation around the beauty shops was how much Amanda resembled Princess Di.

"And they were both taken from us so violently and so young," commented one letter to the editor.

All in all, the prospects for Ted's getting a fair trial were slim. I took perverse pleasure in hearing that Browne's office phones were jammed with vilifying calls and his home number was now unlisted. His moneyed clients were undoubtedly hectoring him for being associated in such a sordid mess. Every cloud has a silver lining.

Until three weeks after the story broke, my name was never mentioned. Fine with me. Then Janice buzzed back to say that Art Honnecker, the *Leader*'s crime and courthouse reporter, was on the line. I wanted to dodge the call very badly. But Art and I had a symbiotic relationship. I fed him news about my cases, at least the ones I won. So he got something to fill his column. He spelled my name right and quoted me. I got free advertising. Good for everybody. I had to talk to him.

"Hey, Art. What's shaking?"

"Hey, Ken. Looks like you picked a good time to duck."

"Huh?"

"The Armbruster case. Listen, I have a source that says you were at Armbruster's the night of the murder. Care to comment?"

"Who is your source?"

"Can't tell you that. Can say that I'm told you were Armbruster's lawyer until you got there, and then you weren't. Browne took the case. The way things look, he did you a favor. Wondered if you had any comment."

"Geez, Art. Just like you can't disclose sources, a lawyer shouldn't disclose representation status. But since you already know, I will say I went in response to a call to be of assistance to Ted. By the time I got there, his neighbor Browne had the case."

"How'd that happen?"

"Beats me. I suggest you talk to M. Stanton Browne, Esquire, or Detective Bliss."

"I've talked to Browne's office. I talked to his secretary. After I gave her my name she said 'Just a minute please.' Ten minutes of classical music later, she came back on to tell me Mr. Browne was 'in conference' and too busy to talk to me. But I could quote him as having 'no comment' to any questions I might have."

He paused to chortle, then went on. "In today's story I quoted him exactly. Listen to this. 'When this reporter contacted Mr. Browne's office with a series of questions after Attorney Browne filed his appearance on behalf of the defendant to confirm representation, I was told "no comment." To the question of guilt or innocence of Mr. Armbruster, Browne's office replied, "no comment." Likewise on the question of what defense would be offered for the brutal killing, the response was "no comment." ' That'll teach him to be such a shit. He should do what you do, just pretend you're not there and have the secretary take a message."

"Hey, Art, I always treat you ink-stained wretches with utmost courtesy. Didn't I take this call?"

"Yeah, and you haven't told me anything."

"Okay. I'll give you something from the guy who isn't his lawyer. Ted Armbruster is innocent."

I could hear Art start to scribble. "Oh, really! Well, you might be the only guy in this town who thinks so. What's your basis for that proclamation of innocence?"

"He told me he didn't do it, and I believe him."

"That's it?"

"That's it."

"So why aren't you his lawyer?"

"Ask Mr. No Comment. Or your undisclosed source, Detective

Bliss. They know more about that than I do."

The conversation went on for another five minutes while I carefully stayed away from "no comment" and stuck to "I don't knows." Then, satisfied that he had gotten all he could out of me, Art rang off, saying, "I'm going to run your claim of innocence, you know."

"Figured you would."

And he did, under the headline:

Fired Lawyer Claims Armbruster Innocent

The story was embarrassing in that it spoke of "setting a new speed record for being hired and fired in a murder case." But at least it described me as "cracker-jack defense lawyer Kenneth Edwards, with a number of surprising acquittals under his belt." So maybe there is no such thing as bad publicity.

I got lots of questions from the courthouse crowd and lawyers at the luncheon round table over at Mr. C's. There were lots of chop-busting cracks on needing to improve my ambulance-chasing skills if I was letting other lawyers beat me to the scene. They also wanted to know how it felt letting M. Stanton steal my client, and whether I was going to go poach one of his medical partnership breakups to get even. I smiled and acted like it was no biggie.

But my fellow bone divers around the table knew I was hurting. Bone diver is a not-so-flattering term for a lawyer who dives for cases in the fashion of dogs diving for a bone that falls from the table. Take what you can get. Gotta pay the bills. Around the lunch table at Mr. C's we were all bone divers of one breed or another. The other mutts knew how much letting an AKC-certified pure blood like M. Stanton steal the meatiest bone I'd ever had my teeth around would rankle. And rankle it did.

I've always had to fight a strong tendency to introversion. I keep a running dialogue in my head and mostly keep my lips from moving. I'm comfortable in my own company and have holed up for entire weekends at the cottage with only Max to talk to with no problem. I've had to cultivate a gregarious side to build a practice and stand in front of juries as their informed but folksy friend, sort of a legal Paul Harvey ready to tell them the "rest of the story." Now the urge to climb into a deep hole and pull the lid over had to be fought daily. I was as close to depression as I had ever come.

As Memorial Day neared things gradually improved. I was going whole days hardly thinking about the case or little Miss Marlboro. Well, I'd have a pang or two, but I was doing better. I represented Gregory Zamnoff on a charge of carrying a concealed weapon in a motor vehicle. The jury must have found my closing argument more convincing than Greg did. While they were deliberating, he split. We took the not guilty with the defendant in absentia. He called me the next day from Toronto and returned to do ten days for contempt of court.

I picked up a good looking auto neg case where my lady had been coming home from volunteering at the old folks home when a well-insured drunk crossed the center line and whacked her. If only she didn't get too well too soon, that should put a few shillings in the coffers. And I got my respondent's brief in to the Court of Appeals one hour ahead of my final extended deadline by driving it to Lansing myself. I'd borrowed Billy's pick-up to make sure the Benz's quirkiness caused me no more grief. That case represented a twenty-thousand-dollar verdict we'd gotten for Gus Tackett when he took a dive in spilled pickle juice at a supermarket two years earlier. All in all, I was slowly getting back in the traces and pulling the plow.

In Michigan the preliminary examination is a probable cause hearing before a district judge to determine if the prosecution has a prima facie case on a felony charge. If the people can show the crime was committed, and that probable cause exists to believe the defendant committed it, the case is bound over to the higher circuit court for trial. Usually the defense offers no evidence. Lazy lawyers waive the prelim. However, I always made it a point to force the prosecutor to give me a sworn sneak peak at his case. Ted's prelim was scheduled in late May, after a couple of delays requested by Browne so he could attend his firm's retreat in the Bahamas. Way to go, M. Stanton, I thought. Go bask in the sun while your client rots in jail.

I wanted to go to the hearing just to satisfy my curiosity and see how much of what was in the papers matched the prosecution case. I also wanted to see how big a buffoon Browne would make of himself trying to handle a criminal case. But to make sure I didn't go, I bought a couple of tickets to a Tigers game and invited my fellow longsuffering Tiger buddy, Harry Gilfeather.

Harry did insurance defense in Saginaw. As my practice was in transition from criminal defense to plaintiff's personal injury, I'd been seeing more of Harry. What I saw I liked. He was courtly in appearance, always immaculately groomed and fashionably attired. He was a bulldog as an opponent, but friendly as a puppy when the whistle blew. Besides, we both followed the Detroit Tigers from a lifetime of devotion. We made it a point to keep the faith even after almost every other fan had long since given up. On the drive down he wondered why I wasn't at the prelim.

"How would that look, Harry?" I asked. "Judge Wilson had to borrow a bigger courtroom to handle the mob. They've got reporters from all over the state. And John Q. Public is lining up in droves to watch the circus. So do I want to be down there fighting for a seat and trying not to notice when people point and ask if that's the lawyer that got booted off the case before he ever got in it? No thank you. Plus I might lose it and duke it out with that arrogant ass, Browne."

"Not your favorite guy, I take it. Always quite cordial with me," Harry said, knowing it would get a rise out of me. And it did.

"Let me tell you something about M. Stanton, don't call me Stan." So I told Harry how I'd wrestled for a week after that night at the Armbrusters' with whether to call Browne about the change in underwear. Finally I decided it was my duty to call.

"So I call, give my name to the receptionist, and ask to speak to M. Stanton, as I have important information on the case. The bastard won't even take my call. The receptionist comes back on the line to inform me 'Mr Browne's quite busy at the moment. He has asked me to connect you to his associate, Miss Lori Teasdale.' "

"You're kidding."

"No kidding. Well, Miss Teasdale is one year out of Michigan Law and she's very prim and proper. Believe it or not, she was more affronted that I'd sneak a peak up a lady's dress then she was interested in where the evidence might lead. So I asked her if she has checked the autopsy to see if there was any semen or evidence of sexual contact. You know what she said?"

"Tell me."

"You mean the autopsy would have that information?"

"No shit?"

"No shit. That's the crack defense team in whose hands Ted's fate rests."

"I wouldn't feel too bad about that. The way I hear it, F. Lee Bailey couldn't do anything with that case. Anyway, what did the autopsy say?"

I shook my head. "Sweet Lori promised she'd call and let me know. Two weeks pass and nothing. Then I caught her over at the clerk's office. Funny as hell, we go to sit in the lobby and she makes a point of pulling her skirt over her knees. I laughed out loud. Anyway, no semen, no vaginal bruising or tearing. But there were a couple of bruises on the thighs. So what do you think of that?"

Harry laughed. "I think you are lucky Browne has the case and not you. It's a stone loser which is going down in spectacular flames."

As we pulled into a vacant lot off Woodward to walk down to Comerica Park, I shook my head quickly, as if weighing what he'd said. "Yeah, you're probably right. I just can't help thinking about it."

"C'mon, let's grab a couple of brewskis and you can think about the Tigers for a while. They're hopeless, but not as hopeless as that damn case."

But the Tigers gave the lie to that. They blew a two-run lead in the ninth to fall ten games under five hundred. And May wasn't over yet.

Lawyer Claims Confession Faked

The headline grabbed me like a bouncer grabbing a drunk. I stopped walking into Mr. C's for lunch and did an about face, fumbling in my pocket for a couple of quarters while standing in front of the *Leader*'s yellow vending box. Instead of joining the boys for lunch, I picked up a sandwich from the Subway and took the paper back to my office. I knew I'd sworn off the case, but this I had to see. Art Honnecker's story, which started on page one and continued for much of page four, made fascinating reading.

> A packed courtroom erupted in an uproar at the preliminary hearing for Ted Armbruster yesterday. Local industrialist Armbruster stands accused of first degree murder for the brutal slaying of his beautiful young wife, Amanda. Until yesterday the evidence against the accused seemed overwhelming. As reported in this newspaper and as presented in testimony before District Judge Edmond Wilson at the hearing, the defendant was found next to his wife's battered body by investigating officers. The pajama-clad Armbruster was covered in his wife's blood. His fingerprints were confirmed by a crime lab technician to match the bloody impressions on the murder weapon. The weapon, a golf club known as a Solarz Super Wedge, was found in the immediate

vicinity of the defendant and his deceased wife. The club was identified as belonging to the accused.

The court also heard what readers of this column already knew. Armbruster only recently had increased a life insurance policy on his wife from $100,000 to $2,000,000. Under examination by assistant prosecutor Tina Botham, the lead investigator, Sheriff Detective Raymond Bliss, offered a signed confession purportedly made by Armbruster within hours of the homicide. Bliss testified that Armbruster, with the advice and consent of his attorney, M. Stanton Browne of the fairly prominent local firm of Butler, Browne, Steele, and Thompson, admitted guilt for the grisly death.

I nearly choked on my sandwich in laughter admiring how Art had stuck the word "fairly" in front of the word "prominent" in describing Browne's firm in the course of skewering Browne for allowing his client to confess. That'd teach Browne to give a reporter the brush-off. Perhaps the arrogant SOB might learn not to get into a pissing match with someone who buys ink by the barrel. I chortled as I returned to the story.

It was on Browne's cross examination of the detective that pandemonium broke out amongst the spectators. In a surprising twist, Browne all but accused Detective Raymond Bliss of willfully altering Armbruster's confession. Browne swore as an officer of the court that his client had told Bliss he didn't kill his wife and that Bliss had mistakenly written the word "did" for the word "didn't." Bliss responded to Browne's attack by swearing he accurately quoted the defendant's admission to beating his wife to death with a golf club.

Before this shocking development the crowd had been murmuring over another curious tactic by the defense. Prior to asserting the confession had been erroneously transcribed, Browne attempted to suppress the statement in its entirety. As reported here a week ago, Lake Pointe's well known criminal defense attorney Kenneth Edwards had been called by Armbruster from the murder scene, the family's country club home on Bonnie Brae. On the stand Detective Bliss admitted Edwards had given him strict instructions not to talk to Armbruster. Yet before Edwards could reach the scene, Browne, who is Armbruster's neighbor, long-term friend, and attorney, appeared. According to Bliss's testimony, Armbruster identified Browne as his counsel on the matter. Before Edwards arrived, Browne and Armbruster conferred and agreed to give Bliss the statement he requested. In his motion Browne sought to have the confession quashed as being taken after Attorney Edwards told Bliss no statement was to be taken. Thus Browne claimed the statement violated the Fifth Amendment.

Judge Wilson couldn't quite conceal his disdain for the defense position when he ruled on the motion to suppress. "No offense, Mr. Browne, but I think your concern for protecting your client's right to silence comes a little late. Might have been a little more timely at the scene of the crime. Motion denied. The confession is admitted."

When that tactic failed, Browne switched to attacking the accuracy of the statement as written by Bliss. But Judge Wilson brushed those allegations aside as well and admitted Armbruster's statement. In doing so he pointed out that, not only had the accused signed the document, but that Browne had initialed it. Courthouse veterans allowed that they'd "never seen anything like it."

Another interesting fact came to light concerning the confession, which observers speculate might give the defense some "wiggle room." The confession was handwritten by Bliss, signed by Armbruster, and initialed by Browne. Thus, it is not in the defendant's own hand. Bliss testified that Mr. Armbruster was in an "extremely nervous" condition so close in time to his wife's death, his hands shaking so badly he couldn't hold a pen. According to Bliss, he'd taped the statement as it was given. But on attempting to replay the tape, he discovered that the tape had broken. So he summarized Armbruster's admissions and submitted them for review and signature.

At the conclusion of the hearing one matronly spectator described it as "way better than TV." Judge Wilson bound the defendant over to circuit court. He will be arraigned June 5th on a charge of first degree murder.

I read the story several times. A number of thoughts raced through my head. Now at long last I grasped why at the scene and jail Bliss had been unconcerned about my threats to suppress the confession. Secondly, I understood why Ted had ignored my instructions to keep silent. He must have told Browne he was innocent. As out of his depth as Browne had been, he never would have let Ted talk to Bliss unless Ted had told Browne he didn't do it. And best of all, it was obvious that Ted would soon be needing new counsel. Once Browne was on record as attacking the accuracy of the confession, he had become a witness. He could no longer serve as Ted's lawyer.

It was hard to contain my excitement over the prospect that the case might yet be mine. I fought the urge to go visit Ted at the jail. After all, I'd been canned once on the case. I didn't need to be rejected twice. I thought of calling Art to see if Browne had given any hint at the hearing that he realized he'd have to get out. Plus, I could compliment him on sticking it to Browne yet again. But I decided I'd look too much like a vulture circling a wounded beast waiting for it to die. The idea crossed my mind to call Ted's mom to see how she was holding up. However, since I hadn't checked in before now, my motives would be pretty obvious. I'd just have to sit tight and let things take their course.

The sitting and waiting proved nerve-wracking. Days passed. No word. A week later Browne appeared at the arraignment entering a plea of not guilty for Ted. The paper quoted him as asking for extended scheduling as "a possibility of a change of representation" existed. A few days later, while over at the jail to meet with a burglary client who'd been caught coming out of an upstairs window with his hands full, the turnkey gave me unsettling news.

"Man, it's been Who's Who in criminal law over here. We've had three big names up from Detroit: D.D. James, Big Jack McCarthy and some black lawyer whose name I can't remember, but who arrived in a chauffeur-driven Rolls Royce. All here to see your old client, Ted Armbruster. And I hear there's another hot shot from Chicago coming this afternoon. Man, those guys have got to cost big time. You don't pay for a Rolls taking criminal appointments."

I wandered back to the office after convincing my burglary client to take a plea to attempted, feeling pretty down. I'd started to get over losing the case. Then the news out of the prelim had rekindled my hopes. Now I was right back on the outside looking in. I picked up my messages from Yvonne and barely returned her cheery greeting. Bet she thinks I'm pretty moody lately, I thought as I wandered down the hall and closed the door to my office.

My office occupied part of the second floor of what many years ago had been Lake Pointe's finest men's department store. The growth of the suburbs and the rise of malls had spelled the end for Damon's long before the advent of online shopping. The building had sat like a sightless dowager in the heart of Lake Pointe for at least ten years. Then the Damon family all died off and the estate, wanting to close up affairs, sold it for a song. I was the guy who whistled up the money to buy it. Then I went whistling to the bank to borrow money to remodel. A year and a half later and at twice my original loan amount, the place looked good. The original oak floors had been restored to their natural luster. The façade on Lafayette Avenue harkened back to the building's glory years. All the grime had been blasted from the brick, and the original stone cutting announcing Damon's, Established 1923, was visible in the cornerstone at street level.

The Subway sandwich shop on the ground floor was steady with the rent, and the smell of fresh bread baking gave the whole building a pleasant aroma. My tenant who shared the second floor, Thomas Thalberg, a.k.a. "Teutonic Tom," was a lawyer with a busy divorce practice. He matched his timely rent payments with a steady stream of tenant complaints. The elevator buttons stick. The drinking fountain leaks. The air conditioning is noisy. The janitorial service stinks. The handrail on the steps is loose. Finally, I wised up and cut his rent by twenty-five percent and made him the building supervisor. A court reporting firm rented half the third floor and I was getting nibbles for the other half. If everything held together, I'd have the place paid off in fifteen years.

My own office was perfect. I'd had the carpenter leave off the doors that were supposed to cover the wooden file drawers he'd built all along the north wall. For a while I filled them with dummy binders to look busy. Now they were reasonably full of paying cases. The interior decorator chose some expensive bamboo grass wallpaper and designed a built-in settee that straddled the southwest corner. Behind it she'd created a little fern garden that had flourished once I turned the watering responsibilities over to my secretary, Janice. The walls were decorated with original oil paintings I had collected on visits to Jamaica over the years.

So with the wood on the floor and cabinets, the wallpaper, the paintings, and lots of plants, the place had a nice, natural feel. Add in the aroma from downstairs, and the place seemed to put prospective clients in the mood to retain me. I sat there thinking, If only I could get Ted over in front of my desk, I could probably land that fish too. But with the audition for high-priced talent going on at the jail, I guessed I'd be better off concentrating on the cases I had instead of the one I used to have. So I picked up the message slips from the desk and started dialing.

One benefit of not having Ted's case was that I had time for golf. With May racing toward June, the weather was becoming more reliably pleasant. In fact, once Michigan gets winter out of its system, it can be quite delightful. With daylight savings time and the approach of the summer solstice, the sun hung around until after nine p.m. So for the last few weeks I had been knocking off at four and heading for the club.

My membership to Lake Pointe Golf and Country Club was a conflict for me. I fashioned myself a champion of the underdog. But at the club I was hanging with the overdogs. My practice was gradually in transition from a high concentration of criminal defense to more time in civil plaintiffs work. The personal injury work paid better. The clientele was less seedy. And since the cases were all retained on a contingent fee, my compensation was in direct proportion to how well I performed for the client. Happy client, happy lawyer. Sad client, lawyer gets one third of nothing, which makes for sad lawyer.

The personal injury work had started with a sprinkling of auto negligence cases. Gradually I was picking up the occasional medical malpractice and a few premises liability cases, slip and falls and such. The club had quite a few docs, businessmen, and land barons. Since other lawyers didn't want to lose their cocktail party invitations and malpractice cases required so much work, none of the local competition would touch them. But sending them over to me for the referral fee and the promise I wouldn't mention their names was becoming increasingly common. If a person wondered why he couldn't get a Wednesday afternoon appointment with his MD during the summer, he need look no further than the club's luxury-car-filled lot. I was definitely becoming the fox in the chicken coop. As you might expect, the chickens weren't all that cordial to Brer Fox.

My bank statement was a midget among giants out there. The monthly dues steadily increased, and there were always special assessments and fees. Range fees, arbor fund, debt retirement, meal minimum, caddy scholarship, shoe shine, all found their way onto the monthly billing. I could afford it, but not without blinking. So each winter when the snow was on the ground and the monthly kept coming, I thought of dropping. But it was such a great place to indulge my addiction for the game. The course was immaculately maintained. The greens were lightning. The practice facilities were first class. And best of all, save early Saturday mornings, you could just show up and play, no tee time required. So I could tolerate the occasional cold shoulder from the members I was suing. I understood their feelings. I wasn't being invited to the cocktail parties anyway.

Thus on Thursday, June 15th, as the clock on my desk ticked to four, I put the file I'd been working back in the drawer, turned out the light and headed for the front to make my escape. "Last-minute appointment with Mr. Green, Yvonne," I said as I breezed past her desk to the door.

"Oh, sorry, boss, but you're going to have to cancel that one. Mrs. Armbruster called not ten minutes ago. She asked me if I would squeeze her in. She should be here right away. She said she was just leaving the jail from visiting her son. I hope that's okay?"

"That's definitely okay, Yvonne."

"What about Mr. Green? Should I call to reschedule?"

"No, Yvonne. I was sneaking out to the golf course."

"Oh, that Mr. Green."

Marjorie Armbruster was a robust, refined matron. At seventy-eight she was big-haired and well fleshed out. She moved slowly but erectly. Her gray hair was surprisingly full and well coiffed around a face lightly browned from her devotion to gardening. She entered wearing a brown two-piece suit with jacket and skirt and lightly frilled ecru blouse.

"Look who's here," beamed Yvonne as she got up from behind her desk and moved to the front counter to greet Mrs. Armbruster. "Boy, we've missed you. How is your puppy, Winston?"

Yvonne was a jewel. Her mother worked part time at the florist's two doors down, so the vase on her desk always contained sprigs and blooms slightly past their prime. If she had a mean bone in her body, it must have been hidden in her little toe. She loved people and loved to chat them up. She remembered family or personal details, and she had a ready smile that crinkled her eyes and engaged her entire face. Many a client would stop by long after their case was concluded just to say hello to her, show family pictures, or simply bask a few minutes in the warmth of her friendliness. If the entire human race had her disposition, war would be a thing of the past, and lawyers would have little to do. Mrs. Armbruster reached into her bag and pulled out a purse to show Yvonne a picture.

"Oh, is that Winston? What a cute puppy."

"He's not a puppy anymore. Look how big."

"Wow, he is big. Look at all the flowers behind him. Are those zinnias?"

"Yes, I've had great luck with them."

I walked up to the counter next to Yvonne and smiled, seeing the juxtaposition of a jowly bulldog surrounded by flowers. Winston looked like he'd be much happier romping and digging amongst the flowers instead of posing with a purple ribbon on his neck.

"What a pleasant surprise, Mrs. Armbruster." I smiled. "How are you?"

Mrs. Armbruster gave me a stern look. "Kenneth, I thought we'd agreed. Please call me Marjorie."

"Yes, ma'am. Nice to see you, Marjorie. May I offer you coffee, a soft drink or some ice water?"

"A nice cup of tea would be delightful, please."

"Sorry, I'm not too sure we have tea."

Yvonne broke in, "Oh, Mr. Edwards, of course we have tea, just for clients like Mrs. Armbruster. One cup of Earl Gray coming right up. A spoonful of sugar and no cream, if I remember right."

Marjorie beamed. "Yvonne, you're a treasure. Ken, are you sure you are paying her enough?"

"Quite generously. Right, Yvonne?"

"Well, Mr. Edwards..." A pause to consider and a mock reproachful glance for me. "Oh, yes, Mr. Edwards, quite generously."

I followed Marjorie down the maroon carpeted hall past the kitchenette toward my office. She still had a decided limp on her right side, a lifetime reminder of her urologist's misguided application of the bone hammer. I settled into my chair and watched as Marjorie skeptically eyed the modernistic chairs. "Perhaps you'd find the couch more comfortable." She nodded and brushed a frond aside as she sat. After a few minutes chatting about her hip, health, and well-being, she squared herself to me on the couch and leaned forward.

"Ken, I guess you know why I am here."

"I'm not sure I do."

"Ted needs your help. Desperately. They are going to execute him for a crime he didn't commit."

"Marjorie, we don't have capital punishment in Michigan."

She thought for a moment. "Might as well. Prison will kill him in no time."

I nodded. "Why do you say 'a crime he didn't commit'? What do you know that I don't?"

She leaned further forward, put her hands on the comer of my desk and brought her brown eyes directly to bear on me. "He told me didn't."

"Yes. He told me that too."

"Then why are you just sitting there? Why aren't you helping Ted?"

"He has a lawyer. He hired M. Stanton Browne."

"He told me that he asked you to assist M. Stanton."

"Never work. I told him that. Then he chose M. Stanton."

"Are you going to let your pride stop you from helping Ted?" She looked and sounded like my 11th grade literature instructor, scolding me for sloppy work. I sat back in the chair and glanced out the window at the traffic on Lafayette, considering a response. I put my elbows on the desk too and looked back into her eyes.

"Marjorie, pride has something to do with it, I'm sure. But I am not built to work with co-counsel, even if I'm lead counsel. I am definitely not built to sit second chair to M. Stanton. We are very different. Frankly, I don't like him, and he looks down his patrician nose at me. We'd spend more time fighting a turf war than helping Ted. I'm sorry. I just don't work that way. I won't do it."

She held my gaze a few seconds, then she nodded. "I expected you'd say something like that. What do you think of M. Stanton's handling of the case so far?"

The words "piss-poor" came to mind. Instead I replied, "I make it a policy not to comment on another lawyer's work."

She smiled. "Very diplomatic. I'll take that to mean lousy. If so, I agree."

I held my hands up. "Hold on a second. I did not say lousy."

"But you were thinking it." I shrugged my shoulders and she continued. "My husband Marvin used old Whitley Butler for both his business and personal legal affairs. M. Stanton was his junior associate. When Whitley passed on, M. Stanton took his place. Marvin thought M. Stanton a bright young man. Stanton and Ted were friends growing up. He was sharp, but a little too sharp for my taste. On my hip case, he was put out that I came to you. He called to say he had a chap he referred cases to who had much more experience than you. When I told him I was quite happy where I was, he was rude."

"Rude. How?"

"Oh, once he saw there wasn't a chance he could make a buck off me, his exact words were: 'It's your decision. I respect your decision even if it's a mistake.' "

I shook my head in disbelief. "Did he happen to mention that Dr. Hogart was his client for personal and professional affairs?"

The surprise was obvious on Marjorie's face. "No, he certainly did not. Although he did say he couldn't handle it himself and would refer it to a highly qualified colleague who specialized in malpractice."

I laughed. "I'll bet he didn't tell the good doctor either that he was out angling for a referral fee for steering a case against his own client."

Marjorie reddened. "Why, that rascal. Isn't that unethical?"

"If it isn't, it should be."

Marjorie leaned forward on the couch and spoke in a conspiratorial whisper. "Ted asked me not to mention this. He knows I'm here, by the way. He's been meeting with some lawyers over at the jail. After that fracas in front of Judge Wilson at the pretrial—"

I interrupted, "Preliminary hearing."

"Whatever. After that, M. Stanton said he couldn't keep the case much longer, as he would perhaps need to appear as a witness about the statement Ted gave that awful detective. He was staying on long enough to explore plea negotiations with the prosecutor. He said he and Bliss got on well enough and Miss Botham might be a candidate at his firm one day. So we waited. I thought he'd come back and say the whole thing would be dismissed after he pointed out to them that the detective transcribed the statement in error."

I didn't have the heart to tell her that she was dreaming. So I just asked, "How did his discussions work out?"

She sat straight up. "He wanted Ted to plead guilty to second-degree murder. Said they would cap his sentence at twenty years. Can you believe that?"

Actually I was surprised the prosecutor would offer such a good deal. So I answered truthfully, "No, I can't believe it."

"My Ted would be over seventy-five years old before he got out, if he lived that long, which he wouldn't."

"So Ted told him no?"

"Ted told him he wanted to consult with other attorneys. M. Stanton had some kind of list of the best criminal lawyers. I called a bunch of them. Most wouldn't come, but the ones who did come were not the answer. Two of them thought he should take the deal. The other two wanted an incredible sum of money just to get started. After what we had already paid M. Stanton, I couldn't afford it. Just simply can't. And if I could, I'm not sure I would. Those fellows are so full of themselves, what my Marvin,

God rest his soul, used to call 'city slickers.' I think a jury from these parts would see through them right away. So here I am."

I shrugged off the slight of being the lawyer of last resort and squelched my temptation to ask what the big guns wanted as a retainer. But I did need to know what M. Stanton had socked them. "How much has been paid to Mr. Browne?"

"Ted paid him $20,000."

Less than I thought he'd sting them. "That was a one-time retainer for the whole case?"

"Oh, I don't know about that. Ted paid him the twenty and I cashed some bonds for the other eighty."

That sounded more like the M. Stanton Browne I knew and loathed.

"One hundred thousand?"

She nodded and went on. "And with what those out-of-town sharpies are asking, we don't have it. You know Ted's business is in trouble and I just don't have that much money, but whatever I have left, you can have it. Will you take his case?"

"Money is not the issue, Marjorie. But Ted is the one who should be asking."

She shook her head in frustration. "Ted wants you. That's why he called you that awful night. Then M. Stanton told him he could handle it and to leave you out of it. And Ted thinks you are really mad at him because of his letting M. Stanton take over. Are you?"

I thought it best not to tell her the agony I'd been through. So I just waved my hand as if it were a mere bagatelle hardly worth mentioning. Instead I concentrated on the operative words. "Ted has sent you to ask if I'll take his case?"

She looked at me as if I were a little slow. "Why else would I be here? I just need to know how much," she said, pulling a checkbook from her purse.

I held my hands up in a stop sign. "Put that away, Marjorie. First I'll need to meet with Ted and see if we are good to go. If so, I have an idea how we can get Mr. Browne to make any further cash outlay unnecessary. How would that be?"

"Oh, you are such a clever lad. I tell everybody that."

She stood up and I stood to escort her to the door. Before I reached for the handle, I had something I needed to ask. "Marjorie, a minute ago you said hang for a crime he didn't commit. Besides Ted telling you he didn't do it, how do you know he didn't?"

Marjorie looked me straight on. "I know my son. He's not capable of murdering anyone. He loved Amanda more than life itself. In spite of the troubles in their relationship, he would never hurt her."

"Troubles?"

"Well, she was much younger. After his operation I don't think Ted was quite the same."

"Operation?"

"Prostate surgery. I don't know the details, but, well, I think he was limited. I believe he had tried Viagra with at best mixed results. I had heard stories that Amanda was active outside the marriage."

"Oh. That's not too helpful. Jealousy is a powerful motive."

Marjorie's eyes bored into me. "I understand that. But not in Ted's case. He wouldn't hear gossip or rumors or anything bad about Amanda. I think maybe he knew on some level and understood. All I know is he adored her. She was the love of his life and his best friend. He wouldn't hurt her. I know that."

"I'm sure you've read that he confessed to Detective Bliss with M. Stanton Browne standing right there. And yet you still believe he didn't do it?"

She looked at the floor, briefly gathered herself, and looked back up at me.

"I know all the horrible things they are saying about my son. I'm his mother. I asked him if he hurt her. He told me no. I believe him."

At least I had one witness for the defense. "Okay, Marjorie. I'll go talk to Ted. I'm not saying I'll take the case, but I'll talk to him. It's late in the case. It's always dangerous to switch horses midstream. I need Ted to understand that. I'll call you tomorrow and let you know. Okay?"

"Not okay. Call me tonight, so I can get some sleep."

"All right, I'll call tonight."

Bliss stood in the jail parking lot next to his plain brown Chevy and a yellow Corvette, so new it still had dealer tags on it. He and two deputies were swapping stories and laughing in the last light of a warm beginning-of-summer evening. As I approached, I could hear the bray of Bliss's laughter before I rounded the comer of the building. My adrenaline surged as I prepared to see him for the first time since Amanda's death. On rounding the building I had a mental picture of Bliss as a shark and the deputies as pilot fish, hanging to feed on his leavings. The deputies, Doyle and Meeks, worked the graveyard shift and were the scourge of drunk drivers. Their high arrest totals of bar patrons were a steady source of income for the criminal defense bar.

Bliss held his sport coat draped over his shoulder by one finger. His blue shirt was only partially tucked in. His gut hung over the belt. Somehow, he'd managed to stick his left hand between the waistband and his belly. The circle of sweat under his armpit extended below where his shoulder holster lay against his ribs. His tie was loose and askew over his shoulder, where the breeze had left it. He whispered something to his brown-uniformed cronies that must have been a real knee-slapper. I suspected I was the subject of their mirth. As I approached, I watched his lips curl in a sneer, displaying nicotine-yellow teeth in a feral smile. As he was standing right next to the entrance sidewalk, I had no choice but to pass by him. He stepped toward me, the corners of his eyes wrinkled in mirth, and extended his hand in greeting.

"Good to see you, counselor, been awhile. Check out Meeks' new wheels."

I could see no alternative but to reach my hand out, as to refuse a handshake, even with the devil, was bad manners. My parents had been relentless on the subject of manners. I felt my hand being enveloped in his massive paw. Even though I'd been schooled in the importance of a firm handshake and looking the other person straight in the eye, nothing prepared me for the vise-like squeeze he was applying. Still, I kept the wince to a minimum and my voice from cracking as I lied through my teeth.

"Nice to see you too, detective. Nice car."

Bliss turned so the deputies could hear him and in so doing pulled me forward. "Rather than you standing outside our door waiting for clients, why don't you just give me a few of your cards? I'll see if I can hustle up some business for you. Things are a little slow, I'll bet, since the Armbruster retainer slipped through your fingers."

The aroma of sweat, stale coffee and cigarettes nearly gagged me. The deputies chortled along with Bliss. By effort of will I kept my tone even. "Thanks for the offer. But not necessary. Business is looking up. Working on something that should keep me real busy."

His smile faded a little and the grip slackened enough for me to retrieve my aching right hand. I resisted the urge to wipe it on my trouser leg. "What, you finally managed to catch an ambulance?" His smile was a veneer over the cauldron of animus, seething just below the surface.

"Nah, just another wrongly accused wretch in need of justice," I said as I walked around the unmoving Bliss and pushed the jail entry buzzer.

"Anybody I know?" he asked.

The door buzzed. I grabbed the handle and stepped in. Then I looked back, pausing as if I was considering his question.

"Perhaps," I answered and let the door close behind me.

Ted hugged me like a drowning man hanging on to a life preserver. "Thanks for coming. Thank you so much. I didn't think you would. After

I got you out of bed and then chose M. Stanton, I thought you'd be too angry with me."

"Not an easy night for you, Ted. You did what you felt was best at the time."

"And before you say I should've listened to your advice and kept my mouth shut, I know you were right about that now. For all the good it'll ever do me."

"Wasn't gonna mention it. Spilt milk now."

I extracted myself from his embrace and we walked through the wood and glass door to the jail's attorney conference room. I sat in the old secretary's swivel chair, reminding myself not to lean on the broken back. Ted pulled up a wooden-back chair with faded floral upholstery. We sat kitty-corner around a table engraved with the initials of various guests. From where I sat I could look through the door glass across the hall and see the turnkeys gathered, talking and pointing in our direction. My visit must have been a news blip on a dull day. I watched as Christine, the senior matron in charge, picked up the phone and began to talk animatedly. When she saw me watching she swiveled her chair so I could no longer see her face. No doubt Bliss would soon know the purpose of my visit. I turned my attention back to Ted. His physical condition had deteriorated significantly since I had last seen him in the intake holding cell the morning of Amanda's death. His formerly salt-and-pepper hair was, in less than six weeks, mostly gray. Where once it had been immaculately groomed, it now was long, shaggy and unruly. His face sagged under the weight of the bags beneath his eyes. His color was pasty. The orange jumpsuit sagged on him.

Nonetheless I asked, "How are you feeling, Ted?"

He smiled, the teeth still pearly white. "Better, better now that you are here. Can you help me? Will you help me?" His voice quavered.

"That's what we're here to talk about. I'm afraid my answer about working with M. Stanton is still no."

He nodded. "Mother told me you'd say that. I'm a little disappointed in M. Stanton. Nothing he has told me would happen has happened. I'm still in jail. My case is set for trial for first degree murder. The newspapers are sure I killed her. M. Stanton doesn't come to see me. He sends his associate, Lori Teasdale. I don't think she likes the jail much. She gets pretty nervous and has a hard time answering my questions."

I thought of Lori covering her knees. If I made her squeamish, then visits to the jail to meet a man accused of bludgeoning his wife to death probably rocked her to the core. This was duty they probably didn't mention in the job interview at Butler-Browne. If I were accused of murder, she wouldn't be my first choice. I exhaled a small breath of disgust. Just like M. Stanton. He wouldn't like getting the grit of criminal defense underneath his fingernails. The dingy, confined space of the attorney-client conference room in which we sat was nothing like a corporate boardroom or executive office.

"You haven't seen M. Stanton at all?"

Ted shook his head. "Not much. Over at the courthouse those three times. He really fought on that confession issue. The deputies would hustle me back after each hearing and he promised he'd come here. But it was always Lori. Then after the arraignment, he was trying to work things out with the prosecutor. He came here a week ago to tell me about the plea deal. Here, I wrote it down."

Ted reached in the pocket of the orange inmate jumpsuit and handed me a crumpled scrap of paper. "Plead no contest to murder two. Minimum ten years—maximum twenty."

I examined it. "What did you tell him?"

"I told him I couldn't plead guilty because I didn't do it. He said that's why he bargained for no contest. What's the difference between guilty and no contest, Ken?"

"In your case, Ted, not much. You'd go to prison for at least ten years. If you're convicted of first-degree murder you'd go for life. Do you think you'd survive ten years in the penitentiary?"

Ted shrank inside the baggy jail uniform "I'm not sure I can survive another ten weeks till the trial in here. Everybody treats me well, but I just don't have much appetite and I can't sleep. I keep thinking this is a nightmare and I'll wake up soon. But it's real. All of it is real. Can you get me out of here?"

The desperation in his voice was obvious. I hated to give him more bad news. "Honestly, Ted, no. You will have to remain here until the trial. The bond issue is resolved. And even if I take the case, I can't promise you that you'll ever get out. From what I read and hear, the prosecution has a strong case. A very strong case."

"You mean it's hopeless. I'm going to prison for something I didn't do."

I chose my words carefully, as I didn't want to push Ted any closer to the edge of total despair. "Well, Ted, Bliss claims you confessed with your lawyer standing right there. How are we going to explain that?"

His face constricted in concentration. He shook his head as if the right answer was nowhere to be found. "I'm not sure exactly what happened. I told M. Stanton I hadn't done it. He told me that it might be wise to remain silent, unless I was sure I had done nothing wrong. I hadn't, and if I didn't talk to Bliss, Stanton said he'd have to take me down to the station. And you weren't there yet. By the time you got there I had already said it was my fault."

"I'm sorry I was late, Ted. The damned car wouldn't start. By the time I'd gotten a jump it was too late. But why did you admit killing her if you didn't? I don't understand that."

Ted wrung his hands together and contorted his face as he thought back. He spoke slowly. "I'm not sure of what I said exactly. I know I wouldn't have said I killed her. I've seen the statement. I did say her death was all my fault."

"Your fault? How?"

"I was a mess. After I called the police I just sat there next to Amanda. I remember feeling like it was all just a dream and I'd wake at any minute. But it wasn't."

He lost his composure and tears ran.

"All I could think was if I hadn't left her with that stranger at Heather Hollows, if I hadn't drank so much, if I hadn't lost my temper, none of this would have happened. When I said it was my fault, that's what I meant. I think, I'm not sure, but I think I did tell them what I meant. But with the tape recorder not working, maybe Bliss didn't write that part down. Really, the next thing I remember is sitting with you in jail, you leaving and M. Stanton telling me everything would be all right."

His voice trailed off at the end.

"Did you ask M. Stanton if he heard you try to explain?"

"Yes, yes I did. But he said he was so shocked when I said it was my fault, and he was telling me to be quiet and asking Bliss to stop the interview so he could talk to me, and Bliss was talking and I was trying to talk. He didn't hear what I was trying to say. What a mess!"

This sounded better already. I much preferred a client who maintained his innocence than one who felt confession was good for the soul. I put my hands on Ted's shoulders. "So are you telling me you didn't kill her?"

"I did not." He looked unblinkingly back into my eyes.

"Do you know who killed her?"

"Probably the Italian guy. He was the last guy with her. I told Stanton about him, but he said it was a dead end. The guy dropped her at home and left."

An image of the foyer from the night of Amanda's death floated into my head.

"Ted, what were you doing with that banned sand wedge and those other golf bags in your foyer?"

He shrank as that horrible morning came back to him. "Every year a bunch of guys from the club go up north the first nice weekend of spring. This year we were going to stay at Garland. You know it?"

"Yep. Played it. Nice resort. Who was going?"

"About sixteen guys. I was driving our foursome, my member-member partner, Randy Dykes, as well as Jim Simpson and Stanton."

"I only remember three bags in the hall."

He was about to disagree when the answer came to him.

"That's right. Stanton was in Chicago or someplace and was flying back late. Randy, Jim, and I played at the club that afternoon. Remember, I saw you there?" I nodded. "Anyway, I was driving to Garland. So when we finished playing, we loaded our clubs in Randy's Explorer. Jim and I were going to play some gin, and Randy dropped them off at the house.

We checked the bag room and Stanton's bag wasn't at the club, so they must've been in his trunk or garage. He's right next door, so it wouldn't slow us down in the morning."

"What about the sand wedge? Who had one?"

"All of us used to have them. Until they got banned last year, everybody played them. The pro said if he caught anybody playing them at the club he'd drop that person's handicap five strokes. Randy could perform magic with that club, and when I called him he asked to waive the rule for our little junket. Randy and Jim had theirs in their lockers and stuffed them in their bags when we were loading up. Mine was in the garage, and if I hadn't seen the clubs standing in the hall when I came downstairs before going to dinner, I would have forgotten it. Amanda waited in the car while I ran it in. I just leaned it against the bags."

"What about Stanton? He still have the club?"

Ted rested his chin on his hand in concentration. "I don't know. They got banned last year and we've hardy played this year. I'm not sure what he did with his."

I considered this for a minute. My thoughts were interrupted by a pounding on the door. The ruby color of Bliss's face documented a blood pressure problem and obvious displeasure. He yanked the door open and stood towering over Ted and me. "What the hell are you doing with Mr. Armbruster? He's not your client. Does Mr. Browne know you are interfering with his client?"

I make a quick decision as I leapt to my feet. "Mr. Browne's ex-client. Mr. Armbruster has retained me and is discharging Mr. Browne. So I'm asking you to get your intimidating, unwashed and overweight form out of here. This is an attorney-client meeting and you're way out of line."

Bliss was torn with indecision. Should he throw me against the file cabinet now, or wait for a better opportunity later? The faces gathered at the control center glass may have convinced him he couldn't damage control that many witnesses. With obvious effort he reigned himself in, lowered his tone and spoke evenly to Ted. "Mr. Armbruster, is Mr. Edwards your lawyer?"

Ted looked back up at Bliss and smiled. "Yes, sir. Thank God he is."

Bliss glared over at me so we were standing eyeball to eyeball. I could see the wheels turning. "I wouldn't be so quick to thank the Lord for your deliverance, Armbruster. We've got you trussed up like a Thanksgiving turkey. You're going down for the count for the murder of your wife. Even this so-called legal Houdini you've got here can't get you out of this box. Against my better judgment, I told the prosecutor okay on her little deal that would have spared you the rest of your natural life behind bars. I only did that because I promised Mr. Browne if you cooperated I'd go to bat for you. Now all bets are off. You can fry in Hell for what you did." He paused, caught his breath, and looked over at me. "As for you, hotshot, we're not finished." He looked at his watch. "Attorney visiting hours ended twenty minutes ago. You get no special treatment. You've got two minutes to hold your client's hand and then I want your ass out of here. Got it?"

I managed to say "Nice seeing you too" before he slammed the door in my face. I hardly had enough time to sit down and take a breath before I could see two turnkeys standing at the door looking sheepish and pointing at their watches. I told Ted I'd call Browne and give him the news and that I'd be back to see him as soon as I had a chance to read through the file. As I got up to leave, Ted reached out to shake my hand, gripping my right elbow with his left hand. He looked remarkably calm considering the tension in the room seconds before. When he spoke, his voice had much more timbre. "I wasn't going to take that deal anyway. I didn't kill her. You'll prove that for me, won't you?" he asked as if it would be a piece of cake.

"I'll try, Ted. I'm sure going to try."

With that the deputies escorted me to the elevator and out of the building. As I walked back to the office I found myself whistling the old Dinah Washington standard "What a Difference a Day Makes."

10

I should have expected no better from M. Stanton. I showed up on time at one at the offices of Butler, Browne, Steele, and Thompson. The firm's offices perched atop the Whittaker building with a commanding view of the shoreline. When the elevator door opens to the penthouse, you know you have entered the rarified atmosphere occupied by only the finest legal eagles. "B&B" was artfully and deeply engraved into the platinum name plates on both sides of the massive mahogany entrance doors.

In my briefcase I had the substitution of counsel form signed by Ted and myself, needing only Browne's signature. At 1:35 Browne breezed in from lunch with a couple of his junior associates. I didn't even have time to get off the couch to shake hands before he breezed down the hall, tossing over his shoulder, "Be right with you, Ken. I've got a couple of calls that are urgent, including one from Mother Nature. Just be a minute."

Now it was 1:55 and I had an appointment of my own back at the office. An hour was plenty of time to steep in the refined splendor of the law office of Butler-Browne. I had time to read the brochures describing with pictures and text that this was no ordinary law firm. "At B&B we are not just attorneys, but counselors at law." And I had left "counselor at law" off my yellow pages ad to save a few bucks. "We recruit our associates only from the top of the class at the nation's finest law schools." No poor Wayne State night-school riff-raff like me allowed. "We counsel our select clients in every aspect of business, corporate, estate, and personal planning." Must be nice to have only "select" clients. I expected that to qualify as "select," a client need only be able to pay the $300 an hour fee required. At $75 an hour, I was obviously a legal K-mart compared to this top-of-the-line Tiffany's.

The receptionist was dressed and coiffed as if for a formal dinner. She sat behind a mahogany counter-desk. The ringing of the office phone was so muted as to be barely audible. She spoke in quiet and precise tones. She apologized for Browne's tardiness, saying he'd been besieged with calls. To make up for the wait she offered me tea. "We have oolong, chai, and mandarin dream to choose from."

I declined and noticed her looking askance at my shoes. The antique furniture was much better polished than they were. The massive coffee table had the latest *Fortune* and *Time* magazines mixed in with *Conde Nast Traveler*, *National Geographic*, *Country Living*, and the *Nation*. Not a single *Reader's Digest*, *Sports Illustrated* or *People* to be found. The last two issues of Barron's were in an antique newspaper rack next to the couch. The cover of one depicted a dancing lady, martini glass held high, asking "Are you rich yet?" If you had to pay their fees for long you soon wouldn't be, I thought to myself.

Finally, M. Stanton's secretary entered the reception area through the glass-paneled door that gave entrance to the offices. "Mr. Browne will see you now."

The small, cool smile she gave me and the way she turned on her heel for me to follow meant she knew I wasn't a "prestige" lawyer or client. M. Stanton barely looked up from his custom built desk console as he waved me to a client chair. "Oh, Ken, please have a seat. Be right with you. Just finishing a few adjustments in an estate portfolio, interest rate changes, you know."

I didn't know, and after an hour's delay, I didn't care. "Excuse me, M. Stanton. I have an appointment with a new client at two. I had hoped to spend an hour with you getting up to date on what you've done. So let's get started."

He looked up, distracted and slightly annoyed. "Oh, that won't be possible. I've got a limited partner's closing at the bank at 2:30. The

Water's View Condo Development. You've heard about it?"

"Afraid not."

"Nice, nice deal. Forty condos on the lake starting at $250,000. Twenty pre-sold. It qualifies for inner city redevelopment tax credits. The depreciation passes through to the limited partner on an accelerated schedule. Sweet. Maybe we can consider you for the next one. Assume you are in the top bracket?"

"Let's talk about that another time. I'm here to see you about Ted."

Suddenly he looked like an undertaker standing with the bereaved at coffin-side. "Ah, Ted. Poor Ted. I'm afraid your coming back on the case seriously gums up the works. I spent hours meeting with Miss Botham, a bloodthirsty vampire, that one, but also with her boss, Alvin Corliss. Thank goodness I've had Alvin up to the farm skeet shooting a few times. Finally got a deal that would've kept Ted from spending the rest of his life in prison. Murder two, no more than twenty years at the maximum and only ten at the minimum. I had Lori research it. You know Lori, Michigan Law?"

I nodded. "Yeah, I've met Lori. A little green for a murder case, don't you think?"

"Very capable. Very bright. Hey, and pretty nice to look at, wouldn't you say?

"'Nice to look at' kinda fades when you are facing life in prison."

"With good time Ted could've been out in as little as eight years. Not bad for bludgeoning your wife to death, you must agree."

I tried to conceal my contempt. "At fifty-eight, what do you think Ted's chances are to reach sixty-five at Jacktown?"

The way Stanton bristled, I could tell I wouldn't be called on the Lake View II. He spoke in a clipped, forceful manner. "A damn sight better chance of getting out than if he gets convicted of murder one and gets mandatory life without parole." He softened a bit. "Listen, Ken, you've got to make the best of a bad situation. Cut your losses. I had to spend a couple of hours with that dreadful Cro-Magnon Bliss to get his okay on the deal. I can probably save the package if you stay out of it. He hinted as much this morning."

I sat up then. "You talked to Bliss today?"

For an instant, a guilty look crossed his brow. He covered it by pushing back his swanky red leather swivel and rising.

"Oh, yes. He was waiting in the parking lot for me to arrive. Had to send the maintenance guy out to sweep up the cigarette butts. Very uncouth fellow, really."

He continued around the desk and opened an antique armoire to extract his suit jacket, talking over his shoulder. "Quite upset with you, me, Ted, the world. Accused me of being in cahoots with you, said this was a deal breaker. In fact, his exact words were 'you can take that deal and shove it up your ass.' Rude man, very rude." He stood in profile before the mirror inside the armoire door and shot his cuffs. For a second it was as if I'd ceased to exist while he admired his image. He nodded in satisfaction and moved behind me toward the door.

"Anyway, I got him calmed down; assured him this is the first I'd heard of it. I'd look into it and get back with him. I think there is still a chance for Ted on this murder two package."

I turned in my chair to stare at M. Stanton in amazement. He was so self-assured that he seemed to be taking no offense at being fired. Rather, he was talking like a camp counselor addressing a young camper who had taken a wrong turn in the woods. Still time to correct our mistake and go back.

"M. Stanton, murder two sucks if you're not guilty. Hasn't Ted told you he didn't do it?"

He shrugged his shoulders, unfazed. "Ken, Ken. You'd know more about this than do I. But don't all criminal defendants proclaim their innocence? In fact, Lori showed me a Harvard Law School psych study showing many of those people actually begin to believe they are innocent after a while. So yes, Ted has told me he didn't do it. Once or twice it sounded like he wasn't so sure. 'I couldn't have done it,' he said. Unfortunately, he told Bliss he did do it. That's on paper," M. Stanton said with innocent finality.

I couldn't resist. "Who has he got to thank for that?" I said, rising.

Browne crooked his arm theatrically to look at his gold Rolex with obvious concern. "Oh, I'm going to be late. Can't keep the bank and the investors waiting."

"Hold your horses a minute. Beside the circumstances surrounding Ted's giving the statement, did he at any time before or after Amanda's death say anything to you that could be incriminating in any way?"

He let the arm fall to his side and we stood facing each other. In the silence I noticed for the first time the metronomic ticking of a gilt grandfather clock in the corner. He gathered himself and appeared to be checking his memory banks. Then he waved the question away as he would a fly. "No, not a thing." He started for the door and turned back for a few last words.

"I think you're being very unfair. Isn't hindsight wonderful? You fail to show up and want to blame me for trying to help. Bliss told me he'd have to arrest Ted unless Ted could explain a very bad-looking situation. He let me take Ted aside for ten minutes and Ted told me he had nothing to do with it. He was very afraid of jail. I was completely shocked when he blurted out his guilt to Bliss. What would you have done any different?"

I shrugged. "Spend more than ten minutes with my client before he talked to anyone."

Coolly, Browne bent to pick a scrap of lint from the Persian carpet. He inspected it between thumb and forefinger, considering his reply. "Isn't the retrospectoscope marvelous? Anyway, I have had Ted's complete file copied. My secretary has it on her desk for you. Why don't you speak to Lori if you have any more questions?"

It was obvious I was an unpleasant and non-billable part of his day that he wanted over quickly. "Just one thing before you rush off, counselor. You need to sign the substitution of counsel form," I said as I pulled the form from my newly labeled Armbruster file.

Distractedly, Browne pulled his reading glasses from the front pocket of his suit coat and scanned the short document. He walked back to the comer of his desk and bent over to sign. Peering over the top of the half-glasses, he looked over his shoulder at me. "I had Lori go over to talk to Ted this morning. She tried to talk some sense into him. He seems bent on his own destruction. Who am I to stand in his way?" He signed with a flourish.

As he walked past me, he handed me the form and kept moving down the hall. I fired a weak parting shot. "Too busy with high finance to go see your longtime friend, neighbor and client yourself, were you?"

He opened the door to the reception area and walked out without giving any indication he'd heard me. I found Alicia, Browne's long-time secretary, who handed me the file as if it contained something slightly toxic. Her nose actually wrinkled. I got directions down the paneled, sconce-lit hallway to Lori's office. But her secretary was sorry to advise me that Miss Teasdale was out for the rest of the day. I left a message for her to call me and walked out myself. On the way through the waiting area the receptionist called softly from behind her desk. "Oh, Mr. Edwards, your trousers are riding up on your right leg."

Oh my, they were indeed. My socks were $1.98 Hanes with a small hole by the heel. Definitely not silk stockings, not at all. I fixed the pant leg, said thank you, and walked back out into the world. M. Stanton's case file on Ted was thick, but not thick enough for a murder case which had been ridden hard for over a month.

It was ten p.m. by the time I had thoroughly reviewed, notated, and reorganized Ted's file. Obviously M. Stanton had been too preoccupied by his big condo deal to review or sanitize the file before it was copied for me. The time sheets and ledgers were copied along with the police reports, autopsy, lab reports, and witness interviews, such as they were. The first ledger entry reflected receipt of the $100,000 fee days after Ted's arrest. The time sheets were kept in meticulous hourly billing form. All phone calls were rounded up and billed in 1/4 hours. The cell phone companies had nothing on Butler-Browne. At $300 an hour, rounding a five-minute call to fifteen cost the client fifty dollars for ten minutes not spent on the file. Everything from dictate letter to prosecutor (1/2 hour) to review letter from prosecutor was billed. I checked the May 18th billing date to see what weighty epistle would be worth $150 of attorney time. It read:

> Sirs:
>
> Enclosed please find our appearance on behalf of Mr. Theodore Armbruster in the above entitled matter.

Sincerely,
M. Stanton Browne

The margin on the right side of the time sheet contained the initials of the attorney performing each itemized service. The initials L.T. for Lori outnumbered the SB's for M. Stanton by about 3 to 1. So Ted was paying a lawyer one year out of law school $300 an hour to handle the defense of murder charges. In my first year of private practice I took $50 an hour if I could get it. And I must've missed the advanced billing class in law school. I didn't charge for phone calls and I didn't list postage under costs. Of course, the chairs in my waiting room were none too comfy, and if we had tea, it wasn't oolong. So one of my first acts was to dictate the following letter to M. Stanton:

Dear Mr. Browne:

Having deducted your itemized billings to date in the amount of $19,372.25 from the initial retainer of $100,000, I find Mrs. Armbruster is entitled to a return of retainer in the amount of $80,627.75. Please remit that amount to her forthwith. I find no form signed by the Armbrusters consistent with MCR 729.3 allowing the charging of a non-hourly single retainer. Your meticulous time records clearly indicate an hourly billing practice. Thus, I trust you will have retained the unused balance in your office trust account, as required by the rules of professional responsibility, and will be able to remit a check from said account upon receipt of this letter.

Thanking you for your kind and prompt attention, I remain,
Very truly yours,
Kenneth M. Edwards

I guessed since M. Stanton had never descended to the depths of criminal law, he had never heard of the professional responsibility rule, which required that if a criminal retainer was to be one-shot, nonrefundable and not hourly, the client must sign an acknowledgement form. Lori was probably too green to know any better. Thus M. Stanton and his partners had probably distributed the retainer upon receipt. A sudden call for eighty G's probably would make for a little indigestion with their morning coffee. Both Ted and Marjorie had signed my form calling for a $50,000 non-hourly retainer, which was a record for me. After paying me they'd still have a $30,000 refund from M. Stanton and hopefully the best defense possible from me. At least that was the plan.

11

I was excited about a $50,000 fee. But I figured the next three months would belong to the case. I planned to earn it. The review of the file demonstrated that not much had really been done to earn the $20K at B & B. Lori's interviews with Jim and Jillian Simpson revealed that the scene at Heather Hollows had been even uglier than Ted had told me. A few quotes had been highlighted by Lori:

"Never seen Ted that angry."

"He kind of lost it. It was embarrassing."

"Amanda was in tears, pleading with Ted to settle down."

"Ted pushed Gianfranco when he tried to calm Ted down."

"Gianfranco was a perfect gentleman."

"Ted was slurring his speech, unsteady on his feet, loud and red in the face."

"When the bartender came over to quiet things down, Ted told him to 'mind his own fucking business.' He never talks like that."

"Amanda was afraid to leave with Ted. Mr. Firenze said he would drive her home."

"If we hadn't physically walked Ted out the door, the police would've been there to arrest him. I'm sorry they didn't. Maybe none of this would have happened."

"Ted hasn't been himself lately. Under a lot of strain. Work, health, marriage. I think it all built up. Then the dam burst."

This stuff would be less than helpful, particularly coming from Ted's friends. Lori's typed summary of her interview with the Latin lover boy Gianfranco Firenze was brief:

> Met Mr. Firenze at the offices of Firenze Metals Recovery on Industrial Drive in Saginaw. He declined a taped interview. Told me quite busy and had told the police everything he knows. Learned the following in ten minute interview:
>
> 1. President of Firenze Metals. Scrap metal yard.
> 2. Barely knew deceased from United Way breakfasts before night of her death when she invited him to join group at table.
> 3. Had played golf with friends at Heather Hollows. Finished at sunset and retired to bar for drinks and settle bets.
> 4. Husband came in very upset. Wouldn't shake hands. Pushed him ("Lucky I didn't rearrange the old duffer's face").
> 5. Stayed till closing to calm Mrs. Armbruster. Drove her home. Did not enter home. Did not see or hear anything after she closed the front door.
> 6. Terminated interview when asked about marital and family status. "None of your business."
>
> Impression: Fancies himself a ladies' man. Offices very nice for scrap yard. Real leather furniture. No condolences for fate of Mrs. Armbruster. "Seemed like a nice lady. Tough luck." Knows something he's not telling me.

I picked up the phone and called Saginaw PD to speak with Detective Avery Bond. We went back to my days as the prosecutor of an arson for fun and profit ring which we'd put out of business. He was a big, handsome, slightly graying black man who looked like Sydney Poitier and sounded like Yaphet Koto. His voice boomed over the phone. "Counselor. Calling to confess your sins as a defense lawyer and come back to the true path?"

I laughed. "No, I'm doomed to spend my days confined to the outer darkness. How are you, sir?"

"Been better. Just had my only witness on a drug killing end up on the bone pile this morning. What can I do for you?"

"What can you tell me about Gianfranco Firenze?"

The voice took on an edge.

"Trouble. Stay clear of him. Why?"

"He was the last person with whom my client's wife was seen still alive."

I could hear the wheels turn and the lock click open.

"What? Armbruster? I saw Bliss at an FOP meeting. He said you had been shitcanned on that one in record time. Said the perp had hired some big-shot society lawyer I never heard of. Bliss took a lot of pleasure in describing the look on your face at the scene when you found out your client had confessed and you'd been replaced all in the time it took to get a jump start for your car. Can't you afford a car that starts? That's what you get driving a fancy foreign job. Told you, this is UAW territory. Get yourself a trusty set of Detroit wheels." As his voice wound down I could picture his toothsome "I told you so" smile.

"Yeah, yeah. The world keeps turning over. One day you're down, the next day you're up. Mr. Silk-Stockings is out. I'm back in. So what've you got on Gianfranco?"

"He's a minor lieutenant in the Rosselini crew. They're big in Detroit. He's their local branch manager. He started out as muscle for loan sharking and bookmaking. I guess his collections were good 'cause they moved him here five years ago when old Tony Rosselini died. Hang on, I'll type him into the LEIN system and see what we get. While we're waiting, I can tell you what I hear. He's primarily a money laundering center. The scrap business is okay. But not okay enough to pay for the palace he owns out in the township. He and I both have something in common. We both were rejected for membership at Aurora Golf and Country. For me it was the color of my skin they didn't like. With him it was the color of his money."

I could hear the computer printer revving. Then Avery spoke again. "About what I thought. Convicted in 1979 at age eighteen of A&B. Probation. Uttering and Publishing, 1982, 1991. Case dismissed. Wayne

County Attempted Extortion. '89, receiving and concealing stolen goods over $100. Pled to misdemeanor under $100. Probation. '93, assault with intent to do great bodily harm. Directed verdict of not guilty at trial. Witness non-appearance. Lots of arrests followed by dismissals. Oops, almost missed a concealed weapons beef in Oakland County in 1993. Let me see, all of those are Detroit or Wayne County. Last entry, another receiving and concealing in Lansing, 1994. Nothing over the last five years."

"Whoa, slow down there, partner. You're talking faster than I'm scribbling. How'd he get charged with stealing and receiving and concealing the same car in Lansing?"

"Beats me. Maybe they caught him with the car and he claimed he got it from somebody else. Maybe they caught him driving one hot car and in possession of another. Being in the scrap business offers a tidy way to clean up your mess after a car's been stripped."

"I suppose so. Anyway, you were saying nothing recent?"

"We hear his name from time to time, but nothing solid. I've seen him at Saginaw High football games. He's got a son who is one hell of a linebacker. Pretty blonde wife, and a couple of little girls. Active in church and charity. I think he's under orders to be very respectable. But my take is, there is still a bad guy not far below the surface. How did he know your client's wife?"

"I'm just back in this, so I'm trying to figure it out. He told the police here she'd gotten friendly with him after golf at Heather Hollows. He gave her a ride home after Ted, my client, and Amanda, the deceased wife, had a fight in the bar there."

"Yeah, that sounds like the Italian Stallion. He's a skirt chaser. We've seen his Town Car in the parking lot of a couple of hot spots close to closing. If a girl likes them muscular, toothy, hairy, with lots of cologne, he'd fit the bill. I'll keep my ears open. And you, my friend, you keep your eyes open. That shark has teeth. Hear me?"

"I hear you. Thanks, buddy."

I got out the phone book and noted the address for Firenze and stuck it in my pocket. I'd drop by for coffee tomorrow and meet Romeo.

When I arrived at Firenze Metal at 8:30, the sun was shining and the trucks were lined up out front, waiting for the chain link gate to swing open. There were battered old pick-ups, dump trucks, flat beds, push carts, and even a child's wagon, all laden with scrap metal. The wagon had a car bumper hanging from front to back. Everything from old washing machines, sheet metal, structural I-bars, and cannibalized car parts was crammed chock-a-block in the beds of the trucks. The drivers were checking in and waiting to be weighed on the scales. So I parked a block away and walked in past a rusty Chevy Silverado that looked like it was ready itself to be crushed and recycled along with its contents.

"Hey, buster, where the hell do you think you're going?"

I turned and squinted into the sun to see a monster of a man striding toward me, remnants of a well-chewed cigar hanging out the corner of his mouth. His tattered denim jacket was cut off at the armpits, leaving the tattoos visible. A Devil's Disciples logo decorated the massive expanse of a bicep. Incongruously, his stained T-shirt urged me to "Save the Seals."

"Attorney Edwards here to see Mr. Firenze," I tossed out as a morsel to slow the onrushing watchdog. He paused to chew on it, the cigar stub bobbing. I looked the part, suit and tie, briefcase, tasseled loafers.

"He know you're coming?"

"Yeah, the Armbruster matter."

His mental muscles were less developed than the bulging and rippling sinews stretching his t-shirt. He pushed his shoulder-length hair back over his shoulder with both hands, lost in indecision. He had a gate full of delivery men and a long walk to the office and back. "Yeah, well. Office is around the corner of the blue building. Next time check with me. Don't just walk in like you own the place. Got that?"

"Yes sir, thank you for your help."

I gave wide berth to the crane affixed to a railroad flat car swinging its magnet over to unload scrap from a semi-trailer. By the time I reached the office entrance, my newly shined shoes were covered in dust. I stood on one foot and rubbed each shoe against the calf of the opposite leg. The pants were ready for the dry cleaners anyway, and no other option suggested itself. I pulled open the tinted glass door and walked into the office area. What a contrast. Outside, dirt, grime, clamor and industry. Inside, expensive-looking cream tile with blue and green patterned insets. Plush leather furniture and Andrea Bocelli on the sound system.

The tableau behind the reception desk grabbed my attention. A huge painting of the Trevi Fountain adorned the wall behind the desk. A raven-haired Mexican girl no older than nineteen leaned forward, her elbows on the desk. Her loose peasant blouse allowed a view of ample cleavage. Behind her a man who matched Bond's description of Firenze was administering a neck and shoulder massage. Must be part of the benefits package. She looked up, her dark eyes visible through cascading tresses. His dark Mediterranean orbs were sharp and attentive. Firenze didn't stop immediately, but finished working his large hands over her shoulders while I stood and watched. Finally I broke the mood.

"Mr. Firenze. Good morning. Ken Edwards."

He reluctantly finished his ministrations and straightened up. "Yeah, and what's a Ken Edwards?"

"Lawyer from Lake Pointe."

"Oh. I've heard of you. Sent a couple of my boys to you for receiving and concealing over in Lake County. They said you got them off but didn't charge enough to be any real good."

"Oh, Dempster and Restonga. They worked for you? Better to get the job done and charge too little than drop the ball and charge too much, don't you think?"

He smiled and walked around the reception counter and stuck out his hand. "Gianfranco."

My dad had taught me to give a firm handshake and look the other fellow square in the eye. But he hadn't prepared me for the trash-compactor grip into which my hand disappeared. My hand was still recovering from Bliss's attempt to break a few bones in his greeting outside the jail. I wondered what else the two of them had in common as I tried not to wince or blink and kept smiling at him. His smile back at me would have lit a small arena; a poster boy for the new whitening agents. I managed a "nice to meet you" without my voice cracking. When it was obvious I wasn't going to plead for mercy, he released me and let the smile drop from the corners of his mouth.

"What can I do for you?"

"I've got a case I was hoping you could help me with. Can we talk for a few minutes?"

He glanced at a shiny Rolex nestled amongst the hair of his forearm. I wondered whether he and Stanton shared the same jeweler. "I can give you five or ten minutes. Come back to my office. Rosita, bring us some coffee."

He turned and I followed him down a short hall to a door with a metal plaque announcing "The Boss." He sat behind his battleship of a desk and motioned me to one of the tan leather chairs in front. The light coming in through the east window behind the desk was bright and it took a few seconds for my eyes to adjust. Perhaps on purpose, the light created an aura of light around his head.

When my eyes adjusted, I noticed the multiple framed family photographs on his desk and the office shelves. If you didn't know better, you would've thought he was the family man of the year. A younger Gianfranco in a tux and a petite, beautiful blonde in a wedding gown, ready to cut the cake. Mother and father holding swaddlings in their arms. Gianfranco and a large family of Mediterranean folk all dressed up fancy with a matriarch and patriarch seated in the middle. Gianfranco dressed in a baseball uniform, his hands on the shoulders of a twelve-year-old replica of his father. The son, now four years older and man-sized in a football jersey, staring at the camera, helmet in hand, as if a quarterback were holding it. A pretty brunette in a confirmation dress, looking sideways from a piano bench. Mixed among the photographs were numerous trophies, some topped by a golfer in mid-swing.

"Good looking family," I offered. "Your son plays football, I see."

"No, man, Johnny doesn't just play football, he excels at it. We've already got two full-ride scholarship tenders, one from State. More to come. He's an animal at linebacker. The all-conference running back he hit last year went from the #1 recruit in the state to no offers after Johnny took him out at the knees. Man, that kid can hit."

The look of fatherly pride was all over Dad's face. Then his tone changed. "You said you needed my help?"

"Yes, yes I do. I'm now Ted Armbruster's attorney. I need to talk to you about his wife's death."

All the warmth went out of Firenze. His feet came off the desk and he eyed me like I was a rusty piece of scrap unworthy of recycling. "Look, counselor. I've been through this twice before. First the police come to my house and get my wife all upset. Then that wet behind the ears lady lawyer sat right where you are sitting and wanted my time. I'm not going over this shit again."

I kept my voice even. "Mr. Firenze, I appreciate your taking time to talk with me. My client is charged with murder, a crime he claims he didn't commit. According to the police reports, you were the last person to be seen with Mrs. Armbruster while she was still alive. I hope you can see why I need..."

His hands went up. They looked like they could stop a train. "Listen here, counselor. The way I got it, your client was the last person to see the lady alive. And he beat her brains in with a golf club. So don't be sitting in my place trying to put me in that picture. Try insanity. Try self-defense. Try intoxicated, cuz he sure was that. But don't try my patience. It's not good when I lose my patience. Know what I mean?"

I dropped my conversational tone, sat up and replied, "No, what does it mean?"

"Best off you don't find out. We're done talking." He reached in his pocket and held a five-dollar bill out to me. "Here, get your shoes shined. You look like a bum."

I shook my head as I rose. "No thanks. But you're leaving me no choice but to subpoena you for the trial. I know you are a business man and figured you didn't want the publicity associated with this trial. Lotta media coverage of this one. As a family man, I was thinking you'd like to avoid that."

The rising blood turned his face a darker shade of swarthy. "What do you mean, family? Are you cracking wise here? You are way out of your depth here, mister."

I realized the double meaning of family and wise. Was he subtle enough to intend the pun? "No, I can tell you are very proud of your wife and children. I wanted to save them any embarrassment. So the better I understand your testimony, the more discreetly I can handle things."

I watched the calculator reflecting in his eye movements. The tension in his posture eased, and he waved me back into the chair.

"Mr. Edwards, the last guy you want on the witness stand is me. Your client, Mr. Armbruster, was a nut case. He yelled. He screamed. He swore. When I tried to calm him down he pushed me. Nobody pushes me." He looked meaningfully at me. "But I was cool. I just stepped back. His wife was crying. He told the bartender to fuck off when he tried to cool things down. If his friends hadn't dragged him out of there, the police would've. I know the bartender called them. No, I don't think you want me as a witness."

"Did he threaten her?"

Firenze thought for a minute. "I don't know if it was a threat. Something like 'I've had all I can take. I won't stand for this anymore.' Is that a threat? In light of what he did to her, I guess it was."

"What time did you take her home?"

"I don't know, a little before midnight."

"Stop anywhere on the way?"

"Whaddya mean, stop? Where would we stop?"

"I don't know. The ME has her time of death at around 2:30 a.m., give or take. She was still in the hall dressed. So I figured maybe she was just arriving."

"Sharp. I heard you were sharp. I'm surprised neither the cops or the lady legal-eagle didn't ask about that. The lady was upset. She didn't want to go right home. She was afraid her husband would be still awake and they'd fight. So I took her back to my place to let her settle down."

"What about your family?"

"They were in Detroit at my wife's sister's."

"So what happened at your place?"

"Happened? Nothing happened. I put some music on, mixed a couple of drinks. I let her pour out her troubles. A shoulder to cry on."

"Nothing else?"

"What are you getting at?"

"She was wearing a different set of panties when she got home than when she started out. I think I just figured out how that happened. Your wife missing a pair of red panties?"

He was obviously startled, but kept his hard face slack in a childlike innocence. "How do you know what color panties she had on? You some kind of peeping Tom?"

"She had green undies on when she started out and red when she ended up. So I am asking what happened?"

Gianfranco was back on the muscle. "Okay, so I boffed the broad. So what? You try to make something of this in court and embarrass my family, you're going to regret it. The lady liked it rough. Her dainty underthings didn't hold up. The stockings and belt went in the trash. I don't know why she cared, but she didn't want to go home with no panties. So I found an old pair of my wife's in the bottom of the drawer. That what you wanted to know?"

"It's not a case of want to know, it's have to know if I'm going to do my job. So what time you take her home?"

"A little after two. I know I felt like shit the next morning." He pointed a thick finger at me and dropped his voice to a whisper. "Look. I had nothing to do with what happened to that woman. And if Joanna, my wife, finds out that the broad died in her underpants, I'm going to experience a very unhappy period at home. If I'm unhappy, you're going to be unhappy. You understand?"

I nodded.

"Now beat it. I don't know why I told you this shit, but you're probably smart enough to have figured it out. So better we have our little chat here than it comes out in court and a lot of people get hurt. We want to avoid people getting hurt, don't we, counselor?"

I watched his hooded eyes as his head moved slowly, rocking back and forth for emphasis. I felt like a mouse staring into the eyes of a cobra. I shook my head quickly to break the trance and turned for the door. "I'd like to avoid that too if possible."

I walked past Rosita, who had straightened her blouse and brushed her hair neatly. "*Buenos dias, senorita.*"

"*A usted tambien.*" She smiled, and I was out in the clamor, dust and grit of the junkyard. A rusted-out Chevy dangled from the magnet on its last ride to the crusher. Unbidden, a vision of me lying trussed in the back seat frantically trying to scream through a gag came into my head. Firenze had told me more than I had expected. He'd also proven himself a bragging liar in light of the autopsy report saying no sex. But he probably wasn't lying when he told me how I could avoid getting hurt. I glanced again as the crane load fell into the crusher. No, we definitely didn't want anyone getting hurt. Especially me.

The woman was humiliating me in front of a crowd. As she was to be the presiding judge in the biggest case of my career, Judge Alexandra Kingsdale's obvious hostility was not a good omen. This woman, before getting elected judge, had professed undying love and affection for me. In response I had thrown caution to the wind and followed my heart in committing myself to her. Not long after I had helped her to win the judgeship, she tossed me overboard as excess baggage. The pain and despair of being used and discarded had led to a dark period of drinking, one-night stands, and withdrawal.

Now three years later I had climbed back out of that black hole. Judge Alex's comments and tone stimulated painful nerve endings which only lately had settled into a dull ache. Now, in front of a packed courtroom, she was using my simple motion to substitute for Browne as defense counsel to make sure anyone who held onto the outdated notion that we had a special relationship was disabused of that misconception.

Since it was a Monday, motion day, the courtroom was full of lawyers, clients and people with nothing better to do. As my motion dealt with the "Country Clubber" case, the media was out in numbers. The press chased the Armbruster case like a pack of dogs after the neighbor's cat. No development in the case was too small to miss an opportunity to rehash the lurid details, show the pictures of the beautiful victim and the so-called admitted killer in cuffs and jail issue jumpsuit. My motions were rather mundane. Nevertheless, the fourth estate frothed and jostled at the rail that divided courtroom spectators from combatants as if a jury were about to pronounce guilt.

I accompanied my motion to substitute as counsel for M. Stanton Browne with a request to adjourn the trial so I'd have more prep time. The woman making life miserable for me had once made me very happy. She had been my lover and I had thought then, perhaps, someday my wife. Now she was neither. She was the judge and she was taking the legal rolling pin to me with a relish that would've done any boarding house proprietress proud.

"Mr. Edwards, why are you asking me to allow you to substitute yourself for a highly qualified lawyer like Mr. Browne when you are not prepared?"

"Because Mr. Armbruster has faith in me."

"Didn't he have faith in Mr. Browne?"

"You'd have to ask Mr. Armbruster, Your Honor."

Those eyes I knew so well found Ted's. "Mr. Armbruster, changing lawyers in any case shortly before trial is risky. Changing counsel weeks before the start of a murder case is worse than changing horses in mid-stream, very dangerous. Are you aware of the dangers?"

Ted stood and looked straight at the judge. "I understand, Your Honor."

"Mr. Browne has many years in practice and is the managing partner of a well-respected firm with many associates and is happy to assist in your defense. Mr. Edwards comes from a one-lawyer firm with, I don't want to say limited resources, but let's call it fewer resources. Do you understand that?"

"Yes, Your Honor, but Mr. Edwards is good."

This brought a cackle from those in the audience who shared my opinion of the vaunted Mr. Browne, but the judge was not laughing. She banged the gavel and called for order.

"Mr. Armbruster, I warn you. I am familiar with Mr. Edwards' reputation and I am also familiar with his razzle-dazzle tactics. There will be none of that in this courtroom. This is a court of law, not the stage of the

Lake Pointe Players. There will be no theatrics. You are to face trial for the murder of your wife. I will not be distracted, nor will I let the jury be distracted from the gravity of the crime by legal sleight of hand. Is that clear?"

"Yes, Your Honor."

I felt I must interject. I moved from behind the defense table and positioned myself between my client and the judge. Her eyes followed me. Mine met hers directly for the first time in years. For a second there was no one else in the room. Their was no compassion in the steel blue eyes that challenged me to come no further. I pushed the past away and tried to keep anger from my voice.

"Do your last remarks indicate that you have a preconceived notion of my client's guilt, Your Honor?"

She pulled her long blonde hair over her ears, the black robes sliding to her elbows as she reached up and back. I'd known that subconscious gesture well once.

"Mr. Edwards, I am addressing your client on the issue of whether he is making an intelligent decision in the matter of his representation. I am not speaking to you. Please step back so I may see him." I held her gaze just an instant short of contempt before retracing my steps to stand with Ted behind counsel table. There were raised eyebrows in the gallery, as if to ask "What's that all about?" Judge Alex bit on the corner of her lower lip, which I knew to be an anger management device. Then she continued:

"I am of course familiar with the news accounts of the brutal killing of Amanda Armbruster and the things which Mr. Armbruster is reputed to have said and done following the killing. I make no finding as to his guilt or innocence, nor need I make any, as a jury has been demanded. I do know that Amanda Armbruster was a fine woman who contributed much to her community, and that she died most horribly, so I wanted Mr. Armbruster to understand that this court is going to hear this matter with the utmost gravity. There will be no legal shenanigans, is that clear?"

"All too clear. I wonder then if this court has preconceived notions about me that would preclude my client's having a fair trial. The reason I ask is because your comments here today about shenanigans, razzle-dazzle, and sleight of hand evidence a distinct prejudice against me. I am at a loss to understand them." The red flush rising from above the collar to suffuse her neck and face were a seismic warning I'd seen before. The volcano was rumbling. I stood next to the cone and dared it to explode.

"And if that is so, I need time to consult further with my client to caution him that such an attitude toward his counsel could have a material adverse effect on his chances for a fair hearing. Further, I must consider, if you are so prejudiced against the defense, whether a motion to recuse is in order."

Her eyes narrowed and her jaw muscles tightened as she reined herself in. Maybe dealing civilly with me was as hard for her as it was for me to deal with her. Her voice was taut.

"Are you questioning my ability as judge, counsel?"

"No, I am questioning your attitude toward me, as it might impact on my ability to zealously defend my client when faced with the most serious charges known to our law."

She looked down for a few seconds at the papers on the bench. I watched as her full head of flaxen hair formed a curtain around her downcast face and remembered how lush and silken it was to the touch. I knew from experience she was practicing her yoga techniques of anger management. Her shoulders rose and fell in accompaniment to deep and even breathing. It must've worked, because when she looked up the redness had drained away and she looked serene.

"Mr. Edwards, I don't have any attitude toward you. I have spoken to other judges who had regrets that they allowed you sufficient license to steal a jury's vote with appeals to passion or misdirection. That will not happen in this courtroom. I want your client to understand that before I sign the order of substitution of counsel. Do you understand, Mr. Armbruster?"

"I understand, Your Honor." Ted spoke clearly.

"In light of what has transpired here today, is it your decision, in spite of the warnings I have given, to discharge Mr. Browne and have Mr. Edwards act as your lawyer?"

"Very definitely, ma'am."

"So ordered."

All this fire and smoke over what should've been a simple motion in light of Browne's preliminary exam statements making him a witness. But I couldn't argue that for fear she'd rule my presence at the scene meant I too should be a witness. So this whole show had been elaborate kabuki to show no love lost between us and to show me who was boss in her courtroom. Assistant prosecutor Tina Botham tried to keep the smirk from the corner of her mouth as she watched me twist in the wind. She had a slam dunk case and a judge who looked ready to call all the fouls on defense counsel if he tried to obstruct her way to the basket.

"Now, Mr. Edwards, you have a motion to adjourn the trial date. Please speak to that motion."

Which I did. I explained that this was a very complex case, that a number of investigations required pursuit, that I had motions to make regarding evidence, in particular to suppress the confession, and I needed more time than the five weeks before the scheduled trial date in August in order to prepare.

Her response went like this: "The case doesn't appear so complex. Somebody killed Mrs. Armbruster with a golf club, a sand wedge, I believe. Your client said he did it. Now he says he didn't. A smart man like you can figure out those facts in a month. As to your motions, I have already calendared time two weeks from now for the hearing of these motions. I suggest you get busy so that the prosecution and the court have time to read and prepare for hearing. If you can't be prepared for trial, why did you ask the court to allow you to substitute for counsel who has had the case for months now? If you and your client thought you could postpone justice by a late-in-the-game switch of lawyers, then you are wrong. I told you legal tricks will get very short shrift in this courtroom. No adjournment. Get ready or get out. I have not signed the order of substitution. Do you want to withdraw your motion?"

"I do not."

"Very well. I am signing the order of substitution. Ms. Botham, do you have an order denying the request for adjournment?"

"Right here, Your Honor." My opposing counsel beamed as she approached the bench.

I said goodbye to Ted as the detective handcuffed him and escorted him to the elevator. I tried to sneak out the back door of the courthouse to avoid the press. No such luck. They had all the doors covered.

"Mr. Edwards, weren't you Mr. Armbruster's lawyer the night he murdered his wife?"

"Ted didn't murder his wife, and the police made it impossible for me to speak to Ted before they extracted the so-called confession out of him. Mr. Browne was his lawyer before I could meet with Ted."

"Are you saying the confession is bogus?"

"Yes."

"In what way?"

"Ted didn't kill his wife. Detective Bliss claims he admitted doing so. I don't believe Bliss accurately recorded Ted's statement. Ted loved his wife. He would not hurt her."

"Are you calling the detective a liar?"

"I'm saying he was inaccurate."

"If Ted didn't kill her, who did?"

"Get yourself a seat at the trial. I don't want to ruin the suspense."

"What's going on with you and the judge? What did you ever do to her? Why is she so hostile to you?"

I make it a point to only speak favorably of the judiciary publicly. Anything else is professional suicide. "Judge Kingsdale is a fair judge. I supported her candidacy. You can see that she hasn't entertained me with any favors. I can only guess that she had heard erroneous reports of my trial tactics and wants to assure a fair trial for both sides."

"Right, right, but she doesn't seem to like you much. Can you explain that?"

I shook my head, squinted in mock concentration, looked up, and then said, "Beats the heck out of me. Gotta go." And with that I pushed through the note pads and microphones and walked back toward my office. As I did I searched my mind for the thousandth time for the answer to the reporters' last question. I sure as hell had no explanation for what had come between us.

The next day's *Leader* local section headline read:

Fireworks Precede Murder Case

That afternoon Janice interrupted me in the library as I was yellow highlighting the autopsy report. Just as Lori had said: no evidence of sperm, no evidence of recent intercourse, just some light bruising mid-thigh. I wondered why Gianfranco had made it sound like he'd had his way with her when from the autopsy, that seemed unlikely. Yet why would he say she was wearing his wife's underwear if she wasn't?

Janice intruded into the library with a smug smile on her lips. "Where do you want these? And who is G.F? I don't recognize the initials in the client rolodex. New girlfriend?"

I looked up at the large vase of lilies she carried. "Put those on the corner of the table, please." I looked at the florist's card stuck between the tines of a plastic stick. "Thinking of you. G.F." was the only message. The coincidence of my thinking of Gianfranco with the arrival of his message that he was thinking of me was eerie. Janice looked over my shoulder as the impact of the message sank in with me. Then she broke the quiet as she turned to go back to her desk. "Boss, you've dated some strange ones. But this lady's got to be weird. Lilies are for funeral homes, aren't they?"

"Yes. I believe they are," I answered to the walls of the now- empty library.

Three nights later I'd been working until eight trying to get my hands around the case. My car had long since had its solenoid extracted and replaced with a very expensive, brand new Bosch part. As I headed out to the beach on a perfect summer evening with the top down and the radio blaring Bob Seger's "Night Moves," I had convinced myself the repair was worth it. I'd also decided I should've become a sports car mechanic. Less stress and the money was better. When I pulled into the drive my neighbor, Billy, was waiting. "You switching from cable to dish?"

"No, Billy. Why?"

"There was a truck here this afternoon. Had a picture of a satellite or something on it. When the guy tried to get into the back yard, Max went crazy. I've never seen him act that mean. He wasn't just barking. He had his lips pulled back and was showing lots of teeth. I was in the back yard, so I walked over to the gate. The guy was wearing surgical gloves, and he reached into his overalls and pulled out a baggie with some raw meat in it."

My heart started to race. I hadn't received Max's usual greeting of racing around to leap up and put his paws on the gate, with tail wagging furiously. "Did Max eat it?"

"Nope. I told the guy you had strict rules. Nobody feeds your dog but you. He claimed that was on his order sheet on how to get into the yard to do the hook-up. I told him he better come back when you were home. He argued a bit, said you would have to pay for another service call. So I told him I'd take Max into my house. When I got back he was gone."

"Max is okay?"

"Yep, but my cats aren't. Misty is on the top shelf of the hall closet, and I haven't found Sniffles yet. Plus, he cleaned out their food dishes. What's the deal with that guy? What was he doing here if you didn't order satellite? Did I do the right thing?"

"Yeah, Billy. You did exactly the right thing. I think he was trying to poison Max."

Billy looked startled, then angry. "That SOB. Who would want to hurt Max? He's a great dog."

As we walked over to Billy's front door to retrieve Max, I wondered the same thing. Gianfranco and a certain overbearing detective came immediately to mind. "I don't know, Billy. But thanks, buddy. If it weren't for you I think I'd have a very dead dog on my hands about now."

I collected Max, offered to pay for the screen door he'd shredded and arranged for Billy to keep Max with him while I was at work. Then I called the state police. Trooper Karen Williams, who arrived a half-hour later, loved dogs. She filled out a complete report, including a description of the suspect. "Late 20's, buzz-cut blonde hair under a light blue baseball cap that matched the overalls. White van with a blue star or satellite or globe on it. Had some lettering, but I was working in the yard without my glasses on," Billy reported. When she asked me if I had any idea who would do this, I considered the likely suspects and how much evidence I had that it was either one of them.

"No, ma'am. I'm afraid I don't. I just took a case that's not very popular."

The light of recognition came on behind her eyes. "Oh, you're that Edwards. You poor schmuck. You're supposed to be a bright guy. Why'd you grab a deck chair on the *Titanic*?"

Before I could answer, Max started barking at the gate to the back yard. She looked over and smiled at him. "Oh, aren't you the handsome one? Better interview the prospective victim before I finish my report. Does he bite?"

I shook my head. "He's more of a lover than a fighter."

With that she strolled over to the gate making lovey noises and let herself into the back yard, where she bent down to pet Max and ruffle his mane. "Hey, how come the hair on the top runs back to front?"

Billy and I walked over to the gate to watch the lovefest between dog and trooper. "He's a Rhodesian ridgeback. That's where the name comes from."

Max was a glutton for attention, but he went over the top with his new lady friend. His tail wagged in joyful cadence. He licked her face each time she leaned over, and he rubbed himself against her uniformed leg when she made ready to leave. Max was demonstrating good taste in women. The trooper was a very pretty young woman, late twenties, I guessed. Her strawberry blonde hair was thick and full, albeit trimmed short so that it angled along a strong jawline. Freckles dotted her face around a slightly upturned nose. The hazel eyes were alert and looked right at you when she talked. Beneath her blue uniform it was obvious she was wearing a vest, but judging from the nicely shaped behind, she probably looked enticing in a dress. When she turned from Max to the gate, she caught both Billy and me in mid-ogle. She stiffened and her smile died aborning. When she spoke after shutting the gate behind her, she was all business.

"Nice dog. I'll make a complete report and keep an eye out for the satellite van. But I've got to tell you what you already know. There's not much to go on here. Anything comes up, we have your numbers. Any questions?"

I was too busy worrying about how foolish I had looked checking her out to think of anything to ask. Billy, who normally would talk the ears off a deaf man, was also silent. She closed the metal top over her report pad, stuck her pen in her uniform pocket and closed the interview. "All right then. Thank you both for your cooperation. Have a nice evening."

She headed for the dark blue patrol car. Both Billy and I watched her walk back down the driveway and waved as she drove off. Then Billy gave out the old wolf-whistle. "Fills out the uniform quite nicely, that little filly. If I'm going to be busted, she's got the bust to do it."

"Looks a little young for you, pardner. Heck, she looks young for me, and I'm a couple of years your junior."

"Never hurts to dream. You see that little turned-up nose and those freckles? I've always been partial to strawberry blondes. Did I ever tell you about Molly? Now there was a spitfire. Why, she..."

I held up my hands and smiled. "Save it for next time, neighbor. I've had a very long day and I haven't eaten yet. Thanks for being so alert. Max and I both thank you." At the sound of his name Max came back from the lawn nearby and followed me into the house. I sorted through the pot-pies in the freezer and stuck a "creamy chicken chunks" in the microwave. I pulled the half-full half gallon of skim milk from the fridge.

It was two days past the "use by" date. With trepidation I unscrewed the light blue plastic cap and took a whiff. Not overpowering. I looked left and right, as if my mother was there to catch me, and took a swig. Just starting to go but not gone yet.

I left the jug on the table and went out in the back yard to search for Max's dish. He stood on the cement back porch watching me, his tail wagging slowly to see how long it would take me to discover where he had left it this time. Right at the base of a maple tree, it leaned well-chewed and dirty, but easy enough to find. Once I started over to get it, he bounced happily at my side.

"Geez, Max, this hidey-hole is not up to your usual standards. Ah, but you were otherwise occupied today. Weren't you?"

He looked at me with his ears cocked as if trying to comprehend, then bent his head down, placed the dish in his mouth and pranced happily back toward the house. As far as Max was concerned, life was great.

That night as I lay sleepless, staring at the ceiling and wondering whether I was in over my head with Ted's case, Max slept soundly. He lay on his side atop the old quilt he'd had since he was a puppy. His stentorian snores rattled the windows. I knew once I dozed he'd make his move for the bed. I smiled, taking comfort in our well-established routine.

Actually, the close call had worked out pretty well for Max. I decided rather than accept Billy's offer, I would get Max further out of harm's way. So I contacted Esther Grimes, from whom I had bought Max as a puppy, and explained the situation to her. As a breeder of Rhodesian ridgebacks for over twenty years, she couldn't stand the idea of somebody trying to hurt "one of her grandchildren." She lived on a thirty-acre farm and wasn't far out of my way to work. I agreed to pay her sixty dollars a month plus feed costs. For that Max got a ridgeback's idea of heaven in day care: lots of room to roam, a sister, a brother, an uncle and a cousin to romp with, and lots of squirrels, pheasant and woodchuck to chase. Plus he got two car rides a day. And rides were definitely his idea of a good time.

The sight of Max and me sitting in a top-down two-seat convertible was a real attention getter. At 110 pounds he filled the bucket seat with no room to spare. Since puppyhood he'd been carefully conditioned to remain seated, no matter how fascinating the scenery or passing dog show might be. With me in jacket and tie and Max with his ears straight out in the wind, we were quite a sight. As a way to meet girls, it was an inspiration. Everybody wanted to talk about him at traffic lights. Little kids and grandmothers pointed as we passed. In fact, Max got me pulled over by the cops.

Shortly after picking up Max at Esther Grimes' one night, I was speeding down Townline Road. "Oh, shit. I don't need another ticket," I thought. I pulled to the shoulder and watched the red lights of the dark blue state police cruiser flash in my rearview mirror. In the glow of the parking lights I could see the figure of the trooper approach. It wasn't until the officer reached the driver's door and spoke that I recognized Trooper Karen Williams.

"What's the rush, counselor? I've got you going 64 in a 55."

"Good evening, Trooper. Actually, it's two hours past Max's dinnertime." At the sound of Karen's voice and the mention of the word "dinner," Max lost control. He broke his sit command and stepped across the console, putting a huge paw squarely on my vitals. I grunted and tried to push him back. But he wasn't moving anything except his tail as long as Trooper Williams was petting his head and making girlish sounds.

"Hi, Max. Oh yes, hi, hi. Aren't you just the biggest lovey-dovey? Oh, a nice big kiss for me. Aren't you nice..."

"Hey, can we break this love-fest up? Max is none too dainty on his feet. Ooph. Come on. My mom's hopes for grandchildren are in jeopardy here. Max. Sit! Sit!"

Finally I got Max back in his seat, but by then Trooper Karen was having way too much fun to write me a ticket. "This is the first time I've let someone go because their passenger stuck out their tongue at me. But Max is a good character reference for you, so I'm going to give you a break."

"Hey, thanks, I appreciate that," I said with relief, knowing my insurance agent was thinking to drop me if I got one more ticket.

"Don't thank me. Thank Max. Plus, there is a string attached."

I raised my eyebrows. "Oh, and what would that be?"

"Nothing you can't handle. Just want visitation with Max. My apartment allows no pets. I've always had a dog. Could I drop by every so often to check on him? Maybe bring him a bone. That be okay?"

I was relieved that her catching Billy and me in mid-ogle on our first meeting hadn't completely poisoned the well.

"Sure, sure. Fine. But I'm not leaving Max at home during the day. I've got him at Grimes puppy farm."

"Yes, I know. Drove by your place a couple of times to check on him. He wasn't in the yard. Your neighbor told me where you were keeping him. So I sort of expected you'd be coming by."

"Ah, entrapment. You knew I'd be coming."

"Yep, but how was I to know you'd be speeding?"

That was the start of an easy friendship. Karen got off at ten p.m., and she'd drive by once a week or so to see if there were lights on. On the first visits she was still in uniform, navy blue shirt atop grey slacks with black striping down the outer seam. Max liked her better than any of the other ladies I'd dragged home. Come to think of it, I did too. It wasn't just the bones and scraps she'd bring him. Max really took to her. He would start prancing and tail wagging the moment she entered the back yard to play with him.

The first few visits she'd stay in the back yard and refuse my offers of a soda or a beer, like she'd drawn a line, this far and no further. But then one Friday night she was wearing jeans, a sweatshirt, and a faded Tigers cap. I took this as a good omen and pressed her again to stay for a drink. She shrugged her shoulders, nodded her head and said, "Why not? What kind of beer you got? Is it cold?"

"Labatts, and icy."

"Well, all right then. Thanks."

So we dragged two padded canvas chairs down to the sea wall and sat and listened as the gentle waves of Lake Huron washed the shore. No moon, so plenty of stars. We sat in silence for a while. Max, the traitor, curled up at Karen's feet and began to snore.

When the silence was broken I learned that Karen's dad was a Detroit Metro cop who'd been killed in the line of duty while she was attending MSU as a pre-law student. With her dad gone, mom devastated and two little sisters, she switched immediately to a criminal justice major and applied to the Michigan State Police Academy. The state police were still eagerly recruiting females, and she was immediately accepted. So she cut her class load at State and finished fourth in her class at the Academy. That was six years ago. After postings in the Upper Peninsula and the Thumb, she'd transferred to Lake Pointe five months ago. Her college boyfriend wasn't very understanding about her schedule, and their plan to marry after the Academy got dropped. She'd almost married a trooper in Bad Axe. But this time she changed her mind before wedding bells chimed.

"We were too much alike. When he spoke I could hear myself talk. That was getting old, and we hadn't even started living together." Unbidden, I imagined us keeping house and me walking in to catch her stepping from the shower.

She'd completed her college degree at night a couple of years ago and was targeting law school for fall a year from now. "I figured the police need a good lawyer in the prosecutor's office to keep guys like you from getting the bad guys off. And, by the way, doesn't it bother you?"

"What?"

"Using courtroom tricks and technicalities to get people off when you know they are guilty."

"None of my clients are guilty. They're just misunderstood."

"Yeah. What about Mr. Armbruster, the 'Country Clubber'?"

"That's what you call him? Probably best we don't discuss that one. Let me just say there's a whole lot more to the story than what you read in the paper."

"What, you think I'm trying to pump you for defense strategy?" She sat forward and put her beer on the ground next to her cap. In the dim light from the house I could see her face in profile. She had a strong face over firm but feminine bone structure.

"Nope, it's not that. Although my big mouth has gotten me in more trouble than I care to remember. I'm still working on a defense strategy. A lot of things in this case look one way at first blush and a different way on more careful review."

"Yeah, like what?" I had her full attention now. She had turned on her charm, and I could see the twinkle of interest in her hazel eyes even though it was pretty dark.

"I'll let you know when I get it figured out."

Max and I escorted her to her cute yellow convertible, and I held the door as she slid her athletic five-foot-eight frame behind the wheel. I'd been working up the courage on our way to the car. "Listen, Max is too shy to ask, but he wants me to invite you out for a steak barbeque next week. He said you guys can ditch me after dinner and go for a walk on the beach. Plus, he gets a bone out of the deal. You're off Thursdays, aren't you?"

She pulled the door shut, turned on the ignition and rolled down her window to smile impishly at me. "Tell Max I thought he'd never ask."

I felt an old familiar feeling begin to stir as Max and I headed back into the house. Thank God my batting average in court was way better than it has ever been in romantic relationships. In love I was zero for life. The fiery passion that had driven Jackie and me to the altar within three months after meeting cooled to a cinder within a year of wedlock. At twenty-two neither of us knew the difference between love and lust. When the lust was sated, we both discovered we didn't really like each other all that well. She was a neatness freak. I was a messy pig. She loved to run up the credit card on clothes and dinners. My father's message had been, "If you can't pay cash, you don't want it." She liked weepy romance movies. I thought John Wayne and Clint Eastwood were worth watching. She'd switch the channel from the ninth inning of a close Tigers game to watch ice dancing and dare me to change back. I'd say tomato. She'd say tomahto. We both agreed to call the whole thing off.

Before Jackie, my high school and college romances would seem to be going great until I finally uttered the magic "I love you" words. Then, having won me over, my paramour would lose interest. Before you knew it, I was on the receiving end of one of those "Why can't we just be friends?" conversations. I took a vow after Jackie to keep the magic words to myself. And that worked fine until Alexandra. She was the unkindest cut of all. Alex, now Judge Kingsdale to me, had taken my heart to places I'd thought were closed to me. Then, right after I'd given all I had to the normally impossible task of helping her defeat an incumbent circuit judge, she'd dumped me.

"My family and friends think it best if we put our plans on hold while I settle in to the judgeship."

How's that for a kiss-off? In the years since Judge Alex had taken the bench, she'd bent over backwards to make it obvious to all that she owed me no favors. Now I would be trying the biggest case of my career in front of a woman who, as near as I could figure, was mad at me for her decision to break things off.

"Thanks for getting me here. Your services are no longer required. Is that it?" I'd fired over my shoulder on my way out her apartment door. If I'd stayed a second longer she would have seen the first tears I'd cried since my father died.

In the years since, I had contented myself with relationships of convenience, some lasting months, others only for a night or two. My mom had stopped asking about who I was seeing as she lost hope for grandchildren from me. I'd envy my married friends with young families but was coming to accept that somehow I'd missed the boat.

I grabbed a pot pie out of the freezer, stuck it in the microwave and marveled at how happy I was feeling about my barbeque date with Trooper Karen. I reached down with both hands and ruffled the thick fur around Max's neck and said, "Better be on your best behavior, old buddy. This one could be a keeper." His brown eyes stared up at the micro as his nose wrinkled with the first scent of chicken cooking.

"Members and accompanied guests only. You must be 18 to enter," reads the sign on the door to the men's locker at the club. When I walked in after practicing my chipping and putting to prepare for the member-guest tournament later in June, Big Lou was in his customary position behind the well-burnished mahogany bar. He pulled the pretzel he was munching from between his teeth and smiled. "Hey, stranger, long time no see. What'll it be?"

"Let me have one of those Goose Islands on draft, please, Lou. Been pretty busy with Ted's case." Instead of sitting at a table, I stood at the bar to jaw awhile..

"Yep, yep. That's not exactly the first time it's come up out here. Sorry about Ted. Always liked him." Lou surveyed the room conspiratorially. Seeing only two members huddled over a gin game at a corner table, and with the wall-mounted television blaring the day's stock market wrap-up, he decided to go on. "Bad shit, Ken. Ted was one of the good guys out here. Always polite, pleasant, friendly, you know. Took good care of me and the guys tip-wise, unlike some other cheap bastards I know. And his wife, what a looker! I been reading the paper, and let me tell you, she wasn't quite the angel they make her out to be."

I unscrewed the lid on the glass jar full of giant cashews and poured some into the bowl Lou supplied. "What do you mean, Lou?"

He stepped back and busied himself rearranging glasses. "Nothing.

Just saying. People think me and the guys are just part of the furniture. They think we've got no ears, got no eyes. We hear stuff. We see stuff. All I'm saying is, ask around. Mrs. Armbruster had an active social life. Know what I mean?

"Can you give me any names?"

He shook his head determinedly.

"Okay, Lou, thanks for the tip."

"Way I figured it, Ted finally wised up and lost his temper. Heat of passion. I read lots of books. Can't you turn that into manslaughter instead of murder?'

I swallowed the last of the beer, pulled the chit over, adding an extra tip, and signed it. "Think about this, Lou. Ted says he didn't do it. Maybe one of Amanda's social contacts did. Ever think of that?"

Lou laughed and shook his head. "Ain't buying that. I've read where they got him with blood on his hands and his fingerprints on the murder weapon. Man, did Ted love that club! Before they banned it he showed it to me, bragging it took two strokes off his handicap. Jacking the insurance and confessing to the cops. No sir, I may have been born yesterday, but not late yesterday. Your only hope is to dig up the infidelity dirt and have Ted say he lost it. Hell, I hear she was with that scrap yard mobster over at Heather Hollows that night and they had a big fight. There you go." He wiped a rag across the counter. "If she was cheating on him and rubbing his nose in it, the jury will cut him some slack."

I headed around the end of the bar to go to my locker. "All right, Lou. I'll think it over. See ya."

The shower at the club was much better than the trickle coming from the nozzle above the curtained bathtub at the cottage. So I showered there. By the time I'd finished and was sitting on the bench at my locker, the place was quiet. As I bent to tie my shoes, I asked myself what I was doing out there with a murder case coming to trial in less than six weeks. The answer was, I was as hooked on golf as I had been on cigarettes. With that thought, a little devil inside my head prompted me to thoroughly search my locker for an old pack. None there.

I was there that night because the invitational was next week and I didn't want to be a complete albatross for my partner. My brother Matt and I had a long-term tradition of my playing in his club's Invitational and him in mine. Invitationals were a gas. Three days of dining, drinking and hoopla woven around competitive golf. Matt and I would be teammates instead of adversaries on the links. And what with the weather that spring and then being back on Ted's case, I needed a golf fix. That's what golf is for me, a fix.

I've played fifty-four holes on a single day. I've played in the heat at plus one hundred and in the sub freezing cold when the snow on the green collected around the ball while putting. I have been out in downpours, gales, and sleet storms. I'm too foolish to come in out of the rain and too stubbornly optimistic to recognize my limited talent for the game. I'm a lifetime eighteen handicapper. What a curse that is!

Quality golfers playing at a handicap under ten have their love for the game requited. Alas, the poor lost souls like me with a handicap near twenty are doomed to a few quick flings, when the game rewards devotion. Oh, you can play well for nine holes, maybe even a couple of rounds, enough to move the handicap down. But it doesn't last. You keep chanting the same mantra: "Full shoulder turn," "Back elbow in," "Swing down the target line." But the mind-body synergy breaks down. You've developed a reverse pivot, or your hips slide, or you come over the top, or, or, or. It's always something. And there you are again at the end of eighteen, reaching for your wallet and attesting to a triple-digit score.

A rational person with senses not addled by addiction would, after countless Sisyphian trips up the mountain of golf improvement, wake up in the morning with the boulder back at the bottom of the hill and decide the rock looks just fine where it is. Maybe he decides to take up jogging for outdoor exercise. Not the golf junkies. Like Sisyphus, we are condemned. After all, just before evening we are close enough to glimpse the apex. Maybe another lesson, more time on the range, try the swing tips from Tiger Woods in this month's *Golf Digest.* Then we will be able to wrestle the rock all the way to the top this time. It's a fool's dream, a golfing fool like me. Besides, how many excuses does a grown man get to wear short pants, wildly colored shirts, and funky caps, doing what his mother implored him to do as a boy? "Go outside and play for awhile."

Two bad things and one good came out of playing in the Invitational. I missed a three-foot putt on the final hole that would have sent my brother and me into a playoff. He still rides me about it. On day two of the tournament I caved in on smoking. His Marlboros had been winking at me from the dash of the cart for two days. After hitting a sweet drive on number 4, I winked back. Forty-seven days of self-denial and ten pounds added around the waist went up in smoke. The first couple made me dizzy. By post-round cocktails, nicotine was meeting me in all the old familiar places. It was embedded back in all my neuro-circuitry like a worm in a computer.

The good thing was the putting lesson from Grayton Lansdale. Leaving aside the final hole yip, his tips really helped. In fact, I'd been making all the easy ones and a surprising number of long ones throughout the tourney. Nowhere does success breed success like on the putting green. Make one and you think you will make the next. Make a bunch and you stand over the next, knowing it is going in. All of the technique books, videos, and lessons not withstanding, golf is a mental game. That is what Gray told me on the practice green two nights before the tournament. What he told me in the bar after the lesson would prove more important.

Gray was a gregarious two handicapper who strove diligently to reach scratch. At age forty-five, he was tall, athletically wiry, and handsome. His tanned face had the leathery look of a smoker who spent his share of the time in the sun. The laugh lines were etched in crow's feet around his eyes beneath his full head of wavy, prematurely gray hair. He had inherited and expanded the family's construction business and was friendly to everyone.

Gray leaned on his putter and watched me miss a series of five-footers. "Need a little help?"

"Ah, more than a little, I'm afraid."

He stepped closer. "You are trying to guide it with your hands. Let the shoulders rock and roll the ball. Here, watch me." He bent over at the waist and demonstrated by hitting three balls to the back of the cup. Still hunched over, he glanced up at me. "The less moving parts, the better. Grip the shaft lightly, keep the wrist firm and let the big muscles do the work. Here, you try it."

He spent a very patient and instructive half hour with me. By the finish he had me in a repeatable three-step putting routine that was sending the ball to the hole with confidence.

"Gray, this really feels good. Thanks for your patience."

"No problem, Ken. Putting is half technique and half confidence. Believe in this approach and you'll be surprised." Gray walked over to his bag beside the large old oak at the side of the practice green and put his putter away. Then he knelt down to tuck the balls into his bag. He squinted up at me into the last light of the setting sun. "Say, I saw your name on the board playing with your brother in Invitational. How are you going to do that with taking over Ted's case?"

"Tell you the truth, I feel a little guilty. But my brother cleared his schedule and trial is still almost a month off, so I can manage. Hey, if Stretch is still there, let me buy you a beer as payment for my lesson."

"Sounds good to me," said Gray as he lifted his bag over his shoulder. We carried our bags back under the upper deck porch overhang to the unattended bag room.

Stretch, a six-foot-four bean-pole, was still behind the bar sorting through the members' chits for the day. Otherwise, the place was empty. He looked up and smiled. "Just made it, gentlemen. I was ready to close. Can I get you something?"

We both replied, "The usual, please."

Within a minute, Stretch was there with a frosty schooner of Goose Island draft for me and a tall gin and tonic for Gray. He set the chit down and said, "If you want food, I think it's too late. The kitchen closes at nine and it's after that. But I can check."

I signed the bill and said, "Don't worry about it, Stretch. We're just going to have a quick one and go. If you're done, don't wait for us."

He looked at the clock. "If you don't mind, I'm going to go. I'm already a half hour late for a date." He held the TV clicker in his hand

and pointed it at the soundless TVs. "Want the ball game on?"

The upper left hand box of the screen showed the Tigers getting thrashed by Kansas City, 9 to 2 in the eighth. I shook my head. "Shut it off if you want." The screens went black. Stretch grabbed his keys, said good night and was gone. We had the place to ourselves. I held my glass up to Gray. "To all those who wish us well," I offered.

"The rest of them can go to hell," he replied as our glasses clinked. The beer was cold and refreshing and I took a hardy swallow. Gray took a generous pull on his drink, set the glass on the table and asked, "How's Ted's case going? From what I'm reading and hearing, can't be too good."

"Gray, maybe you heard. Judge placed a strict gag order on the case. I'm not supposed to talk about it. But, since you asked. It's not as bad as it looks."

He laughed. "Be hard to be that bad, wouldn't it?"

"The paper loves the 'rich country club big shot kills trophy wife for insurance proceeds' angle."

"Add the jealous husband angle off the brouhaha at Heather Hollow, and I could argue the prosecutor's case," laughed Gray.

"How'd you know about that?" I asked.

"Everybody out here knows about it. You know Jillian. That girl loves to talk. The paper knows too. But, since they've painted such a saintly picture of Amanda, they're keeping that under wraps."

"Do I look suicidal? Would I take a case where there was no hope?"

He nodded and laughed. "You bet. Your name is on the front page every other day. Last I looked, you can't buy advertising on the front page. Everybody knows Ted's guilty. So when they convict Ted, nobody blames you. And if somehow you pull it off, which I rate about even with your chances to win the Masters, your career is made. I just smile when I hear the guys saying what a stupid move it was for you to take the case back."

I looked at Grayton with new respect. He had it nailed. "Pretty cynical, aren't you? You've got the odds of a defense victory a little long, don't you think?"

He shook his head while taking another sip. "Don't think so. They had Ted without the confession. With it he's sunk."

"Remember, the so-called confession isn't on tape and isn't in Ted's hand. It's Bliss's summary of what Bliss says Ted told him. Ted denies it. We've got something to work with."

"That's it? That's your defense?"

"Among other things. I'm working some angles. We'll see. Plus I'm a better lawyer than I am a golfer."

Gray sputtered on his gin and tonic to the extent that some landed on the table. "I hope so," he said, dabbing at the spill. "No offense, but Ted's going to need a scratch lawyer, not an eighteen handicapper. Who are you calling on his behalf?"

I handed him another napkin for the drink on his chin. "How about you, Gray?"

All humor left his face. "Me? I was in Elkhart, Indiana at a builder's show the night he killed her."

I sighed. "Thought you were his friend. He says he didn't kill her. You just toss that out the window?"

He held his hands open. "Okay then, I was still in Elkhart the night she died."

I moved my beer to the side and leaned my elbows on the table. "Look, Ted was a member here thirty years. He was friendly. He volunteered for every committee with some dog shit job to do. If memory serves me right, that gap on the wall between the pictures of the 1992 club president and the 1994 club president in the entrance foyer used to be occupied by his picture. Now, nobody knows him."

Gray ran his fingers through his thick gray hair. "Yeah, I thought taking the picture down before the trial was tacky. The ladies were having a charity fashion show and a group of nonmembers were gathered at the sign-in table below the presidents' wall. The ladies were all talking and pointing. Mary Delano, the wife of the president-elect, thought this just wouldn't do and told her husband so that night. The picture was gone the next morning. It's chicken shit. But what are you going to do?"

I leaned further forward in my chair. "You think that's chicken shit?

I had Ted give me a list of ten character witnesses out here to interview. I've talked to nine of them. Know what his best friends told me? 'I'm sorry, I'll be out of town that day. When is it?' 'My company wouldn't like it.' 'I'd feel very uncomfortable.' 'My cat's getting spayed that day,' etc. We've got a real group of standup guys out here at the Club."

"That's a shame. Ted was always a real gentleman. Who is number ten?"

I looked him in the eye. "You, Gray."

"Oh, shit. Knew you were going to say that." He paused, shifted uncomfortably in his seat, sighed, and looked back at me. "What do I have to do?"

"Just testify to what you know. Was he a man of good moral character? Was he honest? Did he have a violent nature? Was he a good citizen? Did he love his wife? That kind of stuff. Will you do it?"

Gray rested a cheek on his fist and stared down at the table. Finally he answered, "Ken, I build homes for the gentry. The same folks who took his picture off the wall. They probably won't approve. But I've known Ted for a long time. Heck, I remodeled his house. Whatever reason he did what he did, I was his friend. Count me in."

"Thanks, Gray, it'll mean a lot to Ted. I didn't know Amanda that well. But I've been picking up rumbles that maybe she won't be next in line for sainthood. You know anything?"

Gray looked at his watch, took a gulp to empty his glass and stood up. "I think Ted loved her with all his heart. Amanda loved him. But more as a father figure. Quite an age difference, you know. Some of her other needs may have gotten taken care of away from home. That's all I'm saying." He turned and walked around the corner of the bar and back into the locker room. I followed. When I caught up, he was sitting on the bench in front of his locker and loosening his golf shoes.

"C'mon, man, you can't leave it at that. What do you know?"

"Listen, Ken, I'm already in this deeper than I should be. I agreed to be a witness, which I will probably regret. I don't really know anything. Let's just leave it at that."

I took my foot off the bench and started for my back corner locker.

"Gray, I appreciate your agreeing to help. If you know something and can tell me, nobody will know where I got it. Think about it with the idea that maybe, just maybe, Ted didn't do it." I walked back to my locker, switched shoes, picked up my suit hanging on a wooden hanger, and slipped the strap of my sports bag over my shoulder.

Only my convertible, Gray's Explorer, and the night man's clunker dotted the empty parking lot. The western sky retained a tinge of purple. As I was trying to lay my suit evenly in the trunk, Gray drove up behind me and leaned out of the window. "If you say you heard it from me, I'll deny it. Early in April I went into the pro shop to return a putter. It was ladies' league night. The shop was empty, but Sonny's office door was open. I walked to the door and saw Amanda sitting on the desk. That fresh out of college assistant, Chip, had his back to me, but I think the instruction he was giving emphasized the hip turn."

Before I could say anything, he took his foot off the brake and drove out the exit. As I rode home I thought to myself, if I were like M. Stanton, my trip to the club would've been billable hours.

15

July mistook itself for August. The temperatures were in the high eighties with the humidity building from morning to afternoon. Only the odd gusty thunderstorm provided relief. The office air conditioner decided to get an early start to the weekend. At two p.m. one Friday, my tenant, Teutonic Tom, called to say he had a man on the way, but with the heat, ours wasn't the only system down. I congratulated myself again on making him building superintendent and let the girls go home early. So I sat with my office windows open, sleeves rolled up, and a portable fan vibrating on the wooden floor. My plan, with trial now a month away, was to take inventory of Ted's case and schedule what witnesses I needed to go see. Other than Big Lou's reference to Amanda's fooling around and Gray's sighting of the assistant pro in flagrante delicto with Amanda, my list of somebody else to blame was very short. I needed a scapegoat.

It looked like Gianfranco would have to be the guy. I thought of him as my kamikaze defense. Try to blame him, and however it played with the jury, it could well have fatal complications for me post trial. After he'd sent the lilies to my office and then the attempt on Max, if that's what it was, things had been quiet. Oh, I'd gotten so many post-midnight heavy breathing calls I'd taken to unplugging the phone. Those calls were as likely to originate with members of the public as from king of the scrap heap. I was hopeful I could find some other angles from which to focus a defense.

I was convinced that Ted was on the conviction express unless I could sidetrack the bloodhounds on the jury with other possible suspects. One of the best ways to create reasonable doubt was to seed the path to conviction with the scent of others with motive and opportunity. Oh, I planned to confront Chip and subpoena him if he didn't have an airtight alibi for April 28th. But somehow I didn't see the pro shop tryst providing a motive for murder. But you never know unless you try. Since my shirt was welding itself with sweat to my back, I decided there was no time like the present to go talk to Chip. So I closed up shop, peeled the convertible top down on the Benz, and headed for the club.

The club pool was full of splashing, squealing youngsters. I could hear the calls of "Marco" answered by "Polo" as I walked along the well landscaped sidewalk separating the pool from the clubhouse. Mothers lounged on recliners or sat in groups of three or four at umbrellaed tables. The smell of French fries and hamburgers mixed with the coconut smell of suntan lotion in a most pleasant concoction. I swung by the pro shop in search of Chip only to learn he was playing in the Boyne Mountain pro-am for the weekend.

My initial purpose scuttled, I headed for my locker, hoping I'd left my swimsuit from the Invitational. I said a few hello's to the gin players and the CNBC stock market cabal on my way through the bar. By now the claws of the bear market, which had started in March of this year, were beginning to draw blood. Eighteen years of a bull market capped with a two-year parabolic tech-spec bubble had created a lot of paper wealth. It had also created a group of self-styled market geniuses in the clubhouse. This selloff was burning paper profits and confidence in a hurry. But Thad Granger's repetition of the bygone bull market mantra "Buy The Dips" was all I could glean from the stock players in passing. Heading toward my locker, I wondered if the thousand-point swoon over the last three months hadn't changed the watch words just slightly. "Dips Buy." Since I had so little money in the game, it wasn't keeping me up at night.

A couple of members clad in the club's logo towels were standing in front of the wall length mirror applying talc, deodorant and hair spray from the mantel beneath the mirror.

"Hey, Kenny. Give you a chance to get your money back." I looked down the aisle of lockers to my left and saw Freddie Hildebrandt tucking his pink golf shirt into white shorts. Freddie was a golf buddy; that is to say, we had lots of contact and phone calls during the season. When the snow fell I never saw nor heard from him. He'd expanded the family's nursery business to the point he had hired a full time manager and had lots of free time. Golf filled much of it. But for some reason, his handicap hadn't dropped to reflect the time and attention he was giving the game. I suspected he was only turning in the score cards from his lousier rounds so as to remain at the fourteen handicap he used to win virtually every bet I made with him. He'd shoot 78 and then exclaim, "Best round of my life. Never played so great." Some of the other pigeons confirmed Fast Freddie was having lots of career rounds.

I smiled at him. "No thanks, Freddie. Too hot for me. Just going to leap into the pool."

Three and a half hours later I missed a measly little four-foot putt to lose match, medal, and overall bets for the grand total of thirty bucks. Some tuxedoed high school senior standing at the rail of the upstairs patio had a grandstand view of the green on eighteen. He convulsed his chums with "Miss it, Noonan" just as I took the putter back. And miss it I did.

Freddie suggested we have a drink on the upstairs patio. As was our tradition, the winner buys. So at least I would get a free drink out of the deal. A ten-minute shower later, I walked through the late season graduation party, headed for the patio. The joker nudged his date and pointed at me. They were both laughing as I walked outside. Freddie was seated at a wrought iron table near the rail. The sun was reluctantly hanging by the horizon, and the course was bathed in the last light of day. The sprinklers went tocketa-tocketa, making their slow rotation to shower the greens. Fish surfaced for bugs, leaving concentric rings on the surface of the pond that guarded eighteen. When the waitress, Veronica, opened the door, bearing our drinks on a tray, the coolness of the air conditioning and the babble of teenage voices wafted out to us.

"Oh, Mr. Edwards. Mr Hildebrandt said to put these on his tab.

You didn't lose to him again, did you?"

"'Fraid so. Think it's time to report him to the handicap committee?"

She smiled a prim Mona Lisa smile as she set our drinks on the table. "A generous tipper like him? Never."

With that she left the chit in front of Fred, curtsied, and left us alone. We had a couple of rounds, and when Ronnie said she could still arrange a sandwich if we acted right away, we ordered hamburgers. As dusk turned to dark Freddie's jaunty demeanor suddenly turned contemplative. I looked over my shoulder to see what had grabbed his eye. Just below, his first wife, Joyce, was climbing into a golf cart for the ride home with Leo Jackson, a successful veterinarian and her husband for the last five years. They smiled and waved as they drove off.

"Christ, Ken! How could I have been so stupid? That woman really loved me. She gave me two beautiful daughters who barely speak to me since the divorce. She knocked herself out building the business. What do I do? I trade a real woman in for eye candy. My marriage to Lisa lasted about thirty seconds. And the way things are going with Nicole, she won't beat that by much. Shit, Nicole is only three years older than my eldest."

Freddie needed to talk and I provided an ear. I stopped my beers after three. But Freddie was on his fifth gin and tonic when he gave me what would prove to be a whole new angle for Ted's defense. After bemoaning his marital fate, he thanked me for listening and asked about Ted's case. I gave him an update and asked him if he had any thoughts. "No idea, man. One beautiful woman gone south. Just was getting to know her through being on the Dressler Foundation Committee set up to find the missing half mill. Oops, forget I said that."

I came fully alert. "What half mill?"

"I didn't say anything." He shook his head, suddenly realizing the impact of the drinks.

"C'mon, man. Don't tease me. Give."

"I'm sorry I mentioned it. I took a pledge of secrecy. Just forget you heard it."

No amount of prying and cajoling would move him. Suddenly we had nothing more to say, so we walked down the stairs to the sound of the party band, uninterrupted by further conversation. Watching him weave over to his Jag, I offered to drive him home. "No thanks," he slurred. "I'm just around the corner. On Dressler, just drop it." He waved his hands exaggeratedly. "I'm in deep shit if anybody hears I mentioned it."

Watching the highlights of a rare Tigers victory on Sports Center before sleep, I made plans to be at the jail first thing Saturday morning. I wanted to see what Ted could tell me about Amanda and Dressler's missing money.

I was brimming with curiosity as I sat down with Ted in the familiar dingy confines of the jail's conference room. A matron had favored us with fresh coffee. Ted was excited for my unscheduled visit until I told him the purpose. Suddenly he withdrew behind a mask of apprehension.

"I'd rather you didn't get into that." His tone was distant.

"Why not?"

"You could do a lot of harm without doing me any good."

Since I'd come back on the case he'd treated me like his knight in shining armor. Maybe that's overdoing it. I was at least his dusty paladin charged with fighting for his freedom. He'd been open, warm, and trusting. Now I could feel his chill. He sat back in his chair, furrowed his brow and nervously started rubbing his index finger on his thumb.

"Ted. What's going on here? You tell me you didn't kill your wife. Can you tell me who did?"

He shook his head.

"Okay. If I am to have any chance at trial, I've got to give the jury someone else as a possible suspect. You understand that?"

A brief nod.

"All right then. A missing half million dollars leading to the death of a woman investigating where it went has me pretty excited. So give."

Instead of answering my question, he gave me the almost seventy-year history of the Foundation. Turns out the Dressler family had made very big money during the logging era in and around Lake Pointe. When timber played out, the next generation of Dresslers lent sizable money to Will Durant as General Motors was struggling for a foothold in the car business. The loans were paid back with stock, a large piece of which formed the endowment for the Foundation. The Foundation had been doing philanthropic work in the tri-county area for generations. Among many other things, the Foundation had built a home for unwed mothers, a cancer wing on the hospital and a band shell in the park, and endowed an extensive college scholarship program. I watched him sip his coffee.

"Ken, you have no idea the good they do around here. Makes the United Way look like the Little Sisters of the Poor. There are only two Dressler heirs living. Both sisters moved to New York years ago. But under the Foundation's deed of trust, those sisters have all the say so on where the money gets spent. Over the years there has been talk they might want to move the funds focus to needy folks out east. One whiff of scandal here and they might do that."

"All right," I conceded. "I'll tread softly, but you told me the most important reason why you are fighting this case is so that whoever killed Amanda doesn't get away with it. Am I right?"

He softened some and took a more relaxed posture. "Okay. I'll tell you what I know." I smiled and reached for my pen and legal pad. "But only on one condition," he added forcefully.

I dropped the pen. I wasn't liking my client's new attitude. "What's that, Ted?"

"You use none of what you learn without my okay."

The coffee went untouched and cold in the cups while we sorted out who was boss, a challenge I had to win. I even suggested maybe he wanted to start looking at some of those lawyers he'd interviewed in the transition from Browne to me. "I'm not going to fight your case with my hands tied behind my back."

"It's too late for that and you know it. The judge wouldn't let you off the case this close to trial even if you wanted out. And I know you well enough now to know you don't want out," he threw angrily back at me. His dead-on appraisal of the lay of the land startled me.

And so it went, until we compromised, agreeing I'd keep him posted on what I learned and I'd let him know before I brought it out in court and then "we'd decide."

After tempers cooled, I asked him why he had reacted the way he did. His answer impressed me at the time. "Ken, I was on the Dressler board quite a few years back. They do an unbelievable amount of civic good. More than you or I could ever do in five lifetimes. I don't want to drag them, and some of my friends who are on the board now, into the mud in a desperate attempt to save myself. I'd almost rather go to prison for something I didn't do. Can you understand that?"

I stared at him while I considered it. "Yes, I think I can. And I admire you for it. But what if the killing had to do with the missing money?"

He shrugged as if that was a dubious proposition. "Ask away."

"So what was Amanda looking into, and who else was commissioned to investigate with her?"

"Amanda swore me to secrecy, and even then she wouldn't tell me much. She was appointed to a committee with fellow board members Freddie Hildebrandt and the accountant, Brenton Eubanks."

"When was she appointed?"

He paused to think, wrinkling his lips as he tasted the cold coffee. "Best guess, late January, early February. I think something came up on the Foundation's year-end accounting."

"What was her assignment?"

He got up and stretched, twisting his torso. "Boy, my back kills me every morning since I've been in here. The bed is like sleeping on lumpy towels. Her assignment? I'm not sure. She had a couple of meetings, and she went out and bought a leather attaché to keep her documents." He was behind me as he paced to work out the kink in his back. At the mention of the valise I jumped from my chair to look at him.

"Where's the attaché, Ted?"

He pursed his lips in thought. "Probably in the den-office we set up at the back of the house."

"Did you ever see what was in the case?"

He started shaking his head, then caught himself. "Once I walked in to get an address and she had papers all over the desk with the case open on the floor. She kind of scooped a bunch of papers together when I came over to use the rolodex."

"Any of them catch your eye?"

"Not really. I did see the cover page of an S.G. Hayden Securities statement with the Foundation name on it. Amanda had a bunch of sticky notes custom made with butterflies on them, and I could see a bunch of those sticking from the pile of papers. That's about it."

"Ever look inside the attaché?"

He recoiled as if I'd asked him if he'd cheated on his taxes. "Certainly not. That was her business. Plus the case had a combination."

"Ever ask her what was happening?"

He moved back to the chair, sat slowly and wiped some of the dust off the wooden table. He nodded. "I was curious. In the couple of weeks before she died, she was on the office phone a lot so I wouldn't overhear. I'm guessing those calls had to do with the investigation, as she usually used the cordless in the kitchen. When I asked what all the phone conferences were about, she told me I had to stay out of it."

We sat for another ten minutes while I asked every question I could think of, but got no further information except that the keys for the office file cabinet should be in the upper right hand drawer of the desk. He seemed relieved when I said, "That's all for now," and made ready to leave. He took my hand as I went to the door to signal for a turnkey.

"Ken, sorry about the disagreement. It's just that I put a lot of heart and soul into that Foundation over the years. I know how many lives it changed for the better. Be careful. Be discreet. Please."

17

By that afternoon I had gotten the house keys from Marjorie Armbruster and was sitting in the drive on Bonnie Brae. The landscaping service lawnmowers were roaring in both the front and back yards. The cottonwood seeds were drifting like a summer snow flurry in the gentle July breeze. I sat in the convertible parked in front of the portico and thought that everything on the outside looked as if nothing had ever happened. Only the remnants of a yellow police tape wrapped around one of the columns gave hint that things had changed forever.

Once inside, the house had the feel of a ship abandoned in mid voyage. The air conditioning was a quiet whisper. The fridge hummed softly. Dust motes floated in shafts of sunlight. But the place felt empty. The marble tile glistened, and no residue remained where Amanda had fallen, green and white, in a pool of red. The mirror was gone from the staircase. I noticed a few small specks of red on the wall near the first step that the police photos hadn't captured.

As I walked through the living room toward the back of the house, the French doors offered a view of the pool and patio area. A teenager on a riding lawnmower traversed the lawn behind. I walked over, unlocked the doors, and stepped onto the flagstone surrounding the empty pool. Blue tarp covered a grouping of overturned deck furniture for which summer had never come this year. From there I heard the click of club hitting ball and a shout of "Be the right stick!" I had a glimpse of the number 15 fairway through the trees, but not the players. I was delaying my move to the den to allow the excitement simmering since Ted had told me of the attaché to come to a boil. Would I find the keys to his freedom in that briefcase? Somehow, I was sure I would.

The louvered shutters in the den were closed, the room dark. My eyes had to adjust to find the light switch and then again to the brightness when the lights came on. A well furnished home office lay before me, with a large oak desk in front of the shuttered windows. A brown leather couch faced a custom built audio-visual center of the same oak. The plush burgundy carpet cushioned my step as I moved to the three-drawer file cabinet in the corner to the left of the desk. But no attaché. I checked the closet near the credenza to find only a couple of windbreakers and an umbrella. The shelf yielded only dusty fingertips as I stood on tiptoe and ran my hands back and forth. I got down on the floor to look under the couch. Nothing.

Opening the desk drawer, I found the cabinet keys Ted had told me would be there. The lock in the upper right corner was already unlocked, the key mechanism standing out. I made a note to ask Ted whether it was normally locked. The hodgepodge of file dividers in the top drawer rekindled hope. But an hour of leafing through them revealed only tax documents, deeds, correspondence dating back twenty years, and other personal marginalia. The second drawer was jammed with owners' manuals for everything from the pool pump to the garbage disposal.

The bottom drawer was empty, but with a clear rectangular pattern where dust had been dislodged. Had the attaché left that pattern in the dust? The desk contained stacks of butterfly sticky notes in the center drawer among the pens and paper clips. The side drawers were filled with phone books and stationery and an old dictation recorder. There were no cassettes.

I spent an hour or so wandering from room to room, feeling like a jewel thief as I rifled drawers and closets to no effect. A search of the cabana, garage, and basement proved equally disappointing. I locked the front door in the quiet late afternoon and gave the departed maintenance service credit for a job well done. The landscape was a testament to gentrified country living and gave no hint that uncivilized violence had come calling on the lady of the house only a few months ago.

My suppertime return visit only took Ted away from his macaroni casserole for a few minutes. The file cabinet was always locked, and Amanda had kept her attaché in the bottom drawer from time to time. He seemed at a loss to explain the attache's absence until he mentioned the family cabin on Lake Huron near Oscoda.

"I didn't go up there in the winter. But Amanda liked the solitude. Two Saturdays before she died she spent the night there. Whether she took that case with her, I don't know." He also mentioned something I should have thought of myself. "Did you check the trunk of her BMW?"

I'd looked in the passenger cabins of both the Lincoln Town Car and the green sports car parked in the garage, but not the trunk. He pointed out that the key ring given to me by his mother had keys for both cars and the cabin as well.

On my way home I wheeled up to the KFC drive thru and ordered a large bucket of chicken for me and a side of extra gravy for Max. I could stretch that gravy for a week pouring just a little over his Pedigree. Whatever the Colonel put in his gravy sent Max to the moon. So my faithful companion cavorted and leapt when the aroma reached him on my arrival at his doggie day care. I had to put the bag of food in the trunk to drive home. His head was in my lap while I worked on a Sunday *Times* crossword and ate my chicken at the backyard picnic table by the lake. Water and jet skiers zoomed by, in close to shore, and the sun was still high enough that the first wave of mosquitoes was an hour away. Evenings like this made the cold loneliness of the wintertime worth the trouble. The puzzle got so greasy from my finger-lickin'-good fingertips that the pen wouldn't work. So I fed Max and lit up a post-dinner Marlie to plan my approach from here. I was on the half pack a day plan since my collapse at the tourney. But the discipline was waning.

I decided to talk to Thad Granger at S.G. Hayden Securities before I spent a day driving to the Armbruster cottage. I'd also go see Brenton Eubanks, who just happened to do my books. One of them should be able to help. If not, I'd lose another thirty bucks golfing with Freddie and try to get him looped enough to tell me more. He'd opened the door while getting soused on the patio after our last round before slamming it shut again. Maybe I could recreate the scene. I sat there lighting smoke after smoke, trying to see through the mist shrouding the Dressler file. Ted seemed to think it was unrelated to Amanda's death. But it seemed more than coincidence that the murder had happened so shortly after Amanda's appointment to the board investigating missing money. For me, coincidence was an explanation of last resort.

Five hundred thousand seemed like a lot of money to misplace. Surely, by now, somebody had a pretty good idea where it had wandered off to. Ted's fear of jeopardizing the fund's staying in town seemed a good explanation for why the whole thing was hush-hush. But it didn't explain why Amanda's file had disappeared. Or did it?

My conjectures ended with the first squadron of dive-bombing mosquitoes. Max and I went inside. As I gathered the chicken packaging, I had a very small fit of domesticity and pulled out a new barrel-sized trash bag, which quickly filled with two weeks of newspapers, food wrappers and unemptied ashtrays.

"Why don't you keep this place cleaned up, Max?" I asked as he followed me into the bedroom. I let my clothes fall in a heap.

The next morning the S. G. Hayden brokerage offices were without other clientele when I came looking for Thad. In fact, he came out to greet me as soon as the receptionist buzzed him. I'd just sat down with this week's *Barrons*, a picture of a drunken bull, ice pack to his head, on the cover. The tag line was "Is the party over?" Thad was wearing a dapper, light-blue striped, seersucker jacket over a pink silk tie and dark blue shirt. His bronze tan nicely topped off his ensemble. No hair of his magnificent mane of swept-back auburn hair was out of place. And, to judge by his smile, the party was definitely not over. He reached a handshake to me and in so doing helped me out of the plush chair into which I'd just sunk.

"Hey, partner. How are you? You know, I looked in my planner. I've called you nineteen times over the last three years trying to get you in here to open an account. Just goes to show you: never give up. I've got most of the attorneys here in town, Judges Tedorski and Kingsdale included. Be nice to add you to the list at last. C'mon into my office."

We walked by some other brokers sitting in cubicles, staring at their computer screens or talking quietly on the phone, on the way back to Thad's office. Thad's office was no cubicle. Glass looking out over the rooftops to the lake. Finely polished furniture and lots of artwork adorning the walls. The shelves were filled with plaques attesting to his unfailing attendance at Rotary and Lions Club as well as numerous golf trophies. A picture of his still pretty wife, Jeannie, perched on his desk so that both he and his customers could bask in her portrait smile. After he got us both a coffee, he settled into his swivel chair, took a sip, careful of his pink silk tie, and smacked his lips.

"Real Jamaican Blue Mountain. Only the best for our clients. So, ready to take advantage of this little sell-off? What are you thinking? Some of these Internet funds have dropped twenty, thirty percent in the last few months. Might be the perfect time to hop on board before the train leaves the station."

"Actually, Thad, I came to ask you about the Dressler fund account."

Now the party was over. His cheery demeanor vaporized. He stiffened and sat back in his chair. "What do you know about Dressler?"

"Only that Amanda was on the audit committee looking into what I'll just call an irregularity of some sort. I know they had accounts with you. So, as Ted's friend and neighbor, I came to see what light you can shine on what happened."

"What makes you think they had an account with us?"

"They did, didn't they?"

"I'm not allowed to disclose customer identity by exchange and firm rules."

"What? Didn't you just mention Judge—?"

His face turned red, clashing with the pink tie. He held up his hand and interrupted. "My mistake. I shouldn't have. I cannot and will not discuss whether the Foundation has ever done any business here. Now, is there something else I can help you with? I'm kind of in a hurry."

"Okay." I set my cup on the table. "Gosh, Thad. You seemed so happy to see me not two minutes ago, and now you can't wait to get rid of me. What gives?"

"Nothing, just a lot of things on my plate."

I could see the first little glow of perspiration on his forehead. So I pushed on. "Let me save you the trouble of telling me whether you have the account by saying I have it on unimpeachable authority that you do. So, now do you want to tell me whether you were interviewed by Amanda as part of the audit?"

A vein on his left forehead stood out. "Listen, Edwards, you're way out of your depth here. You're fishing in waters where something nasty could bite you and, if I talked to you, bite me too. That's all I'm saying. If you don't mind, I've got calls to make."

He stood to emphasize that our chat was over. I rose too, noting the steam still rising from the cup on the desk corner. "Gosh, great coffee, Thad. At least the one sip I got. I'm here trying to help your neighbor and you're giving me the bum's rush. This is how you help your friends?"

He held his office door open. I watched him take a deep breath, hold it, and consider before answering: "Nobody who'd do what Ted did is a friend of mine. So don't expect any help from me."

I got two steps down the hall with him standing in the doorway to see me leave when I turned and fired a little torpedo to take his mind off stocks for awhile. "Do you want your subpoena served here or at home?"

Just the briefest flicker of fear crossed his eyes before they hardened. "Do what you have to do."

The door shut behind me. The cheery receptionist glanced up with surprise as I passed. "Leaving so soon, Mr. Edwards?"

I adopted a quizzical expression. "Afraid so. Mr. Granger seemed so bearish this morning. Is he usually like that?"

"Not like that at all."

I shrugged and moved out to the sidewalk beyond the office with its finely polished furniture, Chamber of Commerce plaques, and artwork. The sound of morning traffic replaced the hum of the electronic ticker. I didn't know what I had with Dressler, but whatever it was, it was something big and something scary. Scary enough to turn one of the jolliest gladhanding guys I'd ever met into Mr. Cold Shoulder in a flash. Now what could do that?

The barbeque with Karen had been perfect. As the summer solstice had just passed, the sun hung around till almost ten p.m. She drove over in her yellow Miata and let me take it for a test drive. Cornering around back country roads, the car was nimble and responsive. She reminded me of the speed limit every time I tried to wind it up. On more than one occasion I found myself glancing over to glimpse her profile. Her strawberry blonde hair streamed in the breeze coming over the top of the sporty convertible. When the evening sun broke through the canopy of trees, it dappled her freckled face. Her profile looked girlish yet determined. We chatted and laughed and she instructed me more than once to keep my eyes on the road.

Max forgot his disappointment at missing a car ride upon our return. But instead of greeting me on the driver's side, he pranced over to the passenger's side, his tail wagging a mile a minute, until Karen climbed out and bent to pet him. His large pink tongue lavished kisses on her face. I even felt a little jealous watching the bond between them; of her for getting all the attention from my one-man dog, and of him for his license to smooch. As we walked around to the lake side I looked at her yellow convertible parked next to my red one. Unbeckoned, the image of the two of us sharing a garage on a long-term basis entered my head, which made me wonder how far gone I might be, upcoming trial or no trial.

As the steaks grilled I watched Karen and Max playing at the shore.

She threw sticks into the lake and Max tirelessly bounded into the cool waters to retrieve. She wore blue jeans and a red and white checked shirt. Seeing her out of uniform, she was, as Billy had originally speculated, well put together. Long legs, girlish hips tapering into a trim waist, and a bust which tightened her shirt as she reached back to toss another stick. I wondered, considering our age difference, if I dared to even hope she'd have much interest in me.

The Merlot she had brought went well with the T-bones. A full moon made a spectacular appearance, rising over the lake as we sat at the outdoor picnic table and chatted. We sliced the few remnants from the bones into Max's dish and sat on the same side of the table, enjoying the moon rise. "Ken, that was nice. Thank you."

"Glad you liked it. But barbeque steaks and baked potato pretty well covers my culinary talents."

"Can I ask you something?" she asked, turning more serious.

"Fire away."

"How can a lawyer defend someone knowing he's guilty?"

I must have stiffened, because she added, "After my father's death and the tricks the shyster used to try and get the killer off, it made my mother and me so upset I just had to ask."

"Are you asking in general, or about me and the Armbruster case in particular?"

"Both, I guess."

She seemed sincere. So I thought about my answer while I emptied the last of the wine into our glasses. "Well, in a way it's easier when you know the client is guilty. At least then if he's convicted you don't feel so bad, and most of the time you try to find some way to mitigate the circumstances to get the best plea deal you can. As a defense lawyer it's part of the job to keep the system honest, like if the police seized the crucial evidence through an illegal search and your client walks. Then you feel good, because you are protecting John Q Citizen's Fourth Amendment rights from police intrusion. You've been around cops long enough to know, if there were no consequences for crossing the line, the line would keep getting crossed."

She cocked her head as if to say okay, and held her wine glass up to me as a peace offering. I touched my glass to hers and went on.

"Plus, there are usually at least two sides to a story. From when we were kids, 'He hit me first' is a good defense to getting caught hitting back. So it's the defense lawyer's job to tell his client's side of the story as best he can and let the jury decide. Our whole system turns on presumption of innocence and proof beyond a reasonable doubt." I turned in my chair to look directly at her. "It all started with people fleeing arbitrary kings in Europe who were dragging the peasants in at their whim. So lawyers are set up in the battle between individual and state to protect everybody. The system requires us to raise the burden of proof high enough that sometimes the guilty go free so the innocent are not convicted. The defense lawyer keeps the system vigorous and honest by making the police and prosecutor work before the accused gets locked up. Is that so bad?"

She sipped her Merlot. "You can't think something like the O.J. verdict was a good thing."

I shrugged. "System is not perfect. It's just the best available."

"What about you and the Country Clubber?"

I put my glass down and looked over at her. Her hazel eyes stared earnestly back at me. I knew she was wrestling with her job and my job, and I decided to give her the best answer I could. "Karen, this case scares me like none I've ever had. I'll confess I wanted it because with all the publicity, it could make my career. But the deeper I get into it, the more worried I get that I'll blow it and Ted goes off to prison to die for a crime he didn't commit. I'm not sure how I'll live with that."

She screwed up her face in disbelief. "C'mon, Ken. You aren't talking to the jury here. You can't really believe he's innocent with all the evidence, the confession, and then jacking the insurance just before he killed her. Give me a little more credit than that."

I felt a wave of melancholy at her words. Most believed them. Quixotically, I'd hoped she'd believe in my truth. "That's what scares the shit out of me. He looks guilty as hell. But he's stuck to his claim of innocence since I talked to him on the night his wife died. I'm not a walking lie detector, but I believe him. And unless I come up with something really good, he's going down for a crime he didn't commit."

"So what have you got?"

I shook my head, tempering it with a smile.

"Please don't take offense, but they would take my bar card if I talked defense strategy with a cop. I will say the so-called confession is bogus. I think Bliss heard what he wanted to hear, and in a state of shock over his wife's death, Ted signed it."

"Yeah, what about his lawyer, Browne, initialing it?"

"Don't get me started on Browne. But you know he's told the court Bliss got it wrong."

"Right, right. You believe that? Still, I'm not too crazy about Bliss either. He's what I call a boob talker."

"You mean a talking boob?"

"No, a boob talker. I've seen him at a couple of interagency meetings. Talked to him on a couple of occasions. His eyes never leave my chest. If men only knew how women felt when they do that."

I made a mental note to make a greater effort to keep my eyes on the face in the future. I wanted nothing in common with Bliss, particularly in how Karen saw us.

We went down the stone steps to the beach, taking Max with us. As we sat on the bottom step to remove our shoes and socks, Max stuck his muzzle in to hurry us along. He loves walks. Karen gave me a playful hip check five minutes into our moonlit beach stroll where the wet sand sloped steeply into the lake, then laughed heartily as I fought to regain my balance in the water. My jeans were soaked to the knees. Max barked and rushed in to join me. Karen danced away from my retaliation splashes but couldn't escape the shower as Max rushed out of the water to chase her down, then gave himself a thorough shake while right next to her.

A neighbor a few cottages down flipped on his yard light and opened a squeaky screen door to peer out in reaction to the ruckus. We both made childish shushing noises at each other with our index fingers held up to our mouths. I wondered as we strolled whether our occasional bumps into each other were strictly due to the uneven footing. I debated taking her hand the next time it brushed mine but didn't want to ruin the moment.

We stood in the drive under the now fully-leafed oak and said our goodnights at 1:30. "How did it ever get so late?" Karen asked. "I've got to be at the range for the seven a.m. slot tomorrow. I hate to think what kind of marksmanship score I'll get. This was fun, really fun. Thank you so much."

Again I hung between the desire to kiss her and the fear of rejection. The longer the moment extended, the stronger was my desire to taste those full lips. So, while telling her how much I'd enjoyed the evening, too, I leaned to close the gap between us and put my hands on her shoulders. Her eyes twinkled as she let me draw her closer, but our lips touched only for an instant before she backed off, smiling, leaving me with a shimmer of their sweetness.

"Let's take this nice and easy. I like to touch all the bases. And when it comes to kissing accommodations, I prefer non-smoking. Are you okay with that?"

"Sounds good to me." I tried to keep the disappointment out of my voice. Apparently I failed, as she stepped over to hug me just long enough to leave an indelible impression of her firm body etched into mine. She bent to pat Max, allowing him more face time than she'd given me. Then she hopped into her convertible and backed out of the drive.

Pulling the garage door shut behind me, I followed Max into the kitchen. Once inside, he looked quizzically over his shoulder as if to ask me "How did it go?"

"Good, I think, old buddy. At least I hope so," I said, crumpling a half empty pack of Marlies.

Brenton Eubanks was exactly what the mind pictures upon seeing the letters CPA. He was a gnome. His five foot frame was hunched over from what I fancied to be long years bent over the ledgers. His short-cropped gray hair receded from a prominent forehead. Nearing sixty-five, he'd risen to second from the top at Williston, Reed, Eubanks and Downing, LLC. In the world of international corporate accounting, they weren't even a speck on the radar. But for northern Michigan, a twenty-member, home-grown accounting firm was big. He was a man I respected. Understated, pleasant, and rock solid honest, he knew the tax code intimately. He made sure you didn't send Uncle Sam any more than you owed. But he'd tolerate no flimflams to send less.

Brent had been handling my personal and office returns for the twelve years I had been in private practice. I'd met him while still taking parts at the Lake Pointe Players, as he was a big booster of the local theater group. At the cast party for my stage debut in *The Man Who Came to Dinner* ten years ago, he'd presented me with a beautifully framed picture of me trading dialogue with the E.B. White character. It still sat on my dresser beneath the mirror, serving as an odometer to the miles I'd traveled since I was a fresh-faced law school graduate. Brent had offered to keep my books and keep Uncle Sam off my back, and I accepted. I had to be his smallest account.

The firm had taken an old Jefferson Avenue lumber baron's mansion and lovingly redecorated and restored it to showplace standards. Wooden floors, gaslight candle sconces, and wainscoting made one feel like one had stepped back a hundred years on climbing the steps to enter. Brent came out to greet me with a look of surprise on his face, adjusting his half-glass bifocals to make eye contact. His eyes were bright, still elfin in spite of his age. "I had to check my calendar to make sure it wasn't April fourteenth. That's the only time I see you these days. C'mon in."

His office had once been the upstairs parlor, and it was appointed with antique furniture that matched the vintage of the home. Except for the computer and telephone on small tables behind him, everything was from a bygone era, including the uncomfortable straight back chair in front of his desk.

"Coffee?" he offered. His voice was deep and weighty, as if asking whether I could document my deductions.

"No thanks. Just had a little." I smiled, thinking of my brief stay in Granger's office a few days earlier.

"Didn't get one of those little brown envelopes from our friends at the IRS, did you?"

I squared myself, trying in vain to find a good way to sit in that chair. "Actually, Brent, I'm here to see you about Ted Armbruster."

He tilted his head to the side with a puzzled look, acquired over years of practice. "Don't know how I can help you with that. Terrible thing. Both such nice people. Can't understand it. Can you get him a deal?"

"Actually, Brent, Ted says he didn't do it."

The skeptical furrowing of his brow matched earlier times when I'd tried to claim deductions for such things as three-piece suits under the uniforms deduction. "Okay, how can I help?"

"I need to know what you, Amanda, and Freddie Hildebrandt were investigating over at Dressler."

His reaction was less icy than Granger's. He rested his cheek on his fist and used his pinky to scratch between lip and nostril while he looked appraisingly at me. "What do you know?"

"Know half a mill went missing. Know the three of you were on a committee of the board appointed to look into it. Know Amanda got killed not long after that. Know that her investigation file is missing. What do you know?"

He gazed evenly at me. I could almost hear the abacus discs sliding up and down the columns in his head. Finally, the calculations complete, he spoke.

"Technically I can tell you nothing. I will only say that the accounting matter was resolved well before Amanda's death. I give you my word on that. So, if you are trying to tie the two together you are definitely gone astray. I tell you this so you don't waste your time and energy on a dead end that cannot help your client. I tell you also in trust that you will not use it as a red herring in Ted's defense that can only hurt lots of innocent people without helping Ted."

"Brent, sometimes a red herring works quite nicely in getting a jury's nose off the scent of the accused."

Now he looked put out, and his voice reflected it. "I've heard lawyers do that. But Ted was a very active Foundation board member for many years. Their good works are too dear to his heart for him to want you to create a scandal as a diversion. I'm certain of that." He paused and looked over my head out the window behind me as if searching for the right words. He pinched his lower lip, released it and looked me directly in the eye. "I am sure Ted would be opposed to dragging the Foundation into it. Very sure."

I marveled at how well he'd captured the sense of the lawyer-client chat Ted and I had had the day before. So I sat and listened as Brent extolled the Foundation's importance to the community and reiterated a long-standing worry that the Dressler sisters might move the largess east. He would answer no questions about the "accounting matter." He did say he wondered about the file materials Amanda had had, and that discreet inquiries had indicated they were lost. He wouldn't tell me who had given him that information. He was polite, professional and firm. Unlike Granger, he was never hostile.

He walked me out to my car. As I reached for the door handle he squinted up at me, his deep, sincere tone attesting to his concern. "Ken,

I've always liked you and stood up for you when others said you were a rascal. I think I'm a good judge of character. I am confident you will not damage our community when I've told you there is no connection to Amanda's death."

He didn't wait for my response. He just held up his right hand, either to prevent one or in benediction, and walked back up the steps.

I sat in my car, listening to the traffic on Center, fighting the temptation for a contemplative smoke to help in my deliberations, and tried to figure what to do next. The missing money was better than a jilted lover as a motive for murder. It had to be more than coincidence that Amanda had started to look into where it went and ended up dead not long thereafter. But I trusted Brent. And he had just told me it was a waste of time. And Ted was eager I leave it alone. So, for that matter, was Thad Granger. What about it could turn Thad from Mr. Warm to Mr. Chilly in a heartbeat?

Finally, after maybe ten minutes, I knew I had to find out and turned the ignition key. The old childhood saying popped into my head as I drove back to the office. "Curiosity killed the cat."

They say you are not paranoid if somebody really is out to get you. Within a few days of my meetings with Eubanks and Granger, I began to suspect I was being followed. The plastic rear window in the 280 was slightly frosted with age, making identification of vehicles at a distance behind me difficult. But now it seemed there were an awful lot of tan Fords and light green Chevys going wherever I was going. I'd gotten jumpy enough to try sudden turns into back streets and driveways, only to watch the cars drive on by on the road I'd left. Just when I'd think it was my imagination and a day or two would pass without incident, there would be a set of headlights following that looked familiar, or a tan or green car a couple of cars behind in traffic.

One evening a beat-up, red Chevy wagon had trailed me on the dusty dirt road to Esther Grimes' puppy farm. The same car was behind me fifteen minutes later when Max and I headed home on a road that might see twenty cars a day. Paranoia? Maybe. But I didn't think so. When I confessed my fears to Karen, she listened sympathetically but didn't attribute much concern to them.

"You think maybe you're getting a bit stressed?"

"That, too."

20

For July the evening weather was cool. I leaned back in my leather office chair with my feet resting on an open desk drawer. The windows behind my desk were cranked open, admitting the street sounds from Lafayette Avenue one story below and letting the smoke from a borrowed Marlie escape. Since as far as my secretaries knew, I was off the weed, the ashtrays had been washed and stored away. My Subway soda cup stood in for them.

Every so often, the boom of a maxed-out car stereo echoing off downtown walls would interrupt my eight p.m. reverie. Ted's file was spread across the desk and spilled onto the floor by my feet. Yellow legal pads containing my every thought on the case were stacked on the credenza behind me. The appellate court volumes I was citing in my trial brief sprawled split-spined on my couch. With only two weeks until the start of trial, I had the pad with my to-do list before me. Still lots to do and little time to get it done. Panic was setting in.

I reviewed what I'd checked off the list as done: Been through all the police reports many times. Interviewed Jim and Jillian Simpson. No help for Ted there. At Heather Hollows he'd been "drunk, crazed with jealous anger, and threatening." But I still needed to talk to the bartender out there. He'd been avoiding me. Gianfranco interviewed. He looked like the best one to blame. But blaming him was going to prove more injurious to my health in a much shorter time than the cigarettes the

Surgeon General had warned me about. Interviewed Chip, the assistant pro. After strenuous denials and threatening to beat the shit out of me, he'd acknowledged the pro shop tryst, saying: "The lady made me an offer I couldn't refuse. The way she strutted her stuff, I'm sure I wasn't the only one. But if you drag me into court they'll can my ass. Boffing the members is a definite no-no under PGA rules. Give me a break here."

The interview had taken place on the driving range, after Chip finished his lesson with a twelve-year-old who was already a better golfer than I could ever hope to be. Chip had walked over to schedule my lessons before the member-member tournament coming up in August, in his usual jovial mood. By the end of our chat he was decidedly distant. When I wouldn't promise to leave him out of it, his parting words were, "Maybe you should find somebody else to try and fix that swing of yours. It's beyond my talents."

I felt resurgent guilt over my decision to play in the club's biggest tourney in the middle of a murder trial. My regular partner, Judge Ernest Schroeder, had invited me as his member-guest partner before I joined the club, and we'd remained a team for the member-member since I'd joined. He was understanding but disappointed when I told him I was out after Ted rehired me. He was elated when he called me into chambers a week later. "Great news, Ken. Just had a chat with Judge Kingsdale. I was giving her hell for holding a murder trial right in the middle of the tournament. Told her her priorities were screwed up. Guess what she told me?"

I felt a surge of hope that the trial would be moved back to its second trial date in September. I could use the additional time to prepare. Judge Ernie, like me, was a Michigan State grad and had his two daughters sucking tuition and room and board out of his bank account at an alarming rate. His office was decorated with green paint on the floor skirting and white on the ceiling molding. Spartan memorabilia lined his shelves, including autographed photos of the judge with the head basketball and football coaches. It was fun with out-of-town counsel, unfamiliar with the judge's reputation for impartiality, to mention during in-chamber conferences their Wolverine background, then watch them pale as the judge raised his bushy eyebrows in mock disapproval.

"I don't know, Judge. What's she got in mind?"

"A wedding, that's what."

My jaw dropped. Even though Judge Alexandra Kingsdale had dumped me within weeks of getting elected to the circuit bench, I guess I still carried a candle for the woman who'd been the love of my life. Ernie knew the history.

"No, not her wedding. Her sister's. Alex is to be the maid of honor in her sister's wedding the weekend of the tournament. She's adjourning trial on the Thursday and Friday to fly to California. So we can be partners."

I was uncertain. "Geez, Judge. I don't know. Right in the middle of a trial I probably would have trouble concentrating, and who knows what will have come up that needs my attention? I sure wouldn't want my client on trial for his life, hearing I was out playing golf while his case hung in the balance."

Ernie laughed. "Look, partner, the only thing that should be hanging is your client, if half of what I hear is true. Ted was an avid golfer. He knows how big the member-member is. Ask him."

When I asked Ted, he was insistent that I play. "You can't miss it. It's the biggest tournament of the year. You're already looking stressed and tired, and the trial hasn't even started. A little break in the middle of trial will let you recharge your batteries. God, I wish I could play. Wonder who Randy got to replace me?"

I didn't have the heart to tell him his steadiest of golf buddies and tournament partner for nineteen years, Randy Dykes, was one of the character witnesses who had begged off, claiming, "Sorry, Ken. Be bad for business. Please tell Ted I wish him luck though."

I told Ted I could use the time mid-trial to work on his case, but he was insistent. "Play, by all means, play. My only condition is, let me take vicarious pleasure through you. Give me updates on how you guys are doing."

In the end I accepted Ted's clearance and told Ernie I'd play, subject to having to pull out if the case required. But as dusk settled over the city,

I couldn't help but feel I'd be letting Ted down. I didn't realize at that moment the impact the tournament would have on Ted's case.

21

The police report file was always open on my desk. Sometimes it was stacked in a corner with a file clip holding the pages together so I could work on some other matter. Now the yellow-highlighted pages covered the desk top. A circular coffee cup stain on one page alternated with smeared ash on another. I'd read and reread the file countless times, looking for something I'd missed. The only remaining anomaly was Geraldine Chambers. The 911 log from the night of Amanda's death reflected her two calls reporting a suspected prowler within an hour of Ted's call asking for an ambulance. I stared again at the highlighted sections of the 911 log.

> **02:21:** 1612 Bonnie Brae. Geraldine Chambers reports prowler. Frightened. L.C.S.D. to inv.
>
> **02:49:** 1612 Bonnie Brae. Mrs. Chambers reports burglar escaping with sack of stolen property. Heard glass breaking. L.C.S.D. adv.
>
> **02:52:** 1608 Bonnie Brae. Ted Armbruster reports wife attacked. Assailant unk. Vic not moving. Amb disp. Det Weston L.C.S.D. notif. Unit 347 en route.

I'd listened to the tape of Ted's call repeatedly. If the prosecution didn't put it in evidence, I would. He sounded frantic with worry and desperate for the ambulance to arrive. But the tape of Mrs. Chambers' calls had not been preserved. By the time I'd gotten back on the case, it had been erased under the department's policy to keep tapes thirty days and then recycle. When I'd asked Jamie Dawson, the sheriff's chief dispatch officer, about it, she'd told me it was long gone.

"Kinda surprised me, what with the next door neighbor calling about a prowler at the time of the murder. But prosecutor Botham had me preserve the Armbruster section of the tape and said to let the Chambers call just go on the thirty-day rotation. That other lawyer never asked for it. So it's been taped over."

I'd filed a motion before Judge Kingsdale to dismiss or otherwise sanction the prosecution for destroying potentially exculpatory evidence. Browne had filed a boiler plate discovery request asking for all exculpatory information. The judge seemed a little put out until Tina gave her the history between Geraldine and 911 dispatch. "Judge, dispatch officer Dawson has over ten 'suspected prowler, burglary in progress' calls in the last eight months since Mr. Chambers died last year. So far the police have found exactly one cat up a backyard tree and been offered lots of plates of cookies and cups of hot chocolate. Geraldine Chambers is an eighty-two-year-old widow who is frightened and lonely and panics at every bump in the night. Moreover, we gave the defense the 911 log as soon as Mr. Browne filed his request. If they wanted the tape preserved, all they had to do was ask."

Motion denied. Since then I'd been trying to talk to Mrs. Chambers with no luck. I'd made repeated visits to her ivy-covered, brick, Tudor-style home, which stood between the Armbrusters' and the Brownes'. I'd stand on the front step listening to the doorbell play Beethoven's "Ode to Joy," knowing she was in there. The upstairs curtain would move. But no one came to the door. She would answer the phone, but hang up once I identified myself.

My last recourse was subterfuge. The Chambers' backyard separated itself from the number 15 fairway with a short fence overgrown with a tall hedge. The sign on the white wooden gate proclaimed

Private Property—No Trespassing

Over the years I'd been warned that it was best to abandon wayward second shots that came to rest in her yard. Freddie Hildebrandt had cautioned me the summer before as I moved to recover my ball from her yard. "Not worth it. Ralph jumped the gate for a new Pro-V fresh out of his bag. The crazy old bat came after him in her nightie swinging a broom. Old Geraldine in a nightie is not a pretty sight. Ralph tore his pants going back over the gate. I nearly broke a rib laughing. You should see the collection of golf balls she's got on wooden racks in the garage. She hasn't been right since her husband died."

But since nothing else was working, I decided to take the Ralph approach. It took me three shots to land one in her yard. Surprising, given how easy it was to hit one there when you weren't trying. It was 7:30 on a late July Thursday. The course was empty. The light breeze carried the laughter and smell of steaks cooking from a barbeque a couple of yards down. I looked to make sure no one was looking and tried to lift the latch on the gate. Locked. So, with visions of how painful a failed vault of the picket-fenced gate might be, I braced myself and went over. With my golf cap pulled low over my face to avoid recognition, I started beating about the hedge to make noise. Actually, my ball was plainly visible near a stone birdbath.

"Get out of my yard, you hooligan!" A shrill voice over the screen door slamming shut. I kept my back to her and continued rustling in the hedge, pretending not to hear. Mrs. Chambers approached, waving spindly arms to shoo me away.

When she was close enough, I reached in the side pocket of my golf slacks and turned, handing her the subpoena. "Sorry, ma'am. You left me no other way."

She looked at the order to appear and looked up at me with surprise, giving way first to anger, then tears. I felt like a schmuck making a little old lady cry. She took off her glasses and fetched a hankie from the pocket of what I guessed to be a long used gardening dress. She had a dowager's hump that caused the dress to ride up in the back and expose varicose veins in her legs above footies in worn Converse tennis shoes. She dried her eyes and peered balefully up at me, her five-foot frame still trembling. "What does this mean?"

"It means you will have to come to court in a week or two for your neighbor Ted's trial." I stood there feeling like Simon Legree as her eyes welled anew.

"But Miss Botham said they wouldn't be needing me. Please, please, young man, don't make me go. I don't know anything about that dreadful murder, and I get very nervous."

It had been a long time since anybody had referred to me as "young man." All a matter of perspective, I thought. From eighty plus, I was about half her age and probably seemed like a whippersnapper. I smiled and tried to calm her. "I'm Ken Edwards, Ted's lawyer."

"I know who you are. I've seen your picture in the paper. But this is a private club. How did you get in?"

"Actually, ma'am, I'm a member."

This seemed to soothe her. She relaxed and stuffed her hankie in her pocket and fitted her specs over her eyes to examine me more closely. "Well then, as a gentleman you should understand about not putting a frightened little old lady on the witness stand. I'll just faint dead away. I know I will."

"Perhaps if we talked awhile I could better decide if I need you in court."

She pondered that, saw an elusive ray of hope, and brightened. "Do you like chocolate chip cookies? I just made a batch and they're still warm."

"They're my favorites."

The kitchen was bright and airy. The cookies sat on a large platter on a marble countertop. Their aroma filled the room, and I kept asking her for just one more. She fetched me a glass of milk and told me how she "just loves a man who can eat." I took the gentle approach. To begin, I talked about Ted as her neighbor.

"Wonderful man. After my Lester died he'd check on me. Fixed the garage door when it was stuck. Always very thoughtful. That's why it's so hard to believe he did such an awful thing to poor Amanda."

I emphasized Ted's repeated claims of innocence to skeptically raised eyebrows. "You've known Ted for decades. Did the kind, helpful neighbor you were telling me about suddenly turn into a monster?"

She was sitting across from me at a dining nook and fussed with her teaspoon before looking up at me. "That's what troubles me about everything I hear and read. It all seems so unlike Ted. I've even thought of visiting at the jail, bring him some cookies or a cake. I can't imagine he's eating very well there. But after what he did to poor Amanda, I just couldn't even bring myself to send him a note. I still can't believe he would do such a thing. He was such a gentleman."

"Ted tells me he did not kill her and has hired me to prove that."

She shook her head. "But all the neighbors say, and the newspaper and the TV, well, they say he's guilty."

"I understand. But that hasn't been proven in a court of law. And yes, many people have turned against Ted based on what they've heard. I know he'll be very saddened to hear that you have too."

She looked slightly abashed and bent down to stroke a calico cat weaving itself between her feet. As she sat erect again she stammered, "I'm not judging... I didn't say..."

"Mrs. Chambers, you appear to be an intelligent woman. Do me a favor. Imagine, just imagine for a minute that what Ted is saying is true, he didn't kill his wife. Then imagine the grief he feels over her death and the loneliness of having all his friends desert him, while the real killer gets away with murder."

She looked stricken with guilt as she considered what I had said. Then another thought crossed her mind. "But both Miss Botham and that big ape of a detective—oops, sorry, Mr. Bliss—they said they have a confession."

"That's what they claim. I say he didn't confess because he didn't kill Amanda; but if you won't speak to me I'll report back to Ted that I tried. Thanks for your time and the wonderful cookies, and I'm sorry to have frightened you."

I began to rise. She reached a birdlike hand across the table and touched my forearm. "Sit a spell. Miss Botham said I didn't have to talk to you. She didn't say I couldn't."

"Can you tell me about what you saw and heard the night Amanda died?"

I watched her compose herself, old and alone and anxious. "I haven't done well since my husband died. I have trouble sleeping. I get scared in the night. I had the landscaper come and trim the trees around the house because the noise from branches rubbing sounded like an intruder. The police have come so many times I know them by name. They've been so nice, but I'm sure they think of me as the old biddy who cries wolf. That's why I hesitated to call that night."

"I understand."

"I heard a rustling. My bedroom looks over the back yard and onto the golf course. It was one of the first warm days in April, so I had the window open. I got out of bed and looked out and couldn't see anything. But I was sure somebody was out there. I thought I'd also heard glass break. But, funny what happens to your hearing when you get old. You don't hear things that are there, and you hear things that aren't. So I can't really say for sure."

"Don't worry about it. What else did you notice that night?"

"I thought I saw a shadow." She seemed hesitant to go further, her eyes faded behind tear-smudged glasses.

"Go on, tell me about the shadow."

"Well, the first time was by the hedge. I thought I saw one. But my eyes aren't what they once were, and sometimes I guess I see things that aren't there; but the second time, after I'd called the police again about breaking glass and put the telephone back, I was sure I saw a burglar."

"How do you know it was a burglar?"

"He had a sack on his back, but he was on the outside of my gate, on the golf course."

"A sack?"

"All I saw was a shadow, running—no, not running, walking fast. I know this sounds stupid, but I thought of Santa. I could see the profile stooped over with a sack over his shoulder. Since I'm a little old to believe in Santa, I thought it was loot he'd stolen."

"Could you be sure it was a man?"

She paused, her native intelligence surfacing. "Not really. My eyes. I had my glasses on as I do now, but I still can barely pass the driving test.

I don't even drive at night anymore."

"This person, which way was he or she going?"

Again she hesitated in concentration. "Oh, boy, I should know that. I can just see the profile. I want to say away from Armbruster's, but maybe that's because of what happened. I'd have to say I'm not sure."

"Did you tell the police about this?"

"I'm sure I would have. I know I talked to the deputy in the morning, but what I told him I can't say for sure. I was pretty upset."

"Tell me about breaking glass."

"I heard the rustle, I called the police, but they know me at dispatch. I could tell they were being polite. Then I looked out the window for a while and everything was quiet. I began to think I was just being silly again and went back to bed. I remember thinking I had some fresh brownies for when the police came. It must've been a half hour or so after I heard the rustling. And then I heard the sound like a window breaking. I panicked and ran downstairs to make sure all the doors were locked even though I always double check before bed. I grabbed a butcher knife from the kitchen and ran up to my bedroom and locked the doors. I sat in my chair by the window but sort of behind the curtain. That's when I heard what maybe was whispering voices, but it might have been the breeze. The police said maybe it was Ted on the phone to them. I don't know, I was pretty agitated. Then I peeked from behind the curtain, and that's when I saw the shadow. I got scared again and called the police. After that I didn't look out anymore. I was afraid the burglar would see me and not want any witnesses. So I was just frozen in my chair till the police cars started arriving next door."

"Did you recognize any of the whispered voices?"

"No."

"Male or female?"

She shook her head.

"Anything else unusual?"

"That's enough for one night, isn't it?"

"Yes, ma'am," I said, smiling. "I guess it is." I drank the last of the milk and rose to leave. "You've been very kind, Mrs. Chambers, thanks for the cookies."

As she opened the gate to let me back out onto the course, I shouldered my bag and started to angle back toward the clubhouse. I had almost cleared the trees between her yard and the fencing when she called me back.

"Most of the members ride in a cart. I guess I don't see many walking. But as you were walking away and got sideways to me—well, that's when the shadow looked like Santa. But nobody plays golf at two a.m., do they?"

"No, ma'am, not even me, and I'm pretty fanatic."

I considered everything she had told me as I cut across the fairway to reach 18 and the clubhouse. Did she actually see or hear any of what she was telling me? Why wasn't any of it in the police report? Who was the shadow golfer? I could figure why her statement to the deputy had ended up on the cutting room floor. It didn't fit with the nice, neat package of guilt in which Bliss had Ted wrapped.

I swung by the Armbrusters' and found the trunks of both the Lincoln and the BMW empty. One more thing off the list. Still needed to go up to their cottage and see if I could pick up the trail of the missing Dressler Foundation file.

22

In the week or two before trial my anxiety level steadily rose. Not only was I torn between different defenses—an unhappy lover, Gianfranco, or the missing Foundation money—but also, I wasn't getting much sleep. Even though my number was unlisted, I was getting repeated two and three a.m. calls. I guessed they were coming from a bar or club, as I could hear music, the sounds of a pool game, and voices in the background. Sometimes a throaty voice, sometimes a deep bass, always raspy breathing. Whatever the voice, the message was never friendly.

"Oh, did I wake you? Ask the wrong questions and you'll get all the sleep you'll need." Click.

"You've been warned, mouthpiece. Don't mess where you shouldn't mess." Click.

"Just called to say hi, asshole." Click.

"If we're looking for you, there's no place to hide." Click.

"Think anybody would really care if a certain jerk off lawyer had a bad accident?"

"Want to buy some insurance, pally? You might need it soon."

Most of the time it was no message, just breathing, a laugh and a hang up. I had caller ID, but all it showed was "incoming call." In terms of the effect on my sleep, it may as well have read "incoming grenade." I talked to Karen about it and she arranged a trace, but the five-second calls didn't allow enough time. Finally I just unplugged the phone at night.

I had a pretty good idea who to thank for these calls: Gianfranco. So I called Firenze Metals one morning after a sleepless night. Gianfranco sounded quite chirpy.

"Morning, counselor, you're up early."

"Early birds get the worm."

"What can I do for you?"

"Somebody's been making late night calls to threaten me. I wondered if you knew anything about that."

"Probably one of your many fans. I hear you're not that popular with John Q Public. Trying to get off Mr. Big Shot Country Club guy for killing his Saint of the Charities wife. If you can't stand the heat, get out of the kitchen. Why are you crying to me? If I'm the closest thing to a friend you've got, you're in big trouble."

"No, I thought maybe you knew who might be making the calls."

He laughed. "Me? Come on. I'm a legitimate businessman. Harassing phone calls must be some kind of crime. Why would you think I'd have anything to do with criminal behavior?"

"Just a guess."

"Guess again. Maybe I should report you to that tight-assed prosecutor for calling to harass me. Harassing a witness has to be more serious than crank phone calls. You know the prosecutor's subpoenaed me?"

"Yep. Way I figure it, about the time their subpoenas went out is the time I started getting the calls."

I could hear him swivel his chair and his feet hit the floor. The joviality left him. "Well, figure this then. Crank calls are cute. Nothing I do is cute. I'm what you call an 'all in' kind of guy. Know what I mean?"

I tried to keep my voice even. "No, can you explain that for me?"

"You're a bright guy. You'll figure it out. On the stand I'm going to testify to my brief contact with the deceased, the nut case client of yours losing it in the bar, and me giving the lady a ride home. Anything that might embarrass me or upset my wife, I'd have to do what you lawyers do, object."

Before I could say any more, he'd hung up. My hand was shaking as I put the receiver back in its cradle. He'd scared the hell out of me without saying anything that could be called a threat and while maintaining a pleasant tone. In essence, he'd squashed me like a bug. To think I'd actually been happy when the case came back to me.

That morning offered a break from the life and death wars of defending a major criminal case. The final pretrial conference on my biggest car accident case was scheduled before judge Ernie. I walked over to the courthouse to calm my nerves. The county courthouse was a classic example of Depression-era public works architecture. Its nine stories of Russian wedding cake architecture housed all the county offices as well as the courts. As Lake Pointe's tallest building, its upper stories were visible for miles. From two blocks away the sun brightly lit the monolithic white walls.

My chat with Gianfranco had elevated my fears that this building would be the scene of my undoing on both a personal and professional level. It was difficult to concentrate on the civil case that was the subject of my meeting with the judge and opposing counsel. I felt a premonition that I'd lose Ted's case. My client, whom I was beginning to think might really be innocent, would go to prison for the rest of what would be a very short life. That would be a heavy cross to bear. But, if my futile efforts to save Ted embarrassed Firenze, I probably wouldn't have long to carry the cross. Damned if you do. Damned if you don't.

I was pretty distracted at the conference, but Judge Ernie was so excited about the upcoming tournament he covered for me. After Al Martin, opposing counsel for the insurance company on a pick-up truck striking my bicycling client case, had chatted football long enough to make for a full billable hour, he checked his watch and left. Ernie took me aside in the hall.

"Ken, you all right? You look like you've seen a ghost."

"I have, and it was me."

"What?"

"Oh, nothing. Just the stress of prep for the Armbruster case."

Ernie wrapped his arm around my shoulder and said, "Relax. Do the best you can, lose gracefully, 'cause everybody knows it's a loser. No one will fault you except to wonder why you went back into a case you were well out of. But I'm expecting you to fight like hell once the member-member starts."

"Yes, Your Honor." I managed a smile and headed back to the office, the bicycle accident case in the file under my arm and out of my head.

As I climbed the stairs to the second floor, Tom Thalberg was on his way down. Known to his colleagues at the bar as Teutonic Tom, Tom the Terrible or Testy Tom, and to his clients as Tom Terrific, Tom Thalberg was an enigma. Built on Falstaffian lines and fastidiously attired, he looked like a young Jackie Gleason. His thick black hair lay in curls on a massive head. He spent more on three-piece suits than the national budget of some small countries. He could be by turns ebulliently cheerful or darkly brusk. He was the scourge of the divorce practice. Many a philandering spouse found their worst legal nightmare incarnate in Tom. The cost of trashing the old model for a new trophy wife was exorbitant when Tom represented the woman scorned.

He was relentless in extricating the details of hot pillow romances. He tracked hidden assets like a malnourished truffle hound. By the time he had finished with the ambidextrous anesthesiologist at trial, Tom's name was legend among doctors' wives. Seemed that the good doctor, after administering the anesthetic, had stood back to peer over the operative field from behind a scrub nurse and a candy striper. His feeble claims of accidentally brushing their gluteus maximi turned to ether when they both took the stand. The nurses described, in detail, extensive and prolonged palpations while they'd stood frozen side by side. The manual ministrations were punctuated by periodic pelvic thrusts. When an LPN he'd been boinking in the 3 West linen closet came forward, it was Dr. Allenbee who took enough gas to leave him financially comatose.

Another of Tom's not so gay divorcees, a nimble-fingered matron of thirty married years, worked out the frustrations and psychological trauma of her Dow VP husband's foray into the secretarial pool by doing needlework during her six-month divorce. When her ex had been completely drawn and quartered in court, she came to Tom's office to pay the final installment on her legal account. Beaming, she presented Tom with her work of art in a silver frame, depicting a young lad with his trousers down over his mother's knee. Mom, sitting in a rocking chair, had her right hand raised ready to spank again. The little miscreant's tortured face was so lovingly rendered, you could almost hear him howl as the tears poured. In bold, red, old English letters, Tom's battle cry was woven: "Gonna play? Gotta pay!" Tom drove a nail into the wall and hung it behind his desk before Mrs. Jackson had a chance to get out the door.

I greeted Tom as I was halfway up the stairs. "Mr. Biggs. What's up? Thought you were on a diet?"

Tom, clutching a briefcase in one hand and the last bite of a donut in the other, smiled as he popped the final morsel into his mouth. He held up his right index finger while he chewed and swallowed. "Behold, the lazy landlord. Speaking of tasty morsels, have I got one for you." A couple of crumbs spilled from the corner of his mouth onto the vest of this three-piece, navy blue pinstripe. He scrupulously brushed them away. "I'm late for a custody hearing now. But check with me after five tonight. Might save your Mr. Armbruster from the gallows."

He continued past me and down the stairs. "Tom, don't leave me like this," I called after him. "If it's that good, tell me now."

Like the rabbit in Alice in Wonderland, he looked at the watch hanging on a gold fob at his waist and said, "I'm late, I'm late, for a very important date." With that he disappeared around the corner and was gone.

23

Tom's teaser had my mind spinning as I mounted the stairs and walked down the hall to my office door. I straightened the artwork in the hallway as I passed and wondered, not for the first time, if Tom wasn't the one who kept nudging them askew. Was he fooling with me now? The glass entrance door to the office squeaked on its hinges as I entered. Yvonne looked up from the counter where she was collating copies and smiled. "Hi, boss."

"Hey, Yvonne. Anything new? Charmed anybody today?"

"Not so far. Lots of calls." She pulled a stack of pink message slips out of their nest and handed them to me.

"Okay, well, let me sort through these messages and see if anybody is just bursting to send me a large check." I turned from the front desk to walk back toward my office.

"Oh, I just took a call from Terry O'Shea at Midwest Casualty."

I turned, and she handed me one more pink slip. "That was the one I was looking for." O'Shea was the claims adjuster for the bike case in the file beneath my arm.

Ted's case was occupying all my time. The retainer was my largest ever. But the way his case was distracting me from other work, I was beginning to think I'd go broke getting rich. Keeping a law office up and running was like keeping a stable of polo ponies: expensive. Secretaries, process servers, court reporters, books, phones, insurance, supplies, etc.

They all wanted to be fed whether the cash was coming in the door or not. Ted's case engaged my attention waking and sleeping. The publicity couldn't hurt. But the rest of my practice got bare maintenance. Depositions, motions, and trials got adjourned. I tried to return client calls in the evening. Yvonne was trained to recognize promising personal injury case calls and set the appointments in the evenings and on Saturdays. But since Ted had rehired me, pickings had been slim. His retainer, which had seemed large at the time, was rapidly being consumed in operating expenses.

Terry O'Shea's call could represent a sizeable load of hay. Having just handled the case at the pretrial, it was fresh in my mind. My client, Trisha Evans, was a scholarship volleyball player at CMU and had excelled at both academics and athletics all her life. She was tall and charming. During the Thanksgiving break last year, she was marathon bike riding near West Branch to stay in shape. Mr. O'Shea's insured, one Waylon Forsyth, clipped her with his F-150 pickup's passenger side mirror. He fractured her L-1 vertebrae and the L-2 spinus process. After the insertion of two Harrington rods, running from the base to the top of her spine, Trisha was able to walk after extensive therapy. But at age 21, she was done with sports. The waitressing job she'd held to pay for college was out, as she couldn't stand on her feet for more than a half hour without spasm and pain. Early traumatic arthritis had already begun to appear on x-ray. By the time she was forty, she would have the back of an eighty-year-old woman.

We filed suit within a month of the accident. Terry O'Shea had tried to settle pre-suit for $100,000 of Forsyth's $250,000 policy and said he couldn't go higher. I could see no point in holding further suit pending further discussions. Once suit was joined, Forsyth claimed in his deposition that Trisha had swerved from the right-hand edge of the road just as he started to pass her. The Ogemaw County deputy had done a thorough job. When Waylon told him his swerve story at the scene, the officer searched for and photographed the gouge marks the bike had made in the pavement right next to the shoulder of the road. When my investigator found Jim Drummond, a pharmaceutical salesman, who had been headed southbound when the northbound Forsyth had hit Trisha, the liability questions were resolved.

"I couldn't believe it. I'm watching the girl on the bike, cute Spandex biker's outfit. Next thing I know this idiot came up from behind her and pulls out to pass her. I'm right there. I swerved to the shoulder or he would have hit me. What's the hurry? He could have just slowed for a second or two to let me go by, then pass. I don't think he ever saw me until the last second. His head was turned. He was admiring the young lady from behind."

That testimony had the ring of truth. Trish made a compelling witness. Great determination to rehabilitate herself. Heartfelt longing for competitive athletics and the camaraderie of her teammates. Now she watched the volleyball games from the stands, feeling left behind.

So I picked O'Shea's message from the pile and called him. "Terry, Ken Edwards. How are you, sir?"

"Good, Ken, good. How's your murder case looking? Need an adjournment of our trial?"

"No thanks, Terry. Looks like we'll probably be done in time. Since you and I are not going to settle, I don't want to lose the trial date." Always a key mistake for a plaintiff lawyer to take his foot off the accelerator by adjourning a trial date.

"Yeah, well, I think the company has done an agonizing reappraisal. I took your mediation summary to our monthly settlement authority roundtable. I played the last five minutes of the doctor's testimony for them. Say, you got that guy on your payroll?"

"Nope. Terry, you know that doctors don't like lawyers and they don't like lawsuits. This guy is no exception. But the good doctor picked an awful lot of bone fragments out of Trish's cauda equina, and he really admires how hard she's worked to come back. She's a beauty, Terry, jury is gonna love her!"

"Yeah, I know, I know. All your clients are wonderful. But Al Martin says she makes a nice appearance. What's it gonna take?"

"Terry, if I don't get her the $250,000, they'll want my law license."

"Come on, Ken, I said agonizing reappraisal, not complete capitulation. The jury is not going to know Mr. Forsyth is insured for a quarter mill. We'll dress him like the hayseed he is, and they'll think they are doing you a favor for $100,000. Now, what will you take?"

"The jury may well think a million is not enough, and since your boy, Waylon, inherited a rather large farm when his mother passed away last year, we've got a place to collect. I'm sure Midwest Casualty wants to deal in good faith and stand behind their insured, who was spending his time admiring my client's behind. Two-fifty."

"Goddamn it, Ken, be reasonable. Give me a little something here."

Eureka! "Little" was the operative word. "It's your move, what have you got in mind?"

"Two hundred thousand, and that's tops."

Another five minutes of the mating dance of the ruffled grouse, and we agreed on $225,000. Trish was ecstatic when I called for her okay. I hung up and danced around the office singing parts of The Rascals' "It's a Beautiful Morning." When Janice cracked the door, I laughed and explained. "Just chased the wolf from the door for another month or two."

The settlement relieved my guilt about not devoting enough time to Trish's case and meant I wouldn't be walking directly from a criminal case into a civil case with no rest or prep in between. For the first time in weeks, I felt things were looking up. Now if only Tom the Terrible had a silver bullet for Ted's case.

It was 5:45 p.m. by the time I had returned all my calls. Thank God for answering machines. "You called. I called back. You're it."

I climbed the stairs to the third floor. Acme Reporting was closed and dark at their end of the hall. I walked toward the front end of the building and Tom's oak and glass door. The reception area was empty, but there was a light showing through Tom's paned office door. As usual, he had the phone fixed to his ear. No smoking in Tom's office. But that didn't prevent him from sticking a fat, unlit Macanudo between his teeth. He pulled it out to wave me to a chair. Looked like this one had been pretty well chewed over.

I surveyed the eclectic decor of his office. Massive oak desk, credenza behind his swivel rocker, feet perched on open desk drawer, vest unbuttoned, tie loose and askew, chair canted back, Tom staring at ceiling. Grunting, "eh, a huh, a huh, a huh, yup, a huh," out of the side of his mouth opposite the cigar. Framed cartoons from the *New Yorker*, obligatory degrees, family pics of his wife with a bright, open smile, and his daughter, who got her good looks from her mother. A hand-carved boy fishing, perched on the corner of his desk so it could bob up and down. Classical and jazz CDs stacked neatly in their jewel cases by his CD player. Sounded like Thelonius Monk, but the volume was too low to be sure. I stared at the needlepoint of the wayward client getting spanked over his mother's knee.

"Fine, fine, Mr. Goins. But you continue to ignore my bill and I'll have no choice but to move to withdraw. I've got the motion right here in your file." Tom's eyes went back to the ceiling while he listened. "Right, right. Well, I hope so." A pause. "And good evening to you, sir." He swiveled to replace the phone back on the receiver behind him. "God, but I hate deadbeats. Owes me $2,500 for over three months and he's got two motions he wants filed yesterday. How's it going, Ken?"

"Looking up, Tom, looking up. You?"

"Same ol' shit, different day. Hey, at least it's Friday. How's about a beer?"

"Sounds good."

Tom lifted his massive frame out of the chair and appraised his stogie. "They last a lot longer if you don't light 'em. My third week on this baby." He picked a couple of leaves from between his teeth and his lip. "Should I try for four?"

I shook my head as he walked across the waiting area to the kitchen and pulled a couple of Molsons from the fridge. By the time he'd handed me mine and returned behind his desk, half of his long-neck bottle was gone in two draughts. "Ah, cold enough for you? Keep them at exactly 38 degrees."

"Perfect," I replied after the first swallow. "And now, my good man, you said something about a juicy tidbit."

Tom raised his eyebrows and smirked. "Not just a friendly social call?"

"Always love your company, Tom. But you did drag the lure past the weed bed. I'm biting. What have you got?"

He opened a side drawer in his desk, fished around for a long pair of scissors, and made a studied effort to prune the branches on his scraggly cigar. I was sure the meticulous effort was just to keep me hanging a little while longer. When finished, he held the wreck of the cigar out at arm's length toward the windows to examine it. He rolled it in his fingers and then stuck it back into the corner of his mouth. He adjusted his lips to hang onto it and spoke out of the other side.

"Well, my friend. By the scuttlebutt around the courthouse, you and ol' Teddy Boy are sinking fast. So I figured you could use a little life raft. I think you are headed for Davy Jones' locker anyway, but it might keep you afloat a little longer."

He stopped and peered over his dark-framed glasses to check my level of interest. He had my attention.

"Yeah, yeah, whatta ya got?"

"You know the matrimonial bonds of Mr. and Mrs. Calvin Salomon have been downgraded from AAA to junk status?"

I shifted in my chair, wondering why this would be of any interest to me. "Nope, didn't know that."

Calvin was a car dealer and past club president. I knew he was a scratch golfer and he liked gin, the card game, and gin, the liquor. I'd seen him sitting with his card playing cronies around the corner table of the Club Room. I'd heard him curse the bartender for giving him Gilbey's instead of Bombay. Not much else. Calvin's wife, Suzie, was a short-haired, athletic blonde whose form could be admired on the tennis court two or three afternoons a week. I knew they were elaborate party givers from clubhouse talk, but I was not on the guest list. In fact, Cal, who stood six foot three, would walk past me going to or coming from the locker without even a grunt of acknowledgment. Not very friendly for a car dealer, I thought. Until I remembered I'd sued him for a car accident on one of his loaner vehicles under the Owner's Liability statute before the legislature gutted it.

"I'm not in on Cal and Sue's innermost thoughts. So?"

Tom paused for a second, and then a smile jiggled the stogie. "Here's the dirt. Suzie stopped by the dealership unannounced about two p.m. one Wednesday afternoon to get some shopping money on her way to the mall. She walked right back to Cal's office. Cal's secretary, the young Crystal Evans, might have warned him, except she was in taking dick-tation. If you know what I mean. Sue walked in to find Cal reclining in his Lazy Boy, arms crossed behind his head, satisfied smile on his face and Crystal's head in his lap. After Suzie gave Crystal a solid boot in the ass, she told Cal he'd 'pay big time.' She retained Billy Joe Brimley to file the divorce. Appropriate, don't you think, hiring old B.J. for catching her hubby in mid header?"

I snorted to acknowledge his remark but couldn't understand what this had to do with a life raft to delay Ted's and my descent to Davy Jones' locker. "Fascinating little piece of Americana, Tom, but I fail to see how its going to get Ted and me safely away from the *Titanic*."

He waved his soggy torpedo in the air. "Wait, wait. That's the back-ground. Here's the nugget. Cal is fighting fire with fire. He gave his dep-osition this morning. When Brimley asked him to explain what Miss Crystal's face was doing in his lap, he testified as follows." Tom shuffled through the leaves of a yellow legal pad for a minute or two. "Aha, here it is. And I quote: 'Same thing my darling wife's face was doing in Amanda Armbruster's lap. Giving head.' "

All of a sudden my level of interest had picked up. I put the beer on an old *Lawyer's Weekly* so as not to mar Tom's side table. "Tell me more."

"I can't tell you more. Old Brimley looked like he'd been hit by a board. Mrs. Salomon stood up, threw the contents of her glass of Pepsi at Cal, and said, 'You lying bastard! You promised you'd never tell,' and she left the room, not to return. I believe Cal's parting shot was: 'This is war, you silly bitch.' Brimley decided to terminate the deposition. The rest of what I know Cal told me after. It's pretty juicy."

"So, let's have some juice."

Tom shook his head and answered, "No can do. Privileged. But if I were you, I'd go and see Mrs. Salomon. She drinks a bit and if you catch her at the right time, she might be chatty."

"What about your client, can I get a few details from him?"

Tom waved off my request with the well-chewed cigar. "Nope. I asked him if he would talk to you. His answer was, 'I'm in enough trouble as it is. No way I'm getting involved in that mess.' I believe the reference to the *Titanic* originated with Cal. I convinced him to let you in on what's on the transcript by telling him it is public record anyway. Plus, he doesn't seem to mind having his life partner, who, by way of terms of endearment he calls 'that gold-digging slut,' squirm a little."

I tried through the rest of that beer and another to pry a few more details out of Tom. You could see the mirth in his eyes as he dodged, evaded and declined. Walking down the street to my car, I thought about the nugget Tom had handed me. I turned it over in my mind's eye. Real gold or pyrite? I needed to know more. But how?

Suddenly I remembered. I knew where I could find Suzie Salomon. The ladies' member-member was this weekend. My plans had not included attending the deluxe seafood buffet, which was a tournament staple. I definitely didn't plan on making the "Women of the Club" fashion show that followed dinner. But when I remembered seeing on the tournament program that Suzie Salomon was fashion show coordinator, my plans changed. I headed home to shower and change. I had seen Suzie seated at the upstairs bar on more than one occasion. Maybe I could slide onto the stool next to her and try to loosen her lips with a cocktail or two. Nothing ventured...

"Sailor buy the lady a drink?" I asked as I sat on the barstool next to Suzie. The music and laughter of the dinner dance crowd pulsed in waves from the main dining room into the piano bar. I had been chatting with a couple of members by the piano, standing so I could keep an eye on Suzie at the bar. She was seated where Amanda was when last I'd seen her alive. Suzie and Abigail Woodcock had been absorbed in conversation for the twenty minutes I'd talked golf with the boys and listened to Archie, the pianist, sing the greatest hits of Mel Torme. Archie had been a clubhouse fixture since the place was built. He played well but didn't sound much like the Velvet Fog. From habit I kept patting my pocket for a smoke. But since my ten-a-day nicotine diet plan had failed so miserably, I was back to total abstinence.

Then Abigail suddenly got up and headed for the dining room. After a couple of steps, she turned her head and snarled something nasty to Suzie. Abigail didn't wait for an answer. Her six-foot-one, 220 pound frame was through the door to the main dining room and gone. I quickly excused myself from my conversation with the boys and moved to fill the spot vacated by Mrs. Woodcock.

"You're no sailor and I'm no lady, but if you're buying, I'll have another White Russian," Suzie said, looking appraisingly over her left shoulder at me. Although Suzie's husband Cal wouldn't give me the time of day, Suzie made a point to smile and say Hi in passing. Last year her steady duplicate bridge partner, Julie Upshaw, had had the flu and couldn't make the third Wednesday of the month group at the last minute. Suzie was desperate. So when she saw me heading for the range to hit some balls, she chased me down. I learned the game from my mother, who was a life master. Although I wasn't near Mom's equal, I could play and enjoyed the game.

At first it was a little awkward being the only male amongst 23 females, but since I was the necessary ingredient to get the game rolling, I had been warmly welcomed. My skills, while better than novice, were far from expert. However, I'm a card magnet. That day, the magnet was working and Suzie and I had done well. Thereafter, Suzie would kid me about getting a wig and a skirt so I could be a regular in the ladies' monthly group. I enjoyed the game, but wasn't prepared to cross-dress in order to play.

As I situated myself on the stool next to Suzie, Eddie, the upstairs barman, set Suzie's White Russian on a napkin next to the drink she had been working on. As he reached his hand to pick up the old soldier, Suzie touched the back of his hand to delay him and gulped the remnants out of the glass before allowing him to remove it. "Well, counselor, to what do I owe the honor of your company?"

"Let's correct the record first," I said. "I may not be a sailor except in a sense. I sail uncharted legal waters and am headed for the rocks, according to most observers. You, Ms. Suzanne, are every inch a lady, and a very beautiful one at that. Why would you deny it?"

Suzie picked up the fresh glass and turned to me. Her watery eyes made it apparent that the drink before her was not her second of the night. "A lady doesn't tell Ms. Abigail Winters Woodchuck that she is a moose upon whom no designer dress would fit, let alone make her look attractive."

"You said that?"

She nodded glumly. "Sure did. When she told me I was being replaced as fashion show chairman, I told her she could stuff the show up her big behind."

I noted the slur in Suzie's speech. "Wow, no wonder she seemed in a bit of a huff leaving. You're right, not very ladylike. That doesn't sound like you. What's going on?"

Suzie looked across the bar at the mirror behind the shelves of bottles and absentmindedly fingered the loose, short blonde hairs around the base of her right ear. Her fine bone structure in profile was a testament to how beautiful she must have been as a young bride. Even now she was as pretty as diligently applied cosmetics would allow. She was apparently deciding whether she wanted to tell me more. Obviously, she needed to talk to somebody, and I was there. She nodded slightly when she got the hair back into place. "I don't know what's happening to me, Ken. I seem to be burning a lot of bridges lately. Ever since Amanda..." She stopped herself. "I don't want to talk to you about Amanda. You're representing that bastard who killed her. I shouldn't even be talking to you."

I needed to paddle quickly, or my chance to talk to Suzie was going to be washed out to sea. "Let's agree, we won't talk about either Ted or Amanda. Strictly off limits. Let's talk about your friend. What did you call her, Mrs. Woodchuck? She's rather large for a woodchuck. What happened there?"

Suzie hesitated, trying to decide whether to brush me off. She looked up and down the bar to see if she had a better audience upon whom to vent her frustrations. Apparently no one caught her eye. And she had just started the drink I'd bought her. "That self-righteous old cow. Her nose is out of joint. I wouldn't let her model in the show. We had three stores supply outfits, Jacobson's, LaBelle Boutique and The Fox Shoppe. Nobody had anything close to her size. I even tried Lady Big and Tall, but they wouldn't participate. They probably thought Abigail wouldn't be a boost to sales. Anyway, she blamed me. Said I ruined her summer. We have four women whose husbands are executives at Woodcock Manufacturing who had already picked outfits, bought shoes and accessories. When I couldn't find anything for Abigail, she made them drop out of the show. Boy, did I have to scramble for replacements. Anyway, she said the show stunk. According to her, the ladies' beachwear segment was like amateur night at the tittie bar with all the men whistling and clapping. She claims she already has the votes to kick me off next year's committee."

I laughed. "Wow, she works fast. Speaking personally, I loved the show. You looked quite fetching in that yellow two-piece with a lacy parejo. I liked the music, and the pace of the whole thing was fun. I'm glad I decided to come tonight. Plus, that seafood buffet was killer. If I ate one more oyster on the half shell, they'd have had to wheel me out on a gurney."

Suzie smiled. "Thanks, I'm glad somebody liked it. It was a lot of work. But better be careful with those oysters, aren't they supposed to make you virile?" She raised her eyebrows and looked me right in the eye while trying to keep hers in focus.

"Sitting next to you is a far greater aphrodisiac than any old mollusk. But the combination could be dangerous."

Suzie turned in her seat, cocked her head and raised an eyebrow, giving me a frank appraisal. I tilted my head down and looked back up at her earnestly, like a puppy eyeing a frog, until the corners of my lips turned up.

"Oh, Edwards, I heard you were a bullshitter."

"Man's gotta earn a living, you know. But I'm not telling you anything you haven't known since you were a girl. I'll bet the boys started sniffing around you early and often."

She laughed and then got a wistful look in her eye. "I've spent a lot of time and money staying in shape—makeup, clothes, spas. Not easy looking good after three children. If I had a dollar for every tummy crunch, freeweight rep, and toe touch, I wouldn't need Cal's money. What's it gotten me? A husband who chases every sweet young thing in sight. Three grown kids who have moved away and whom I have to call if I want to talk. A bunch of biddies at this stupid club spreading rumors that when the divorce is over, I'll be out of the club with few real friends. Amanda was… oops, that's a no no, right?"

"You're getting divorced?" I asked as if this were news to me.

"Didn't you know? Everybody knows. I caught my devoted husband, Cal, getting a header from his twenty-three-year-old secretary at the dealership. After he promised me for the third time no more fooling around. Heck, I was in your building today. I saw your name on the door. It was Cal's deposition. What a fiasco! That lying son of a bitch, he..."

She suddenly choked up. Tears began to fall. "Oh, God, I'm such a mess. My whole life is a mess."

She ran around the corner of the bar through the piano room toward the ladies' room. I sat at the bar for ten minutes. Man, I was so close, if I could just get her to talk a little more. But she didn't come back. Maybe she'd left through the back parking lot door. I couldn't go into the ladies' room to look for her. I declined Eddie's offer of another drink.

Just as I was signing the chit, Suzie came back around the corner and stopped behind my seat. There were no tears visible on her face, but her eyes were red and her makeup streaky. "Ken, I'm so sorry for the scene. Everything I do is out of control. I'd better go home. I'm in no shape to drive, so I'll just walk home across the course. Good night. I'm sorry."

I stood. "Don't worry about it. Sometimes it helps to have somebody to listen. How 'bout if I give you a ride?"

"No thanks. I need the fresh air, the walk will do me good."

"Well then, I'll be your chaperone. You've already been attacked by a woodchuck tonight. I hear there's carnivorous squirrels, moles, and groundhogs out there, not to mention lions, tigers and bears."

She looked ready to refuse, tightly clutching her purse, until I got to the *Wizard of Oz* stuff. "Lions, tigers and bears, oh, my! You'll protect me?"

"With my life, brave Dorothy."

"Okay then, you may accompany me."

We slipped out the back, her first and me two minutes later. We met at her car, where she was still straightening out her makeup in the rear-view mirror. As I approached, she slid out the driver's side, favoring me with a nice shot of thigh. "Oops." She giggled, pulling her light blue dress back down over her knees. "You didn't look, did you?"

"Who, me? Why, no."

"Never?"

"Almost never."

We walked hand in hand between the cars, past the cart shed, and around the pool so as not to have to go near the clubhouse again. The moon was almost full, but just as we stepped out behind the eighteenth hole to cross the course, it disappeared behind large clouds. Away from the club and its lights, it was suddenly dark. I squeezed her hand. She responded in kind, and we followed the fairway in a comfortable silence. We reached the tenth green as the moon broke from behind the clouds.

"It's such a perfect summer night. Can we sit for a minute and enjoy it?" she asked, steering me to the bench next to the eleventh tee. We watched the clouds float across the sky. A comfort was developing between us as we sat in the warm air in the midst of the manicured meadow. The muted lights from the courseside homes and the clubhouse seemed far removed. I let Suzie talk and sensed a first trust, a tremor of intent to share private things.

She was an only child of a minister and a pharmacist in Xenia, Ohio. As I suspected, she had been a cheerleader in high school. The time and effort she'd spent to stay in shape had paid dividends. She was slim, trim, and firm. In the moonlight, the crow's feet around her eyes vanished and her white smile brightened the darkness. She'd received a band scholarship to go to Michigan, met Cal, and married him while in her senior year. She graduated with a B.A. as a music teacher. Cal started out in sales at his uncle's car dealership in Standish, Michigan. They had two boys and a girl within four years of marriage before she said enough. By the time their daughter, Karla, arrived, Cal was selling enough cars that she didn't have to go back to teaching. By the time the boys were seven and five, Cal had bought his uncle out and they could afford a house at the country club and a nanny.

"It was then I stopped being a serious person," she said, her voice catching. As she cleared her throat to continue, I glanced and saw her eyes glistening in the penumbral moonlight. "I played golf. I played tennis. I played bridge. I joined the investment club, this charity, that committee. We were always going to parties, giving parties. We formed a travel group and went to Jamaica every year. That's the first time I ever caught Cal cheating on me. Remember the Skileses?"

I shook my head no. She described discovering her husband and Marge Skiles sneaking off for a moonlit beachside tryst at two a.m. "He promised never again. Never didn't take long in arriving."

As we walked across the bridge over the stream that bisected number 11 fairway, she recited the litany of lies and betrayal that had destroyed the Salomon marriage. By the time we reached Salomon manor behind the eleventh green, she had cried herself out. She dried her eyes and managed a smile as she invited me in. "Cal's been living in a condo since the divorce," she said, spying the concern on my face.

She poured me a beer in a glass and herself another White Russian over ice. We sat on the leather circular couch that surrounded the sunken fireplace area. Diana Krall's "Breathless" emanated softly from the surround sound. She turned the gas logs on low, switched off the the rest of the lights and asked me to dance. "Do you mind? I'm not trying to seduce you. I just haven't had much human contact lately." We swayed wordlessly for two or three more of Diana's offerings. Then she patted a spot next to her on the couch. The condensation from our glasses sparkled in the firelight. She fiddled with the top button on her blue dress, lost in thought. Then, having come to a decision, she looked over at me. "Can I trust you?"

I met her eyes and replied, "I believe you can. Why?"

"Because I feel so much better having told you so much already. I want to clean the slate and see if it helps. I haven't told anybody else because my so-called friends are just that. I've been hurting so bad since Amanda died, and the only one who could understand why is Cal. Believe me, he couldn't care less. Can you promise to keep it confidential, like lawyer-client?" I hated to make that promise, but could see no other alternative.

There, with the moonlight coming through the windows and Diana singing "Temptation" in the background, she told me. She described a loveless marital bed and her fears of catching a social disease from her husband. She told me how years of being golf, tennis, and fitness partners with Amanda had made them inseparable friends. She recounted Amanda's background of being abused by a stepfather at a tender age, concluding by saying, "When her mom sided with her stepdad, it warped Amanda. She had sexual issues that no amount of counseling could cure. You know she treated with Dr. Felton for years?"

"No, I didn't know that." I knew the psychologist, who looked like a rumpled college professor and who made a living shrinking the well-to-do.

Suzie smiled slyly. "There's lots you don't know. Did you know he tried to get Amanda on the couch for more than just counseling?"

I sat up. "Didn't know that either. What happened?"

Suzie laughed. "That little wimp. Amanda has had self defense training, and when he tried to grab her she flipped him on his back and had her knee on his throat while he cried like a baby." I wondered how much of a fight Amanda had put up at the end as Suzie finished, "Yeah, she stopped seeing him. But she told me she'd catch him following her after that."

I added Felton to my list of jilted lovers and asked Suzie, "How did Amanda's problem affect her relationship with Ted?"

"She had appetites that Ted couldn't satisfy, what with the prostate surgery and all. And she wasn't that particular whether it was a man or woman she used to satisfy her appetites."

When I looked surprised, Suzie pushed on as if afraid she'd run out of courage. "As her best friend, she kept me up to date. I wasn't too surprised when she came on to me after golf one night, right here on this couch. You know, I think I'd been hoping she would. Anyway, I didn't resist for long." She paused to gauge my reaction: rapt attention. She shook her head at me. "Just like most men, lots of girl-girl fantasies, huh?"

"Not me," I lied. Her face told me she wasn't buying it. "Okay, maybe once in a while."

She laughed derisively. "That's all the details you're getting. It's the closest to a loving relationship I expect I'll ever get. I was getting uncomfortable with the whole thing even before Cal caught us in the bedroom. He promised he'd never say a word if I broke it up. Lying swine! From then on, anytime I'd say anything about where he was, he'd ask, 'What's new with your lady friends?' And then he testified about it in the divorce. Now everybody will know. How can I live here with all the gossips at the club?" Her face filled with anguish and the tears flowed.

I slid over and put my arm around her shoulders. "Don't worry, kid.

Nobody will hear it from me. Tom Thalberg is my tenant. I'll make sure he keeps it quiet. Nobody has to know."

"Really?" Daring to hope. The firelight was both kind and unkind to her. From a distance the pert, pretty face of the high school cheerleader was still in evidence. But up close, as she peered earnestly over her shoulder, the tiny lines around her eyes and mouth gave testament to intervening years filled with heartache.

"Really." I nodded and squeezed her shoulder.

She smiled through the tears and extricated herself from my arm to go powder her face. "Be back in a sec." Her blue dress swirled about slender hips as she moved away.

How much different is her story from mine? I wondered. Youthful dreams rusting on the reef of reality. The corrosion caused by the salty air of disappointments and moral accommodations so gradual as to pass unnoticed. I thought of the early days Lake Pointe Players photo on my dresser, and how I looked in the morning mirror these days. Truth be told, on the outside Suzie was showing less wear than I was. I consoled myself, feeling the steady thrum of my internal power plant. With Ted's case I had something to keep me motivated and busy. I had purpose and hope. I could feel the tide rising. I was underway.

Suzie came back, fresh makeup restoring color to her face. She flipped the switch on the table lamp behind the couch and sat a cushion apart from me. In the light she looked less like the teenaged cheerleader she once had been, and more like the empty nest divorcee she was struggling against becoming.

"Coffee's on. You've got a long walk back and ride home." Nervously she checked to make sure she remained all buttoned up. Then she looked up to me, her embarrassment obvious. "Why did I tell you all that about Amanda and me? I hardly know you. You must think I'm some kind of deviate."

I did what I could to ease her anguish. "Not at all. I think you're a very caring woman with a lot to give, who got shortchanged in the husband department. I'm thinking your life is richer for that relationship. You deserve some happiness."

She gave me a wan smile and crooked her head.

"Yeah, but with another woman?"

"No biggie to me. I gather she was quite a woman."

She nodded in recollection as she got up to fetch the coffee, placing mine before me and returning to sit.

"That she was. She was also the best friend I ever had, and you are representing the man who killed her."

I tasted the coffee and asked softly, "What makes you so sure Ted killed her? Didn't he always treat her lovingly?"

She nodded acknowledgement. "Jealously makes people do horrible things. I know. But it's hard to imagine it of Ted. I think he knew, at some level, about Amanda's needs. Needs he knew he wasn't meeting. But she never rubbed his nose in it. In fact, they were always the perfect couple together. And Ted was always a gentleman, but he confessed. What else is there?"

I looked straight at her. "Suzie, trust me on this. The confession is a phony. Ted was in total shock. He hears something. He wakes up. There's his wife lying bloody on the floor. His hands were shaking so badly he couldn't write. So Detective Bliss wrote it for him. Bliss added a few things that Ted didn't say and subtracted a few he did. For example, if you drop the letters 'n't' from 'I didn't kill my wife,' what have you got?"

She looked stunned. "Why would Bliss do that?"

"I don't know, Suzie. Maybe he didn't hear Ted correctly. Maybe he heard what he wanted to hear, maybe it all looked open and shut to him, maybe some other reason. I don't know."

She thought for a moment. "Why did Ted sign it then?"

That was the question I was going to have to answer to the jury's satisfaction. I might as well give it a dress rehearsal with her. "His mind was in the hall with Amanda. He was so shook up, he couldn't see straight. I doubt he more than glanced at the statement. Bliss wouldn't let me near him. Then his asshole neighbor, M. Stanton Browne, attorney at law, comes over and tells him it's okay and he signs it. Browne wouldn't know a criminal law book from a Betty Crocker cookbook."

At the mention of Browne's name, Suzie startled. "What was Stanton doing there?"

"He handled Ted's legal business and was a close golf buddy and his neighbor. Anyway, I'm called out of bed at three a.m., rush over there to try and prevent Bliss from talking to Ted, only to be told that Stanton's got the case and if I don't get out of the crime scene, I'll be arrested for obstructing justice. They still had to have two deputies haul me out of there. Why did you jump at the mention of Stanton's name?"

"I've never liked Mr. Fancy Pants. I like the lovely Annabelle Browne even less. It can't hurt to tell you why."

"Please do."

"It was about six months before her death that Cal came home and found me and Amanda together. The bastard is never early except that one night. He made me promise to break it off or he would divorce me and make sure everybody knew the reason why. My kids are all grown, but I couldn't stand the idea of them ever hearing. I told Amanda that it was over. She thought I was a wimp, but said she understood. In truth, I'd been thinking about how to end the sex part. I don't think I'm really a lesbian no matter how it sounds. Anyway, I kept my part of the bargain. For awhile I'd still play tennis doubles with Amanda. She was outwardly friendly, but then she stopped calling altogether. I couldn't figure out why until I saw Amanda and Annabelle together."

"Oh. How together were they?"

"Lips locked together. It was the charity ball in January of this year. Were you there?"

I shook my head.

"Well, it was at the Conservatory, and there's this ladies' room right next to the cloak room. Nobody ever uses it because it's upstairs and the party is downstairs. I left a recipe in my jacket pocket I'd promised Marge Lyons. Long as I was up there, I thought I'd use the ladies'. They were standing in front of the mirror embracing each other. Amanda's hand was on Annabelle's behind. It was more than just a holiday hug."

"What did you do?"

"I said, 'Oops, excuse me' and turned around and walked right back out the door. The whole thing upset me to the point I took my coat back down, told Cal I had a migraine, and insisted we go home."

"Annabelle Browne? She's a real goody two-shoes."

"That's not all. Maybe you heard about Amanda and Chip Stevens at the club?"

"Yes, I heard he was giving her very careful instructions one evening in the pro shop. Amanda was a lot busier than I would have ever guessed."

Suzie got up and cleared our glasses from the coffee table. On her way to the kitchen, she looked over her shoulder. "You know, I'm not sure Amanda could help it. Anyway, somehow, Annabelle heard about Chip. From what I heard, she was jealous and insistent that Amanda stop. Annabelle told her to knock it off or else. And Amanda chose the 'or else.' "

I considered this while Suzie was in the kitchen. I could hear the sink running as she was washing out the glasses. The list of potential suspects was growing. When Suzie came back into the living room, I asked, "How long was this ultimatum before she died?"

Suzie stopped for a moment to think. "Oh, I don't know. Three weeks, more or less. Why? You don't think...?"

"I don't know. What do you think?"

She bit at her lip. "I guess I don't know what to think." She gathered our cups and headed for the kitchen.

Suzie's cleaning up of the premises was a pretty clear hint, but there was one last question I wanted to ask. I followed her into the designer kitchen and leaned against the double-wide sub-zero fridge. Her back was to me as she rinsed the cups.

"Amanda ever mention anything about a Dressler fund audit?"

The way her back tensed told me she had. She glanced at me appraisingly over her shoulder and paused before turning to face me. "Enough confession for one night. What little she told me was in confidence. I won't break my word to her, even if she is dead."

"Even if it got her killed?"

She moved to open the door, shaking her head. "A jealous husband got her killed." Her resolute expression made clear that further probing was pointless. When I shrugged acknowledgement, she softened and pulled me in for a hug on the patio. Her blonde hair tickled my nose.

"Thanks for listening, Ken. I feel better having someone know how much Amanda's death hurt me and why. Remember your promise. Everything confidential."

I kissed the top of her head and said goodnight. I'd played my share of radar golf, finishing after sunset. But I'd never been alone on the course in the dead of night. The ramic shadows of trees in the moonlight would disappear into total darkness when the clouds eclipsed the moon. I almost stepped into the marshy pond between the green on fifteen and the tee on sixteen. My head was spinning and I wasn't watching where I was going. I felt squeamish at using Suzie's vulnerability to build Ted's defense. But I'd have felt worse if I'd passed up the chance. With the clubhouse parking lot lights as a beacon, I followed the cart path and considered all the new angles of defense I had gained.

Amanda's sex life, for reasons that were now more clear, was a fertile field ripe with jilted lovers. Suzie, prissy Miss Annabelle, Chip, probably more I knew nothing about. What was I going to do with all of them? If only I had gotten together with Suzie much earlier, I'd have more time to investigate these things further. Now I was days away from jury selection. All of the suspects were double-edged swords. How could I use them to good effect? How could I protect my source? I owed Suzie that. I'd set her up to trust me. I wasn't going to betray that trust.

New suspects with juicy motives. New dirt that might cause the jury to wonder about Amanda, but it was all so dangerous. As much as these people with motives might create a reasonable doubt about Ted, they could cement conviction if the jurors found all this sleazy information to be the motive for Ted to kill her. Years of wifely philandering coming to a head. Ted can't take any more humiliation, and his jealousy overflows in violence. How much of this did Ted know about and not tell me?

As I neared the now-darkened clubhouse, I used the parking and security lights as a compass. There were two cars left in the lot, my Benz and the night watchman's '83 Malibu sitting in opposite corners of the lot. I knew I'd have to make time to confront Ted with this new information. I'd probably gone too easy on him in the past regarding his feelings for his wife. I had accepted his telling me that Amanda was a wonderful woman, faithful and true, because it was what I wanted to hear. That view from the mourning husband left him without the lover's triangle motive for murder. But he had to know more than he was saying if Amanda was as active as it seemed.

Driving home, I left the top down so I could watch the skies clear for moonset. Sunset gets all the romantic press., but watching the moon grow larger as it approached the horizon before being devoured by the earth was worth staying up for. I thought about the seafood buffet and fashion show. So much going on. So much hidden away behind the latest chic couture, glittering jewels, deep tans, and capped-tooth smiles.

26

At 6:30 a.m., I hit the snooze. Again at 6:40 and 6:50. At 7:00 a.m., I was out of bed feeling slightly the worse for wear. I panicked. Where was Max? Then the fog cleared. He'd been on an overnight at Mrs. Grimes' puppy farm.

I stumbled into the bathroom. The face looking back from the mirror had even more lines and wrinkles than I recalled while sitting on Suzie's couch last night. There was more salt than pepper in the bird's nest of hair atop my head. The receding hairline around the widow's peak must have snuck back an extra inch without my noticing. The bags beneath my eyes were threatening to become valises. Must have been an awfully good-sized crow that left his footprints by the sides of my eyes. All this at thirty-eight.

Over the years I had sold myself on a self image of ruggedly handsome. Just now, plain rugged seemed more apt. I remembered watching as the stress and strain of office had taken its toll on Jimmy Carter and Bill Clinton. But that was over a period of years. The haggard face staring intently back at me gave testament to the pressures of the last few months since I'd joyfully stepped back into Ted's case. At this rate I'd be getting the senior citizen discount by the time the trial ended.

Two hundred and fifty stomach crunches, forty push-ups, a shower, and a shave seemed to help. Dressed in khaki slacks and a navy blue golf shirt, I looked more like a legal eagle and less like a down-on-his-luck night watchman who drinks a bit. I was presentable.

I made it to the jail by 7:45 a.m. and waited for breakfast to be finished. Ted was surprised to see me. As always when he shook my hand, he looked me straight in the eye and smiled. "Counselor, what brings you here today? Thought you'd be out warming up your swing."

As I took my seat across the table in the conference room, I smiled back at Ted. "To quote F. Lee, 'the defense never rests.' Ted, I wanted to talk to you about something that's bugging me."

Ted smiled openly. "Sure, Ken, what's up?"

"Well, you know we've talked about whether Amanda had always been faithful to you. In the statement, Bliss quotes you as saying you'd heard rumors. I'm sure the prosecutor will pound on that part of the statement. I need to go over that again with you."

As I spoke, the friendly smile dropped into a tight-lipped frown. "Ken, I won't have them tear Amanda apart in public like that. I just won't. They can say whatever they want about me. I'll deal with it. But I never let others speak ill of my wife when she was alive. I sure as hell won't now that she's dead and can't defend herself. Tell Ms. Botham that's off limits." This was the angriest I'd seen Ted. His eyes danced with agitation. The muscles of his face tightened and his hands curled into fists.

"Calm down, Ted. It's just you and me talking here, and there is no off limits when you take the stand. I can give you Ms. Tightbottom's opening statement: 'For love or money.' She's claiming she's got two motives for murder, the insurance money and jealousy. She's saying your business was in trouble and you needed money. And without an infusion of cash, you soon wouldn't be able to afford to keep Amanda in the style to which she had become accustomed. She will use the two oldest motives in the book, money and jealousy. She'll claim you were afraid that you were losing her to other lovers."

"Object. Make them leave Amanda's memory alone." He was shouting. I reached across the conference table to touch his jail-orange-uniformed arm and felt his muscles contracted and tense. We just stared at each other for a while until he gave in and sat back in his chair. Tears formed but did not fall from his eyes. "God, I wish whoever killed her had killed me too. I'm not sure how much more of this I can take." He rubbed the orange sleeve over his eyes, gathered himself, and looked back at me, under control again. He nodded for me to get down to business.

"Okay, so we need to talk about it. The prosecutor is content to rely on your statement to show you heard your wife was fooling around. She doesn't want to throw so much mud at Amanda to have the jury let you off on the Texas defense."

He looked quizzically at me. "Texas defense? What's that?"

"That she had it coming."

He leaped out of his chair. "How could anybody say she had it coming? She was a beautiful person. Nobody deserves what happened to her. To be left like that..."

Now profuse tears streamed over his cheeks as he was apparently reliving Amanda lying bloody and disfigured on the floor. He sat and collected himself. "I'm sorry, Ken. I think I'm going crazy. My first wife killed by a drunk. Amanda killed by a maniac. My business is going down the drain while I sit here rotting in jail, accused of this horrible thing." He stopped and stared down at the table, thinking God knows what. Then he went on. "I don't know if I can handle sitting in the courtroom while they drag her name through the dirt. All of that crap will end up in the papers, won't it?" His shoulders slumped and he appeared to visibly shrink before my eyes. "Can I just plead guilty to something and be done with it?"

I had discussed with Ted the possibility of a plea at various times since I had replaced Browne. Assistant Prosecutor Botham had at no time offered anything. I knew she wanted to make her name on this case. But the prosecutor, Alvin Corliss, was a realistic veteran who knew no case couldn't be lost. If I had really lobbied, I might have been able to get the original Murder Two deal Browne had offered.

But that was the last thing I wanted. Ted had vehemently maintained his innocence and his unfailing faith that I would get him off at trial. In Michigan, conviction for Murder One, willful, deliberate and premeditated, leaves the judge no discretion. Your sentence is life in prison without parole. Murder Two provides for a sentence of any term of years up to life and is parolable. Realistically, at Ted's age, a conviction of either would probably mean that he would spend the last days of his life in the state penitentiary. At the rate he was fading while incarcerated, I doubted he'd last more than a year or two in prison.

If Ted had told me he had done it, I could have considered manslaughter. Maybe I could even sell the lesser included offense of manslaughter to the jury. The jealous rage, provocation, mental strain from his wife's infidelity, failing business, heat of the moment anger could leave a jury sympathetic. I knew the prosecutor in this well-publicized case could not afford to come all the way down to manslaughter, which was probationable. Anyway, no judge who had to run for re-election would have put him on probation. Even with manslaughter, Ted would have to do enough time against the fifteen-year max for manslaughter to be equivalent to a life sentence anyway. The jury would be instructed on Murder One, Murder Two, and manslaughter. But I could hardly argue to them that my client didn't do it and in the next breath say, but if he did, it was in the heat of rage. I had gone over all of these things many times with Ted, and he had never indicated any interest in a plea. Here we were, at the eve of trial, and he was asking me about a plea.

I waited till he gathered himself and asked him, "Did you kill her?"

He lifted his head and looked me in the eyes and answered slowly, "No, I didn't."

"Then why are you talking to me about a plea?"

He shook his head a couple of times. "I don't know. Being here in jail so long gets to you. I'm just really down today. It's the weekend. I've had a lot of time to feel sorry for myself. How much longer till this is done and I can go home?"

"Wow, Ted, I appreciate the vote of confidence. You sure I can get you off?"

"I'm not guilty. You've gotten guilty people off before. I have faith in you."

"Thanks, Ted, but it's not that easy. That's why I'm talking to you. To give us the best possible chance. I haven't lost my faith in you, and I believe you. You know how the evidence looks. They have motive, opportunity and means. Good old M.O.M. If that's all they had, I'd feel a lot better about it. But it's the confession that that SOB Bliss is going to testify to that makes the hill that much harder to climb."

Ted pulled at his orange sleeve. "I wish I could be more help to you on that, Ken. I don't remember my exact words to him. I just remember sitting there feeling numb. While we were talking, he was writing things down. His handwriting is a little like yours. It's hard to read. I couldn't concentrate when he handed it to me to review and sign. M. Stanton had been right there and he said okay, so I signed it. I can only tell you I didn't kill her and so I can't imagine I would have told him that I did. There is no way. I just wouldn't."

I got up from my chair and walked over to the file cabinet and leaned against it. Mistake. Years of accumulated dust covered my slacks and shirt. I cursed and brushed myself off before continuing. "We talked about this before, Ted. I told you that if the jury believes that Bliss accurately wrote down what you told him in that so-called confession, then they are going to convict you. If you tell me that the confession is true, and that you killed her, there is still time to change our defense so that we would have a shot at manslaughter. We can argue that you did it in the heat of the moment, under strain and with provocation. Manslaughter would mean that you would have a chance to get out of prison sometime within your lifetime. If, as you've told me from the start, you didn't do it, then we've got to go for broke. I wasn't there, so I have to hear it from you."

Ted let me finish, took only a few seconds to consider what I had said, and spoke softly. "Ken, I did not kill my wife."

I sat back down. "Good, I didn't think you did. Now the question is, do you trust me to do what's best?"

"Of course."

"Well then, I want you to trust me on this. I've investigated. I've learned things. Things about Amanda and who might have had reason to kill her that could really help improve your chances."

"What sort of things?"

"The sort of things you just told me you don't want to hear. That's why I need you to trust me. I'm doing my level best for you. But I can't fight with one hand tied behind my back. If I can show the jury that other people had relationships with Amanda, relationships that gave them motive for violence, this takes away a major part of the prosecutor's case and gives us a way of arguing to the jury. Can you say, for example, Annabelle Browne was not jealous, hurt and angry? Can you say beyond a reasonable doubt that she didn't kill Amanda?"

Ted's jaw dropped. "What? Annabelle Browne? What are you talking about?"

I responded in a level tone, "Ted, I'm sorry. But I have it on reliable authority they had an affair."

"No way. Amanda and another woman? Amanda and Annabelle, that's ridiculous. It's disgusting. It's not true."

"Good. That's what I hoped you'd say. Knew nothing about it, huh? Let me ask you this. Over the last six weeks before her death, did Amanda and Annabelle see each other at all?"

"See, that proves you are wrong. They had a fight about something and Amanda had me answer the phone. If it was Annabelle, I was just to take a message. She said Annabelle had cheated at bridge by giving signals or something, and Amanda called her on it. They weren't speaking. She hadn't been over to the house for weeks. For awhile, she was here a lot. They were always doing something."

"How often did Annabelle call?"

"Oh, for about a week, it was every day. Then not at all. Why?"

"Because Amanda had found her too possessive and ended their relationship."

Ted was much more animated. He shook his head. "I don't believe it. Who told you this?"

"Just trust me on this. I can't tell you. It's attorney-client privilege. This person knows. This person was also intimate with Amanda."

"Who is it? I demand to know." The color returned to Ted's face with a vengeance. He pushed his chair away and strode to the furthest reach of a room so small it had no far reaches.

"I'm sorry, Ted. I can't. You said you trusted me. Would I lie to you? Would I lie to you and hurt you as much as this is hurting you?"

He paused and thought for a moment and resumed his seat across the graffiti-scarred table from me. "No, I don't think you are lying. I just think you are wrong or the person who told you is lying or wrong or something. Who is he?"

I shook my head. "That's why I'm here this morning. I just learned these things. I have to talk to you about them. And because of how I learned it, I can't tell you who told me. Let's cover something else. You know Chip Wilson, the assistant pro. I have an eyewitness who saw him with Amanda."

"Of course, he was Amanda's instructor. They were friends. They spent lots of time together at the club. I know that."

"No, I mean really with Amanda, in the office at the pro shop."

"Who is this witness?"

"Gray, Gray Lansdale. The only one of your clubhouse friends who is willing to testify for you at trial. Do you think Gray would lie?"

The mention of Gray's name stunned Ted. He sat back in his chair with a sigh. "Oh, God, I don't know what to think. After the first year of marriage, I had prostate surgery. Cancer. But they got it. Anyway, I wasn't very good in bed after that. And, well, Amanda was younger and she was sexually abused as a child. She told me about that even before we were married. She was in counseling for that. I guess it made her sexually active or something before we married."

I reached my hand across the desk and put it on top of Ted's. "Not just before, Ted. I'm not a shrink. But she had an illness. They have a name for it: nymphomania. It's not something that getting married just cures. It's a personality disorder, a mental illness, something a person can't always help. You said she was abused as a child. That often damages a person's sexual self-image. What has Dr. Felton said to you?"

Ted sat back in his chair and tilted his head to stare at the ceiling. Whatever he was looking for there, he didn't find. "I don't know. I don't think much of shrinks in general, and I never really felt good about Dr. Felton. He uses all this fancy psychobabble that sounds good in his office, and then you get out in the car and try to remember what he said and you can't. At least I couldn't."

"I know what you mean. I think they get paid by the number of syllables in a word, with deductions for saying anything the average guy can understand. But do you remember anything?"

This elicited a small upturn at the corners of his mouth. "He was always saying things in her childhood, trauma at a vulnerable age, arrested development, something syndrome, I don't know. You know, I watched Felton sometimes in the office when both Amanda and I were there. I saw how he looked at her. I'm not sure all of his ideas were strictly professional, now that I think about it."

I nodded. "I've heard something like that about him, and not just with Amanda, but, for what it's worth, I understand she wasn't interested in him. Did you ever, yourself, witness Amanda do anything, well... you know?"

Ted looked back at me and paused to consider. "No. I mean, she loved to dance and I didn't. Lots of the guys at the club would ask her to dance. She'd go out with her friends. Work and golf kept me pretty busy. I couldn't and wouldn't insist she sit home like a dutiful little homemaker. I trusted her. I guess I heard whispers. But I loved her so much, and I know she loved me. She was beautiful and I guess a little flirty. She hugged and kissed and touched. But that was just her. Until that night with that mobster guy, she never rubbed my nose in it."

The look of anger and hurt that flooded his features as he recalled the Heather Hollows encounter was something I'd have to make sure a jury never saw. We talked long enough for me to explain I'd have to give the jury a picture of Amanda leaving a trail of broken hearts to show that others had a motive for murder. That is, I'd have to unless I could throw them a bone with the Dressler Foundation. If the only meat the jury got came from the prosecution, then Ted was a goner. I had to dangle something else appetizing as an explanation—lust or loot, or both—if we were to have a chance. Ted didn't seem warm to either avenue, but he told me in subdued tones where the keys to the family cottage were so I could drive up that afternoon and make sure no trace of the Dressler file was to be found there.

While we stood waiting for the turnkey to come and return Ted to his cell, I noticed how little of Ted seemed to be left to fill the baggy orange jail uniform. This once-imposing man was shrinking before my eyes. My news today appeared to have exaggerated the weight on his slumping shoulders. His right leg limp was more pronounced. His parting words as he and the turnkey departed down the hall to the cellblock remained with me as I passed through security back out into a bright August morning. "Do what you have to do. But no mud just for mud's sake."

My vigilance for someone following me had waxed and waned since my meetings with Granger and Eubanks. A few nights back my adrenaline was pumping when a red Chevy pickup followed me all the way to the beach from downtown. I pulled into my drive, jumped from the car with fists curled, ready to fight for my life, only to watch the pizza delivery man pull into a neighbor's drive two doors down. Then I'd admonished myself, "Get a grip."

Now, as Max and I headed east toward the Armbruster cottage on Lake Huron, just north of Oscoda, my sixth sense was in overdrive. The dusty brown Ford Crown Victoria had been in the rearview mirror since I hit the highway. It sure looked like the same car I'd been glimpsing at the far range of my vision over the last weeks. Stopping in a gas station, I saw both front seat passengers' heads turn to look at me as they passed. I didn't recognize either face and put it down to their interest in my car or dog for the next five miles, until there it was again, two cars back.

When I turned north from M72 to M33, they turned north. When I slowed to look for mailbox numbers, they didn't pass. Only when I made a sudden right turn into the cottage drive did they go by again, staring directly at me. Very unsettling. I don't carry a gun. Here I was in the middle of the piney woods on a large private lot, and my only resources were my wits and my dog. Max sensed my agitation and a low grumble began deep in his throat, audible over the rumble of the Benz beneath the canopy of evergreens.

I pulled up to the cedar log cabin and quickly went inside, locking the door behind me. I lifted the kitchen phone off the hook, but the line was dead. No surprise, as Ted had been in jail almost four months now. While I kept an eye out the back window, Max sniffed around the place. The cottage had the same empty feel from lack of use that the Armbruster home had had when I'd searched it for Amanda's missing file. Yet it was easy to see what a cozy nest it had been in happier times. The place was small, with only two bedrooms, a kitchen, and a living room. But the glass windows and sliding doors overlooking the vast lake gave it an open, airy feel.

Having seen no activity out back for half an hour, I pushed open the glass sliding doors onto the front deck. The ground fell away rapidly beneath the deck until it reached the sandy shore. To call Lake Huron a Great Lake is no exaggeration. From the deck it stretched as far as the eye could see. The west wind whispered through the evergreens and was blowing off shore, so there were no waves until about a hundred yards out. I could just make out the smokestack on an iron ore boat near the horizon.

Max bounded around the deck, eager to reach the beach. As all was quiet, I unlatched the wooden gate at the top of the steps and followed him down at least fifty stairs until we reached a landing next to a small boat house.

Max bounded in and out of the water and barked joyfully for me to come and throw a stick. The white sand beach was one hundred feet wide and stretched for miles in either direction. A half mile north I spotted a mother and two youngsters walking in and out of the water. I took off my shoes and socks to feel the crystalline sand beneath my feet. Rolling up my pants, I waded in with Max and was astonished at how cold the water was, even though it was August and we were in the shallows near shore. I quickly abandoned plans to see if Ted had a swimsuit lying around. However, the chilly water affected Max not at all. He raced into it and swam after the driftwood I threw with boundless enthusiasm. With each retrieval he'd wait until he was next to me on the sand, drop the prize, and shake himself, thoroughly soaking me in the process. After fifteen minutes my anxiety about being tailed receded to minor concern.

"C'mon, Max. You've had your fun. Time for me to get to work."

We made the long climb back up the stairs. I closed and latched the gate, leaving Max to sun himself on the deck while I went inside to look for Amanda's Dressler file. Ted had mentioned that his wife had come up to the cottage the weekend before her death and that it was possible she had wanted privacy to work on the file. In light of what I was learning about Amanda's love life, I thought it more likely she had used the cottage as a love nest.

I made a systematic search of the cottage, opening drawers, standing on chairs to see the top of closet shelves, and looking under the four-poster bed in the master bedroom. Nothing, until I was left with only the guest bedroom unsearched. That room too had large windows looking over the lake. Beneath one of the windows, a desk and chair sat between the dresser and the double bed.

I sat at the desk and admired the small framed pictures of Amanda and Ted in happier times. In one they sat in the front deck's Adirondack chairs at sunset in matching sweaters, toasting each other with champagne glasses. In another Amanda ran laughing into the frigid lake, looking sexy in a two-piece. A larger wedding photo captured the newlyweds ready to cut the cake. I couldn't help but feel sad at the devastation since those happy times.

I thought ruefully of my own bedroom, the stage debut photo, a couple of framed playbills, the *Sports Illustrated* cover of Tigers shortstop Alan Trammell over the headline "Grrr-eat!" when the Tigers had won the '84 series, and my mom and dad on their fortieth anniversary. All was in ruin for the Armbrusters now. But the photos before me testified to a happy intimacy that had once warmed their lives. I envied them that.

I thoroughly searched each of the Chippendale desk's three drawers. Nothing out of the ordinary. I rested my hands on the blotter covering the desk top to admire the view one last time before collecting Max to head home. The blotter shifted as I pushed up to turn away, revealing the image of a butterfly on what at first I thought was a piece of woman's stationery. I lifted the blotter and found the paper to be an oversized fancy sticky note on quality paper with butterflies flitting about the edges.

The adhesive kept it stuck to the desk top as I removed the blotter and set it on the floor. The feminine hand spelled out the following cryptic message:

Dressler 500K—Cats went to the dogs—TNPC.

No sooner had I started to consider what it could mean when Max commenced to bark fiercely. I glanced out the window and could barely see him at the edge of the deck with his front paws on the rail, barking in deep, menacing tones. I stuffed the note in my jeans pocket and had raced into the living room when I heard a male shout, "Lewis, shoot that animal before it comes over the rail."

"Noooo!" I screamed, running for the back door. I reached the door and flung it open as the shot rang out.

Stepping onto the landing, my eyes tried to focus in the bright sunlight. I regained sight just in time to watch the muzzles of two handguns turn from where Max had been on the lakeside deck to point directly at me. Time went into slow motion. My knees buckled. For an instant all that registered on my retinas was the gleam of the sun off the nickel weapons as they came to rest aimed directly at me. My focus was so narrow I even saw the index finger twitch on the trigger of the weapon closest to me. My face contracted to a grimace as I waited for the shot.

"Hands up! Hands up now!" came the scream from below.

I raised my arms in a spasm above my head. My field of vision expanded to include two brown-clad deputies standing five feet apart at the base of the back steps, coiled in the Weaver stance with their left hands supporting their right wrists to steady their automatics. The nose of the Oscoda County patrol car was just visible through the trees fifty yards up the two-track drive. I finally managed to breathe. Then I heard a throaty growl from my right. I stole a glance and saw Max, his head sticking through the deck railing, teeth bared. The guns wavered and started to track in his direction.

"Don't shoot my dog! What the hell is going on here?" I meant to sound commanding, but my voice came out in a hoarse croak.

"Control that animal or he's dead," the deputy closest to the bottom step ordered.

"Easy, Max. Easy, boy." I sidled over to the gate giving entrance to the deck and extended my right hand over to him. There was a fresh chunk of wood missing from the top rail of the gate, which must have deflected the shot and spared Max. He let me touch him and his growl subsided to a low rumble.

"I am Kenneth Edwards, Mr Armbruster's lawyer, and I am here with my client's permission and keys. Would you please tell me what this is all about?"

The deputies slowly rose from their crouch and lowered their guns.

"We got a burglary in progress call."

I began to lower my left arm to reach for my wallet in my back pocket, and the guns started to rise again.

"Easy, easy. I'm just reaching for my ID."

"Do it slowly."

I retrieved the wallet, held it in the air, and lobbed it down to them. After they examined my driver's license and state bar card, they holstered their weapons and relaxed. The older of the two, a sergeant by the stripes on his sleeve, pointed at Max, who under my hand had begun to settle.

"He all right? Sorry about that, but the report was that the intruder might be armed and was in the company of a vicious dog. While we were waiting for Lake County backup, the dog spotted us and was coming over the rail. I mighta panicked a little telling Lewis to shoot. But I'm a might chary of big dogs, and that dog's a monster."

My hackles rose at the mention of Lake County.

"Max is fine. He's a teddy bear. He's never bitten anybody. Why would you be waiting on Lake County? Who called in a burglary?"

The deputies started to approach the steps. This caused Max to snarl and show his teeth, so I asked if I could come down there. I left Max sealed on the deck, peering through the slats, as I walked down the back stairs to the sandy parking area. We shook hands and formally introduced ourselves.

"So you're the poor bastard defending the 'Country Clubber.' Damn fine looking woman from the pictures in the paper. What a waste. Why'd he do it?" asked the younger deputy with a narrow, rectangular bronze plate on his breast announcing him to be Cpl. Lewis. Now that he wasn't squinting up into the sun to shoot me and my dog on the porch, he removed his aviator sunglasses and slid one stem into his shirt pocket so they hung loosely to his shirt front.

I could feel my heart returning to normal rhythm and my muscles' tremors subsiding to a quiver. The sarge, a beefy man with a well-trimmed mustache under a bulbous nose, pulled a deck of Marlies from his uniform slacks and held the open flip-top box toward me, thumbing a couple of cancer sticks up for easy access. "Smoke?"

"No, I quit a few weeks ago." But as he stuck one between his lips and fired it with a flip-top Zippo engraved with the Marine Corps insignia, I couldn't resist.

"Yeah, give me one. Not that many folks can claim they faced a firing squad and had their last cigarette afterwards."

It turned out not to be my last one, either. After the dizziness of the first one, the next three or four were greeted like lost companions by my addictive neurons. We moved over to the shade of a mammoth spruce and sat around a lacquered cedar picnic table chatting over the drone of the cicadas in the afternoon sun. Max relaxed and dozed on the porch after satisfying himself the danger had passed. I remembered seeing some eight-ounce Cokes in the old classic bottle sitting in the fridge and opened one for each of us. They explained how they'd been hiding in the forest when Max spotted them.

"We got the call from the Lakies. Seems they had an anonymous caller who reported seeing a burglar with a huge animal. Apparently the witness was from Lake Pointe and knew it was the Armbruster cabin and knew to call Detective Bliss."

At the mention of Bliss's name, I knew he must be the man behind the car that had followed me on my way up. But why? And since Max and I had been there for almost two hours, why the delay?

Soon the answer was clear. Sergeant Jackson went on, "Yep, Bliss said he was trying to get a search warrant for the cabin. Something about motive evidence. Anyway, he asked us to lay back and keep the place under surveillance 'til he got here with the warrant. Said the 911 caller told him the dog looked vicious. And so here we are."

Before I could make further inquiry, the sound of a car crunching brush intervened. Bliss rolled in at speed and jerked to a stop, leaving us covered in a haze of dust drifting in the still air. The driver's door swung open and he levered himself from behind the wheel with a grunt. He reached for the pack of Camels in his breast pocket, extracted the last cigarette, crumbled the pack and tossed it on the ground before lighting up.

"Well, lookee here! A nice little picnic in the woods. Is Edwards the burglar, boys?"

Max showed impeccable taste in people and commenced a guttural rumble at the sound of Bliss's raspy voice. "Warned you about that animal, didn't I?"

I rose from the picnic bench, my face reddening with anger.

"You damn near got both me and my dog shot, you son of a bitch, telling these fellas that I was armed and dangerous and my dog was savage. From the guys you had tailing me, you knew damn well it was me."

He stopped in his tracks and held his hands palm up in a gesture of innocence. "Easy there, Edwards. What guys? All I know is 911 routed a call to me from an anonymous neighbor saying there was a break-in here and he thought he saw the perp with a rifle. Mentioned the dog looked mean. Can't have my brother officers walking in unprepared. Looks like you and the dog are no worse for wear. What's all the fuss?"

"Central dispatch has the neighbor's number?" I asked, knowing the answer would be false.

"Checked that. It's a pay phone at a party store a mile or so up the highway."

"Yeah, right," I spat back. "And you just happened to be working on a search warrant for the cottage when you got the call?"

He chortled, shaking loose some phlegm, which he spat in my general direction.

"Naw, nothing like that. Didn't know Armbruster had a cottage till the caller mentioned it. Figured as long as I was coming up here, I should take a look around and see if maybe your client left any evidence lying around. So I got me a nice little search warrant. Here, wanna see it?"

I looked at the affidavit in support of the warrant. It was obviously cobbled together in haste.

The Fourth Amendment requires that the places to be searched and the things sought be stated with specificity. Moreover, the person seeking the warrant must, in a sworn statement, itemize with particularity the reasons to believe the evidence will be found in the places to be searched. This affidavit was a collection of generalities in which Bliss recounted that Armbruster was charged with the murder of his wife, that in the course of investigations it was learned that a leather bag containing "financial documents" known to be in the possession of the deceased was missing, and that the defendant's confession to the police gave evidence of a financial motive for murder, i.e. troubled business and recently increased policies. A thorough authorized search of the crime scene had failed to locate the valise. A report of a burglary at the Armbruster cabin had raised the possibility that the documents, which may provide motive, were the object of a theft or might be found on the premises. The warrant authorized a search for financial documents evidencing a motive for murder.

I struggled to keep the smile from my face. The bull appeared to have started to break china. This affidavit might be worth more to the defense at trial than finding the valise itself. Bliss was now under oath, swearing that some financial documents contained in a missing pouch could be a motive for murder. Although he'd scripted the affidavit to make it look like the motive would apply to Ted, I knew, and I began to suspect he knew, that it didn't. I thought it best to act dumb, which wasn't that big a stretch for me.

"Bliss, what the hell is it you're looking for? What else would Amanda have that would be worth killing for?"

Bliss crossed his arms over his gut and rested his chin pensively in his left hand.

"You're supposed to be a legal genius. You figure it out. You tell me what you were looking for in there, and if we come across it, maybe we'll hang on to it for you."

"Very thoughtful of you. Actually, it was just a couple of personal things my client felt would help him get through his stay in jail. His father's Bible, which is on the bedside table, and some pictures of his wife. Mind if I go and get them before you start?"

Bliss looked dubious, a man checking an apple for worms before biting. Then he shrugged. "Hell, go ahead. Make a list and show me what you're taking and then get out. We'll drop a copy of the warrant return at your office."

So I collected the Bible, a couple of framed photos and a stack of pictures from the desk drawer. I showed them to Bliss. The sticky note stuffed in the back pocket of my jeans I kept to myself. After all, the search warrant said nothing about searching me.

I grabbed Max's choke collar and leash from the trunk, shook hands with the deputies and accepted their apologies.

"You guys buy me a beer sometime in place of a new pair of undershorts."

Halfway to my car Max made a lunge for Bliss that almost dragged me off my feet. Bliss caught his foot on a tree root in his haste to back away and fell on his duff. The Oscoda guys and I shared a smile and a shrug that told me they didn't much care for the manner in which Bliss had used them. The sarge was pulling Bliss to his feet as I steered around the police cars on my way to the highway. As I sat waiting for an opening in the heavy weekend traffic, I closed my eyes and offered a little prayer of thanks that Max had not been hurt.

"And me too, Lord."

28

As I drove south my mind was awhirl with ideas. I was full of adrenaline and anger at Bliss. He'd nearly gotten me and my dog killed. I didn't for a moment believe the anonymous pay phone bit. The guys following me had to have done so at his instruction. That was a lot of police man hours over the last few weeks, if my suspicions were right. But why? How would he know anything about Dressler? Why should he care?

I didn't believe in coincidence. Ever since I'd started rattling the Foundation cage I'd suspected a tail. Today those suspicions were confirmed. Before Dressler came up, only Gianfranco was making threatening noises. Now Thad Granger had told me to stay away. Brent Eubanks had gently steered me in another direction. My own client preferred I not stir that pot. And now Bliss was having me tailed and rushing a search warrant to get his mitts on Amanda's missing Dressler file. Nope. Way too much going on for coincidence. Now if I could only figure out what.

I'm not sure how long a dog's memory runs. But to look at Max sitting tall in the passenger seat, his ears horizontal in the breeze coming over the windshield, not long. His head turning side to side as we motored down the highway told me he'd already forgotten his near death experience. Not me. I could clearly recall my first look at the business end of a handgun. I felt my shoulders jump in a shudder at the memory.

When cool reason took over, I thought the affidavit stuffed in my glove box might have been worth the trouble. Now I had the chief investigating officer under oath swearing that Amanda's file provided a motive for somebody to kill Amanda. As far as I knew, Ted had nothing to do with the Dressler Foundation. So when Bliss swore that the missing file's contents gave someone a motive to kill Amanda, he was swearing at somebody other than Ted. With trial only days away, I had a whole new angle to come at Bliss with during cross examination. And that warrant would perhaps give me a shot at getting the whole Foundation issue into evidence, as Bliss had made it relevant.

That is, if I decided to ignore my client's wishes and those of everyone else on the subject and get down into the mud on the Foundation money. Until this afternoon I had been leaning toward sticking to Amanda's sex life and her struggle with Gianfranco. But near death experiences have a way of cleansing the mind. It seemed to me now that Amanda's death might have more to do with what was on the sheets of paper in the missing file than with what she'd been doing between the sheets before her death.

The letters TNPC tugged at my memory. I knew I'd seen them before. I rooted around in the attic of my brain to recall where. Their meaning and significance hung just beyond recognition, evanescing on the edge of consciousness. To find the acronym's meaning, I used the same mental decoder I used working crossword puzzles and tried free letter association, blurting possibilities. When I got to "Tarantula Nose Picked Clumsily" I gave it up. The harder I pushed, the more the meaning eluded me. My experience was that if I didn't force the synapses, eventually the memory would bubble to the surface on its own. But with all the things going on in my head to get ready for trial, this one stayed submerged. If Ted hadn't insisted I play in the tournament, it probably would've never reached my consciousness.

On arrival back at the cottage, I let Max off leash. He stood next to the car, his ears cocked, listening to the engine tick away the heat. Then he flapped his ears violently and ran over to greet Billy Starkweather, who was coming around from the lakeside, hose in hand, watering his flowerbeds. Max bounded up to Billy and drank thirstily as Billy held the nozzle at head height.

"Hey, neighbor, where you been? Tried to find you to go fishing. You should see the mess of perch I've got in the freezer. Really nailed 'em." As I walked over I could see the blood and guts from fish cleaning on Billy's overalls. Not all of it was fresh.

"Hey, man, don't you ever wash those clothes?"

"Last time I did I got skunked four straight times. Not a single fish. Nope, like 'em just the way they are. So where were you?"

"Getting shot at."

"What?"

"Damn near got Max killed. And if you want the details, it's going to cost you a beer."

So we sat next to each other on the ratty old sofa Billy left on his back porch year round, a couple of Old Milwaukees in our hands, and I told him about my day. Max romped in the lake for a few minutes and waited until he was right in front of us, as usual, before he shook himself off. Then he lay at our feet and was sound asleep in all of thirty seconds, leaving us to steep in the aroma of wet dog. When I was finished I asked Billy if TNPC meant anything to him. Trans National Pickerel Competition was the best he had to offer.

"But I will say this. Whatever it means, stay after it. Get to the bottom of it, and you'll find whoever killed that country club gal laying in the weeds like a thirty-inch pike with his teeth all sharp and shiny. You can take that as wisdom from the Old Ranger."

Old Ranger was Billy's hunting and fishing alter ego. In fact, since practically all Billy did was to hunt and fish on the comp company's money, I'm not sure how much was left of unaltered ego. He'd say things like "Trust the Ranger. Today you'll catch fish with minnie alone." That meant minnow on a bare hook, no razzle dazzle. Ignore him and watch him catch fish. Heed the Ranger and you could almost keep pace. Or he'd crook his head, sniff the breeze and utter, "Wind from the north. Fish go forth." And he'd head his boat away from shore to the south side of Dyke's Island and catch fish when nobody else could. After years of having Billy as a neighbor and a friend, I seldom ignored the Old Ranger's advice. And today, with the second beer mostly gone, his warning about a toothsome monster in the weed bed had a scary ring of soothsaying to it. I felt a chill even though it was near eighty.

When Max and I got home I called Mama Rosa's. Their pizza won no awards, but their Italian salad was great. Besides, they were among the few willing to deliver out to the beach. I picked up the phone again to follow the Old Ranger's advice.

Timothy Nagalski was a computer nerd. He owed me a favor. He'd been caught hacking his employer's personnel files to delete a reprimand and change his pay grade. I'd negotiated him a free pass in the form of informal probation, and he was grateful. So I put him on computer search for TNPC Investments. In spite of the hour, he was eager to be of service.

"TNPC, huh? That's all you got?"

"That's it. Sorry to have bothered you."

"Wait,wait! I didn't say I couldn't do it. Nothing stays hidden from me. If it's in the ether anywhere, I'll find it. Is it important?"

"Might be, Tim."

I rang off and then left a message for Karen, as she was on patrol. By the time she got back to me I answered the phone with a mouthful of pizza. It took a couple of repeats before she understood what had happened up at the cottage. I left out the sticky note but otherwise told her the whole thing.

"Is Max all right? That poor thing. He must be really shook up."

"Couldn't tell it from the way he wolfed his dinner or the way he's eying the pizza in my hands. What about me? I've never been on the business end of a pistol before."

"Oh, sorry. You sound fine. What kind of a car was it again?"

"Wondered if you'd ask. See, it wasn't just stress fueling my imagination. I'm sure it's the same tan Ford Crown Victoria I've been seeing for weeks. Why?"

"Sounds like one of the sheriff department's plain brown wrappers. I'm sorry I didn't take you seriously before. Are you sure you're all right?"

"Actually, I feel pretty good. Must be something about a near miss that juices you up. Plus, I think Bliss screwed up. He's given me a way to get some good stuff into evidence. I'm starting to think there's an outside chance I might pull this one off."

"As an officer of the law, I can't take that as good news. But I'm happy if you're happy."

"Can I take that to mean you and I are getting somewhere?"

There was a short pause and then a coy girlish tone. "Maybe."

29

Tina Botham's office had once been my office. I'd started in the prosecutor's office for the first two years out of law school. Can't beat the job if you want on-the-job training as a courtroom lawyer. But stay longer than two or three years, and the invisible strands of the spider's web of civil service begin to bind tighter and tighter. So after trying almost eighty jury trials, misdemeanor and felony, in the span of twenty-six months, I got out. I was tired of always seeing the bad in what people did rather than what led them to do wrong. I found jury arguments that were once fresh now cloying with constant repetition. The cops had been sorry to see me go, but the other assistants were glad to see me gone. I was done hogging the glory.

This exalted closet, which had been the first office I called my own, always evoked memories. I had been a hard-charging new lawyer, eager to take on the top guns, when I sat behind that desk in the same county issue swivel chair with a sticky wheel that Tina now occupied. Now Tina was planning to notch her six-shooter by leaving me bleeding in the dusty streets of Laredo.

For an instant I saw myself trapped on the great mandala as it turned slowly through time. The Byrd's song from Ecclesiastes, "Turn, Turn, Turn" popped into my head. "To everything there is a season—" I felt the same angst that had been keeping me awake nights even before Ted's desperate call. Had my time come and gone? Was my star setting and

Tina's about to rise? I shook my head to dispel the clouds of fatalism from my mind as I reached to shake my worthy opponent's hand.

"Ready to dismiss all charges?" The bravado in my voice in no way matched my mood. Stretching her five-foot-two frame across my old desk piled with the ammunition she was mustering for war, Tina pretended to consider while she firmly grasped my proffered hand.

"Nah, can't do that. Tell you what. Plead him as charged to Murder One, and we won't charge him with making a false report of a crime."

The lawyerly banter out of the way, we both sat to get down to business. Again a feeling of a fated hidden universe beyond my understanding seeped into my brain. Tina sat where I had once sat. In between, the great love of my life had occupied that chair. Alexandra Kingsdale had been a fire-breathing young prosecutor when we met and fell in what I'd thought was lasting love. Now Alex was the judge who would referee between Tina and me. The crystal goblet that had been our relationship lay in sharp broken pieces. And my psyche bled any time I stepped near the memory. For reasons which completely escaped me, Alex acted as if the fault were mine. I guess I should've been more understanding when she threw me overboard. Women—a lifetime enigma for me. But how strange that the three principles in the drama about to unfold had all sat in the same chair, earnest, eager, and determined. The same sticky wheel had screeched under us all.

Tina kept the office on the fifth floor landing directly across from the elevator a lot neater than I ever had. She, now three years out of school, had just been appointed chief trial lawyer. Judge Alex had ordered us on this Monday, the eve of trial, to meet and mark exhibits. Tina sat behind my old desk so full of excitement and energy that you could almost hear her body hum. Her suit jacket hung from the coat rack behind the door. She had the sleeves of her white blouse rolled up, but it remained buttoned to the top. Her short auburn hair had some kind of mousse in it and clung tightly to her head. At five-two she used a thin pillow to boost her in the chair. She wore no lipstick or other makeup. If she weighed more than one hundred pounds wet, I'd be surprised. Yet when she removed the tortoiseshell glasses to read the return on the search warrant before handing it to me, I noted for the first time that she was really quite pretty.

"Here you go. They found nothing. Bliss tells me you had a bit of excitement up there. To quote him: 'Edwards will be investing in a new pair of jockeys.' True?"

I glanced at the warrant return—"No evidence seized"—and looked back at my opponent.

"Shame on you, Tina. What kind of question is that for a lady? Bliss exaggerates. I was a might bit shook, but managed to avoid that kind of embarrassment. Have you considered that Bliss might have opened some interesting doors with his little foray into the north woods?"

Her smile vanished. "Like what?"

"Like I'll tell you later."

She chewed on that for a minute, then shrugged as if to say "no big deal."

"Ken, I want you to take this the right way." She paused to consider her words. "I'm gonna whip your butt. Browne had me scared 'cause I thought he was going to plead and rob me of the biggest case of my career. Then along you come, riding to the rescue. Thank you. Thank you. Thank you."

I smiled, remembering what that kind of eagerness felt like. "That confident, are you?"

"Best dead bang case I've ever seen. Why did you take it?"

"Because it looks like the best dead bang case I've ever seen." I let that hang for a minute and then, as part of the ritual of combat lawyers, I tried to seed a little doubt. "Imagine how good it'll look if he's found not guilty."

The quizzical look that crossed her face told me she'd never even considered the possibility. It didn't last long, but I knew she'd glimpsed the abyss of a spectacular defeat for just an instant. Then she straightened her neck, replaced her glasses and smiled confidently.

"Never happen on my watch, counselor."

I raised my eyebrows and smiled back. "We'll see."

By the time Tina and I had catalogued over a hundred exhibits, the county building was empty. The night janitor, Gordie, had been mopping floors before I came to town and was still mopping them ten years later. His graying hair was thinner. The Michigan "Go Blue" t-shirt was more frayed, and if possible, his eyebrows were bushier. But his broken-tooth smile remained the same.

"Well, I'll be. Old home week. Hey, Kenny. In there begging for a last minute deal? Evenin', Miss Botham."

I stuck out my hand. "Hey, Gordie. Long time no see. Nope, no deals. Trial starts tomorrow."

His face lit up. "Great. I don't want to miss a day of it. Think you've met your match, Kenny? Miss Botham don't lose many. The guys down at the Moose Hall say your client is guilty for sure."

I laughed and said as we climbed in the elevator, "You tell them Mr. Edwards says hello, and if they ever need a lawyer—" The door shut, and I admired Tina's trim calves as she pushed the button for the ground floor.

She used her key to let us out into the empty parking lot on a humid, dog days of August evening. It seemed like the weatherman had misplaced Savannah, Georgia's climate for the last week or so. As she reached her very sensible Volkswagen Jetta, I stuck out my hand."Luck."

She cocked her head and her thin lips parted to reveal perfect teeth as she put her hand in mine. "Luck."

Neither of us specified the kind of luck we were wishing the other.

She drove off, giving me a beep and a wave. The last friendly gesture I could expect from here on out. I walked back to the office for a meeting with the Witches of Endor, a meeting for which I was already late.

30

Climbing the red-carpeted steps to the second floor, I used the handrail which Tom had made certain was firmly embedded in the wall. Normally I ran briskly up the steps for exercise. But on the eve of trial I was without energy. Exhausted. And battle had yet to be joined.

Instead of turning right for the office door, I turned left for the restroom. The face in the mirror looked tired and careworn. I splashed cold water over my face and toweled dry. I ran the hairbrush through my hair and noticed the brush was full of strands that had opted for early retirement. A last glance in the mirror showed improvement but was still miles from the fresh-faced youth in the theater cast picture on my dresser. Was it that long ago?

Janice, who had stayed late to keep the office open for the Moondrake sisters, looked pointedly at her watch as I swung the office door open. She was a crackerjack secretary and a real workhorse. But her loyalty to me was a distant second to her devotion to her eight-year-old daughter, whom she was raising on her own.

"Had to get the neighbor to sit with Jamie, and she's got bowling. I've got to run. The ladies are in the library." Her voice dropped to a whisper as she brushed past me for the door. "Bit odd, aren't they?" As the office door squeaked shut Janice pulled it open again. "Oh, boss." I looked over my shoulder. "Good luck." I made a mental note for the hundredth time to complain to Tom about the door and turned into the library.

This was my first experiment with jury consultants, and I'd used five thousand of my retainer for the sisters I referred to as the Witches of Endor. As I surveyed them, unnoticed in the library doorway, I wondered not for the first time what I'd gotten into. Graciella and Lydia had pushed my Supreme Court volumes aside on the table and were engaged in some video mortal combat on their laptop to the sound of machine gun fire and animal roars.

"Evening, ladies. Sorry I'm late."

Neither looked up. Instead Gracie raised her hand to wave. "Almost got him. In the underbelly, Lyds. That's it. Oooh, there he goes!" To the sound of a primordial death rattle, they pushed back their chairs and stood to greet me. The lawyer who had referred me to them told me they were Romanian. Looking at them was a study in the gypsy gene pool. Their coal black hair tumbled in wild curls to their shoulders. They weren't twins, Gracie being older by a year, but they could've been. Tall and slender, with olive skin, dark eyes and prominent noses, they reminded me of a young Cher. Lydia wore an Old Navy sweatshirt cut off at the sleeves over faded denims. Gracie dressed her heritage in a floor-length peasant dress. A broad black leather belt cinched an off-the-shoulder white blouse. Ruby orbs dangled from gold chains beneath her ears. My face must have reflected my concern.

"Don't worry, Ken. We clean up real nice for trial." Gracie smiled, taking my hand, laughter in her onyx eyes.

I grabbed everybody a soda while they rebooted their computer to bring up the jury evaluation they had done for me. Jury consulting is a booming legal mini-industry. Others swore by it, and since the art of jury selection had always been merely guess work for me, I had decided to try it. No sense trying to sell bikinis to nuns, as I had found out on a couple of post adverse verdict jury interviews. My penchant for letting pretty women grace the jury box had cost me more than once. Matrons, dowagers, oddballs, and ugly ducklings seemed to find me more persuasive. Go figure.

I had Fed-Exed the jury questionnaires to Talisman Associates in Detroit as soon as I got them from the clerk's office last week. Now it was time to see what I was getting for my money. Lydia opened a brief-case and spread the forms on the library table after moving my formerly well-organized research books into a hither and yon jumble on the empty chairs and floor.

"Okay, Ken. We've rated each prospective juror from plus five to minus five," Lydia explained as she bent her spare frame over the table to organize the piles. "Your client's mom would get a plus five. The prosecutor's wife a minus five."

"Actually, the prosecutor's a she and she's not married," I said. The sisters shared a look of surprise.

"Oooh, you didn't mention that," Gracie murmured. "Probably have to change a few ratings as we go through them then. Not to worry."

But I began to worry. I'd spent little time poring over the questionnaires, leaving it to the hired pros. But their being from out of town was already proving a disadvantage.

"Explain your methodology again."

Lydia adopted a serious look. "Well, first on a moonless night we take juror forms out under a baobab tree and mist them with essence of bat wing—" She must've seen the panic on my face. "Kidding, just kidding. Relax, will you? Both of us have master's degrees in psychology. Gracie has a subspecialty in group dynamics, and I have made a life study of graphology." She saw the question mark in my raised brow. "The ability to identify personality through handwriting. Yes, it's a science. The FBI has its own section. If you study pressure, slant, open or closed letters, loops, t crosses and i dots, you can learn a lot about people through their handwriting. Then I apply Myers-Briggs and LeSenne typology to classify each potential juror. You know what that is?"

"Afraid not. I'd like to learn, but not tonight, with trial starting tomorrow. Gracie, what arcane arts do you practice?"

She tilted her head so that the tresses fell from her right shoulder and brushed the table. "Nice and simple. I am a human mixologist. Group dynamics allows me to look at a mix of people and tell you who are the dominant leaders and who are the followers. When your jury is chosen, I'll write down three names and I guarantee one of them will be the foreperson. I can tell you whether a person is a sympathetic listener type or a skeptical get-down-to-business type. There are no sure things, as this is art as much as science. But we'll improve your odds." Over the next few hours I began to believe they just might.

It was after eleven by the time the ladies headed for their hotel. By the time we'd covered each questionnaire and they'd explained their thinking on why Miss Jones was a plus three and Mr. Smith a minus four, I was beginning to think they had something better than my old gut feel method. I threw the Chinese take-out boxes in the trash and wandered back to my office. Even from behind my desk the place smelled sweet and sour.

It was zero hour, and I had to decide whether to give my opening statement or reserve it. I'd never reserved before. The wisdom is almost universal that most cases are won in opening statement. To let Madam Prosecutor have the floor to herself was risky in the extreme. But I could see no other way.

My problem was that at this late stage, I wasn't sure of what my defense should be. To have a glimmer of a chance I had to give the jury a possible suspect other than Ted. Should I go with the jilted lover angle, headed by Gianfranco as suspect number one, with Annabelle Browne, Chip Wilson, and Dr. Felton in lesser roles? That could work if any of them confessed on the stand, but that only happens on TV. Could work if the jury decided Amanda wasn't the angel portrayed by the media and rather was a tramp toying with people's affections. Could blow up big time if the jurors thought I was heaping mud on the deceased, who could no longer defend herself. However it played to the jury, it would be painful for Ted.

I was more tempted by the Dressler and TNPC angle. A headline-making scandal could do what my client, and others such as Brent Eubanks, were urging me not to do: create a jolly good circus. While the jury was distracted with financial elephants and legal trapeze artists, Ted and I might slip out of the tent with a not guilty verdict. Misdirection works great for magicians. And I knew magic was needed.

The problem here was that I'd come back into the case late. I had only a very strong intuition that Dressler, TNPC, and Amanda's death were intertwined. In spite of taking a jackhammer to my brain, nothing would shake loose from memory as to what TNPC stood for. I had a mental picture of Tina interrupting my opening statement, objecting to the relevance of the scandal, and Judge Alex hitting me over the head with her gavel as I responded to the objection.

"Judge, I've got a strong feeling about this. Let me wave this red flag in front of the jury, and as soon as I have it figured out, I'll let you know."

Right. I knew that Amanda had died while looking into missing Foundation money. But I didn't know where the money had gone. I had the "cats to the dogs" memo but no idea what it meant. I had Bliss's affidavit for the cabin search saying finances were the motive for murder. Again, no clue why Bliss would care about Foundation money. He was from the other side of the tracks and had nothing to do with the community big shots who sat on the Foundation board. In short, I had way more questions than answers. So I'd reserve my opening statement and hope like crazy I had the answers when it came time to put on a defense.

I flipped off the lights, locked the squeaky entrance door and trod down the stairs, exhausted and very anxious. "What have you gotten us into, Ollie?" I muttered to the empty street as I stepped into a muggy August midnight that was even more oppressive than my mood. Wilson Pickett's "Midnight Hour" greeted me when I fired up the Benz in an empty parking lot.

The tourist bureau calls the Eastern shore of Michigan the "Sunrise Side." Tuesday, August 11, Max and I were up in time to catch the first rosy fingers of dawn. In fact, it had been so still and close at the cottage I'd hardly managed any sleep. We dashed in for a five-minute swim just as the sun climbed above the horizon. I showered and dressed in my lucky suit. Others called it my ice cream suit. It was an off white, linen three-piece which I superstitiously had worn at the start of every big case since law school. Even the best of dry cleaning couldn't hide the fraying at the cuffs or the trace of a coffee stain on the left inseam. The suit reminded me of Gregory Peck in "To Kill A Mockingbird."

As I stood before the mirror adjusting my tie and stringing the gold chain that held my most treasured possession, a pocket watch from my father, through the buttonholes in my vest, I noticed my craggy visage and high forehead weren't all that far off Gregory's. I bowed my head in silent prayer asking for wisdom and courage, took a deep breath and headed off to war.

I dropped Max at Esther Grimes' puppy farm and wished we could trade places as he romped off, tail wagging, to frolic with his doggie pals. Esther stood by the car as I put the top up. The air was so heavy with moisture, rain seemed a foregone conclusion.

"Do your best, Ken. But I must say, I'm hoping justice gets done."

I had to laugh. "Thanks for your support, Esther." I stopped at the

Lazy Farmer party store and grabbed a coffee and the morning *Leader.* Oh-oh. The headline read,

Trial Of The Century

I leaned against the car, making sure not to dirty my suit, and scanned the front page story. Right away I wished I'd kept my mouth shut when talking to Art Honnecker over a beer last Friday. I thought we were just having a friendly chat at the Dew Drop Inn, the local courthouse dive. With a newspaper man there is no such thing unless he commits to being off the record. The lead paragraphs read:

> Defense counsel Kenneth Edwards promised, "This will be the trial of the century. We've turned over a few rocks in our investigation and some dark and slimy things crawled out. By the end of the trial my client's innocence will be clear."
>
> When pressed, Armbruster's attorney would offer nothing further. Prosecutor Tina Botham shrugged off Edwards' remarks, telling the *Leader*, "He's whistling Dixie and doesn't even know the tune. We have an overwhelming case, as the jury will soon see."

The rest of the story rehashed old news and opined that public interest would assure a full courtroom. A sidebar referred readers to the editorial page debate on reinstituting the death penalty. Oh boy. The first thing on the docket for this morning was my renewed motion for change of venue, and here I was fanning the flames of media coverage. In building my practice I was shameless about media self promotion. But even if it was only August 2000, Trial of the Century seemed a bit of a reach even for me. What was I thinking, even hinting the defense might have a surprise or two? Loose lips sink ships. How many beers did I have?

I had planned to park in the county building lot during trial so as not to be lugging heavy briefcases back and forth. However, my drive past the courthouse disabused me of that notion. An hour before court was to begin, a crowd spilled down the courthouse steps and into the street. A patrol car was arriving at the curb to deal with the mob. And there wasn't a parking space to be found anywhere in the usually half empty lot. I guess nobody wanted to miss the trial of the century. So I parked behind the office and entered to the aroma of the morning's first loaves baking.

Stuffing my files in my satchels, I noticed the message light on my answering machine blinking. Two messages. The time of the first message was a few minutes after midnight last night. I must have just missed it. I hit play.

"Uh, Mr Edwards. It's me, Tim. Found something on TNPC. I'll call tomorrow."

The second message was ten minutes ago. Karen's contralto message was short but reminded me this case wasn't my whole life.

"Hey, big guy. Missed you at home. Missed you here. Missing you. Made up my mind. I'm pulling for you. Go get 'em, tiger. Oh, remember, I'll be at Quantico the next ten days. I'll call you when I have a number." Karen was working to become one of the state police department's youngest female detective sergeants ever. This training session at the FBI facility in Virginia was a big step along that path. I was excited for her and wouldn't have seen much of her anyway with the trial.

I left a note for Janice to have Tim in the office at six and started trudging the four blocks to the courthouse, my arms straining at their sockets from the weight of the briefcases. Even at 8:30 the heat and humidity were overwhelming. I had to stop after each block and rest and was soaked by the time I neared the back door to the courthouse. So much for my cool-as-a-cucumber look. The rear basement entrance required a swipe key, which every lawyer had. As I was pulling mine out of my wallet, a guy on the front sidewalk wearing a baseball cap shouted, "There he is. That's Edwards."

As the door closed behind me, two radio guys and four or five spectators started pounding for admission. I shrugged "no can do" and climbed on the elevator. On the first floor the door opened to admit three ladies wearing juror buttons. I stepped to the rear and nodded good morning. Only one managed a slight nod in return. Not a good sign.

When the elevator doors opened on four, pandemonium reigned. The vestibule that separated the courtroom from the jury assembly area was jam packed. The three ladies were frightened by the crush. I saw

Larry Wilson, Judge Kingsdale's bailiff, trying to maintain order. I waved at him and mouthed the word "jurors," holding three fingers up. He created a lane and escorted them to the juror assembly doors. The lady who had nodded looked back before entering and mouthed, "Thank you."

I stood holding the elevator till Larry came back, and he grabbed one of my bags and then yelled, "Clear the way. Officer of the court. Make way."

He ran interference as we headed to the hallway that gave entrance to the judge's chambers. Suddenly I felt a hand on my sleeve and turned to see a bird-faced man with broken teeth. As he opened his mouth to call out, I was overpowered by the smell of onions.

"Rot in hell, shyster. The Lord will punish you."

A teeny lady, incongruously dressed in a white pillbox hat and matching gloves, pressed closer to say quietly, "Shame on you. That poor woman."

The rest of the crowd closed in with shouts. None was friendly. Somebody held a poster above the sea of heads: "Justice for Amanda." I almost tripped on a large boot a burly, bearded man stuck in my path. Larry reached back to steady me and dragged me into the hall behind him. Only in the hall did I realize how frightened I was. My heart raced. I was breathing hard. I was scared, worse than when the deputies had pointed guns at me. At least that was over quickly. This was just beginning.

"Whoa, Larry. What's going on?"

He looked shaken too. "Never seen anything like it. They mobbed the judge on her way in. She called the sheriff and the chief down at City PD. They're meeting now to discuss crowd control."

"Sounds good to me." I followed Larry down the hall. When he turned right to enter the judge's office, I opened the door on my left and entered the unlit courtroom. I set the satchels at the defense table and finally caught my breath.

The courtroom was a throwback to the classical era. Oak paneled walls were topped by ornate metal light sconces. The judge's bench sat on a riser and dominated the room with its ornate girth. Behind the bench a massive metal frieze of a helmeted, military-looking robed justice stood with a sword held in her hands. The ceiling was two floors above, as there was a second story of spectator seats that could only be reached from the fifth floor. Dust motes swirled in the shafts of light coming from large, high windows surrounding the upper level seating. I could hear the rumble of the crowd and turned to the back of the courtroom to see faces pressed against the narrow glass panes in the solid oak doors. I imagined myself to be a captured Gallic gladiator waiting in the amphitheater for my Roman opponent. It sounded like the crowd outside was pulling for the hometown gal, not the suddenly frightened Gaul.

I jumped at the sound of the judge's hall door opening. Tina ushered the Moondrake sisters in.

"These ladies claim they're with you. I thought you were a sole practitioner." Tina held her hand up to usher the women in.

"New associates." I introduced Gracie and Lydia, who towered over Tina. All three women were dressed in jackets and skirts, strictly business attire. Tina nodded knowingly and stepped back into the hall. She had apparently dealt with jury consultants before.

I pulled up two additional heavy wooden chairs to the defense table, which was of a size to accommodate three comfortably. The sisters had their wild manes of last night corralled in tight pony tails falling over the collars of their jackets. They looked very professional.

"Morning, ladies. You do clean up nicely for trial."

"I'll have to add a chapter to the thesis I'm writing on group behavior to include lynch mob mentality," breathed Gracie as she put her briefcase next to her chair and sat next to me. Her musky perfume wasn't strong, but it reached olfactory receptors I didn't know I had. I was going to ask her what it was to get some for Karen, and then realized Karen was more a fresh-from-the-shower type. Lydia slid into the chair on my other side, and it was obvious the sisters shared scents.

"Wow," Lydia said, "we've done some high-profile cases before, but I've never seen anything like this. They're all the way out onto the street jockeying for seats. You've got your work cut out for you. Did you see the 'Avenge Amanda' poster out front?"

"Nope, missed that. Hey, you guys are supposed to be my secret weapon, not soothsayers of doom."

The women shared a look, with me in the middle. Lydia nodded at Gracie to go ahead.

"Not a very scientific sampling, Ken. But have you thought of a change of venue? With the emotional vibes we got in just a few minutes, it might be hard to find an impartial jury."

I nodded. "First order of business today is to renew my motion. Judge has denied it once. But this morning's chaos may change her mind."

Promptly at nine the court reporter and bailiff followed Tina and Bliss into the courtroom. Ted's seat was empty next to me. Larry Wilson signaled to a deputy in the upper gallery and walked to the back of the courtroom. Both the doors on four and five were unlocked, and Larry stood collecting numbered stubs to let the public in. No placards allowed. The public squeezed into every nook and cranny, with maybe fifteen standing against the wall of the fifth floor gallery.

Once the rumble and hum of the seating subsided, Larry called out, "All rise," and the door to the judge's chambers swung open. Judge Alex strode purposefully to ascend the bench, her tawny tresses floating above her black robes. Unbidden, an image of Alex robed in a see-through negligee the night we first made love filled my head, fresh as yesterday. Seated, she peered over her half glasses to inquire, "Where's the defendant?"

The bailiff stepped smartly to face the bench. "Still in lock-up, Your Honor. We were afraid for his safety. We've seated one hundred and fifty members of the public, but we've got at least that many in the hall waiting for someone to leave. Judging from their reaction when Mr. Edwards got off the elevator, many of them are hostile to the defense. I've only got three extra deputies here, Your Honor. I didn't feel sure we could safely bring Mr. Armbruster through."

The judge paused to consider and then said, "Clear the halls of all spectators."

She then scanned the crowd jamming her courtroom. "Ladies and gentlemen. I believe in public trials and am loathe to discourage any member of the public from attending. However, the order of business is to hear a defense motion and then proceed to jury selection. We have well over one hundred prospective jurors in the assembly area. When it is time to pick the jury, you will be required to give up your seats."

Just as the outcry of anger crescendoed, she banged her gavel to silence the crowd.

"This is a court of law, not a football game. Any more outbursts and you will be removed. You have the slips the deputies handed out. After jury selection you will be readmitted. Bailiff, bring in the defendant."

Larry signaled to the door next to the jury box, and a turnkey accompanied Ted over to counsel table. He recoiled from the hostile buzz coming from the gallery and wobbled so that the turnkey had to take his elbow to steady him. Ted was wearing an eight-hundred-dollar suit topped with a fifty-cent jail haircut. The suit hung on him like it belonged to a bigger brother. The ladies and I rose to greet him, and Lydia slid back to sit in a chair at the rail.

The judge had telegraphed her decision on my change of venue motion when she outlined the day's agenda a minute earlier. But I gave it the old college try to preserve the issue. She slapped down my reference to today's crowd scene and all the pretrial publicity and saved a backhand for me, which I richly deserved.

"Mr. Edwards. I might have given more credence to your motion if I hadn't read your grandstanding play in today's paper." An approving murmur from the spectators punctuated with a male stage whisper: "You tell him, judge." She quieted the crowd with a raised eyebrow and continued. "I am imposing a gag order on both counsel for the duration of the trial on penalty of contempt. I am going to exhaust every effort to find a jury of fair-minded Lake County citizens, which I am confident we can do. Because of the notoriety of this case, I will allow more latitude than usual as part of voir dire. Motion denied."

Good news indeed. Since I was reserving opening statement, the more room I had to sell my case during jury selection, the better.

She had the now-reinforced deputies clear the courtroom of spectators and replace them upstairs and down with the blue-and-white badged prospective jurors. I stood with the sisters next to the rail and watched the jurors file quietly in. All three of us painted pleasant smiles on our faces. Only a few reciprocated.

"Tough crowd," Lydia whispered in my ear.

"In the matter of the *People of the State of Michigan vs Theodore Armbruster*, one count of murder in the first degree. Are the People ready to proceed, Miss Botham?"

Tina Botham stood and looked very professional in her light grey suit with a frilly blouse, but her voice cracked as she answered, "We are, Your Honor."

This was even bigger than either of us had imagined. I'm always nervous at the start of a case, but with all the attention this was getting and my fears that my innocent client faced a very big risk of being convicted, I was as jumpy as a cat.

"Mr. Edwards, is the defense ready to proceed?

"We are, Your Honor," I lied.

Jury selection took four full trial days. The jury clerk had to round up jurors from next month's panels. Two hundred and six of the two hundred and forty potential jurors were excused either for cause or by exercising preemptory challenges. To get a juror excused for cause a party must show bias, prejudice, contact with witnesses, and so forth. At least sixty of the prospective jurors admitted their minds were made up. They knew who did it, and he was sitting right next to me. Another forty knew family, friends, witnesses or had personal or business exigency that would make it impossible to sit.

Among those that remained, the most difficult were the ones who had made up their minds, but wanted to sit to see that justice got done. They were smart enough to figure out what gets people kicked off for cause and tailored their answers accordingly. Some say cases are won or lost in opening statement. Some say it's closing argument. For me it's jury selection. If you are selling ice, don't pick a jury panel of Eskimos. I'd already had my share of Eskimos, dressed up as good-looking blondes.

Preemptory challenges allow the lawyer to do social engineering. You need give no reason for excusing up to twenty prospective jurors. Don't like the cut of their jib, they're gone. Problem was, I wasn't always very good at deciding which way a jib should be cut. That's why I was willing to ante up for the Moondrake sisters. They were earning their keep.

As the procession of jurors marched in and out of the box, both were fully focused. While I tried to plant the seeds of reasonable doubt and presumption of innocence through my questions, they studied body language, facial expressions, and voice inflection. The prospective jurors, particularly the males, studied the sisters in return. The judge had introduced them as "with Mr. Edwards' firm." When the three of us would put our heads together, my thinning mane between thick, lustrous pony tails, after questioning a prospective juror, some of the men were obviously thinking the practice of law had some great fringe benefits. Little did they know those fringes were costing a grand a day.

The sisters would watch the interplay between the lawyers and each juror, looking for subtle body language. They examined and reexamined the juror's questionnaire, consulted their laptop and each other. They'd share their cryptic thoughts in whispers in my ear or notes on scraps of yellow legal paper slid beneath my nose.

"Dropping Mr. Ekkens from plus one to minus two. Smiles at you; all teeth, no eyes."

"Miss Lewis up to a three. More open to you than Miss Botham."

"E-6, Thames, hates you. Arms folded any tighter, he stops breathing."

During the breaks they'd keep running computer calculations of the plus-minus status of the jury information. An example of their value was juror D-16, Elaine Moffat, a leggy medical transcriptionist, who seemed responsive to me, laughing at a couple of my lame little jokes designed to win friends and influence people. Plus, I thought she'd make nice window dressing during a lengthy trial.

Lydia countered my arguments to keep her. "She's setting you up. She can't wait to stick the knife in you. She smiles to your face, but you should see the looks she exchanges with Mr. Larue when your back is turned. Get rid of them both. Trust me."

No sense paying for advice if you don't use it. I dumped her just before lunch on day three. As I was walking out of the courthouse to grab a bite, Miss Moffat was waiting at the bottom of the courthouse steps. Her tone at first was cordial.

"Why did you excuse me after I sat for three days?"

I shrugged. "Nothing personal. Just a hunch."

Then the venom. "Lucky for you. If you were any more like my ex-husband I'd swear you were twins. You sound sincere, but it's all style, no substance. And I am not the only juror who thinks so." As she stalked off I decided those legs were nice, but not that nice. After lunch I dumped Mr. Larue.

Over the four days I jealously guarded my twenty preempts, trying to get the hostile ones to admit enough to get rid of them for cause. There was nothing newsworthy in jury selection and no spectators allowed. So the surging mob of day one was gone. By the time I'd exercised my twentieth and final preempt, the sisters were actually upbeat. With the seating of juror N-19, Robert Zack, a first grade teacher, their cumulative number rating system broke into the plus column for the first time.

And then Tina screwed up big time. She'd been lying in the weeds throughout, only using four of her preempts. She'd rise after I booted another juror and announce with equanimity, "People are satisfied with the panel."

She wanted to create the impression that her case was so strong that it didn't matter who sat in the jury box. I knew she was waiting for me to exhaust all twenty preempts to preserve the venue issue for appeal, and then she'd customize the panel to her taste. After the sisters and I shared a little glance of pleasure at Mr Zack's seating, I waited for the axe to fall on my favorite jurors. Instead, Tina stood and breezily repeated the people's satisfaction.

Judge Alex, who had been around the track enough to understand what Tina had been doing the last four days, looked surprised. The judge looked down at her desk, where she kept an accurate count showing all my preempts were exhausted, then looked to me.

"Mr. Edwards, according to my calculations I believe you are satisfied, too."

I stood and said, "Yes, Your Honor. We'll make no further challenges to panel."

"Good. Then we have a jury. The balance of the prospective jurors are thanked and excused."

At this point Miss Botham was looking confused and distressed. "I'm sorry, Your Honor. I think I made a computational error. I have Mr. Edwards having used only nineteen, and so, well, I'm, I'm not sure I would've passed the panel. I mean, I would like to exercise a preemptory."

But it was too late. The last few jurors were like horses let out of a corral. When the judge said "excused" they were out of the door and gone. The judge looked perplexed.

"Miss Botham, we've been at this four days. Some of these jurors have been in the box for much of that time. If you had misgivings you had plenty of time to act. You just told me 'I'm satisfied with the panel.' Mr. Edwards passed the panel. We have a jury, twelve jurors and four alternatives."

Tina turned ashen. She grabbed her jury seating chart and stared at it. I could see the upper right-hand corner of the sheet. She had the numbers one to nineteen crossed out. Somehow over four days she'd missed one little stroke of the pen. On such little things momentous events hinge. "For the want of a nail—" I mused.

After the panel was sworn, the judge turned to them to excuse them for the weekend with a very stern warning not to read, listen to, or watch any news accounts of the case. She threatened to sequester them for the lengthy trial on the hint of any violation of her instructions. None of them liked that idea, and all nodded very positively when asked to promise not to discuss the case with anyone, including family and friends, on penalty of a long stay at the Holiday Inn. I watched them as they gathered their purses and paperbacks to file out. They weren't great, but they were better than I had hoped for in the commotion four days ago. And they were sure a lot better than if Tina had used sixteen preempts to customize them to her taste. All in all, a good start.

I walked out with Grace and Lydia and invited them into the dark and dingy confines of a rundown lumberjack-era hotel next to the courthouse for a farewell drink. The decrepit Fox Hotel was missing bricks from its first floor and paint from the rotting lumber on the second. Four rooms upstairs were rented by the week. The electric sign above the entrance, due to unreplaced bulbs, advertised the joint as Ox Hot. For as long as I'd been in town it was called simply "The Ox." The place was a dive, but the burgers were the best in town, and right next to the courthouse, the location couldn't be beat. A Christmas tree stood in the corner of the bar year round and twinkled through a miasma of stale smoke and dim lighting. It was definitely not to Lydia's taste.

"What a dump," she said as she dusted off her chair before sitting at our corner table.

"Hey, but it's got history. If you walk up front with me to the stairs, I'll show you the bloodstains on the carpet Gus Culver left when his best friend shot him coming downstairs with the barmaid."

"No thanks. What happened to the barmaid?"

"She hid behind Gus and was back at work the next night."

After their fancy cocktail orders met a clueless look from the waitress, they settled on the house white, which from their moues on first sip left plenty to be desired. I played it safe with a Labatts. I wanted to celebrate with a smoke, but having done my penance of heeby jeebies for last weekend's relapse at Ted's cottage, I didn't want to go through that again. So I ignored the siren's song from the corner cigarette machine. Plus the sisters had become my nicotine-anon helpmates when I'd explained my hyperactivity and box after box of Good 'n Plentys by telling them I had quit. I couldn't let them down.

"Way to go, Ken. You've done better than we dared hope. That panel grades out at plus .73. Grace and I were thinking after day one you'd be doing great at minus two. You may even have a chance now. What was Madam Prosecutor thinking?"

I laughed and shared what I'd seen on her jury roster. "I can't believe she let that happen."

The sisters shared a look and then Gracie leaned in to whisper conspiratorially.

"Actually, Ken, we put a hex on her. Just an old Romany chant up in the hotel room involving lizards and frogs." Lydia nodded affirmation, her big dark eyes wide as she looked meaningfully at me. Then they broke the spell with gales of laughter.

"Had you there for a minute, didn't we?" Gracie giggled.

"Actually, I was worried about the spells and incantations surcharge." I laughed at how easily they'd suckered me. For just an instant I'd seen an image of the two of them with a portable cauldron steaming up their room at the Holiday Inn.

"No extra charge for that, but we will send you a bill for the fourth day of jury selection. We quoted three, remember?"

I nodded. "No problem. You ladies were great. You saved me from myself more than once. Heck, Miss Moffat alone was worth the dough. And I want to thank you both for how kind you were to Ted." They had treated him like an old friend or long lost uncle rather than someone accused of a brutal murder. They'd smile at him, touch his arm in conversation, and give him their full attention when he talked. Ted responded like a flower lifting its wilting stem to a soaking rain after weeks of drought. By the end of the week his posture was erect, color had returned to his cheeks, and there was timbre in his voice.

Lydia cocked her head, looking pleased. "That was easy. He's a very nice man, a gentle man. Hard to believe he'd do such a thing."

I feigned offense. "Remember, ladies, he didn't."

Lydia's coloring turned even duskier in embarrassment. "No, no. I mean I'm beginning to think he didn't. He doesn't seem like he's capable of that."

Gracie nodded thoughtfully. "I agree. But if he didn't, who did?"

"I'm still working on that," I replied.

We chatted and laughed, me relieved to be out of the arena for three days, the ladies' work finished. They even forced down a little of their untouched wine in a farewell toast: "Success."

I saw them to their black Lexus, and they spurned my handshake for hugs and cheek kisses that left all my senses reeling.

I'd been making progress tracking TNPC as the week of jury selection dragged on. Each day after court I'd do a little digging. On the first night, Tuesday, I met Tim Nagalski at the office. Approaching the glass office entrance door next to the burnished plate announcing in raised letters that this was the legal lair of Kenneth Joshua Edwards, I saw that Tim had made himself feel right at home. He had sprawled his six-foot-four beanpole frame across our waiting room couch. His sneakered feet dangled over the arm, keeping fast time to the earphone feed from his CD player. His nose was buried in the *Sports Illustrated* swimsuit issue he'd ferreted out of our magazine rack. The heavy metal was audible the minute I swung the door open. I shuddered to think what he was doing to his eardrums.

He jumped when I tapped the soles of his sneakers and spilled something called Jolt from the can on his chest. As we walked down the hall to my office, I grabbed a paper towel from the kitchen, which he used to swipe at his yellow t-shirt emblazoned with a black lightning bolt and the words "Cyber Punk."

Sitting across the desk from me, Tim was a bundle of energy. His long fingers tapped busily on bony knees jutting beneath faded khaki shorts. The left temple on his black frame glasses was missing, so they canted at an angle on the bridge of a beak-like nose. His acne seemed under better control since last I'd seen him a year ago.

We chatted about his mom and his efforts at finding a new job for a minute before getting down to business. "What have you got for me, Tim?'

He dug into the pocket of his shorts and pulled a crumpled sheet of paper out.

"Not much. But it's something. I know every search engine and all the magic queries, but this still took a while. Finally got a hit at someplace called OffshoreInvestors.com." He straightened what looked like a page ripped from an old high school ruled essay book on his leg and handed it to me. Scribbled there was the following:

TNPC Investments. Suite 14 Caribe Landing, Grand Cayman West Indies. 345-392-8786.

Xavier Westphal, Managing Director.

"That's it?" He looked hurt. "Sorry. I mean, was there anything else?"

"That site had a hypertext link, but all I could get was 'This page no longer available.' Trust me, man. I tried everything I know. It was just on an index at OffshoreInvestors.com. That place advertised itself as a clearinghouse for stuff like leveraged tax shelters, offshore assets and something called hedge funds."

After making sure there was nothing more he knew or could do, I rose to get the office checkbook to pay him for his time. "What's fair, Tim?"

"Oh, dude. You're kidding, right? After what you did for me, my mom would throw me out of the house if I charged you a dime. No way."

We argued all the way to the door, and I finally managed to press him to take a fifty for "dry cleaning." He stuffed it in his pocket and sauntered down the hall, leaving me with what I'm sure he meant as a compliment.

"Mr. E, for an old guy, you're pretty cool."

During the lunch hour recess the next day, I dialed the number and was thrilled to have it answered after a series of clicks and buzzes associated with antiquated overseas lines.

"TNPC Investment group. Antoinette speaking. How may I help you?" A lovely Jamaican accent.

"Good afternoon. Kenneth J. Edwards here calling from Michigan. Is Mr. Westphal there, please?"

"Sorry, sir, Mr. Westphal is off the island."

"When is he expected back?"

"I'm sorry, Mr. Edwards, I don't have that information. Perhaps you would leave your number. If I hear from Mr. Westphal, I can have him contact you."

"Is there someone there who can help me? I have some interest in a leveraged tax shelter."

"Actually there is no one in office at the moment. Could you leave a number and the name of your referring party?"

"Referring party?"

"I'm supposed to note that down. You have a referring party, don't you?"

I thought for a second and gave her the name of William Starkweather and spelled his last name three times.

"What if I flew down next Monday? Would Mr. Westphal or someone be in the office then?"

"I'm not sure I'd recommend that. The company policy is that all meetings are appointment only."

"Yes. That's what I'm trying to do, set an appointment. When in the next two weeks could I have an appointment?"

"I really can't say, sir. You will have to await a return call."

"When might I expect one of those?"

"I really can't say, sir."

"Can you say anything about the company, its investment programs or products?"

"I'm not at liberty to do that, I'm afraid."

"Antoinette, you sound very pleasant, but I'm not getting much information from you. What can you tell me?"

"I've noted your call. Please have a nice day." Click.

I hung up the phone and shook my head. What was that all about? On a whim I dialed the number again, but changed the last digit to seven instead of six. The usual click and switches that probably meant an expensive call and then, "Santa Maria Holdings, Antoinette speaking. May I help you?"

"Hi, Antoinette, Mr. Edwards again. You're pretty busy working two jobs at once."

A nervous laugh that caused me to picture a sultry Caribbean lass with brilliant teeth smiling from an ebony face beneath tight curly hair. "Oh, Mr. Edwards. Aren't you the clever one. How can I help you?"

"Promise you won't tell me you 'can't say' again."

"I can't say yes to that."

"See, there you go again. I tell you what. I'll give you your job description and you tell me if I'm right. Can we try that?"

A pause. "We can try that."

"You sit in a small office and answer phones for a number of businesses. You take messages. You collect mail. Am I right?"

I heard the sweetest little giggle. "I can't say," and she hung up.

Maybe to be a Cayman corporation you had to maintain an office and a phone number. Maybe to do business in this tax protected foreign atoll with more banks per square foot than Zurich, you needed to maintain the pretense of a headquarters, and maybe you needed an Antoinette to not tell anybody anything they didn't already know. If so, that girl deserved a raise.

I kept my mind on jury selection that Wednesday afternoon, but as soon as 4:30 rolled around I took hasty leave of Ted and the Moondrake sisters to try to reach my broker buddy, John G. Nash at Smith Barney, before he closed shop for the day. The TNPC spoor was faint to the point of evanescence. But I'd gotten a whiff. I had to get closer.

As I waited for John to come on the line, I stared at the inscrutable butterfly sticky note. Ted had confirmed it was Amanda's handwriting. He too thought TNPC sounded familiar, but couldn't place it. As to the cats and dogs, he had no clue.

John G. Nash was an old law school buddy who'd taken a fork in the road halfway through law school. He quit night school and kept his day job as a stockbroker. He was a big bear of a man with an outgoing personality. He would greet all and sundry with a hug and warm embrace.

He loved to sell and was bright enough to sound like he knew what he was talking about. However, over a few beers during the '87 crash, when asked what was going on, he replied, "Don't look at me, Ken. I've never figured this shit out." Even though the great bull market of the '90's had made John and his clients rich, he still didn't pretend to be a genius.

"Buy good stuff. Hold on to it. Sell the losers quickly."

This advice was contrary to my inclinations to sell my winners and let the losers run, hoping for a comeback. The net effect was that John and his clients had investment portfolios. My portfolio, if you could call it that, was an investment casting call for the night of the living dead, a number of stiffs and mummies that staggered about in the subterranean darkness of a Wall Street graveyard. Most of his clients were stockholders. I was a stuck holder.

If I weren't his friend, I doubted John would even have me as a client. I didn't listen to him. My portfolio was chump change compared to the big shots and corporate 401(k)s and retirement accounts he managed, but he always took my calls.

"Hey, Ken. What's up in the world of legal eagles? Making any money?"

"Keeping the lights on, John. Secretaries paid most of the time. If I'm careful till Friday I can probably buy myself a steak and a six-pack. Things are fine. How's the market?"

"The sun is up. Feathers are down. Lead is trading heavily. And the old lecher in the elevator with the secretaries is feeling for a bottom."

I laughed. John knew every market bromide ever coined. "Listen, I need your help. Ever hear of something called TNPC investments?"

"Nope. What is this, another of your hot story stocks?" I could hear him punching in the letters on his computer. "Nope—nothing. I get Trans Canada Pipeline, TCP. Probably a good buy. I like the pipeline business. Nice dividend. Is that it?"

"Uh-uh. This is some offshore tax shelter located in Cayman. Ever heard of that?"

"No, but there are lots of those around. One of these days Uncle Sam is going to take a good hard look at these offshore tax dodgers. Are you in a tax bracket where you're thinking of taking that risk?"

"Regrettably not. I've got a murder case where the name came up, so I called down there in Cayman. They completely brushed me off. Sounded like an answering service for multiple offshores."

"Yes, that's how they do it. But I don't handle that kind of stuff. I'll check our tax shelter guys in New York and see if any of them have heard of it. Let me put you on hold." So I listened to Smith Barney's message on the many ways they could help me manage my non-existent wealth for two and a half trips through the loop. Then John came back on.

"Hey, Ken. The guys in New York checked their indexes. It's a small arbitrage fund. Last report about fifty million in assets. They sell limited partnerships offshore. Not registered in the USA. So we don't offer it and it's too small anyway. What's it got to do with murder?"

"Some money is missing from a foundation. My client's wife was on the committee looking into where the money went, then she ended up dead, bludgeoned with a golf club."

"You've got that case? I read about it in the *Free Press*. Some lawyer named Browne had it. They caught the husband red handed. No?"

"Yep. Only he didn't do it. Mr. Browne got the boot, and here I am. Anyway, I found a note she made just before she died. Here, I'll read it to you." He listened.

"Cats and dogs, eh? That sounds like your portfolio. Wait a minute. CATS, eh? You know what CATS are?"

"Four-legged felines that eat mice."

"Could be that it's an acronym for Covered Arbitraged Treasury Securities. They have these mathematical formulas for the difference between T-Bills rather than, say, investment grade corporates or LIBOR rates, or Euro-bond rates. Then they do what's called a carry trade. Know what that is?"

"Sure don't."

"I'll make it real simple. They borrow by going short on low interest rate bonds in a strong currency like Japan and use the sale proceeds to go long in high interest rate, tax free bonds denominated in another currency. Got that?"

"Sorta. Sounds risky."

"The key is leverage. For every dollar of capital invested, they have ninety-nine dollars borrowed. At one hundred to one leverage, an eighth of a point differential in yield spread equals a twelve percent return on capital. Not bad, huh?"

"If they're so great, why don't you handle them?"

"Like you said, they are risky. They have a tendency to blow up. At that kind of leverage even a little miscalculation can spell disaster. Remember Long Term Capital Management about three years ago? Everybody thought those guys were geniuses, but every so often something outside the formula happens and you can get crushed. That is what happened to LTCM when the Russian ruble collapsed." He paused and I could hear the wheels turning. "CATS going to the dogs, huh? I'll bet that's what it means. Somebody's black box model failed. An overnight currency devaluation like the Brazilian dollar. An interest rate zigged when the model guaranteed it would zag. Something like that. Make any sense?"

"Some. That could explain what the note means."

"I've got a prospectus for one of the tamer partnerships we do handle. Half a million minimum, interested?"

"In the prospectus, yes. As for the investment, I'm about four hundred and seventy-five thousand short."

"I'll get it out to you and see if anybody in New York knows of any of the little CATS getting their tails caught in the door lately. Okay, buddy?"

"Hey, thanks, John. I appreciate it."

"Oh, yeah, and if your client yells 'Fore!' I suggest you duck." He was still laughing when we hung up.

On that weekend, with Karen gone, Max and I spent a lot of time together. I took him into the office with me both Saturday and Sunday mornings. I was still looking suspiciously at cars. But since the near death experience at Armbruster's cottage, my tail seemed to have disappeared. Each day at noon I'd buy two sandwiches from my tenant's sub shop, and Max and I wandered around Lakeside Park three blocks away. The meatball sub, I ate myself. I separated the meat from the bun on Max's favorite, the triple meat combo, and fed him little strips by throwing them up in the air for him to catch. He dropped less fly balls than that season's edition of the 105-loss Tigers. Lots of people were down by the lake to escape the heat. A banner advertised next weekend's celebration of Lake Pointe Heritage Days.

When I'd come up to interview for the assistant prosecutor job fresh out of law school thirteen years ago, I'd never laid eyes on Lake Pointe. All I knew was that it was "up north." I'd gotten to know its history since. In fact, the park in which Max and I were sitting had once been a massive sawmill. Lake Pointe in its youth had been a Sodom and Gomorrah of the Northlands. In the early 1800s Michigan had been carpeted in hardwoods. To supply a growing nation's insatiable appetite for lumber, most of those hard-woods were mowed down by multi-ethnic gangs of lumberjacks who spent months at a time in isolated lumbering camps. The wood they harvested would float down the river until arriving at Lake Pointe, then a major port on the shores of Lake Huron.

After the timber became lumber, it was loaded onto ships that carried it throughout the five-pearled necklace of lakes that comprise the Great Lakes, arriving in Chicago, Detroit, Buffalo, and through the Erie Canal out into the Atlantic. Shipbuilding grew up side by side with sawyering. By the mid- to late-nineteenth century Lake Pointe was a boom town. Great Lakes sailors traded stories and punches with lumberjacks, carpenters, mill hands, and ship builders in bars and bordellos that stretched a "Devil's Mile" along the waterfront.

The lumberjacks coming in from the wilderness, where the bosses allowed no booze and no women, were a rough and ready crew. Their pockets would bulge with pay from months in the woods. Three-night bacchanals would leave them hung over, bruised, rife with social disease, and broke on their way out of town.

Over time, a sizeable merchant class rose from the commerce in lumber, shipbuilding and shipping. Ready access to fresh lumber allowed the town to grow like topsy. The population burgeoned from twenty-five hundred souls to over sixty thousand in less than two decades. The lumber barons, bankers, and captains of industry competed with each other to build larger and more elaborate mansions as monuments to their prosperity. One of the larger of these palaces stood within my sight a half mile down the shore. Erected at the peak of the boom in the 1890's, it had been home to Leland H. Dressler and his family all the way up to the late '50s. It was Dressler largess that had endowed the Foundation which now, so many years later, was the focus of my driving curiosity.

Not long after the building of Dressler Manor, the bubble had burst. The lumber barons had no interest in reforestation in those days. All of a sudden the seemingly endless supply of hardwood near navigable streams was gone. The barons returned to their homes in the East. The lumberjacks went west. The staccato pounding of hammer on nail faded away. In the quiet, Lake Pointe fell asleep, not to be wakened again until the internal combustion engine and the auto industry roared north from Detroit, looking for new plant space.

I smiled, reflecting on the characters from the town's past while sitting on the top of a park bench, ruffling the thick folds of skin and fur on Max's neck while he sniffed the empty sandwich bag, hoping I had overlooked a morsel. I didn't realize then that one of the storied characters from the town's past would play such a big role in the outcome of Ted's case.

When I first came to Lake Pointe I had rented the cottage out on Sunrise Beach, thinking of it as a temporary way station on the road to marriage and a home of my own in town. More than a decade later, I was still paying rent. The retired minister I rented from resisted my every offer to buy.

After all this time I had become, as my neighbor Billy put it, a lifer. I loved the solitude in the winter and the beach parties and crowds in the summer. All you had to do was look at which direction the V of honking geese was pointing to tell if the upcoming season involved crowds or isolation.

I loved having the water right outside my back door, even if every time you jumped into Huron's chilly waters you risked heart stoppage. Even if the place was drafty—and it had been a long time since Pastor Munson had put any real money into it—it was my home. I had begun to send down roots here. Plus, there was lots of room for a one-hundred-pound dog who loved to run. Each of those torrid August weekend days, both Max and I were happy to close up shop at the office and take a convertible ride back out to the shore, where it felt at least fifteen degrees cooler. Saturday Billy provided the steaks. Sunday I made a run into the Kentucky Colonel's.

Both nights Billy whupped me but good at backgammon and crowed about it to the point that I bade him good night and took Max across the back yard to home. "Having a hard time concentrating with the trial and all" was the best excuse I could muster.

"You're moonin' cause Trooper Karen's out of town" was his diagnosis. I suspect we were both right.

That Sunday night was the first for a recurrent dream that haunted me throughout the trial and beyond. Experts say dreams are a mechanism for solving problems that remain unresolved during waking hours. It's like walking away from a crossword puzzle and doing something else.

While the conscious mind is otherwise occupied, the unconscious keeps turning the problem over and over. Then, an hour later you sit down with the puzzle and you know where you wrote in "eland" for an African grazer in 105 across is wrong. The correct answer is "okapi." Once the false assumption is erased, the whole blank corner fills in a heartbeat. I knew my dream was trying to show me something. I just couldn't figure out what it was.

Each night the dream was the same. I was sitting on the seawall in Lakeside Park at evening. I heard a faint feminine voice calling my name. I turned to see a dark-haired woman with a white skirt and red top beckoning to me from the stage at the park's band shell. I ran over but was running in slow motion against a crowd moving away from the stage, making no effort to get out of my way. By the time I arrived, the woman had gone around behind the band shell. I followed and was surprised to see that, where in reality there stood a concession and loading area, in my dream there was a grassy lawn. The woman was standing at the entrance to gardens where the pathways between the flowers were lined with low hedges. She smiled and slowly motioned me closer. Just as I got close enough to be sure it was Amanda, she turned and walked into the garden, saying over her shoulder, "Come. I will show you." Before she'd moved away I had been close enough to see that the red of her blouse was blotchy stains.

The further I followed her, the more the light failed and was replaced by a misty vapor. The path narrowed, changing from grass to rough stone on my feet, now strangely bare. The flowers were gone, and the hedge on either side of the path stretched well above my head. The once-straight path now made sharp turns, and I'd lose sight of her. I struggled on bloody feet to keep up, but each time I'd catch a glimpse of her, she'd be further away. Then the path straightened and I could see her faintly through the mist, standing in a meadow of fresh cut grass. She bent on one knee to pick up something at her feet and held it between her thumb and index finger, examining it closely. Then she held it out toward me. It glimmered with a light of its own. Now on smoother ground, I rushed forward. When I reached where she had been standing, she was gone.

I'd lie in bed while the dream was still fresh and try to decipher it. When the dream would come again, I would not resist, hoping each time I'd get close enough to see what she was holding out to me. Always it would end with me on the ground where she'd been standing, groping about the short grass, hoping she'd left the object behind. Always feeling lost, alone, and empty-handed.

34

When trial resumed on Tuesday, the public was back. But it was like a ballpark for the second game following opening day: lots of empty seats. The media was there for opening statement, but the judge had ruled no cameras in the courtroom. So most of them left a stringer with a cell phone in case of any surprises. Art Honnecker approached me outside the courtroom's back door with his right hand extended and a pen-clipped notepad in his left.

"Hey, Kenny. Got anything for me before the fireworks?" Art had to be nearing sixty and had been covering the police courthouse beat since I had come to town. His gray hair was thick on the sides and thin on top. His round face bore creases of skepticism. A few years ago, after a few beers, he'd told me his editor had caught him pulling a flask out of his desk at press time. Since then his career had stalled. He didn't seem to mind.

I shook his nicotine-stained paw and smiled ruefully. "Art, after last week's story, if I give you any more than the time of day, I'm going to jail courtesy of Her Honor's gag order." I made a show of pulling my father's watch from my vest pocket and said, "It's 8:14, and you can quote me on that."

He patted me on the back as I entered the courtroom and wished me luck. As the heavy door swung shut I heard him mutter, "You'll need it."

Tina was seated at the prosecution table poring over her notes for opening statement. I set my satchels next to my chair at the defense table and finally got her to look up and acknowledge me by asking, "Can I help you with that?"

She gave me a sideways sneer. "I can manage. Thanks anyway."

The doors at the rear opened, and I had to look twice to be sure it was Bliss. He hadn't attended during jury selection. They'd given him quite a makeover. His hair was neatly trimmed. He was wearing what looked like a new lightweight gray summer suit over a blue oxford shirt that actually fit at the collar. His hands were full of files, and despite myself, I stepped forward to swing the doors at the rail open for him. As he passed me, his normal aura of sweat and smoke had been replaced by the aroma of Old Spice Red Zone. He was close enough for me to notice that the barber had trimmed the hairs that had once sprouted from nose, ears, and eyebrows in undisciplined profusion. "Thanks, Edwards," he muttered as he brushed by.

The bailiff brought Ted over and I greeted him warmly. The prosecution table reacted as if he didn't exist. Promptly at 8:30 the judge took the bench, checked to be sure all were accounted for, and ordered the jury brought in. Many of them had been sitting in the padded swivel chairs in the jury box much of last week. Yet today they looked nervous and unsure, like sixth graders on their first day of junior high. They surveyed the spectator section to see it only partially full, with five or six preferring the upper deck seats on the fifth floor. When the rustling quieted, the judge smiled and addressed them.

"Good morning, ladies and gentlemen, and I see we are evenly divided between ladies and gentlemen. You are about to perform the most solemn duty our country asks of its citizens: to sit and decide the guilt or innocence of your fellow citizen, Theodore Armbruster. To perform that duty properly you must devote your full attention to the evidence which comes to you in open court. Anything you know, or think you know, about this case from out of court must be put aside and forgotten. Am I clear on that?" The heads bobbed. "Today we will hear opening statements designed to give you each side's expectation of what the facts will be, and what those facts mean in light of the charge involved."

The judge was departing from the scripted opening instructions and in so doing was putting me in a spot. The defense is allowed to reserve opening statement until the close of the prosecutor's proofs. Here the judge was telling them to expect mine today. Ted tapped me on the shoulder to whisper, "You told me you were waiting on yours."

I whispered back, "The judge missed the memo."

My mind was in turmoil. I'd never deferred opening statement before. I hated the thought that by the time I gave it, a week or so from now, the train would have long since left the station and the jurors' minds long since settled on conviction. While the Dressler angle was beginning to take shape, I needed more time before I let that genie out of the bottle. So I stood to interrupt the judge as she went on to instruct the panel on how they were to regard the parties' openers. "May we approach, Your Honor?"

She gave an exasperated nod. When Tina and I reached the side of the bench furthest from the jury she asked, "What is it?"

"Actually, Judge, I am planning to reserve my opening statement."

If looks could kill I'd be dead. "Why didn't you tell me?"

"Sorry, Judge. I expected you to follow the script mandated by the court rules, which specifically refers to the defense's right to exercise that option, and caution the jury to keep their minds open." She relaxed. I had her. She didn't like it, but I was right.

"All right, what do you want me to do?"

"Ask me my intentions. I'll reserve, and then please carefully instruct the jury that this is proper and they must not decide the case before the proofs are in."

As we walked back to our respective battle stations, Tina whispered, "Are you crazy?"

I whispered back, "Like a fox."

The judge bent over backwards to say that what the defense was doing was completely appropriate, and even though all the jury was going to hear today was the prosecution's side of the case, they must remember there was another side to the case and arrive at no conclusions until the defense presented its side of the story. Now all I had to do was figure out which story we were going tell by the time the prosecution rested.

After that the judge opened the red binder of pretrial jury instructions and followed them to the letter. For the next hour she instructed them on evidence, objections, evidentiary rulings, presumption of innocence, burden of proof, and all the other ingredients of a fair and impartial trial.

I listened to Alex's authoritative voice and marveled at her commanding presence on the bench. This was the young prosecutor I'd risked my career to help get elected judge. Her blonde hair had once adorned my pillow. The generous body beneath the robes had for many months been mine to pleasure and explore. We'd sat under the stars on the beach in Negril, Jamaica, after she'd finally given herself to me, and we talked about how many children we wanted. Then four years ago, a few weeks after her election, she'd cut me out of her life. Oh, the words she had used had been kind and thoughtful. But she couldn't have cut me deeper if she'd used a butcher knife. As I fled her apartment to keep my tears from her, my last words to her outside of a courtroom had been to tell her, "Have a nice life."

Somehow since then she'd treated me like it was my fault. She made it painfully obvious to all who came before her that she would be doing her former lover and campaign manager no favors in the courtroom. Every close call went the other way. At social gatherings you could look for us on opposite sides of the room. After I got over the drinking and self pity, I wanted to call her to have her explain what had happened in greater detail. But by the time I'd dried out, we were a long ways down the road from what she once had called "hopelessly in love."

Watching Alex now, I could see she had grown into the job. Oh, she was still achingly beautiful, even cloaked in judicial robes. The four years had added an aura of wisdom and character to her softly chiseled face. I could feel the old scars beginning to tear loose in my psyche and got my mind back to business.

The judge closed the book upon concluding and looked to the jury with a smile.

"I must ask your kind indulgence and patience. I am a stickler for promptness, and the lawyers will tell you I do not grant adjournments or delays easily. But next week my older sister, Lorraine, is getting married in California. Since we were girls we promised we'd be each other's maid of honor. No man has sought my hand, alas!" For a millisecond I thought of objecting to that fib. "So we will be taking a break in trial Thursday and Friday of next week. Please plan accordingly. Now we'll take a short recess, and the prosecutor may then give her opening statement."

Good old sister Lorraine. It was Mom and sister Lorraine's advice that Alex had mentioned when she broke my heart. "They think we should give each other space while I settle into the judgeship. Can we put our plans on hold for now?" That's when I walked out.

"All the best, Lorraine," I said to myself, rising to watch the jury be led out.

Tina was a dynamo as she stood to address the jury. Last week's gaff in jury selection was a thing of the past. I'd tried two earlier cases with Tina, each of us having to give the other the time-honored congratulatory handshake. I'd seen her style. So I warned Ted that the feisty little welter-weight would be in his face as she outlined her case in opening statement. And she was. Her heels lifted her to five foot two inches. She looked smart in a navy skirt and jacket over a white blouse. She'd modulate her tones as she stood near the jury box and then strut back to stand in front of the defense table, her arm extending and index finger pointing at Ted in "J'accuse" fashion.

Her voice filled the courtroom. "This man left his defenseless wife in a pool of her own blood on the marble tiled floor at the base of the stairs."

"This man ignored her pleas to stop."

"This man bludgeoned Amanda to death, turning a golf club into a war club."

"This man, who confessed to the brutal slaying on the night of the crime, comes before you now to deny his guilt."

For almost two hours she laid out the prosecution's case in intricate, gory and damning detail. Softly and in almost a whisper when describing what a lovely and caring person Amanda had been. Forceful and con-demning as she pointed at the beast who could turn a living saint into a lifeless heap. To his credit, Ted never cowered, grimaced, or glared. Rather, he looked back at her with compassion and understanding. When I asked at the break how he managed, he replied, "I agreed with everything she said, except that I had done it. I just imagined that the real killer was who she meant, and it was easy."

I congratulated Tina as we broke for lunch. "Heck, you almost convinced me." I could feel the residual juice as she shook my hand and said thanks. I couldn't make myself eat the tuna sub I'd bought. I liked to see good lawyering. I just didn't like to see it from the receiving end. The jury had been nodding like the choir in a revival tent as she made her points. I felt tempted to abandon my plan and make my opener to remove some of the certainty from their faces. But the die was cast. Good plan. Bad plan. I was going with it.

The story in the paper captured the essence of Tina's opener. Under the front page headline:

Love Or Money

Assistant prosecutor Tina Botham mesmerized a hushed courtroom as she laid out the case against Theodore Armbruster today. Armbruster stands accused of beating his wife Amanda to death with a golf club in the entrance hall of the the family's stately country club home in the wee hours of April 28th. Mrs. Armbruster, age 35 at her death, was prominent and active in many social causes and charitable affairs, including a stint as United Way chairwoman and on the board at the Dressler Foundation.

Botham told the sixteen jurors selected over four days last week that the defendant had strong motives for murder, including anger over seeing his wife dancing innocently in another man's arms the night before. She told the rapt panel, in addition to letting love turn to jealousy, Mr. Armbruster had much to gain from his wife's death. "Only months before he killed her, the defendant jacked the limits on his wife's term life policy from a modest $100,000 to a whopping $2,000,000. Just the amount he needed to save the failing family business from collapse." Botham told the jurors of a signed confession obtained the morning of the crime

> from Armbruster while "his wife's still-warm corpse awaited transport to the morgue." She claims that facing the enormity of his crime, the defendant has recanted the confession and accused seasoned detective Raymond Bliss of erroneously transcribing his words. "Desperate acts by a desperate man" is how she described the conduct.
>
> Surprisingly, veteran defense counsel Kenneth J. Edwards reserved his opening statement until the close of the prosecution's proofs. One courtroom observer told this reporter, "He's probably still trying to figure out a defense." Another, overhearing the first, said: "Edwards is a wily rascal. He's got something up his sleeve." Last week, before Judge Kingsdale imposed a gag order, Edwards told *The Leader* that evidence at trial would prove his client innocent and made vague reference to bringing "dark slimy crawly things" out from under rocks. None of our sources had any idea to what he referred. Although, a criminal defense lawyer who asked to remain nameless commented, "Edwards is a master of showmanship and misdirection. I wouldn't put anything past him."
>
> The afternoon was taken up with testimony from the first officers on the scene and medical first responders. They described a grisly scene of blood-spattered floors and walls surrounding the lifeless but still warm body of the deceased. Detective Philip Weston testified he found the defendant seated on the staircase next to his wife's body, his pajamas covered in blood. The murder weapon, a sand wedge, lay between the defendant and the deceased.

I subscribe to the less is more school of cross examination. Go in and get what you can and get out. Don't allow the witness to repeat the damning testimony from direct. So that first afternoon of testimony, while Tina soaked the courtroom in blood, I tried to put a tourniquet on as best I could.

On cross, the first on-the-scene deputies all testified Ted was cooperative and was most concerned that attention be given to helping his wife.

Deputy McIntyre was as helpful as he could be. "Mr. Armbruster was crying. He begged everybody to do something for her. 'Help her! Help her! Call the doctor!' he kept saying. He kept going over to her, calling her name. I told him that help was coming. When Detective Weston got there and said she was gone, he lost it. He started moaning, 'Oh my God, no. Oh my God, no.' Over and over."

"Did he ever admit in your presence that he had harmed his wife?"

"No, sir."

After Tina took Sara, the paramedic, through a graphic description of Amanda's injuries, I had her describe Ted's mental status.

"We saw him after the interview with Detective Bliss. He could barely stand up coming out of the living room. He had the shakes real bad. He was pale. His pupils were dilated. He looked shocky. He wanted to ride in the ambulance with his wife, but Detective Bliss said he was going to jail. I thought a doctor should see him, but the detective said they'd watch him at the jail. I did offer him a sedative, but he told me he'd taken sleeping pills before bed."

"Would you characterize him as alert and in full possession of his faculties?"

"No. Right on the edge of losing it completely would be more like it."

"Was he indifferent to his wife's condition?"

"Just the opposite. We'd tell him there was nothing we could do, and two minutes later he'd be begging us to help her. He broke down completely when he realized he wasn't going to be able to ride in with her. As we wheeled her out he kept calling out her name."

Her male counterpart supported Ted's shocky state and described his physical exam of Ted before Bliss took him away. "Low blood pressure. Tachycardia—that means racing pulse. He had a bruise on his forehead, and it appeared that his right ring finger was broken, like I told the prosecutor a few minutes ago."

"Let me ask you something she didn't. Did you take a history from Ted as to how he injured himself?"

"Of course. Got it right here in my notes. Fell on last few steps trying to reach his wife."

Then I pulled the bow a notch too far. "And his injuries were consistent with that history?"

He looked thoughtful for a few seconds and answered, "Suppose so. But also consistent with being in a bar fight. You tell me."

I thanked him and let him go. Then I asked the judge to excuse the jury so I could renew my motion to suppress the confession.

"Judge, for a confession to be admissible it has to be given as the result of a knowing and intelligent waiver of one's Fifth Amendment rights. From the testimony before the court, we have a man with all the physiological signs of shock. Per the paramedics, he couldn't grasp the information on his wife's condition they kept repeating to him, in spite of her lying right before him. How then, leaving aside the detective's circumventing my clear instructions not to interview my client, could this man be said to have heard and understood abstract rights?"

Tina rose to answer, but the judge stayed her with an outstretched palm.

"Mr. Edwards, I have previously ruled the confession is admissible. I have before me a signed waiver of Miranda which Detective Bliss swears was carefully read to and understood by the defendant. Having said that, I might still be tempted to give your motion greater consideration were it not for Mr. Browne's appearance at the defendant's side when the waiver was signed and the confession given. Miranda was designed to afford a defendant the right to confer with his attorney before talking to the police. Mr. Armbruster had that in spades.

"It is for the court to decide legal admissibility of a confession and for the jury to decide whether the defendant knew what he was saying and doing at the time it was given. Motion denied."

When the day was over, I gave my secretaries a brief recap in response to their "how did it go" question. "I've had better days." Then I plopped my exhausted form into my desk chair and wondered how I could feel so drained. After all, Tina was carrying the fight. All I was doing was counterpunching. When I had started trying cases at age twenty-four, a day like today would've been a light sparring match. Now, at thirty-eight, I felt as if I'd been hanging on with Sonny Liston for fifteen rounds.

Could time do so much?

I had been halfheartedly prepping for the next day for an hour or so when my private number rang. It was my member-member partner, Judge Ernie. "Not much more than a week until the tourney, partner. How's your game?"

"Hey, Judge, what game? Maybe you heard I've been a little tied up elsewhere."

"Yeah, yeah. Heard things are a little rough down the hall. Reserved your opener. What were you thinking?"

"I've got a plan."

"It better be a dandy. Anyway, I'm just saying to get your priorities straight. I want to win that damn tournament so bad I can taste it. I'm counting on you."

"The way things are going, I'm not sure I'll be much help. Haven't touched a club in weeks. Maybe you should get a new partner."

"No way. You're my man." I told him I'd try to find time to work on the game and rang off.

Since I was getting nowhere fast at the office, I drove out to the club and hit range balls in the fading light of evening just to relax. The trip to the course was anything but relaxing. A light green Ford sat three car lengths behind me on the expressway. I got nervous when it followed my 280 up the exit ramp without signaling. When it imitated my three left turns ending in the country club lot, my pulse was racing. The lot was nearly vacant, and yet the car parked right next to me.

I swung my door open and leaped out in a fighting crouch. Scared the heck out of a grandmother and two pre-teen girls who were coming to retrieve a charm bracelet left by the pool earlier that afternoon. My lame excuse about a hornet in the car satisfied them, but only barely. I stood slowing my breathing as they walked toward the pool, the two girls pausing to look back and point.

"Get a grip, man. Get a grip," I admonished myself.

"Newest style in golf attire?" commented Sven Riklis, the only other figure on the range at that hour. My suit jacket, vest, and tie were draped over my golf bag. My dress shirt was glued to my torso in the muggy heat. I liked Sven. At thirty, he was one of the younger members. He and his brother Daj were strapping Swedes whose wholesale lumber supply business was going great guns. Both were open, funny, and friendly. Both could hit the ball a mile off the tee. Their short games were another matter.

"Hey, Sven. Saw you and Daj made the tournament this year. Bet we end up in the same flight."

"That would be great. Daj and I tried to get in the last two years, but the darn thing was always oversubscribed and so we had to wait for some of the old fogies to die or move to Florida. Just squeaked in this year. I'm pumped. The last few weeks both of us have been playing in the eighties. Better watch out. How's your game?"

"Non-existent. Just snuck out to get reacquainted with my clubs."

"Hey, I was watching. You're making great contact with the irons."

Actually, the time away had caused me to forget a bad habit or two, and I was striking the ball well. It was refreshing to flush the case from my mind. We hung around until the assistant groundskeeper chased us away so he could retrieve the range balls before darkness set in completely. We grabbed a beer in the men's locker and headed into the empty parking lot long after the sun was gone.

Other than my convertible and Sven's F-150 pickup, the only other car in the lot was a rusty, dusty Olds 98 of early '80s vintage. I assumed the greenskeeper hadn't finished his chores yet. At the stone entrance gate to the club, Sven honked as he turned left. I returned the salute and turned right along the unlit country road. My mind was on the case, and so I hadn't noticed the lights behind me until they went on high beam and filled my mirror. At the same time, as I struggled to see through the reflected glare, the sound of Steppenwolf's "Born to Be Wild" at full volume and the roar of a poorly muffled engine reached my ears.

The horn blew and the old faded Olds I'd seen in the parking lot swung out from my tail to pass. I was so startled I overcorrected to the right to let the gas-guzzling dinosaur from a bygone automotive era get around me. My right wheels chattered on the gravel shoulder. By the time I'd gotten back on pavement, the Olds was neck and neck with me. The old biker tune blared loudly. Instead of passing, he kept pace with me. I looked to my left, but on the dark country road I could only make out a shadowy bulk behind the wheel. I yelled, "What the hell are you doing?"

The shadowy skull turned, and I noted the outline of a pork-pie hat and a cigar jutting with a glowing tip beneath the brim. I heard a guttural bellow over the music. "Fuck you, asshole," and then the Olds started to edge right.

I had little room to maneuver. In that part of the county, deep drainage ditches lined the road. I was already half on the road and half on the shoulder. Any further right and the next stop was fifteen feet down. The Olds just kept nudging right.

I could see the streetlight over the intersection with Sycamore Drive a quarter mile ahead. I had to hang on till then. On the other side of the intersection the ditch culvert was covered by lawns. I accelerated and managed to get a half car length ahead. By the time the Olds pulled even and started to squeeze right, I bounced over the crown of Sycamore and onto the lawn of the farmhouse on the corner. My car, with the wheels turned right, slewed sideways, gouging deep ruts in the grass, and almost turned over. Instead it came to a rest pointed north at the end of the deep furrows I'd left in the newly mown lawn.

As I took my first breath in at least a minute and tried to calm the trembling that gripped my body, the porch light came on. The Olds had slowed to a crawl in the center of the road, maybe a hundred yards ahead. When the homeowner turned the porch light on and came out, the Olds accelerated away. I could hear in the quiet of the country night the loud guitar twangs of "Born to Be Wild" fade into the distance.

"What are you, drunk? Look what you did to my yard."

I was startled. In the time I'd followed the fading lights of the Olds, the irate homeowner had come to stand next to the front of the car. He wore what I took to be pajamas, an oversized Detroit Lions jersey with number 20 on the back over a pair of brown shorts. If his face were any redder he'd have been on fire. I was speechless after my near death experience.

"I'm calling the cops."

"Please do," I managed.

While he ran inside, I took a couple of deep breaths and got out of the car. I inventoried both myself and the Mercedes. Amazingly, we both seemed to be in one piece. As I was examining my rutted skid path across the broad expanse of his lawn, I heard the siren and then saw the blue flashers of the patrol car over my shoulder. They stopped on the side of the road. Just my luck—it was Doyle and Meeks who got out of the sheriff's cruiser.

"Doing a little off roading, counselor?" croaked Meeks as they walked over.

"Not by choice, deputy. A homicidal maniac forced me off the road. He was trying to nudge me into the ditch back there, and I just managed to make it to this poor gentleman's lawn."

"Hey, Doyle, that's a new one. The maniac made me do it. No deer ran across the road? No swerve to avoid a jogger, and I suppose you haven't had anything to drink?"

I sighed in frustration. "Yes, I have had exactly one beer."

Doyle smirked. "Usually when we find a drunk on somebody's lawn, he at least admits to two. You want to plea bargain to two beers? You look pretty shaky standing there, counselor, for only one beer."

Now the adrenaline coursing through my system not only made me a little unsteady, but it overwhelmed my patience. "Now listen to me. I'm not drunk. Somebody just tried to kill me, and you guys are auditioning for Comedy Shack. Get your PBT out and let's get this settled."

"Sounds like a plan," said Doyle and he went back to the patrol car to retrieve the roadside Breathalyzer. I blew a .02 on two separate tests. They were obviously disappointed.

"Okay, you're not drunk, but driving all over somebody's yard looks like reckless driving at the least, and malicious destruction of property. Over $100 at the high end. What do you say, Jim? Give him a break and just write him up for careless?"

The homeowner, who identified himself as Kenneth Utermallen, had come from his porch to stand next to the deputies. "Who's going to fix my yard?"

"I'm sorry about your yard, but I didn't do this for fun. Somebody in a big, rusty Olds 98 tried to force me into the ditch to the tune 'Born to Be Wild.' I'm lucky to be in one piece." I turned to the deputies. "I'm making a complaint of felonious assault. The Olds followed me out of the lot at the country club, and he tried to kill me back there. So if you guys are done playing with me, maybe we could look into catching this guy."

Doyle stepped aggressively toward me. "Look here, Edwards, we're not buying your bullshit…"

At that point Utermallen spoke up. "Excuse me, deputies, he might be telling the truth. I did hear that biker song through the window. When I got to the porch there was a big old car sitting in the middle of the road a couple of doors down. When I came out and turned the porch light on, the car drove off."

The deputies were again disappointed. I wasn't drunk and the complainant was corroborating my story. "Stay right there. We'll call this in and get back to you."

"You might mention in your call to be on the lookout for an early '80s Olds 98, light blue and rusty."

They went back to the patrol car without responding, and I apologized to the neighbor, gave him the name of my insurance agent at State

Farm, and promised I'd make arrangements to see that they took care of his claim. I also thanked him for coming to my aid.

"Well, now that you mention it, I did hear the music, and the engine noise sounded louder than that little flivver of yours could make on its own."

The deputies came back and took Mr. Utermallen aside for about five minutes. Then they came back to me. "Well, the complainant backs your story up, although we still have our doubts. Besides, you lawyers always cover for each other, so the judge is going to believe you. So we'll let you go, but watch it next time."

I couldn't believe the attitude. "Watch what? For a guy trying to kill me with his car, or two deputies who can't be bothered to take the complaint when I have an eyewitness to support me?"

So they took a complaint form out and handed me a clipboard on which to write. When I was done, Doyle looked it over. "Did you get a plate number?"

"No, deputy, I didn't. I was too busy trying to save my life, but there can't be too many old gas-guzzlers like that with a cigar-smoking gorilla in a pork-pie hat on the road. Can you check and see if anybody spotted the car?"

They looked at each other sheepishly.

"You did call it in, didn't you?"

"We'll do it right now. You want a wrecker?"

I shook my head. "No. I think I can drive it back onto the road, but I'll make sure to tell the sheriff what a fine job you guys did of trying to catch the man who tried to kill me."

They shrugged and turned back to the parked car. "You do that, counselor." They started toward the patrol car. Doyle looked over his shoulder. "Oh, and have a nice day."

"What's with those guys?" Mr. Utermallen asked.

I shook my head in disgust. "I'm on the other side of a case involving their department, and I think they were so disappointed they couldn't arrest me for something, they forgot their manners."

"Edwards? Oh, you're the guy with the country club murder. How's it going?"

"Gets more interesting by the minute."

I thanked Mr. Utermallen for his help, got into my car and drove carefully back to the road. As I hit the pavement and started down the road, I could hear the clods of dirt come off the tires and thud against the wheel wells. I sat through two entire stoplight sequences until my body's shaking slowed. In the two months since I'd taken the case, I'd had more threats of death and near death experiences than in my preceding thirty-eight years combined. I'd obviously stirred a hornet's nest. Now, if only I could find the tree from which the nest hung. I said a silent prayer of thanks and let out the clutch.

As I drove slowly home I tried to think who was behind the attack. Was it Bliss? It seemed like the deputies had gotten there awfully fast. Was there enough time for the neighbor to call and dispatch to reach them? Or did they know ahead of time to expect a vehicular mishap, and to come as soon as the Olds had passed the intersection of Old Parish Road and M-20? They certainly were in no hurry to put a description of the car over the radio.

Was it Gianfranco? The form behind the wheel looked like the kind of ape I'd seen at his scrap yard. He'd already sent me a warning with the flowers. Was this his way of getting me to start pushing up daisies of my own?

What about somebody from TNPC? Seemed my life had become more precarious once I'd started following that scent. Had I touched a nerve that jeopardized the local elite to the point that a tragic accident seemed like a good solution.?

I had lots of questions, but the only answer I had was that I was making serious enemies at an alarming rate. The price of poker was going up. I was in over my head, but getting up from the table was not an option. I hoped that when I looked at my hand I wouldn't find aces and eights, the dead man's hand Bill Hickock died holding.

When I got home I popped a Labatts and called Karen at the the hotel number she'd given me in Virginia. I needed to talk to a friend, and they were in short supply lately. But her room phone went unanswered. The depressing image of her in the hotel bar dancing with some athletic

G-man filled my head. So I rounded up the best pal I had, Max. Mrs. Grimes had scolded me about picking him up so late. When I explained the reason for my delay, she was much more understanding. "You poor man. Best be careful now, or that case is going to be the death of you."

I hoped her skills as an oracle were nowhere near her talents in dog breeding. Half finished beer in hand, I took Max for a starlit stroll along the beach. I apologized to the young lovers on a blanket he interrupted, and we turned back home. "Quite a day, Max," I said, turning off the light and falling into bed.

The next morning I recognized the three women walking to the courthouse steps as jurors and stayed a respectful distance behind. Ahead of them, his back to us, stood Bliss with one foot on the courthouse steps. Instead of using the sand-filled receptacle next to him, he flipped his butt on the sidewalk. The ladies gave him a wide berth. I could only hope they were nicotine Nazis who hated litterbugs. Just in case, I grabbed the smoking detritus and flipped it into the receptacle without checking to see if the jurors noticed.

He turned to grin at me when I reached the steps. "Heard you had a little accident last night, counselor. Hope yer all right."

My suspicions kicked in before my brain. "How did you—" Then I realized it was his deputies who were on the scene. "I'm fine, thanks. Your boys have any luck finding the guy who tried to kill me?"

He feigned a puzzled look. "I just glanced at the report this morning. Something about you drinking at that fancy club of yours and losing control was all I caught. Sounds like the boys cut you some slack."

My mouth engaged before my judgement again. "Listen, detective, I was wondering—is being a jerk something that comes naturally for you? Or is it like smoking, a bad habit you acquire a taste for, then become addicted?"

The color rose in his face. Instead of answering he formed his right hand into a pistol, bobbing his index finger at me.

The bailiff announced there would be approximately an hour's delay in starting, as Her Honor was on a conference call with the state court administrator's office. Ninety minutes later Tina and I were escorted into chambers. The office was dominated by a large mahogany desk with matching arm chairs for her visitors. As I sat, I noticed on the credenza behind her chair a gilt-framed picture. Alexandra, adorned in a red Christmas gown to highlight her blonde hair, was smiling up at a distinguished gray-maned man in a tuxedo. He had his left arm draped possessively over her shoulder.

A spasm of nostalgia mixed with jealousy filled my brain. Those shoulders were home only to my arms once. I wondered if the glow on the face of Mr. Justice Kevin Haley, chief judge of the Court of Appeals in Lansing, was due to holiday cheer or the pleasure of Alex's company. She'd obviously moved onward and upward since our parting. Even four years later I felt a longing for what might have been.

"Listen, I must ring off. I'll be here when you can conference in the clerk of the Supreme Court." She replaced the phone and smiled pleasantly at us. It had been a long time since that smile was turned in my direction.

"Sorry, counsel. Can you believe it? I'm the circuit court representative on the statewide judge's panel to cut court backlog. And here I am keeping you and a jury waiting while I talk with bureaucrats who just love long conferences. I wanted to apologize and tell you I'll be back to the case as soon as I possibly can." With that we were excused. Courtroom practice was like that. Hurry up and wait. Be late because of some pressing issue and endure the wrath of Khan for wasting the court's time.

So I went back to the lock-up and hung out with Ted. He listened with concern about my highway adventure last night, but seemed more interested in my golf swing and the upcoming tournament.

"Man, I'm going to miss that. It was under my presidency that the week of the member-member became the club's largest gross for food and beverage and pro shop sales. Nothing else is close." I didn't mention the blank spot on the wall of presidents. "I wonder if I'll ever play in it again." I had an image of him standing on the first tee garbed in an orange jailhouse jumpsuit. "Stupid thing to worry about when you're on trial for murder, but man, I loved to play in that thing. Pointed all season for it." He pinched his wedding ring, spinning it loosely about a skinny ring finger. "I'm really glad you decided to play. I bid for your team the last couple of Calcuttas. I wish I had a piece of you and Ernie this year."

I tried to dissuade him, reminding him I'd hardly played all summer. But he expressed the same ungrounded optimism he had for my trial skills. "You're a gamer, Ken. The competitive juices ooze from your pores. Whatever you lack in talent, you make up for with grit."

So I finally agreed to sell him a half of my action on our team. "Wow, that's great. I'll have a rooting interest. Keep my mind off my troubles while the judge is gone. Say, weren't you two an item once?"

"Long time ago, Ted."

It was after lunch before we were back before the jury. Like I had done with all the witnesses on the prosecutor's list, I had tried to interview Detective Weston pretrial. Since I knew him from my prosecution days, he'd agreed to meet me in the squad room the same day I was interviewing the deputies. Weston was maybe two years from full pension. The newly minted detective I knew from twelve years ago, brimming with enthusiasm, was now a tired old veteran just counting the days. Fresh off the road then, he was lithe and trim. Now a small potbelly bulged his buttons to expose the t-shirt beneath. The eyes on either side of a large hooked nose had no luster. When my first question was how Bliss had ended up with the case when Weston was the on-call detective that night, he sighed tiredly and rose from his chair. "Best you ask him" was all he said as he left me listening to the fresh coffee drip into the pot he'd offered to make before we got started. Between Weston and Thad Granger, I had a running start kicking caffeine.

So when Weston took the stand, I hoped I'd finally have an answer to that question. Before my chance came on cross, Tina took the jury for another wallow in the gore. Weston identified some fifty of the hundred photos he'd taken at the Armbrusters'. As is the custom, Tina handed each to me after moving their admission. She was so intent on getting the evidence before the jury that she seemed not to notice or care about the effect they were having on the man sitting next to me.

From the first shot of Amanda, white linen skirt hiked, green blouse stained red, looking like she was trying to rise to her knees on the black and white checkerboard tile, the tears began to run down Ted's face. By the third exhibit, as the witness described the area of injury the picture detailed, Ted had turned away, sitting hunched in his chair, shoulders heaving. He tried to muffle his sobbing, but I could hear hushed keening. "Ooooh-oooh." Ted had not been permitted to attend the funeral. This was his final viewing, his final goodbye.

The jurors had a difficult time with the pictures as well. A couple of women in the back row looked ill by Exhibit 20, and just passed the remainder with hardly a glance. Gordie, the county janitor, had a seat in the front row next to the jury box. As the first few pictures were passed among the jurors, he'd stood to get a peek. After the first few he remained seated. Heck, I'd studied these photos a hundred times, looking for answers, and they still nauseated me. One of the early exhibits had captured the profile of Amanda's face, which haunted me from the scene. She looked like she was just in repose, Sleeping Beauty.

At around exhibit number 30 I stood to break the rhythm. "Objection, Your Honor. Enough already. The exhibits already in evidence give a full depiction of the scene and the victim. This photograph is merely cumulative and designed solely to inflame and prejudice the jury."

Tina stood before the bench, a pile of serially numbered photos on the evidence table before her.

"On the contrary, Judge, this picture clearly depicts the gaping wounds behind the victim's ear."

Even the judge winced as Tina demonstrated the picture to her.

"Overruled. You may continue, Miss Botham."

When I raised the issue again at number 50, the judge halted the carnage. The jurors seemed relieved. But they looked at Ted, who had quieted by then, with open antipathy. Any sympathy they might have had for his grief was gone.

On cross exam I turned immediately to the questions Weston wouldn't answer at our abbreviated interview. I stood in a blue striped seersucker next to the witness stand. That close, I could see that Weston chewed his nails and had a missing button on his left cuff.

"Detective, you were the on-call detective the morning hours of the 28th?"

"I was."

"Tell the jury how the on-call system works."

"The department has two senior detectives who would handle a homicide, myself and Detective Bliss. We are on a rotation schedule, so if there is a homicide on the odd numbered day, the deputies would call Detective Bliss. On the even numbered days they call me. Simple."

"And the 28th is an even numbered day, so the deputies called you?"

He shifted a little in his chair. If he hadn't wanted to discuss this with me privately, he was even less eager here. "They called me and I responded to the scene."

"Was Bliss there on your arrival?"

"He was not."

"Did you call for his assistance?"

He paused, as if considering a lie, but he must have realized I had access to the 911 transcript. "I didn't, no."

"Did you instruct any other officer to do so?" He shook his head.

"That's a no?"

"Yes, it's a no."

"So how did he come to be there?"

His slightly bucked teeth bit into his lower lip. "You'd have to ask him."

"Before Bliss arrived, you were the officer in charge at the scene? It was your case?"

A nod. "I was."

"After Bliss arrived, who was in charge?"

"Detective Bliss. He's my senior in the D.B. by almost nine years."

"How long after you were on scene was it until Detective Bliss came?"

Before he answered, Tina rose. "Objection, Your Honor. Irrelevant. What does this minor police procedural issue have to do with the defendant's guilt or innocence?"

The judge looked at me with the same question I'm sure the jurors had. "Why are we taking the court's time with this, counsel?"

"Judge, the prosecutor waved a so-called confession as proof positive of my client's guilt in her opening statement, a confession handwritten by Detective Bliss when, strangely, his tape recorder malfunctioned. A challenged confession, taken by an officer who had no business on the scene, if normal department policy had been followed. This line of questioning is foundational testimony in support of our attack on the so-called confession and the motives of the man who took it."

I could hear Bliss muttering as I finished. The judge's blonde hair swayed side to side as she weighed the arguments. "I'll allow it." Not bad. In responding to the objection, I got to give an important part of my opening statement. The jury had that aha! look, like they had figured out what I was doing at last. And maybe I had planted a seed of doubt that would flower when Bliss took the stand.

So I moved quickly to finish with Weston, establishing that within five minutes of arriving on the scene, he went from being the officer in charge of the biggest case of his career to a minor role carrying water for Bliss. His resentment seeped through when he answered. Such a thing had never happened to him before in over ten years as a detective. I suspected Bliss wouldn't be the featured speaker when Weston retired in a year or two. To finish, I walked from standing next to the witness stand back to counsel table as if I were finished, then turned, feigning a Columbo moment.

"Oh, by the way. You never heard Mr. Armbruster ever say he had hurt his wife."

"No."

"Did you speak to him at all?"

"Yes. When I first arrived, he was on the floor next to his wife. The deputies were trying to move him away. I took him by the hand and pulled him to his feet. As I seated him on the bottom stair, I asked him to tell me what happened."

"And?" I knew if it was bad it would've been in his report, but I still held my breath.

"He kept repeating, 'I don't know. I just don't know.' "

"Thank you, Detective."

He and Bliss exchanged a look as Weston filed out between counsel tables. Weston wouldn't be Bliss's guest of honor either.

During the afternoon recess a cute little pixie of a redhead approached me in the hall. "Mr. Edwards, my name is Elizabeth Townsend. My friends call me Lizzie."

"Hi, Lizzie. I've seen you in the courtroom. What's your interest?"

"I graduated third in my class from Central High in June. I start prelaw at Michigan in the fall."

"Poor kid." She looked hurt. "Just kidding. I'm a State guy."

The elfin smile returned. "Oh, ha-ha. I just wanted you to know I think you're doing a good job. It's my dream to handle a big case like this someday."

I thanked her and told her, "Be careful what you wish for."

Trying a case is like being on a big ocean in a small boat. One moment you are on the crest of a swell and everything looks great. The next you are in the trough between walls of water, waiting to be swamped. Weston's testimony and a few kind words from Lizzie were the crest before the waves got high again.

Jim Schenkel, a slender, dark-haired, studious man, had been doing fingerprints at the crime lab since before my time. He was a pro and sounded like it, describing the eleven points of identification matching Ted's prints to those found on the murder weapon. The sand wedge introduced through Weston leaned against the evidence table wrapped in a heavy see-through evidence bag. The jury hadn't wanted to touch it when it was introduced, and they were content to let Schenkel stand in front of the jury box as he pointed out the various places on the grip and shaft from which he had lifted prints. Only when he removed the club from the bag to show a latent on the shaft did the jurors notice the dried blood and white gray matter on the heel of the club. Three jurors, including one male, heaved, barely keeping their lunch down, and a half hour recess ensued. I felt a little queasy myself.

Presenting a case is a little like trying to make a bid at bridge. When your partner's hand is exposed, you need to count your losers and give them up gracefully. I suspected Tina played no bridge. She played her evidence cards with a heavy hand and refused to concede her losers. Her handling of Schenkel was a case in point. He'd described the multiple matching fingerprints he'd found on the club's grip. Then at the finish she went in for the kill after he pointed out two latents on the grip with no blood.

"So if the defendant told police he had handled the club when he found it lying on the floor next to his wife, you can say with scientific certainty he gripped it before the first blow was struck?"

"Yes, ma'am."

She sashayed from center court back to counsel table as if we ought to throw ourselves on the mercy of the court right now. "Nothing further."

What a gimme! I rose but just leaned on the counsel table. "And would you be at all shocked to find the fingerprints of the owner of a golf club on the portion of the club designed to be held in his hands?"

"I would not."

Mr. Jackson, one of the alternates in the back row, raised a hand and asked to write a note to the judge. She looked doubtful but nodded. The bailiff picked up the scrap of paper and carried it to the bench, where the judge showed it to counsel at sidebar. "Which hand are the clean prints? L.? R.? Golf glove?"

Without asking our okay, she told the jury, "Sorry, folks. Our high court is undecided on the issue of jurors' asking questions. Until they do decide, I am going to err on the side of caution and not allow it." Since I knew the answer and wasn't crazy about it, I asked Mr. Jackson's questions for him rather than leave them for Tina.

"Left middle and left pinkie," Schenkel answered.

"You play golf?"

"I confess." He smiled.

"Right-handed golfer wears his glove on the left hand?" He nodded. "But lots of people take their glove off to putt and then pick up their sand wedge, which they've left near the green?"

"Except when they forget the wedge and drive off without it. Lost two that way."

Mr. Jackson bowed his head slightly to me, recognizing that the three of us, Schenkel, me and him, were all members of the golfing fraternity. I had satisfied his insider curiosity with insider knowledge.

That night when Max and I arrived in the drive, Billy was waiting on his porch, wanting all the details. I had put the Arby's package in the trunk before picking up Max. But the scent was driving him crazy. So I sat on Billy's seedy veranda couch, beer in hand, with Max sitting between my legs, his soulful brown eyes following every movement from hand to mouth. I had overloaded my second sandwich with sauce and a glob fell on the bridge of Max's nose, where his long pink tongue couldn't reach it. When I leaned forward to dab it away, the sandwich got irresistibly close to Max, and without touching a finger, he snarfed half of it in one gulp. Billy laughed so hard he spilled his beer all over his coveralls, which made me laugh.

Man, I needed a laugh. I could feel the tension leave my body. So I accepted a second beer and watched what passed for waves on another August night without a breeze. Billy listened to my case update and seemed more interested in Lizzie than anything that had happened in court.

"You old lecher. She can't be older than eighteen."

"Uh-huh. Eighteen's legal," he leered.

"You're beyond hope," I said, taking Max across the yard to my cottage. I was hoping for a message on my machine from Karen. The light on the phone blinked to indicate two messages. The first was from my friends and family regular calling group.

"You're dead." Click. Couldn't tell for sure, but it might have been Bliss disguising his voice.

The next was Karen. "Hi, you. Seems we're ships passing in the night. Don't try to call. Going out with the guys. Probably be late." Despair. Then a note of cheer. "Remember, I'll be home Friday. If it's not too late I'll drive out." Light at the end of the tunnel. Two more days in court and then the weekend and Karen.

My head hit the pillow, but sleep eluded me. What if the guy with the death threat wasn't just trying to unnerve me? What if the caller was an oracle of fast-approaching doom?

I finally administered a bromide. "If you're dead, you'll have nothing more to worry about." Amazingly, that thought relaxed me enough to sleep.

38

The next two days it was pretty dark in the tunnel. The Simpsons, James and Jillian, were the worst kind of witnesses. They wanted to help Ted, and it was obvious. That just made their testimony about Ted's drunken and irrational behavior at the bar that much more damning. Jillian was demurely dressed in a below-the-knee blue summer dress. She had toned down her penchant for jewelry to a single strand of pearls. With her blonde pageboy freshly coiffed, she brought to mind Doris Day. She touched me on the shoulder and smiled at Ted before standing in the witness box to be sworn. She described their dinner at the club and mentioned that both Ted and her husband had followed a day of beers on the course with a couple of highballs before and during dinner.

"I had this really nice Dover sole in a light cream sauce. Oh, you don't care about that, do you? Anyway, the men had an unfinished card game, so they went down to the locker after supper. Amanda and I waited in the upstairs bar. We even saw Mr. Edwards and his brother. Didn't we, Ken?" I nodded. What are you going to do? She was as light and cheerful as if she were making small talk at a children's dance recital.

"Then those darn fellows never came to fetch us. So Amanda and I took her car. It's the cutest powder blue BMW." The Chevy millwright on the jury raised an eyebrow at that.

"We told Eddie, the bartender at the club, to tell the men we'd be at Heather Hollows. And Amanda knew this Italian chap who was sitting at the bar, Jean Carlo—no, Gianfranco. Anyway, very handsome. She'd met him at some charity thing, and she invited him to sit in our booth. Very charming man, I must say."

Finally Tina reined her in and focused her on Ted's arrival.

"When Jim and Ted got there, Ted was very impolite. Not like his usual self at all. He's always such a gentleman. Not that night, though. I think he lost quite badly at cards, kept going double or nothing till the club closed." My pained expression at her hearsay must have been apparent. "Well, that's what Jim says. Anyway, Jim shook hands with Gianfranco and sat down in the booth. But Ted wouldn't shake and he sort of pushed Gianfranco when he tried to calm Ted down. It was very unpleasant."

"Then what happened?" Tina asked as if she had some control over this runaway train.

"Well, Ted started yelling and swearing, and the bartender came over and I think Ted might have pushed him. He left to call the police and Jim tried to get Ted to let him drive him home, and Ted was mad and then that's all I know."

"Did Ted leave at some point?" Tina asked.

"Oh yes, of course."

"And what did he say on leaving.?"

Jillian looked pained at the memory and answered so quietly Tina had her repeat her answer.

"Oh, I don't know, something like 'How can you do this to me? I've had all I can take.' I'm not sure exactly."

She went on to say that she and Jim left shortly thereafter and that Gianfranco offered to drive Amanda home after she'd had a chance to calm down.

"Very thoughtful of him, wasn't it?" she finished.

I trod very softly on cross and just had her testify that Ted was a loving husband and enjoyed a reputation for good character, but she even screwed that up. "He sure did, until this happened."

Jim, a commercial plumbing contractor, wore a blue short-sleeved shirt over tan slacks, and was positively laconic compared to his breathless wife. His testimony matched hers in every detail, and I stuck to a few short character questions on which he did the best he could.

"Ted was a devoted husband. He would never allow a bad word about Amanda. I don't care what anybody says, I'll never believe he hurt her."

The next nail in the coffin was Ted's insurance man. Phil Anschutz looked like he could think of places he'd rather be. A career as a top producing life insurance agent hadn't prepared him to be a witness in a murder case. He was attired in a very professional gray pinstripe suit with a conservative dress-for-success maroon tie over a white oxford cloth shirt. He had the rheostat on his one-hundred-watt smile turned down to forty watts. As he walked past our table to take the stand, he started to extend his right hand to Ted. Whether it was an act of support or an insurance agent's hardwired reflex, I don't know. But in mid reach he apparently thought better of it and turned his right hand over in a little wave as he went by.

In his left hand he carried a manila folder brimming with dynamite. The explosive was Ted's insurance file. As she pulled each stick and lit it, Tina was obviously enjoying herself.

"And so, Mr. Anschutz, the defendant has been a client for over twenty years?"

"He has."

"And until her death, was Mrs. Armbruster also insured with you?"

"She was since she and Ted got married. I was at the wedding."

"Until this year, how much life insurance did you carry on Amanda Armbruster?"

"We had her insured with a whole life policy in the amount of $100,000."

"Who was the beneficiary?"

"Mr. Armbruster."

"Was her coverage increased within the last twelve months?"

"It was. Actually, it was converted to a different type of insurance policy called a term policy."

"By whom?"

"By Ted. I mean, Mr. Armbruster, I mean, Armbruster Manufacturing actually paid for it."

"And who was the beneficiary?"

"Armbruster Manufacturing. It's called a Key Man Policy."

"What sort of policy is that?"

"Uh, yes. Companies usually purchase them in case a key employee dies. Key employees are assets to their companies, so the policy replaces that lost asset."

"How much was the death benefit to Armbruster Manufacturing?"

"In the event of a qualifying death, two million dollars." The jurors all busily scribbled on their yellow note pads. The spectators, now less than thirty, and all on the main floor gallery, began to chatter and whisper. The judge reached for her gavel and they subsided.

"Did you say two million?"

"Yes, it's the largest death benefit under our Key Man policy I'm allowed to sell."

"A qualifying death?"

"That means death by accident or natural causes. Suicide is excluded."

Tina was pacing in front of the witness, her high heels raising her to five foot two and clicking on the marble courtroom floor. Her tan two-piece suit stayed remarkably wrinkle free as she paced between the jury box, which was just above waist high on her, and the witness stand, where she'd have to stand on tiptoe to be at eye level with Mr. Anschutz. She was enjoying the tennis volley of question and answer. She would remove her glasses to lob a question. Then she'd replace them as she scurried over to the note pad on the corner of the prosecution table to make a note whenever she wanted to highlight Phil's answer. Her diminutive form meant that she didn't need to bend to write. I reminded myself not to stand on objection when she was too near so as not to allow my lithe six-foot frame to appear intimidating to the jury.

Now she paused to walk to the far end of the jury box so their heads would swivel following each question and answer.

"What about murder? Is that an accident within the meaning of the policy?"

"Oddly enough, it can be. However, if the murder was committed by the corporate policy owner, or an officer of the company, coverage is excluded. But if the murderer is not related to the company, well then, the company receives the policy amount."

"So, if Mr. Armbruster is found not guilty, the company in which he is the sole shareholder will receive two million dollars as a direct result of the murder of Mrs. Armbruster?"

Somebody in the back made an audible stage whisper. "Never happen."

The judge pointed to the heavyset, bearded man in a "The Lord Is My Shepherd" T-shirt who had tried to trip me on day one. A deputy escorted him through the rear double doors. Phil waited until he was gone and answered.

"I can't speak for the company. When I notified Employers' Benefit Life, they put a hold on the claim pending the outcome of this trial."

"I see. Just a few more questions, Mr. Anschutz. Was the deceased actually an employee of the company?"

"Oh yes, she had to be to qualify for the policy. My file shows she held the title of executive vice president and was a member of the board of directors."

"What did she actually do that made her such a key employee? How many hours a week did she work at Armbruster Manufacturing?"

"I wouldn't know. You'd have to ask Ted. Oh, I'm sorry, I shouldn't say that." He looked sheepishly at the defense table, giving us all one hundred watts of the insurance salesman's smile, then plowed the rut deeper. "I don't know how this works, right to silence, Fifth Amendment and stuff. Can you ask him? If he testifies you could. Are you going to testify, Ted?"

He asked as if the question was, soup or salad? In fact, we hadn't finally decided yet. An expectant silence fell over the proceedings. The jurors turned their eyes to Ted. The standard wisdom is to keep your client off the stand in a circumstantial case and attack the circumstances. Testifying defendants had a way of clearing up reasonable doubt in favor of the prosecution.

Ted resolved any lingering doubt by speaking for the record for the first time since he had uttered the words "Not Guilty" at arraignment.

"Yes, Phil, I mean to testify."

Another decision I wouldn't have to wrestle with. Tina made a note and the jurors all nodded as if to say, "Lucky thing. And it better be good."

Then Tina went for the kill.

"How long had Mr. Armbruster been insured through you?"

"Oh, twenty or twenty-five years at least. He was one of my first policies after I joined the club. I don't play golf, but I joined as a social member, meet some people, you know, build the business. Ted was my third customer after I joined."

"And how long had Amanda had the whole life policy you described in the amount of $100,000?"

"Since they were married, eight years, nine."

"And so when, then, did the amount on the policy increase to two million?"

Anschutz opened the folder on his lap, his shiny Rolex glinting, and pulled out a document. "Got it right here. February 22, 2000."

Tina strutted, heels clicking her way back to her chair, running her hand through the short wet-look hair, and made ready to pound the final nails in Ted's legal coffin. Her voice gained timbre and resonance with each word of the question. "So the policy was $100,000 for eight years of their married life. Then suddenly, barely two months before Mrs. Armbruster is bludgeoned to death, the amount payable on her death to Armbruster Manufacturing jumps twenty times to two million. Is that right, Mr. Anschutz?"

"Well, yes, but…"

"And who asked you to increase the limits?"

Phil by reputation was one heck of an insurance salesman. But he wasn't all that quick on the draw. It was only now that it appeared to dawn on him that he was the chef cooking Ted's goose. The smile disappeared and his eyes shifted to me as if I could save him. When no help was forthcoming he said quietly, "Ted."

"Your witness."

During the recess I saw Lizzie in the hall, looking pretty downcast. I couldn't let my one-person cheering section go without succor.

"Hey, Lizzie, why so low?"

"Doesn't look good for Mr Armbruster."

"Oh ye of little faith," I tossed off jauntily and headed for the men's. Truth be told, I wasn't feeling all that jaunty. But an old warrior had told me, "Never let them see you sweat." So I went with jaunty.

The ferret-faced guy in jeans and a madras shirt I passed as I entered the john didn't do much for jauntiness either. "The noose is tightening, hot shot. Let's see you wiggle out of this," he sneered as I held the door for him.

"Watch me," I answered as he walked off. The guy washing his hands didn't really look very jaunty in the mirror as he prepared to return to battle.

But I went back into the courtroom and did what I could to create a little wiggle room in the noose. I took Phil through his long history with Ted, then got down to brass tacks.

"Mr Anschutz, I don't really understand much about life insurance in spite of the times you've cornered me over the years." A couple of jurors nodded, imagining how relentless Phil could be with a bona fide prospect in his sights. "Tell the jury the difference between whole life and term insurance."

This was his métier, and he launched into an insurance for dummies explanation. I let him go on a bit, then brought him up short. "Actually, one big difference is price, right?"

"Definitely. Term is far less expensive than whole life." Then it was like a light went on in his head and he remembered what we had discussed when I interviewed him. "In fact, that's why I suggested the policy change to Ted. See, Ted wanted the key man insurance on himself. He was in his late fifties. The company depended on him. He had the big contract coming up and I guess there was quite a bit of debt, what with the old business slowing down and the new contract yet to kick in. So he wanted to make sure if something happened to him, the company could pay its debts, the workers keep their jobs and they could get that valve contract up and running. That's the kind of guy he is."

"Uh-huh. So how did his wife get a policy?"

"Oh yeah. Well, when I quoted him the premium on his, it was pretty high with his age and all, but for Amanda, at thirty-five and being a female non-smoker, it was a fraction of the cost." He dug in his file and pulled out a piece of paper.

"Here it is. On Ted, the two million renewable term was almost four thousand dollars a year, but for Amanda it was less than fifteen hundred. So I pointed it out to him. She was paying almost that amount for the $100,000 whole life. If she converted to key man term with the two million death benefit, her premium would stay about the same for all that extra coverage. I told him she'd have to change from him as beneficiary to Armbruster Manufacturing as the beneficiary. He said fine. That's my job, you know, let the client know what's available. When I showed him that, he said he'd talk to Amanda and let me know."

"And did he let you know?"

"Yep, next day he called and said they had talked and go ahead—both policies."

"Did Amanda know about this?"

"Of course. She filled out and signed the application, and the insurance company nurse came out to the house and did the physical." He dug around in the folder and pulled it out. "Yep, copy of the physical exam report right here."

"So if I'm hearing you right, the idea for Amanda to have a two million Key Man policy was Phil Anschutz's, not Ted Armbruster's. Is that correct?"

He nodded. He liked the way this was going much better.

"I think that's fair to say."

"Oh, by the way, did Ted come in February out of the blue?"

"Nope. That's his renewal date. I like to have my clients in for an annual review. Kinda like your annual checkup with the doctor."

"So Ted didn't come in asking you, as Miss Botham would have it, to jack his wife's policy. Rather, during his annual checkup with Dr. Phil, the insurance doctor"—he brightened at the sound of that—"you suggested how the same premium could buy more coverage for Amanda?"

"Yes, I did."

"And in the event of Amanda's death the policy would not pay money to benefit Ted, but to the benefit of his business and employees. Have I got that right?"

"That's exactly right." Phil was beaming now. The chef's hat was gone. He wasn't going to be cooking his longtime customer's goose. And the Anschutz agency wasn't going to be linked to a murder for profit story. He was on a roll now and kept talking without my prompting.

"And one more thing. Miss Botham was asking about Amanda's working at the company. Like I said, I don't know the details of how many hours a week Amanda was at the plant, but Ted was telling me about how valuable she was on that big valve contract with some big wheeler-dealer cowboy from Texas. Well, Ted said Amanda had him eating out of her hand, calling her Miss Amanda this and Miss Amanda that. Ted said if it weren't for Amanda, he doubted they ever would have gotten that deal. In fact, that Texan sent his private jet to bring Amanda to El Paso so he could show her around. I don't think Ted got a ride on the Lear Jet. He sent Amanda as the goodwill ambassador, and she must've been a good one cuz when she came back, wasn't but a week later the deal got signed."

I looked at Ted. He was beaming at the memory. At the same time he was dabbing at the comers of his eyes. I had an idea of the salesmanship skills that Amanda must've used. Satisfied with the damage control, I turned Phil's attention to reputation testimony.

"Are you familiar with Ted's reputation for honesty, Mr. Anschutz?"

"Ted? Honest as the day is long. Everybody trusted Ted. If he told you he'd do something, by golly, he did it."

"How about his reputation for being a law abiding citizen?"

That seemed to puzzle Phil for a minute. Then he brightened. "Oh, very good. Can you believe I'm in insurance and sometimes I forget to buckle my seat belt? Ted made sure I did. And oh yeah, he never entered an intersection on yellow. We were late for a YMCA board meeting and he coulda made it through on yellow. No sir, not Ted. Slowed right down and waited it out. Very law abiding."

"How well did you know the relationship between Ted and Amanda?"

"He adored that woman. After Jane, his first wife, died in that accident, well, he was pretty low, I mean quiet like, but when Amanda came along it was like a new lease on life. Put a little pep in the step, you know what I mean? I was at the wedding. Handsome couple. Well, he was older, of course. People had their doubts. Not me. I could just see they were made for each other."

"Now, they were married almost nine years. Did that relationship ever change?"

He sat forward, warming to the topic. "If it did, you couldn't tell by me. They held hands. He always offered his arm to her, opened doors for her, always a gentleman. You know what? He listened to her. Some fellas, when their wife starts talking, they can't wait to interrupt as they are not really paying attention. Not Ted. Amanda was smart and witty. He'd just look at her when she was talking with a little smile on the comers of his lips, kind of like a father at his daughter's piano recital. You know, proud. I never heard a cross word between them. It was always honey, dear, sweetheart, that kind of thing."

I could see the ladies on the panel reassessing Ted. They liked the part about not discounting or interrupting, but I didn't want to lay it on too thick. So I thanked Phil and sat down. Whatever help it was with the jury, Phil's testimonial was the first kind words Ted had heard in a long time. I lent him my hanky to dry his eyes.

When I turned to watch the prosecution's next witness enter the courtroom, Lizzie flashed me a smile and a subtle thumbs up. Mr. Ferret scurried toward the door. Harold Chapman entered without a look back.

39

The shrill whine of the office cleaning lady's vacuum assaulted my already frayed nerves. The ring of the phone, a backfiring car, a door slamming, all made me jump. The occasional threats sprinkled atop my steady diet of trial-related nerves were taking a toll. Now, as the cleaning lady moved the vacuum back and forth from carpet to oak floor, it set my teeth on edge. "Am I getting too old for this game or what?" I wondered.

I had closed the door to my office thirty minutes ago to try and regroup. It had not been the best of days in court. Most of the damage control I'd done with Phil Anschutz had been undone by the next witness.

Ted's banker had been a compelling witness against Ted precisely because he didn't want to be. Harry Chapman had been a young loan officer for Lumberman's Bank when he started working with Ted's father at Armbruster Manufacturing. The company was his biggest account back then. Harry had steadily risen at the bank till he became president and chief executive officer some five years ago. The bank had grown and prospered. The Armbruster account had not. Yet Harry had kept the account, for sentimental reasons and because Ted was his friend. He had known the Armbrusters, father and son, from the beginning.

Harry was a local legend. Local boy makes good. He'd been raised by his widowed mom in a small bungalow in the city's first ward. He'd delivered the *Lake Pointe Leader* on his bike to the largest paper route in the city. He'd been honorable mention all state as a point guard on Central High's best basketball team in the last forty years. He'd graduated near the top of his class at University of Michigan's Business School. Yet he came home to Lake Pointe to work so he could take care of his mother He'd risen rapidly at the bank, and the bank had risen rapidly once he took the helm. His accomplishments netted him two paragraphs in a *Forbes* magazine article on regional banks. In the story Harry was credited with pumping the money, effort and advice necessary to transform Lake Pointe from a town dependent on the auto industry to a boating, sport fishing and tourism mecca.

At fifty-five, he looked sharp. His full head of lustrous black hair framed an angular face with a straight nose and prominent brow. His blue pinstripe suit fit smoothly over an athletic six-foot frame. Harry Chapman was a local celebrity, and the jurors sat up and took notice as he walked confidently through the swing door at the rail. They saw him make a point to touch Ted on the shoulder as he passed. That was kind of him.

Under Miss Botham's exam he chronicled his long history with Armbrusters—father, son and company. He admitted that he considered himself a long-standing family friend. Then with straightforward banker's delivery, he described the decline and fall of Armbruster Manufacturing.

The company had grown from twenty employees under Ted's father to a peak of 225 ten years ago with Ted at the helm. The company was a machine tool and die shop that had become almost completely dependent on one customer, General Motors. When the auto giant had instituted single sourcing and tightened centralized purchasing controls, Armbruster had gone from growth to decay. First, profit margins shrank, and then volumes declined. Ted had been resistant to the bank's urging to cut payroll.

"These people count on me to feed their families," Ted had told him.

Mr. Chapman recounted ruefully Ted's resistance to a changing marketplace. International competition was changing how his main customer did business. Local purchasing agents at the Chevy plant no longer had the authority to keep giving Armbruster the work, no matter how good the quality, nor how much they liked Ted. It was all a numbers game now being played in Detroit or New York. The tide was going out for small local providers. He summed it up succinctly. "Oh, GM would still throw him a bone now and then, but each bone had less and less meat on it." He shook his head sympathetically, as if describing the last illness of a beloved relative.

Ted had been slow to adapt: "He thought it was just part of the cyclical ebb and flow of the car business instead of a major sea change." Harry recounted how, when four years earlier the black ink at the company was replaced by a sea of red, Ted finally got the message. He looked compassionately across the courtroom to meet Ted's gaze. "He was a man possessed. He wasn't going to let the family business wither and die. He finally agreed to some layoffs, although less than I recommended, and he went on a crusade to find a new line of work outside the auto industry."

He stroked his chin in recollection and brightened at a pleasant memory. "Doggone it, if he didn't find something a year and a half ago. Two large conglomerates had merged and they were selling off a small non-core fluid control valve business for a song. Armbruster could have the business for ten million cash and assumptions of the company's eight-million-dollar debt. Ted was so excited when he came to see me about it he could hardly sit down. The business was kind of a neglected stepchild, but it was still marginally profitable."

He ran his hand through the thick hair beneath his part and continued. "It would not only let him hire back the laid-off employees, it would allow him to expand. So we looked at it and I even went to Odessa, Texas, a couple of times to kick the tires. I told him if he could get it for eight million and put up two million himself, we'd lend him the other six million. The business was marginal and maybe I wouldn't have done it for someone else, but I knew if anybody could make it go, Ted could. Lord knows, Lake Pointe could use the jobs. So we said yes."

I admired Harold's style, comfortable yet commanding. I also admired his Brooks Brothers suit, also comfortable yet commanding. My new Gentlemen's Warehouse special suddenly didn't seem so special.

Miss Botham listened to him and asked, "Did the deal go through?"

Chapman shook his head sadly. "I guess you could say it did and it didn't."

"Please explain."

He covered his mouth with his fist as he summoned the memory.

"The seller didn't like the price we were willing to bank. So it took a long time negotiating. I even called the President of Artech Industries and finally convinced him that two million dollars was a blip on the radar screen to him and would mean a lot to Lake Pointe. At first he told me no deal. Ted was devastated. Ted's auto related business was disappearing faster than my kids when it's time to do the dishes." The jury laughed.

"But then Mr. Pickering at Artech called me back. It seems Ted's wife had made quite an impression on him. He said it was coming up to year-end and the accountant wanted the business off the books, and he'd take the eight million. Ted was happier than he'd been in years. He'd have to throw in virtually all of his personal finances to make it go, but he was willing."

"And then what happened?"

"Well, we ran into some snags. The accountant had some serious questions about some receivables and some intangibles on the valve company's books. Some inventory that was supposed to be in a warehouse was an obsolete low-volume valve instead of the current model. There was some faulty accounting in the actuarial assumptions on the pension plan. These kinds of problems happen, but these were more than usual. We had to renegotiate the price based on these things coming to light. The lawyers were slow. Mr. M. Stanton Browne blamed the lawyer in Texas; the lawyer in Texas blamed Mr. Browne. Anyway, things dragged on, and time was something Ted did not have. The black ink at Armbruster had turned to red. Ted was injecting his personal down payment cash for the valve deal into Armbruster Manufacturing just to make payroll and expenses, and the deal was looking less and less credit-worthy with each passing month."

"So what did you do?"

"I hated to do it, but back in February of this year I had Ted into the office and told him he had used up his entire line of credit on Armbruster, that he was in technical default on the loan agreements, and unless he could come up with another couple million of capital to refinance Armbruster, we'd not only have to back away from the valve company acquisition, we'd have to foreclose on Armbruster Manufacturing."

"What was his reaction?"

"Well, of course, he was very upset. His whole world was threatened."

"Did you check your calendar for the date of that meeting at the bank?"

Chapman reached inside his suit jacket pocket and pulled out an index card. "February 12th." Again the jurors scribbled on their little yellow pads, many exchanging knowing looks. Obviously, the close proximity to the policy increase was not lost on them.

"Would you say he was desperate?"

The banker put his chin in his hand for a moment and glanced over to the defense table. "Yes, I guess I would. He was of course concerned about his own finances, but the idea of losing the business his father had founded and letting the employees go who'd worked for the company for years—this had him pretty desperate. He wasn't dejected. He said he had some ideas of how to raise money and would I give him some time. I gave him to June first. I wouldn't have done it for anybody else, but sometimes even as a banker you've got to put your calculator aside and give a man a chance." He finished, holding his palms open.

"Did he tell you where the money would come from?"

"Yes. He planned to go to friends and local businessmen and sell them shares, a percentage of his ownership in Armbruster. I even gave him a list of names he could try."

"Was he successful in raising the money?"

"No, he wasn't. I know he was trying, because I had calls from potential investors doing due diligence. I was truthful with them and told them if they could make it over the hump, the first year of transition, it looked like it could be a good business. He had a couple of fellows on the fence, and then Amanda died, and with her death the deal died."

Tina had watched from behind her desk as Chapman described

Armbruster Manufacturing's slide toward the abyss. Now she strode purposefully to stand in front of the jury and paused for effect. The little sparkplug, notebook in hand, looked for all the world like a junior high child addressing her father as she looked up to the witness.

"Let me ask you a hypothetical question, Mr. Chapman. If as of June first Mr. Armbruster had a firm commitment for two million dollars, would the bank have backed off on foreclosure and gone ahead with the valve deal?"

Chapman cocked his head curiously, bending his banker's brain around the question. "I am unaware of any investor that was prepared to inject that sum of money, but to answer your question, Miss Botham, of course. We at the bank stand by our commitments."

"So two million would've saved the day."

"Certainly. All he needed was to show me investor commitment of two million, and we would've done the deal."

"Were you aware that in February of this year, about the time you were telling the defendant that foreclosure was looming, he took out a two-million dollar life insurance policy on his wife, Amanda?"

It was obvious that Mr. Chapman knew where this was going and didn't like it. He looked down sadly from the stand at Tina. "I was not aware of it at the time, no."

"But you know it now?"

"I read the papers."

"And you have described the defendant during the spring of this year as a desperate man, a man whose dream to save the family business was evaporating with each passing day and who, with each passing day, edged closer to corporate and financial ruin, have you not?" She was rocking from one foot to the other with the rhythm of an examination where the lyrics matched the tune in her head. I could watch the calf muscles on either side tighten and relax under flesh-colored stockings.

The witness gave Miss Botham a look he probably reserved for bank employees late for work.

"Miss Botham, I have told you Mr. Armbruster cared deeply about the family business and its employees. He was experiencing difficult times and was very concerned. Does that satisfy you?"

She glanced down at her legal pad and asked with a touch of impertinence, "Didn't you use the word 'desperation' just a few minutes ago to describe him?"

Harry looked resigned. "Perhaps I did."

"Thank you, Mr. Chapman. No further questions."

I did the best I could to minimize the damage. I walked up to the witness stand to emphasize the solidarity between one of Lake Pointe's noblest citizens and my client. Standing at Chapman's side, I could feel his calm self-confidence and hoped I could catch some by osmosis. The banker gave a great character reference for Ted.

"One of the finest people I know."

"An honest man."

"Loving husband."

"Hardworking and more concerned about his employees' welfare than his own."

Then I drew the bow back too far.

"Madam Prosecutor has tried to paint a picture of a man so desperate to save his business that he killed his wife for the insurance money. Do you believe that of Ted Armbruster, the man you've known for so many years?"

Chapman gave me a sideways glance and wrestled with the question just long enough for me to believe I was going to regret asking it. And regret it I did.

"I wouldn't like to think so, Mr. Edwards. Ted was under a lot of stress, and he was consumed by saving his family business to the point he had put all of his personal wealth at risk, against my advice. Things were going badly, and he was under a lot of pressure." He paused, not liking where this was going any more than I was. He shook his head slowly. "I just don't know."

Miss Botham saw no need for further questions, and Chapman walked out looking sad. But not as sad as I felt walking back to the office, kicking myself for that last dumb question.

40

Mrs. Potter, the cleaning lady, turned off her vacuum, stuck her head in to say good night and was gone. The office was empty and quiet but for the ornamental clock on the corner of my desk. I was alone with my thoughts and fears.

Why had I pushed my luck with Chapman? I could tell it had hurt him to answer as he did, but so could the jury, which made the testimony all the more damaging. I was tired, depressed, feeling like I was trapped in a maze. I had been staring at a case to use as authority for proposed jury instructions for ten minutes and couldn't tell you which side of the circumstantial evidence instructions it stood for. Not because the case was foggy, but because I was.

I looked at the gold octagonal clock that sat on my desk. It wasn't expensive, but it was the best my teenage shoplifting client could get her hands on after the jury found her not guilty. It's not nice to ask if she paid for it. So I didn't.

The air conditioning compressor kicked on and I jumped. The trial, the trial strategy choices, and the people who felt threatened by what choice I might make who were threatening me were wearing me down. I'd planned to work until ten p.m. But now at 8:15 p.m. I knew I could do nothing more productive. So I shut the casebook, got up from by black leather swivel rocker, and headed for the light switch. No sooner had I turned the lights out than the after hours number rang. I almost walked away, but thinking it might be Karen, I walked back to the desk and picked it up.

"Man, you are hard to catch up to. Don't you return your calls?" It was Freddie Hildebrandt, the man who had over post golf cocktails first mentioned Amanda's role investigating missing Dressler Foundation funds. Then he'd clammed up and disappeared from my social radar screen.

"No harder than you are, Freddie. I've been trying to reach you for over a month. For a guy who usually can't wait to get into my pocket on the golf course, you've been pretty scarce."

The pause told me what I already knew. He'd been avoiding me. "No, no, man. Really busy, out of town, up to my armpits in crocodiles. Listen, I was out to the club with my regular member-member partner, Dr. Ramirez. We saw Judge Ernie on the range. I was surprised to hear you'd be playing this year, what with the trial and all. Anyway, you know how me and Doc and you and the judge always have a warm-up match, all betting windows open on the stag day before the tournament?"

How could I forget? For the last five years those two sandbaggers had taken Ernie and me to the cleaners on the day before the tournament began. "Yeah, but I'm afraid the bank's closed this year, Fred. I'll be in trial next Wednesday."

"I know. I know. That's why I'm calling. The three of us set the match for this Saturday. Can you make it?"

I had other things to do on the case planned for Saturday. But I really wanted to talk to Freddie.

"Okay, but not till afternoon. I need to work in the morning."

"That's what Ernie expected. So we're set for a four o'clock tee. See you then."

He rang off and I mulled how I could get enough drinks into Freddie to pry the door to Dressler open a little wider.

Friday court was called on account of weather. The humid, still air that had clung to Lake Pointe relentlessly for over a week was about to break with a vengeance. As I dropped off Max, dark thunderclouds gathered in the sky far to the northeast. But not even a current of breeze disturbed the prisms made by the sun in the moist air. By ten in the morning, as Bliss took the stand, the air conditioning in the courtroom was straining to keep the place from becoming a sauna. The judge granted counsel permission to remove jackets, and to the great delight of the jurors, issued them oriental fans. Apparently the bailiff had treated the missus to dinner at the Lotus Dragon the night before. The cheap, corrugated handheld fans were compliments of the house. Madame Chen was only too happy to do her civic duty and donate twenty for the jurors. Even Ted laughed as the female jurors did their Madame Butterfly act.

No sooner had Bliss squeezed his beer belly between the witness chair and the documents desk than the wind and rain crashed against the fifth floor windows, blowing a couple open. The gusty rain soaked a slow-to-move spectator who preferred the solitude of the fifth floor gallery. The gale whistled through and around the fifth floor, creating a mini-cyclone where we stood on the fourth, scattering papers and rattling the pictures of retired jurists on the wall.

Within seconds of the initial shock, a bolt of lightning lit the arena and was almost immediately followed by crashing thunder. And the place went dark. The straining air conditioner spooled down to silence. The only sound was the wind-driven rain cascading against the upper floor windows. We were in recess long enough to determine that a one-hundred-year-old elm had taken out downtown's power feed. The power company was making no promises. So the judge sent us all off for a long weekend. I took wry satisfaction in hearing Bliss ask Tina: "What am I supposed to wear Tuesday? I bought this expensive suit just to testify."

I hung around the courthouse for an hour after the deputies took Ted back to the jail, waiting for the downpour to abate. When I went outside the temperature had dropped almost twenty degrees. The rain was gone, but the flag was rattling its halyards as a steady nor'easter poured a taste of Canadian air into Michigan. The storm was a blessing in that I had extra time to prepare to cross examine Bliss. It was a curse in that around four that afternoon, Karen called to say her connection from Cleveland was grounded. She wouldn't be back till tomorrow. Saturday was a work day, and all she promised was that she'd try to come by after her shift. "Oh, I miss Max so much. Give him a hug."

"Hey, lady. What about me?"

"Oh, you." Her voice register dropped to a throaty whisper. "I'll give you your hug myself."

I tried John Nash to see if he had anything on the Cayman hedge fund. But I was disappointed to hear his secretary, Julie, report that John and his wife had left for a weekend of pleasure in San Francisco prior to company meetings there the first part of the week. Julie had no clue when I asked her if John had left any information for me on TNPC.

"Never mentioned it to me." When I asked if she could check his desk for anything from the head office hedge fund department with the name TNPC on it, she cried out in mock horror.

"You want me to wade through that jungle at 4:45 on a Friday? I might get trapped by an avalanche of prospectuses and miss the whole weekend."

"Please?"

"Okay, for you, Mr. Edwards. But if I'm not back in an hour, call security and have them bring the jaws of life."

She was back in less than five minutes.

"Sorry. Moved everything around. Didn't see anything like you described."

I wished her a nice weekend and closed up shop. Even though I had put the top up, the seats and the floor in the Benz were soaked. There are many wonderful things about owning a thirty-two-year-old convertible. Weathertight roofing isn't among them. So driving home in the crisp, cloud-free air, I got the soaking I thought I'd missed waiting out the storm that morning.

It was chilly enough at four on Saturday that I pulled my wind jacket from my bag as soon as it was produced from the bag room. As I pulled my head through the jacket, around the corner came Stanton and Annabelle Browne. They both carried tennis rackets and, in spite of the cool weather, were dressed in tennis whites. Stanton featured a salmon-colored light sweater draped over his back with the arms tied beneath his neck. Annabelle, statuesque at five foot ten, swished her racket like a cat would its tail. She replaced the initial moue of distaste upon recognizing my head, as it appeared from the jacket, with an artificial smile.

"Should think you had more pressing things than golf, what with the way Ted's case is going. Don't you think it would have been better left in Stanton's capable hands?" she asked icily. She squeezed her husband's elbow and looked fondly at him. I thought of asking her if her hubby's hands were so capable, why did she feel the need to find release in Amanda's, but restrained myself.

Stanton moved his arm around his wife's waist and gave her an "atta girl" squeeze before chiming in, "Now, now, dear. I'm sure Edwards is doing the best he's able." He looked over my shoulder toward the tennis courts and finished, "Oh-oh. The Jordans are waiting. Wouldn't do to keep the president of the school board waiting after we finally got the district's account. Gotta run."

I stood and watched their athletic forms stride toward the courts, heads together, sharing a laugh. For a guy who was supposed to be quick on his feet, I hadn't been too impressive. Not a word had left my lips.

Freddie, Ernie, and Dr. Ramirez were handicap haggling as I reached number 1 tee. Esteban Ramirez was tall and lithe, with a well-trimmed mustache under a conquistador's nose. I let Judge Ernie negotiate the bet while I swung to loosen up. He was much tougher arm-twisting settlements and pleas than he was at getting us favorable terms. I pretended shock that we were only getting four a side from these clearly superior golfers. Really, it felt so good being outside to play in the clean washed air, I couldn't care less. Plus, if I could get the drink cart lady to stop enough times before she checked out at six, maybe Freddie's tongue would loosen.

The format we played was the same as that in effect for the upcoming tournament: team match play, two man-best ball. That meant we took the best score on a hole between Ernie and me and matched it against the best between our opponents. Whoever wins the most holes wins the match. So, when Ernie made eight on the first hole, only my five counted. Unfortunately, Doc and Freddie each made four. Down one after one.

Perhaps the long hiatus from golf was good for me. I played pretty well, including sinking two thirty-foot putts to pull out holes. And Ernie steadied. We were giving them a good match and began to entertain hopes for an upset. The course was nearly empty at that hour. Most members preferred early Saturday tee times. So Kim, the drink cart girl, had few other foursomes to look after, and her cart made regular visits. I had a Labatts and then switched to O'Doul's. More than one beer and my shaky grip on the game is gone. Ernie avoided booze on the links. But Doc and Freddie never passed on Kim's visits, loading up with a six pack of Michelob when she announced last call nearing six.

If Doc hadn't asked to mark my ball on number 18, I might never have detoured around the blocked memory synapses.

My second shot to the par-four finishing hole was a well struck six-iron headed at the pin. Unfortunately there was still enough strength left in the northerly breeze to stall its flight just short of the green. My cry of "Be the ball" died in my throat as the ball trickled into the bunker. Once sand-wedged onto the green, my ball lay between Doc and his birdie putt. While I raked the trap, he asked permission to mark my ball. He chased after his fifteen-footer, yelling encouragement to within six inches of the hole. We gave him the rest and he flipped my ball, which he had earlier picked up to mark, back to me. I bent to replace his mark with my ball.

His mark was more a piece of jewelry than a plebeian ball marker. It glistened gold in the evening sun. The club's logo, crossed clubs over a heraldic shield, was embossed into the metal. In that respect it matched the cheap plastic markers available free by the handful in the pro shop. But Doc's wasn't plastic. As I lifted it to admire it, the heft made me think it might be made of gold.

I was so caught up in needing to make the putt to tie the hole, I missed the tiny letters indented into the metal at compass points around the periphery. Without thinking, the marker went into my pocket. I stood over the putt. Ernie waited until I started to rock the putter back for his last-minute advice. "Don't leave it short."

I didn't. The ball rocketed beyond the cup. Ernie groaned. Freddie kidded, "Never up. Never in. Huh, counselor?" We congratulated them on yet another win and retired to the clubhouse for drinks on them.

After seven on a Saturday the men's locker bar was nearly empty. A foursome of gin regulars barely looked up from the machine gun play of the cards to wave and grunt. The two wall-mounted TVs in the corners were carrying the Tigers versus Oakland from the coast. I'm a Tigers fan since boyhood. So as we sat I couldn't resist a check of the score even though my boys were out of the pennant race by mid-May. Hey, they had brought up a couple of phenoms from the minors. Maybe there was hope for next year. No sooner had Stretch set a bowl of plump cashews on the table than their hottest prospect yielded a game-ending solo homer to Oakland's number nine hitter.

"Bah, you dog. Threw him a hanger on an 0-2 pitch," I moaned.

"You still following those overpaid losers?" Freddie asked.

Freddie signed the chit when the drinks were in front of us. "Hey, you guys did great. Might be worth some action in the tourney auction. Sadly, it wasn't quite enough. Thirty bucks each."

Both Ernie and I reached for our wallets. Doc pulled a silver money clip and slipped his winnings in place. As he went to slide it back into his pocket, a look of panic crossed his face. He stood and emptied both pockets. "Oh man! I lost my mark." He started a headlong rush for the door as if he'd left his infant daughter in the middle of traffic.

"Wait, wait. I've got it," I called. As he composed himself and sat back down, I fumbled in my left pocket and pulled the heavy nugget out. "Wow, nice!" I said as I studied it in the light. It was then I noticed what I had missed on the green. Two golf clubs formed a cross on the embossed shield. The letters LPCC were divided one into each quadrant. That I'd seen before my putt. It was the four tiny letters exquisitely etched into the gold border that got my heart thumping. TNPC.

Suddenly the dam in my memory broke free. I reached across the table to return his precious marker. "Pretty fancy marker, Doc. Almost looks like gold."

He took it quickly. "It is gold, 24 karat."

"Let me see that," Fred interjected, intercepting the handoff. He felt its substantial weight and admired the markings. "That would be at least a brow lift or half a tummy tuck right there, eh, Doc?"

"It's not the money," Doc replied, smiling. "You have any idea how long it took me to get into that club? Eight years."

"What club is that?" I asked, trying to sound casual. He looked at me as if I were asking Sir Lancelot what the Holy Grail was.

"It stands for Thursday Night Poker Club, Ken," Freddie explained.

I knew that. Why had it taken me so long to make the association? The cedar-chipped flower bed between the green on the par-three 16 and the tee on number 17 contained a small pedestal with a bronze plaque on top inscribed: "Donated by the Thursday Night Poker Club, 1987." More than once I'd overclubbed on the par three, landing in the garden. There had even been a debate whether the pedestal was an integral part of the course or an unnatural obstruction allowing free relief. The issue was resolved when the ladies auxiliary insisted the whole area be free relief to protect the evergreens and flowers.

Freddie continued, "Been around for almost forty years. Invitation only. How'd you get in, Doc? No offense. I asked a couple of the guys about joining five years ago. M. Stanton told me he'd get back to me. Five years and I'm still waiting."

"It's really exclusive, ten guys, eight past presidents of the club. Ken, only your colleague, M. Stanton Browne, and I have not been club president. Five dollar, ten dollar games once a week in the winter. Play down here in the club room from eight to midnight. Dinner at seven. Poker starts at eight. Old Horace tends bar while we get down to business. It cost me a lot of money to earn that marker. I can't believe I almost forgot it out there."

"They have a big initiation fee?" I asked.

Doc nodded. "You could say that. From the time Thad Granger asked me to sub for him eight years ago, I've played as a substitute about once a month. Until six months ago when Hiram Furst died and my spot opened, I lost twenty grand just as a substitute. Even after Hiram died I wasn't sure I'd get invited to take his spot. Any member can blackball you. I dropped M. Stanton as lawyer for our medical practice a few years ago. He was billing the bejeezus out of us. So I was sure he'd deep six me. Anyway, Cal Salomon, the car dealer, sweet talked him into letting me in. I gave Suzie a little face lift a year or so ago and waived the co-pay. You know Suzie? Looks nice, huh?"

Oh, yes, I know Suzie, I thought. Before I could reflect further on our post fashion show get-together, Doc continued.

"The way I heard it, M. Stanton finally relented, saying, 'It'll be good getting back into Doc's pocket on a regular basis.' "

"So, if you kept losing steadily, why did you want in so badly?" I asked.

Doc thought for a moment, pursed his lips in contemplation and then spoke. "I'll tell you, but I don't know why I'm telling you. My family was poor. We lived in a poor town in southern Indiana. I wore my brother's hand-me-downs to school. I had horrible acne as a teenager, which is part of the reason I went into plastics. I never got picked on sports teams." He was talking nonstop, looking more over our heads, out the window, than making eye contact. "Danielle Graham, the girl I ached for all through high school, actually laughed as she hung up the phone when I asked her to the senior prom. I worked as busboy at a club like this outside of Chicago to supplement my scholarships. I got rejected at the medical fraternity at University of Michigan med school and I ended up in Lake Pointe. In short, I've spent my whole life on the outside looking in.

"Now I have one of the best practices in upstate Michigan. I've got a nice home over on the front nine, married a cute nurse, got two nice kids, a three-car garage and the cars to fill it. I'm a member of this club, not washing dishes here. All it takes to join the club is money and somebody to sponsor you. But TNPC is invitation only. Ten guys out of three hundred. It's the creme de la crème. All old money. All movers and shakers, smart guys, really smart. And I'm in." Now he seemed to come back to himself and looked at us. "Does that sound stupid?" he asked.

Freddie shook his head. "Not to me, Doc. Sounds like you were born in the rough, worked your ass off to improve your life and are sitting pretty right next to the pin in regulation. Congrats. Keep me in mind if you need a substitute next winter. I'm still trying to get my foot in the door."

I wanted to keep him talking without scaring him off. "What games do you play? Dealer's choice?"

Doc laughed. "Yep. Dealer's choice as long as it's five card draw and five and seven stud. No split pot games, no wild cards, no baseball, no high-lows, no criss-cross, just real poker. Three years ago they voted to allow Texas hold 'em. That's it."

"I'm not sure it's such a privilege to be let into a game where you lose twenty grand," I offered.

"Oh, I'm getting better. I bought a couple of books. Reading one on tells now. You know what tells are?"

"Uh-uh."

"Little habits, twitches, tics, biting your lips, eye movements, looking at your hold cards, that sort of thing. Our esteemed hospital president tugs on his left earlobe when he's got a good hand. Tug, fold. No tug, see him and raise him. Know what I mean?"

"Really. Are you doing better?"

"Starting to, but I'd keep paying just to be around those guys. They're smart, they're connected, they're in on deals, they make things happen."

Now I had my opportunity. I took a shot in the dark. "Now that you mention it, don't they have some kind of investment fund?"

The look on Doc's face was like I'd walked into the surgical suite without scrubbing. He frowned and started to pull at his mustache with his right thumb and index finger. I made a mental note to see and raise the mustache stroke if I ever was sitting across a poker table from him.

"How'd you know?" he sputtered. "Don't know anything about that, not in that. What do you know about it?"

I was surprised by the sudden chill in Doc's demeanor. "Nothing, really. I was just asking. Heard some mention of it."

"Who was talking about it?" he came back quickly.

"Can't really say." I recalled my long-distance Caribbean friend's stock answer. "So is there such a thing?"

Doc's eyes were a tell. They darted left and right. "Not that I know of," he finally answered. He's bluffing, I thought. Before I could think of anything else to say, Doc looked at his watch, swigged the last quarter of his gin and tonic and stood up, collecting his things and putting his ball marker in his pocket.

"Gotta run guys, lotta fun. Good match. Night, Judge."

And he was gone. Ernie, who knew when I was fishing, had sat silently through the whole exchange. While Freddie had turned to watch Doc's departure, he raised his eyebrows to me as if to say, "What was all that about?"

I screwed up the right side of my mouth and nodded over my shoulder quickly twice for him to amscray and leave me with Freddie. And he did. Freddie made to leave as well. But I dangled irresistible bait in front of him.

"C'mon, Freddie. It's early. How about a couple of hands of gin? Give me a chance to get my money back." I'm a lousy gin player, and Freddie is a pro. His eyes lit up, and I had Stretch bring us each another beer with the cards and score sheet. I knew my losses would be an unbillable expense, but duty was calling.

Shutout on all three streets is gin parlance for a shellacking. But I took it for the team and reached for the last one hundred I had on me. Freddie let me owe him twenty so I could buy gas. As we settled up, I tried for a return on my investment.

"Say, Freddie, I was talking with Brent Eubanks a while back and the name TNPC investments came up in connection with the Dressler audit. Think the poker club's investment arm somehow got mixed up with Dressler?"

The victory smile melted from Freddie's face. He checked to see if the other table of gin players was listening. Satisfied they were engrossed in their game, he looked back at me. His watery eyes told me all the beers I'd been buying were taking hold. It was taking him a while to choose his words.

"Listen, Kenny. I told you we were sworn to secrecy on the Dressler thing. I can't believe Brent would talk to you about it. I'm not going to. I'll just tell you to leave that angle alone. If you think somebody killed Amanda over it, what makes you think they'll stop there?"

With that he headed back to his locker to change his shoes. He dawdled around, kibbitizing with the other gin sharpies, hoping I'd go on without him. But I waited for him by the club room door and we walked silently into the parking lot. As he unlocked his Jaguar, I broke the silence.

"Are you saying Amanda got killed over Dressler?"

He delayed sliding into the brown leather bucket seat just long enough to respond. "I didn't say that. I don't know anything about that. As far as I know, Ted killed her. I'm just saying be careful. That's it."

I made a last stab at it. "Dressler—Cats going to the dogs. TNPC, all mixed in together—ring any bells for you?"

He pretended to search his brain. "Nope, no bells at all." With that he slid into the low slung seat and turned the ignition.

I scouted the parking lot for a beat-up Olds and was relieved to find none. These days I was hypervigilant. Most of my life I've dwelled inside my head, lost in an internal dialogue with my thoughts. My awareness of the world around me has usually been just good enough to keep me from moving my lips or tripping over things. The drumbeat of threatening calls, funeral flowers, and homicidal drivers had changed all that. I was now so tuned into the world around me that each shadow and every sudden noise had my adrenaline flowing. I hoped being able to share my concerns with Karen would loosen the strings that made my scalp feel so tight.

It was almost 9:30 by the time I got home. Max bounded over once Billy opened his back door. When a hundred-pound-plus dog decides to greet you by jumping up, you better be braced or expect to end up on your behind.

"Down, dog! Down! Yes, yes, I missed you, too." If only Karen could be that happy to see me. Billy trailed along behind, finishing an ice cream sandwich by popping the last third into his cheeks.

"Hey, I agreed to dog sit so you could play golf. Whadja do, play a double header?"

"Nope. Had to do a little research on the case."

"At the country club?"

"As it turns out. Scene of the crime, you know."

I fended off Billy's questions and begged off, reminding him of Karen's return that night and the need to shower and clean the joint up.

"Think you'll get lucky?" he leered, chocolate clinging around the corners of his mouth.

"Already got lucky." He looked shocked. "Got you as a neighbor, don't I?" He shuffled home, waving off my thanks for watching Max.

I undertook the formidable task of cleaning a place that had gone untouched since Karen's last visit two weeks ago. Stacks of newspapers, fast food boxes, junk mail, and completed crossword puzzles filled a pail. With my windows staying open in the summer heat, a patina of dust coated every surface. A rag was not to be found. So I grabbed a t-shirt from the drawer and gave the place a lick and a promise.

Even with the breeze from the lake, there was a funny smell which traced back to the fridge. Cottage cheese that looked like green curd and milk that looked like cottage cheese were the culprits. By the time I cleared the beyond date stuff from the fridge, the shelves were conveniently empty for wiping with a soapy dish cloth. I did find a beef pot pie in the freezer and stuck it in the microwave before remembering the cottage's vintage microwave had given up the ghost three days ago in a sizzle of sparks and crackle of electricity. Meant to replace it today but was otherwise occupied. So I had to figure out how to work the gas stove. I thought I'd used it a couple of years ago, but couldn't remember for what.

In the bedroom I peeled off my golf clothes and threw them onto the odiferous mountain spilling from the closet. Been a while since I'd made it to the cleaners. That stop was on the list for today also. At first I planned just to shut the bedroom door. Then I remembered Billy's get lucky question and thought, "You never know." As a former Boy Scout, I decided to be prepared and loaded laundry into a couple of hampers and stashed it on the back porch. Having gone that far, I couldn't stop my preparations short. So I peeled the sheets from my bed, which had neither been changed nor made recently, and found replacement sheets which neither matched each other nor the pillow covers. But they were fresh. In my boxers, I inspected the premises and found satisfactory improvement. As I had countless times in my bachelorhood, I vowed to keep things neater.

The shower was the cottage's worst feature. The shower head had been an afterthought long after the four-legged tub had been plumbed. The pipe running from the tap to the head was exposed and held to the wall with rusty brackets. Just to get over the high walls of the free-standing tub was a giant leap for mankind. The shower curtain hung from a circular rod suspended from the ceiling. Its yellow sunflowers against blue sky and green landscape had faded. The plastic was covered with curious black dots which seemed to be multiplying with the passage of time.

The water burped from the head in an uneven and unenthusiastic trickle. I vowed for the thousandth time to call a plumber and redo the whole thing. But the pastor had called the tub a family heirloom a few years ago when he vetoed my last remodeling plan. Toweling off, I resolved to act without Pastor's blessing. After all, "The Lord helps those who help themselves."

I was making comparisons between my mug and the faces of Humphrey Bogart, Montgomery Clift, and Gregory Peck in the pitted medicine cabinet mirror, none of them favorable, when the phone rang. The towel wrapped around my waist came loose in the dash to the phone. It was Karen.

"Ken, I'm really sorry. I've been chasing a little weasel of a burglar by a farmhouse in the west end of the county. Just arrived at the jail with him. Gotta finish booking him. And I'm a mess. Had to chase the bugger through five miles of woods and marsh. I'm covered in mosquito bites and mud. By the time I get home, showered and cleaned up, it'll be too late. I'm really sorry." She sounded exhausted. She also sounded sorry. So I took a chance and begged.

"Gosh, Karen. I told Max you were coming. You should see his tail at the sound of your name. I just cleaned the whole place top to bottom in your honor. I've been slogging through the legal wars all week knowing I'd be seeing you this weekend. What a downer."

"I know. I know. Me too. But I'm a sweaty dirtball. I don't want you to see me looking like I do. Plus, I'm working tomorrow so I can have next Saturday off for the dinner dance after your golf tournament. You should see the dress I found. With your trial and everything, I guess we'll have to wait till then."

Hearing the regret in her voice, I played the last card I had.

"Karen, I don't care how you look. I need to talk to you. Somebody tried to kill me last week. Ran me off the road. To top it off, the sheriff's deputies tried to arrest me. My phone number must be close to 'Dial a Threat' with the number of calls I'm getting. I could use a friend." Pathetic, I know, but I was desperate. And it worked. She said she was on her way.

When she arrived she looked like the one who'd had a near death experience. She had branch scratches on her forehead and her left cheek. Her uniform trousers were muddy and torn at the knee, and she had red welts where the mosquitoes had been feasting on her. I took all this in as I held the door open and Max went bounding across the porch and halfway up the walk to greet her. She ruffled his ears and then pushed him away when he stuck his muzzle in her crotch. They arrived at the doorstep together, Max's metronome of a tail on full allegro. She brushed a matted lock of hair from her forehead and smiled wanly at me. "Warned you. I'm a wreck."

Then for the first time in a long while, I picked the perfect thing to say to a woman. "You look absolutely gorgeous. A lot of women can look great after they've spent hours dolling up. The test of real beauty is, how does a woman look when she's at her worst? Boy, do you ever pass that test. It's great to see you."

Then she did something unexpected. She walked up to me and put her arms around me and just held me nice and close. I could smell the mixture of perfume and perspiration. I could feel her firm breasts against my chest. I could see the wisps of strawberry hair on the nape of her neck covering a small, almost heart-shaped mole I'd never noticed before. We stood like that wordlessly for a couple of the finest seconds of my life to date. Then Max was so insistent on being part of the hug he almost knocked us over. That broke the spell. Karen laughed and when she looked up, I saw a little moisture in the comers of her eyes.

"God, Ken, somebody really tried to kill you? I'm so glad you're okay. I had time to think about your being dead on the way over. I didn't like the thought, not at all."

"Me neither, but a hug like that was worth a close call. Thank you for caring enough to come."

I popped us each a beer and we sat with our shoulders, hips and knees touching on the couch. Max made a tight circle until he could easily place his one-hundred-pound-frame touching all four of our feet. Then he lifted his eyebrows, looked up at me, sighed heavily, and dozed off.

I went over all the details with Mr. Porkpie Hat for her. She pulled her notebook from her breast pocket, flipped a few pages and then asked me, "How sure are you about the time?"

"Pretty certain. I had a beer with Sven. It was just before ten when we left."

"When did you tell the deputies about the blue Olds and the guy with the porkpie hat?"

"Right away, but I had to put up with their hassle and bullshit for a while. They were sure they had me for DUI. Only after I volunteered for the PBT and the neighbor backed me up did they ease off a little."

"How long did that take?"

"I don't know, five minutes, why?"

"I called you from the jail, and after you mentioned somebody tried to kill you, I went to dispatch and looked at the call sheet." She looked down at her notebook.

"They still have it under 'Suspected DUI,' by the way. Neighbor calls at 9:57. Deputies Meeks and Doyle dispatched at 9:59. And they are out at the scene at 10:02."

"Boy, I thought they got there fast. I didn't realize it was that fast."

"They called in your plates and license number at 10:03."

"That could be right."

"Well, the clear the scene, no arrest, and BOL—be on the lookout for an 88 blue Olds—isn't till 10:45."

Now I sat up. "That can't be right. The rigamarole with hassling me and giving me the PBT wasn't ten minutes. Then when Mr. Utermallen backed me up on the car in the road, Doyle said he was going back to the car to call it in. That couldn't be later than 10:15 at the latest. Hell, I was back home around eleven. So what gives?"

She thought about it a minute. "Sometimes you finish your paperwork in the car after you clear the scene and toward quitting time, don't call in on channel 80. You can head back to the barn without getting another call and overlap onto the next shift. But I think those guys work ten p.m. to six a.m., so I don't know."

Now I was hearing alarm bells. "Either those guys just don't like me, and with this case there are guys in that department who don't, or they wanted to give Mr. Porkpie Hat plenty of time to clear the area, and now I think it's a combination of them all."

Concern furrowed Karen's brow. "Ken, I'm taking enough heat for dating a hot shot defense lawyer. We are dating, aren't we?"

I squinted in thought for a second, and she punched me lightly on the shoulder. "Hey, I sure hope so."

She turned to look me in the eye. "Then you need to be more careful. Do you have a gun?"

I shook my head. "More likely to have it go off in my pocket than at some bad guy."

She touched me on the knee. "Ken, no offense, but sometimes you are pretty oblivious. Did you even notice me on any of the three nights before I stopped you for speeding bringing Max home from Mrs. Grimes'?"

I perked up at that. "You mean that wasn't just happenstance?"

Her eyes twinkled and lips curled. "I'd call it targeted enforcement." Then the smile vanished. "Promise me you'll keep your eyes open. I'm worried that you are stirring up a nest of vipers."

We paused and looked intently at each other. I considered the significance of her admitting she had gone out of her way to meet me and the depth of concern for my safety. She wiped a smudge from her cheek and returned my gaze as if she could see the wheels turning in my head. We both realized that we were crossing the line from where Max was her primary male interest at my address, to me taking his place. Sorry, old buddy.

We leaned in and kissed for the first time. My God, was she sweet. Oh, I could taste the Labatts, but beneath that, something—a taste of honey. Her lips were soft and full. It was like my lips had been trying on the lips of all those women for all those years, and I finally found the perfect fit. These thoughts and sensations had about five seconds to surface, and then she pulled back gently. She looked a little shocked and then she smiled.

"Hi, you."

"Hi, yourself," I answered.

We talked over who might want me dead and why the deputies had delayed the BOL call for quite awhile, then she yawned, patted the couch pillows and pushed herself up.

"Okay, Big Shot. I'm exhausted. I'm going home, take a nice hot bath, put cream on my bites and climb into bed."

"You could do all those things here, you know. Plus, I'd have a trained law enforcement officer on hand to protect me."

She cocked her head and gave the impression she was giving the idea serious consideration.

"Not tonight. You've got Max to protect you and keep you company. Leave the phone off the hook and the doors locked."

With that she bent over to pat Max goodnight and in so doing gave me a good look at the sexy bottom which wouldn't be in my bed tonight. I walked her to her car. As she turned on the ignition, I rested my elbows on the driver's window frame.

"Well, what about a nighty night kiss then?"

She gave me a little elfin smile. "You've had that already. I'm so glad you're all right."

With that she reached for the gearshift and backed out of the driveway. I stood there, watching the taillights disappear as she turned from Beachside, knowing we had just crossed a threshold in our relationship. I couldn't wait to find out what lay on the other side.

Lying between my clean sheets and under a couple of blankets in the suddenly fall-like air, I tried to puzzle through why the deputies had delayed calling in Mr. Porkpie. But I couldn't keep my mind on the problem. Instead, my mind kept turning back to the nape of Karen's neck and how very much alive I'd felt in her embrace.

42

Sunday I spent at the office working through the piles of correspondence, motions, notices, and briefs on the files I'd been neglecting while in trial. What a lawyer gets paid for on an all-consuming case is not just what he does on that case, but also what he is not doing on his other files. So I reviewed and dictated responses, many of which were pleas for adjournments.

Monday at six I headed out to Heather Hollows. Walter Hackett would be testifying this week, and I still had not interviewed him. I'd barely known Walter when he tended bar in the country club's upstairs lounge. That bar bridged between the main dining room and the piano lounge. One of the ten plush maroon leather barstools that fronted on the black marble bar top was where I'd last seen Amanda alive. But by that time Walter, don't call me Wally, had long left the club's employ. The story was that Walter was becoming his own best customer. When he was called in by the club manager, the dialogue went something like this:

"Walter, I know you've been with the club for ten years, but we can't have you drinking the Jack Daniels on the job."

"Okay, boss. No problem. I'll switch to Jim Beam."

Whereupon, Walter was forced to seek another employment opportunity. He'd gone down the road to Heather Hollows and had been the head bartender ever since. It was from that vantage point he'd witnessed the turmoil between Ted, Amanda and Gianfranco the night Amanda died. Tina Botham had chosen to separate his testimony from James and Jillian Simpson's, so that it would be an end of trial echo of the rancor between the defendant and his alleged victim a few short hours before her death.

I figured a Monday evening at six was my best opportunity to catch Walter while the bar at Heather Hollows was quiet. I had my pick of barstools. Walter treated me as if I were just another customer.

"What can I get you?"

"Just a Coke, Walter. I'm Ken Edwards, Ted Armbruster's lawyer. I wanted to ask you a few questions."

"I know who you are, and everything I've got to say I already told the cops. It's all in my statement. Why don't you read that?"

"I have, but there's just a couple of things I'd like to check up. Like did you see Mrs. Armbruster dancing with the Italian gentleman, Mr. Firenze?"

"Look, counselor, it was a Friday night, the place was packed. I've got waitresses backed up yelling orders. I've got customers two deep waving their empties at me. You think I got time to notice who's dosi-doeing who?"

"Have you see Mr. Firenze in here before?"

"Maybe."

"Does that mean yes or no?"

"It means I'm not paid to notice who our guests are. It's not like the club, where I have to learn everybody's names so they can all feel like big shots. And they don't pay me here to be chewing the fat with some hack lawyer trying to get one of those big shots off for killing his wife. So if you'll excuse me, I've got work to do."

With that he put my Coke and the tab down in front of me and moved over to the bar sink and tried to find a few glasses to wash. I picked up my glass and followed him.

"Look, Walter, I've got a job to do here. Why the attitude? What did Ted or I ever do to you?"

He looked up from the sink. The ruptured blood vessels on his nose beneath lifeless eyes were obvious at close range. I could see the flush of anger redden his forehead and cheeks. "Listen, Edwards, the pay here doesn't match the club, but at least here I don't have to make nice to a bunch of snobs who look down their noses at me. You, I hardly know, but your client, I think he's one of the ones who got me fired. So I owe him nothing."

"Why do you think that?"

"Cuz maybe I took a little nip one time while he was at the bar. He was on the board of directors. I can add two and two. He was drunk that night, the night he killed his wife."

My patience was wearing thin. "You see him kill her?"

He rolled his eyes and straightened from the sink. He placed his hands on the bar and leaned closer to me. Close enough for me to smell the aroma of whiskey on his breath and to see that his teeth had gone too long without the dentist. "Listen, I heard him threaten her that night. That's when I called 911. After what he said, I wasn't exactly shocked to read that he killed her."

"What were the words he used exactly?"

"I told the cops. I don't need to waste my time telling you again. That lady prosecutor says I don't have to talk to you. Read the police report. That's what you get paid for, isn't it? I got to go in court and testify. You'll hear exactly what he said from the witness stand and not before. As I stand here I don't remember exactly whatever it was I told the cops." He turned abruptly and walked to the other side of the bar with his back to me. I left him three bucks for my dollar fifty Coke and walked out to my car smiling. The tip wasn't for his friendly demeanor. But wanting to hurt me, he could only help me. I could only hope he testified exactly the same in court.

I spent two hours in the office looking at pictures, pictures I'd seen one hundred times before. The police scene photos and the autopsy shots still stimulated the gag reflex in spite of repeated exposure to them. Something about the wound shots from the morgue had been tapping at the door for understanding since I'd first looked at them. That night, with the autopsy report open next to the pictures, I finally found the right door. Or so I hoped.

When court resumed Tuesday morning, the judge reminded the jurors it would only be a two-day week, as she was flying to the coast for sis's wedding. Somehow, the kiss from Karen acted as an analgesic for me. I could look at Alex, and the toothache of loss that had been throbbing dully for years in my subconscious stopped pulsating. Only the absence of pain made me realize how badly I'd been hurting.

Bliss had been called back to the dugout. The next witness to come to the plate was Dr. Rudolph Zimmer. I guess last week's rainout had changed the batting order for the prosecution. From way back in my assistant prosecutor days, I knew the doctor was a heavy hitter. Knowledgeable, fair, prepared, and authoritative. Jurors ate up the local version of Quincy, ME.

"People call Dr. Rudolph Zimmer."

As the prosecutor called his name, the good doctor lifted his stocky frame from the chair behind the prosecution table. He withdrew a file from his briefcase, snapped the case shut and plodded slowly to the witness stand. Nearing sixty and carrying well over two hundred pounds on a five-foot-nine frame, he moved ponderously. He didn't waste money on fancy suits and jackets. Rather, he featured a white lab jacket over charcoal slacks. Tina looked like an elf next to Santa as she escorted the doctor to the stand. As he turned to be sworn, the stem of his signature meerschaum pipe peeked from his breast pocket. Bulldog-like jowls hung from a face creased with years of study into human depravity. He removed his reading glasses from their case and slid them well down his broad nose, peering over the glasses to swear to tell the truth.

Tina returned to counsel table while she took him through his extensive credentials as a forensic pathologist. For the first time I could recall, she was wearing a dress rather than a business suit. I wondered idly whether at her height she had shopped for this little blue number in the girls' or women's wear section. I quickly reminded myself that no matter how small the package, she was a determined opponent bent on my client's destruction. And in extracting her pound of flesh from Ted, she'd take no small satisfaction from leaving me bloodied and beaten in the legal arena.

A forensic pathologist spends much more time amongst lawyers and cops than with doctors and nurses. Mostly, they stand alone in vigil with the deceased, a scalpel in one hand and a recorder in the other. They focus on the injuries that transported the victim from the land of the living to the realm of the dead. Some are sloppy and some are thorough. Dr. Zimmer was the best I'd seen. He wrote a concise but thorough post mortem. He reviewed the case, the tissue slides, the photographs and the physical evidence before he walked in the courtroom door. He was understated but firm. He was patient but not slack. He'd been in court so many times over so many years that he'd see it all.

Tina was nearing the end of her case and wanted the jury to wallow in the bloody details one more time. Dr. Zimmer was the perfect instrument with which to wallow. I tried to avoid his stomach-turning testimony by stipulating Mrs. Armbruster had been killed by blows to the head with a golf club. Miss Botham was too smart for that. She felt the jury would want the benefit of the doctor's scientific analysis.

"How the victim died is at the core of this murder case. Plus, the doctor's testimony will give the jury insight into the defendant's state of mind at the time of the killing. So we thank Mr. Edwards for his offer to stipulate, but elect to proceed with our proofs."

I didn't like the sound of that. Tina was looking pretty smug. The hem of her little blue number was below the knee and swirled about girlishly as she sashayed up to the lectern to begin her examination. She bent to pull a wooden step out so she could see comfortably over the lectern. A few of the jurors smiled indulgently at her. She'd long since come to grips with her height and knew how to use it to her advantage. She cocked her head in acknowledgement of the jurors and commenced to wallow.

Tina exhibited many of the bloody photos, and it was obvious they had not lost their jury impact. The doctor described the rich supply of blood to the scalp as explanation for the extensive bleeding and went on to say, "In fact, the amount of bleeding from her non-fatal wounds allows me to state with medical certainty that the victim lived some minutes before the fatal blow to the back of the head was administered. That and the large contusion to the right forehead clearly point to a time interval."

"Can you describe and sequence the blows the victim received?"

Using picture after picture, the doctor described each injury and how it had been inflicted. By the time he finished, three spinster regulars in the gallery had slipped out of the courtroom. From the jurors' faces, many wanted to join them.

"Can you say, doctor, whether the victim saw what was coming?"

"It is certain she saw the first blow. If you will hand me, please, the exhibit showing the injuries to her right arm. Mrs. Armbruster has what I interpret to be a defensive wound to the dorsal or upper side of her right forearm."

"Why do you call it a defensive wound, doctor?"

"Because it is consistent with her raising her arm to fend off a blow from a blunt object, and it matches the dimensions of the shaft on what I'm sure is the murder weapon."

"What was used as what you called the murder weapon?"

He looked down at his notes. "Ah, Mrs. Armbruster suffered blows from a golf device called a Solarz Super Shot Wedge. The final blow to the left occipital area proved fatal as it penetrated the skull, displacing bone fragments into the subdural gray matter of the brain. The blow penetrated to the brain itself, resulting in massive subdural hematoma, rapidly increasing cranial pressure, and death."

Miss Botham paused to let the graphic details sink in. I glanced at the jury. Three of the ladies and one of the gentlemen looked on the verge of illness. Others were staring at Ted, loathing evident on their faces. Miss Botham gave them all the time they needed to be thoroughly revolted before continuing.

"Yes, doctor, that's quite a bit of technical information. Can you explain in layman's terms?"

"Indeed. Mrs. Armbruster received three blows from this golf implement."

"Excuse me, doctor, you call it an implement, but it's a golf club, is it not? I mean, it was certainly used by your description for a club, was it not?"

"Ha, ha. Yes. Forgive me. I have never played that game. Much too difficult, time consuming, and frustrating, from what my colleagues tell me. Is it not?"

I noticed smiles and nods from three male jurors. They were loving Dr. Zimmer.

"I hear that, doctor," Tina said, the hem of her dress swirling a minor celebration. "Anyway, you were describing the effect of the blows from the club."

"Yes, yes, simply put. The fatal injury was caused by what I am told is called the heel of the club, proceeding with a most forceful downward blow to the left rear of the head, fracturing the bone, tearing the dura, or lining of the brain, and bruising the brain itself. The force of the blow and the bone splinters penetrating the gray matter of the brain caused massive bleeding and fluid flow to the area of injury, a subdural hematoma. The rapid build-up of fluid in the closed areas of the skull created intense intracranial pressure, causing the brain to shut down. Death."

"Doctor, you mentioned a most forceful downward blow. How are you able to say that?"

"Considerable force was required to cause the depressed, pushed in, and fragmented fracture to the skull. The entry wound matches the back portion of the club. You have that exhibit, no?"

"Yes, I do. Your Honor, exhibit number 25. May I demonstrate it to the jury?"

The judge glanced at me. I had plenty of objections, but none were valid. So I nodded acquiescence. Whereupon the forearm shot was replaced by an ugly close-up of the matted hair on the back of Amanda's head.

"Ah, yes. Notice the swelling and the extruded extradural material. My analysis also demonstrated brain matter."

An audible gasp from the audience. Miss Botham then switched the light on an x-ray view box with three x-rays across the top. As she stretched with a pointer to indicate each x-ray, a penumbral light from the view box haloed her prim mouth. "Now, doctor, showing you x-rays 26-28. These are post mortem x-rays. What do they tell us?"

The doctor got up from the witness stand and plodded over to stand on the opposite side of the illuminated x-ray box from Tina. His massive girth, five o'clock-shadowed jowls, and gray hair were juxtaposed against Tina's petite frame, girlish complexion, and pixie cut hair. "Ah, number 26, see the little white spots and lines. They are bone fragments beneath the skull. The blow must be forceful to cause that degree of fragmentation.

"And number 27. See the multiple dark, jagged lines in the bone of the skull; these are referred fractures departing from the area of force, like you would get if you cracked an egg."

Nods of understanding from the female jurors. One woman flinched.

"And number 28. See at the bottom of the main fracture, around here?" He reached into the side pocket of his lab coat, retrieving a red marker to circle the area illuminated on the x-ray. Then he drew an arrow.

"Now, look at the larger depressed fracture traversing the skull toward the atlas. The direction of that fracture matches the shaft of the club, so that tells me a downward blow of sufficient force for not only the head of the club to penetrate, but also a small portion of the shaft to disrupt bone. You can also see the non-displaced hairline fracture over the ear, an injury we have yet to discuss."

"Yes, yes, doctor. We will come back to that." I made a note that she'd better or she'd wish she had. "But first, please tell the jury, what is the atlas and where is it located?"

"The atlas is the first vertebrae of the neck, which carries the weight of the head." He touched just below the bone of his skull. "Here is the atlas. Now the depression left by the shaft is here." He reached up and touched three and a half inches higher on the left back of his gray-maned head. "And we also find longitudinal front-to-back contusions on the scalp. That is to say, we find what we call a train track."

"A train track?"

"Yes, parallel lines caused by a rod or stick. The force of the blow does not break the skin, but crushes and ruptures blood vessels. The pressure of the blood displaces the blood sideways, so we can see the dimensions of the instrument."

"Ah, and did you compare the so-called train track to the Solarz sand wedge, exhibit 5?"

Miss Botham approached the evidence table in front of the bench and retrieved the golf club. The club looked quite large and yet benign in her grip. The head was covered and sealed in a plastic bag, as was the grip. The doctor took the club from her, still standing near the jury box.

"Yes, the dimensions of the bore of the shaft are entirely consistent with the train track contusion."

He held the club up for the jurors to see. They stared mesmerized at it, some talisman of evil.

"Thank you, doctor. Before you return to the witness stand, can you tell the jury the position of the victim prior to the fatal blow?"

"Yes, I can. I can show them." Whereupon he walked to the open area between the counsel table, labored his stocky bulk into a crouch, and then lay prone on the floor with an audible "Oooph." The judge and jury craned forward and the spectators stood to watch. He lifted his head, his glasses precarious on his nose.

"I believe the victim had been knocked to the floor by the second blow to the left side of her head behind the ear. I believe the large contusion or bump upon her forehead was caused by her head striking the marble floor after that blow. I believe she lay there for some time, at least minutes, and then she attempted to rise onto her hands and knees, like so." He pushed himself halfway to a hands and knees position. "She then turned her head to look over her left shoulder, whereupon her attacker approached from behind her and to the right and delivered a most forceful downward blow, the blow that proved fatal. If the detective will take my place, I can demonstrate."

Bliss looked surprised and uncertain, but got on his hands and knees, carefully trying to preserve his new suit.

"No, detective, not quite up on your knee. Like you were doing a half push-up, now look behind you to the left. Ah, just so."

The doctor took the club over his head. A few gasps were heard, but he brought it down slowly and held it inches above the back of Bliss's head. "Something very close to this. You see the heel of the club strikes here, the shaft leaves a train track toward the atlas, or center of the base of the skull. You see?"

Miss Botham nodded and so did everybody in the place. "Thank you, detective, you are spared. Thank you, doctor, please return to the witness stand." The doctor brushed off his white lab coat and assisted Bliss, who dusted the knees of his new suit pants as he rose. Tina stood between them, a pygmy among giants.

"So, doctor, you are saying Mrs. Amanda Armbruster died on her hands and knees by a blow from behind?"

"True."

"Would she constitute any immediate threat to her attacker in such a position?"

"No, she was helpless. She had probably lost consciousness briefly from the second blow over the left lower parietal bone, over and behind her left ear, or from striking the floor as she fell. She could pose no threat."

I could hear the murmur of anger and disgust in the gallery. So could the judge. Alex rapped her gavel gently. "Order." Her face was a mixture of profound sadness leavened with righteous anger.

The murmurs quieted to a whisper, and with one look from the judge, vanished. With order restored, Miss Botham ran her hands through her short dark hair and headed for the finish line.

"Can you sum things up for us, doctor?"

"It is my considered opinion that Mrs. Armbruster saw her attacker and had her arm up to fend off the first blow, which still lacerated the forehead. She received a second blow behind the ear, which knocked her to the floor, where she lay bleeding for at least a matter of minutes. I cannot say whether she was conscious throughout that time. However, I'm certain she was conscious as she got to her knees when the final fatal blow was struck."

"Can you tell us how much time passed between the first blow and the final fatal blow she received on her knees?"

"Conservatively, five minutes. I say this because she has what we call raccoon eyes. The first blow to the forehead caused the eyeballs to jolt in their sockets with attendant micro tears to the blood vessels in the eye sockets." He rose to walk in front of the jury box, demonstrating the photograph of Amanda's face as she lay on the autopsy table. My mind recoiled at the contrast between the sightless eyes in Amanda's bruised and bloody picture and the woman I'd seen only hours before the picture was taken. In the club bar Amanda's eyes sparkled with excitement, allure, and mischief. I felt a slight spasm of vertigo considering how thin the line between the quick and the dead. When I recovered, the doctor was moving to conclusion.

"See, around both eyes, but particularly the right, the beginning of bruising; we sometimes call it a spectacle hematoma. I believe the first blow, which left the golf club impression on her forehead, also caused the extravasations, or internal bleeding, which led to the beginning of raccoon eyes, spectacle bruising, same thing. Based on that, the bleeding, and the hematoma, I am comfortable with five minutes from first insult to fatal injury."

"So whatever passion, anger, madness led to the initial blows, there was time, five minutes, for the attacker to consider what he had done?"

"Objection, Your Honor." I rose to break the steady drumbeat to the gallows. "The doctor has not said that the attacker was male."

The jury looked at me in disbelief. Wasn't it obvious the attacker was the male seated next to me?

Miss Botham waved her hand as if at a fly. She looked like a demented munchkin. "I'll rephrase, Your Honor. He or she had about five minutes to consider and deliberate before inflicting the fatal wound."

The doctor nodded. "I'd say so."

"And was the wound willfully inflicted? By that I mean, any possibility the fatal wound was accidental?"

The doctor removed his reading glasses in a sweep of truth. "No, ma'am."

"So, per your careful forensic science, you are able to say the killing was willful, deliberate, with time to premeditate and reconsider."

"I cannot see inside the mind of the killer, Madam Prosecutor. That is for the jury. I have told you what my medical findings demonstrate."

And then Tina pushed for maximum effect. She strode back to her desk, twirled, skirt swishing, and with her voice on the verge of breaking, finished.

"Doctor, in the last moment of her life, Amanda Armbruster was on her knees, begging for mercy, only to have her pleas answered with a vicious blow to the back of her skull?"

I leapt to my feet and objected. "Highly prejudicial and speculative. There is no evidence of begg—"

Before I could finish Tina interrupted. "Withdrawn."

The judge added, "Jury will disregard the last question."

Yeah, right! I fumed as the jurors filed out for the lunch break. Most looked like the only appetite they had was for vengeance on my client.

As the courtroom cleared, Tina quickly headed off Dr. Zimmer, who was coming over to renew old acquaintances with me.

"No fraternizing with the enemy, Doc."

"No enemy. Mr. Edwards and I are old friends since you were a schoolgirl, Miss Botham. Eh, Mr. Edwards?"

I smiled and stood to shake hands. "I have learned much from Dr. Zimmer over time, but it's hard for me to imagine the formidable and ferocious Miss Botham as a playful schoolgirl, doctor."

He laughed and she pretended to as she led him away. Larry, the bailiff, broke the rules and let me back into the courtroom with my lunch from the basement vending machines: a soda, two Snickers bars, and a package of peanuts. If you are what you eat, I was a ticking time bomb of glucose. Alone in the silent chamber I meditated on what Tina hadn't asked. If the omission was intentional, I thought I knew why.

I was a bundle of energy by the time the doctor retook the stand after lunch, and it wasn't all due to the Snickers bars. To this point all I'd been doing was counterpunching and jabbing, bobbing and weaving, hoping to avoid a knockout punch. Tina's neglect to cover the ear injury, willful or inadvertent, left her open for a haymaker if all went according to plan.

"Hello, doctor, nice to see you." I stood to begin.

"And you, Mr. Edwards." He looked at the jury like a favorite uncle, raising his bushy eyebrows, a prelude to informality. "I've known Mr. Edwards since he didn't have a gray hair on the side of his head. We go back to the days when he used to sit in the chair where Miss Botham is now. A very clever boy." As if the jury needed any more reason to be guarded with me.

"Thank you, doctor. You've noticed I've grown older, but sadly, not much wiser. Do you mind if I ask you a few questions Miss Botham overlooked?"

He sat back and beamed at me. "I should be most disappointed if you didn't."

"First, as part of the autopsy, did you examine Amanda Armbruster's genital area for recent signs of intercourse?"

"Yes, that's standard procedure. Our findings indicated no semen and no vaginal indication of intercourse in the last forty-eight hours."

"What about any trauma in the vicinity?"

"Still reading the autopsy protocol carefully, I see. The victim had bruise marks on the upper left thigh consistent with pressure from a human hand." The jurors perked up.

"Are you able to tell the jurors how long before death the bruising occurred?"

"I can say with confidence that the injury occurred within one to three hours pre-mortem."

"Are these kind of bruises found in rape victims?"

"Sometimes."

"Good. Now if I understand you, doctor, you positively identified exhibit 5, the sand wedge, as the object which struck the fatal blow to the back of Mrs. Armbruster's head?"

"Indeed, I did."

"Can you testify to a medical certainty that my client, Ted Armbruster, was the one swinging the club at the time?"

He adjusted his reading glasses, looking down at the file, eyebrows twitching. "No, I cannot, but I have here the fingerprint lab's report showing his prints all over the grip, including a clear right palm impression in blood."

"Aha. The fact that his fingerprints are on the grip of a golf club is hardly surprising, since that is where the clubs are meant to be held."

He looked up sharply, jowls firming.

"That is true. But I doubt he was playing golf at the time the bloody prints were left."

"Further, it is true that if my client came downstairs after his wife had been injured and touched the club, his fingerprints would be in the blood on the grip, just as they are?"

Skeptically, he answered, "That could be so."

"Then if the jury is looking to the learned Dr. Rudolph Zimmer and asking, can you say beyond a reasonable doubt that Theodore Armbruster swung the blows that injured or killed his wife, you would have to tell them, 'I can't say that.' "

He shook his head and chuckled. "Counselor, I see you have not lost your touch. I have my opinions, indeed, but for me to say to a scientific certainty that your client swung the club at the time of injury..." He paused. "You've got me there, I can't do that. The jury will have to look at all the evidence to decide what happened."

"Thank you for your candor, doctor." I turned from where I stood at the far end of the jury box and walked toward the defense table, deciding not to waste any more time on preliminaries. If I was going to dispel the devastation from his direct exam, now was the time. I turned back, reaching into my repertoire of practiced expressions for curious.

"Now, doctor, something else I didn't hear you say on Miss Botham's questioning. Did you identify the golf club, exhibit 5, as having inflicted all wounds, left forehead, right arm, behind the left ear, and the fatal wound to the back of the head?"

"No, Miss Botham did not ask me that."

I raised my eyebrows and donned a quizzical look. I could feel the first little pulse of positive jury energy. They were checking their notes and sitting up, taking notice. I glanced over my shoulder and saw Tina looking down and trying to look busy with her legal pad.

"Okay then, doc. I'll ask you. You have told us that exhibit 5 inflicted the fatal wound?"

"Of that I am sure."

"Because?"

"The damage to the bone matches the heel of the club. The club head contains residual brain tissue and a fragment of bone. The shaft near the clubhead is distorted or bent from the impact that left the so-called train track impression. I am sure exhibit 5 struck the fatal blow."

"Uh-huh, but you are not sure it struck the other blows?" I held my breath.

The doctor nodded and a wry look crinkled the comers of his lips beneath the full gray mustache. "See, I said you were clever. I'm glad this is coming up for discussion." He glanced over to the prosecution table. Neither Bliss nor Botham looked back. Aha, Mr. Law and Order and Miss Prim and Proper had been caught with their hands in the cookie jar.

"I am a little troubled about the non-fatal wounds."

"Tell the jury then what troubles you, doctor."

"If you hand me the golf club and the close-up pictures of the club face, I'll demonstrate."

The courtroom hummed with a silent expectancy.

"The club's face on exhibit 5 looks new. I'm no expert on golf clubs, but I have a friend at the crime lab who is an expert on tool marks, that is to say, metal impressions. His name is Paul Fredericks. I showed him the club and the abrasions on Mrs. Armbruster's right forehead as well as the smaller marks over her left ear."

"Yes, and what did you learn?"

Miss Botham rose slowly, as if unsure she really wanted to object and look even guiltier of trying to hide something. I saw Bliss reach and touch her left sleeve as if to pull her back, but too late. She objected anyway, albeit apologetically.

"I object, Your Honor. This testimony calls for hearsay from Mr Fredericks. Mr Fredericks is on nobody's witness list." She sat back in her chair.

The judge looked to me. I cloaked myself in righteous indignation and answered forcefully.

"Mr. Fredericks is on nobody's witness list because, in direct contravention of this court's disclosure order, Miss Botham kept his name to herself. Moreover, as I suspect the information we are about to hear would be exculpatory, her suppression of evidence as evidenced by her staying away from this area in Dr. Zimmer's direct examination would appear willful. Accordingly, I am moving for dismissal of the charges. The integrity of our judicial system, the rules of ethics, as well as the U.S. Supreme Court ruling in *Brady vs. Maryland,* 373 U.S. 83, require no less."

All of a sudden the courtroom came alive with excited whispering. Tim Honnecker from *The Leader* stirred from his post-luncheon nap. To a one, the jurors were apprehensively on the edge of their seats. Everybody knows the guilty go free on legal technicalities. This can't be happening here. Can it?

The judge gaveled the hubbub to near quiet and excused the jury. As they left, looking confused and concerned, Tim grabbed my arm. "Have you got something here? Would she really toss a murder rap?"

I shrugged. "We'll see."

"We will have order or we will not have an audience." A tense quiet returned. Judge Kingsdale looked at her protege Tina with a much less amiable visage.

"Miss Botham, you will please fully and forthrightly explain why I should not grant Mr. Edwards' motion for dismissal. We will not have a defendant's right to a fair trial sullied by hiding witnesses and evidence."

I glanced over at my opponent. The sashaying avatar of cool control was gone. Her face was pale and her hands trembled. Her voice quivered.

"Judge, I just learned of Mr. Fredericks this morning as the doctor was about to take the stand. I didn't have time to digest what he was telling me nor understand its importance, and I'm not sure I do now. Anyway, I discussed it with Dr. Zimmer during the recess, and we agreed if Mr. Edwards didn't bring it out, then I would cover the area on re-direct. Is that not so, doctor?" She looked imploringly at him.

I could tell he didn't want to be responsible for the dismissal of a murder case and the cratering of a legal career. I could also guess he felt she was putting a bigger ribbon on the package than it deserved. Probably he'd told her she should have brought it out on direct and that she should ask to re-open direct prior to turning the witness over to me. She must've made the grave tactical error of waiting to see if I would turn over the right rock. As a defense lawyer, I make my living turning over rocks.

But the doctor nodded and said, "Yes, we both agreed this evidence might be important, although it's not conclusive, and I just talked to Mr. Fredericks yesterday afternoon because I saw him on another case. I had the pictures of this case to take home to prepare for trial today. If it is anybody's fault, it is mine. I am ignorant about golf, and I had this nagging question that occurred to me when I did the initial autopsy, but since there was no preliminary exam testimony required of me, and I have so many cases, I must confess I forgot about it until I pulled the file last night. In all fairness, I'm still not sure that the evidence is exculpatory, nor really what it means, and I'm fully ready to disclose it in my testimony today."

"Mr. Edwards?" The judge seemed to be reappraising me at the same time she reappraised the defense.

"Judge, if Miss Botham was so eager to disclose the information, why didn't she take me aside during recess and tell me? Why did she make the hearsay objection?"

"Good points. Miss Botham?" Judge Alex looked down at Tina like an elementary teacher at a pet pupil caught cribbing on a spelling test.

Tina caught the look and knew her fat was in the fire. She went to her most contrite-little-girl-gone-slightly-astray look. Maybe the dress helped. "I'm very sorry, Your Honor. This morning was so hectic. You know from your experience what it's like trying to get witnesses and evidence organized. The storm last week threw everything out of whack. I had a hall full of witnesses that I was rescheduling and explaining to, and the doctor's reminder about Mr. Fredericks didn't sink in. I'm still not sure I understand the significance. As for the objection, that was just a reaction without thinking. I intended to tell Mr. Edwards and let him decide if he wanted to call Mr. Fredericks. It all caught me off guard. I'll withdraw the objection. I shouldn't have made it."

The judge gazed sternly at her, giving no clue as to her thoughts. I remembered that look in reaction to some of my early courtship antics. It seldom boded well. Tina made a desperate plea for mercy. "I'm sorry, this is a very big case and I'm under a lot of stress and well..." her voice trailed off. "Lastly, I'd say the People shouldn't be punished for my mistake. Punish me. Remove me from the case. But the killer of Amanda Armbruster should not go free because the young prosecutor in charge of the case was overloaded, besieged by unhappy witnesses, and made a mistake."

The judge looked sympathetically at the near trembling prosecutor. It wasn't so long ago since she had been in her place, trying to manage a thirty-person witness list and one hundred and forty exhibits. "Mr. Edwards, I find Miss Botham's and the doctor's explanations to be satisfying. I am denying your motion. I'm glad this has come up now, far better than finding out later and having to retry the case. I am admonishing Miss Botham on the record that this court means business about full disclosure, but since you appear to have found the key to the door I am going to rule no harm, no foul. I'll allow you considerable latitude." She nodded meaningfully at me. "Bailiff, bring the jury back in, please."

The jurors filed in, eight along the top tier of swivel chairs and eight along the bottom. They looked curious. Something significant had happened. The patina of righteousness surrounding Miss Botham had vanished. She had tried to keep something from them and gotten in trouble with the judge. They wanted to know what the fuss was about. I was about to show them.

"Mr. Edwards, you may continue."

"Thank you, Your Honor."

I walked over behind the prosecution table to stand next to the jury box rail to continue questioning the doctor. If you want impact from a witness, this is a good place from which to question. Put the jury in the middle of the conversation.

"Now, doctor, just before the objection you were saying you showed the wound close-ups and the club head close-ups to Mr. Fredericks, a specialist in markings on metal at the state police crime lab."

"Yes, yes I did." The doctor remained assured. He felt he was on the right side of this and was interested in the topic.

"When did this meeting with Mr. Fredericks occur?"

"Yesterday afternoon at the courtroom in Flint. We were both waiting our turn to testify. He asked me why I had two files, and I mentioned I had the Armbruster case to take home with me in preparation for today. He'd heard of the case. He is a most enthusiastic golfer, and when I mentioned the abrasions matching the club head, he wanted to see the pictures."

"You obliged?"

"Of course."

"And?"

"Interesting, very interesting."

"Don't keep us in suspense, doctor. What did he say?"

This was blatant hearsay, an out of court statement offered to prove the matter asserted. I glanced at Miss Botham, who looked for the entire world like a child having a first taste of spinach, but she now had no choice but to swallow it without further fuss.

"He felt that the forehead abrasions did not necessarily match exhibit 5, Mr. Armbruster's golf club. He could not say for certain either way, but he had some questions."

"The nature of the questions?"

"I've described abrasions as a tearing of the skin. Often when the skin is torn by an object, the object leaves an impression from its surface. For example, we can tell whether a person was struck by a baseball bat made of ash from one made of hickory. I compared the abrasion on

Mrs. Armbruster's forehead with the club face. I could see that the pattern matched and the measurements matched the clubhead. The club contained traces of blood, hair, and bone splinters, so I assumed the club that struck the fatal blow also struck the non-fatal blow, you see. But Mr. Fredericks thought perhaps the defendant's club was too new to leave the mark we see here on the forehead."

The courtroom hummed with a quiet buzz. The jurors exchanged looks, and from where I stood, I could see the pad on the lap of the juror closest to me.

"Too new?" So that was the next question I asked.

Dr. Zimmer grabbed a couple of photos from the pile on the fold-out table leaf in front of him. I met him in the middle of the jury box and held each photo as he explained. Every juror bent forward to study the photos.

"Mr. Frederick's opinion is that the photograph of the club head on the defendant's club, exhibit 5, shows a very new club which has hardly ever been used. See how sharp the ridges and grooves are?" He held up the close-ups of the club face.

"And the abrasions on Mrs. Armbruster's forehead differ from what you'd expect if exhibit 5 had inflicted them—how?"

"Toward the middle of the club face, what Mr. Fredericks calls the sweet spot, the abrasions are flatter, less pronounced. He feels that the wounds were inflicted with exactly the same model sand wedge but might have been, and I repeat *might have been*, inflicted with a club that had been played more often, much more often, to the point where the center area ridges and grooves are more depressed and smooth."

"What do you say, doctor?"

"I say I wish I had known more about golf and sweet spots when I was doing the autopsy. I attributed the less pronounced ridges toward the midline to the glancing blow and there being less contact in that area. I still think that may be so."

"But the bottom line is, you believe there is a genuine scientific possibility that exhibit 5, Mr. Armbruster's club, did not inflict the forehead wound?"

He paused, considered and replied. "I must admit that to be so."

Everything he had just given me was a bonus. That was not what I had seen in the pictures at my office the night before. Now I was going to try for a little frosting on the cake, and in the process add a little salt to Tina's wound.

"I remember you saying you would discuss the wound by the left ear and Miss Botham saying we will come to that later. Did I miss it and she did come back to it?"

The way he lifted his bushy right eyebrow over his glasses to glance at me standing on his left, and the curl at the corner of his lips, told me he knew I was sticking the blade into Tina's side. He did his best for her. "No. I must have forgotten." The exchanged looks in the jury box told me they were blaming Tina, not the doc.

"However it happened, let's bring it in front of the jury now. The forehead abrasion and arm bruising are from the initial blow."

"That's my opinion."

"And the fatal wound to the back of the head was the final blow?"

"Definitely."

"How do you believe the wound behind the left ear occurred?"

"Likely as she turned away after the initial attack."

"Please select whichever exhibits best demonstrate the injury by the ear." He turned and rifled through the exhibits at the evidence table, found two photos, and then came back to stand beside me in front of the jury.

"I want you to look at number 35, where you have cleaned the wound and pushed the torn skin back in place. That shows the impression left by the bottom edge of the club face and leaves a mark from the hair-line upwards to the ear, where the laceration becomes very deep, true?"

He nodded. This was the picture that had been tapping at my door.

"Can you take the marker and put a circle on the area which you believe was injured by the bottom leading edge of the club?"

He did so, and showed it to the jury. They looked, but seemed to have had their fill of wound shots.

"Now, doctor, right before the wound gapes open there is a little V mark, do you see that?"

"Ah yes, just where I thought you were going with this."

"Would you point that out for the jury?"

"I'll just draw a little arrow to it." As he did so, the jurors' interest overcame their squeamishness and they craned to see. I asked him to hand the exhibit to the jurors.

They stared over each others' shoulders and pointed as they passed the picture down the front and up the back. I waited till they were done, took the picture from the last juror at the back, and stood next to the doctor, who was now seated in the witness chair. In my hand I had the golf club, exhibit 5, and various close-up pictures of the club head.

"Now, doctor, can you demonstrate to the jury on any of the pictures, or on the club head, a deformity which would match the little V mark above the victim's ear."

He barely looked at the exhibit before answering. "I cannot."

"Why not?"

"There are two possibilities. The first, and what I thought by far more likely before talking to Mr Fredericks, is that when I attempted to re-approximate the wound, I distorted the skin with my fingers."

"And the second possibility?"

"There was a second club of the exact same model used to inflict injury on Mrs. Armbruster."

Probably some in the audience or jury had seen it coming. Nevertheless, the whole court gasped in shock. Miss Theary, the librarian, raised her hand and asked the judge if they could please see exhibit 26 and the club picture again, which the judge allowed. The courtroom was quiet while the jurors did their own sleuthing. This was good, very good. Finally. Something to slow down the rush to judgment express.

"Do you know what could cause the V-shaped distortion on the club that inflicted injury above the ear?"

"I do not. But Mr. Fredericks suggested a stone nick caused by striking a piece of rock embedded in the ground while swinging the club." A couple of male jurors nodded as if they'd had a similar experience on the links.

"So if Mr. Fredericks, the crime lab's tool mark and trace evidence expert, is right, then the wounds were inflicted by two different clubs. Have the police provided you with that club for evaluation?"

"They have not."

"Where did it go?"

"I have no idea, sir."

"Who took it?"

"I cannot say. Nor am I prepared to say there was in fact a second club. Only that there might have been."

I allowed him to return to the witness stand, grasped my chin as if in thought while he situated himself, and then took the jury along the path my thoughts were traveling.

"To conclude then, doctor, there exists a very real scientific possibility that two clubs were used?"

"True."

"Two different people could have wielded the clubs?"

"Also true."

"Or one person could've struck Amanda with the worn sweet spot club with a stone nick, and then, during the five minutes or so you describe proceeding the final blow, grabbed Ted's club to make it look like Ted did it and cover their tracks?"

Miss Botham was out of her chair. "I object, Your Honor, this calls for pure speculation by the doctor."

"I'll rephrase, Your Honor. Is there anything about the wounds and physical evidence that we have just been discussing inconsistent with that scenario? The killer used the missing club in the initial attack and switched to use Ted's club sometime during Amanda's last five minutes."

The doctor gave Miss Botham a few seconds to launch another objection. When none was forthcoming, he put his glasses in his pocket, scratched his nose in deliberation and answered, "I have only acknowledged the possibility of two clubs as a possibility I am unable to eliminate. If you assume that possibility to be true, then your hypothesis is possible."

"And if it is possible, then you can't eliminate it beyond a reasonable doubt?"

"That is true."

"Thank you, doctor. Wonderful to see you again." I said it and meant it as I sat down.

Miss Botham redirected and got the doctor to rehash his direct evidence. But the jury was only listening with half an ear. Somehow the case that had seemed so certain contained a mystery. Their expressions told me they were turning that mystery over in their minds like a Chinese puzzle box. And if they were puzzled, there was hope.

As I made my way to the elevator I even noticed the hostility of the spectators begin to thaw. An old timer in a John Deere hat and coveralls came over and shook my hand. "Still think the husband did it, but you're giving me something to wrestle with. You've got the second club stashed somewhere, eh?"

" 'Fraid not, old fella, but if you find it, let me know."

Lizzie smiled and gave me a thumbs-up as the elevator doors closed on a carload abuzz with speculation.

Wednesday early, I was the only customer sitting in a yellow plastic booth at Subway. Coffee and danish before me, I noted the case was back on the front page of the *Leader*.

"Mystery Killer? Set up?"

read the headline. Art Honnecker was making amends for getting me in trouble with our pretrial chat at the Dew Drop Inn. His story described the prosecution's case as "springing a leak." It referenced prosecutor Botham "receiving a stern judicial reprimand for withholding evidence." The story recapped Dr. Zimmer's testimony, highlighting the second club theory, and concluded, "Edwards' cross exam focused on a missing weapon and a mystery killer who had used the defendant's club to frame him. Further fireworks are expected today when Detective Bliss takes the stand." Couldn't have said it better myself, and I hadn't said a thing.

I knew dealing with Bliss would be no piece of cake. But I had a couple of ideas. Plus, after today I could be a boy again. My three-piece suit for the next few days would consist of shorts, golf shirt, and cap. I could go outside and play. It seemed like months instead of weeks since we'd started jury selection. I was excited to have made a crack in the prosecutor's case. But my reservoir of adrenaline was getting low. I needed a break. Three days of golf with my old pal, Judge Ernie, seemed to be just what the doctor would order, provided I were the doctor.

Meeting Ted in the courthouse lockup prior to going in to trial revealed that our improving prospects were quite visible on Ted. His cheeks had color. His eyes were animated.

"Boy, Ken, I think we're getting somewhere now. A couple of jurors even made eye contact with me as they were leaving yesterday. Maybe you won't have to get into that sex stuff with Amanda and can leave the Dressler thing alone."

"Careful, Ted. Reading juror expressions is like reading tea leaves—prone to misinterpretation. Say, any idea where a second Super Wedge might have come from?"

He shook his head. His eyes blinked rapidly in a way I hadn't noticed before. "I lay in the cell trying to figure it out half the night. No idea. Do you think the police have it, but they're covering it up?"

"Seems unlikely. Make me a list of everybody you know who has one."

"That's about everybody at the club. They were hotter than a pistol until the PGA banned them. Speaking of golf, remember I get to buy a piece of your team. If that's still okay."

I laughed at him, worrying about a golf tournament while on trial for murder. On the other hand, I was about to go play golf for three days in the middle of a murder trial. I hoped I was doing the right thing and said so.

"Don't even think about it, Ken. Frankly, I've been worried about you. You look like you aren't getting enough sleep or enough to eat. You seem pretty wired up, you know. I think your getting a little break from the case is definitely in my best interest. I insist."

As the players took their marks for today's drama, I took a minute to appreciate my client. He seemed more worried about my well being than his own. Throughout he'd always been a gentleman. His confidence in my talents exceeded my own. I hoped I wouldn't let him down.

Detective Bliss cleaned up surprisingly well. The prosecution was nearing the end of their case. Like a fireworks display, they had saved their biggest pyrotechnics for the end of the show. In the presentation of a case, you want to start with an impact witness and finish with one. You bury the losers in between. After their conviction juggernaut began to lose a little momentum yesterday, they needed Bliss to deliver. Although the circumstantial evidence looked bad for Ted, it was, after all, circumstantial. It could lend itself to interpretations consistent with innocence.

You can make inroads on eyewitnesses. Are they biased? Do they have a motive to lie? Were they in a position to see or hear? Were they looking? Was it too dark? Was the sun in their eyes? Were they too far away? Did it happen so fast they didn't form a true impression? Were they drunk or on drugs or asleep? Had the prosecution given them the 20 pieces of silver in the form of a plea bargain so they'd say anything to please the master who held the keys to the cell? Lots of different ways to come at an eyewitness.

But a confession is different. This is your own client admitting he's done it. What are you going to do about that? The best thing is to keep it out. Get the judge to suppress as being taken in violation of the client's Fifth and Sixth Amendment rights to silence and counsel, and/or prove that the procedural niceties had not been observed. But I'd tried that already and lost. Judge Alex rejected my motions as firmly as she had my attempts to bed her early in our relationship. On the circumstances, I thought we might have a shot on appeal. But in Michigan, the governor's appointments to the Court of Appeals and Supreme Court were as conservative on the rights of the accused as they were stingy with the rights of injured plaintiffs in civil cases. Plus, it would be just my luck to draw her date for last year's Christmas ball on the appeals court panel.

We'd be fighting a strong headwind. And by the time the appeal process was done, Ted would have spent at least two years in the state penitentiary at Jackson. The massive prison they called Jacktown was not designed for the country club set.

Seeing how four months in jail had aged and worn Ted down, I very much doubted he'd ever survive to celebrate the unlikely event of a High Court reversal of his conviction. It was now or never.

Apparently Prosecutor Botham realized this too. She had cleaned Detective Bliss up to the point he looked almost avuncular. His perpetual five o'clock shadow had been shaved to leave only the pock marks from what must have been a nasty case of teenage acne. Gone were the nape of the neck curls that used to spill over his collar. His bushy eyebrows were mown close to the skin. The tufts of hair sprouting from his nose and ears had vanished. She must have insisted he go an 18 ½" neck size blue oxford shirt so that the wattles wouldn't protrude above the collar and he'd resist the temptation to unbutton at the top. His new suit had been tailored so his massive shoulders and thighs didn't leave bunches and ripples in the material.

In short, he didn't look much like the menacing ape who had loomed over many a suspect throughout his career. He looked more like a large-boned realtor or car salesman who could stand to lose thirty pounds rather than the bull of a man who could grab a perpetrator by the scruff of the neck and carry him bodily across a lawn to a waiting squad car.

"Now, Ms. Botham, you may call your next witness," Judge Alex announced after the jury settled in.

As Bliss pushed away from the table, his styrofoam water cup teetered. As he went to grab it, it tipped over on the table, spilling on Tina's legal pad. The word "shit" formed on his lips but he swallowed it. You could see the flash of frustration in Tina's face for a split second, but she gathered herself. When Bliss pulled a handkerchief from his back pocket and leaned over the table to mop the water up, he got some on the crotch of his new slacks.

Well, I thought, not such a bad start for their star witness, but when I looked at the jury I detected more sympathy than mirth, so I kept the smirk off of my face and offered a couple of paper towels from under my water carafe.

Once on the stand, with his damp lap concealed from view, Detective Bliss was a model of professionalism. He sat relaxed but erect in his chair. He looked at the prosecutor when she questioned him and glanced at the jury when answering. He spoke clearly and in a well-modulated tone, totally unlike the harsh rumble I had heard him use on subordinates and on me from time to time. Talk about taking a nice pill! He must have been well past the recommended daily allowance.

Miss Botham came around in front of counsel table and leaned comfortably back against it. "Tell the jury your full name and occupation."

"I'm Detective Lieutenant Raymond W. Bliss. I'm employed with the Lake County Sheriff's Department and have been for 27 years."

"What positions have you held with the department over those 27 years of service, Lieutenant?"

"After I graduated from Lake Pointe Central High School, I attended Northwood State University on a football scholarship. I obtained my degree in criminal justice. Then I took a job at the sheriff's department, starting out as a road patrol deputy investigating accidents and doing traffic enforcement for my first five years. I was promoted to corporal on the daytime shift inside the jail. About a year after that, I was selected for the Criminal Investigation and Evidence School put on by the FBI in Quantico, Virginia, and was detached for three months to complete that schooling."

Ms. Botham looked like this was all news to her and acted quite impressed. "Did you receive any degrees for your schooling?"

"Yes, I got a bachelor's in criminal justice from Northwood and I received my certification in Techniques of Criminal Investigation from the FBI."

"Did any of the schooling involve the proper and legal methods for obtaining a statement from a suspect?"

"Oh, yes, ma'am. Both courses devoted considerable time to the rights afforded our citizens under the United States and Michigan Constitutions. I'm thoroughly trained in these areas and have kept up to date with seminars and refreshers put on by your office since then."

I wanted to puke. Here was old "slap it out of them Ray" sounding like the best friend the Bill of Rights ever had.

"Are you married?"

"No, ma'am. I'm a widower. Not long after I got back from the FBI Academy, a drunk driver killed my wife." He and Ted shared the same misery. How strange. "I raised our two young sons on my own."

The three middle-aged ladies in the front row in the jury box whispered to each other. I had no trouble reading the lips of juror No. 3, Mrs. O'Shaunessy. "Poor man."

My office building tenant, Tom Thalberg, was handling the divorce for Angeline Bliss at the time of her fatal accident. In her divorce pleadings, she alleged physical and mental abuse. After their daughter's death, Angeline's parents had fought for custody of the boys, who had been living with their mother at the time of her accident. But Michigan is not too big on grandparent rights, and custody was awarded to the father. Angeline's parents had achieved much more success in the civil suit on behalf of their daughter's estate against the drunk driver and the tavern where he'd gotten a snoot full.

I'd heard that the deeply bereaved Detective Bliss had been in the law office of Fenton Farley the day after the funeral, seeking big bucks, seeing as how he and Angeline were on the verge of reconciling on the eve of her death. But her parents hired Barney Whitehead from Saginaw as soon as they received notice of Bliss's attempt to be appointed personal representative of Angeline's estate. Apparently, they were prepared to testify to repeated bruisings of their daughter at his hands and to his womanizing habits. So ol' Barney and Fenton sat down and had a heart to heart. The insurance company for both the driver and the bar couldn't wait to write checks for policy limits. This attitude would change once any dirty laundry was aired. So a deal was done where all the money went into trust for the boys except $40,000 for the bereaved widower. The parents took nothing and the lawyers split the fee. The dirty linen stayed in the laundry bag.

I knew all of this stuff about Bliss but had no idea how I could get it in. So I had to just sit there while the jury felt sorry for the "poor man." I figured Tina had to know at least some of this history but, since it suited her purposes to canonize him, Saint Raymond he became. If people only knew how legal sausage got made!

After the preliminaries of establishing Bliss as a well trained officer dedicated to the rights of the accused and who carried his own personal burden of grief with dignity, Tina got right down to the heart of the matter.

Wearing a trim outfit of matching herringbone jacket and slacks over a blouse with white ruffles at the collar, she looked quite businesslike as she stood on tiptoes once she moved behind the podium. I wondered idly if she had a boyfriend. Unbidden, an image of her tarted up in black leather, fishnet stockings, and stiletto heels flashed into my head. I'd read somewhere that the average American male thinks of sex every forty-five seconds. Sounds about right. This was hardly the time or place to be confirming that statistic. I got my mind back to the business at hand as Tina got down to cases.

"On the night Amanda Armbruster was beaten to death, did you obtain a statement from her husband?"

"Yes, ma'am. I did. Except it was the early morning hours of April 28th."

"Quite right, detective, pardon me. Describe for the jury the circumstances."

"Well, on my arrival, the defendant was seated on the bottom stair. As the other witnesses testified, he had considerable blood about his person. The golf club lay on the floor between Mr. Armbruster and his wife. Out of concern for his emotional state, I asked him to accompany me to the living room so he didn't become more agitated. Detective Weston advised me the defendant was the only person on scene when deputies arrived. He felt the evidence pointed to Mr. Armbruster and that we should arrest him."

"Did you do so?"

"Oh, not right then. I feel it best not to jump to conclusions. I like to give every citizen a chance to tell their story." I felt the danish turn over in my stomach. Bliss sounded like Mr. Rogers. So calm. So pleasant. So thoughtful. So fair. The menacing growl that usually punctuated his speech was gone. This man's tone was measured, dispassionate, professional. If you were ever going to be arrested for murder, this was the understanding public servant into whose hands you would want to fall. Just the kind of father figure to whom a guilt-wracked murderer could unburden his conscience.

"Please describe for the jury your actions at the scene."

"Well, after making sure Mr. Armbruster was kept under observation, I reviewed the evidence gathered by our department and conferred with Detective Weston. We agreed that as I am the senior detective, I would handle the case. Mr. Armbruster appeared quite shaken. The last thing I wanted to do was to compound the grief and distress by arresting the husband if he had no responsibility. However, my instincts and training told me he was our number one suspect, so, like I mentioned a minute ago, I took him aside from the trauma of his battered wife into the living room."

"Did you interview him there?"

"Not right away. I made sure he had a moment to gather himself. I got him a glass of water."

"That's true" read the note Ted pushed in front of me while Bliss continued.

"I waited a minute and asked him if he could explain what happened. At first he said he didn't know; he had heard a noise, came downstairs, found his wife on the floor, and called 911. I told him unless he could give us more information, I would have no choice but to book him for suspicion of murder."

"What was his reaction?"

"He broke down. He was bawling, begging to be with his wife. Wanted to go with her in the ambulance. I told him I needed much more information before that could happen. He agreed to answer all my questions, but asked if he could have an attorney there with him. Normally I would have the attorney see him at the jail, but because of Mr. Armbruster's standing in the community and the level of his distress over his wife, I made an exception and agreed to let him call Mr. Edwards. I wanted to give the man the benefit of the doubt."

"Did Mr. Edwards come to the scene?"

"Yes, but not until much later. I found out Mr. Edwards drives one of them fancy foreign jobs which gave him a spot of trouble." The two Chevy workers on the jury panel nodded, indicating it served me right and that my stock had just touched a new low with them. I had to admire Bliss for the cheap shot.

"So did you wait for Mr. Edwards to get his automotive problems resolved?"

"No, in fact, we were making ready to take Mr. Armbruster in to the jail when deputies notified me that the neighbor, M. Stanton Browne, was at the front door claiming to be the defendant's attorney."

"Did you permit Mr. Browne access to the defendant?"

"Certainly. They conferred in the library portion of the living room. I remained in the room as I needed to keep Mr. Armbruster under observation. Would be embarrassing if I left a murder suspect alone and he killed himself or his attorney or just ran off. But, as the room was quite large, they had their privacy."

Wow! Bliss was pushing all the right buttons: careful vigilant cop, empathetic to the suspect's needs. And oh, by the way, the suspect is a big shot with a huge living room with a library, no less.

"Did there come a time when the defendant agreed to speak with you?"

"Yes, he and Mr. Browne conferred for about ten minutes, and then lawyer Browne told me his client had nothing to hide and was willing to talk."

"Did you advise Mr. Armbruster of his Miranda rights?"

"Of course. I read them on tape, and both Mr. Armbruster and Mr. Browne signed the form acknowledging they understood those rights."

Tina held up the tape cassette and had him identify it. Then moving away from the podium, she asked, "Is the statement you obtained on the tape?"

"No, ma'am. I read the rights, then rewound the tape and replayed that part to make sure everything was working. Then I took his statement thinking the recorder was working. I also kept notes of my interview. After he finished I realized, although the little red light was working on my recorder, the tape itself had broken right where I left off with the rights. I put another cassette in, but by that time Mr. Armbruster was going into shock. He was trembling and crying and making this funny gasping noise. He said he just couldn't go over it again. So out of concern for him, I let him and lawyer Browne go with a deputy to the bathroom and wrote up my notes of what he had said. When they got back from the bathroom he was still shaky, but both Armbruster and Browne were given the statement I wrote from my notes. They reviewed it and I asked them to sign. Well, Mr. Armbruster signed and Mr Browne initialed to the statement's accuracy."

I objected to the statement's admission to preserve my objection for appeal, thereby incurring jury dirty looks. But in came the statement. And unless I could do something to undermine its credibility, it would be the torpedo to sink our ship. This is what the torpedo looked like:

> My name is Theodore Armbruster. I'm 62. My wife Amanda and I had been married eight years. We have no children. Tonight my wife and I went to the club for dinner and drinks with the Simpsons. After dinner, Jim Simpson and I went downstairs to finish a gin game left over from the afternoon. Amanda and Jillian stayed upstairs in the bar. The game dragged on and on and I ended up drinking quite a bit. I ended up losing $1,500.
>
> When we finished, I came upstairs to get Amanda and go home. But she left a message with the bartender that she and Jillian had gone to Heather Hollows. Jim and I went to pick them up. Amanda was with Jillian and some lounge lizard in a booth and wasn't ready to come home. I didn't want to stay because I had to get up early to go up north with friends for a golf outing. We disagreed about her staying. I was upset when I left. I drove myself home. I am responsible for her death.
>
> Got home at about 12:15 a.m. and went to bed. I heard some noise downstairs, saw her at the foot of the stairs. I ran downstairs yelling. I grabbed the golf club. I hit her with it. There was blood everywhere. The club must have broken the mirror. The club is called the Solarz Super Wedge. It's mine. That's Amanda's blood on it. Where you found it is where I left it when I held her and tried to help her. About two months ago, I increased her life insurance policy from $100,000 to $2,000,000. My company is the beneficiary. During our annual insurance review my agent suggested we could increase her policy through the company account. Business has not been good recently. My bank line of credit comes due in six weeks.
>
> I had heard people say she was cheating on me. But I didn't

> tolerate that kind of talk. I loved her. I never wanted to hurt her. I didn't want to kill her. I don't know what happened. I never hit her before. It all seems like a dream, a nightmare.

Ted's scrawled signature was barely legible at the bottom. Even Browne's initials were a little shaky.

Tina asked some follow-up questions but kept it short. The jurors couldn't wait to get their hands on the statement, and the judge agreed to their note asking to take it into the jury room over the lunch hour. Coming back to the attorney's conference room with two bags of chips and an orange soda, I could see the wake of the torpedo as it bore down on me. If I didn't find an evasive maneuver, the good ship *Defense* was taking a hit amidships and going down by the stern with no survivors. I had known from the moment I came back into the case that this moment must come. But still I was nervous as a cat. I could only manage half a bag of chips. I had to tarnish the halo of St. Raymond. I had to cast some doubt on the statement. I had to keep us afloat. Otherwise the remainder of the trial would be no more than picking through flotsam and jetsam.

When I rose to examine, Bliss smiled at me as if we were lodge brothers. Bliss and I had crossed swords in the courtroom before. Then, his distaste for lawyers in general and me in particular had seethed just below the surface. I could only imagine the time Tina had spent in the woodshed with him sanding off the rough edges. I added a whip to my earlier fantasy image of Tina. I stood three or four steps directly in front of the witness stand, matching Bliss's phony smile with one of my own.

During the lunch recess I'd asked the bailiff to run sixteen copies of the statement to hand out to the jurors. Prior to beginning cross, the judge granted my request to distribute one copy to each of the jurors with a slight "you must be crazy" look. Since it was in evidence anyway, there was no sense in treating it like wolfsbane. That would make me the wolfman.

"Afternoon, detective. In whose hand is the statement written?"

"Mine."

"Other than his signature, not a single word was written by Ted Armbruster—true?"

"No, but they were spoken by him."

"Spoken by a man you described as going into shock?"

"You could say that."

"Were your notes word for word verbatim of what he said?"

"No, but I was listening very closely."

"Could you have missed a word or two?"

"Yes."

"How about a little word like the word 'never'?"

"He didn't use that word."

I grabbed the statement from the evidence table, walked over beside him and felt him tense as I got close. Holding my finger on the bottom line of the statement, I started to ask. "Look here, detective, at the bottom. He used the word 'never' not once, but twice, in 'I never wanted to hurt her,' and then next sentence, 'I never hurt her before.' "

He barely let me finish in his rush to answer. "Yes, yes, I forgot that. I thought you were going to ask about earlier."

The danger in overcoaching is that the actor thinks he has heard his cue line from Act Two while you are still in Act One. Tina had prepared him for where I was about to go next, and he had jumped the gun. I was sure she would have warned him, since the statement was in his hand and was his synopsis of what Ted had told him, that I would try to change the whole meaning of the statement by adding or subtracting a word. The first beads of sweat glistened on his forehead. I stepped away from the heavy scent of Old Spice and tried to capitalize on his mistake.

"You have studied and reviewed this statement in preparation to testify, have you not?"

"Yep. I mean, yes sir. I have."

"You did so a number of times with Miss Botham?"

"I guess."

"As recently as this morning?"

"No."

"Last night, then?"

"Yes."

"And yet after numerous reviews, you forgot the word 'never' was spoken by Ted twice within that statement.."

He seemed a little flummoxed, reaching into his suit coat for a hanky and mopping his brow, and finally must have remembered another planted stock answer.

"Gosh, Mr. Edwards, the courtroom is your beat. Not mine. You make me a little nervous."

"Really?" I asked skeptically, raising both eyebrows. "You've testified in court over a hundred times in the course of your career?"

"Thereabouts."

"Uh-huh. Let's go back to the use of the word 'never' you thought I was going to ask about."

I moved back into the area right next to the witness stand and leaned my right shoulder on the rail. At that range the stale smell of tobacco and what I guessed had been lunchtime sauerkraut broke through the miasma of cologne. Neither one of us liked being that close to the other. He stiffened. He knew where I was going and that he had hurt himself by jumping too soon earlier.

"See right here, detective, where you wrote 'I grabbed the golf club. I hit her with it.' " He nodded.

"You would agree with me that if you forgot the word 'never' between the words 'I' and 'hit,' this would be no confession at all. Would it?"

The look he gave me beneath the craggy arches of his eye sockets should be reserved only for slugs and maggots. But this was the question he was prepped for. So he swallowed the bile of animus and answered pleasantly.

"I reckon so. But he never used that word." He paused. "At that point of the statement, I mean."

"Never say never, huh, detective? Anyway, if I heard you right, if you made the same mistake the night of Amanda Armbruster's death that you made here in the court a minute ago and forgot the word 'never,' then, instead of a confession, this statement is a declaration of innocence, isn't it?" I cocked my head and moved away while he answered.

"That didn't happen. Anyway, are you claiming where he said 'I am responsible for her death' that he really said I am never responsible? And where he said he grabbed the club, then said he hit her, that he grabbed the club to never hit her? C'mon, get real."

I smiled. This was more like the Bliss I knew and loathed. The veneer of amiability was peeling away. There was an argumentative edge to his voice.

"I don't know what he said that morning, detective, only what you claim he said. And we've already seen that you, like the rest of us, can be a little forgetful. Haven't we?"

He pursed his lips like he was tasting a lemon. "Whatever."

I had him produce his notes from that night from which he had composed the statement and showed them to the jury. They were a hodgepodge of shorthand covering three pages of a pocket spiral note pad. Everything that was on the statement was in there, just not in the same order as written in the statement. He acknowledged that to be true, explaining, "I put them in order so they would make sense. Something wrong with that?"

"Not so long as you admit what the jury is holding in their hands are words written in the hand of Ray Bliss and put in an order that made sense to Ray Bliss. Do you admit that much?"

Asking him that, I moved near him again. I noticed that each time I stood next to him, his temperature seemed to rise. He probably wasn't used to being crowded and didn't like it. Tina objected that I was badgering the witness. Before the judge ruled, I asked him.

"Detective, do you feel scared of a skinny beanpole like me?"

He snorted and managed a comeback that broke the courtroom into gales of laughter. "Never."

When she quit smiling, the judge ordered me to stand a little further away. Her smile at this interchange triggered a flash of nostalgia. I remembered Alex telling one and all that she'd fatten me up after we married. I shook my head to chase the memory as I backed away from Bliss. The extra space was a relief, as the smell of sweat had begun to admix with the sauerkraut, tobacco and after- shave, triggering an olfactory gag reflex.

Once the no-man's-land between us had widened, Bliss explained that getting a second tape from another officer wouldn't work because it was obvious that Ted was on the verge of collapse, adding that "the EMT wanted to take him to the hospital, but since he'd just confessed to murder, I told her we'd watch him closely at the jail."

"So you took a statement from a man who was shaking, gasping, crying out in grief, on the verge of collapse. I take it his speech wasn't clear and distinct between the sobbing and gasping?"

"I had him repeat some things."

"Which things?"

"Don't remember exactly."

"And you agree that the handwriting of his signature on both the Miranda warning and the so-called statement is so shaky as to be almost illegible?"

"I don't know what his hand normally looks like."

I confronted him with Ted's signature on the insurance documents, and he grudgingly acknowledged there was quite a difference.

"So in conclusion, on this statement you got Ted's signature from a trembling man on the verge of collapse, in such bad shape you couldn't do a retape, and where qualified medical personnel thought he ought to be in the hospital. Am I right?"

"He knew what he was doing. He answered my questions. Whatever shape he was in, how do you explain a fancy lawyer like Mr. Browne signing his initials if I didn't get it right? How about that, counselor?"

"Guess we'll have to ask Mr. Browne, won't we? You know, by the way, lawyer Browne stood up in court at the preliminary hearing and denied the accuracy of this statement?"

"Lawyers," Bliss sneered, as if that word explained all that was wrong with the justice system. I let the viscous animosity of his last comment congeal before the jury. A glance to the panel revealed they were sitting tense with their hands gripping the swivel chairs. I could only hope they could see that St. Raymond had a darker side. To break the tension, I walked to counsel table and took a sip of water.

From the front of counsel table I took the cross exam in a different direction. I asked him why, on the night of the murder, there was a discussion of Ted's business and his insurance. Probably not my best question.

"Part of my training. I'm trained that most murders are, like Miss Botham said to the jury, for love or money. I always ask about insurance and marital problems. Two million bucks is a lot of motive."

I had done what I could on the statement. So I turned to a couple of other areas to finish. Cross exam should be a raid on pre-selected targets, not a full frontal assault. Get in and get out. Hopefully alive. I strolled over toward the jury box, letting the silence serve as a punctuation mark for a change of direction.

"You remember arranging for a couple of deputies to take a shot at my dog up at the Armbruster cottage?" I asked. This caused a stir with the jurors and spectators. Even Judge Alex removed her glasses and looked concerned. But not with Bliss.

"Never happened," Bliss tossed off as it were nothing. "All a misunderstanding. Had a report of a burglar with a vicious dog. That animal of yours is closer to a lion than a dog. Knocked me over. Anyway, nobody got hurt."

"No thanks to you," I fired back, my anger obvious. He folded his arms across his chest as if to say, "What are you going to do about it?"

We stood like that, glaring at each other, before the judge interjected. "You have a question for the witness, counsel?"

I collected myself and nodded.

"Detective, I was just wondering about the affidavit you swore out authorizing a search of the Armbruster family cabin, where the shot was fired. Says you were looking for 'financial documents in possession of the deceased.' What kind of financial documents are you referring to, detective?"

"Nothing in particular. We knew of a leather valise belonging to the deceased we couldn't locate at the family home. Just tying up loose ends."

"Your affidavit says, in your own words, that these documents 'might provide a motive for murder.' Are you saying you had information that financial documents could provide a reason for someone to kill Amanda?"

He examined the affidavit to study his own words. He was obviously stalling while working on an answer. When none suggested itself, he played dumb.

"You got me there, counselor. Maybe something about the money troubles the Armbrusters were having. We got a call about a burglar at a cottage I didn't know the Armbrusters had, and so I kinda rushed that affidavit. So I'm not sure what I was thinking." He held his hands palms up as if to say "What's the big deal?"

I grabbed my earlobe and debated with myself whether to ask the next question. By the time I resolved the issue, I found that I'd wandered all the way back to the defense table. I turned and asked it, holding my chin pensively and looking straight at him.

"Those financial documents might not concern a certain civic board for whom Mrs. Armbruster was investigating misplaced funds at the time of her death, would they, detective?"

A lot of things happened all at once. Tina rose and began objecting. The jury looked dazed, like this was one surprise too many so soon after lunch. The crowd began to buzz. And just as I saw the fleeting look of uncertainty cross Bliss's face, Ted was pulling my sleeve with such force I couldn't ignore it. I leaned over to have him whisper forcefully in my ear.

"Ken, you promised not to drag Dressler into this without my okay. I took your word. What are you doing? I don't want this. If I can't trust you, just let me plead guilty." I had to pry his grip from my sleeve, as the judge was addressing me in an angry tone.

"Counsel. This is the third time I'm asking you. Do you have a response to Miss Botham's relevance objection?" I tried to slow things down long enough to fashion an answer in the midst of an angry prosecutor, a perturbed judge, and a client who felt so betrayed he wanted to plead guilty.

"Sorry, Your Honor, I was conferring with my client. I meant no disrespect. I think for the present I'll withdraw the question, subject to exploring the matter further, should the need arise." I temporized the best I could while standing on the quicksand of an angry client who was threatening to bail out.

The judge was less than satisfied. Her neck reddened in a way that in the past had meant trouble. Her voice trembled with suppressed rage.

"Mr Edwards, I've warned you about courtroom theatrics. I won't have that in my courtroom. I'll await the end of the trial to consider sanctions." She turned to the jurors and substituted firmness for the displeasure with which she had addressed me. "You will disregard the last question completely. Is that understood?" To a one, the jurors nodded like chastised first graders. But I made a mental bet that this was one white rabbit not so easily forgotten.

I marked the affidavit as an exhibit, but the judge wouldn't admit it without even waiting for Tina's objection. "You just don't give up, do you? The affidavit is an out-of-court statement and therefore hearsay. Moreover, no sufficient showing of relevance having been made, it is not admitted. Move on, counsel," she ruled with an imperious wave of her hand. I felt an eerie parallel with her dismissal of me as no longer relevant all those years ago. This was a lot of grief for one question I almost didn't ask in the first place. I gathered myself and moved on.

"You heard Dr. Zimmer testify to wound marks indicating a second club?"

The uncertainty was long gone. Nobody enjoyed watching me roast on the spit more than Bliss. The sweat was gone. He looked calm, cool as a cucumber.

"Don't know anything about that. Way out of my area."

"As the detective in charge, did you inventory the scene looking for a second club?"

"Yes, the murder weapon, the one with the victim's blood, bone, and brains on it, was on the floor between the body and where the defendant sat on the stairs, and is now in this court. The police report and photos show three golf bags against the wall. I watched while every club in each bag was pulled and inspected. Two of them had a similar wedge. The defendant's wedge was on the floor. None of the clubs in the other bags had any bodily fluids or flesh on them. We took them into evidence anyway."

"Did you send them to the crime lab for comparison?"

"Nope. We had the bloody club, the defendant's confession, him with a bruise on his head and a broken finger like he'd been in a struggle. Two of your country club buddies were begging to get their golf sets back since the weather turned nice. I called lawyer Browne and the prosecutor, and they both okayed release. Since Dr. Zimmer's testimony yesterday, I sent a deputy to go retrieve the wedges from Mr. Simpson and Mr. Dykes. They are at the crime lab as we speak. Good enough for you?"

"We'll see." Then I played the last strong card I thought I had.

"Say, detective. You heard your fellow detective, Phillip Weston, say that in all his years he'd never had the non-duty detective pull rank and take over a case from the duty detective. Seemed a little put out by it. Ever happen before?"

Bliss had been prepped for this too. He answered comfortably.

"Sorry Phil felt that way. But technically, I had the first call on the case."

I was surprised by his answer.

"Wasn't the 28th Weston's night?"

"It was. But you see, I was put in charge of a unit the department got federal funding for about a year ago. After what happened to my wife, its mission is very important to me: stopping drunk drivers. Deputies Doyle and Meeks work eight p.m. to four a.m. and report directly to me. They called me after the bartender called from Heather Hollows. Told me of the scene between Mr. and Mrs. Armbruster and reported that Mr. Armbruster was drunk and refused to let anyone drive him home. They wanted my authorization to go to the house and test him for sobriety. God forgive me, I told them no, since they hadn't actually seen him drive. So when the call came in of domestic violence at the Bonnie Brae address, they called me back to notify me. I dressed and drove out there, praying it wasn't what the radio traffic sounded like. I had first responsibility, and that's what I told Detective Weston. Plus, I had my own guilt to deal with for letting him go on the drunk driving. Me of all people." The last he said with a sigh of sad resignation. I asked him why this information was nowhere in the police reports.

"Probably should have been. I guess the deputies didn't want to make me look bad for going easy on the guy."

"Why does the dispatch log make no reference to your contacts with Meeks and Doyle?"

"They called on a cell phone."

"Don't department regulations require you to go through central dispatch so there is a record?"

He shrugged, canting his lantern jaw and stroking his cheek. He must have neglected to tell Tina this detail, and so had no rehearsed answer.

"Technically, I guess they do. But I've got a standing order in the DUIL unit to call me if they have any questions. I'm in charge. I made that rule. Okay?"

I mucked around a minute or two with his ignoring my instructions and granting Browne access and giving me the bum's rush, but he pounded that back over the net without much trouble.

"I let the defendant make his call. I agreed to wait till you got there. Mr. Browne showed and the defendant decided to go with him. I'm not in the lawyer referral business."

On redirect Tina had Bliss swear up and down that Ted had admitted striking Amanda and that he knew the difference between admission and denial. He concluded by saying, "I gave the statement to Mr. Armbruster to review and sign. Then I did the same for his lawyer. What more can a police officer do?"

Judge Alex thanked the jurors for their indulgence and understanding about her sister's wedding, to amiable nods from the jury box. She reminded them there would be no court until next Tuesday, and instructed them to discuss the case with no one and to avoid the media. With that we were free for the next six days.

Only I wasn't free. I had an angry client who felt I had broken faith with him. I needed to know if I still had a client, and if that client was still willing to fight the charges. The deputies were none too thrilled at the delay in transporting Ted back to jail, but agreed, once Ted was done in the bathroom, to leave us alone in the fourth floor lockup. I sat staring at the "My Lawyer Sucks" graffiti carved into the table as I waited for Ted.

As strung out, exhausted, frightened, and nervous as I had been feeling, the prospect of Ted's caving panicked me. "Please, Lord," I began to pray, but then the metal-grilled door screeched open. Ted looked tired and sad. He slumped into the wooden chair across from me, staring at the floor. We sat in silence, a couple of lost souls. I flashed back to that first night in the jail holding area.

Finally, I broke the ice. "Ted, what's this plead guilty crap? I'm giving everything I've got because I believe in you. And you want to fold?"

He didn't answer right away. But he did look up at me, his eyes resigned and very weary. At last in a whisper he spoke.

"You lied to me. We had an agreement. Nothing about Dressler without my okay. Why would you do that?" His gaze was soul-searching.

Rather than argue about the need for me to have my hands completely free to fight for him, I acknowledged I'd made a mistake.

"Ted, I don't work with a script. I just go where the witness lets me go. I felt like Bliss was coming unglued and he might be on the verge of revealing something major. I agree. I should've asked you beforehand, but in the heat of trial, sometimes you ask questions first and shoot the bull about it later. Know what I mean?"

I don't think I breathed as I awaited his response. He took a deep breath, exhaled, and smiled. Man, was I glad to see that smile.

"You were worried I'd plead and rob you of your chance for glory." I started to protest, but he held his hands up as a stop sign and went on. "That's why I wanted you. God knows why, but you love this stuff. I was and am very disappointed you crossed a line we agreed on. But I'm not going to plead guilty to killing the woman I love when I didn't do it. I spent my whole life trying to follow in my father's footsteps, be a man of character. And I'll be damned if I'll throw a lot of needy folks who depend on Dressler into the gutter just to save my own skin. I'm not like that. Can you understand that?"

We discussed the potential value of Dressler to his defense, with him agreeing, if I could prove that it was the motive for Amanda's murder, it came in. I agreed that I'd get his okay before I opened that box in court again. In the last few minutes before the deputy rattled the door, we talked golf. The tournament, and his having a piece of the action, brought color and life to Ted. I promised him daily telephone updates, and thought, as I rode down the elevator in the silent courthouse, that he probably was going to get more vicarious pleasure out of my playing than the actual pleasure my overwrought psyche would allow me to have.

I felt no elation sitting in my office waiting until it was time for the tournament kickoff dinner that night. I'd kept up a brave facade for my secretaries, Janice and Yvonne, when they wanted their daily update from the front. But the truth was that my commando raid of cross exam on Bliss had exacted heavy casualties on our forces without doing equal damage to theirs.

Bliss had been on the verge of losing it and displaying his true colors at the time I had asked the Dressler Foundation question, which nearly cost me my client. After that hullabaloo, Bliss was like a pitcher who had survived a bases loaded jam. He found his rhythm for the next inning. His regret over reining the deputies in on going to the Armbruster house from Heather Hollows had restored some of the luster to St. Raymond's halo. Plus, Tina had nicely timed Bliss's appearance so that the jurors would go home for the next six days thinking "He confessed. So why are they fighting it?" They'd probably answer that question the same way Bliss had when confronted with Browne's disavowal of the statement. "Lawyers."

45

Driving out to the club for the tourney kick-off dinner, I tried to switch gears from the life and death combat of the legal arena to the frivolity of a golf tournament. I'd play both to win. However, the consequence of one so dwarfed the other as to make it seem meaningless. I wondered what Lizzie, with her starry-eyed dreams of becoming a lawyer, would think if she knew her avatar was fooling around on a golf course instead of concentrating on the case. Hell, I didn't think much of it myself.

Every time I tried to put the trial to bed, a little voice in my head kept pushing it into my consciousness. "You are missing something. Pay attention!" I'd thought with the revelation on Dr. Ramirez's ball marker about TNPC, that I'd seen what Amanda was trying to show me in my dream. Yet she continued to haunt my nights, saying, "Follow me. I'll show you." Try as I might, I couldn't grasp it.

As I reran Bliss's testimony in my head, I kept coming back to my regret about giving him the opening to humanize himself with his remorse over keeping Meeks and Doyle on a leash. As I turned into the jammed club parking lot, the image of that shark and his pilot fish that day outside the jail floated to the surface. And what did that fleeting look of panic in the shark's eyes signify, when he was asked, yesterday on the stand, about an investigation into missing money at a civic body?

Then the fanfare and hoopla of the tournament took over. Man, what a used car lot. Continentals, DeVilles, BMWs, Vipers, Jags, Benzes, Navigators, Grand Cherokees, all new and shiny. I found a sliver of a parking spot near the chipping green, where an errant shot could leave a dent, and parked my thirty-year-old relic. Brightly colored pennants hung from wires crisscrossing the lot. They flapped and shimmered in the last breeze of day. A huge "Welcome Contestants" banner hung above the entrance.

Halfway across the lot, I stopped to drink it all in. The sun lit an empty course. The fertile aroma of freshly mown grass filled my nostrils. I could hear the gang mower humming nearby. A lone golfer stood silhouetted on the range, whacking soaring iron after soaring iron in a rhythmic cadence.

With the trial, I hadn't gotten cranked up for the tournament this year. But now, I could feel the competitive sap begin to rise. Thank you, Judge Alex, for having your sister get married. I need a break, and this tournament is just the ticket. I marveled at my relief that it was Alex's sister and not Alex who was tying the knot. Why should I care? The chances of rekindling that relationship were less than the odds of winning Ted's case.

But there I was, standing among all the horsepower in that parking lot, and the image in my head was her spur-of-the-moment detour into a bridal shop years ago. We'd stopped at the mall to pick up toiletries when she took my arm and turned into the store, a coquettish smile curling her mouth. She left me with the saleslady while she went to try on a wedding gown. When she came out, the saleslady commented, "Oh, my God, you look radiant." And she did look radiant on that day only months before we were finished. The image was as clear now as when I had stood there gaping at the woman whom I foolishly thought had just said yes before I'd even worked up the courage to propose.

I shook my head to banish the memory. I inhaled the country air, lightly scented with fertilizer, savoring the freedom of being outdoors and on vacation from responsibility. "Let the games begin," I whispered, grasping the brass ring handle on the heavy oak main entrance door.

The hum, buzz and clatter from within engulfed me. Laughter, loud voices, and hilarity were the order of the day. My lunchtime bag of chips was now only a faint digestive memory. The smell of cooked beef reached out like a shepherd's crook, drawing me in. As I entered, the blank space on the president's wall of photographs stood out clearly. The dining room was full from one end to the other. Circular and rectangular tables were surrounded by diners, most still in golf attire from Stag Day. The staff moved among them like hummingbirds, bobbing to gather salad plates and moving on. Good, I hadn't missed dinner. The head table stretched north and south across the front of the room, which was backed by floor-to-ceiling windows looking east over the course. The leaves of the trees were dappled by the setting sun.

I looked over the sea of members. Over in the right corner I saw Judge Ernie's right arm raised as he stuffed a cinnamon sticky bun in his mouth with his left hand. I started to work my way through the tables and staff, fending off wisecracks all the way.

"Hey, it's Clarence Darrow."

"How's it going, F. Lee?"

"Ted better hope you're a better lawyer than you are a golfer."

"Checking out the scene of the crime, counselor?"

I smiled, shook a couple of hands and kept moving. My salad plate was just disappearing into a server's hands as I sat down.

"Not quite done with that, Sally," I said, intercepting it. "Hey guys, what did I miss?"

Ernie was in high spirits. He grabbed the back of my shoulders. "All right, boys, I got my horse. I'm going to ride him all the way. Right, horse?"

"Neigh," I replied.

Retired probate judge Lenny Unser sat next to Ernie. Lenny got full value from his membership. If it wasn't raining, he was playing golf. At his age, his ball didn't travel far off the tee, but from one hundred yards in, he was money. He patted the open seat to his left and reached for my hand. "Feel like a little action between our teams?" Lenny missed a wagering opportunity as often as he did a golfable day.

"You haven't got enough of my money already? Let me see who is in our flight."

I grabbed one of the tournament programs and started from the back, looking for our flight. The program was like a racing form, rating each team's chances against the other seven teams in the flight. The tournament committee was supposed to flight the teams by handicap, but you could tell who had friends on the committee by where their team was flighted. Looking at the form, I guessed I had pissed somebody off. Ernie was distressed by the seeding.

"Oh my God, Ken. We're all the way up to fourth flight. There's real golfers in here." I noted that Judge Lenny and his partner, Sam Fretter, were in the flight with us.

"Shit, what are you two sandbaggers doing back with Ernie and me?" They were, at worst, 14 handicappers and had won in lower flights.

Sam pretended offense and replied, "Lenny and I have been playing horribly for a month now. Check our scores on the computer or in the book. We stink."

Ernie spoke up. "I looked. Seems like every year for a month before the tournament, you two guys go into the tank. Then comes the tournament, and it all comes back to you. And I see the handicapper has you guys picked to win." I glanced at the sheet. Sure enough, Team Five, Lenny and Sam, was described "Can't Miss."

I scanned the rest of the flight to find M. Stanton Browne and his partner, Dr. Richard Richmond, an ob-gyn, were the second favorites. Richmond, alternatively referred to as "Baby Doc" and "Richie Rich," was rumored to turn off his beeper and cell phone during big matches, leaving nurse midwives to fill in at delivery. The handicapper's comments read:

Dr. Richard Richmond—"Can Deliver."

M. Stanton Browne—"Will Chip In."

Pick number three was the brothers team of Sven and Daj Riklis. Either of them could make my best drive look like a nine iron. Needless to say, Ernie and I weren't among the favorites. The notes behind our names read,

Hon. Ernie Schneider—"Judged To Be At His Best."

Ken Edwards—"Trouble Defending."

It was a relief to have my mind on something other than the case and my stomach full of succulent steak. I laughed and kidded with the other guys and even let my partner talk me into a bad bet with Lenny and Sam.

The highlight of the evening was the team auction that followed twenty minutes of off-color jokes from the club president. Every team in every flight is auctioned off in something they call a Calcutta, for reasons which escape me. Perhaps because of the teeming babble of shouting and hucksterism.

The members love action. They form syndicates large and small. They pool their money and knowledge. They study the handicap book, looking to see whether a player was getting better or worse. They know who has a bad back or whose putter is AWOL. Some syndicates have twenty members each putting in $500. Some have four who each ante up $2,500. They devise intricate strategies designed to bid up the price of teams they don't want and leave somebody else holding the bag, thereby enriching the betting pool for that flight. The whole thing is akin to horse players studying a racing form. I remembered Ted to be an eager punter in years past and lifted my Labatts in a silent toast to him.

In each auction, a team could bid to buy itself. If somebody else was the top bidder, the team then had until tee time the next day to buy one half of the team's action for one half of the auction sale price. The syndicates knew which teams were determined to buy themselves and how to bid them up, causing that team to pay top dollar. This too, served to expand the pool.

The auction was great theater. The cheapest pool in the worst flight would total $4,000. In the championship flight, the prized teams would go for $1,500 to $2,000 and the total pool would exceed $10,000. The winning team got 45% of the total pool; second place, 30%; consolation bracket winners, 15%; Thursday winners, 5%; and Friday winners, 5%. Egos were involved. Rivalries and cliques clashed. By the time the auction started, everybody was pretty well liquored up.

Ernie and I always talked ahead of time about how much we would be willing to pay for our team. So, during the auction for the fifth flight, he and I walked back to the upstairs bar.

"Ken, whose wife did you screw to get us in this flight? We don't have a chance," Ernie muttered

"Looks like winning last year didn't help us," I replied.

"Yeah, but two flights? We were in the sixth flight last year with a bunch of eighteen to twenty handicappers. Now we're playing with fourteen to fifteens. We're going to get killed."

"1 think we are in a little over our heads. These guys aren't Jack Nicklaus or Arnie Palmer, you know. They are better than us, but not that much better. We'll really need to ham and egg it."

The trick to success in this format is for at least one partner to play well on every hole. You can be ball in pocket on a hole as long as your partner is making par. Then when he's in trouble, you make the par. This is called playing ham and egg or Mutt and Jeff. You don't want to play Frick and Frack, where you both disappear on a hole together.

"I checked. We went for $700 last year and paid $1,400 to win," said Ernie, showing me last year's form. I looked at it and remembered how sweet it was to finally win. For years we had been the runners-up or consolation winners. Good for a small payoff, but not exactly the thrill of victory. Last year we had won it all. Ernie wedged out of the bunker on No. 17, turning disaster into a one-up birdie. The opposition was demoralized. My bogey on eighteen tied the hole and secured the victory. The trophy and the cash were ours. The green blazer hung in my closet. We had relived the match about twenty times over beers while the snow covered the ground last winter. But that was then. The price now was that we'd been moved up by the handicappers to the point where we weren't likely to repeat.

"At least we'll go cheap," I said.

"Let's not spend over $300," replied Ernie.

"Okay, whatever. Let's play loose and have fun."

By the time we had gotten back from the bar and sat down, they were ready to auction our flight They started to auction each flight worst to first. Sure enough, the emcee, Jeff Stallings, started with us, Team Six. He sounded like a tobacco auctioneer.

"Last year's winners, albeit a flight or two lower. They are stepping up in class. These two are gamers. Outside of doctors, who else has more time to work on their game than a judge and a lawyer? Saw Judge Ernie the last couple of nights on the range. Shot after shot. What do I hear? Let's start out at $200."

Silence. I waited a discreet period and raised my hand. Jeff recognized me.

"They know something, boys. Last year's winners for $200. Come on now, do I hear $250?" I saw M. Stanton's Rolex ride his right arm into the air two tables down. Bastard, just raising the cost of poker. He didn't want a piece of our team. He just wanted it to cost me more. Jeff recognized the bid.

"Smart bet by lawyer Browne. You got $250. Do I hear $300?" Then he paused.

"Three going once, going twice..."

I raised my hand on going three times and Jeff pointed at me.

"Team bids $300 for itself. They are stealing it, fellas! Looking for $350, looking for $350."

Up went the Rolex again, this time accompanied by a smirk. Jeff pointed at him.

"M. Stanton Browne at $350. Smart buy, smart buy, going once..." I raised my hand.

"We've got $400." Ernie, who had been looking over his shoulder at the podium, looked around to see who was crazy enough to bid $400. Perhaps M. Stanton saw Ernie's body language indicating we'd spend more money for our team over his dead body. The Rolex stayed in his lap. We had it for $400.

"Shit, Ken, we agreed not more than $300."

"I got a little carried away, Ernie. I promised Ted half of my interest. I couldn't let M. Stanton have it. Anyway, you wouldn't want to win this whole thing, and for only $50 a man have only one half of the team."

"I somehow doubt that's going to be a problem," Ernie sighed.

I put my arm on his shoulder and said, "Hey, if you prefer, I'll pay $250 for five-eighths of the team and you pay $150 for three eighths."

Ernie considered that proposition for a minute, shook his head and said, "Nah, we're partners. But make a couple of $50 shots, would you?"

I reached across and shook his hand. "You got it, pard."

Our pool was pretty big at $6,100. M. Stanton and the Baby Doc went for $2,200, followed by Lenny and Sam at $1,900 and the Riklis brothers at $1,000.

My extra $100 looked a little better when they drew cards to decide which teams would play in which brackets. This random selection resulted in the number one and two seeds ending up in the same bracket to meet Friday if they both won Thursday. We were matched against the Riklis boys for the opening round. Win or lose, we'd play one of the other two budget-priced teams on Friday. Since it was win Friday or go home, that, at least, was good news.

Neither Ernie nor I were sticking around for the stripper and late night games of chance going on in the men's locker room bar. As we walked down the circular drive, I put my arm on his shoulder.

"We're in pretty good shape considering the shape we are in, hey pard?"

He smiled wanly. "At least with the seeding, we'll just get beat instead of getting killed."

I drove home with the top down and the radio off. Passing the spot where Mr. Porkpie had forced me off the road, I noticed the newly seeded area on Mr Utermallen's lawn. I shivered at the memory. My agenda for the next few days might be fun and frivolity. But there was nothing frivolous about the intentions of those who felt threatened by my trial strategy. I wondered what dark scuttlings my "civic board" question to Bliss might be causing. And I wondered how far someone might be prepared to go to discourage further inquiry in that area. I flipped the radio on to chase away the goblins of fear. Bob Marley's "Easy Skanking" was a good antidote.

The sun was getting out of bed later as the month of August wore on. It was just lifting its head above billowy pillows of clouds on the lake's eastern horizon as the Benz rumbled to life. My head was still clouded from restless sleep. I'd woken in a sweat when Amanda again held up the shiny object and beckoned to me. Was there something the phantom in the bloody blouse was still trying to tell me? Or was it just that I was about to spend time back at the club, where I'd last seen her, looking so beautiful and alive? Did she have any inkling then of the murderous evil gathering on the near horizon? Did her killer know Amanda's fate as we had chatted in the club bar? Or was it just a sudden spasm of rage from a jealous husband? The last thought was hardly conducive to my job as Ted's lawyer. So I pushed it away.

Pulling my golf shoes from my locker at seven a.m. on Thursday morning felt like playing hooky. I felt a pang of guilt over my priorities, which had me pulling on cleats instead of working Ted's case. The rest of the world was on their way to work. I was going out to play.

In the club room, many of the contestants were sitting around the tables with platters heaped with scrambled eggs, bacon and sausage. I stood in the doorway from the locker, rubbing the last of the sunblock into my neck, and gazed at the members. Was there one among them who had killed Amanda and could still play down number 15 as if nothing ever happened? Did any of Ted's former golf cronies look at me and feel any guilt for deserting their friend when he needed character witnesses? Who among the contestants knew of and felt threatened by Amanda's findings on the Dressler audit? None of the grown men dressed in short pants and colorful shirts looked much like a murderer. Rather, they mostly appeared to be a bunch of men wanting to be boys again.

I wasn't there an hour early to eat. I'm lucky if I can remember what I am doing with a club in my hand from one swing to the next, let alone from one day to the next. I was there early for a visit to the "rock pile," a.k.a. the driving range. As I headed out of the locker room to find my caddy and bag, I heard my partner, Ernie, call out, "Hey, partner, saved you a seat." He was seated near the window with the Riklis brothers. I strolled over to shake hands and started the banter.

"What are these two ten-handicappers doing down in our flight? If they hit the ball any further, you'd need binoculars to see it land."

"Oh, bullshit, Ken," Sven piped in with a smile. "If we hit it any wilder, we'd need radar to find whose backyard it landed in."

Daj added, "Gonna eat?"

"Nope, nope, too nervous about the beating we are going to get. I'm going to grab a coffee and head for the rock pile and try and find some kind of swing. But Ernie and I would be happy to sponsor you guys for a couple of Bloody Marys to get the morning rolling, right, Judge?"

My partner grinned. "Heck, yes. In fact, couple of doubles would probably relax you guys, keep you nice and loose. What do you say? It's on us."

"Nope, no thanks, but nice of you guys to offer," Daj replied.

I left them and found my bag at the caddy rack. Joshua, the caddy I wanted, was not available. My old pal M. Stanton had one-upped me again. As a club board member, he'd gotten first pick and snapped him up. My second pick, Kirk, was gone too. Most of the caddies were standing behind the bags they would carry. Mine was unattended. Josh was organizing the clubs in M. Stanton's bag.

"Morning, Mr. Edwards."

"Hey, Joshua, how you doing?"

"Good, good. The caddy master told me you asked for me?"

"Yeah, I did. You're my lucky caddy. Apparently Mr. Browne beat me to it. Who'd I end up with?"

"I think you got Tommy. He's new this year."

"Is he any good?"

Josh smiled. "He's new this year."

"Oh," was all I could think of to say. The caddies are all high school kids whose parents aren't members of the club. Nice way to avoid nepotism. Some, like Josh, were seniors and played a great game of golf. Some just needed a summer job. I'd miss Josh. He knew the greens like the back of his hand. More important, he knew my limitations and would make excellent club and shot suggestions tailored to the golfer I was, not the one I wished I were.

I hoisted my clubs and headed over to the range, and as a lefty, chose a spot on the far right of the range tees so that my left handed backswing wouldn't become entangled with the righties'. The eight iron I grabbed to loosen up felt foreign in my hands. Here it was mid-August and I had barely touched a club all summer. But the layoff seemed to be doing more good than harm. The faults that dogged my game—sliding hips, flying left elbow, and reverse pivot—seemed to have lost my scent during the long hiatus. I worked my way down to the five iron and noticed the quality of contact begin to fall off.

As I turned to pull out the driver, I saw a Munchkin wearing a caddy's green vest standing not much taller than my bag. The vest hung halfway to his knees. The bill of his cap rested on his horn-rimmed glasses. He smiled shyly.

"Sorry I'm late, Mr. Edwards. My mom's car was out of gas. The neighbor gave me a ride."

I extended my right hand. "Don't worry about it. You're Tommy, I take it."

"Yessir. I didn't want to be late. This is my first tournament."

Oh, great, I thought to myself, but said, "Forget about it, Tommy." I handed him the five iron and told him, "Just don't give me an iron with a number lower than a five no matter what I say. Okay? Let's try the driver."

I hit the driver okay, missed a couple of fairway woods, and told

Tommy to put the fairway woods on the protected species list with low irons. Tommy suggested we could take all those clubs out of the bag so I wouldn't be tempted.

"No thanks, Tommy. Shows you are thinking, though. Is that bag too heavy for you?"

He grunted as he wrestled it over his shoulders to follow me to the chipping green. "No, I can do it. I'm stronger than I look."

"Boy, I hope so," I thought to myself.

I hit a number of nifty flops over the bunker and onto the chipping green. Suddenly, I realized that my lob wedge was very similar in style and purpose to the club used to bash in Amanda's head. "Enough of that," I said, handing the club to Tommy. I had enough trouble playing golf with a clear head. I began to fear that being this close to where Amanda had died and constantly holding implements similar to the murder weapon would prove to be more cognitive dissonance than my shaky game could handle. Just as I was wishing for the umpteenth time that I'd told Ernie no, the head pro, Sonny Raines, lifted his megaphone.

"Match play, gentlemen. Let's keep pace. One slow group holds up the field. If you are out of the hole, pick up your ball and cheer for your partner. Keep it moving."

The format for this tournament is simple and makes for great competition: two-man teams flighted by the handicap of the low handicapped player on the team. A six handicapper with a twelve for a partner playing against a five and a six is dead meat. Thus, you and your partner have to be close in skill level. Eight teams in a flight. Two-man best ball. If Ernie makes four and I make ten and Daj and Sven make five, we win the hole. Ties wash out. The match is over whenever one team leads the other by more holes than are left to play. Thursday winners advance in the winners' bracket. Friday losers go home. Saturday, two teams play for the flight championship and two contest for the consolation "weepers' bracket." If you're still playing on Saturday, you're in the money. It's a shotgun start. For reasons unknown to me, we always seemed to draw the farthest tee. Today it was number 12. Anything farther away was off the golf course. We rounded up our caddies and started walking.

There is something special about that pre-tournament stroll across the dewy fairways to the first hole with your caddies flanked beside you. You haven't hit a bad shot yet. Anything is possible. It's a Thursday morning and you are at play instead of work. You are wearing short pants instead of a suit and golf shoes instead of wing tips. This was a beautiful, sunny August morning with the first telltale traces of fall cooling the air to the mid 60s. Ernie started singing a few bars from the old James Browne classic: "I feel good!"

The Riklis brothers zoomed by in a cart, calling out, "Don't exhaust yourselves on the way to the tee, boys." The long walk and Ernie's enthusiasm lightened my mood. The starter's horn sounded just as we reached the tee box. We shook hands with our opponents and spun a tee to see which team went first. We stood back to watch our opponents tee off. Sven stepped up, took a mighty cut and cursed. He topped a dribbler into the rough for forty yards.

"Don't worry, bro, I got you covered," said Daj as he bent over to tee his ball. He hit a 270-yard blast, 140 yards out and 130 way off to the right. He was over on the fairway on number 11. "Oh, shit. Sorry, pard."

This was their first member-member. They had been on the waiting list for two years. They were obviously a little cranked up. Golf requires a Zenlike state, not an adrenaline rush. Ernie and I had started the same way our first time in the tournament, falling so far behind before we settled down that we never recovered.

That was the story of this match. Sven and Daj steadied after four holes, but by then they were down four with fourteen left to play. I almost let them back in it. My game disappeared as we played number 15. I stared at the lifeless windows in the Armbruster home and thought of Amanda's lifeless eyes where she'd fallen in the foyer. As Tommy handed me my wedge, I got lost wondering about the second weapon that had disappeared from the scene. I shanked my chip into the woods and was out of the hole. Fortunately, Ernie stayed focused and kept us in the match. And once we'd moved from the back side to the front, the ghosts seemed to vanish and I began to contribute.

Thank goodness, because by the fifth hole the Riklis boys started using their Bunyanesque stature to mash drives 300 yards down the middle. But they gained on us only slowly as Ernie and I played conservative course management golf, just trying to tie holes, while they went for low percentage hero balls to catch up.

Nevertheless, their superior athleticism let them close to one down with two holes to play. They had us in their sights.

"Judge, is that the french toast you ate at breakfast, or are your shorts binding? You look a might peaked," teased Sven as he grabbed his driver from the cart and strode to the tenth tee.

Ernie laughed. "Ken, just checking, where do we stand?"

"One up, Your Honor, one up."

"That's what I thought. Couldn't feel better, Sven, have at it."

Number 10 is the number fourteen handicap on the course. It's a relatively easy 350 yard dogleg right with no trouble unless you go left off the tee. A marshy stream separates number 10 from the number 6 fairway. Sure enough, Sven hit a monster push. We watched the ball bounce right off a willow and careen down the slope toward the footbridge and then the water. "Shit," he yelled, beating his driver into the tee so hard that it was covered with a clump of sod."It's up to you, Daj." His violence with the club stirred unsettling images. "Get a grip," I told myself.

They held a team summit, Sven trying to get Daj to hit a four iron up the middle for safety and Daj wanting to blast a drive over the left fairway bunker to leave an eighty-yard chip shot in. Daj prevailed and stepped to the tee with his driver and hit it well. But he had gotten under it just a little. By noon, the wind had come up out of the south. The ball ballooned a little in the head wind as it followed its trajectory over the trap. "Go, you son of a bitch," he yelled, but it was to no avail. The ball hit the lip on the fairway bunker and rolled back down to lay in the middle of the sand. Ernie and I exchanged smiles with our caddies. Both our drives landed in the fairway well short of the bunker.

Sven took his penalty drop by the stream and hit a marvelous punch low under the willow, bouncing in front and rolling onto the green, leaving a fifteen-footer for par. "Nice shot, you dog," I yelled and said quietly to my partner, "Not out of the woods yet. Let's make a shot here."

Both of our approaches made the dance floor. But neither were within twenty feet of the hole. Daj shanked his pitching wedge from the bunker off to the right. He was still cursing when he stood over his chip shot and hit that fat into the green side bunker. After he bladed that sand wedge over the green, he was ball in pocket.

Ernie and I stood at the back of the green as Daj stormed over to pick up his ball. I spoke quietly to my partner. "Judge, we don't need birdie. Let's just get it close. Sven's got a ten or fifteen foot side-hiller and he's got all the pressure."

Our two balls were to the back of the green, downhill to a mid-green pin. Ernie's ball was about two feet left and behind mine. His putt streaked toward the hole. "Hit a house," I yelled. It hit the hole, but with way too much speed. It popped up and spun away another eight feet left of the hole. Oh oh! I walked down past the hole and looked back up at my ball. It was steeper than I had thought. Think speed. Think speed. I took three or four practice putts to get the feel for how hard I wanted to hit it. I moved over the ball.

Just as I exhaled to relax and make a smooth stroke, the image of Sven pounding his club on the tee flashed before me. Except this time the club wasn't covered with sod, but with gore. I stepped away.

"Little tense, are we?" chirped Daj. I stepped back to the ball. Rock and roll. The ball felt right coming off the club, or maybe I'd hit it too lightly. I didn't want to be left with a down-hiller for par. But the slope kept it moving and it came to rest two feet beneath the cup without ever threatening to go in. I breathed a sigh of relief.

"Nice putt," Daj offered. "Gotta make this one, partner," he said to Sven. The two of them studied his side-hiller from every angle. They plum-bobbed. They debated whether it was two or three balls above the cup. They decided on three. At the speed Sven hit it, it was two. The ball missed just high and died just past the hole. We conceded the bogey. I looked at Ernie.

"Make it, partner, and I'll buy you a beer." My putt was short, but I didn't want to have to make it as my hands felt trembly from my vision over the last putt.

Ernie had watched Sven's putt and hit his one ball above from shorter range. Nothing but net.

I whooped and we exchanged high-fives. Upset winners, two up with one to go. We shook hands with Sven and Daj and agreed to meet them in the clubhouse for lunch and beers. As we started to walk the short distance back up the tenth fairway to the clubhouse, Tommy piped up.

"How come we're going in? We've only played seventeen holes."

Ernie's caddy, Nathan, looked at Tommy like a bug in his salad. "Match play, Tommy. Two up, one to play. Game over."

I put my arm on the judge's shoulders. "Thank God Sven missed that putt. I didn't want to play any more golf today. We've been hanging on by the skin of our teeth."

"Amen, brother."

"That extra fifty doesn't look so rash now, does it, pard?" I teased.

Ernie finished where he'd started, humming James Brown.

Man, that walk back felt good. To walk eighteen holes is to go for a five-mile hike. I felt the delicious muscle tiredness mix with the mental relief of victory. I needed that. I'd grab a shower, a burger and a beer, and I could still get six hours of office time in. So when Ernie started with James Brown again, I joined in. "I feel good!"

After a shower and a shave, I threw my sweaty golf togs in the bag. I pulled on a blue blazer over a light-blue oxford shirt and khaki trousers. My cordovan deck shoes had been waiting at the foot of my locker, shined up to look new. My summer convertible short hair required only a couple of passes with a brush and I was good to go. I borrowed Ernie's cell phone to call the jail for Ted's promised update, but the switchboard reported that the prisoners were at lunch. The operator promised to convey the following message: "Beat the Riklis boys two and one."

Over lunch we commiserated with Daj and Sven over their slow start.

"Ken and I did that our first year," said Ernie. "You get all pumped up and before you settle down, you're in a deep hole."

Sven shook his head ruefully. "Yeah, we played pretty well from number 16 on. In fact, we beat you guys from that point on. After my birdie on number 9, I was sure we were going to catch you."

"Heck, yeah, we play you guys ten times, you guys win nine," I replied. Daj finished his last bite of burger, took a deep swallow of his beer, and let out a belch that turned a few heads at adjacent tables, in spite of the raucous babble of other players reliving their matches. He looked sheepish, excused himself and said, "If only my drive on ten goes one more foot."

"If only. Biggest two words in golf," I said, standing, pushing my chair out to go. "Great job, partner. Good luck to you gents tomorrow. Duty calls. I gotta go." Handshakes all around, and I was gone.

47

Top down, Credence Clearwater's "Proud Mary" playing on an oldies station, and Judge Ernie and I with a victory under our belt, I felt pretty good. Heavy clouds were forming on the southwest horizon, and I wondered if the afternoon groups would get wet. I reflected on my many-year golf relationship with Judge Ernie. He was a true golf buddy.

There are friends and then there are golf buddies. Friendships are fashioned of multiple strands of shared experiences woven together with a needle of filial affection. The fabric of friendship has many textures and hues. Friends find a connection in humor, common obstacles overcome, history, mutual ethos and shared interests. Friendship is an ornate tapestry.

Golf buddies, on the other hand, can fashion a decades-long relationship from one primary thread, a shared character flaw. They are hooked on golf. Thousands of dollars of bets can move between them over the years. But with handicap adjustments to the balance of trade, the net surplus or deficit can be $10. They call each other at two p.m. on a sunny Wednesday, identifying themselves to each other's secretaries as "Mr. Green," "Chip Schott," "Shivas Irons," "Sandy Bunker," etc. The pink phone slips carry cryptic notes: "Wants fair way to resolve matter"; "Hopes to iron things out"; "Re driver error"; "feeling trapped." Late afternoon appointments get moved to nine a.m. tomorrow.

Judge Ernie was my number one golf buddy and had been since long before he was a judge. We were friends, too, but foremost we were golf buddies. His eighteen handicap matched mine. Just good enough to think you could get better. Just bad enough to wonder if limited recreational time couldn't be better spent.

The pride of Ernie's game was a laser-like 5 iron with a low trajectory which as often as not could travel 190 yards. Direction was often a variable. He'd forward press his hands and take a mighty downswing, excavating huge divots known as beaver pelts. When he had it working, the ball would sizzle toward the target. When he didn't, the divot would go further than the ball.

Ernie was a likeable, gregarious fellow who, before becoming a judge, had a successful business in municipal law practice. He referred personal injury and criminal cases to me, and I sent the contract and commercial disputes to him. This, too, was in the tradition of the fellowship of golf. All things being equal, if you can steer something to a golf buddy, you steer it.

The voters had installed Ernie five years ago when a new seat was created. Ernie was a good choice. A farm boy, he had been getting up with the cows all his life. So unlike his judicial brethren, he didn't have lawyers on his 8:30 a.m. hearings milling about the halls at 9:30 a.m. looking at their watches and smiling pleasantly, "Good morning, Your Honor," as the judge strolled imperiously off the elevator. The judge's beauty rest creates a great moral dilemma: "Whom do I bill for this hour spent cooling my heels?" The answer is usually that the poor client pays $100 for the judge's extra shut-eye.

Then of course, the whole day's schedule backs up an hour. Lawyers arriving for an eleven a.m. motion get paid to watch the ten a.m. lawyers argue their case. Since the judge has a noon Rotary meeting, the lawyers are told to come back at 1:30 p.m. By the end of the day, twenty or thirty lawyers are billing their clients an aggregate $2,000 or $3,000 because His Honor hit the snooze button. Not with Judge Ernie. Be there at 8:15 a.m. for your 8:30 a.m. If your opponent is there, you are underway at 8:15 and out of there by 8:30. Be there at 8:35 and pay $100 for your tardiness. Judge Ernie is of German heritage. On his railroad, the trains run on time.

On my way to the office I swung by the jail. Jamie Dawson, the supervisor of central dispatch, had told me she'd be working until three when I'd called yesterday to set an appointment. I'd asked her to double check to make sure she didn't have the tape of Geraldine Chambers' suspected burglar calls. The last of those two calls, spaced a half hour apart, preceded Ted's 911 call by only five minutes per the dispatch log. Jamie was a twenty-year veteran of the department who'd seen sheriffs come and go. She stayed because she remained non-political and competent. Strands of gray mixed with her curly auburn hair. She'd given birth to six children, so the brown uniform fit her snugly. Since my days in the prosecutor's office she'd always been nice to me. Spotting me from the glass-walled confines of the dispatch office, she spoke to a seated operator and came into the hall.

"Hey, Ken. Keeping your head above water or going under?"

"Swimming as fast as I can. The crocodiles haven't eaten me yet. Any luck?"

She shook her head. "Told you yesterday the same thing I told you a month ago. That tape was taped over thirty days after April 28th. Just for you, I checked one more time. Long gone."

"Thanks for double checking." Now I got to the real reason for my visit, which I hadn't wanted to tell her on the phone. "What is departmental policy about all radio traffic and communications about a case coming through the dispatch?"

She looked curiously at me. "What are you getting at?"

"Just wondered if my memory was right from my days in the prosecutor's office."

We stood aside to let a couple of deputies pass us in the hallway. They gave Jamie a disapproving glance for fraternizing with the enemy. Me, they ignored. She waited until they turned the corner.

"It hasn't changed since then. Keeping a log of all communications on a call is for officer safety and really helps when sharpies like you try to pretend in court that something didn't happen when it did or vice versa."

"Uh-huh. And cell phones haven't changed that?"

"Nope."

"Hey, thanks, and here is a little something for you." I extended a subpoena, which I had told her to expect.

"No problem. Call fifteen minutes before you need me and I'll be there, although I have no idea what good I'll do you."

"Just routine. See you next week, and thanks again."

I took the elevator up to the jail floors and found Ted refereeing a basketball game for the younger inmates. As he left to meet with me, they called after him.

"Hang in there, Pops."

"Edwards will get you off."

"Keep the faith, baby."

While in jail, Ted had become a favorite of the turnkeys. They extended him privileges somebody doing ninety days for shoplifting didn't get. They indulged his weakness for Nestle Crunch bars. They brought him books and a *Wall Street Journal* regularly. Old Thaddeus Heath, the head turnkey, brought his chess board from home. The two of them would sit in the attorney conference room well past lights out with chins in hands, staring at the board.

While many of his country club buddies had distanced themselves from their fallen comrade in irons, his comrades behind iron bars had become a sizeable cheering section. Inmates like not guilty verdicts much more than the population on the outside. It gives them hope. The turnkeys and a couple of my other incarcerated clients had told me Ted was very popular. He was teaching literacy classes a couple of times a week. Other youngsters he helped prep for the GED. For a lot of the guys, he was the father figure they'd never had.

"Too bad these guys weren't in the jury pool," I quipped as we sat in the confined conference room. Ted didn't want to talk the case. He wanted to talk golf.

"Got the message. Great start. Tell me all about it."

He couldn't get enough of it, wanting a shot by shot replay.

"God, I miss playing in that. Did the guys ask after me?"

I lied and told him yes. With few exceptions, like Grayton Lansdale, the country club set now treated Ted as a good '50s-era communist would treat a purged party leader: pretend he never existed.

Then I turned to business. As the date for his testimony approached, I went over and over his memory, trying to keep that separate from the recurrent dream he had told me haunted him nightly. But I also let him retell his dream in case some subconscious memory might bubble to the surface.

"I keep having the same dream. I hear Amanda crying for me to help her. But I feel like I've been drugged. I'm all tangled up in the covers and I can't get free. I'm moving in slow motion. I hear a sickening thud just as I get to the bedroom door. I try to run to her but it's like I'm moving in molasses. I see the sparkle of the glass. It's like one of those old disco globes flashing lights. Then I see Amanda reaching to me out of the mirror while I'm standing at the top of the stairs. She's all covered in blood. She's crying out. But I can't hear anything.

"Then I break out of the molasses and I run down the stairs to her, but it's too late. She's on the floor, not in the mirror. And her face is all blood. I feel it all over my hands and on my chest. I'm calling her name and calling her name, and then I'm awake. I wake up covered in sweat instead of blood. Then I just lie there with my heart racing and try to catch my breath. I'm afraid to go back to sleep and have to relive it another time."

"Ted, explain how the golf club came to be on the floor between you and Amanda."

He startled. "In the dream?"

"No, from memory."

He paused, considering his words. "I remember, I fell coming down those damn marble stairs. My pajamas got under my foot, I think. When I fell I must have bumped my head and broke my finger. I probably missed three steps, I was in such a hurry to get to her. She was lying on her face with the shaft of the club under her, near her, under her right arm, I'm not sure. I just moved it aside. I didn't pay attention to where I left it. And I don't know how it got there."

At that moment Thaddeus Heath knocked and opened the door. On the table he set a couple of cans of Coke cold enough for condensation to drip down the sides.

"Sorry to bother you gentlemen. Figured you could use a little liquid refreshment with all your legal strategizing. Don't forget, Ted, Kasparov versus Fisher at ten. And Kenny, if you tell anyone I said this, I'll deny it. A lot of us are pulling for Ted. So don't drop the ball."

"Trying to avoid that," I replied as he swung the door shut. I turned back to Ted.

"You might testify next week. Let's do another run through. So, tell me again, what are the rules for being a good witness?"

"Oh, Ken, how many times do we have to go over this?"

"Just until the day after you've testified." Ted gave me a resigned look and then recited his litany:

"Tell the truth. If you don't know, say you don't know. Don't guess. Be polite, yes sir, yes ma'am. Be pleasant. Look at the attorney who is asking you the question, and then look at the jury when you answer. If you don't understand the question, ask to have it repeated. Short answers are best. Answer only the question that you are asked. Don't argue, but you can respectfully disagree. There, how's that?"

"Perfect, you'll do fine. Let's go over the statement again. Our friend Prosecutor Botham will be waving that like a flag in cross examination."

I reached into my file and pulled out my copy.

"Is that your signature, sir?"

Ted responded, "Yes, but I was too upset to read..."

"Ted, you already forgot three rules: one, don't argue, two, answer the question asked, and three, give short answers. The right answer to that question is 'Yes, it is.' I guarantee you'll have a chance to explain the circumstances. Trust me on this."

"Sorry, Ken." And so it went.

For the fourth time in five days I took him through all the questions I thought he would be asked both by the prosecutor and myself. He was an intelligent man and made fewer mistakes each time through. His recurrent mistake was to talk too much. A witness who does that gets himself in trouble.

Ted seemed to get the message. After an hour and a half, he looked worn out and I had things to do back at the office. I told him I wouldn't see him Friday. I had work to do in the morning and round two of the tournament in the afternoon.

"Who have you got tomorrow?" he asked eagerly.

"Paul Peters, the electrical contractor, and Frank Phelps. They beat Lynch and Tatum."

Ted's face brightened. "Oh, you can beat those guys. Paul can hit it long, but he's erratic. He's always trying hero shots from the trees instead of a safe little knockout."

"Yeah, I've played a lot with Paul. He hits it as far as anybody out there. But his short game is kinda iffy. Frank Phelps I don't really know."

"Watch out for Fluffer," Ted said with a smile.

I had heard the guys call him Fluff but didn't know where it came from. "Is that after Tiger Woods' former caddy?"

Ted laughed. "Heck no. He's been Fluffer Phelps since before Tiger was a gleam in his father's eye. He's always improving his lie. He noodles the ball around with a club so it sits up nicely. If you don't call him on it, he'll do it all day. I don't think he even realizes he's cheating."

48

With Ted's words of encouragement and advice, I said so long and headed for the office.

"Hi, stranger. We don't see you around here too much these days. How did you and the judge do this morning?" Yvonne smiled and looked up from her desk in response to our squeaky entrance door.

I held my left hand out flat like Caesar and started to slowly turn my thumb down. Her bright smile began to evaporate. It returned instantly as I flipped the thumb up. "We got them. Big upset victory for the good guys."

"Good for you. Congratulations!" she beamed. "Oh, John Nash from Smith Barney called for you a few minutes ago. Said he had what you've been waiting for." I grabbed the note and hurried back to my cluttered desk to return the call. Whatever my strengths may be, neatness and organization don't head the list. Ten minutes of rifling papers and files were required to find the TNPC legal pad containing the notes of my earlier conversations with Tim Nagalski, teenage cybernaut, and John Nash, middle-aged market maven.

John's secretary informed me he was "down the hall doing some research." I recognized the code for a call of nature and agreed to hold. He was his usual ebullient self on picking up.

"Hey, Kenny. What's happening in the world of legal eagles?"

"We're on a wing and a prayer. Did you find something for me?"

"Whoa, no niceties? No how was your trip? No how's the market?" He affected offense. But I knew John loved his little market bromides and would be hurt if I didn't request the special du jour.

"Sorry, sorry. How was your trip? And please give me the latest from Wall Street."

"Trip was great. Landed two new big corporate accounts. As for the markets. Recreational drugs are hitting new highs. Cattle futures are making new lows, and airlines are leveling off." After the cow pun sunk in, I laughed in spite of myself.

"Don't you ever run out of new material?"

"Never. Got a million of 'em. And I've got something for you." He waited to make me beg.

"So don't keep me in suspense."

"Your friends at TNPC, appears they stepped in a serious cow pie. Okay, here are my notes. They got caught in a perfect storm. They had borrowed heavy short term at the LIBOR rate. They were using the leverage to buy Government of Chile Assured Treasury Service Notes. The LIBOR rate jumped 25 basis points on the Bank of England's unexpected tightening of interest rates. The Chilean peso lost ten percent the same week in a massive narcotics corruption money laundering scandal that reached to the top government echelons. Lots of resignations, including their Secretary of the Treasury. That's a nasty combination, but they should've been okay, except their hedge's counterparty defaulted."

I was scribbling furiously.

"Government of Chile what?"

"Assured Treasury Securities. They're government bonds."

"Do they ever call those kind of bonds CATS?"

"Don't do much Chilean bonds myself. Here, like I told you last time, we call them treasury bonds. But everybody on Wall Street is big on acronyms. So, maybe."

"You were saying something about hedges. Explain that in English for me."

"They are derivatives. Derivatives are getting bigger all the time. Could bring the whole house of cards down someday. Anyway, if you are borrowing one currency to buy a higher yielding other currency, you have to protect yourself from the currency you borrow going up and the currency you buy going down. The way you do that is to buy a call option on the borrowed currency, here the British pound sterling, and a put on the currency you're buying, here the peso. Got it?"

"Sorta. It's like an insurance policy on currencies rising and falling?"

"Exactly, except we call it hedging. That way you supposedly take the currency risk out of the deal. Which is exactly what TNPC did."

"So where is the problem?"

"The hedge counterparty, the seller of the put and call options, went belly up. They kind of specialized in the niche market between English and Chilean currencies. So for them the combo of a sharp rise in the pound and collapse of the peso was Armageddon. It would be like you paying Allstate for house insurance and finding out when your house burns that an earthquake in 'Frisco wiped them out."

"Yeah, but there is usually government insurance for failed brokers, right?"

"Yep, if it's a U.S. licensed brokerage firm doing business with the public. But these guys are offshore, non-registered, and doing business only with sophisticated institutions. No security blanket there. None."

"What's the name of the failed counterparty?"

I could hear John shuffling papers on his desk. "I'm looking for the name, ah, here it is, Dumbarton Oaks Guaranteed Securities." Bingo. The name hit me like a bolt of lightning.

"Dogs, Cats. Cats go to the dogs, that's it. So what happened?"

"Dumbarton defaulted. The Chilean peso bonds were put to them and they were swamped, they couldn't pay. So TNPC loses their insurance policy against disaster. They are forced to liquidate the bonds, the CATS, for eight-five cents on the dollar to pay back their British LIBOR loan. At ninety-nine to one leverage, that kind of a hiccup gives you major indigestion. You getting any of this?"

"Enough to smell a rat among the cats and dogs. What does all this mean to TNPC?"

"My note says British banks called the LIBOR loan when they felt threatened and TNPC came up short. Way short. A petition has been filed in Cayman to appoint a receiver. Near as I can tell, TNPC completely cratered. Nothing left. The Brits are pretty tight with their former colony in Cayman and pushed the government in Cayman to go after the fund manager there. This is where it gets really interesting. His name is Xavier Westphal, a U.S. ex-pat formerly of Lake Pointe."

I was stunned. "He's from here?"

"That's what the boys in New York tell me. Thought you'd find that fascinating. Good stuff, huh? How's that for full service brokerage?"

"You are the greatest. How big was the deal or fund or whatever you call it ? What do you call it?"

"It was called TNPC Voyager Three. It's called a limited partnership leveraged investment trust. Total investor capital was two hundred and fifty million. Fifty partnership units at five million a pop. All of it vaporized. Oh, and Mr Westphal. He's vaporized too. They've been looking for him for almost a year. What with all the cats and dogs, that bird done flew the coop."

"That explains why his secretary informed me he was off the island when I called. Your boys have any idea where he might be?"

"Nope. They tell me that the Cayman banking authorities contacted our SEC and the FBI with a formal extradition request. He must have a pretty good hidey hole if those boys can't find him."

"You said a year ago. When did all this happen?" I could hear more papers shuffling and remembered that John's desk was as cluttered as mine. His phone buzzed a couple of times, and he bellowed "Message" and kept digging.

"Aha. Knew I had it. Partnership formed January 5th, 1999. Monies invested March 19th. Crater job the week of October 12th. Why is it that October is the month for market disasters? Have to figure that out sometime. Let's see what else. Receiver appointed for TNPC December first. That's it. Oh, I even have a little item from page 34 of the *Wall Street Journal,* December fifth. It's hardly a paragraph reporting appointment of the receiver. I'll fax it to you."

"Great. You've really helped. Thanks. One last question. From what

I hear, our local foundation is only out five hundred thousand, and you were saying five million a unit in this deal. Any idea how that fits?"

I heard John hum tonelessly. If he was playing poker, it would tell me he was considering his next move carefully.

"All right, you didn't hear this from me. Huh?"

"Right, right."

"On these leveraged funds, partnership units, hedge funds, they are all supposed to be only for the very rich who can afford to take the beating if something like this happens. But five million is still a lot of money. Everybody's talking about the great returns. Everybody wants in. What happens a lot these days is the unit gets subdivided two ways, five ways, ten ways maybe. The fund manager winks and looks the other way. That's all I'm saying. Plus, I've got five calls backed up from real paying customers. I've got to go before the market closes. Ciao, baby."

The phone went dead before I could even say so long. I stared at the frantic scribblings on my legal pad. Cats, dogs, a fund called TNPC run by a former local boy. When Amanda connected the dots, she ended up dead.

Two minutes later Janice dropped the brief blurb John had faxed me onto the desk. I barely looked up as she came and went. As she was shutting the office door, she asked, "Boss, you okay? You look a million miles away."

"What? Oh, fine. Just thinking. Say, you got all our subpoenas out, right?"

"Yes, boss. In the hands of the process server day before yesterday. He called today to say they'll all be served by Saturday."

"Good. Thanks."

I glanced at the fax and continued to marvel. Buried in the bowels of the financial paper of record was a report about a failed Cayman hedge fund in December. From what John had told me, the tendrils surrounding that failure stretched across the Atlantic to London and across the equator to Santiago. The Brits decide to raise interest rates at the same time as a narco corruption scandal hits Chile, and presto, a beautiful woman ends up bludgeoned to death in Lake Pointe the following

April. I had an eerie feeling, as if someone had peeled back the facade of reality and behind it were all these unimagined strings of causation. I shuddered with the realization that those same strings had controlled my life ever since April 28th.

49

My mind was awhirl as I drove out to pick up Max. The skies had cleared without a drop falling, much to the pleasure, I'm sure, of the afternoon contestants. The radio was promising fair skies throughout the weekend. I was so distracted trying to fill in the gaps in the Dressler-TNPC enigma that I ran a country stop sign to the irate extended honk of a sugar beet truck. The Grim Reaper's scythe missed me by about twenty feet or one second. Scary. How weird would that be, if I got killed wondering about what had gotten Amanda killed? I offered a little prayer for my deliverance and decided to concentrate on my driving.

Max heard the throaty roar of the Mercedes and bounded across open fields and leaped a drainage ditch to meet me as I pulled into Esther Grimes' driveway. "Wow, what a magnificent beast," I thought, not for the first time. Against the rules, he placed his front paws on the driver's side and licked me before I could get my seat belt off. Feeling pretty happy to have averted death minutes before, I waived the rules and endured a thorough face cleaning. Esther came out to tell me her lovely bitch, Hannah, was pregnant and to ask if I wanted second choice of the litter at a special price. I loaded Max up and said I'd think about it. If I got another of these monsters, I'd be paying for the puppy, which my budget could handle, and a new SUV, which it couldn't.

Billy Starkweather shocked me with his appearance as I pulled into the cottage drive. He stopped himself from climbing into his nicely waxed and polished pickup and moseyed over.

"Hey, neighbor. You are still my neighbor, aren't you? I never see you."

"Little busy these days," I said, opening the passenger door for Max, who promptly went over to pee on Billy's front tire. "Hey, why the fancy get-up? They change the dress code at Coco's bar?"

A changed man Billy was. His trademark haystack of unruly blonde hair looked professionally cut and styled. Gone were the coveralls, to be replaced with new khakis and a pink polo shirt with a blue horse and rider on the pocket. I noticed the store tag at the nape of his neck and had him turn to yank it free. At that range whatever fancy cologne he had bought was overpowering. As he covered his "aw shucks" smile with his hand, there was no dirt beneath the manicured nails.

"C'mon, give. What's going on?"

"Got a date," he mumbled.

"Yeah, with who?"

"Louise."

"Where did you meet her?"

"Haven't yet."

"What?"

"Online dating service called E-Harmony."

"You're shitting me."

"Nope, been e-mailing and sending pictures and stuff for about six weeks. She finally agreed to meet me. I don't mind telling you I'm a little nervous. Spent some money on these duds. What'll I do if it doesn't work out?"

"Relax. Actually, you dress up pretty good. She'll fall head over heels. Let me know how it works out."

He beeped and waved as he pulled out. I yelled "Luck" and went to help Max find his dish, which turned up on the other side of the sea wall. Max loved this little game and stared at me with his liquid brown eyes as if to thank me for playing along.

We both raced in to catch the phone, Max keeping his supper dish in sight. It was Karen.

"Just on my dinner break, so I thought I'd see if I could catch you. How'd the match go? Still in contention for the championship?"

Boy, did her voice sound great. Maybe a near death experience heightens your appreciation of things. I told her so and updated her on our golf victory.

"Plus, I think I'm onto something that could blow this case open, maybe."

"Really? I don't want to hurt your feelings, but the paper tonight makes it look like Bliss came across pretty well yesterday."

"Was that only yesterday?" I asked, walking with the cordless to the door and grabbing today's *Leader*. The headline was grim.

Confession Solid

"Yeah, I guess that was yesterday. Anyway, I'm onto something else that looks promising. The whole thing is such a yo-yo. One day you're down. Next day you're up. Hearing your voice, I'm up. Ready for the dinner-dance?"

She purred, "Oooh, you're going to like my dress. Almost didn't get to wear it though."

"What? Why?"

"Desk sergeant had me in for a little chat as I was coming on shift this afternoon. Seems he and the post commander have been hearing about us. Thought maybe it didn't look good for a troop to be dating a guy defending a high profile criminal case. Suggested I give it a rest till the trial's over."

I didn't like the sound of this. "What did you say?"

"Told him about the dinner-dance and he went ballistic. Said that's way too public. No way."

"Oh, shit."

"Don't worry. I told him I laid out almost three hundred bucks on the dress and I was wearing it unless he could show me a departmental reg that banned defense lawyers off duty. He couldn't, of course. So he fussed and fumed a while and told me to cool it. How's that?"

"You're my heroine."

I felt very happy after hanging up. We hadn't gotten beyond a soul kiss or two, and yet she was prepared to fight to be my date.

"Might have something here," I told Max as he watched expectantly to make sure I scooped the full allotment of Pedigree into his bowl.

I felt good enough to treat myself to a home cooked meal. Rummaging around in the cupboards for the Kraft macaroni package, I found a pack of Marlies that had fallen behind the soup cans. Being off the weed for almost three weeks, I thought I had climbed out of the morass of addiction. The bright red and white package set off neurons of craving I didn't know I had. A giant hand reached to my core and dragged me back to the swamp. The cellophane wrapper was off without thinking.

Superstition saved me. I was sure if I sinned, I'd be punished. Minor punishment would be to lose in the tourney. Capital punishment equaled losing the case. Couldn't risk that. Saying "Get thee behind me, Satan," I ran tap water on the smokes to prevent backsliding and threw them in the trash on my way to bed.

Max and I went for a 6:30 swim to start Friday morning. Lake Huron seemed oblivious to the calendar's report that it was August. Even the near shore waters remained cold enough to cause major shrinkage. Dressed in golf togs for the afternoon round, I headed with Max for the car. Even though it was only eight a.m., Billy had the hood up on his F-150. He'd reverted to his normal fashion statement, raggedy cutoffs, faded NASCAR t-shirt, and a Tigers cap. Max ran over to greet him and I trailed behind.

"Car problems?"

"Nah. Preventative maintenance. Hey, I'll be home all day. You can leave Max with me."

"Great. So how did it go? Should I take today's fashion statement to mean your cyber date was a bust?"

"*Au contraire, mon ami.*"

I choked and spat out the sip of coffee from my traveler mug. "What?"

"Louise is a fine little lady of French Canadian extraction. She taught me that when I was apologizing for being a poor dancer. What do you know? I got to use it right away." Billy looked pretty smug.

"Is she cute?"

"As a button. She can't be over five foot two or a hundred pounds, but man, that woman can dance. We closed the Elks." The image of a fairy princess dancing with Shrek crossed my mind. After learning that she was a single mom who waitressed to support her five-year-old, and that they had a date for next week, I left Max with Billy and drove, top down, into the office.

I caught the phone on the last ring and sat at Yvonne's desk admiring the framed family pictures surrounding her work space. At 8:30 I was the first one in.

"Morning, Ken. Your secretaries take to the lifeboats before your ship sinks?"

"Morning to you, Madam Prosecutor. Nope, they're out buying gowns for the victory celebration."

"They better hope the store has a liberal return policy after Bliss testified," Tina crowed. "You hardly laid a glove on him."

"Busy counting unhatched chickens, are we? To what do I owe the pleasure?"

"I talked with the boss. We're willing to go with the same deal we offered Browne, murder two and a fifteen-year minimum. Interested?" Why would she be making such an offer after Bliss had sailed through? Must be a wrench in the works somewhere.

"I'll take it to Ted. But I doubt it. Anything else on your mind?"

"Yep, got the crime lab report on my desk, which I'll fax you. The bottom line is the tool marks guy, Fredericks, says neither of the two other clubs made the forehead or above the ear marks. He also says, quote, 'There is enough discrepancy between the club face of Mr Armbruster's sand wedge and the wounds to the victim's forehead and left parietal area to leave a possibility that a second, similar make club inflicted the wounds. Without a suspect club to compare, no positive identification can be made."

"That explains your plea offer."

"Whatever. I'm calling to ask that you stipulate to the admission of the report without Mr. Fredericks' having to appear, as he and his family have a pre-paid vacation to the Ozarks next week. Can do?"

"Probably, send me the report and I'll let you know. Anything else?"

"Yep. I'm happy enough with the way our case has gone to rest my case. So I'm asking you to excuse the rest of the witness list we promised to produce, Firenze, the bartender Hackett, and Geraldine Chambers. Firenze and Hackett will only be cumulative on Armbruster's rage at Heather Hollows in light of the Simpsons' testimony. So I thought I'd cut you a little slack rather than pile it on. Firenze has been driving me crazy, begging to be excused. I gather he hasn't mentioned his little tryst to his wife. He said he has talked to you and thought you'd agree." An image of Greeks outside the gates of Troy crossed my mind.

"Tell him he thought wrong. If he's talked your ears off, he's threatened to remove mine in a more violent fashion. He's a real piece of work. He was the last person seen with the victim alive. Produce him. I'm sorry, but you will also have to produce Hackett and Chambers. Each of them might prove useful. But thanks for thinking of me and offering to go easy." I could think of a number of reasons why Tina would like not to have to call those witnesses. None of them included doing the defense any favors.

"Whatever, we should still have this thing wrapped by the end of next week. What the hell is your defense, assuming of course you have one?"

"That's a good assumption, Tina. Have a nice day."

Before I'd gotten two steps from the desk, the phone rang again. It was Brent Eubanks. No niceties were observed.

"I got a subpoena yesterday. Why are you doing this to me? I thought we were friends."

"Sorry, Brent. My first obligation has to be to my client."

"Ted would never countenance the destruction of Dressler. He said—" Eubanks stopped in midsentence.

"He said what? When?" I was on alert.

Brent cleared his throat. "I meant he has always said that Dressler is the best thing this town has going for it." His tone softened to that of a teacher dealing with a slow learner. "I told you that the missing money had been replaced weeks before Amanda died. So it could've had nothing to do with her death. To create a scandal, a scandal that could ruin a lot of good people, me included, just as a sideshow is irresponsible."

Yvonne walked in, hands full with the morning mail, and stood looking bemused at me sitting in her work place. She started to talk, but I covered the mouthpiece and waved her off. "Go make some coffee, please."

"Right," I said to Brent, "but you didn't tell me that Dressler's missing money had to do with a Cayman hedge fund that happens to have the same name as a local high profile poker club. Nor did you mention the head of that hedge fund was from Lake Pointe. Why is that, Brent?"

I could hear his swivel chair creak as he sat up.

"Where did you learn that? Who told you?"

"Not you. Want to tell me about Xavier Westphal and why he's hiding out from the Feds?"

During the ensuing silence I imagined the beads madly sliding up and down on his mental abacus. Finally, in an almost pleading tone, he replied, "Just give me a couple of days. Don't go public with your half baked suspicions. I promise a complete explanation, an explanation that clearly shows Dressler was not the cause of that woman's death. Before you toss a grenade into a crowded restaurant, at least give me the chance to prove that you'll be blowing up innocents. Can you do that?" I'd never heard the Spock-like Brent Eubanks speak in such an urgent tone.

I respected Brent and felt his panic. "I'll hold off as long as I can, Brent, on your promise to lay the whole thing out. But I've got an opening statement to give and a defense to put on next week. If I have to choose, I'll go with what I've got to help my client. I hope you understand."

"I'll get back to you." He rang off without saying good-bye.

50

I spent the morning trying to concoct an opening statement. That wasn't easy as I didn't know whether to blame Gianfranco, TNPC, or other jealous lovers like Annabelle Browne. I envisioned M. Stanton's blood pressure rising when, not only was a subpoena dropped on him, but also on his snooty wife. I was making enemies at a remarkable rate and losing friends like Brent equally fast. If I blew the whistle on Dressler, taking down the lambs with the lions, I'd be, at best, a pariah. If I went after Firenze, I could end up as recycled metal. If I blamed them both, my sudden disappearance would be the cause of little mourning.

Fear makes for an amazing writer's block. All I could manage were crumpled sheets of legal paper surrounding the wastebasket my shaky shots couldn't find. Sure hoped I'd putt better this afternoon.

I had to give the jury somebody else to blame, or Ted was going down on Bliss's testimony. But who? For the umpteenth time I tried to create a motive for Bliss to lie. There was something more than his sad tale of guilt for letting a drunk driver go. But for the life of me, I couldn't fathom what it was. I had discovered no ties between him and Firenze. He wasn't a hedge fund sort of guy. He didn't hang with the country club set, let alone the crème de la crème in the Thursday night poker group. I was missing something, unless my client really had confessed. That was a line of thought very inconsistent with offering a good defense. So I shoved it back down like I'd done a hundred times before.

Once in trial, a defense lawyer must remain convinced of his client's innocence. Otherwise, he'd have no chance to persuade the jury. I suspected that was at least part of Tina's motive in making an offer she knew we wouldn't accept. She wanted to create doubt in me by making me reevaluate the case so I could properly advise my client. Plead and get out in fifteen years, if you live that long. Or get convicted and have no chance to ever be free.

Her ploy had succeeded to the extent that I had to reconsider the possibility that Ted had really done it. Doubts would sap my effectiveness at trial. But the strengthening sense of powerful forces stretching around the globe to claim a woman's life in Lake Pointe felt so true that the doubts easily fit back into the mental hatch I'd created for them. I secured the bolts on that hatch and headed for the golf course, lamenting how little I'd accomplished.

51

“Here it is, Mr. Phelps,” Tommy, our caddie, called from the deep rough left of number 2 fairway. Round two and we had all played number 1 well, three pars and a bogey (mine). Match all square. We were well past the five-minute time limit searching for Fluffer’s second shot on the par five. He’d pulled it left toward the farmer’s field, which was out of bounds. The last fifteen yards before the field was high grass that gets thicker the closer you get to out of play. I started walking back from where I’d been looking as Paul Peters and Frank Phelps raced by in their cart toward Tommy. Paul was an electrician wired into golf. Frank Phelps was a semi-retired real estate broker. They stopped near Tommy, and Frank got out of the passenger side to peer down into the ankle-deep grass that obscured the ball from sight.

“Are you sure it’s mine?” he asked Tommy.

“Oh, yes, sir, I watched it when you hit it and, see, if you push the grass aside,” which Tommy bent to do, “you can see the Nike logo.”

Phelps bent down to pick up the ball without announcing his intention to Ernie and me. This is a stroke penalty under the rules. Once he had it in his hand, he did say what we already knew.

“Lift to identify. Yep, yep, that’s mine.”

He leaned down and gently placed the ball at least a foot from where he had found it and sitting up so that more than half of the ball was visible above the grass. Ernie and I exchanged glances. Ernie shook his head to signal me to keep my mouth shut, so I did.

Sure enough, Fluffer hits his third shot onto the green, two putts for par, and they won the hole after both Ernie and I three putted. They motored off to number 3, congratulating each other, whilst Ernie and I trudged over.

"Damn it, Ernie," I grumbled. "It's bad enough we both three putted, but to lose to a guy who blatantly improved his lie, that's crap."

"I know, I know, but this is a golf tournament, not mortal combat. Relax, we're only down one and we've got sixteen holes to go. We can beat these guys."

I shook my head. I'd grown up with four brothers, and what I lacked in athletic talent I made up for with competitive juice.

"You know, Ernie, they don't call this guy Fluffer Phelps cuz of his work with pillows. He cheats. Next time I'm going to call him on it."

"No, Ken. Let me deal with him. Fluffer helped me get the realtors' endorsement last election and a hell of a lot of yard sign placements. His partner, Paul, is one of your golf buddies. You want to piss them both off?"

"Nah. It's just bullshit, that's all."

Sure enough, our opponents used their tainted victory on number 2 as a springboard to go on a tear. Paul relaxed, swung easier and started lacing his driver down the middle. They reeled off five straight pars, two of which Ernie matched, to leave us a desperate four holes down coming in to number 8. I was useless, as my mind was on the unfinished opening statement on my desk and on the info John Nash had given me. Fluff and Paul were as jovial as a couple of magpies at a bird feeder. Ernie and I trudged along as if on our way to the gallows. Four down, even if it's still the front nine, is a very deep hole, as the Riklis boys had found out yesterday.

As we walked over to the eighth tee, Ernie pulled me aside under a stand of evergreens.

"Pard, you look like you're a million miles away. Something bugging you?"

"Sorry, Judge. This case is getting to me. Lots of stuff going on."

Ernie squared to face me and grabbed both my forearms gently.

"Listen, Ken. I know how you get during a case, but I've never seen you this wired. If you don't relax and help out here, our goose will be even more cooked than your client's. Could you just let the case go long enough to beat these turkeys? Please?"

I took a deep breath, exhaled, and smiled.

"That's an order, I take it?" He nodded, smiling back.

"Yes, Your Honor," I replied, resolving to sweep the case-induced turmoil into a mental corner.

Approaching the tee on number 8, a short par-three, 150 yards over water to the pin, Tommy looked up from under his green caddy cap and offered, "Not looking too good, eh, Mr. Edwards?"

"Not at the moment, but you never know when the worm will turn."

Sure enough, Paul tried to juice a pitching wedge with the following breeze and swung so hard he almost fell over. In doing so he shanked the ball into the reedy marsh between tee and green. One down. Frank, the golf antithesis of Paul, had a smooth short swing. He threw a handful of grass in the air to gauge the wind and conferred with his partner. "Six iron, seven iron, what do you think, partner?"

"Plenty of breeze to help you, maybe even an eight."

"OK, I'll just hit the seven."

The selection seemed perfect. He took his short, effortless swing; the ball went "click" off the club and soared toward the center pin placement, but in the time it took for Paul to say "Way to go partner, that's right at it," the wind died and quartered the ball right over the fattest part of the trap. Instead of carrying over the bunker that protected the front of the green, the ball hit on the lip of the bunker, popped up, and then fell back into the trap.

"Tough break, Frank. That ball was looking perfect," I offered as I took his place on the tee.

"I knew I should've used the six iron," Frank muttered as he walked back to his partner.

"Aha, a little dissension in the opponent's ranks," I thought as I pushed all the case-related demons aside. Plenty of club, just finish where you want it to go.

When you strike a golf ball correctly, you don't have to look up to know it. Your hands feel the clean contact off the sweet spot. Your ears hear the solid click of metal on ball, and your muscles recognize an effortless transition from back swing to follow-through. Then you can look. For me the sight of a well-struck high iron rising toward the target is the most satisfying aspect of a frustrating game. This one was perfect. It hit twenty feet below the hole, turning left to right, and climbed the hill up to the cup, stopping less than a yard from the hole. Ernie and I exchanged high fives. He too hit his ball onto the putting surface, but well above the hole.

As Tommy backpacked my bag next to me over to the green, I asked, "Hear that, Tommy?"

He cocked his head to listen.

"What? I don't hear anything."

"Oh, you've got to listen closely if you want to hear the sound of a worm turning."

He smiled in comprehension.

"Oh, I get it."

I didn't get upset or say anything as Fluffer grounded his club in the trap prior to swinging (loss of hole in match play), nor after he made a beautiful bunker shot which just missed going in and came to rest inside my ball. All I managed was, "Great shot, Fluf—Frank. That's good. Nice sand-save par."

I had hoped he'd give me mine, which was maybe six inches behind him. But the idea apparently never crossed his mind.

"Thank you, sir." He snatched his ball and walked to the side of the green to watch Ernie and me putt. Ernie babied his putt and left himself a good twelve feet downhill and side hiller, which he missed, going well past the hole.

"Sorry, pard."

"No sweat. You've been carrying us all day. My turn now," I replied.

I was sweating. All of a sudden my two-and-a-half-footer uphill looked a little more daunting. It was steep, so I had to hit it firmly, but too firm and I'd be looking at a twisting downhiller to tie. We didn't need a tie anyway. We were down four after seven holes. I needed to sink this.

"Back of the cup. No prisoners," I told myself as I stood over the ball. Somewhere behind my eyes Amanda smiled. I took a short back swing and finished firmly through to the hole, almost too firmly. The ball raced at the hole, slammed into the elevated bed of the cup, popped up a little and fell with a satisfying rattle to the bottom.

"You're the man," Ernie rejoiced.

I let out an audible breath.

"Thank God I didn't miss. Who knows where that freight train would've stopped?"

Down three after eight. It looked like we were going to give it right back. I was so distracted by the feeling of Amanda looking through my eyes on the last putt that I overswung off the ninth tee, hitting a massive slice into the wind. It ended up in the marsh that had swallowed Paul's ball on 8. By the time we reached the hole, I was ball in pocket. Ernie was on the fringe in the throat of the green in four. Both of our opponents were on in three and maybe fifteen or so feet from the front pin placement. I stood off to the side, staring at the clubhouse, imagining cigar smoke hanging over intent poker players staring at a pot full of golden ball markers. I barely heard Ernie call to his caddy or speak to me. "Alex, bring me the putter and pull the pin. Gotta go for it, Ken."

Only his jubilant whoop as the ball took one last roll and died in the hole brought me back. I looked at him in pleased amazement. He stuck out his hand and walked over.

"Mutt, I'm Jeff."

I clasped his hand firmly and replied, "Great to see you, Jeff."

Our opponents were sufficiently rattled that they both missed their putts. Bogey tied the hole. Down three after nine. Ernie's heroics were a catharsis. The new life he'd given us broke the dam on my competitive juices, and they washed over my case-related preoccupation. As we strolled over to number 10 to begin the back nine, I felt good. Surprisingly good for being down three. I could envision momentum, old Mr. Mo, taking off his electrician's tool belt and red realtor jacket to try on a judicial robe over a three-piece suit.

"Looking sharp, Mo, looking sharp," I whispered.

"Pardon me, Mr. Edwards, who's Mo?" asked Tommy.

"Huh? Oh, just a fickle guy I know who is trying out new team colors."

"What?"

"Nothing, Tommy, nothing."

Ernie birdied 10 after a marvelous approach. Down two. My bogey tied the par-five 11. On 12, a 375- yard par four, Mr. Mo showed he really liked the fit of his new duds. Our opponents went for a safari to the woods on both sides of the fairway. My tee shot was my best of the day, 225 yards down the middle, but I got cute with the eight iron third shot to the green. Instead of playing for the middle, I aimed at the left side pin and pushed my shot just enough to be pin high in the bunker. I was too far away to be sure, but it sure looked like Fluffer had noodled his ball around the rough prior to chipping within ten feet.

Oh-oh, the left greenside bunker had a wall five feet high between me and the pin. I waded in with my sand wedge, feeling a singular lack of confidence. I am normally just happy to get out of the sand and onto the green somewhere. This one had to be close.

I took my stance and glanced at the imposing height of the bunker wall. I was at least even money to hit that wall and still be in the bunker in three, but then I noticed about an eight-inch area where the sand made a smooth transition from lip to fringe. If I could putt the ball firmly there, it would pop up and maybe land safely on the adjacent green.

"Tommy, let's have the putter."

As I traded clubs with the caddie and tried to gauge how hard to swing the putter, I heard Fluffer say to his partner, "What the hell is he doing?"

"Oh, he does that sometimes. Sand game not so good," replied Paul.

I stroked the ball hard to get over the sand and up the wall. It must have gone three feet in the air coming over the lip, but when it came down it hit in the edge of the fringe, kicked left and rolled down to within six inches of the cup.

"I don't believe it," Fluffer muttered.

"You asshole," was Paul's form of congratulations.

"Unbelievable! Way to go, partner," shouted Ernie, nearly falling over jumping to follow the ball's path toward the hole.

"Good, boys?" I asked.

"Yeah, take it, pure luck," grumbled Paul.

"Sometimes it is better to be lucky than good." I smiled as I leaned over to pick up my ball.

Fluff was so rattled he stubbed his putt. We won a hole we had looked destined to lose only minutes before. But that's tournament golf, playing two-man best ball in match play with high handicappers. Anything can happen. I'd snatched defeat from the jaws of victory often enough to know how they were feeling.

"Wow, only down one! Their daubers are down. We're on a roll," beamed Ernie, a definite spring in his step as we trailed their cart to the next tee.

But instead of rolling, we settled into a stalemate. The next four holes all ended in draws, three at bogey and one at double bogey. Lots of bad golf and missed opportunities on both sides.

As we approached 17, time was running out. We were one down with two to go. I had the awful feeling that our comeback was going to fall one short. I kept thinking that if I had called Fluffer on number 2 we wouldn't be in this mess, but here we were. That kind of thinking caused me to swing too hard on my drive, a booming wind-aided slice that hit off the left side of the fairway bunker and jumped left, out of bounds.

"Up to you, pard. Keep us in it," I said sheepishly to my partner.

Keep us in it, he did. Dead solid up the middle for 240 yards on the 390-yard hole. Paul matched him plus twenty yards but was in the rough, and Fluffer used the wind to good advantage, carrying past the two hundred yard marker. After my reload was yanked into the knee-high grass right, I was a cheerleader for my partner. Fluffer hit a very solid three wood that threatened the green but ended up in the right front sand. Paul hit his off the toe and it skipped four times in the right pond before sinking from view. The pin was front center. If Ernie could put it on, we should be in business.

"Whaddya thinking, pard?" I asked as we stood in the sunshine in a group of four with our caddies.

"I just paced it off. It's 163 yards. I think a smooth seven."

I could see the concentration on Ernie's face. He wanted this one as bad as I did.

"Go with the eight. Wind's at your back. The pin is in front. Fluff's is in the trap and Paul's is in the drink. If you're short you'll be right in the throat, an easy chip and a putt. You don't want to go over the back. It's tough coming back."

He considered it and grabbed the eight, took a couple of practice swings and shook his head.

"No, I feel better with the seven. I'll just hit it smooth."

"Okay, you're the judge."

Well, he hit it smooth. Smooth and hard. He got all of it. Carried by the wind, it sailed over the pin, bounced on the upper body of the green and rolled over and off.

"Guess it was an eight, huh?"

"You just hit it too good. No sweat, partner."

While we walked up, Paul took his drop next to the water, lying three and chipped over in four. He was out of it. He cursed and climbed into the cart and drove over to inspect Fluff's bunker lie. As we approached, Fluffer was reaching down to pick up a small twig that the breeze must've blown into the bunker. His ball had come to rest against it.

"Should I mark my ball in case it moves when I lift this stick?" he asked.

"Sorry, Frank, can't do it," said the judge. "That twig is a loose impediment. Can't move those in a hazard."

"That's not fair, I didn't put that there. I've never heard of such a thing," remonstrated Fluff, his face taking on a decidedly roseate hue.

"I'll bet you haven't heard of it," I thought, but I kept my mouth shut. My partner had said way back on number 2 that he'd deal with Fluffer, and by golly, he'd picked a good time to do it.

"Paul, is he right?" Fluff turned to his partner.

"Frank, I don't know, it's never come up before."

The caddies, sensing the friction in what had been a friendly match, took a couple steps back. But Ernie called to his caddy, "Reach in the right side pocket of my bag. There's a rule book there."

And sure enough, out came a pocket-sized paperback entitled *USGA Rules of Golf.* Ernie looked at the rules and then turned to the definition of "loose impediment," which includes stones, twigs, branches, etc. He read it aloud. Then he flipped over to rule 13-4, which prohibits removing loose impediments in a hazard.

Before he'd gotten two words into the recital, Fluff blurted, "All right, all right, so that's the rule. It's still bullshit to call it on me."

"Play it as it lies," said Ernie with judicial aplomb as he moved off to locate his overshot behind the green.

I stepped back with the caddie to watch Fluff's shot. So far today he had gotten out of every bunker with no problem. But now I could see a vein on his forehead throbbing and the muscles of his left arm tightening. Whether he was trying to miss the twig or just too tense, I don't know. But he picked the ball clean out and sent it sailing over the green into the bunker on the other side. He stomped wordlessly over and underhit the next one, which only reached the fringe. He two-putted from there for six, and Ernie's five won the hole. All even.

"There goes the realtor vote," I said to Ernie as we walked to eighteen tee.

"Fuck the realtor vote! Next election is four years away. Let's finish the job," uttered Ernie, his soft face set in grim determination.

You could have cut the silence on number 18 tee with a knife. I slowed my swing way down and hit the ball perfectly. It came to rest in the garden spot in the fairway left of the bunker and right of the pond. Ernie's ball wasn't far off mine. After leading all day, our opponents came to the tee tied, tight, and in trouble. We had taken full advantage of first position on the tee and put some pressure on them. They were tense and it showed.

Fluff swung way faster than his normal rhythm and pulled a grounder to the shortstop. Paul swung under his, hitting a pop up to short right center. Fluff's second was in the pond, and Paul's, while carrying the water, was well right of the green. Both Ernie and I hit smooth irons to the putting surface. Two good lag putts and a tap in later, we were in in four. Paul's five was the best they could do. The only time we'd led all day was after 18. The best time. Winners, one up.

To their credit, they were gentlemen, offering handshakes and congratulations. After the second beer, all animosity was forgotten, and they wished us luck for the championship in Saturday's match. Amidst the camaraderie I felt my gaze drawn to the large corner table used for big poker games. For an instant, the jovial golfers laughing and drinking peeled away to reveal a table full of visored gamblers intent on a glittering pile of gold. I shook my head and the room returned to the faces of today's winners and losers. Looking four tables over, I could tell from the expressions who we'd be facing for the championship. Lenny and Sam looked exhausted and deflated. M. Stanton and Baby Doc were all smiles.

Standing in the locker shower, I could hear the banter of the other golfers echoing off the tiled walls of the adjacent stalls. But my mind was elsewhere. The torrent of water made such a nice contrast to the trickle from that relic at the cottage. I just let it beat on my back while I tried to think of who could enlighten me about a Lake Pointe boy named Xavier Westphal.

The answer was obvious. Retired judge R.T. Halley had found me my first job. He was a hometown boy, born and raised. And he was still my friend, an increasingly endangered species. I let the water beat on my shoulders while I reflected on my long history with R.T.

Fresh out of law school, I had sent my resume all over the state. Judge Halley was looking for a law clerk. My interview was set for 4:30 on a Friday. A law clerk's job was very low on my career shopping list, but I'd been looking quite a while with no luck, and my bank account was running on vapors. His chambers were those now occupied by Judge Kingsdale. They were replete with University of Michigan regalia, maize and blue everywhere. As an MSU green and white man, the profusion of maize and blue made me feel like Clark Kent doing an interview in a kryptonite mine. But the rivalry got us off and running conversationally. By the five-minute mark we had twenty dollars on that year's game, me getting six and a half points. If I didn't find a job soon, he might have to take my marker if the Spartys failed to cover.

He asked me what kind of a lawyer I wanted to be, and I told him a trial lawyer, to which he replied, "If you want to be a player, what are you doing applying for a spectator's job?"

I shrugged my shoulders and said, "At the moment, beggars can't be choosers."

He told me that he'd interviewed a studious U of M graduate that morning and he was probably going to offer her the job. Then he told me to "keep your eye on the ball. You want to be a trial lawyer, take a job that'll get you into the courtroom."

We talked fishing, about his thirty years in private practice before appointment to the bench four years ago, and life in Lake County. It was 5:30 when he glanced at his watch, jumped up and grabbed his sport coat, reached across the desk to shake my hand and said, "In trouble now, supposed to have picked up my wife at the bridge club fifteen minutes ago. C'mon, I'll walk out with you."

Standing on the courtroom steps in the late afternoon sun, he smiled and said, "For a Moo-U grad, you seem all right. I've got your number and your resume. No promises, but the prosecutor and I are golf buddies. You play?" I nodded. "Thought you might. I can always use a new pigeon. No promises, but I'll talk to Alvin Corliss. He's been prosecutor here since Moses. I'll put in a word for you."

True to his word, he did. A week later Prosecutor Corliss's secretary called to set up an interview. At the interview the first question was, "I don't need another nine to fiver. Are you ready to work your ass off?"

"Yes, sir, I am."

"Okay. The judge says he's got a good feeling about you. I'll try you for two months. If you can't cut the mustard, you're gone. Fair?"

"Fair."

"Be here at 8:30 a week from Monday, ready to go to work."

I was floating on air and already heading south on I-75 when I realized I had no idea what the job paid.

After that the judge took me under his wing. He'd critique my performance in front of him. He'd tell me what the other judges were saying. I remembered a time early in my career when he'd taken me aside in the hall to teach me. "Lesson one, don't piss a judge off. Don't make him look bad. Last week in that misdemeanor trial downstairs in front of Judge Benson, you stood up in front of the jury and told him he forgot to instruct them on the elements of the offense. Don't do that. Ask him to approach the bench and remind him off the record. You embarrassed him, and he's pissed."

So I went downstairs and apologized, explaining I was new and didn't know the ropes. After a frosty initial reception, I was forgiven, and he confessed that with his wife's illness he was having a hard time concentrating. A floral arrangement sent to her hospital room, and presto, a friendly forum. Judge Halley had been my mentor since then.

Judge Halley finished out the four years of his term and retired, but over that four years he tutored me like a senior partner would a favored new lawyer in the firm. He beat me senseless on the golf course, but I looked on it as tuition for a course in advanced trial practice. I kept his ten commandments taped to the bottom of my desk drawer so they were always handy.

1. Don't piss off the judge.
2. Learn all the jurors' names and address them by it. No sweeter sound than the sound of your own name.
3. Keep questioning short. Know what you want to get from the witness. Once you got it, sit down.
4. Don't promise more in opening statements that you can deliver. Keep some goodies in the bag for later.
5. Find a hook, a theme, and weave it like a thread through the case from start to finish.
6. Fight the case on your hill, not theirs. Make the case be about a point you can win, not one you are going to lose.
7. Preparation and pizzazz are the ingredients of a good trial lawyer. Preparation will beat pizzazz more often than not. So be prepared.
8. Know the law. The law is the suitcase into which you fit the facts. If you don't know the law, you're going to have a hard time packing.

9. A trial is a form of theatre. Direct and choreograph to interest, entertain and convince. Know what actors you've got in the cast and use them well.
10. Act like you deserve to win. Believe in your case by the time you get to the courtroom door, or nobody else will.

There were others, but I never started a case without opening my drawer and doing inventory.

Once the judge retired I'd see him much less often. His tee times changed from 3:30 p.m. to 10:00 a.m. We played in a poker group once a month, and every so often he'd need a fourth for bridge. But if I was stuck on something or needed a sounding board, he was there for me. So when the name Xavier Westphal came up, I knew whom I could call to get help. After dressing and sprucing up at the wall length mirror, I used the locker room phone to call him.

"Well, if it isn't the big star of the criminal defense. Now why would he be calling me at 7:30 on a Friday night just as me and the missus are walking out the door for a weekend with friends?"

"Missed you and need your wise counsel. Hoping to buy you a beer and pick your brain. When will you be back?"

"Sunday late."

"Could you meet me at El Sombrero at five on Sunday?"

"What's so important, and what's all that racket? It sounds like a frat party."

"I'm at the club and it's tournament time. Can't really explain now. Will you meet me?"

"Let me check with she who must be obeyed." R.T. had adopted that *Rumpole of the Bailey* moniker for his wife of forty years. I could hear a brief muffled conversation. Then he was back on the line. "Better be important. Donna's none too happy about coming back early." I wished I'd thought of him earlier.

By the time I'd hung up, the locker room bar was beginning to clear, with the members going upstairs for the rib barbeque. Ernie and Paul were locked in a gin battle, and Fluffer had gone to pick up his wife. The scanty remains of two burger and fry combos lay on their plates, reminding me I had hardly eaten all day. So I munched on pretzels, waiting for my burger to arrive, and watched the staccato play of two scratch gin players. After eating I reminded Ernie, who was starting to get into Paul's pocket, of our early tee time, shook hands, and left.

Not long after I'd bored Billy with a replay of today's match, Max and I sauntered home. The delicious exhaustion of a full day had me nodding on the couch when the phone rang. I considered ignoring it, but thought it might be Karen, so I stepped over Max's prone form to catch it on the fourth ring. I wished I hadn't.

"Evening, asshole." Gianfranco's menace was immediately apparent.

"How'd you get my number? I've changed it twice since you and your pals started calling."

"That friendly little secretary of yours gave it to me when I told her I was your star witness and had important information to tell you." I made a mental note to tell Yvonne to be more careful, then erased it, thinking she had probably done the right thing.

"What kind of information?"

"You're going to be sorry you're making me take the witness stand. That prosecutor broad told me she was willing to excuse me, but you wouldn't let her. You got a death wish?"

"That sounds like a threat. Want to say it again so I can record it?"

"I don't make threats, only promises. And I promise you, if you go where you shouldn't go, you'll regret it. I'm telling you that nothing I've got to say from the witness stand is going to help your client. That's all I mean. You'd be stupid to have me on the stand. You're not that stupid, are you?"

I considered my stupidity quotient and answered, " 'Fraid I am. Show up on Tuesday."

"It's your funeral." With those parting words, the line went dead. It was quite awhile before sleep would come again.

53

"You fellas want to make a little bet?" Dr. Richard Richmond asked as he straightened after teeing his ball. The doc's picture would appear in the dictionary right next to silver spoon. He was tall, athletic and had a full head of short, cropped blonde hair. His nickname as a boy had been Richie Rich, owing to his father's patent on some method for bubble wrap packaging. He'd grown up in California as a surfer boy, attended UCLA for undergrad and Stanford for medical school. If it weren't for the girl he married, Lake Pointe would never have crossed his consciousness. While at Stanford he'd met Lake Pointe Central's former homecoming queen and valedictorian, Becky Jevitzki. She was majoring in health care administration and was the only child of two diabetic parents. She agreed to marry Dr. Richie only if he'd move to Lake Pointe so she could be near her parents.

His ob-gyn practice grew by leaps and bounds. His charm and good looks made him the delivery man to the well-to-do. His wife rose from chief of personnel to hospital president and CEO over the next twenty years. Baby Doc, in spite of the number of new doctors he brought into his practice and then pushed out, became chief of staff. Dr. & Mrs. Richmond were the Juan and Eva Peron of the medical world, except that they wasted little attention on the *descamiscados*. They were on the top of everybody's social A-list.

Today Baby Doc was nattily attired for the links. Like Payne Stewart, he featured plus-fours with red and white argyle socks. His white golf shirt bore a red Stanford Cardinal and was tucked to accent his flat belly. A scarlet tam sat jauntily on his head. His smile to Ernie and me was as artificial as his earlier pre-match handshake. I had whacked him in front of Judge Ernie for $200,000 for an unnecessary C-section that had been hurriedly sewn up, leaving nasty keloid scarring. Apparently he had a plane to catch and didn't want to let nature take its course. The labor charts and nurses testified to a slow dilating delivery without fetal distress which ended abruptly by C-section, just in time for the doctor to catch the Chamber of Commerce flight for the Las Vegas weekend blow-out.

Baby Doc didn't like lawyers to begin with. He was so sure that his charm and medical genius would wow the jury, he'd refused to sign off on a $100,000 settlement recommended by his malpractice carrier. After the carrier dropped him post-trial, his new company had doubled his premium and the judge had denied him a new trial motion, telling him he should have settled as follows: "You rolled the dice and lost." His smile from the tee was more that of a shark showing its teeth to a school of halibut than that of a well-meaning fellow competitor.

"Hey, what do you say, gentlemen, a little action to spice things up?" added M. Stanton. His smile was as genuine as his partner's.

"What a pair," I thought, seeing M. Stanton looking every bit the well dressed linkster in new khaki shorts beneath a country club logo navy golf shirt. His bald pate was covered by a Nike cap.

"What do you have in mind?" asked Ernie.

"I dunno, something more than chump change. Say one hundred dollars per man per side, and one hundred dollars overall. You've already made that much by reaching the championship. How does that sound?" M. Stanton offered with a smug smile.

Ernie and I looked at each other and shook our heads. We'd looked at the handicap book, and both M. Stanton and Richie had a long-established habit of turning in high scores for the month and a half before the tournament. After the contest their scores would drop back into the low 80's from the high 80's and 90's. Ernie had heard they both missed a lot of putts in the last five holes if things were going too well in the weeks leading up to the tournament.

"Nah, thanks anyway, we'll pass," I said as I compared the bounce on a couple of Maxfli noodles off the cart path.

I was going to play a Slazenger with the cougar on the label, but M. Stanton, who had won the tee, suggested in typical style that I change balls because "I always play cats and we have the honor. Sorry, old boy."

"No confidence, boys? We hear you've been playing great." Baby Doc tried again.

"Nope, you guys are just too good. Why do you think your team sold for twice as much as any other team in the bracket?" Ernie replied.

"Suit yourself," Doc said to us and then looked back at his partner. "Seems like these guys are beat even before we start."

Then he struck a smash 250 yards down the middle that soared over the rocky creek and traversed the fairway on number 1, leaving himself only a sand wedge to the hole. His partner followed suit, coming up only ten yards short of Baby Doc.

"Didn't really get that one, sorry, partner."

Golf should be played with a calm, relaxed mind. Mine was anything but. Here I was approaching the tee, my skin recently greased with sun-block on a beautiful sunny morning. Meanwhile, my client was turning pale after months in the county jail.

I stepped away from the ball as a guilty image of Ted languishing in irons in a medieval dungeon replaced the sight of my grip on the driver. My drive drifted a little left of center and had just enough momentum to trickle into the front edge of a fairway bunker.

"Gee, tough break, Ken," M. Stanton offered with all the sincerity of a used car salesman.

"Yeah, too bad, you hit it just hard enough to roll in," added Baby Doc, whose ball was 50 yards closer to the hole and sitting smack in the middle of the fairway. But Ernie tied into one himself and ended up just short of M. Stanton.

"Nice shot, Judge," they muttered as the caddies saddled up the bags and we set off down the fairway on a particularly overcast and almost windless 73-degree morning. The absence of wind was a rarity at the club and should make scoring easier.

When M. Stanton's caddie hung back to walk with Ernie and me and our caddies, M. Stanton promptly motioned him over.

"C'mon, Joshua, who are you working for? Didn't I tip you good yesterday?"

Josh looked sideways at me and then hurried forward.

"Coming, Mr. Browne."

Neither of their wedges stopped in birdie range, and Ernie was able to two putt from the back fringe to tie the hole.

The match in front of us was still in driver range on the par five second, so we waited for them to clear. M. Stanton decided to use the break for more mind games.

"Ken, I hope you have better luck getting Ted out of the hazard he's in than you did getting out of that fairway bunker." Both he and Doc found that amusing enough for him to push on.

"You know, I could've gotten him Murder Two if you'd kept your nose out of the case. Judging from what I hear, you'll be lucky if either of you comes out of that trial alive. I heard early on that the spectators are openly hostile to you, and somebody ran you off the road down from here."

Doc chimed in, "What's one lawyer more or less, eh, Ken? They're cranking them out of law school like cockroaches anyway."

Ernie spoke up while I struggled for a polite way to tell them both to get bent.

"Dr. Richmond, I think you'll agree a good lawyer helps to keep the medical profession healthy, kind of like a lion thinning out the diseased and lame from a herd of antelope, eh?"

Doc looked like he'd taken a chomp out of a lemon. I couldn't resist a salvo.

"Stanton, judging from your genius in letting your friend and neighbor Ted give Bliss a complete statement within ten minutes of your arrival on the scene, probably best you keep your comments to yourself. Oh, by the way, we put the $85,000 retainer in Ted's client trust account. Thanks for sending it over. Glad we didn't have to take that up with the ethics commission. Ted appreciates your seeing the light."

The smile vanished from Stanton's face. They walked to the far side of the tee, but just far enough away so you couldn't miss the stage whispered "—destroy these assholes" from Doc. So much for friendly competition.

The Collinses had built a huge white colonial house occupying two of the "manor lots" that ran along the fairway's left side. Maybe when the trees grew in it would look less like a mausoleum and more like a manor. Their house was in long distance driver range, and they already had replaced all the windows on the golf course side with some kind of shatterproof glass.

We could see the matched set of Jack Russell terriers sunning themselves in the yard as M. Stanton teed off. I guessed our little chat must have juiced him, because he pull hooked his drive, causing it to bounce in the rough and come to rest just beyond the white out-of-bounds stakes and into the Collinses' yard. Whereupon, Ruff and Ready awoke from their doze and, yipping and yapping, ran over to the ball. Ruff picked it up, and Ready chased him around to the front side of the house. Without thinking, I said the first thing that came to mind.

"Hey, M. Stanton, looks like your cat just went to the dogs."

Both of them startled and looked at me.

"Whadda you mean by that?" Baby Doc demanded as if he were reprimanding a nurse for handing him the wrong instrument. Stanton's gaze moved quickly from where his ball had disappeared to stare at me. I could see alarm in his expression.

"I meant Ruff and Ready ran off with Stanton's OB Slazenger. Why, what does that phrase mean to you?"

They exchanged glances with each other, and I could detect a minute shake of M. Stanton's head, telling Doc to leave it. He looked back at me.

"My ball was a foot or two inbounds. The dogs came onto the course to get it. Those dogs are an 'animate and outside agency' under rule 19-6. I am entitled to a free drop."

Ernie, ever a student of the law, asked, "The dogs are a what? There's a rule that covers that?"

M. Stanton reached into his bag and pulled out the *Rules of Golf* from a side pocket, and while he flipped to the page, I chimed in, "Counselor, I don't doubt there is such a rule, but I'm sure it applies to balls still on the course. Looked to me like your ball was clearly in the Collinses' yard, and I know they have one of those invisible fence things to keep yippy and yappy off the course."

Stanton started to redden right to the top of his bald head.

"Are you calling me a liar? I saw the ball stopping inbounds. Am I right, Rich?"

"That's how it looked to me," Baby Doc offered without batting an eye. "Judge, what do you say?"

"Hell, I can't see the ball once it gets one hundred yards out. It's your call, boys, in or out?"

Without hesitation Stanton said, "In." Golf presupposes its players to be honorable and thus leaves to the player striking the ball, not his competitors, the duty to make this kind of call. The game's founders must not have known anyone like Stanton.

So Stanton took a drop next to the white line along the edge of the course and smashed a five wood over a tree and out into the fairway. I nudged Ernie while we watched Stanton hand his club to his caddy and stride proudly down the fairway. Ruff and Ready had come racing back around the house, both wearing red collars with the shock boxes associated with the electric fence dog control. They stood barking excitedly side by side, two feet away from the flags that marked the electric fence at the edge of the OB. Ernie smiled in understanding and said just loud enough that it might have reached M. Stanton, "Cheaters never win."

"I hope not," I added.

Hole number 2 was an exception to the rule. M. Stanton's five wood had left him a 30-yard bump and run up the throat to the pin. He left his shot less than two feet short and tapped in for a birdie. Down one.

For the next seven holes hardly a word was spoken between opposing teams. Nobody gave anybody a putt with the exception of Ernie, who gave Stanton a seven-footer for bogey, which was three feet behind his partner's four-footer for par. Baby Doc misread the putt and played break when none existed. So we won the hole.

"Good thinking, partner," I said as we walked to the next tee following Ernie's par putt.

At the turn the match was tied. We weren't playing that well, but they were off form. They were coming off the tee great, but their short game was shaky. Stanton, who prided himself on his dexterity with wedge shots, left nothing close to the hole. Twice shots over greenside bunkers ran low and lay well past the hole. Another time from 80 yards out the ball bounced hard near the front pin and ran to the back. Doc, who bragged of his surgeon's hands with the putter, missed eight-footer after eight-footer, leaving us very much alive in the match.

As the foursome in front was playing like molasses, and still on number 10 fairway as we walked off 9, we took a clubhouse break. Ernie and I walked in to use the bathroom and stopped at the bar for "Arnie Palmers," an ice tea-lemonade combo. Big Lou, standing behind the bar in the empty locker room, looked up questioningly at us, turning his thumb up and then down.

"Well, how's it going?"

I held my hand flat. "Even after nine."

He smiled. "No kidding, you're holding your own with those two sandbaggers? They should be one, maybe two flights higher."

"So far, so good," Ernie offered, grabbing a handful of large pretzel sticks from the jar. We walked back out, handed the caddies their Gatorades, and headed for number 10 tee.

Tommy spoke up. "Thanks for the drink. You're playing good. You can beat those guys."

"Thanks, that's the plan."

We waited five minutes for our opponents. I could see the two of them over by the flagpole, with M. Stanton talking agitatedly on his cell phone. Their caddies had already come to the tee with their bags. Josh was looking at me kind of funny. Before I had a chance to ask "What's up?" M. Stanton came stalking over, his face florid.

"Edwards. I never liked you. Now I know why. Why the hell would you subpoena my wife to that circus? She just called me on the phone all hysterical. I'd like to smash your face!"

I put down my driver and prepared for what looked like it might be an imminent attack. "I'm right here."

But Ernie stepped between us, and I think M. Stanton was used to fighting all his wars with words anyway, so he just spat the anger at me.

"You asshole. What does Annabelle know about the case? What difference can she make? Your client's going down, and you are going with him. Why would you call her?"

"I'm not going to discuss my strategy with you, counselor. When you get home, ask your wife why I'd call her."

The anger still boiled in him.

"I told you not to call me as a witness. I warned you not to waive the attorney-client privilege between Ted and me. But you went right ahead and sent me a subpoena. You are a fool, and I can guarantee you now that when I take the stand, you are not going to like it."

I realized by now that M. Stanton was going to deliver his punches with words and not fists, so I added a little fuel to the fire.

"Am I hearing you right? My sending a subpoena to your wife changes your testimony? Your anger at me means to hell with Ted, a man who has been your friend and neighbor for twenty years? A man who was your client until you did everything but gift wrap him and hand him to Bliss and the prosecution?"

"Fuck you, Edwards. I'm twice the lawyer you'll ever be, and I've got the law firm to prove it. What have you got? A little hand- to-mouth hole in the wall operation and a couple of lucky courtroom wins? You're strictly flash in the pan, all glitter and no gold. I've hired and fired a dozen hot shots like you. My office will have a motion to quash not only my wife's subpoena, but mine as well, and I'll let the judge and your client know in open court that I've warned you that my testimony could be the last nail in Ted's coffin. You are going to be sorry you messed with me, and even sorrier you dragged my wife into it."

I waited to make sure he had run out of gas. The caddies took a couple of steps away from us, staring in fascination. I could see heads turning on number 9 and 18 greens in response to M. Stanton's tirade. So I calmed myself and then said as if nothing had happened, "All square. I believe we still have the tee."

I took a three wood instead of my driver in the hopes I could control the adrenaline tremors. But now we were on the back nine, where images of the case had haunted me in each prior round. To my right was the clubhouse where I'd last seen Amanda alive. Ahead was the fairway where Suzie and I had held hands on the night she told me of Amanda's short-lived fling with Annabelle Browne. Further ahead, number 15 passed the back yard of the Armbruster home. Whether it was ghosts or just my marginal golfing skills, I'd butchered that hole each time.

Standing behind me, jingling coins in his pocket, was Ted's neighbor, M. Stanton Browne. A man who had gift-wrapped Ted for the police and then had the nerve to critique my handling of the case. His anger seconds ago made me imagine him lifting his driver to strike me down while my back was turned. I shuddered, stepped away and looked behind me. Stanton's hand quit stirring coins in his pocket.

"That bother you? Little tight, are we?" he sneered.

I shrugged and his hand came from his pocket. His driver was still in the bag. I took a deep breath and tried to clear my mind. That didn't work too well, as I got way under the ball and popped it high in the air for all of 100 yards. Luckily, Ernie came through.

M. Stanton was so wired he almost whiffed on his drive, barely knocking the ball five feet off the toe of the club. But his partner, like mine, came through. After a couple of violent hacks, M. Stanton and I were reduced to spectating. I cheered my partner as he sank a downhill fifteen-footer to save a tie with Baby Doc.

Baby Doc took M. Stanton aside between the tenth and eleventh tee. I could see him attempting to calm and soothe his partner. Ernie did the same with me but couldn't resist asking, "His wife? I assume you've got a reason?"

"Yep. A good reason."

"Okay by me. Now, do you think you can get your head back into this match? I really, really want to beat those bastards."

"You got it, pard." I nodded.

Both pep talks must've worked, because M. Stanton started playing well, and I played eight of the best holes back to back I had ever played. I played those eight holes at three over par. I was in a zone. I swung slow and with a nice easy tempo, like I was on the range instead of in the match of my life. I struck a six iron on number 13 within six inches for birdie and chipped in for birdie from off the green on 15 to tie the hole. I had banished the ghosts on the "Armbruster hole" by remembering Ted's telling me he was starting to get less hate mail and more letters of support with each jailhouse mail call. "You must be doing something right, counselor," he'd told me at our last meeting.

On the holes I bogeyed, my partner rose up to make par. M. Stanton had become a horse. His short game returned. His ball would hit and stick on the green, sometimes spinning backwards. His flop shot over the green side bunker on 17 slammed on the brakes right behind the pin and almost backed up into the hole to tie Ernie and keep the match all square with one hole to play. Ernie's "Nice shot. That's good" were the first words exchanged between teams since the tenth tee.

It was to play like this in a big tournament that I had hit all the range balls, read *Golf Digest* faithfully, and spent hours on the putting surface. This was a big match against opponents we desperately wanted to beat, and now it was coming down to the last hole.

The wind from the southwest had been building all day and was blowing at least 25 mph straight down the fairway to the green 360 yards away. Just beyond the red disc marking 100 yards to the center of the green, a stream crossed the fairway. The pond from which the stream flowed guarded the entire left side of the fairway. On the right was knee-deep rough in which few balls were found, let alone found hittable.

"Ernie, I'm going with the three wood. Lots of wind up there."

"I think I'll just hit a five iron. With that breeze, that should get me in reacher range."

"Okay, pard. Let's do it."

Tommy pulled my driver and I shook my head. "Let's have the three wood."

I could hear Baby Doc humming tunelessly as I addressed the ball. I lifted my head to look at him. "Sorry," he said but didn't mean as the humming started up again as soon as I stood over the ball.

I stepped away, reminded myself to take a full, loose, easy swing, and moved back to address. I took a deep breath and hit it perfectly. Two hundred and thirty yards up the middle, right at the cart path bridge over the stream.

"All right, partner," said Ernie, and his five iron got up in the breeze, rolling to a stop fifteen yards behind mine. We had two shots in position. Things were looking good and were shortly looking even better as Baby Doc decided to try and carry the stream with his driver, but got a bad break when the ball hit near the bridge and jumped right into the stream.

"Son of a bitch," he muttered, "can you believe that? Sorry, pard."

M. Stanton, with quiet determination, walked over and stared at his bag. "Gimme the five wood."

What a great swing under pressure. His ball soared on the wind and came to rest five yards past mine, 115 yards to the center left pin placement. Ernie went with a pitching wedge and hit it well, too well, to the fringe on the back of the green top right.

That resolved all doubt for me. I took out my sand wedge, which will go 100 yards when well struck, and left the wind to do the rest. I took a couple of practice swings, stood behind the ball and took dead straight aim like you are supposed to, then stepped up to swing. The contact felt perfect.

"Good as I can hit it, it's right at it," I exclaimed, looking up to follow the ball's flight.

"Be the right stick," shouted Ernie.

"Carry ball." I began to worry that the left side bunker would capture it. The ball listened all too well. It carried the bunker, then hit a down slope and ran twenty or thirty feet past the pin. Baby Doc took his penalty and dropped behind the stream. His next shot ended in the right side bunker. He was done. We were going to win this thing.

I stood with Ernie as M. Stanton readied his shot. He hit a high wedge that started up the throat of the green and drew a little left in spite of the wind. The ball hit near the hole and spun backwards, stopping not two feet from the stick.

"Unbelievable." Baby Doc literally jumped on M. Stanton's back.

"You the man! You are the man!" he exulted.

To our credit, both Ernie and I hit our putts hard enough to go in, but neither did. I tapped in for par. We made M. Stanton putt his. Had to after coming this far. It was a short uphiller that he couldn't miss. Nevertheless, I found myself praying for a miracle. M. Stanton waited for us to concede the putt. We were as silent as mummies. Finally, he snorted in disgust and stepped over the ball. He was tight as a string, and he almost decelerated enough to push the ball wide. The ball teased us by hanging on the left edge for a millisecond before dropping. Match over.

We walked over to shake hands. Baby Doc was all smiles and "great match," etc. M. Stanton shook Ernie's hand but just stared at mine like it was rancid liver.

"How do you like them apples, asshole?" he snarled.

M. Stanton and Richie Rich strode across the green toward the clubhouse, arms on each other's shoulders. When they reached the fringe, M. Stanton broke away and turned back to extend his arm and pointed his index finger at me.

"I'm not finished with you."

I smiled.

"Always the gentleman, eh, Milt?" He flushed at the sound of the name with which his parents had christened him. Before he could respond I went on. "Well, I'm not done with you either. He who laughs last..." Before I could finish Stanton substituted his middle finger for the index and turned back toward the clubhouse with his partner.

"Gee, I thought this was a gentleman's game," Ernie said, handing his putter to his caddy.

"Yeah, well, I thought you said cheaters never win. Remember him out of bounds on two?"

Ernie shook his head. "As a lawyer, you know there is an exception to every rule." Then he stuck out his hand. "Great match, partner. Gosh, we played great. We didn't give it away. They just came and got it."

I grasped his hand and smiled back. "Hell, you're right. That's the best we can play. What a great effort. You were a pleasure to have as a partner. Too bad we had to lose to those jerks, though. Anybody else but them."

Ernie shook his head and then said, "Nah. Losing sucks, period."

"You got that right, pard," I replied as we moved over to the caddies. All four of them were standing on the fringe putting gloves and balls back into the bags. Tommy looked like he might cry.

"Mr. Edwards, I'm so sorry you lost. I didn't like those men. I'll never caddy for them."

I patted him on the back.

"Thanks. You were great. You can caddy for me anytime."

Josh walked over, also looking less than happy at the outcome, even though he was probably in line for a great tip.

"I know I shouldn't say this, but all us caddies were hoping you'd win. Looked for a minute like you had, and then..." He looked troubled, as if there was something he was deciding whether or not to say. Apparently he decided against it.

"Anyway, well. Good match."

He and Billy hoisted their bags and headed for the clubhouse.

Club tradition requires in tournament play that the winners buy the losers a drink. I tried to steel myself to sit politely for five minutes with our opponents, but I could see as we entered the locker room bar I wouldn't have to endure the final indignity. Our opponents had crowded two chairs around the small table of the foursome in front of us. Doc was obviously regaling them with a recap of their victory. M. Stanton looked over his shoulder at us and guffawed, turning back to his group to make some remark that had the whole table in stitches. No invitation was forthcoming. Thank God.

Ernie said without much enthusiasm, "Feel like a beer, partner?"

"Only with a hemlock chaser. Let's get out of here. M. Stanton might say something and I might do something and it all could end up badly."

So we showered, dressed and went to visit old Jack in the pro shop to collect our runner-up money. But he'd apparently taken ill and the prize was upstairs in the club office. Betty, the office manager, was on the phone and held up five fingers to ask us to be patient. So Ernie and I stood in the hallway. I pointed out the blank space where Ted's picture had once hung among the more than fifty photographer portraits. Ernie agreed that yanking Ted's portrait was pretty shabby. "At least let the jury convict him first."

We were looking along the row of pictures, picking out faces we recognized among the more recent past presidents, when I noticed the name Lawton X. Westphal etched into a metal plaque beneath a thirty-year-old picture. His high forehead and prominent nose sat beneath a luxuriant ebony mane. Dark, alert eyes looked at the camera intently, and his smile just curled the lips above a prominent chin.

"Judge, you know this guy, Westphal?"

"Name rings a bell. He was before my time. Mayor, president of the school board, some kind of big shot. Don't remember exactly. Why?"

"Just wondered."

Ernie let that hang for a second or two and let out a sigh. "Listen, while we're here, let's tell Betty were canceling our dinner reservation for tonight. I don't think I could sit there and watch those two jerks going up to get their green jackets. I'm plumb out of good sportsmanship. And if you and Stanton get a couple of cocktails in you, it could turn ugly. The only trouble is, Nancy has got a new dress she's all excited about. We've got to go somewhere nice. Is that cool with you?"

"Absolutely. I hope my date will understand. She just spent big bucks on a new frock. Wherever we go has to be classy and have live music so we can dance. But I do want you to meet Trooper Karen, my new lady friend. She's a knockout."

We settled on the Embers in Mt. Pleasant as nice enough to mollify the women, and agreed to meet there at eight.

I went back to the cottage to work on my opening statement, and in the quiet of a cicada-buzzing Saturday afternoon, started to make real progress. Maybe the tournament had served as a sorbet to my brain's palate.

Depending on how I did with Gianfranco, he would be my number one suspect. If I decided to put M. Stanton's wife, Annabelle, on the stand, and she was deceitful enough in her denials, maybe Suzie would agree to testify to impeach her. There was no love lost between those two. At least it would give the jury another bone to chew on. I reminded myself that my antipathy toward M. Stanton was no reason for me to humiliate his wife. Dr. Felton had a great alibi for the night of the murder, as he was at a shrink conference in Tahoe. The assistant pro might have enjoyed Amanda's favors. But for all I could tell, that was strictly a one-shot deal with no strings attached.

So that left the mysterious shape emerging from the mist, TNPC. I could tease the jury with cloaked allusions to it. But if I couldn't tie the investment to the poker group and then to Amanda's discovery about the missing Dressler money, the judge would stop me even before I got started.

I had spent more time with Alexandra in the last few weeks than in the last few years. Yet she was still an enigma to me. This woman with whom I'd shared my hopes for a distinguished trial career now seemed poised to derail my best shot to rise above being a courtroom journeyman. And she knew me well enough to anticipate my moves in time to cut them off at the pass. I shook my head to chase away her knowing steel-gray eyes. Time spent trying to understand that woman was time wasted. Back to my opening statement.

Westphal's picture on the wall at the club had convinced me I was getting closer to the truth with each passing day. The question was, were there enough days left?

I double checked the answering machine in the office and at home to see if Brent Eubanks had called. No luck. Except for a new round of threats and hang-ups on the home machine, there were no other calls. I called the phone company to change my number again, but was told by a computer after pushing five different prompts to call back Monday if I actually wished to speak to a human. I was so lost in thought over the missing fund money that I forgot the time and was late picking up Karen.

She knew from my earlier phone call that I was in the dumps about losing the golf match and accepted my apology with a smile. God, she looked great. Short strawberry blonde hair gave her face an elfin look, pert nose set off by sparkling blue eyes, light makeup subduing her freckles. The slinky black chemise showed off all the curves that her uniform only hinted at. I remembered to keep my eyes above the string of pearls resting on the swells cresting above a low-cut neckline. As I stood on the doorstep offering my lame explanation for tardiness, her full lips turned up to expose perfect white teeth.

"So what are you staring at, counselor?"

"Uh, you. Wow. You're beautiful! It's taking me a second to realize somebody so gorgeous is my date for dinner. You were right about the dress—stunning!"

Her face reddened slightly. "I clean up pretty good?"

"I'll say."

Taking my arm, she turned us around and we headed back toward the convertible, still with the top down.

"C'mon, don't stand there gaping. It won't do to keep a judge waiting. Surely you should know that, counselor."

As she sat to swing her legs into the low-slung car, her dress rode up, and I found myself admiring perfect legs in sheer black stockings. Again I must've been way too obvious.

"Now what are you looking at?"

"Oh, nothing. Well, actually, your legs. I think I've only seen you in trooper pants or jeans. The uniform doesn't do you justice."

She laughed.

"I know your reputation, old silver tongue. Flattery might get you somewhere, but not so fast. Remember, I give tickets for speeding."

I actually felt like a schoolboy caught sneaking a peek up a cheerleader's dress. I stammered, "No, no. I wasn't trying anything. I mean, what I was saying is, you look nice. Very nice. Is that okay for me to say?"

She smiled. "That's okay. Now quit gaping and get in. We're late."

The forty-five minute drive proved to be a blessing, as we talked nonstop. She'd fetched a scarf to protect her hair and given me the nod to keep the top down on this perfect seventy degree evening near the end of summer. I'd glance over as she told me of her dreams, which included law school and the bench with a stop as a state police detective sergeant along the way. The scarf framed her face nicely, allowing the wind to nibble at only a few strands of her bangs.

"What about becoming a wife and a mother? Doesn't sound like there's much time for that?" I asked, surprisingly interested in her answer.

"I'll make time for that. Family is number one for me. What about you? Confirmed bachelor?"

"More like a condemned bachelor. One failed marriage." I paused to concentrate on passing a semi as the wind wake from the behemoth pushed the lightweight car toward the shoulder. "One great romance gone south. And time marching on. When you reach my age, the roses with dew still on the bloom have all been picked."

"All of them?" She glanced over at me with a pouty look painted on her face.

"Well, maybe not all." Her face brightened and we laughed.

I felt close enough to ask her if I could talk about my case, to see what I was thinking by hearing myself think it. She said as long as I wasn't confessing any past crimes, or planning any new ones, she would keep things confidential. So I practiced my opening statement. She interrupted regularly to ask questions or suggest different phrasing. She thought "the mob guy" would make a plausible suspect. She was not too keen on dragging Annabelle through the mud. As I downshifted to exit the expressway she asked, "What have you got on her besides a failed relationship?"

"Not much. Just motive and opportunity. She lives right next door. They had a falling out."

"Sounds like grasping at straws. If you start crawling down in the sewer you can't help but get slimy yourself."

Before I mentioned Dressler she said, "If you don't give me a reason to disbelieve Bliss, and I'm a juror, your guy is going down."

"Thank goodness there are no cops on my jury." But I knew she was right.

As I told her about the missing charity money and the Cayman hedge fund with the same name as the country club poker group, she grew wide-eyed. "Wow. That's hot stuff. But what's that got to do with Bliss?"

She was sharp. That was the same question that haunted me. Find that connection, if there was one, and Ted would likely be a free man. Continue to grope about in the dark, and the hot stuff would never see the light of day in front of the jury. We were in the middle of that conversation as we pulled into the restaurant.

A stiff Jack Daniels followed by a couple of glasses of Merlot gave me a nice glow. Dinner was perfect. I was famished, and the scaloppini with a side of noodles alfredo nicely filled the void. When Ernie attempted to pass the Merlot for me to join him in a post prandial, Karen interrupted. Smiling sweetly, she leaned close to whisper in my ear, "Miles to go before we sleep." Her breathy tone caused a stirring of hope that tonight would be the night. Alas, she was merely acting as my personal breathalyzer.

Ernie's wife, Nancy, and Karen hit it right off. Ernie liked pretty women even more than golf, so he chatted Karen up enthusiastically. She could count on a warm welcome testifying in his court. The ladies imposed a complete table embargo on golf talk, so we didn't waste time, energy, and a good mood crying over what might have been.

As the ladies went off to powder their noses, Ernie's eyes closely followed Karen's departing figure. "Well, counselor, quite an upgrade from the last couple of doxies I've seen you with. This one actually has a brain. This relationship going anywhere?"

"Too early to say, Your Honor. But it's an idea worth exploring."

Karen had traded shifts with a morning shift troop and had an early wakeup. So, while she gave me a memorable clinging kiss to send me on my way, on my way I went. The old Rascals song "Groovin' " was on the radio as I motored home. Kinda fit my mood.

I was up early Sunday morning. I awoke in a panic. All I remembered of the dream that had chased me from sleep was the jury foreman saying, "We find the defendant guilty." Time to get back to work.

Max and I took an early sunrise swim, which helped to clear the cobwebs. I gave the half-gallon of milk in the fridge the sniff test. It passed, but only barely. A bowl of cereal and a banana later, I was collecting Max and congratulating myself that I'd be in the office by 7:30. Max loved my office. My scent was everywhere there. I think it seemed to him to be a room of the house that he couldn't quite remember how to find. He was more than happy to accompany me on weekends, although the cleaning lady scolded me for the dog hairs she had to vacuum off the carpet in the reception and secretarial area.

I patted myself down for wallet, car keys, office keys. Shit. My office keys were in a little compartment in my golf bag. I remembered them mingling in my pocket with golf tees and ball marks early in yesterday's round, and I'd slipped them in my bag. In the excitement of the match and final hole, I'd just turned my bag over to Tommy, completely forgetting them.

I'd lose an hour at least driving out to the club and then back into the office. But there was no avoiding it. Max didn't mind the extra drive. But as I pulled into the nearly empty club lot, I realized I had a problem. Max would definitely not be popular strolling through the clubhouse to get to the bag room. So I pulled over to the cart barn, which also housed the caddy shack. I could see a number of green-vested caddies lounging in various carts. Maybe I could get one of them to dig my keys out of my bag and bring them to me.

As I got out of the car, Josh walked to the passenger side and started patting Max's head and ruffling his ears.

"Mr. Edwards, what are you doing here? Didn't you get enough golf in the tournament?"

I shook my head. "Yeah, Joshua, more than enough. But I left my office keys in my bag. Would you mind running over to the bag room? They're in the top left pocket."

"No problem, be right back." And he was gone. I got Max out of the car and walked over toward the chipping area. He lifted his leg on the bag drop rack and sniffed eagerly in the plush grass. I scanned the empty course and parking lot. Quite a contrast to the beehive of tournament time. If you want your pick of Sunday morning tee times, the day after a three-day tournament is perfect. All the junkies have had their fix, and the golf widows have a long list of "honey-do's" and "your turn with the kids" to mete out as penance.

When Josh came back, he handed me my keys, looking troubled. "What's the problem, buddy? No loops today?"

He shrugged, looked over his shoulder to be sure no one was near. "I feel bad about you and the judge losing. Mr. Browne gave me a $100 tip, but still I wished you guys had won."

I shrugged. "Thanks, Joshua. That's the way it goes. Ernie and I played our best. Those guys are just better."

I thanked him and reached for a fiver to tip him. He shook his head.

"No thanks, that's okay." He patted Max and started to turn away. Then he turned back. "Can I tell you something and not get in any trouble?" He stuck his hands in his pocket and slumped a little.

"Sure, we're friends. What's up? Having trouble in school?"

"No, no. Nothing like that. I don't want to lose this job. I might get the Evans Scholarship, and I'm going to need it if I want to go anywhere but the local Juco."

I looked at him with more interest and could see he was very conflicted. The Evans Scholarship was a full ride to either MSU or U of M for caddies who could really play the game and had good grades and winning personalities. Josh qualified on all three fronts.

"Hey, I hear you've got a great chance for the scholarship. Did you do something that might cause a problem with that?"

"No, but—well, Mr. Browne's on the scholarship committee." Max had taken a seat at Joshua's feet, and and Josh stroked his ears distractedly.

"I'm afraid I don't have much influence with him, Joshua. You could probably tell yesterday we're not exactly friends. I'd help you any way I can. But me going to him on your behalf could only backfire."

The pace of the ear scratch picked up as the youngster looked perplexed and uncertain. Finally his hand stilled and he went on.

"No, that's not it. I want to do what's right. But if I tell you, I could get in trouble and lose the scholarship. My mom's got all her hopes on that scholarship. Me too."

"Tell me what?"

"You won't say I told you?"

"What is it?"

"'I think Mr. Browne cheated yesterday."

I laughed. "Oh, you mean that ball that was out of bounds yesterday that he called in. Not much we can do about that."

"Not that."

"What then?"

"He switched a club after nine holes. I know the rules. You can't change any club in your bag in the middle of a round. I looked in the rule book last night to be sure. It's rule 4-4. The penalty in match play is loss of two holes. So instead of losing by one, you guys should win by one. Should I report it to the pro? I wanted to tell you yesterday, but well, the scholarship and all, and then I could hardly sleep last night. He cheats and wins. If I do the right thing I'll get punished, and if I do the wrong thing, like keep quiet, I'm okay. Life's not supposed to be like that, is it?" I could see the agony on his face.

"No, it isn't. You didn't do the wrong thing. If anybody was wrong, it's Mr. Browne. Don't worry about telling the pro. It's not worth it. I'm already over losing, but how do you know he switched?"

He looked at me like I was dumber than he thought. "I'm his caddy. He always hands me his clubs to wipe off and put back in the bag. Except on the back nine he kept putting his wedge back in the bag himself. When I pulled it out to clean it, I knew it was not the one he'd used on the front side. Plus, you could see how his wedge shots were spinning and stopping on the back nine. That must be some club."

Now I was really interested.

"Wedge, what kind?"

"Well, his irons are all Pings. This was something called a Sunny or something."

"Oh yeah, a Solarz Super Wedge?"

"Yep, that's it."

That dog M. Stanton. When Dr. Zimmer had raised the second club possibility, and the wedges belonging to Jim Simpson's and Randy Dykes' clubs proved no match, I had called M. Stanton to ask if there was any chance his club had been at Ted's for the next day's golf trip up north. He got very stuffy and told me, "The rules prohibit play with that club. I'm a guy who plays by the rules. I'm not sure if I still have it." I reminded him that the other guys had agreed to waive the rule for their junket. His response: "None of those guys are in a profession dedicated to following the rules."

Then I thought he was a self-righteous prig. Now I realized he was a lying self-righteous prig. I looked back to Josh.

"Is it still in his bag?"

"No, I looked when I went to get your keys. His regular Ping is in there now. He must've gotten the super wedge out of his locker when you guys took a break after nine holes, then put it back after the round."

"You think it's in his locker now?"

He shrugged. I handed him Max's leash.

"Hold Max for a minute. I'll go check."

I went to the locker room bar. Big Lou wasn't there that early on the day after a tournament, but Stretch was. He was used to me forgetting my locker key and gave me the master without hesitation. The locker room was virtually empty, so I proceeded to the row where M. Stanton's locker was. The director's plaque made finding the right locker easy. The row was empty, so I inserted the key and opened the oak door.

Sure enough, leaning against the back comer was the wedge. I pulled it out and looked at it. For an illegal club, it had gotten a lot of play. The grip was worn and the clubface had stone nicks. My heart was rushing. I felt guilty in somebody else's locker and wanted out of there fast. So I closed the door, held the club by my left leg and dropped the keys on the end of the bar. I waved at Stretch on my way out the door and walked directly into the bag room. It too was empty, and it didn't take too much wandering to find M. Stanton's bag.

I examined the club for half a minute and slid it into his bag. The shaft had a sticker wrapped around it with the club logo and M. Stanton's address and phone number on it. Handy, as wedges get left by greens all the time. As I walked back toward the parking lot I thought to myself, "Gotcha, you bastard. The last laugh is coming quicker than you think. And it will matter much more than the laugh you got at beating me for the green jacket in the fourth flight."

Two other caddies were over talking to Josh and playing with Max when I came around to the chipping area again. "Hey, guys. Thanks, Josh, for holding Max. Got what I needed. Joshua, mind walking Max back to the car? He seems to like you."

We walked over to the car with Max prancing happily on a loose leash.

"Found it?"

"Yep. It's in his bag now. Listen, kiddo, I don't care about the match, but that golf club may be important in that murder case I'm trying for Mr. Armbruster. I might need you to come to court."

Josh stopped and his well-tanned face lost all color. "Oh, my God, I can't do that. I'll lose the scholarship and be fired for sure. Mr. Browne will kill me."

"No, no. Just listen. I'm going to serve a subpoena on you. That's a court order that forces you to come. You have to tell the truth in court.

So it's nothing he can blame you for. I'll also subpoena Jackie, the bag room guy, to bring Mr. Browne's bag to court. All you have to do is identify the sand wedge as being the one Mr. Browne used in the tournament. Has he been using it much?"

"He used to all the time. Yesterday was the first time I've seen it this year."

I considered the implications of that. "Will you do it? I'll make it look like I noticed, not something you told me."

He looked doubtful.

"Will it help Mr. Armbruster? He's a nice man. I can't believe he killed his wife."

"He didn't, Joshua. And this might help me prove it. What do you say? This is doing a very important and right thing, and I'll give you my word, it won't come out bad for you."

He nodded his head slowly. "Okay then. Can I tell my mom?"

"Yep. Tell her, but nobody else, and if she wants to talk to me, here is my card. I'll write my home number on it too."

Max and I climbed back into the car and headed for the office. I had some serious thinking to do. Was this the second club? Almost had to be. How did it get from Ted's back to Browne's? How did the police miss it? Why would someone use one club to inflict the initial injuries to Amanda's forehead and a second club for the fatal wounds to the back of the head? Were there two assailants? If Browne was one, was Ted the other? If not, who?

On Sunday the downtown streets were deserted, so I swung the 280 to the curb right in front of the office. No sooner had I let Max out of the car than he began to growl and strain at his leash. Pulling in, I had noticed no one. But Max had sensed the young man who'd come out from the shadows of the pharmacy. He was now crossing the street and jogging in my direction with something in his hand. I went into a defensive crouch.

Usually Max was people friendly. Not today. Max doesn't bark. He woofs. He woofed in a basso profundo that echoed off the downtown buildings and stopped the man in mid-street.

"Looking for me?" I called out.

"I'm an intern with Mr. Browne's office. I have a notice of hearing to serve."

I relaxed, but Max didn't. When a determined one-hundred-and-twenty-pound dog is using his low-to-the-ground power, he can pull you off your feet. I stumbled forward a couple of steps before I could brace myself. The kid turned tail and retreated to the far curb. It took a minute for me to get Max under command and to turn him for a short walk up the sidewalk.

"Leave it on the bench over there. I'll consider myself served."

"But Mr. Browne insisted I hand it to you personally." The youngster's voice was uncertain.

"Tell him if he loves big dogs so much, to come and do it himself. I'll be here all afternoon. Otherwise, leave it on the bench. I won't raise any service issue."

I let him get a block away before Max and I walked across the street to pick up the papers. As promised, it was a motion to quash my subpoena for his wife, alleging vindictive and harassing motives to me. For good measure he moved to quash the subpoena for his testimony, citing attorney-client privilege and accusing me of "gross professional incompetence." Talk about the pot calling the kettle black. If he hadn't let Ted talk to Bliss in the first place, I wouldn't have needed his testimony to try and undo the damage. The emergency motion was set for Monday at 4:45.

Although the music at El Sombrero was strictly south of the border stuff, it was nevertheless the spot where couples met to do the tryst. There was not a window in the place. The rheostat for the candelabra lights was attached to two suspended wagon wheels hanging between the bar, and the booths' setting was always turned down low. The leatherette booths were always in shadow. It took a minute for my eyes to adjust from the bright sunlight outside before I could scan for R.T. Halley.

Near the rear of the restaurant a slender, middle-aged man took the arm of a younger blonde and scurried out the back door. My eyes hadn't adapted well enough for me to recognize him. But I bet he recognized me. I was half tempted to slip out to the parking lot to see who it was, but I figured my quota of new enemies for the month had already been met. So I took a seat at R.T's normal booth and ordered a Dos Equis.

I once asked R.T. why he'd chosen this spot as his watering hole. He told me that it was close to home, he loved Mexican food, and he loved the floor show provided by the furtive couples. The next time the front door opened to light the stygian darkness, it was R.T. who stood waiting for his eyes to adjust. After a warm handshake, he slid into the booth across the table from me and motioned for the barmaid. She sauntered over, her peasant outfit swaying in time with her syncopated hips.

"*Buenos noches, Juez. Como estas?*"

"*Muy bien, Carmelita. Y tu?*" They exchanged pleasantries in Spanish, with him ordering for both of us and telling her to "*Da la cuenta a eso hombre.*"

R.T. was nearing seventy. Yet he looked younger now than when he'd retired at sixty-five. He was rotund and jolly. The semicircle of baldness reaching the crown of his head was framed by wispy gray hair in back and along the sides. Before he would say a word about the case or the purpose of our meeting, he waxed eloquent on on his new greenhouse.

"I've got the best collection of orchids for miles around. My Red Queen Dendrobium has got to have twenty purple and mauve blooms at least three inches in diameter, and my Vuylstekeara Cambria is finally in flower after two years of waiting." We were through the first beer and had our meals in front of us before he wound down. He asked how Ted was holding up.

"About as well as can be expected when somebody kills your wife and you're waiting in jail for the jury to convict you," I replied.

"Same old bullshitter." R.T. laughed and took a deep swallow of the Dos Equis, so well chilled the bottle had a thin layer of ice near the neck.

His assessment of my case after I updated him and answered his questions was, "You're down by a couple of touchdowns, but there is still time on the clock." After settling on the terms of our Michigan-Michigan State bet for the fall, he asked, "What do you need from me?"

"A little history lesson. Do you recognize the name Xavier Westphal?"

He put down his fork full of chicken fajita and cocked his balding head. "That's a blast from the past. I knew him, or better to say, knew of him. Only then he went by the name of Lawton X. Westphal. Why do you ask?"

The plaque under the photograph in the country club entrance came to my mind. "Name came up in the Armbruster case."

R.T. laughed. "I know you've been working on creating as many suspects as you can to feed the jury. But Lawton will never fly. He's been gone twenty years. He left Lake Pointe for the Caribbean about the time Amanda Armbruster was in high school. I doubt he ever knew her."

"The Caribbean?"

He picked up his fork and ruminated while he chewed. "Yep, one of those little banking islands. Probably not much more than fifty-five when he left. Big family money in shipbuilding was becoming smaller family money when the market for Great Lakes freighters dried up. Still, he was a mover and shaker. Head of the Chamber of Commerce, county commission, a director on at least a couple of corporate boards. I think he was chairman of the Republican party when Republicans could still get elected around here."

"So why did he leave?"

"He got divorced. Still had a pretty good pot of money left. Was some kind of Wall Street whiz. Hated Michigan winters. Went off to a sunnier clime to manage his money is what I remember. If he's been back in town since, I haven't heard of it. Now tell me what hare-brained idea you have that could possibly involve him."

So I swore him to absolute secrecy and told him everything I knew about CATS, DOGS, Dressler, and TNPC. He let the rest of his meal grow cold and gave me his full attention without interrupting until I said, "That's it. What do you think?"

"Holy Shit! That's quite a little bombshell you got there, son. Makes watching the lounge Lotharios here seem pretty dull. Might just wander back to the courthouse myself to watch the show. How are you gonna get it in? Judge Alex runs a tight ship. Say, didn't she make you walk the plank a few years back?" he concluded, his pleasure at his play on words dimming as he saw me wince.

I shrugged, trying to minimize the pain. "Something like that. Anyway, I'm pretty close. I can show Amanda wrote the note within weeks of her death. I can show what it means. I can claim it's at least as good a motive for murder as the insurance policy."

"Yeah, but are you going to claim ten poker players all stood around taking a whack at her? If it wasn't Ted, who was it?"

I told him about M. Stanton's club and his eyebrows arched.

"Little Lord Fauntleroy? Never liked that pompous swine. But murder? Doubt he has that in him. I'll definitely be there to watch him squirm, though. Still think the judge will keep it out as too speculative. Heck, I would, and I like you. I bet Judge Alex says no go. Sorry about the tasteless remark a minute ago. I know you had a bad time for a while after the break-up. What happened there?"

"Ancient history. Tell you sometime, if I ever figure it out. And whatever happened between Alexandra and me, she treats me like it was my fault. So she won't be cutting me any slack. Anyway, I need something good, or Bliss's confession testimony probably sinks us."

At the mention of Bliss's name, R.T. stopped in mid swig from his beer. A look of concentration crossed his face.

"What?" I asked.

He ignored me for a minute. "The memory isn't what it used to be. Heck, I can't remember where I left my glasses five minutes after I take them off." Saying that, he patted his shirt pocket to assure himself of their whereabouts. "There is something rattling around in my head involving Bliss and Westphal, but I'll be darned if I can think of what it is."

"Oh, Judge, if you've got something there, I'm in business. Think, man, think." And he did, stroking his jaw and staring at the wagon wheel chandeliers. Then he shook his head.

"Nothing. But I find if I walk away from something like this and forget about it, sometimes it just pops up. I know a couple of guys who were around back in the day. I'll do what I can. Meanwhile, before you pull the pin on that Dressler thing, think about the harm you could cause. Sometimes it's best to let sleeping dogs lie. You know, if they put the money back and all."

"Even if the sleeping dogs woke up long enough to kill her?"

"Nope, not then."

I caught the check and walked out to the parking lot as the sun headed for the horizon. The breeze from the north was chilly enough for me to wrestle the top up on the Benz. Change of season was in the air.

57

M. Stanton's motion had been appended as the last item on the judge's docket. When it was reached at 4:45, the only people in the courtroom were the judge, her staff, Browne, and Miss Botham seated at counsel table with him. "Strange alliance," I thought. I asked that Ted be brought over, as the judge might want his on-the-record acknowledgement of my position.

Judge Alex looked great. A week in California with family had agreed with her. She was rested, relaxed and even managed a smile at me. The years since our break-up had been kind to her. Then she was a pretty young thing. Now she was reaching full bloom as a confident, beautiful woman. I shook my head at what might have been.

Browne got up to argue his motion. Stretching his arms, he shot his cuffs, presumably so all could marvel at the solid gold seahorse cufflinks. Then he launched into his diatribe about his responsibility to his former client and how my calling him would constitute a waiver of the attorney-client privilege between Ted and himself.

"Mr. Edwards' desperate grandstanding will force me to reveal confidential communications which can only have devastating consequences for my former client. Even a first-year law student should know better than to waive attorney-client privilege."

I took the bait. "Even a high school drop-out should know better than to let his client give a statement to police at the scene of a murder within minutes of his arriving there. Now Mr. Browne is my only witness to impeach that so-called confession. Believe me, Judge, considering the regard in which I hold my brother at the bar, if I could avoid calling him, I would."

The judge tossed her thick mane of hair and asked if I had carefully considered the danger of putting Mr. Browne on the stand. "Mr. Edwards, I know you well enough to know your propensity for risk taking. Have you considered the devastating perils such a tactic exposes your client to?"

"Very carefully, Your Honor. I don't intend to ask him about private conversations between himself and Ted. I have Mr. Browne's statement to the court at the preliminary hearing that the confession does not accurately reflect his hearing of what was said."

Browne jumped up. "But Judge, part of the foundation for my remarks at the preliminary was my private conversation with Ted before I let the detective speak to him. And once we get into that conversation, then the door is open to all other conversations. I state on the record now that I had a confidential conversation with Mr. Armbruster on a date shortly before the murder which, if revealed, could prove quite damaging."

The dog. He had told me when I took the file back and discussed his testifying that at no other time had Ted told him anything incriminating. Either he had lied then, or he was lying now.

"I intend to avoid privileged communications, and as the file was returned to me from Mr. Browne, I asked him quite explicitly if there were any conversations with Ted I should know about. He assured me there were not, so naturally I'm shocked to hear about some quite damaging conversation for the first time today in court."

Browne looked a little undecided as to his course but then decided to forge ahead.

"I don't remember any such conversation with Mr. Edwards. He seemed in quite a hurry to get this front-page news case back and have the balance of the retainer sent to his firm. I would've gladly shared the additional information if he had bothered to ask."

"Mr. Browne's memory of the meeting and mine are distinctly different." That's lawyerese for "He's a liar."

"As to the retainer, Mr. Browne used up more than I have in four weeks of trial by showing up in court for a total of two hours. I'd suggest that unless he'd like to spend a few days with the Ethics Committee, he keep his mouth shut about fees."

The judge shook her lovely head.

"Enough, gentlemen. This is not a schoolyard name-calling match. It's a court of law. A court of law concerned with a very significant case and a very delicate legal matter regarding waiver of the attorney-client privilege. Mr. Browne, I'm going to deny your motion. Mr. Armbruster can waive the attorney-client privilege if he chooses to do so. I'll make a separate record if it comes to that. I see Miss Botham is here making copious notes, and I suggest, Mr. Edwards, you proceed very carefully. I think you may be on thin ice. Understood, gentlemen?"

"Understood, Your Honor," I said. "Please caution Mr. Browne only to answer what he is asked and not to blurt out things that can create a problem."

Browne glared at me. Then in a measured, dignified tone, he said to the judge, "I expected your ruling, Your Honor, but I felt I had to make a record to protect my reputation and myself from Mr. Edwards' reckless conduct, and I want it to be clear I had no part in this legal maneuver and have opposed it all along."

"Gee, Judge," I said, shaking my head in disbelief, "he is pretty slow on the trigger. I told Mr. Browne I'd have to call him when we had the conversation in his office that he doesn't remember. Then he said he'd be happy to do it. I sent him a subpoena four weeks ago at the start of the trial, just in case he decided he had important business out of town when I needed him, and now here we are at five o'clock on a Monday on an emergency motion. Would the court please order Mr. Browne to disclose to me in private what damning evidence just bubbled to the surface of his memory since yesterday's motion filing?"

"So ordered," said the judge, shuffling papers. "Now, Mr. Browne has asked that his wife's subpoena be stricken. Is this somehow related to the privilege issue, Mr. Browne?"

M. Stanton straightened his tie and looked to the judge. "No, Your Honor. I believe this subpoena is a tactic by Mr. Edwards to harass and annoy me and my family. Perhaps he is seeking revenge for my earlier embarrassing displacement of him as Mr. Armbruster's counsel."

"Is that your purpose, Mr. Edwards?"

I held my hands upturned at my sides and shook my head in denial.

"Judge, I'm trying to give Mr. Armbruster the best defense I can in a very difficult case. The last thing I'd do is call a witness that could jeopardize that task for some petty personal vendetta. Besides, Mr. Browne's handling of the case during his short tenure at the helm should be more embarrassing to him than anything I could ever do."

The smack of the judge's gavel resonated loudly in the empty courtroom.

"Enough. Quit your infantile bickering, the both of you, or I'll fine the both of you in an amount you will feel for a while. Mr. Edwards, will you tell the court the reason for calling Mrs. Browne?"

"I'm sorry for my unprofessional bickering, Your Honor. I'd prefer to keep my reasons to myself as a matter of defense strategy. I think it would be unfortunate if the unpleasantness between Mr. Armbruster's past and present counsels provided Madam Prosecutor any advantage. I assure you as an officer of the court that Mrs. Browne's testimony deals with matters at issue in the case and is not designed to harass and annoy."

The judge looked cross at being left in the dark. I had seen that look before when we were dating and I had been evasive about nights out barhopping with my fellow bachelors on the lawyers' softball team. "Then I'll deny Mr. Browne's motion, but I'll be very ready to impose sanctions if I find after hearing her testimony that your motive was improper. Moreover, I am directing you to disclose to Mr. Browne your reason for calling her so his wife will know the expected area of inquiry." She then rose from the bench and stared down at us over her reading glasses.

"Dismissed."

I needed to use the restroom, so I told M. Stanton I'd see him in the attorney-client room in five minutes. He glared his acknowledgment at me and walked out of the courtroom.

When nature's call had been answered, I walked back out into the elevator lobby outside the courtroom, only to see M. Stanton sitting with Tina Botham on the bench across the lobby. They were a strange-looking couple. Even seated, Stanton towered over her petite form. However, his rich navy pinstripe nicely matched the same color and pattern on the skirt and jacket she wore over a lace- topped blouse. Browne was talking quickly and sotto voce. Tina had a legal pad in her lap and was making notes. On hearing the squeak from the men's room door closing, they both looked up guiltily. Conversation ceased as I rushed over.

"Counselor, neither I nor your former client have waived any privilege at this moment. If you have disclosed anything to the woman who is trying to convict him of murder, I'll have you before the State Bar Grievance Committee so fast you won't believe it. And when they're done with you, I'll sue your ass for every penny you've extracted from your clients over the years. Nothing personal, you understand."

At the mention of a threat to his pocketbook, I saw his ferret eyes flicker for an instant. I'd touched him where he lived. I could see him wondering if he had said something to Tina out of his animosity for me that could cost him. Tina looked like a teenage girl who had just gotten the bottle out of the liquor cabinet as her parents pulled into the garage. She spoke up.

"Now, Ken. You know I want to win this case, but do you think I'm stupid enough or unethical enough to try and get Stanton, I mean Mr. Browne, to violate a confidence right out here in the hall with you gone for just a minute, do you?"

"No offense, Tina, but I do know just how much you want to win this case. I'm not saying you'd climb the forbidden tree to get an apple, but if one just fell into your lap, I think you'd bite."

Her eyes averted from mine to the side just long enough to see I'd hit the mark. Then the professional mask closed over her face again. She closed the note pad on which I could see three or four lines of notes. She got up and headed for the stairs, smoothing the crease out of her skirt, her high heels echoing on the stone floor. She turned and looked at me as if trying to think of the right thing to say, gave up and merely said,

"I'm sorry you feel that way," and she was gone.

"Damn it, M. Stanton! What the hell are you doing? Get even with me any way you want, but Ted Armbruster's been your friend and neighbor for twenty years, not to mention your loyal client about as long. What is the matter with you? Are you so eager to see me fail that you're prepared to throw him overboard to do it?"

M. Stanton was still seated. He covered his mouth and chin with his hand as if in thought for half a moment, then he looked up at me.

"Screw you, Edwards, and the horse you rode in on. I told her nothing, nothing that won't be coming out in court anyway. So make all the empty threats you want. Now let's get this meeting over with. I've got a hospital board meeting in an hour. I don't want to be late. They pay me more in a one-year retainer for once-a-month board meetings and a few consultations than you're going to earn for knocking yourself out day and night on this case for two months steady."

He grabbed his briefcase and we walked down the hall toward the conference room together. There was a wall of animosity two feet thick between us. I shook my head and couldn't resist asking, "So that's all your ticket is to you? A license to print money?"

He snorted. "And yours isn't? It's just that you're not too good at it, that's the only difference between us."

The room was small. We sat on opposite sides of a rickety table with graffiti etched into the top. The leaf on my side bore a message I often wondered at: "Mea Culpa." I hoped one of my clients wasn't the artist.

"All right, M. Stanton. You're in a hurry. What's this missile you're about to launch at Ted, and why didn't you tell me before?"

He looked smug. "You never asked."

"Okay, I'm asking now."

"Six weeks or so before Amanda's death, we had a sunny Sunday in March. Ted and I snuck through the back fence to play golf even though the course wasn't officially open. He's better than you, by the way. But that day he played lousy. He had a flask of vodka and was taking nips to stay warm. Didn't help his game or his mood.

"Anyway, I invited him into my trophy room for a post match drink.

By the way, I just added the one from last weekend to the mantel."

He looked to see if that last remark would get a rise out of me. I pretended it was no biggie. "Yeah, you were saying?"

"Right. So I asked him what was eating him." He paused to catch the apprehension on my face.

"And?"

"Well, he told me how hard business was. They had that big contract promised, but the bank said it couldn't wait much longer on the deal. He had used all his available cash, and the company would go under if something didn't come up soon. He actually had tears welling in his eyes about his employees losing their jobs, and when he started talking about Amanda, he bawled like a baby right there in front of me."

"What about Amanda?"

"He said he loved her so much it hurt, but the way she'd been acting, he thought he was going to lose her too. She seemed more distant. She was out a lot, that kind of stuff. You know, I think the only guy in town who didn't know Amanda was fooling around was Ted. And I think he was beginning to suspect."

"Did he say that?"

"No."

"So what's the big deal?"

"Well, the big deal is—" He paused to draw out the agony, and I swear he licked his chops. "When he got up to go home, I told him to cheer up, things would get better. He looked at me, shaking his head, and these are words I'll never forget. He told me the only hope for the company was to collect on that life insurance policy. I was worried about suicide. But now after what happened—"

"Oh, shit," I thought. What I said was, "That it? Any other little bombshells you haven't told me?"

"Nope. That's enough, isn't it? Actually, I called him the next week at work to make sure he wasn't suicidal. He sounded better and when I asked about the company's finances, he said he had an idea he was working on."

"Anything else?"

"Nope."

I looked at the ceiling. M. Stanton was trying to manufacture a look of rueful concern for Ted, but he couldn't help enjoying in his smug way the sight of my legal ship taking on water.

"How much of this did you tell Madam Prosecutor?"

"Nothing." His eyes wouldn't meet mine. I knew he was lying.

"M. Stanton, I'm warning you. I saw she was taking notes. I'll subpoena them if I have to, and lest you think your natural male charm has warmed Tina's heart, she told me she thought you were an arrogant jerk who didn't know his ass from his elbow in a criminal case. So don't expect her to save your butt. How much of this did you tell her?"

Now he looked shaken. "Nothing, really," he muttered.

"What's nothing really?"

He paused, considering whether to tell me now or have it out with the judge, considering that Tina might not be such an ally after all. Finally he decided. "All I said is if I had to testify, I might have to disclose conversations about insurance. That's it, no details."

"That's enough, isn't it? What's the matter with you? Ted was your friend. You know, M. Stanton, you've got all the qualities of a dog, except loyalty."

I saw the muscles in his jaw tighten. "Hey, fuck you. It's your idea to call me. Don't call me and it doesn't come out."

"Well, if there was any other way other than calling you to attack that confession, believe me I'd use it. The statement to Bliss is not privileged, so don't you volunteer anything about the pre-confession chat with Ted. I know you want to bring that up to explain how you could do something so stupid as to let Bliss interview him at the scene, but don't. I'm telling you we are not waiving the privilege."

"Okay, what am I going to do if she asks me about the post-golf conversation about insurance?"

"You turd, you did tell her about that conversation?"

He realized he'd already said too much. "No. Well, I told her where and when, but not what he said."

I shook my head in disbelief. This guy, for all his fancy trappings, made me feel sleazy being in the same profession with him, let alone the same small room. I started on damage control.

"You've been Ted's personal and business lawyer for twenty years?"

He nodded.

"Nobody else was there for the conversation in the den?" I held my breath.

"No."

"You've discussed confidential business and personal matters with Ted in social settings before?"

He thought for a second. "Definitely."

"You were reviewing the status of his business and domestic situation as his trusted legal advisor?"

He curled his lip up as if he considered my approach dubious. But his opinion on criminal procedural matters meant nothing to me.

"I guess you could say that, although I didn't bill him for it."

"This may come as a shock, Stanton. You don't have to be running the meter to be acting in a privileged lawyer-client relationship."

He thought about that for a moment, then he brightened.

"I am on an annual retainer with the company. I do tell my clients that the retainer makes me available whenever they need me. You're right, I was listening to his problems and counseling him, so it's privileged, and I didn't tell the prosecutor what he said, I swear."

"Good, keep it that way. Now is there any other dynamite you're holding?"

"Nope, that's it. Now that we got that cleared up, will you release Annabelle from her subpoena?"

All buddy-buddy again. I shook my head.

"Sorry, M. Stanton, I can't."

"You fucker, why not?" So much for buddy-buddy.

I looked at him. "You have no idea why I'm calling her?"

"Except to piss me off, no."

"Okay. I feel very uncomfortable saying this. I have it on reliable authority your wife had an affair with Amanda."

"You bastard. I'll kill you!"

He was out of his seat like a shot and came across the table at me. It broke under his weight and my chair went over backward, so I was on the floor with him on top of me. His hands were closing around my throat. In spite of being a fop, he worked out and was in shape. I was losing the battle to pull his hands away and started to panic as my air grew short. Black floaters were filling my vision. I mustered all the strength I had and brought my knee into his groin, hitting pay dirt. His grip loosened and I was able to roll him into the corner and go to the opposite side of the tiny room to gasp for breath. He was curled over in great pain, but he looked like he was steeling himself for another attack.

"Stanton, goddamnit. Before you kill the messenger, go ask her," I croaked. "I didn't make it up. I got it from someone who knows." I crouched in the corner of the small room in case his efforts to stand proved to be a prelude to another assault. Instead he grimaced and leaned, muscles still tense, against the wall in the far corner, catching his breath and glaring at me.

"Who?"

"Ask her. Ask your wife if it's true. Ask her about the coatroom in the conservatory at the bar party last year."

That must have struck a responsive chord. Maybe Annabelle had been upset at the party, because the tension evaporated from him. He slumped back against the wall.

"I'll ask her, and if you're lying to me I swear I'll make your life miserable any way I can. My number one goal in life will be to ruin you. But even if it's true, which it's not, why humiliate her? Why humiliate me like this? What good can that do Ted?"

I pulled my tie from over my shoulder. The wrinkles testified to the force he'd applied to my neck. "I'd rather not have to, believe me, and maybe I won't have to. Got another angle I'm working on. But the prosecutor's motive, in addition to money, is jealousy. Your wife got dumped by Amanda. She was jealous. She stalked Amanda for a while. Did you notice they stopped seeing each other?"

Again I struck home. I could see him checking his memory bank. "They had a falling out over some golf course thing."

"Just take your wife aside and sit her down and then ask her. Tell her you need to know the truth, all right?"

"All right, I'll ask her, but either way, you can't put her on the stand. The gossip will kill her. It'll ruin both of us. I can just hear the guys snickering in the locker room. Oh my God." He was talking to me but fixated on the grease spot his jacket had acquired from the floor.

The potential damage to his social standing and perceived macho image seemed more deflating to M. Stanton than the idea that his wife had been involved in a lesbian affair. As he contemplated the magnitude of professional, social, and dry cleaning disasters, all his tension evaporated. He licked his fingers and concentrated on the sartorial blemish to his suit jacket, his mind so preoccupied it was like I wasn't there.

I picked the chair up and set it on its legs, but there was nothing to be done for the table. "I'll go find the janitor. I'll tell him you lost your balance," I said as I walked out into the hall. I'm not sure he heard me. As the door closed his head was in his hands. I left him alone with his thoughts.

“I choked myself shaving,” I whispered hoarsely to Janice as I entered the reception area and she asked me about the red marks on my neck. I headed straight for my office and shut the door. Trial was like being tossed about on a stormy sea, but the tumult on the surface in this case paled in comparison to the rip tides beneath the waves.

I stared out the window at the street below to calm myself and collect my thoughts. The sunny afternoon was giving way to a violent thunderstorm. A high black wall of cumulonimbus clouds approached, lightning coursing through them. The wind blew dust and papers in a flurry down Lafayette Avenue. The rain fell in blankets, if that’s the next step up from sheets.

I watched a lady trying to manage an armful of bags and a poodle on a leash as she dashed for her car. Running seemed pointless as they were both already soaked to the skin. Apparently little Fifi so decided, because she stopped running at her mistress’ heels and dug her paws in. The leash snapped back in the lady’s arms and the packages spilled onto the sidewalk. The woman stood abjectly staring at her pet. I imagined tears of frustration mixing with the rain upon her face. She looked so forlorn, standing all alone in the tempest.

I felt a kinship with her. The Armbruster case had left me standing alone, exposed to the storm. I couldn’t dash for safety because I had a client who totally depended on me for his deliverance. I’d been threatened and harassed, had guns pointed at me, and been run off the road. Somebody had tried to kill my dog. I'd been vilified personally and publicly for defending someone everyone knew was guilty. An hour ago I'd nearly been choked to death. My practice was in a shambles. All my other cases were growing moss from neglect. I wasn't sleeping well at night. My dreams were haunted with the recurrent vision of Amanda holding a shiny object out to me.

I also identified with the lady's pooch. She'd been dropped into terrorizing lightning and thunder. Her fur was soaked to a frizz on the skin. She never would've done this to herself. The little dog looked like the type who would rather ride out this kind of storm cowering under a bed, but forces beyond her control had pulled her into a nightmare. She'd gone with her mistress trusting that she'd rescue her. With every step forward her misery had magnified, so she'd dug her feet in and stood trembling, wanting to go no further.

I was beginning to wish that option was available to me. This case had dragged me into just such a maelstrom. With each step I was making new enemies. Gianfranco was making threats that if I exposed his dalliance with Amanda, the consequences would be severe and personal. Bliss bore me personal animus mixed with a feral quality that matched his ape-like bearing. M. Stanton felt his whole existence threatened and was vowing revenge. His recent loss of control showed how tightly he was wound.

More than any of these things, the case was dragging me into conflict with my community's whole money-power structure. Whatever the smell rising when I lifted the TNPC-Dressler manhole cover might be, it was not essence of roses. Big money, big power and big social prestige were at risk in the cats going to the dogs. If Ted and I had to be sacrificed to maintain order and protect vulnerable community interests, then the altar would be made ready to receive our blood.

I felt the urge to emulate poor Fifi down below. I wanted to dig my feet in and refuse to be dragged any further into the storm. Then the woman crouched and apparently talked soothingly to her pet. She picked the dog up and carried it to the car, closing the door before coming back for her sodden packages. That's what I needed. Talk reassuringly to me, take me home, rub me dry with a warm towel, stroke me gently in the calm harbor of my mistress' lap, make the storm go away.

My strategy from the start had been to find someone else who might have had motive to kill Amanda. Create another suspect who had the same motives the prosecutor had ascribed to Ted—money and jealousy—and you had the makings of reasonable doubt. Seemed like a logical plan at the time. The problem was I'd found too many suspects. All of them would be hurt by exposure to the light of day in the courtroom. All of them could hurt back. How many others were there whose names hadn't surfaced? What did they all add up to? A lonely-hearts club of moths and butterflies who couldn't resist the flame of Amanda's short-lived passions, and a pack of big shots whose power and status Amanda threatened.

And what of Gianfranco? Him, I must pursue. I could prove he had been at the scene contemporary with her death. The veneer of civilization was thin with him, very thin. With a little witness stand provocation, I felt sure the animal beneath the expensive suits and flashy jewelry wouldn't stay hidden long. The jury might bite on an atavistic gangster getting rough with the society gal. He promised to be rough with me in return if I exposed him. I didn't think he was kidding. In fact, he scared the daylights out of me. I wanted to call him least of all, not out of concern about his reputation or home life, but rather out of self-preservation. Even if it worked and I won the case, I might not be around long to enjoy it.

If it was just about me winning the case, I think I'd have taken the easy way out and let the Latin Lover stay on the shelf. Life seemed a little desperate and miserable at the moment. But it was still life. I wanted to go on living it. Who'd take care of Max? I wondered. An image of Max with his head on Trooper Karen's legs in a cozy kitchen crossed my mind. He'd get over my death quicker than I would. But saving myself at the expense of my client was something I couldn't do. Lawyers take a lot of guff for helping themselves at the expense of their clients, but the truth is, most of us take our legal duty to heart. My duty was to do the best I could to save Ted's skin without worrying too much about my own. So at the moment, it was damn the torpedoes and full speed ahead on Gianfranco and Dressler.

"A fine mess you've gotten into, Ollie," I muttered.

There I sat with my feet up on a pulled-out desk drawer, staring out the window and feeling sorry for myself. The rain had slowed to a steady drizzle. The windshield wipers on the cars below had down-shifted to a relaxed slip-slap. The catch basins had begun to catch up with the curbside flow, but I could still see water rushing through the grate of the curbside drain across the street. At the moment I felt like a leaf being carried along in the gutter current, racing to the edge of the precipice. I watched as a leaf disappeared through the grate, not to be seen again. Events were carrying me, and I didn't much like where I was headed.

Why hadn't I been smart enough to stay out of this case when I'd been put out early? Why hadn't I let Ted and M. Stanton lie in the bed they'd made for themselves? Why was I so eager to get back into a case that M. Stanton's ineptitude had screwed up beyond recognition?

I felt like the belly surgeon called in on a case after the intern before him had caused massive internal bleeding resulting in temporary heart stoppage and hypoperfusion to the brain. I probably couldn't save the patient, and I'd get the blame when he died under my hands. So why did I walk into the OR and agree to try and save the patient?

Because that's what I did. I took the hard cases, and once in a while my patient recovered from a legal near-death experience, and I felt great. So it was time to stop feeling sorry for myself. If I had to get my hands bloody trying to stop the bleeding, so be it. I had taken over the case. I had to stay with it until the jury, the legal bedside vital sign monitor, signaled flat line or full recovery.

As I considered the list of suspects, I had almost forgotten the number one candidate: my client. The police, prosecutor and press were convinced Ted was guilty. What did I think? In the criminal defense business it's not particularly helpful beyond a certain stage to entertain too many doubts about your client's innocence. Once all prospects of plea-bargaining are gone, then it's time to take what the theologian Paul Tillich, in a very different context, calls the "leap of faith." You must, as Coleridge said, make a "willing suspension of disbelief." You must go beyond facts and logic, and trust with an intuitive faith. No matter how eloquent an orator a lawyer is, the jury can sniff out insincerity faster than Max on the trail of a trespassing bunny.

As a lawyer, if you can convey your heartfelt belief in your client, the jury will pay much closer attention to your arguments than if they feel you are just going through the motions. So for weeks before we started picking a jury in Ted's case, I had been selling myself on Ted's innocence. I convinced myself so I would be more convincing to others. I pushed every shred of doubt under the rug. I was on a mission to save a very decent man who had suffered the horrifying loss of his beloved wife. I must prevent a miscarriage of justice that would punish him for a crime he didn't commit. I would brandish the gleaming sword of justice and its bright light would reveal my client's innocence. I would be a hero.

But now, in the quiet confines of my office, watching the streaks of rain trace rivulets through the dust on my dirty windows, I lifted the lid on my own doubts. Ted had enough motive for three murders. The list of people with whom Amanda had shared her favors was long. Normally she had been discreet and not rubbed his face in her affairs. Then, on the eve of her death, she embarrassed him publicly with a stranger in the Heather Hollows bar. Had the doubts and anger from years of whispering reached the boiling point? Had the encounter in the bar been the straw that broke the camel's back?

The increase in Amanda's life insurance policy so soon before her murder was at best an unfortunate coincidence. Coupled with Ted's personal and business financial woes, Ted had two million more motives than my other possible suspects. Kill Amanda and stop the torment of an unfaithful spouse, a spouse who was becoming more brazen? Was she, perhaps, seeing the financial well running dry, making noises about divorce? Kill Amanda and stop the baying of the financial hounds? Save the family business? Save his self-respect? Save his employees' jobs? Save his dignity? Motive? Ted had plenty.

But if that were true, why kill her in such an obvious way, call the cops and confess? If he were found guilty, no insurance proceeds would be forthcoming, and his personal ruin would include a lifetime in prison as well as being broke. That made no sense. Unless, as the prosecutor argued, he'd planned a more discreet death and became impetuous under the humiliation of the confrontation at the bar. Then, faced with the bloody reality of his wife's death, he'd been overwhelmed with guilt and admitted it. Could be right. I just didn't think so.

Ted just didn't seem like the type. My pre-case impression of him as a gentleman to the core had only been reinforced by my close contact with him during the case. He just didn't seem to be cut from the cloth of a man who would scheme to kill anyone for money. Nor did he impress me as a man who would ever strike a woman, let alone bludgeon one to death. Everyone I'd interviewed said that Ted had shut down all rumors and whispers about Amanda as soon as the gossip neared him. As far as Ted was concerned, Amanda loved only him. He would hear no different. He denied killing her. In fact, he was shocked that anyone would think he could ever have done such a thing. The picture hanging on the wall over his jail cell bed, Amanda smiling from beneath a sun hat, told me he couldn't have done it. Would you brutally murder someone, then allow her to haunt you every night?

I'd taken every approach to make it possible for him to tell me if he'd killed her when a plea bargain was still possible. Not even a hint that he was debating revealing his guilt to me surfaced, except one time when I'd asked him if it was possible he'd gone into a blackout rage where he didn't know what he'd done. He thought about that as an interesting possibility and then replied, "If I didn't remember, how could I tell you I did?"

My clients had fooled me before with claims of innocence. And in a sense, I'd let them fool me. It made trying the case much easier. You can't just put your client on the stand to deny he did the deed after he'd already told you "I done it." You have to tell the judge and the prosecutor of your client's desire to testify and that you have reason to believe he may lie. The rules of ethics require the lawyer take a very passive role in questioning. That approach telegraphs to the jury that even his own lawyer knows the defendant is lying.

But I had none of those feelings with Ted. Having spent so many hours one-on-one with Ted, I believed him. And if I didn't figure a way to get the jury to believe him, or at least entertain serious doubt about his guilt, the image of this case would hang on the cell walls inside my head, haunting me for the rest of my life. That prospect frightened me more than any of the other perils I faced.

My crisis of doubt was over. My father's old Irish-Canadian phrase aimed at me as a boy, complaining of a daunting task or offering excuses for possible failures, popped into my head. "Buckle down, Woonsockie." I was warmed by the image of him and determined that if I went down, it wouldn't be for lack of trying.

Just as I was turning out the lights, the after-hours phone rang. Caller ID revealed it was the county jail calling, but not the prisoner pay phone. Had something happened to Ted?

"Hello."

"Ken? It's Ike over at intake. Thought you'd want to know your legal buddy, Mr. Browne, just left. Somebody upstairs extended visitor hours for him to see your client."

"What? When? Who set it up? How long was he there?"

"Whoa! I saw him getting into his fancy ride when I was coming on shift. Darla upstairs told me he met with Armbruster. That's all I know. Thought you'd want the info."

"Thanks, Ike."

What was Browne up to? I looked at my watch, and as it was close to eight, I realized I'd have to wait for the morning to talk to Ted.

59

Having the phone in hand reminded me I was still waiting to hear from Brent Eubanks. I'd tried his office three times that day. On the first call the receptionist had cooed: "Just a minute for Mr. Eubanks, please." Thirty seconds later her voice was more businesslike. "Sorry, Mr. Edwards. I thought he was in his office. But he had to step out." I left a message and called back twice more with no luck. Just as I opened the phone book to try to find a home number, my night number rang again. Talk about ESP. It was Brent, sounding apologetic.

"Sorry, Ken. Couldn't take your call earlier. Was trying to line up some ducks. The ducks are in a row. Can you stop by my office?"

"Sure, sure. I was on my way out, so I'll be there in five minutes."

"Great. We'll be in the main conference room upstairs." He hung up before I got to ask who he meant by "we."

Brent's building was only four or five blocks from mine. As I walked up to the former lumber-era mansion, I could see the light on in Brent's second story office. I opened the double door entrance and climbed the steps. Gaslight-era sconces cast muted light on the stairs and second story hallway. Approaching the conference room, I could hear the reverb of a deep voice behind the red oak door. I knocked.

"C'mon in, Ken."

Brent was seated on the opposite side of the polished conference table. His thinning hair was disheveled, as if he'd been running his hands through it. I'd seen the look each year around tax time, but this was August. He smiled wearily and said, "Thanks for coming."

He then looked to his left. Leaning back in a leather chair at the head of the table was a man I'd never met, but recognized immediately. I was shocked how closely this man resembled his portrait from almost thirty years earlier.

"Xavier Westphal, I presume, or is it Lawton?" My voice was a throaty whisper as a result of my run-in with M. Stanton.

The man rose, a warm smile reflecting a full set of his own teeth or a very good set of somebody else's. He had to be in his seventies, but he looked twenty years younger. His six-foot-two frame was firmly fleshed, and his posture showed none of the effects of age. He was dressed in a blue blazer over khaki trousers and a light blue shirt. He stretched athletically across the table to grasp my hand firmly. Reaching across to meet his hand, I got close enough to notice age lines and wrinkles in a weathered face. I also felt an aura of power and confidence emanating from him. He chuckled and looked over to Brent, still grasping my hand firmly.

"You were right, Brent, our young lawyer friend is sharp. Dropped Lawton when I dropped the trappings of my old life thirty years back. Please call me Xavier. Been looking forward to making your acquaintance, young feller."

"Been awhile since anybody called me that, Mr. Westphal. I'm not sure I qualify."

He laughed, a deep, resonant chortle.

"You get to be my age, pretty near every feller I meet is a young feller, relatively speaking. Just celebrated my 76th a month ago."

"Whatever you're doing down there, it's obvious the tropics agree with you. If I should be so lucky to reach your age, I'd be happy to look half as good. What's the secret?"

"Living in the tropics by the sea. Positive ions from the sea. Swim every day. Play a little polo. Eat fruits, nuts and fish. No meat. A liberal diet of island girls. They'll keep you young. Oh, and hire the best plastic surgeon money can buy. Say, what's the matter with your neck? And your voice sounds a bit raspy."

"Disagreed with a colleague over a point of law. What brings you back to our fair city? I tried to locate you down there with no luck."

Again, resonant laughter. "Antoinette mentioned your call and your sly little call back. Well, son, that's why I wanted Brent to arrange this meeting. I didn't want him to mention my name in case you might have a subpoena handy. My visit here is very hush-hush. I'm in the unfortunate position of having a few creditors and a couple of securities and exchange types looking to make my acquaintance. So I'd appreciate your keeping our little get-together private, but even if you don't, I'll be on the highway and gone as soon as we are done chatting. Mind if I pat you down for recording machines? It'll put my mind at ease, allow our chat to be more informative."

I allowed it and asked as he frisked me, "Might I ask your destination in case I have questions after our talk here tonight?"

Westphal smiled as he folded himself back into the director's chair at the head of the table and motioned me to be seated.

"You may ask." His look made it clear I could ask all I wanted, and then he looked over at Brent.

"Thanks, Brent. I'll stop by your office to say goodnight on my way out."

Brent looked relieved as he headed for the door. Either he already knew the substance of this upcoming meeting, or he didn't really want to know. He nodded and pulled the massive door shut behind him.

"Now, Mr. Edwards, it's nice to meet you. I've been hearing a lot about you, particularly lately. They tell me you're a real firecracker of an attorney." He looked relaxed, and it was hard not be mesmerized by the alert, steely eyes with which he skewered my attention.

"But I'm worried, what with your rooting about where you shouldn't ought to be rooting, that in fact you are going to be more like one of those suicide bombers that those Arabian folks seem so proud of. Trouble with them is, not only do they get hurt themselves, but a whole mess of right nice folks go up in smoke with them. Man, you don't approve of that sort of thing, hurting a lot of innocents for the cause, do you?"

I could catch his drift without running hard.

"As a matter of principle I'd say no, but I expect it depends on how you define 'innocents' and what the cause is. Not to change the subject, but why are you in Lake Pointe, and why are we having this little get-to-know-each-other session?"

He sat back to size me up again.

"Never trade punches with a boxer or questions with a lawyer. You are always going to come out bruised." He exhaled, leaned forward on his elbows and looked right at me. It was all I could do to keep looking back.

"All right then. As I gather you already know, we've got a little mess here in Lake Pointe, and I'm keen to see if I can prevent it from becoming a much bigger mess. I'm sorry to say I had a part in creating the mess. So I thought I'd do what I could to straighten it out. Frankly, your stirring around is creating real concerns that a fixable problem is turning into an unfixable disaster. Not so much for me as for a lot of good folks who trusted in me. I just hate to let those kinds of folks down. So I guess what you and I are having is a defuse-the-bomb session."

I leaned my elbows on the table and looked right back at him. "I'm guessing the fissionable elements in the bomb are a mixture of TNPC Investments and the Dressler Foundation."

He sat back and crossed his legs, showing well-polished deck shoes on his feet. "Yes, sir, a real firecracker. What I'm going to tell you is what I think you've already figured out for yourself, but if you hadn't turned on Brent, our friendly host, and laid a subpoena on him, I wouldn't be talking to you at all. Now Brent and I, and another lawyer, whom I expect you know, all tried to figure how Brent could avoid testifying to what he has found out during his Foundation audit. But, frankly, since Brent seems to have qualms about perjuring himself, I've decided to see if you could be persuaded not to ask the wrong questions."

"Heck, I do that all the time."

"Been following your case pretty closely, as a matter of fact. Knew your client a little, mainly as a youngster, before I left town for the sunnier climes. But I knew his daddy very well. Fine man. Shame, the troubles Ted has gotten into. Ain't it always the way though; Daddy spends his life building the business, and Sonny comes along and tears it down?" Westphal's face was now that of a preacher contemplating the way of all flesh.

I let him chew on his pithy observation for a second or two before replying. "You understand my loyalty has to be to Ted and not all the fine upstanding people you referred to?"

"Yes, I do. That's why I am talking to you now. You strike me as a clever enough lad. So, what we're hoping, what I'm hoping, is if you understand what happened with TNPC and Dressler, you'll understand that it had nothing to do with Mrs. Armbruster's death. With me so far?"

I nodded. "I'm listening. I'm not promising, but I am listening."

He pursed his lips a little, as if having second thoughts, but then went ahead. "Okay, listen carefully. TNPC Investments started out as five fellas playing poker at the country club almost forty years ago. It was almost like one of the investment clubs people form to play the stock market these days. We were all young men just beginning to make some real money. So back in the sixties we'd each put $1,000 a month into the fund on the last Thursday game each month. For a half hour before we dealt the cards, one of us would make an investment presentation. Then we'd vote up or down.

"We invested in local businesses; startups and projects mainly, some in the stock market. Well, at five grand a month, the money starts to add up. Then our group grew to ten. We made some real good investments. You take any money out or miss your monthly payment, you're out of the club. Nobody wanted out. Only withdrawals were guys who died or moved away. The move-away guys mostly just kept sending their checks. Anyway, while I was around, nobody lost money and everybody did well, very well. I got interested in the currency markets, bond carry trade, gold carry trade, leveraged investments. You understand any of this?"

"Some."

"Let me give you the success story of my little offshore hedge fund, the gold carry trade. After Nixon took the country off the gold standard price in 1973, gold went from $35 an ounce to over $850 an ounce. Then gold went into a twenty-five-year-long bear market. So what I'd do is borrow gold from the bullion banks, sell it, invest the proceeds in U.S.

Treasuries at six percent, and then buy the gold back cheaper. We were making money on the leveraged bond investments. Six percent at ten times leverage is 60%. Then add it to the profits on the gold short sale. We had some very good years. Once in a while gold would zig when it should have zagged, but on the whole it was going down, so we did fine. My motto is 'the trend is your friend.'

"Then gold looked like it was making a bottom. So I got the fund into the International Bond Carry Trade. We'd borrow short term at increasingly lower rates and use leverage to lend long on foreign bonds. I developed a strategy of buying options to put a collar around the interest rates, so my rate assumptions were supposed to be fully covered. It worked well, darn well, until TNPC Voyager Three."

"Why the name?"

"TNPC? Sentimental. I founded that poker club. Superstitious in that we never lost money. Plus, in the early years the only people who knew I had the touch were from here. Midas was the name of our gold carry funds. Voyager for bond carry trades spanning the ocean. Three 'cause it was our third. Third time is supposed to be the charm. Some charm!"

"What happened with three?"

He shook his head like a man who still couldn't believe his misfortune.

"Government scandal in Chile, currency collapses, British interest hike, and worst of all, my option counterparty defaulted. Dumbarton Oaks Guaranteed Securities. Everything bad that could happen, did."

I interjected, "Yes, and Amanda Armbruster found out about it. She called it the cats going to the dogs."

He laughed wryly. "So I heard. She sure got that right. The funny thing is that she and that Freddie Hildebrandt feller were put on the audit committee as the two least likely Dressler directors to recognize a fiddle if it bit them in the behind. Wrong about her, I guess."

"Fiddle?"

"British expression for cooking the books."

"Are you willing to explain the fiddle for me?" I looked at him expectantly.

"We'll get to that. Hold your horses. I am laying all the cards on the table to protect a lot of good people who trusted me. I think when I lay it out, you'll see there is no reason to toss that bomb you're thinking of throwing." I started to interrupt. He held a liver-spotted hand up to stop me. "Anyway, as the dear departed Mrs. Armbruster put it, 'The cats went to the dogs.' TNPC Offshore, formerly of Grand Cayman, owes a lot of money. All the investors crapped out on their entire investment, and I've been required to seek dwelling elsewhere. They've seized my home and bank accounts down there, and if they ever catch up with me, that's not all they'll seize. Fortunately, I planned for all contingencies and have another nest with a tidy nest egg to sit on. I doubt they'll find me."

"I'm glad you were forward thinking, but where do the local country club types and Dressler come in?"

"The motto of the poker group was 'Don't play if you can't afford to pay.' All of those guys were limited liability investors, so they got hurt, but they'll get over it. Five hundred thousand up in smoke is nasty, but for most of them they'll just have to work a few more years. The problem, and why I'm telling you, is Dressler."

I adjusted myself in my chair. "I've been waiting for that."

"TNPC Voyager Three required ten investors at $500,000 each to buy a five million dollar unit. The guys in the club told me during the offering period that they had ten members, some past and some present, committed. Then, at the last second, they tell me somebody crapped out, can't come up with the cash. I told them find a tenth or we don't have the five million minimum for them to be in on the deal. In fact, I had two other investors with the five million to complete the total offering of fifty million. Luckily for those other chaps, the local boys came up with the missing five hundred G's. They'd all done well on my earlier deals and they didn't want to miss the party. So certain members of the club who were also on the board of Dressler got the last half million from the Foundation. They decided it couldn't miss and the return would be well above Dressler's normal investment return. Hell, Dressler is so conservative it has underperformed in the market for years. But if I'd known what they were doing at the time, I woulda never taken the money. Little detail they neglected to mention when I got the check."

"Okay, so Dressler loses a half million. They make a bad investment. It happens. What's the fracas?"

"Offshore hedge funds are not within the investments by-laws of the Foundation. Far from it. That's the fiddle. They cooked the books to look like the money was in U.S. Treasuries. Even had a brokerage statement to prove it."

"Thad Granger?" I took a shot. He looked up at me, surprised.

"Why do I get the feeling I'm telling you a yarn you've already heard?"

"I've got some pieces of the puzzle. With what you're telling me, I'm starting to see the whole picture. Let me guess. When the deal blew up, there was going to be no five hundred thousand to pretend was just a treasury bond maturing?"

He nodded appreciatively. "You are right clever. That's what started the scramble up here. All nine of the guys had just lost a half million. Now they each had to come up with another fifty-five thousand each to cover the fiddle. Some were dragging their feet. That's when the audit started. In fact, if they had all just anted up when I told them to, you and I wouldn't be having this chat. The transaction on the Dressler books shows $500,000 in a two-year treasury at five percent. So we'd have been able to show that on maturing, the moneys had been in the Foundation account and everybody goes away happy. This all should've happened before anybody knew it was missing and the Foundation started looking for it. Instead, they dragged their feet." Again the look of the world-weary parson.

"And just why are you telling me all of this?

"So we can put a band-aid on the wound and let it heal without gushing blood all over the place. I had to come back here a couple of times trying to get the sinners to come to Jesus. Had to hit a couple of the mules over the head with a two-by-four. They didn't want to pay their share. So I came back with my securities lawyer and we had a little facts of life session out at the club. We reviewed the meeting at which they all voted to approve making Dressler the tenth partner. Then Gabe Silverstein, he's the lawyer, told them they are all guilty as aiders and abettors for approving it. And he told them by the time they got done paying for lawyer's fees and costs, it would cost them more than just putting the money back. When he got to the sentencing guidelines and explained the only argument was whether they'd do one year or three behind bars, they all got religion."

I had a mental picture of fat cats sitting around a round poker table watching someone walk out the door with their bowls of cream. Then their expressions of haughty resistance changing to abject fear as the door opens and a swarthy bulldog enters the room. I chuckled.

"Yes, I imagine they did. Before we go on, I want to ask you something."

Westphal cocked his head non-committally. "Ask away."

"What happens if the Chilean peso or whatever it is doesn't fall out of bed, and everything goes as planned, what would Dressler have gotten, the five percent Treasury bill rate, or the sixty percent our esteemed captains of commerce were counting on?"

He tilted his head back and guffawed. When he stopped roaring he smiled over at me.

"There may be a future for you in commerce, my boy. If I ever get on my feet again, I'll keep you in mind. But let's get back to the matter at hand. The money is all back in place at Dressler, including the T-Bill interest. The audit is just going to show a bookkeeping error. The widows and orphans will all be fine, nobody harmed. No harm, no foul."

"Not quite. Mrs. Armbruster seems to have suffered a rather flagrant foul, and it seems to me to be more than just a coincidence that she was killed shortly after she started looking into the finances at Dressler."

"You are not listening." The good old boy smile vanished.

"Tell me what is missing."

"By the time she died, the money was all back in place. The $500,000 plus two years of interest had all been wire transferred from the brokerage office back into Dressler's account. We had dummied up brokerage confirms all in place. Brent was head of the audit committee. He was satisfied with restitution, as he didn't want a scandal and loss of good name, not to mention issues of accounting raised. So he called the committee together and announced the missing half million had been found, end of story. Mrs. Armbruster knew that a week or more before her death. You doubt me, ask Brent. So your theory of the missing money as a motive for murder, while right smart, is also dead wrong."

I felt relief and disappointment at the same time. To give myself time to adjust to my great theory springing a leak, I asked out of curiosity, "Who was the lucky guy?"

Westphal looked quizzical. So I added, "You know, the guy who missed the boat, the tenth guy who crapped out?"

He sat back in his chair and ran his tongue around the inside of his mouth, considering. He sat forward as if to begin to answer, paused, then shrugged his shoulders and replied, "Darned if I know. All this trouble and I never thought to ask. Can you believe that?" He must have been one hell of a poker player, because his face said he was telling the truth, when we both knew he wasn't. He sat back again, content to wait for my next question.

"You're saying nothing was missing at Dressler when Amanda died."

Westphal nodded. "Not a penny. You want to ask Brent, ask him."

Another thought occurred to me. "I will, and just how long before Amanda's death had you gotten the band-aid on the wound?"

Again he looked perplexed or annoyed.

"I think the wire transfer happened about a week or so before she died. It was all there when they had that last audit committee meeting. Brent can confirm that too. It was at least four or five days before her death. So check that out with Brent and then let him off his subpoena. That poor man had nothing to do with the money leaving Dressler. I persuaded him it was best for everybody to let them put it back without a big scandal. If you make a stink, he's finished. I got him in this mess. That's why I'm here asking you not to burn him for no purpose. He tells me you were friends. Would you do that to your friend? I don't think the poor man has slept since you served him."

I sat there trying to digest everything I'd heard. Obviously this was bad news for the defense. I had this sensational scandal that could've taken the jury's minds off Ted and onto who else could have killed Amanda to keep her quiet. So now this scent I had been sniffing in the hopes of freeing Ted looked to be going nowhere.

On the other hand, I was relieved. I wouldn't have to drag a lot of influential people and their families through the mud, plus I wouldn't be responsible for the town's biggest charity folding its tent. I was trying to sift my emotions through the facts Westphal had given me. I must've been pretty deep in thought, because he reached over and touched my arm.

"Are you still with me, counselor? Can I tell Brent he can go home and get a good night's rest?"

"Huh? Oh... I need to think about what you've told me. I need to confirm the money was back before Amanda's death. I don't know what you can tell Brent, except I won't blow a lot of people up just to create a diversion. On the other hand, my duty is to my client, and after I think through all the information, if I think, or Ted thinks, 'cause I'm telling him, that the jury needs to hear it, they'll hear it."

He looked disappointed.

"Are you so sure about your client's wishes? I hear your client doesn't want you creating a stink around Dressler."

I sat up. "How would you know what my client wants?"

He leaned over the table as if to let me in on a confidence, then reconsidered.

"Trust me on this. Your client doesn't want you messing around in the Foundation finances." He paused, then added, "Brent tells me Armbruster is very devoted to the Foundation. Donated lots of money and time to it, so I understand. And I have it on good authority—" Then he stopped in mid-sentence.

I wondered at what he had almost told me. Was it merely a coincidence that Brent had called me so soon after Ike's message about Browne visiting the jail?

"You were going to say?" I prompted.

He scratched his cheek a second in reconsideration, and then with a barely perceptible shake of his head, went on. "Hey, I told you this so a lot of good people, people who are my friends, people who make this town go, don't get hurt. Folks told me you'd listen to reason; otherwise we don't have this conversation and we have to deal with it another way. So now that you know that TNPC didn't get Amanda killed, all I'm asking is that you be reasonable. Can you do that?"

"If I weren't reasonable as advertised, what's the other way?"

He paused, shrugged and stood up. He reached for my hand and gripped it firmly, pulling me close and looking me right in the eye.

"Best we don't pursue that. When will we hear from you?"

I held his gaze and gripped back as hard as I could. "I don't know. You didn't give me your number."

He chortled once, nodded his head and released his grip as he headed for the door.

"Let Brent know, soon. I'll be in touch with him."

I stood where I was. A last minute idea crossed my mind.

"One more thing. I understand we share a mutual acquaintance."

He looked over his shoulder. "More than one, I'm sure."

"I'm talking about Detective Ray Bliss. Heard you knew him."

For the first time since I had met him, a look of uncertainty crossed his face, but only for a second.

"Bliss? Raymond Bliss? Isn't he the cop on your case? Don't believe I've had the pleasure. Why?"

"Just wondered."

With that he turned and walked down the hall toward Brent's office. As I entered the hall I could see Brent standing at the door to his office, looking expectantly down the hall at us. I waved to him as I opened the stairway door.

"I'll be in touch," I called out as I headed down the stairs.

I'd stopped at the jail early Tuesday to tell Ted of my meeting with Xavier Westphal and find out what Browne's visit was all about. My disappointment at the drop in the evidentiary value of the Dressler-TNPC fiddle wasn't shared by Ted. In fact, he seemed quite relieved.

"I'm glad we don't have to cause so many people to suffer. The whole thing would've been bad for the community."

I told him I hadn't dropped the approach but was rather "taking it under reconsideration." He sat forward as if to argue, then relaxed, saying, "Remember our agreement. No Dressler stuff in court unless we both agree." I nodded, as the point no longer seemed worth arguing. Then I asked about Browne.

He waved it off. "Oh he's just upset about you dragging his wife into this. I told him I'd talk to you about it. You don't really think Annabelle killed her, do you?"

"Probably not. But a jury might."

"I know you and Stanton don't get along, but Annabelle doesn't deserve this. Please don't drag her through the muck if you don't really think she did it. Promise me."

"I'm not ready to give her up quite yet. Seems what I learn about this case changes every ten minutes."

"Let's agree you don't call her without consulting me and us both agreeing. Aren't I entitled to have some say in my own defense?"

"Yes, you are. Okay, I'll let you know if I want to call her."

"Same as our agreement on Dressler, right?"

I wanted to discuss who would be making final trial strategy decisions further, but he quickly switched to having me recap the tourney. He seemed thrilled to have won $200 as his piece of our team. I deposited the money in his prisoner account on my way over to court.

Riding the elevator, I tried to summon my resolve for the return to combat. Those efforts were undone by the greeting committee waiting for me on the fourth floor.

As I got off the elevator, Gianfranco and two of his gorillas spotted me. I tried to go around them to the chambers doorway, but they angled to intercept me.

"Hey counselor, what's the deal? No time for old friends?" Firenze asked.

"I'm in a bit of a hurry, a couple of matters for the judge before we get going," I lied, my voice cracking as much from nerves as from M. Stanton's bruising my larynx.

"Well, at least let me introduce my associates. They're eager to meet you. Know what I mean?"

Dressed in double-breasted suits with studs and tie pins, they were a strange-looking pair, one tall and lean, the other short and squat. Firenze motioned to the fireplug.

"This is Theo. He's my bad debt workout officer. Theo, shake hands with Mr. Edwards."

As Theo moved closer, his suit appeared ready to tear at the seams. He had hedges growing where his eyebrows should have been and a flattened nose that was the termination point for an old scar starting beneath the left eye. He sneered more than smiled, exposing missing teeth in the lower jaw. He made a point as we shook to invade my personal space, assaulting me with a cloying aroma of cheap cologne and cigar smoke. "Nice to meet ya. But ain't we met already?" he rasped.

Images of the man in the porkpie hat who had tried to run me off the road came to mind.

"I don't know. You drive a beat-up blue Olds 88?"

His lips curled up at the corners. He let the question lie as he relaxed his grip. I made a conscious effort not to shake the numbness out of my hand.

"Nah. I've got a brand new Caddy. Nice. If you want sometime I could take you for a ride, whatta you think?"

I stepped away and answered in a voice more casual than I felt, "I'll let you know."

Theo looked Neanderthal, a caveman in a suit with intellect to match; but his associate, he looked feral. He stood over six feet three to a slicked-back head of thick black hair. His aquiline nose separated penetrating, alert dark eyes that flickered with intensity. He moved like a cat, a tall, tawny, lithe lord of the jungle, as Gianfranco introduced him.

"Meet Vincenzo. He's my director of special projects."

The grip was firm but normal on first contact. Then, just for an instant it turned hard as stone and relaxed again. He smiled pleasantly.

"A pleasure."

"Special projects? What's that?"

The smile broadened. The eyes twitched left and right as if he could see everything in a 240-degree radius.

"Whatever needs doing."

I kept my voice level and turned back to Firenze. He was a handsome guy with classic Mediterranean looks. His gray silk two-piece suit was well tailored and expensive over a gray shirt and pink tie. The stones for the cufflinks might have been real rubies.

"Your associates here for moral support?"

He laughed. If Firenze's large teeth were any whiter I'd have needed sunglasses. Releasing his hand, I could feel the sheen of whatever concoction Gianfranco used to slick back his long, thick mane.

"No, no. They've heard so much about you they wanted to meet you. Get a look at you. Know what I mean?"

I could feel the sweat dripping from under my arms, running down my ribcage. "I'm not sure I do."

The smile disappeared.

"In case we had a problem, needed to find a certain lawyer, they'd know who to look for. Right, fellas?"

Vincenzo remained stone-faced, just staring at me. Theo rambled, "You bet, boss. We got a problem, we know who to look for."

I managed to avoid trembling long enough to answer, "Nice to meet you two. Gotta run," and entered the darkened corridor leading to the judge's chambers.

Once in the hallway it was a different story. My legs felt weak, and breath was tough to catch. I leaned against the wall and wrapped my arms around my chest to still the shakes. I wanted to run. Just catch a plane somewhere and start over as an estates attorney. I thought of reporting the intimidation to the judge, but what did it amount to? Anonymous phone calls, lilies at the office, a shadowy profile behind the wheel and some hallway introductions. Nothing. But as I tried to push the panic down, one thing was clear. I was very afraid of nothing.

I cut through the courtroom using the bailiff's entrance and went across to the attorney conference room. I lifted a couple of *National Geographics*, one dated July 1984, off the blue leatherette couch and sat down for one last review of my options before Firenze took the stand.

It wasn't too late to take the approach of which my life insurance agent would approve, if I had life insurance. I could just let the prosecutor examine him. I could ask some questions about the scene in the bar. I could get Firenze to admit he was dancing with another man's wife. I could develop that he was the last man seen with her while Amanda was still alive. I could pretend to be tough. Amanda's flirtation in front of her husband would tarnish her in front of the jury. Maybe the jury would figure out that this Romeo wouldn't be content with a dance, a snuggle and a kiss. I could act like I was doing my job and live to fight another day.

I had other angles for reasonable doubt. I could still go with the Dressler thing. Stanton Browne, regardless of his threats to incriminate Ted, was on record as saying Bliss had inaccurately recorded the confession. Scorned lovers provided other suspects with motives. Why did I have to commit suicide by embarrassing a man who took embarrassment very seriously?

Ted would be spared the agony of knowing his wife had among her final living acts the sin of near adultery. I'd rationalized all along: no need to tell Ted about Gianfranco's claim of sexual conquest any sooner than when I had to use it in court. In his depressed state Ted didn't need another blow to the memories of the marital relationship. But really, I had been just postponing my gut check, leaving myself an avenue of escape. Now the time was up. I either stayed on the freeway to disaster or took the last exit before the toll bridge. The little get-to-know-you session with Firenze's minions had left me no doubt the toll would be steep.

I was still wrestling with my duties to my client and my instinct when the bailiff rattled the door and stuck his head in. "There you are. Judge is looking for you. Jury is ready. Let's go. You feeling okay?"

I sighed and rose from the couch.

"Yeah, Larry. Tough case and about to get tougher."

I had come to court this morning thinking I'd won the wrestling match with my fears. I walked into the courtroom a lot less certain.

"People call Gianfranco Firenze."

The ladies in the jury box sat up and took notice when Firenze swung the gate at the rail open and strolled past the box. He radiated an aura of animal magnetism. He sat comfortably on the witness stand and smiled pleasantly, teeth dazzling, as Tina took him through preliminary questioning. To hear him tell it he was an avatar of respectability. He'd worked hard to build his metal processing business and was proud to have provided thirty-five people with employment. He'd married his high school sweetheart and she'd blessed him with three wonderful children. His son was all-state in football and his daughter was on the honor roll. He was active on the PTA and in his church. As he put it, "I try to give back to the community that has been so good to me and my family." He testified that he'd met Amanda through The United Way. "We'd met at the tri-county fundraising kickoff. Great lady. Really knocked herself out for the needy."

By the time Tina was ready to get down to business, she had Gianfranco burnished to a shiny all-American rags to riches story. I knew better, and yet I was almost believing it. Maybe sensing his mugs sitting directly behind me in the gallery encouraged that line of thinking.

He testified that on April 27th he'd played golf with customers and had entertained them with dinner and drinks afterwards.

"Then as I was leaving, I recognized Mrs. Armbruster from the United Way. She was in a booth with a lady I didn't recognize. I excused myself from the customers to say hello. She invited me to join them. They bought me a drink, and I had just returned the favor when Mr. Armbruster stormed in."

"What do you mean, stormed in?"

He shook his head, recalling the scene.

"He was crying. He was rude. He was drunk. It was almost like he thought I was trying to make a move on his wife."

"Why do you say that?"

"Right away he had an attitude. Amanda, Mrs. Armbruster, tried to introduce me. I'd gotten up to shake hands and so he could have my spot in the booth, and he grabbed Mrs. Armbruster's arm and said, 'Let's go home now.' I reached over to calm him down, and to make sure he didn't hurt her arm, when he pushed me."

"What did you do?"

"Well, I lost my balance, as I was just standing, and I fell back into the seat. I was so surprised by the outburst I jumped back up and asked him to calm down. I could smell alcohol on his breath. His face was red and he was very loud. I wanted to tell him I was leaving, but I couldn't get a word in, he was so angry."

"Describe the conversation."

"He wanted her to come with him right then. She asked him to apologize to me. He told me to get away from his wife. Mrs. Armbruster and the other couple, the Simpsons, tried to get him to sit down and calm down. He accused her of humiliating him. He was like in a jealous rage. Mrs. Armbruster started to cry. The bartender came over and asked him politely to please settle down. He told him to f— off. The bartender said he would have to call the police and left. The more we said to try and settle him down, the worse it got. Everybody in the bar was looking. I was so embarrassed for her. Then he threatened her and stormed out."

"Threat? What did he say?"

"Let me think. I can't be exact, but it went something like this. 'I've taken all I can stand. When I need you most you are running out on me —running around on me—I'm not sure which. You are going to regret this, really regret it.' Then the Simpsons were trying to take him home, but his keys were in front of Mrs. Armbruster. He snatched them up and said, 'I don't need your help. For what I am going to do, I don't need anybody's help.' And then he was gone."

"What happened next?"

"He couldn't have been gone more than five minutes and the police were there. They asked if I wanted to press charges. I guess the barman said he shoved me. I said I was fine. They were going to go to the house and Mrs. Armbruster pleaded with them not to. She told them he was under a lot of pressure at work and that he wasn't violent. The police left. The Simpsons got up to leave and offered her a ride, but she wanted time to compose herself and for him to go to sleep, so I offered to give her a ride home."

"What time did you take her home?"

"I'm not certain, she was too upset, so we waited maybe an hour. Then in the car she said she still was afraid he'd be awake, so I'm guessing I dropped her off in her driveway around 2:30 or 3."

"Did you see Mr. Armbruster at that time?"

"No, I didn't. I watched her enter the front door, and I went home."

"Thank you Mr. Firenze. No further questions."

I'm not sure exactly what decided it for me. Perhaps it was the self-assured smugness with which he testified. Maybe it was seeing him come across like he could gild the lily as much as he wanted without fear of cross-examination. He was so confident that I was in the bag, cowed by his intimidation, that I posed no threat at all. Whatever it was, I knew that when I stood to cross-examine him, the wolf wouldn't be wearing sheep's clothing when I was finished.

"Mr. Firenze, you've told the jurors about your family and your career, but you didn't tell them about your criminal record. Do you have a felony record?"

His jaw tightened and his eyes narrowed in focus on me. The relaxed posture stiffened.

"Do I have to answer that? I'm not on trial. I am just here as a witness."

Miss Botham stirred as if to object, but didn't rise. Judge Alex looked over at Firenze, re-evaluating him in light of his not so affable tone. I'd seen that look before whilst switching the TV from *Law and Order* to hockey without discussion.

"I'm afraid you do, sir. Previous criminal records, if any, may be used by the jury to evaluate a witness's credibility."

He shook his head as if he wasn't used to having to do anything he didn't feel like doing, but he didn't answer.

I verbally prodded him. "Sir, please tell the jury for what crime you've been convicted?"

"I'm not sure what it was called. It was a long time ago, making threats, something like that."

I pulled his certified conviction record, which had arrests and convictions on a sheet attached to a cover with the state seal on it. I let the sheet with lots of entries, most of which hadn't ended in conviction or had been felonies reduced to misdemeanors, flap loose so the jury could see it wasn't a single entry document. I ran my finger down the page.

"Ah, I think you were referring to a 1985 conviction in Wayne County for attempted extortion."

"Yeah, something like that."

"Others, sir, or do you need me to show you your record to help you remember?"

"It was all a long time ago."

So I stepped up to the witness stand and held it open for him, but he was staring at me, not at the record. I hoped the jury could feel a small bit of the animosity that emanated from him. It made it hard for me to concentrate on the role I had. I had to gather myself and go on.

"Do you remember 1992, this time Oakland County, carrying a concealed weapon?"

He looked down at the sheet, which had come folded in pleats and was now open before him.

"No, that was dismissed, see."

"Not 1991, Mr. Firenze, 1992." He looked confused for a second, perhaps because my index finger had been on the 1991 arrest dismissal. When I slid my finger down the page, he glanced up at me, realizing I'd snookered him.

"Yeah, 1992. Like I said, a long time ago. No jail time. I must've forgotten."

"Oh, then let's try closer in time, 1994, receiving and concealing a stolen car in Lansing, Ingham County."

"Yeah, there was a mix-up over a title."

"A mix-up over a title and you got convicted of a felony?"

"I had a lousy lawyer and he talked me into copping a plea."

I walked back to counsel's table, folding the long printout back under the cover page and laying it on top of the table so the folded sheets formed a noticeable bulge under the top page. Tina was fidgeting, obviously aware of what I was doing but afraid to object lest she call more attention to the record.

"In your current business, you deal with a lot of cars, don't you?"

"Some."

"You receive hundreds of automobiles to crush into scrap? That's a big part of your business, sir, buying cars cheap and reprocessing them and receiving titles in the process?"

"I guess you could call it that."

I let that answer sit for a few seconds, then switched tack.

"Would you say Mrs. Armbruster was a beautiful woman?"

He gathered himself. He could see I was in for a dime, in for a dollar. I was heading where he'd told me not to go.

"I guess. I didn't really notice."

"How about when you were on the dance floor, dancing slow songs with her? Did you notice then?"

"I didn't say I danced with her, who says I did?"

"How about Walter Hackett, the bartender? You know Walt, don't you? This wasn't the first time you'd been in the bar at Heather Hollows, was it?"

"I know Walt. I entertain out there a lot. I play golf there since the blue noses at the country club wouldn't let me in."

"Why would that be?"

Tina finally moved.

"I object, Your Honor, irrelevant."

"Mr. Edwards?"

"Asked without thinking. I'll get back on track. So did you dance slow songs with Mrs. Armbruster?"

"All right, I probably did. In fact, I remember now, she asked me to dance. A gentleman doesn't refuse."

"So as a gentleman, you danced with her to calm her down."

"Pretty much."

"How many dances?"

Now he was aggravated.

"What's this, a meeting of the social committee? How do I know how many? A couple, a few. How's that?"

"Whatever you say. But did you take her straight home after you left the bar?"

"She was still upset, so we drove around a little. She didn't want an argument when she got home, I guess."

"Did you stop anywhere before taking her home?"

Now it was clear I was going where he'd told me not to travel. He pointed his finger at me. All vestiges of that PTA father were gone.

"I warned you, counselor. Don't say I didn't."

"Warned me, what?"

"Not to embarrass my family. I take family seriously, very seriously."

"Was your family at home that night?"

"No, they were visiting my wife's sister in Detroit."

"So in attempting to calm and console Mrs. Armbruster, did you take her to your home?"

He looked at me in disbelief.

"Yeah, we stopped in."

"What did you do there?"

"We talked."

"Let me be specific. Did you have intercourse with Mrs. Armbruster?"

I think the jury must have known where I was headed, but they still looked shocked. Gianfranco just glared. He made no answer.

Tina stood. Her white seersucker dress with blue pinstripes made her look more like a schoolgirl on her way to a church picnic than a sharp-tongued prosecutor bent on my client's destruction. "Your Honor, I object. This is irrelevant. Mr. Firenze is accused of no crimes. This is a sordid attempt to besmirch the name of a woman who can't speak in her own defense. This is mudslinging at its worst."

While the jury was looking at Tina, Gianfranco made eye contact with me. His right hand was at the top button of his shirt as if adjusting his tie. He stuck out the index finger to touch the left side of his neck and pulled his head away, and in so doing, the finger cut across the throat left to right. He raised an eyebrow almost imperceptibly to see if I'd noticed. I glanced at the jury to see if any of them had caught it. Mrs. Doyle had turned a little pale and her mouth was open in an "O" shape. She looked away from the witness to me with a look of dread on her face. If she was scared, imagine how I felt. I had no time to plumb the depths of panic, as the judge was trying to get my attention. For the first time in years there was a look of empathy for me on her face. She must've seen the gesture too.

"Mr. Edwards, I asked for your response. Are you all right, counselor?"

"What? Pardon me, Judge. I will have a matter for the court before this witness is excused. I have no wish to tarnish Mrs. Armbruster. My client will testify that when he last saw his wife at Heather Hollows, she was alive and unharmed. When next he saw her, she was mortally wounded in the hallway of the family home. This witness then is the last person to see her alive and well. What physical contact they had and the aftermath are part of the *res gestae* of the crime. My client is on trial for murder, a murder which he denies committing. I should be allowed wide latitude to cross examine this hostile witness."

"I agree, counselor. The witness is to answer."

"What's that, Judge? This guy kills his wife, gets caught red handed, confesses and now I'm the suspect? There is something really rotten. I'm not answering."

Alex took over. I'd been on the receiving end of this no nonsense tone in my every appearance before her since the break-up.

"Mr. Firenze, you were asked whether you had intercourse with Mrs. Armbruster, not whether you killed her, and so if you refuse to answer the question asked, I will have no choice but to hold you in contempt of court, and remand you to the custody of the sheriff until you do answer."

The tension in the courtroom was palpable. I could hear the goons behind me muttering. The bailiff rose from his seat by the door and moved a couple of steps toward the bench. Clouds of confusion, rage and uncertainty raced across Gianfranco's face.

"Can I talk to a lawyer?"

"I'm not going to hold up this trial. I'll give you fifteen minutes while the court takes the morning recess. Can you reach your attorney by phone?"

"Yeah, he's on retainer."

"Very well then, the jury is excused. We are in recess."

The jury filed out, and you could see in their body language and how far they stayed away from the witness stand that Mr. Firenze had lost all his charm for them. As the door to the jurors' hallway closed, Firenze headed for the main doors in the rear of the courtroom. The judge stopped him.

"Mr. Firenze, we have a possible contempt citation pending. Until that is reached, I am going to ask the bailiff to accompany you to the attorney's conference room. You will have privacy for your call. You are to otherwise remain in the company of the bailiff, understood?"

Firenze teetered, moving from his left foot to his right, looking at the exit doors, which were now closed to him. He shrugged his shoulders and went with the bailiff, who stood between him and those doors. As he passed me on his way to the front of the courtroom, he hissed the words barely loud enough for me to hear: "You're dead."

I recovered and looked up at the bailiff.

"Catch that, Larry?"

He nodded and put his hand on Firenze's arm to steer him to the attorney's conference room.

I was pretty shaken and would've just stayed in the courtroom, but I really had to take a leak. The bathroom off the conference room was unavailable, so I had to walk through the throng outside the courtroom doors to reach the public restroom. When the door swung open, the rest of the voices washed over me like a wave. The spectators were all talking at once in excited tones.

As I headed through the crowd toward the restroom, they parted to give me room, as if it might be dangerous to be too close to me. I overheard a couple of comments they were making to each other.

"Give the guy credit, he's got balls."

"For now. But what about when Firenze's boys are finished with him?"

I opened the wooden door to the john and said to myself as I walked through it, "My thoughts exactly."

An elderly gentleman wearing a light blue jacket with the UAW logo on it was pulling off a towel to dry his hands as I stepped up to the urinal. I'd seen him almost every day since the start of the trial.

"Remember me, Mr. Edwards? I was in the jury pool. There was about ten of us left when the jury got seated."

"Sure do," I said with my back to the man.

"I really wanted to be on that jury. The case sounded so interesting. Just like TV. So I've been coming back every day trying to pretend like I was a juror. Gets me out of the house and away from my wife's honey-do's. Anyway, you're doing great. I started out thinking Armbruster was guilty as sin."

I turned around, zipped my fly and stepped to the other sink to wash my hands. The towel dispenser was right next to me, so as I looked up in the mirror I could see his reflection.

"Hey, thanks. What do you think now?"

He smiled at the eyes, and the jowls on his cheeks crinkled to keep up. "Can't say. Remember, I'm pretending to be a juror. Judge says the jury is to keep their minds open till it's time to decide, but if it's any help, my mind is more open now than it was at the start. Keep pitching, tiger, keep pitching."

With that he chuckled and walked out. I took that as a positive straw in the wind and made my way through the throng to the courtroom door. I could see the slicked back head of Vincenzo and an open space in front of him as he tried to push through the crowd to reach me. I assumed the open space was Theo doing a little blocking, but I was in the door before they got to me.

Ted was waiting for me at counsel's table. He looked tired and sad.

"Gee, Ken, why didn't you tell me about Firenze and Amanda?"

"Did you really want to know, Ted?"

He sighed, "No, I guess I didn't. Be careful. I think that man means to do you harm."

I nodded. "I know he does, but he's been threatening me behind the scenes for a while. Now that it's out in the open, I might be safer."

The news of prior threats startled Ted. "You mean he warned you beforehand and you went after him anyhow?"

"Never a doubt, Ted, never a doubt," I lied.

"I think maybe you have more guts than brains."

"Never a doubt, Ted." This time I wasn't lying.

But as I sat down I found that I wasn't as scared now that the cat was out of the bag. Better to die one painful death of revenge than a thousand little deaths of remorse for running from the fight, or so I thought then.

When Judge Alex reconvened court, the jury was still in the jury room. Her glasses rested atop the crown of her blonde head. She raised her eyebrow to me as if to ask, "You okay?" I nodded and opened my hands as if to reply, "Hope so." Firenze was back on the stand. She turned to him.

"Did you reach counsel, Mr. Firenze?"

"Yes, I did."

"What then, after consultation with counsel, is your decision?"

"He told me to ask you for more time so he could interview me in greater detail."

"Denied. Your intention, sir?"

Firenze exhaled deeply, stared over at me for a second, and answered, "I'll testify, but I'm not going to forget who got me into this mess."

Her hackles were up. A rosy flush rose from her neck to fill her face, and her eyes narrowed. "Are you threatening the court?"

"No, ma'am, no, not the court, not at all. Not your fault. You are just doing your job."

"Who then?" Her tone was sharp.

"Nobody, nothing. I didn't mean anything."

"Very well." She bit her lower lip in thought, then motioned to Larry. "Bailiff, have the jury back in."

Once they were seated, I resumed questioning.

"The question, sir, is did you have intercourse with Mrs. Armbruster the night she died?"

"The answer to that is no." I pretended to be stunned, although in light of the autopsy report, I wasn't.

"So what is all the fuss about not answering? Couldn't you have just said no twenty minutes ago?"

He shrugged without making a further answer.

"Didn't you tell me when I went to interview you in your office at the scrap yard that, as you put it, 'I boffed the broad'?"

"Yeah, but I lied."

"When, now or then?"

"Then."

"Speaking of lying, didn't you tell the police you took Mrs. Armbruster straight home from Heather Hollows at midnight?"

"I might have."

"Was that true?"

"Not exactly."

He was answering my questions in a flat tone, but the antipathy of his demeanor was obvious.

"So you lied to the police, and after your little visit to your house, where you didn't have the sex you earlier claimed you did, you took Mrs. Armbruster home?"

"Right."

"What time, then, was it you took her home?"

"I don't know, 2 or 2:30?"

"Then, if I understand right, you were with her very close in time to when she died, weren't you?"

He shook his head. "Listen, shyster, I didn't kill her, so I don't know what time she died. Got that?"

All the patina of respectability was gone. He was exposed as a dangerous animal backed into a corner with a very short leash on his predatory instincts.

"All right then, sir, why, if you were the last man to be with her within what may have been minutes of her death, would you claim to have had sex with her?"

"I was just bragging, exaggerating, I guess you'd say. We almost had sex. She came on to me and I said no. I told her I was happily married."

"Pretty noble. But why, as a happily married man, were you inviting a beautiful woman into your home in the wee hours of the morning?"

"I told you, she was upset. She didn't want to go home until she was sure her husband was in bed. I wasn't going to just drive around, so..."

"Uh-huh." I walked up to the exhibit table and found the crime lab bag containing the deceased's clothing. It was marked exhibit 19. I rummaged around in the bag until I found the red underwear. I walked over to the stenographer. "Would you mark this as defense exhibit 19D, please."

I held them pinched between my finger and thumb at the elastic band.

"You recognize these, Mr. Firenze?"

"No, should I?"

"Look more closely, sir. See the tiny little monogram, the letters AEF?"

He nodded.

"What is your wife's full name?"

"Angela Elana Firenze."

"Now do you recognize them, or shall I subpoena your wife to identify them?"

He was halfway out of his chair.

"You do and it will be the last thing you ever do, you son of a—"

The judge pushed a buzzer behind the bench that could be heard sounding out in the hall. The doors swung open and two deputies rushed in, hands on their holsters. Firenze sank back in his chair. The judge tossed her glasses on the bench and leaned over to him, her blonde hair framing the determined set of her jaw.

"Witness, I'll not warn you again. This is a court of law. Intimidation and threat have no place here. Anything other than straight answers to the questions and you are on your way to jail right now. Am I clear?"

Nobody had talked to Firenze like that since his mother when he was a boy. He looked off balance and embarrassed.

"Sorry, Judge. I don't want my wife dragged into this mess. I got upset. It won't happen again."

She had the deputies pull up seats behind the witness and sit down. "See that it doesn't. Continue, Mr. Edwards."

"The panties, are they your wife's?"

"Yes," with a sigh.

"What was Mrs. Armbruster doing in them when she died?"

"Well, it was a misunderstanding. Like I said, I was trying to comfort her. We were on the couch, but well, I had my arm around her. Then she's looking up at me. You know how women do when they want to be kissed. Well, it went from there. Everything was fine until I lifted her dress to pull off her panties and she started to resist. I thought she was just being cute, so I kept pulling, and hers got torn and she became hysterical and started bawling, so I backed off. She kept crying and tried to put her panties back on, but they were torn too bad and that seemed to upset her more. So I got that pair from my wife's drawer and that seemed to help. Then I took her home. End of story. I wasn't lying when I said no intercourse."

"Did you argue on the way home?"

"No, she just kind of whimpered about how she couldn't hurt her husband anymore. He'd been through so much and yadda-yadda-yadda. I just drove."

"Weren't you angry and frustrated? She'd gotten you excited and aroused and shut the door at the last minute. You are kind of used to having your way, aren't you?"

He kind of waved his hands in the air, grasping for an answer.

"Yes, but if a lady says no, it's no. I didn't like it, but no big deal, huh?"

"Let me suggest this to you, Mr. Firenze. You'd invested hours in this pretty, classy woman. She'd gone willingly to your home in the wee hours of the morning, then bang, it's over. You were aroused enough to tear her clothes, and leave a bruise on her thigh, then she's sniveling all the way home. You follow her in the door and press your affections on her again. There is an argument and you lose your temper. She yells and you hit her with a golf club to shut her up, and it just got out of hand."

He was vehemently shaking his head side to side.

"No, sir, didn't happen. Maybe up to the driveway that's what happened. I let her out of the car. I drove home. End of story."

"That's the story you're telling the jury, but you've also told these good folks you lied about this case before."

"I didn't strike that woman. I didn't hit her, period. I didn't kill her, and that's the truth."

"Didn't hit? I tell you, sir, that the pathologist called by the prosecution testified to bruising on her inner thigh."

"Maybe I squeezed a little. But I never struck her, not with my hand, and sure as hell not with no golf club."

"You did say you were playing golf that day. Your bag was in the trunk, I take it."

"Yeah, so?"

"And still there when you took her home?" He could see where I was going and took a minute to consider lying, deciding against it. The pause was helpful.

"And that's where it stayed. I didn't touch—I mean, I didn't hit that woman, period."

"So you say. But are you asking this jury to believe you wouldn't lie to save yourself from a murder rap?"

He snorted. "Think what you want. I didn't kill her, so I don't have to lie."

I turned away from him and walked back to counsel table, leaned my hands on the table, then turned back to look him straight in the eyes. His dead-eyed return gaze was chilling. I paused to let the jury feel the animosity and to think whether I could do any better with him, decided I couldn't, and sat down.

"No further questions."

Tina looked shaken, but she tried some damage control.

"Was Mrs. Armbruster injured in any way when you last saw her?"

"No, not at all."

"Did she walk to her front door without any problem?"

"Maybe a little unsteady. She had a lot to drink and was still kind of weepy when she got out of the car."

"Did you go in the house ever?"

"I never got out of the car."

She moved to sit and said, "May the witness be excused?"

"Mr. Edwards?" Judge Alex glanced over as if seeing me in a new light.

I tilted my head in acknowledgement and answered, "Before you excuse the witness, can we put something on the record out of the jury's presence?"

"Bailiff, please take the jury out."

Then, with Firenze still on the stand, I recounted everything from the threats in his office through my introduction to Theo and Vincenzo in the hall that morning. I included the attempted dog poisoning, the threatening phone calls, and being forced off the road by a man who looked like the gentleman seated in the gallery. When I pointed at him, Theo glared back at me. Larry attested to the "You're dead" comment over recess. I did it all under oath, and the judge offered the prosecutor and Firenze a chance to ask questions. They both declined.

I then closed by saying, "I have now asked the questions he warned me not to ask. I believe him to be a dangerous man, and to be perfectly honest, I am very frightened about retribution. I wanted to make this record in the event I should meet up with an accident. At least the authorities would know where to look. Probably won't make any difference, but at least there is a record."

Alex had been watching me intently as I laid out the grounds for my fear. There was a look of anguish on her face. Confessing my fright was draining. Add to that the first feelings of warmth from the woman I had once loved heart and soul, and I almost wept as I finished.

The judge gathered herself and spoke. "Madam Stenographer, I am instructing you to transcribe the record and send a copy to each of the law enforcement agencies in the county and to place a copy in my permanent file." She turned to the witness stand, index finger practically in Firenze's face. "Mr. Firenze, I'm not in a position to prosecute you for attempting to obstruct justice; that's up to the prosecutor's office. I note you've been very clever with your contacts with Mr. Edwards before you came into court. You weren't so clever here in court, so I am cautioning you and anyone who works with or for you. Hope that Mr. Edwards stays healthy, because if anything happens to him, I'll personally see that the law falls on you like an unrelenting ton of bricks. Now get out of my courtroom."

And he was gone in a heartbeat, his henchmen trailing behind him. Ted shook my hand as the courtroom emptied for lunch. "Holy cow! Can't they arrest him for Amanda's murder?"

"No, Ted, but the jury can convict him in their minds and let you go. Maybe then the police can take another look at Firenze, but we've still got to get past this jury. One step at a time, okay?"

"Sure, Ken, thanks."

I walked out to grab a bite. Lizzie was the last person in the hallway. She waved and walked over as I came out the courtroom doors.

"Oh, my God, Mr Edwards! I'm so frightened for you."

"Don't worry, kid. I think the judge just gave him a strong vaccination against doing me any harm."

Riding down in the elevator with her, I prayed he wouldn't need a booster shot.

Tina was smart, motivated and a disciplined worker. What she wasn't was experienced. This was her first truly big case. As the prosecution wound to a close, the lack of experience showed. My training was to open your case with a compelling witness and then to close with one. In the middle you bury your losers. But Tina had left a couple of loose ends in Geraldine Chambers and Walter Hackett, whom she was required to call. She'd tried to get me to agree to waive their production. But I was enough of a hard bitten veteran to be wary of Greeks bearing gifts. I would be very glad that I'd declined her offer "not to pile it on."

The courtroom was obviously a daunting prospect for Geraldine Chambers. The spunky old gal I'd met over tea and cookies was nowhere to be seen. In fact, she leaned on the bailiff's arm and minced birdlike toward the witness stand. Her wispy white hair was newly coiffed. She was dressed in her Sunday best. A lilac jacket loose enough so as not to accent the dowager's hump topped a light green skirt. Miss Botham opened the swinging door in the bar and took over for the bailiff in offering her arm. She escorted her gently to the witness stand. I could hear Tina whispering to her as she passed the defense table.

"Relax, no one's going to hurt you, just do your best, you'll be fine."

There was no smile for me as she passed. I assumed that Tina, as she had with Firenze, blamed me for Geraldine's having to appear.

On Tina's direct her testimony came down to: "I'm a little old widow lady. I imagine things. I thought I heard a noise. I thought I saw a shadow. I got scared, so I called the police two times. I don't really know anything and I'm sorry if I caused any trouble."

When I stood up for cross examination, she cowered as if I were a mugger.

"Easy, Mrs. Chambers, relax. We've met, remember? I ate a whole heap of your chocolate chip cookies. They were the best."

She managed a little smile.

"You have quite an appetite. Always appreciated a man who can eat."

"Remember, we had tea and talked, and I asked you what you remembered about the night Amanda died?"

She shrank back into the witness chair, which already dwarfed her diminutive form.

"I probably said things I shouldn't have."

"Can you tell the jury what you told me?"

"I told you I saw—"

"Objection." Tina was up and Mrs. Chambers recoiled like her wrists had been spanked with a ruler. "Calls for hearsay. What she may have told Mr. Edwards is hearsay. What she actually can remember observing on the night in question is what is properly before this jury."

The judge looked to me.

"I think the experience of being in the courtroom is very unnerving to Mrs. Chambers, and I am simply trying to put her at ease, as she was with me when I interviewed her, so she'll tell the jury what she observed."

"Objection sustained. Rephrase your question, counsel."

"Yes, Your Honor. Did you hear somebody in your back yard that night, Mrs. Chambers?"

She looked over to the judge nervously to see if she should answer. "I thought I saw a shadow, but sometimes I think I see things that aren't there. I thought I heard rustling, maybe I heard rustling. What is it, what did I say before?"

"Didn't you call the police because you saw a burglar moving behind your house in the wee hours?"

"I called them because I was frightened. Since my Harold passed, I get scared at night."

"Did you tell the police you saw a prowler?"

"Objection, hearsay."

"No, Your Honor, this is an exception both as an excited utterance and as an attempt to refresh her recollection of prior statement."

Alex considered. "Well, Mr. Edwards, which is it?" Her blue eyes looked to me. "The first, the jury could use to prove the truth of the matter asserted. The second, they can't."

"I think I'd plead the first, then."

"In which case, you'll need a better foundation."

"Mrs. Chambers, did whatever you saw or heard in your yard frighten you?"

"Yes it did."

"Were you still frightened when you called 911?"

"Oh, yes."

"Did you call right away after you became scared?"

"Well, not right away. Because I know I've called them so many times, and I always promise myself before I go to bed I'm not going to call again unless there is really something."

"So there was really something that scared you?"

"I was scared."

"Tina was up. "Objection."

"I'm going to allow the question even though she didn't act immediately under the effect of what she thought she perceived. Objection overruled."

"Did you tell 911 you had seen a prowler?"

"I guess I did."

"Where was the prowler?"

"Over the back hedge, on the golf course."

"You also called the police a half hour later to report the sound of breaking glass."

"I did call back."

"Because you heard breaking glass?"

"I'm not sure anymore why I called back. I was still frightened."

"If the 911 log shows you reported broken glass, you wouldn't argue with the police report, would you?"

"Well, Miss Bottom—" There was a ripple of mirth not shared by Tina. "Oh, my goodness, I was so worried I'd do that. I'm so sorry, my dear. Miss Botham told me the mirror in the hall of the Armbrusters' house was broken that night, so there was glass breaking for me to hear."

"Mrs. Chambers, what did you do after you called back the second time to report breaking glass?"

"I waited for the police."

"Were you so sure you'd heard breaking glass, and that a burglar was loose, that you ran downstairs to make sure all the doors were locked?"

She nodded. "Sometimes I can't remember if I locked everything before I go to bed."

"Did you grab something while you were downstairs?"

She looked confused. I prompted her.

"A knife."

"Oh—oh—yes, I was scared."

I took a chance.

"On any of the other occasions you called the police, did you go downstairs to get a knife?"

I was lucky.

"No, I don't think so."

"After you checked the door and grabbed a knife, did you return to your bedroom?"

"Yes, I sat in the chair behind the curtain and looked out."

"What did you see?"

"I can't say."

"Can't say?"

"She told me not to mention Santa."

The jury laughed as one, but when the embarrassment reddened Geraldine's face, they quieted.

"That's okay, Mrs. Chambers. I am asking you, and I promise that when you explain, the jury won't laugh."

She didn't like looking stupid, so she shrugged her shoulders and pressed on.

"I saw a man stooped over just outside my back gate in the trees. He was stooped over and had, well, it looked like a sack with things sticking out of it. He was in a shadow, so I could just see him in side profile for a minute—no, a second, really, 'cause I ducked behind the curtain so he wouldn't see me. But, well, I know this sounds stupid, but that profile made me think of Santa with his bag and toys spilling over the top."

"You live between the Brownes and the Armbrusters with your back yard ending at the trees on the fifteenth fairway of the golf course, true?"

"Have for over twenty years."

"Which way was the man with the sack going; toward the Armbrusters' or toward the Brownes'?"

"I just can't remember that."

"Okay, Mrs. Chambers, let me just ask about something else. Mr. Armbruster, he has been your neighbor for many years?"

"As long as we've lived there."

"What kind of person is he?"

"Always a good neighbor, always a gentleman. After my Harold passed, he checked on me. Well, he did until they put him in jail. I'd call him when things needed fixing. He'd take care of it. Nice man."

"Thank you, Mrs. Chambers."

Tina let her frustration show. She'd thought Mrs. Chambers to be sufficiently cowed and timid that she wouldn't give me Santa. Tina wasn't prepared to let Mr. Kringle take the fall. She rose from her chair and ran her hand through her moussed hair. I wondered if her handshake would leave a residue, like Firenze's had.

"Now, Mrs. Chambers," Tina said, "you've been pretty regular about calling the police since your husband died, haven't you?"

Geraldine looked guilty and shrunk back even further in the witness chair. "I guess so."

"You've called the police eleven times in the nine months following your husband's death."

"That many?"

"Yes, ma'am, that many. Each time you reported a prowler."

"I did, I guess that's right."

"How many prowlers did the police find?"

Geraldine just shook her head.

"Ever?"

"Well, no, but that doesn't mean—"

"Doesn't mean what?"

"Nothing." She gathered herself. "Nothing. It doesn't mean there wasn't one either."

Tina looked smugly over to the jury. A couple of them were rolling their eyes.

"When the police talked to you the next day, did you tell them about Santa Claus?"

"No, but—"

"Why not?"

"I didn't want to seem foolish, seeing Santa Claus and all."

"But after you had milk and cookies with Mr. Edwards, now it's not so foolish to tell these good men and women of the jury under oath in a murder trial you saw Santa?"

Geraldine looked ready to cry. All she could manage was, "It was tea. Tea and cookies."

"Oh, sorry. Thank you, Mrs. Chambers."

The judge asked, "May the witness be excused?"

Mrs. Chambers grabbed her purse as she pushed herself up from the chair. She looked ready to bolt for the exit. I hated to make her suffer anymore and almost let her go, but I wanted to salvage what little value I could.

"Just a few more questions. Please take your seat for a moment longer, won't you, Miss Chambers?"

She sadly sunk back into the seat.

"Not only were you kind enough to invite me into your home and let me ask questions, but Ms. Botham has visited your home too, hasn't she?"

She brightened. "Yes, and she ate two pieces of my pecan pie the second time."

"So you met her twice?"

"Twice at the house and in her office last evening."

"Did you tell her about the figure that looked like Santa?"

"Each time."

"What did she tell you?"

"She said I was imagining things. She said if I mentioned it in the trial I'd look like a fool, and she was right. I feel like an old fool. I'm sorry I said anything."

"I'm sorry for your embarrassment, ma'am, but have you lied or tried to mislead the jury?"

She looked offended. "Of course not."

"Are you claiming you saw Santa, or just a shadow with something over his back that reminded you of a Santa shape?"

"Just a shadow with a pack."

"And is that still your testimony now, in spite of feeling foolish?"

She paused and I began to repeat asking the question, but then she came through. "I wish I never mentioned it, but that's what I saw."

"Thank you, ma'am."

Again she started to rise, but Tina wanted to hit the ball back over the net.

"Mrs. Chambers, there is no light on the golf course at that time of night."

"True, but there are houses and streetlights over on Glen Gary Drive on the other side of the course. They make shadows."

"But between your backyard and the fifteenth fairway there are trees and bushes."

"Yes, there are."

"Isn't it possible in that short time you looked out, after running down the stairs to check the locks and get a knife and the ducking behind the curtain, that what you saw was the shadow of a tree or a bush, and you were so upset at that moment that the tree or bush created a shadow that looked like Santa?"

Geraldine didn't have that much fight in her anyway, and what she'd once had was now exhausted. She nodded and spoke quite meekly.

"I suppose so. I'm sorry for all the trouble I caused."

"No trouble, Mrs. Chambers. Thank you."

The judge excused her. She was so shook up she almost stumbled getting off the stand, so I got up and offered my arm to escort her across the courtroom. I wished she hadn't, but she whispered in a stage whisper loud enough to be heard in the back of the courtroom.

"Sorry, young man, I did the best I could."

I patted her on the arm and said in the same megaphonic whisper, "You did just fine. You are a very nice lady." With that she was gone.

That left only Hackett, the bartender from Heather Hollows, before the prosecution rested. During the recess following Geraldine's testimony, I spotted him sitting glumly on the bench across from the elevator. He ignored my handshake proffer, but I sat next to him anyway.

"Nice to see you too. Just doing my job, you know."

He turned his rheumy eyes in my direction long enough to mutter, "Think I care about your job?"

As I moved away he reached into the breast pocket of his white shirt and rattled some Tic-Tacs into his hand. "That horse left the barn already," I thought, the whisky vapors still fresh in my nose. He'd had a bracer or two to steel himself for the witness stand. I made a mental note to have him stand with me in front of the jury box so they could conduct their own breathalyzer test.

Tina was in a hurry to get Hackett on and off the stand. She had him recount Ted's angry outburst and obvious intoxication. He described Ted's aggressive conduct in pushing Firenze and added, "He shoved me too when I asked him to please calm down."

Then Tina tried to gild the lily as I'd hoped she would. "Did you hear Mr. Armbruster threaten his wife?"

"Yep. That's when I figured I'd have to call the cops."

"What did he say?"

"He stuck his finger out at her as his friends were trying to get him to leave and said, and I quote: 'You'll pay for this. You'll be sorry.' "

The jurors grabbed their note pads as Tina pertly pranced back to her seat, cocking her head at me as if to say, "You asked for it."

She was right. I'd asked for it. Now I had to make sure I liked what I got. So I had Hackett come in front of the jury box and demonstrate the pointing and repeat the threat. The front row recoiled from the fumes. And while he was still standing before them I asked, "Were you drinking that night, sir?"

"Of course not. Against the rules."

I let that hang while I scratched my cheek skeptically, then asked him to return to the stand.

"Mr. Hackett, do you remember me coming out to interview you about a week ago?"

"Yeah." His leathery face contorted as if recalling a visit to the dentist.

"And when I asked you what words Ted Armbruster used to threaten his wife, you told me you didn't remember, that it was in the police report, and if I did my job I'd go read the report to find out. Didn't you say that to me at Heather Hollows when I came to talk to you there?"

As Hackett answered, Tina was out of her chair objecting that I was inserting myself in the case, and if I wanted to testify I should be a witness, not the attorney. A perfectly valid objection. But before she'd finished her objection, Hackett answered over her. His answer caused the judge to overrule the objection.

"Yeah, I said that. I told you Miss Botham said I didn't have to talk to you and to go do your job. Something wrong with that?"

"Just wondering when your memory came back. I took your advice and read your statement to the police again. It doesn't say what words you claim Mr. Armbruster used to threaten her. You tell me you don't remember the words a few days ago, and now here you are in court swearing under oath to the exact words. So when did your memory come back?"

Walter Hackett was a dim bulb, but even at his wattage he realized he'd stepped into trouble.

"I met with Miss Botham over the weekend. She helped me remember. She told me to do the best I could from memory, that's what I am doing."

"So was Miss Botham at the bar that night?"

"No."

"So how'd she help you remember what Ted said?"

"She showed me my statement."

"I think we've agreed that the statement doesn't contain any specific threatening words, so how else did she help you?"

"Well, she just told me to remember the best I could."

"So are you admitting now you don't know exactly what Ted said to his wife?"

He held out his hands, palms up. "Okay, F. Lee Bailey, you got me. It was a long time ago. It was loud and I probably didn't hear exactly what he said, but I do know he was angry and he threatened her. He pushed me and he shoved Mr. Firenze. He looked threatening. He acted threatening. That's all I can really say, okay?"

"Okay. Thanks for your honesty. Now, did you see Mr. Firenze dancing with Mrs. Armbruster?"

Walt paled and looked edgier than at any time so far. "I don't think Mr. Firenze would want me talking about him in court."

"You know Mr. Firenze, then?"

"No, not exactly. He came in once in a while. He's a good tipper."

"How's Mr. Firenze employed?"

He looked at me as if I'd asked him from which direction the sun rose. "Everybody knows. He's with the—" He paused to reconsider. "He's in scrap metal or something, I think."

"Aha. So, did he dance with Mrs. Armbruster?"

He looked again at Tina, who had stopped scratching her nose.

"Maybe once or twice."

"Slow songs?"

"Well, both."

"Was he holding her close on the slow songs?"

"He always does."

"So you've seen him with other ladies?"

Walt didn't like the direction this was going, so he just sat back and didn't answer. Finally Tina bailed him out with a relevance objection, which the judge sustained, but I'd made my point. Gianfranco inspired fear.

Okay, enough groundwork. Time to see if he could answer a question that, in spite of hundreds of readings of the police reports and logs, only recently had bubbled to the surface of my mind.

"Whom did you call about the disturbance?"

"The police."

"Any police in particular?"

"The sheriff's department usually gets our 911 calls."

"Did you call 911?"

"Yep."

"Well, I'm wondering how it didn't show up in the 911 call register?"

Walt paused, considered and answered, "Oh, maybe I used the other number."

"What other number?"

"I have a direct number to get the sheriff's department's special drunk driver unit."

"Where did you get that?"

"We serve liquor. We get drunks. We need the police a couple of times a month. Some of the department guys stop in for a drink now and then. They said to use their number and alert them so they can catch drunk drivers before they get on the highway. Kind of a public service thing." He looked a little smug.

"So you call the cops on your customers? Does your boss know about this?"

He didn't look so sassy.

"Well—no. But I mean, they don't bust them most of the time. They talk to them, check them out and call a cab or give them a ride or something. Keeps them off the roads."

"Whose idea was this?"

He glanced over at the prosecution table, but it wasn't Miss Botham he was looking at, it was Bliss, who was suddenly trying to look busy shuffling papers. Walt looked away before Bliss shook his head slightly, but I saw it. "Mr. Hackett, I asked you whose public service idea it was?"

"Well, I'm not certain, but I think it might've been Detective Bliss. He comes in once in a while. I think he gave me the number."

Bliss got much busier with the papers, so I took a shot in the dark.

"And do you receive anything for your participation in this public service operation?"

Hackett now stared at Bliss like a dog caught with his snoot in the garbage. Bliss wasn't looking back. Whatever on-your-feet thinking skills old Walt had once possessed had been eroded by years on the booze. He was smart enough to recognize he'd walked into a minefield, but not smart enough to find his way out. So he just sat there.

"Mr. Hackett?"

"Uh, yes, uh—not really, not much, not all the time. It comes from some fund—they call it a tip fund or something. Kind of like a Crime-Stoppers for drinking and driving, like that. It's not like I'm ratting on my customers. They usually end up leaving their cars in the parking lot so they don't drink and drive. I guess they're pretty thankful not to be going to jail and express their gratitude to the police for letting them off with a warning and calling a cab. So it's good for everybody, and mostly it's people who have money, so nobody really gets hurt."

"How do you know they've got money?"

"Our bar is pretty upscale. The drinks are pricey, and it's my job to know my customers. We get lots of folks from the country club. The bar there closes at ten most nights."

The jury members were on the edges of their seats. Walt hadn't been all that likeable to begin with, but to be violating the bartender-barfly privilege so egregiously in a drinking town like Lake Pointe was shocking.

"Mr. Hackett, let's recap then. You serve liquor to the well-heeled. When they have too much and you're afraid they might drink and drive, you perform the public service of calling a number Detective Bliss gave you?"

Now Hackett looked like a trapped rabbit. The fight was gone. "Yep."

"And you get a reward for tipping?"

"Not all the time, like not the night of the murder."

"Who took the call that night?"

"Well, it was Doyle and Meeks, the usual drunk driving deputies, that came." The memory of Meeks standing next to a new yellow 'Vette popped into my head. I now had an idea how he'd financed it. "But Armbruster had already left," Hackett added.

"No, I mean who answered the phone when you called?"

Again a glance at Bliss, who had stopped looking at his papers and was now staring at a fixed point on the wall near the ceiling.

"Detective Bliss, I believe."

"What did you tell him?"

"I told him Mr. Armbruster was drunk, too drunk to drive."

"So the call wasn't about a disturbance. You were just doing your public service of reporting a potential drunk driver?"

"No, no. I told him Mrs. Armbruster was still there with Mr. Firenze. I told him that the Armbrusters were arguing. I don't know what else."

"What did Detective Bliss say?"

"I don't know. He asked some questions, like how drunk he was, did I recognize Mrs. Armbruster for sure? Who else was there? How drunk was she, that kind of thing. Then he said he'd take care of it. That's about it."

"Did Bliss come to the bar?"

"No, just the deputies. Maybe they talked to him on their cell phone. I think they did."

"All right, Mr. Hackett, that's all my questions. Thank you."

I sat down. I kept the look of satisfaction off my face. Instead I grabbed a legal pad and adopted a demeanor of puzzled concentration, jotting a note or two, while the jury looked over to the prosecution's table. It was no longer the look of the local fans cheering for the home team. The judge finished writing furiously on her legal pad and looked to Miss Botham. "Any further questions, Madam Prosecutor?"

Tina looked daggers at Bliss, who decidedly avoided her gaze. I'm sure she had some further questions, but none she wanted to air before the jury.

"None, Your Honor."

The courtroom was buzzing. Although not all of the seats were filled, enough spectators remained to create quite a stir. Art Honnecker jostled his way to the aisle and made a beeline for the door. The judge gaveled the room to silence and looked at Tina, who was as pale as her white seersucker suit.

"Your next witness, Madam Prosecutor."

"People rest, Your Honor." She spoke quietly. Hardly the high note she'd wanted to finish with.

"Very well. Ladies and gentlemen of the jury, the prosecution has rested. We will begin with the defense tomorrow. You are excused for the day."

While waiting for the elevator, I glimpsed Tina and Bliss heading for the stairwell. Tina had regained her color. She was red in the face. "You stupid bastard," were the only words I heard from this woman who never swore.

Murder Case In Trouble

read the headline in the *Leader*. But the story concerning the defense's creating other suspects "ranging from a suspected mobster with a violent past to Santa Claus" shared equal space with

Sheriff's Shakedown Scam

above a subheading "Bartender Blabs on Bliss."

Not only was I on the front page, I owned it. I'd gotten up early for the paper and was on my second cup of coffee and third reread when the cottage phone rang.

"Ken?"

"Hey, Tina. How are you?"

"I've been better. I can't believe that stupid ape Bliss would do this to me."

"If it makes you feel any better, I don't think Bliss ever expected this to see the light of day. I imagine the two of you are going to be a little uncomfortable sitting next to each other till the end of trial."

"Are you kidding? Bliss is suspended. I've already arranged for Detective Weston to take his place at counsel table the rest of the way. If Bliss had just let Weston handle this from the start, I wouldn't have a perfectly clear murder case all f—, I mean, messed up by a police corruption scandal."

"And you wouldn't have a confession either. Has it crossed your mind that maybe what I've been telling you about Bliss and that confession might be true? Maybe Ted's telling the truth."

She snorted. "Bliss on the take? That's a shock, but what's that got to do with Armbruster's confession? Are you saying Bliss went to the house to shake your client down about a drunk and disorderly and then extracted a phony murder confession, or what?"

"I'm saying I don't know why Bliss jumped into the case, but I do know that the credibility of your star witness to prove the confession just went into the toilet."

If she'd sighed any harder she'd have risked suffocation. "That's why I'm calling. I spent practically all night talking to the boss. He was a hard sell, but in view of recent developments, we'll offer your client manslaughter, killing in the heat of passion, and we'll put a five-year sentence cap on it. Beats the hell out of Murder One. We both know he did it, so it's an incredible deal. What do you say?"

"I'd say my client has been steadfast in telling me he didn't kill her."

"Okay, we'll take a no-lo-contendre plea to manslaughter. The judge can use the record before her to find a basis. The no contest means he doesn't admit anything, but he'd have to agree not to pursue the life insurance claim. I'll be darned if I'll stand by and watch him jackpot on killing his wife. Best we can do. What's your reaction?"

"Not my reaction that counts. I'll take your offer to my client."

"When can you let me know? I've got to prepare to cross examine your client, and I have jury instructions to submit." Tina had gone from supremely confident to desperate in twenty-four hours. Trials are like riding a seesaw. With Bliss's weight gone from her side of the fulcrum, I envisioned Tina high in the air, her short legs dangling far from the ground.

"I'll take it to him now, but I wouldn't stop working if I were you. With what happened recently, Ted may just want to roll the dice."

"Sounds more like it's you who wants to gamble. Remind yourself that if you crap out, life in prison is an awfully long time. Call me when you know. I'm at the office." With that she hung up.

I left right away to convey the offer to Ted. His jailhouse supporters were calling out words of encouragement as we walked from the cell to the conference room.

"Way to go, Edwards."

"Kick ass and take names."

"Bliss is the cop on my case. When do I get out?"

Ted listened as I told him of Tina's offer. He asked me what I thought.

"Damn good offer. You could be out in three years. Up to you."

"After yesterday, will I still have to testify?"

"No way around it. The way things are going I'd maybe rather you didn't. But you told the jury you would testify. Kind of limits our options."

He retreated into himself. His lips moved wordlessly as he thought. After a few minutes he refocused his eyes on me and spoke. "Tell them no deal. If I say I did it, they quit looking for the person who really killed her. If I have to go to prison for the rest of my life to keep the case open, I will. I want to testify. It's time people hear my side of the story."

Pandemonium returned to the spectator seating. The headlines and promise that Ted would be taking the stand had brought out a capacity crowd. They were decidedly friendlier than they had been back at the start of the case. But we didn't start on time. The judge sent her bailiff, Larry, to fetch me to chambers. "Watch out. She's breathing fire," he whispered.

Tina was seated and Alex stood behind her desk as I walked in. She had yet to don her robe. Her blonde hair spilled over a white sundress, just as it had in my dream on the morning Ted's frantic call had awakened me. However, as she turned her head to me, there was nothing romantic about the look she gave me.

"Be seated, counselor. Are you that reckless?"

My posterior had not even settled into the leather chair.

"Pardon me, Your Honor. Isn't it customary to tell me what I'm accused of before asking how I plead?"

"Sit. Sit. Miss Botham advises she offered you manslaughter with a five-year cap and that you refused. Tell me that's not so."

I was still standing as I replied. "It's not so. She made the offer. I didn't refuse it. My client did."

"I can't help feeling he did so with your encouragement. I know you. You're a gambler, and now that the prize is in sight, you want to go for the glory." She held her hand up to stifle my protest. "I'm telling you I think that's unprofessional and very risky. Even if the jury throws out the confession in light of the detective's recent problems, your client still can, and probably will, be found guilty. That's him at the scene with her blood all over him. That's his club that killed her. Those were his friends testifying to the confrontation at Heather Hollows, and his insurance agent selling him a huge policy on her life in an amount just enough to save his business. If I were on that jury, he's guilty. Turning down a five-year max. Are you that irresponsible?"

It was like Tina had vanished. Standing, staring back across the desk at this woman who had hurt me to the core, my scars unhealed years later, I could only see Alexandra, her eyes on fire with indignation. All that pain rendered raw with this new accusation nearly caused me to lose it. I kept my eyes fixed to hers and swallowed the anger. I took a side step toward the door and spoke quietly.

"I can only hope the jury is more willing than you are to listen to the defense before convicting my client. I would also hope they will at least hear me out before deciding I'm reckless and irresponsible. Now if you'll excuse me, I've got an opening statement to give."

"You are not excused. I'm doing this as much for your own good as my own satisfaction. I'm calling in the court reporter and asking Miss Botham to agree that nothing that's said will be used in any way against your client, but I am going to have him say on the record that he is walking away from the best plea offer I've ever heard of on his own accord. So you can stand or sit, but you are not excused."

Ted looked confused as the bailiff brought him in and the stenographer set up. The judge was polite and patient as she laid out the benefits of the plea offer and the risks of conviction at trial. Ted gave her the same explanation for his refusal he'd given me about not allowing the killer of his wife to escape. He thanked Tina most politely for the offer, and the judge for taking the time to explain it all to him, and then looked out for his lawyer.

"Your Honor, everything you've told me Mr. Edwards explained for me when he recommended I take the deal. But I can't. I just can't. I hope you understand why."

Judge Alex turned red with embarrassment and asked me to remain behind as Ted was escorted away. I couldn't be sure, but I thought I saw moisture at the corners of her eyes.

"I'm sorry," she said. "I misjudged you again. Seems I'm always wrong when it comes to you. If your client comes across that sincerely in front of the jury, they might actually believe him. Say, what happened to your neck, and why has your voice been so gravelly this week? You're not back on cigarettes again?"

"Nope. Although I could have used one the last few weeks. M. Stanton and I didn't see eye to eye in the kiss-and-make-up session you ordered Monday."

"Oh my God, really? Are you pressing charges? You want me to hold a hearing?"

I laughed and shook my head. "No thanks. We are both big boys, and I doubt he'll be jumping his show horse for a while. So we're even. But thanks for asking. Can I go?"

I had my hand on the door when she started to speak again.

"Ken, I'm really sorry about—"

I turned and we shared the kind of smile that once was my daily sustenance. "Forget it. Apology accepted."

I paused in the corridor between chambers and the courtroom to reflect. I had told Karen about Alex dumping me and the chilly reception I had gotten in her court. Should I mention that the ice was beginning to melt? Best not.

There were a few moments for Ted and me to talk before the jury came in, and I congratulated him for his handling of the judge. I concluded by saying, "I don't actually remember my telling you to take the deal. I remember saying it was a good deal, but—"

He smiled easily in answering. "I knew from the atmosphere in that room when I walked in that the judge was on your case and why. I don't want you worrying, if this whole thing blows up, that I'll be blaming you, or the judge will give you trouble, thinking you were trying to build your reputation at my expense. If you'd gotten on your knees begging me to take that deal, my answer would've been the same. I didn't kill her and that's that. Answer your question?"

"Very nicely. Thank you."

As the jury filed in I marveled at the insight, understanding, and concern of my client. Really a quality guy. Now all I had to do was make sure the jury felt the same way.

64

As I stood to give my opening statement, lucky cream-colored suit fresh from the dry cleaner, red carnation in the lapel, I was as confident as I had been at any point since the case had come back to me. I was feeling like Tina had felt before the weight of Bliss's testimony had been removed from her end of the seesaw. It wouldn't be long before we'd trade places again and I would be the one up in the air, legs dangling.

Normally when addressing a jury, I'm peripatetic. I range far from the lectern and move away from and then near to the jury as my nervous energy and points of emphasis command. My voice is strong and deep enough to reach my audience from anywhere. Not today. Thanks to M. Stanton, my vocal cords could manage only intimate conversation. So I stood directly before the panel and talked to them in a cracking voice about peeling an onion.

I told them the prosecution's case was like buying an onion at the market that felt plump and firm, only to prove soft and rotting once the layers were peeled away. I told them each brown area of decaying flesh was a basis for reasonable doubt.

"Take Detective Bliss, whom Madam Prosecutor tarted up to be St. Raymond. Peel away the layers and we find a rotting scandal of graft and corruption. There are layers yet to peel if we are to know why he was so eager to violate departmental procedure and take the Armbruster case ahead of Detective Weston.

"Take Mr. Firenze. Again, Madam Prosecutor casts him as the perfect gentleman rescuing a damsel in distress. Peel away the layers and we find him to be anything but a gentle man. Rather, at the core, we find a dangerous man with a violent history who was the last person seen with the victim alive. A man who admits he is the cause of the bruises on Amanda's thigh. Peel away the layers of lies he admits to telling. Can you believe him when he admits violently pressing his affections on her, but denies pressing to the point of killing her?

"Take Dr. Zimmer. There is nothing rotten about him. But how about the prosecution tactic of trying to hide the second club? If their case were solid, would there be a need for hiding evidence?" I cleared the gravel from my throat and in so doing scraped away most of what was left of it.

"Ask yourself why Miss Botham tried to discourage that charm-ing lady, Geraldine Chambers, from mentioning Santa skulking behind her house. Who was fleeing the scene of the crime at the time Ted was calling 911, begging for help for his wife?

"We will do what the prosecution did not: play the 911 tape. Listen to the anguish, anxiety, and concern in Ted's voice. Ask yourself as you listen to that tape and Ted's testimony if he is the cold-blooded killer the prosecution claims, or a man who loved his wife with all his being and found her in mortal peril, and called out desperately for help."

As my voice faltered to a whisper, I promised them they would find Ted a devoted husband who could not and did not hurt his wife. Lastly I told them that I hadn't been able to peel enough layers to find all the dark forces at work in Amanda's death, but that by the time the defense was finished, they would know enough to know the prosecution's case was rotten to the core. They might yet find the real motive for Amanda's killing, and in so doing not only have a reasonable doubt as to Ted's guilt, but also have a pretty good idea who was truly responsible. They all sat forward in their seats throughout so as to hear me, which I took to be a good sign.

The defense started with the 911 supervisor, Jamie Dawson. She admitted that the two calls by Mrs. Chambers to report a burglary came close in time to Ted's call for help, but had not been saved. The jury listened with rapt attention to the recording of Ted's anguished plea to send an ambulance. Nothing on that tape was inconsistent with Ted's innocence. He claimed he thought he heard angry voices, glass break, and had rushed downstairs to find his wife near death. In response to the dispatch officer's repeated requests to stay on the line, Ted closed the call with a desperate plea:

"Amanda needs me. I've got to go to her. Hurry! Please hurry!"

Jamie also confirmed that the cell phone calls between Bliss and deputies Meeks and Doyle were in violation of departmental policy requiring all calls to go through central dispatch.

Grayton Lansdale made a solid character witness. He made a nice prologue for Ted's testimony. Every eye in the courtroom followed Ted's dignified walk to the witness stand. His light gray suit had recently been dry cleaned. I'd had a barber style his full head of hair to his former swept back, company president look. His voice was resonant as he swore to tell the truth. Throughout my direct questioning he followed my instructions to the letter. He would look to me to hear the question and then shift his gaze to the jury box to give his answers.

I walked him from his birth fifty-eight years ago in Lake Pointe to the present. He'd been an all-state wide receiver on Lake Pointe Central's football team. I saw two of the older male jurors nod in recognition when he described his team playing for the state Class B title in his senior year. He'd volunteered for service in Vietnam against his father's wishes, and been awarded a Purple Heart for a Viet Cong bullet he'd taken in the thigh. After an honorable discharge, he'd returned to Michigan to complete his degree at the University of Michigan. The bullet had dashed any hopes of making the college football team.

He described returning home to work for his dad at Armbruster Manufacturing. His description of his mom and dad working hand in glove together brought tears to his mother's eyes as she sat in the first row of the gallery. He told the jury how, since starting as a stock boy during high school, he'd worked practically every job at the business. A Chevy plant worker on the panel nodded approvingly as he mentioned with pride his journeyman's card as a machinist.

Ted told the jury of taking over the helm at Armbruster Manufacturing when his father died young of a heart attack. He recounted the evolutionary decline and fall of the small independent machine shops in the face of automaker one-sourcing and foreign outsourcing. He was making common cause with his audience when he said, "Maybe I'm old-fashioned, but I think American companies should be giving American workers first crack at building products for American customers."

He shouldered the blame for his company's problems. "I feel like a failure. Work that we had counted on based on our four-star quality rating was gone. I had to let men and women go that had been with us for years. My dad took such pride in the business providing so many families with a good living. Our people did not move around, they stayed with us, and I kept many of them on part time even though my banker told me I shouldn't. I kept hoping we'd find something."

Tina Botham stood to object. "This is all very nice, Your Honor, but it's not relevant. Mr. Armbruster is on trial for killing his wife, not for how he managed or mismanaged the family business."

I saw Ted react to the word "mismanage," as did a couple of the jurors who understood what was happening to independent toolmakers.

The judge looked to me.

"Your Honor, the prosecutor has spent the last three weeks claiming that my client killed his wife to collect the insurance money and save the family business. Surely he is entitled to meet that accusation by describing the business and his feelings toward it."

The judge considered that for a moment.

"Very well. Objection overruled, but let's try and get to the point, Mr. Edwards."

"Thank you, Your Honor. I intend to, but since the prosecution has had weeks to paint a certain picture of my client, I trust you'll understand that I'd like the jury to have a few minutes to get to know him for themselves."

The judge looked a little vexed, considered a comeback and then said, "I've overruled the objection, please proceed."

"Thank you, Judge. Now, Mr. Armbruster, I was asking you if you had come up with a plan to revitalize the company. Can you tell me about that?"

"Yes sir, but first, Miss Botham accused me of mismanagement, and I'd like to reply to that by saying she is probably right. I didn't see or anticipate the changes going on between the companies and the suppliers. As we all know, the car business is up and down. I thought we were just in a slump and I was slow to recognize that the world was changing. This hurt the company and our workers. It was my career's biggest mistake, and I deeply regret it." He paused and slowly shook his head. "I'm sorry, I forgot what you were asking me."

I marveled at how well Ted had skewered Miss Botham with her own sword. He'd admitted guilt for something openly and honestly, and truth be known, virtually all of Ted's competitors in the business had not seen the sea change coming either. Lake Pointe, like many auto towns, was dotted with tool and die shops with half-empty employee lots or with the gates locked and rusting. There had to be people on the jury who knew this and knew why. I doubted they'd blame Ted. In my appreciation of Ted's deft handling of the issue, I too had lost track of my question.

"Now where were we? Madam Court Reporter, my last question, please?"

As she spooled the roll back, looking for the question, one of those little straws in the wind appeared. Juror # 6, Miss Tomlinson, the librarian, spoke up.

"His plan to save the business."

"Oh, yes, thank you." The court reporter scrambled to get the steno paper back and transcribe the interchange.

The judge looked at her sheet listing juror names. "Miss Tomlinson, you must not speak unless the court addresses you. I know you were trying to be helpful, but that's not allowed. Do you understand?"

The juror's face had turned red in embarrassment and she answered meekly, "Sorry."

But a juror doesn't help a lawyer if there is no sympathy for that side. If they don't like you or your case, they are happy to see you wallow around in ineptitude. For at least one juror, a hopeful sign. As I began, I looked appreciatively at Miss Tomlinson and gave the merest nod of thanks.

"Yes, Mr. Armbruster, I asked about your plan to save the business?"

"Yes sir. I'm sorry too, Judge. I kind of lost track and I'm a little nervous. Yes, well, when it finally became clear that much of our automotive work was not coming back, I started to search for new work that could save our business. Just when it looked like there was no hope, a friend in Texas called and said there was this water control valve business in Odessa. Safety Valve was a company that went back to the early 1900's making products for fluid control. A big conglomerate had bought them, and that conglomerate merged into a bigger conglomerate and so on. Over time Safety Valve got forgotten, so now they were ready to dump it for not much up-front cash, a percentage of sales for ten years and assumption of debt. Plus, they had a patented reverse osmosis process that purified the water. It was perfect. And the machinery used to make these valves is very similar to what we use, so we could bring their machinery and equipment here, and I could bring a lot of our laid-off employees back to work. Amanda made the deal happen."

"Why do you say that?"

"J.T. Pickering was the man in charge of the deal for the seller. Once he saw what our finances were, and the conditions under which the bank would finance the deal, he lost interest. I was very depressed, but Amanda and J.T. got along great when he was here doing due diligence. He had invited us down to his ranch, and she called him up when it looked like a non-starter and accepted his invitation. By the time she got back a week later, she'd persuaded him and the deal was on."

I could see the happiness of that moment reflected in his face.

"How did she do it?"

"I'm not sure. I know I was getting nowhere with him and she was only supposed to go for a weekend, but she called and said she'd revived his interest and needed to stay a week. At the end of the week we had a deal. It's pretty hard to say no to Amanda when she gets her mind set on something." I had a pretty good idea of Amanda's methods of persuasion. A couple of jurors whispered to each other, making me think they had guessed as well.

The light went out of his eyes as the pleasant memory was replaced with the reality that Amanda's magic was gone. I switched to him describing his marriage to his first wife and how her death had impacted him.

"I didn't handle it well. I just kind of went into a shell, and then Amanda saved me. She was like an angel of light reaching down in the darkness for me. She saved me."

I admitted a series of photographs showing the two of them together, the wedding, walking hand in hand, on the cottage beach, seated kissing in front of Rome's Trevi Fountain, and dancing at a New Year's Eve ball. Ted was animated as he told a little story with each picture. I wanted the jury to understand how much he cared for her.

"Did you love your wife?"

"Very much. I still do." His voice failed him as tears welled.

"Did you kill her?"

He straightened, and as we had planned, he looked me straight in the eye. "No sir. I did not. I loved her more than life itself. I would not hurt her. I did not hurt her."

"Can you tell the jury what happened?"

"Not very well. As the jury has heard, I had a disagreement with Amanda and lost my temper. I drank more than I should've, and I went home and took a sedative to calm me down, so I'd get to sleep, because I was supposed to be up early to go north with the fellows for golf. I'm not sure what woke me. I heard a noise but I was way under, and it took me a while to come awake."

"What was the noise?"

"It's hard to differentiate between sleep and awake. I think I heard the mirror break. I think I heard voices arguing. I was lying in bed thinking I'd had a bad dream, then I heard a door slam. So I got up. When I got to the top of the stairs there was Amanda all covered in blood. Oh my God, oh my God."

His composure was gone. There in public he was seeing her body again. The anguish had him wringing his hands, his face contorted in pain. I let it sit like that for a moment. The courtroom was silent as all eyes watched him wrestle with the demons of memory. When he finally looked up at me again, his face was a whiter shade of pale. He looked lost and frightened.

"Did you see anyone else in the house?"

"No, no, just Amanda."

"What did you do?"

"I ran down to help her. She was in pain. I heard her moan and rasp for breath. I was in such a hurry I tripped on one of the bottom steps and I fell on the marble floor."

"Is that how you injured your hand?"

"Objection, leading."

"Sustained."

"Ted, tell the jury how you injured your hand."

"I don't know for sure. I think I stepped on my pajamas rushing down the stairs and fell. I didn't notice I'd broken a finger and my hand was swollen until I was in the patrol car on my way to jail."

"Did you injure your hand striking your wife?"

"I have never struck Amanda in my life."

I grabbed Exhibit 5, the golf club. "Is this yours?"

I held it up. He recoiled from it. "Yes, it is."

"Did you strike Amanda with this club in the early morning hours of April 28th?"

"I did not."

"Did you touch it that night?"

"I must have. I don't want to say for sure, because I'm not a hundred percent clear. I seem to remember it lying on the floor next to or just under Amanda. I think I moved it when I knelt down to help her."

"Was she still alive when you reached her?"

"I don't know." The pain was obvious on his face as he searched his memory. "I know I saw her move from the top of the stairs. I heard a strange breathing sound like a gasp, then I fell, and when I got to her, I turned her sideways, facing me, and put her in my lap. I called her name, but she didn't respond. I kept calling, nothing, nothing. Then I put my hand on the big artery in the neck. Maybe I could feel a little thread, but I wasn't sure, so I ran to the phone and called 911. By the time I got back there was nothing. She was gone."

He'd been describing at a rapid pace. The last three words came out as a resigned sigh. He was slumped in his chair, as the retelling had exhausted him. I let him and the jury catch their breaths. The jury to a person had their chairs swiveled to face Ted. They gazed at him fixedly. I could not tell from their rapt expressions if they were sympathizing with him for his loss, or loathing him for killing her and lying about it, but at least they were listening.

I let it lie like that for a minute, then I asked, "Did you tell Detective Bliss that you killed her?"

"I don't know. I don't think so."

"You don't know?"

"Mr. Edwards, the whole thing seems like a dream, a very bad dream. When Detective Bliss was talking to me, I must have been in shock."

Tina ventured another objection. "Lack of foundation. He is not a medical witness. Shock is a medical diagnosis."

The judge liked her objection better than the jurors did. Many of them sat back and rolled their eyes.

"Sustained. The jury is to disregard the term 'shock.' "

Ted looked confused.

"Did I say something I wasn't supposed to?"

"That's all right, Ted. Don't worry about it. Just tell the jury what you remember about talking to Detective Bliss."

"Really, nothing. I'd called you. I remember that, and you told me to wait, but then M. Stanton came. We talked and I told him what I knew. Then he went over and talked to Detective Bliss. He said it was okay to talk to him. The detective asked questions on tape, and he was making notes. He let me use the bathroom, and when I came back he said the tape broke. He wanted me to write, but my hands were shaking so bad I couldn't hold the pen. So he wrote up a statement. M. Stanton looked at it and said okay, so I signed it."

"Did you read it before you signed it?"

"I think I must have, but you know, it was like signing one of those forms at the bank with lots of small print on it. You look at it and you don't see it. I thought I had to sign it, then they would let me go to be with Amanda."

I picked up the statement and showed it to him. "Is that your signature?"

"Yes, but..."

For the first time he had broken training. He wanted to jump ahead and explain. I interrupted quickly.

"Mr. Armbruster." If I used his last name rather than his first, he was going astray. "I just asked if that's your signature in the statement?"

"Uh, sorry, yes."

I walked over to stand next to him and pointed to a line in the statement. "Do you see where it quotes you as saying, 'I'm responsible for her death'?"

"I do."

"Did you say to Detective Bliss, 'I am responsible for her death'?"

"I think I did."

"You think?"

"Well, most of what happened after I found Amanda is not totally clear in my memory. I know I felt that way then, and I still believe I am responsible." This caused a stirring in the heretofore silent spectator seats.

"Why do you feel that way?"

Here, the tears again appeared, and he dabbed them away with the handkerchief, which he held crumpled in his right hand.

"Because, because if I hadn't lost my temper, if I hadn't argued with her in the lounge, if I hadn't left her there in the bar, and just waited a few minutes, we would've gone home together, then none of this would've happened. Or if it did I would have been there to protect her, or they would've killed me instead, which would be better. Anything but what did happen."

"Did you tell Bliss you grabbed the club and hit her with it?"

"I'm sure I didn't say that."

"How can you be sure?"

"Honestly, I can't say for sure exactly what I told Detective Bliss. So I take that back. I can say I did not hit her with the golf club. That is the truth. I remember almost nothing about my conversation with Detective Bliss. I remember sitting on the couch and all I could think about was Amanda, what happened to Amanda, all that blood."

"Where it says it all seemed like a dream, a nightmare, is that correct?"

"Nothing could be more correct. Since the moment I reached the top of the stairs, my whole life has been unreal, a nightmare. I keep waiting to wake up, but it just goes on and on. I have thought of suicide to escape, but I can't do that."

"Why not?"

"I am Catholic. I'm not sure my faith can sustain me now, but if I did kill myself, then everyone would be sure I killed her. Then they would stop looking for who really did it. I can't let that happen. I can't."

"Thank you, Ted. Your witness, Madam Prosecutor."

I sat down. The judge excused the jury for the morning break and I watched as they filed out. They seemed to be looking differently at Ted now. At least they were looking at him as they got up and left the courtroom. He'd been good. He'd given them something to think about. Now if he could just hold up on cross examination.

65

The hall in front of the elevators was crowded. Many of the spectators were claiming they had known all along that Ted was innocent. A few snarled, "It ain't over." The bearded brute who had tried to trip me at the start of the case glared, shaking his head. I started to wade through the crowd to ask Lizzie how she'd liked Ted, when I saw R.T. Halley's straw gardening hat waving over the throng. We elbowed our way to meet in the stairwell.

"Hey, Judge, you decided to come. How did Ted come across?"

"Liked him. But direct exam is batting practice stuff. Let's see how he hits the high hard one on cross. That's not the reason I came, though. Was watering the dendrobiums this morning when I remembered. Then I called Central High's long retired football coach."

"Remembered something about football?"

"About Bliss and Lawton X. Westphal."

"What have you got?"

"Westphal was like a surrogate father to Bliss. Bliss's mom ran off with a peddler when Bliss was maybe five or six. His dad was no great shakes, barroom brawler, odd jobs kind of guy. But he raised the boy until he had a stroke and died. Bliss was a starting tackle on the football team in his freshman year at Central High when it happened. Anyway, Bliss was starting to go down the tubes after his dad's death. Missing school, getting into trouble. They were ready to drop him from the team when Lawton Westphal stepped in. This I'm not sure of, but Lawton was head of the Central booster group for a while, and it was probably around that time. Anyway, he took the kid in all through high school, kept him on the team so that he got a football scholarship for college. How about that?"

"R.T., you're amazing!"

"You don't know how amazing," he bragged, pulling two documents out of a manila folder. "This first one is a birth certificate for Raymond Anthony Bliss, October 19, 1951. The second is a probate court certificate documenting Raymond Anthony changing his name to Raymond Westphal Bliss on October 23, 1972, right after he turned twenty-one. How good is that?"

"He changed it to honor his surrogate father," I said, "a father who told me he didn't recognize the name. Outside of you and my client, I can't think of anybody involved in this crazy case who has told me the truth. Now I understand Bliss wanting to take an interest in TNPC and Dressler. He didn't want anybody making trouble for a man he considered his father. Holy shit! Bliss could have killed her to keep her quiet. He had as much motive as anyone. But I don't know if I'm going to use this stuff."

R.T. looked stunned. "You've got to use it. It's dynamite."

"Well, Bliss already lost a lot of credibility with the scandal. Firenze looked like he's guilty of killing somebody, even if it wasn't Amanda, and Ted did great on direct. Some good people, including you and my client, don't want to jeopardize the Foundation. Let me see how Ted does on cross. If he sails through, maybe I won't need it. But thanks, Judge. You really came through. This is great stuff."

He said he'd hang around to watch Tina cross examine. I promised to meet him for lunch.

Ted didn't sail through. Tina knew she had to crack him to save her case. And as is so often the case, there is always something the client thinks the lawyer is better off not knowing.

Tina was wearing a light gray jacket with matching skirt. A heart-shaped diamond brooch graced the lapel of her jacket. Her tortoiseshell-rimmed glasses were perched on her nose as she strode purposefully to the lectern to begin cross.

"Mr. Armbruster, you've told the jury you loved your wife very much."

"Yes, ma'am, and it's true."

"You've also said she was a loving wife to you?"

"Very much so."

"You make your marriage sound like it would've lasted forever, but for Mrs. Armbruster's death."

"She was a wonderful woman, and maybe I'm old fashioned, but I'm Catholic and I took the vow 'till death do us part' seriously."

I felt a chill. Poor choice of words, Ted.

"You don't believe in divorce?"

"I'm not trying to be judgmental about others, but no, I personally don't believe in divorce."

So far so good. Then the axe fell. "Did your wife share your views?"

"I think so. She took the same vows."

"Had she told you that she was planning to divorce you?"

Ted reddened and answered quietly, "No." His eyes darted from Tina to me.

"Your answer is no?"

"It is."

"Do you recognize the name of an attorney from Midland, Diedra Avroms?"

Now Ted looked neither calm nor resolute. He looked like a deer in the headlights, scared, eyes shifting side to side, unable to move. He looked over to me as if I could answer the question for him.

"I have met her."

"In fact, you met her about ten days before your wife's death, did you not?"

Ted slouched in his chair, my posture instructions forgotten.

"I'm not sure of the exact number of days, but not long before Amanda died."

"What was the purpose of the meeting?"

"I asked Amanda if we could all meet."

"Why?"

"I didn't want to lose Amanda. I wanted to try counseling, therapy, anything to keep us together. I didn't want her to file divorce papers."

"Isn't it true that Ms. Avroms already had the divorce papers on her desk?"

"Yes, she did. But she didn't serve them. I was pretty upset. In fact, I broke down in her office. Amanda said to hold off. I begged Amanda to reconsider. She told Ms. Avroms to hold off on filing the papers."

"You realize, sir, that those papers included a petition to grant your wife separate occupancy of the home on Bonnie Brae?"

"No, I didn't."

"You realize, sir, that if granted, you'd be ordered out of your home?"

"I don't know about those things."

The sweat was beginning to bead on Ted's brow. My hopes were sinking fast. How could he keep this from me? Very clever of Tina not to call Deidra Avroms. I would recognize what her testimony would have to be. Much smarter to keep that arrow in the quiver and come at Ted on cross. If he admitted it, it was in front of the jury. Or, way better for her was to have Ted lie and deny the divorce and then destroy his credibility with the mention of the divorce lawyer's name, and stand there reading from the complaint Ted had just denied existed.

"You realize, sir, those divorce papers included a petition for you to pay separate maintenance for your wife?"

"What's that?"

"Alimony, temporary and permanent."

"Oh, that would've been hard. I was having a hard time making ends meet anyway. I think money troubles were causing friction between us. I told Amanda we'd have to resign the club for a while till we got things on the valve line going. I know she was upset."

"You knew, sir, that those papers on Ms. Avrom's desk called for Armbruster Manufacturing to be sold, and the proceeds divided between you and your wife?"

Ted looked aghast. "I don't know what the papers said. Amanda wouldn't have done that. She knew how much the family business meant to me. My father founded the business. The workers trusted me. That could never happen."

"How did the meeting at Lawyer Avrom's office end?'

"Okay, I guess. I made a fool of myself. I apologized for my… my... inadequacy."

"Your what?"

Ted looked completely abashed and ashamed. He squirmed. His color drained. "Ever since the prostate surgery, well you know, the complications. I couldn't get… I couldn't get… well, I couldn't meet her needs. She was younger, so naturally, well, she'd have needs. I thought she understood. I didn't realize how important it was. I promised her to go to the doctor and do whatever was necessary. I told her I'd borrow money from my mother so she didn't have to leave the country club. I told her I'd do whatever I could to keep her happy. I apologized for neglecting her. The pressures with the business... people relying on me. I promised her I'd be better, I told her how with everything else I needed her, really needed her to stand by me." He mopped his brow and eyed Tina, waiting for the next blow to fall.

She strode from behind the lectern to stand in front of the jury box. She had regained her confidence. She was once again the feral huntress, stalking her prey. "Did you threaten her?"

Ted sat back up to meet her advance. As we'd discussed, he looked back over to the jury to answer. But I could see, looking at the panel, that the faces that formerly had looked openly and sympathetically at Ted had shut down. They were staring intently, but now without warmth. I noticed Mr. Billings' head turn over his shoulder to look up at Mrs. Timmons in the second row. His face was cocked and eyebrows rose in a "What did I tell you?" look.

Ted scanned the faces and his head recoiled as if hit by a sudden blast of cold air. He gathered himself. "I did not."

"Mr. Armbruster, did you threaten your wife in the presence of Attorney Avroms, using the words, and I quote them..." Botham made a show of picking up a legal pad and reading from it. " 'You can't do this to me, Amanda. I can't handle it. You'd run out on me when I need you most? I've got nowhere to turn. You will force me to do something terrible. Something even God can't forgive. Don't leave me.'

"Did you make that threat in lawyer Avroms' office not more than two weeks before your wife's death? Did you, Mr. Armbruster?"

Ted just sat there stunned. Tears began to run down his face, and audible sobs could be heard. His shoulders shook. I was wishing I'd been a stockbroker instead of a lawyer. All the days and weeks of time and effort I'd put in to keep Ted's case afloat were exploding with one well-aimed torpedo. If he'd only told me, we could've dealt with all of this on direct. How clever Botham had been to keep Avroms off her witness list, to let me paint a picture of Ted's loving his wife to the point that he could never hurt her.

Then she waited in ambush for Ted to take the stand. If he admits the threat, he is damned. If he denies it, he's twice damned, once for threatening her, and doubly for denying it when Avroms appears as a rebuttal witness. What a chance Tina had taken if the defense hadn't called Ted! I had to admire her gambler instincts, which were paying off big. Why had I allowed Ted to take the stand? We'd punched enough holes in the prosecution's case to create reasonable doubt.

All of these thoughts rushed through my head in five seconds or less, while Ted sobbed, and before the trial lawyer in me kicked in hard. I needed to talk to my client before he answered the next question or two and confessed. I rose.

"Your Honor, my client is obviously very upset. I ask for a few minutes' recess for him to gather himself together."

The judge nodded as if she were going to grant my request, but then Miss Botham spoke up.

"Your Honor, this is a very important part of my examination. I have only a couple more questions on the meeting in lawyer Avroms' office. I think Mr. Armbruster's reaction indicates we are getting very close to the heart of the truth here. Please do not allow this process to be interrupted by a recess and a meeting with his attorney."

How savagely complimentary of Botham. She was sending a message to the jury that I'd use the recess to try and contrive answers for Ted. Nothing complimentary about that, but for her to think I'd come up with something in five minutes that had a chance to float, she obviously overestimated my talent. In any case, the judge made that moot.

"We will allow Miss Botham to continue this line of questioning prior to the recess."

She looked over at Ted, who was trying to collect himself. He used a wadded handkerchief to dab under his eyes and blow his nose. The judge spoke quietly to him.

"Mr. Armbruster, we are going to continue questioning. Do you need a few more moments, or can you go on now?"

I tried to send Ted a message by ESP. "Faint, Ted. Have a seizure, anything. Don't answer the next question."

But he ignored my telepathy. He looked sheepishly at the judge and spoke, his voice husky at first but gaining in timbre. "I apologize for the outburst, Judge. The whole thing, Amanda's death, being accused, waiting in jail, the trial, everything. I thought I could handle it, but I'm not handling it very well, am I? I think I can go on now. I want to testify. I want the truth to come out."

I took that last remark to mean the axe was about to fall, as did Miss Botham. On a signal from the judge, she moved in for the kill. She stepped close to the witness box, waving the legal pad which contained the divorce lawyer's office quote.

"All right, Mr. Armbruster, you say you want the truth to come out. Tell them, is this quite accurate? Did you make that threat?"

"Yes, Miss Botham, I did." Ted spoke very calmly.

"And you carried out that threat two weeks later at the foot of the stairs after you argued with your wife over being with another man."

Time stood still for a split second while I waited for Ted to confess to the jury what he had never told me.

"No, I did not." Quietly but firmly.

Tina pressed on. She, like me, thought that with just a little more pushing, Ted would collapse and confess. So, sensing the blood in the water, she made the mistake every lawyer is warned about. She asked a question when she didn't know the answer.

"Mr. Armbruster, you've now admitted you said the words, 'I will do something terrible, something even God can't forgive.' "

He nodded his head slowly.

"That's a yes?"

"Yes."

"What else could you possibly have meant other than a threat to do violence to your wife?"

Ted answered without hesitation. "I meant I was going to kill myself. I'd refilled my sleeping pill prescription after that meeting. Maybe two nights before Amanda died, I drank a bottle of wine, put on my robe and laid the pills on the bed table. I prayed for God to forgive me and I took a fistful up to my mouth, but I just couldn't do it. I knew from my faith and my prayers that God couldn't forgive that."

Ted paused. I could feel a ray of hope begin to break through the clouds of defeat. I glanced at Tina. The flush of the predator swooping for the kill was replaced with a look of hesitation. She'd had Ted squarely in her sights, if she had just not asked that last question.

Ted continued. "So after a time I put the pills back in the bottle. I got down on my knees and prayed for strength, and I went to bed. Sometimes now I wish I had taken those pills."

Tina took a desperate stab. "So you would've killed yourself instead of your wife?"

Ted looked at Tina like a patient teacher trying to explain a simple point to a slow learner.

"Yes, Miss Botham. The last thing I would have ever done was to hurt Amanda. I wish I had taken those pills because maybe with my funeral, all things would have been different and Amanda would not have been hurt. If I had taken them, I wouldn't have had to see my beautiful wife in such a horrible way, all the blood. I wouldn't see her like that every day, every night, and I wouldn't be sitting here telling the truth, which nobody will even believe. God forgive me, I wish I had taken them."

With the last at almost a whisper, Ted slumped in the chair, all the strength gone out of him.

Botham, realizing she needed to regroup, turned to the judge.

"Perhaps now would be the time for that recess, Judge. Mr. Armbruster looks like he could use a break."

While the judge nodded and started to speak, Ted interjected. "Thank you, Miss Botham, I surely could."

As the jurors rose to file out, Ted rose, but his near death experience on the stand combined with sudden rising left him weak. He almost toppled forward and grasped the rail for support. I was sure I saw compassion for Ted in a couple of faces as the jurors filed out of the jury box, a couple of them close enough to the witness stand that they could almost touch Ted.

What a roller coaster, up and down, almost for the count, and now, thanks to Tina pushing the envelope, at least still in the fight. During the recess I stayed away from recriminations. Ted needed a pat on the back more than I needed to kick him in the butt.

On our return to court Tina waded back in, looking for the knockout punch. Ted retreated and covered like a boxer who had scored early and was now hanging on for the bell. He parried her jabs on signing the confession well. He explained that he'd signed it, but in the state he was in had not really looked closely at it. M. Stanton had looked at it, so Ted had thought it must be accurate.

"All I could think about was Amanda, her lying on the floor like that. I kept expecting her to wake up. I had all these images racing through my head. Amanda as she sat at her dressing table mirror brushing her hair before she went out to dinner that night, smiling and laughing over her shoulder at me when I told her we were late. You couldn't hurry her. She looked so beautiful. Then what she looked like when I came down the stairs; all covered in blood. Oh, oh, I can still see her, glass from the broken mirror sparkling, me holding her. She was still warm to the touch. Oh my God."

Tears welled up and ran down his cheeks. His face contorted with the memory, and his hands clenched and unclenched spasmodically. Whatever had happened that night, there was no doubting that the memory of his wife lying on the floor was horribly painful to Ted.

So Tina switched tack again.

"You don't deny, sir, that shortly before your wife's death you greatly increased your insurance policy on your wife?"

"I do not deny it. I think Mr. Anschutz was quite truthful about how it happened."

"Yes, but Mr. Armbruster, if your company is bleeding cash, if you are having to tighten up expenses at home, why are you spending more money on insurance?"

Good question, and one I hadn't thought to prepare Ted for. I watched as Ted thought before answering.

"You are quite right, Miss Botham, it wasn't practical. The truth is, I increased the amount of insurance on my life as an option of last resort. I had considered that if all else failed on closing the valve deal, I could just pick a rainy day to lose control of my car, hit a tree or slide into a water-filled culvert. The company would collect on the policy, the deal would close, and the workers would keep their jobs, and Amanda would be provided for."

This caused a stir in the courtroom, and I could see Tina feeling a fresh breeze in her sails. "So, you are telling the jury you were prepared to defraud the insurance company of millions to keep your own family business afloat?"

"I cannot deny I thought about it. In fact, one afternoon on I-75, coming home from another failed attempt to raise money, the road had a sheet of snowy ice on it. I told myself this was the time to go into a skid and hit a bridge. But the traffic was heavy, and I didn't want to injure anyone else. Or, maybe, I just couldn't do it. I remember sitting in the garage after I got home thinking how desperate I had become."

"So you chickened out?"

Ted considered it for a moment. "I think it was more complicated than that, but that was probably part of it."

"What you've just admitted, sir, is you were desperate enough to take your own life to save the business and had acted in furtherance of that desperation by increasing the insurance policy when you couldn't really afford it."

"I was desperate enough to create that option as a final resort. I don't know that I was desperate enough to actually do it."

"Then tell the jury, if killing yourself was Plan B, if all else failed, what was Plan C?"

Ted looked confused. But I knew where she was going, and I imagined as the jurors leaned forward that they did too.

"Plan C?" Ted asked.

"Yes, Plan C, kill your wife, collect the insurance, save the business and avoid a divorce that would've left you penniless? Not to mention with Plan C you don't have to pick a bridge to crash into."

I'll give Ted credit, he looked stunned. "That idea never crossed my mind."

"Then why, sir, if you were strapped for cash and couldn't really afford to increase your policy on your own life, did you raise the policy limits and premiums on Amanda at the same time, if you were giving yourself last resort options?"

Good question. I, like the jury, waited for Ted's answer. We didn't wait long.

"I thought it would look better, increasing both policies, in case the insurance company had any questions about my death. And the premiums for her were so much less than mine over the couple of months it would take to find out if I could save the company without having to die to do it."

He hadn't hit that fastball out of the park, but he'd at least fouled it off. Some of the jurors sat back in their seats, looks of contemplation on their faces. At least he'd given them something to think about.

Tina picked up a separate legal pad and walked back to the podium in front of the bench. She took a little time to study what was on the pad, then she looked up at the witness.

"Let's review what we know, Mr. Armbruster. Okay?"

Ted looked weary and a little frightened. "Yes, ma'am."

"What I am asking you to do is give simple, direct, non-evasive yes or no answers to my questions. Can you do that?"

Ted nodded like a prisoner shown the steps to the guillotine and ordered to begin to climb. "Yes, ma'am."

"Armbruster Manufacturing was in serious trouble?"

"It was."

"This company was your life's work and your legacy from your father."

"That's true."

"It was your sole means of support?"

"Pretty much."

"For all of your life it provided wealth and income to support you with a luxurious country club home, a beautiful cottage, fancy cars, boats, travel, the perks of wealth, did it not?"

"It also provided jobs and food on the table for hundreds of employees, Miss Botham."

"Remember, Mr Armbruster, you are instructed to answer directly without arguing, yes or no."

"Sorry. Yes, the business provided well for my family."

"The truth is, sir, that in the last few years under your management, Armbruster Manufacturing was in a major decline."

"If you are blaming me for that, I blame myself too."

"By the time you recognized the changing economic atmosphere and moved to acquire the valve company, your company's finances and your personal finances had been severely compromised."

"They had."

"You were scrambling to raise the funds to keep the company afloat and close the valve deal."

"I was."

"And no matter how hard you swam, the tide was pulling you under. Your banker was threatening to foreclose. Your best efforts to interest investors were meeting with closed doors. True?"

You could see the remembered setbacks in Ted's face.

"All true."

"You were desperate, weren't you?"

He nodded. "I can't deny that. I was very concerned."

"How much money was it going to take to close the valve deal and keep your company going through transition into the valve business?"

Ted answered quietly. He was reaching the top of the steps and could see the guillotine blade glistening in the sun.

"About two million."

"Did you have the two million?"

"I was working on it."

"Did you have it?"

"No. Not committed."

"But you did have Plan B, a life insurance policy on yourself and your wife that you had just purchased as your company's circumstances became more desperate?"

Ted nodded resignedly.

"Answer for the record, please, sir."

"Oh—what? I mean, yes, I bought the insurance."

"The amount of the policy again, sir?"

"Two million."

"Two million you were prepared to kill to get?"

Ted looked shocked and stiffened.

"No, ma'am, I didn't kill my wife."

"So you say. But you also say you were planning to kill yourself if you had to to save the business."

"Oh—oh, well, that was my possible last resort."

"You did more than think, sir. You've told this jury here today you bought insurance that you couldn't afford as Plan B in case all else failed in your desperate attempt to keep the company afloat. Didn't you say that earlier?"

The atmosphere in the court was of tense expectancy. She'd walked Ted to the blade earlier. Would he kneel and bow his head this time?

"I guess I did."

"More than that, you were in furtherance of Plan B, actually considering how to make the crash look like an accident."

"I had those thoughts."

"Those are desperate thoughts, aren't they, Mr. Armbruster?"

Again you could see in his eyes and posture that he was reliving his feelings from back then. "Yes, at that time I felt very desperate."

"So desperate, Mr. Armbruster, you were prepared under Plan B to kill and lie about it afterwards?"

"How would I lie? I'd be dead."

"Oh, but in order to collect, you'd have to stage the death to look like an accident. So your last living act would be to perpetrate a lie on the insurance company."

"I guess looking at it that way, yes."

"But you chickened out. You looked death in the face while out driving, and you couldn't find the nerve to do it, could you?"

"I don't think I'd agree with that. I hadn't exhausted all hope of getting the financing. I wasn't at the end of my rope. I'm not sure that it was fear of death that stopped me as much as fear of damnation under my faith."

Tina paused to consider his answer, her head down. She apparently decided to pursue it. She looked up.

"Yes, as a Catholic you are taught all sins can be forgiven, even murder, if you repent. Am I right?"

"That is my faith."

"But under your faith, one sin cannot be forgiven because you cannot ask for forgiveness."

"I was taught that."

"Do you believe it?"

"I do."

"So Plan B would condemn you to hell?"

"It would, yes."

"But Plan C, for that you could be forgiven?"

I had wanted to object much earlier. Religion and faith are not proper subjects of cross examination, but Ted's testimony had made it relevant. But I too could see the executioner fitting Ted's head into the blocks, so I made the objection to bring him out of his tranced submission.

"I object, Your Honor. Clearly the subject of faith and religious belief is irrelevant and is being used by the prosecutor to incite prejudice."

Tina turned to the bench to answer, but the judge raised her hand to stop her. "That would be so, Mr. Edwards, if your client hadn't introduced the matter to explain his conduct. Overruled."

I sat back down and looked at Ted. The few seconds had given him a chance to regroup a little. His answer was as good as could be hoped.

"There was no Plan C, Miss Botham. Maybe God could forgive me if I killed Amanda, but I would never forgive myself. I loved her."

"You lied to this jury in denying there were divorce papers. You were prepared to lie to collect money from the insurance company by making suicide look like an accident. You finally admitted making a desperate scene in the divorce lawyer's office, begging your wife not to leave you. And then on the night of her death you saw her being friendly, familiar, cozy with Mr. Firenze?"

"I saw her with him."

Tina's index finger practically touched Ted as she pointed accusingly and fired at him in a righteous tone. "And all those angry, jealous feelings spilled over the top. You lost control. You yelled. You argued. You became physically aggressive with Mr. Firenze."

"I behaved very badly."

"You went home in a rage."

"I was angry. When I got home I was just embarrassed. Embarrassed and..." He paused. "Embarrassed and very sad."

"Sad because you knew it was over. You'd seen the divorce papers. Not only were you going to lose her, she was going to take what you had left, your home, your cottage, your marriage."

"No, she had agreed not to file the papers. I had hope."

"What did seeing her in that bar with Mr. Firenze do to that hope, Mr. Armbruster?"

He sat back, all the air leaving him. "It didn't help."

Tina turned so that she was looking at both the witness and the jury box. "So there you are, Mr. Armbruster, sitting at home in despair. Your wife has humiliated you in public and in the process shattered your hopes for your marriage. You've just embarrassed yourself and lost control of your anger to the point of physically attacking Mr. Firenze. Your attempts to save your business were failing. You were so desperate you had Plan B to kill yourself to defraud the insurance company by trying to make it look like you weren't responsible for your death. But you lacked the nerve for Plan B."

Ted started to answer, but Tina just went on. "Hours passed and Amanda hadn't come home. Your mind was filled with jealous thoughts of what she and that gentleman in the bar must be doing. You had those thoughts, didn't you?"

"I tried not to. But it was getting late. I was upset and had some of those kinds of thoughts." Ted was a treed cat, peering from a low branch at the angry hounds below.

"And that's when you went to Plan C. Kill the woman who was leaving you, kill the woman who was unfaithful to you, kill the woman who was going to take all you had left in a divorce, and in the process save yourself, then use the insurance money to save your business. Unlike Plan B, you wouldn't be damned to hell. That's what you were thinking, wasn't it, Mr. Armbruster, in those wee angry hours of the morning, waiting for your wife to come home?"

Surprisingly, Ted seemed to gather strength from having his soul laid bare for all to see. He sat up straighter, and as he answered, the resonance returned to his voice.

"I wanted this trial so the truth can come out. There is truth in much of what you say about my mental state. I had all those thoughts that night. Every one of them except actually deciding to kill my wife. What I did decide to do was to take the sleeping pills and get some rest. Something to stop my mind from racing, and this might sound stupid, but I really wanted to go on the weekend golf trip in the morning. It's something the guys and I have been doing for years. I really enjoy it and look forward to it all winter. I figured with the way things were going, this would be my last year. So I tried to put away the dark thoughts, took the pills and climbed into bed. I will not deny that I looked in the abyss. I thought of what you call Plan B, and God forgive me, I even considered what you call Plan C, but I pushed those evil thoughts back as far as I could and I went to bed. I just went to bed."

"And the man who was found with his wife's blood all over his pajamas, with an injured hand, with his bloody fingerprints on the murder weapon and who confessed to Detective Bliss, who was that, Mr. Armbruster?"

Again, a sigh of resignation. "That was me, Miss Botham." He paused and started to answer further, but she had what she wanted and stopped him.

"Thank you, Mr. Armbruster. That's all." She surveyed the jury to gauge their reaction, ran her hands down the seams of her skirt, and walked back to her seat.

I stood up, my mind a flood with ideas of how to rehabilitate Ted. Instead I just asked, "You were about to say, Ted?"

"But I didn't kill her. In spite of everything, in spite of how it looks, I didn't kill her. I loved her and I still do."

He delivered his answer in a firm, level voice, looking directly at the jury. They in turn studied him. Some looked puzzled. Some looked sad. Some looked doubtful. But none of them turned away. At least they were still listening.

His last answer encapsulated our defense: "I didn't do it." So instead of following up on all the notes I'd made during the painful cross examination, I just said, "Okay, Ted, thanks," and sat down.

The jury was gone. The bailiff had taken Ted. The courtroom had emptied save for Tina and me. She clasped her file to her chest as she passed me seated at the defense table. I tried not to look like I'd been hit by a board.

"Oh, Ken. That offer we made. It's off the table." I listened to her heels clicking on the marble floor and the rear door creak on opening. It felt like our chances had gone out the door with her.

66

R. T. waited for me by the elevator, shaking his head. "I assume the divorce papers were news to you?" I nodded glumly.

He brightened "Speaking of Plan B, I gather you'll be reaching for the dynamite."

"Would you describe Ted as 'having sailed through'?"

He chuckled. "Not exactly."

"Then there's not much choice, is there?"

I begged off lunch to drive over to Brent Eubanks' office. This wasn't the kind of news to deliver by phone. His secretary waved me right down the hall to his office, saying, "He said if you called to interrupt whatever he was doing."

Brent rose from his desk, eyes pleading for good news. When he saw my face, he sank back into his chair.

"But you told me on the phone last night you thought you were going to leave Dressler out. You said things were going well enough that you wouldn't need to use it." His normally emotionless voice was laden with despair.

"That's what I hoped then. I'd hoped Ted would do better on the stand."

"But Ken, after what Xavier told you the other night, what's the point? All the money was back in the Foundation account at least a week before Amanda was killed. You are going to ruin a lot of people, me included, just to create a distraction so you can win your case. Is that all you care about, winning regardless of the cost?" His voice was shaky, like he was on the edge of hyperventilating.

"Shit, Brent, I don't want to do this. The facts are, Amanda starts looking for missing Foundation money. She discovers where it went: TNPC. She ends up dead. And you think I should just look the other way? Maybe somebody was afraid Amanda wouldn't look the other way and killed her. Well, I'd rather look the other way, but then I would be right where you are: having done something unprofessional so that a lot of big shots avoid embarrassment, and looking over my shoulder to make sure nobody saw me do it."

Brent recoiled as if slapped. "You're going to ruin me. I could go to jail."

"I don't think so. You didn't steal from the poor box. You just looked the other way when they put the money back in. You'll come out of this fine."

This last was wishful thinking. His reputation would suffer a devastating hit. He'd allowed the money to be replaced in the Foundation's account and acquiesced in the phony explanation to protect the pillars of the community. He'd done what he'd done for understandable reasons, the foremost of which was to avoid Dressler's leaving town. But for an accountant to put his imprimatur on a set of phonied-up financial records, however good the reasons, was to make a bargain with the devil. It was like watching your partner in a two-man best-ball match fluff up his lie and then hit the hole-winning shot. Either you do what honor requires and have your partner acknowledge he was out of the hole, or you rationalize and tell yourself: "I don't want to embarrass him and I didn't do it and he probably would've hit it there anyhow."

That's where Brent was with TNPC. He'd caught them cheating. He'd watched as they improved their lie, and since the money had been replaced, he'd acquiesced in burying the rules violation.

Now this good, honest man who had nothing to do with the improper taking of the money, who worked diligently to get it replaced, was going to be disgraced along with the big shots. All because he'd seen them improve their lie and had looked the other way. And I was to be the instrument of his destruction.

"Does Ted know you are doing this?"

"We've discussed it."

"He approves?"

"I didn't say that. Anyway, your subpoena requires you at 1:30. I'll see you there. I'm sorry."

He didn't accept my apology, nor my hand stretched across the desk. Nor did he look at me as I walked out. Can't say that I blamed him. Sometimes lawyering really sucks.

By the time I got back to court, the bailiff was rounding everybody up to begin the afternoon session. I begged him to give me five minutes with my client to deal with a "sudden emergency." He brought Ted into the conference room, where the broken furniture from my scuffle with Stanton lay in the corner. I told Ted that in light of his failing to tell me about Ms. Avroms and the divorce papers, his Plan B of suicide, and last-minute contemplation of Plan C, I had to go with the Dressler-TNPC connection. He forbid it. I told him the damage his little secrets had caused made it non-negotiable. He raised his voice. I raised mine.

The bailiff knocked to announce, "Judge says right now!"

Ted told me he'd fire me on the spot if I did it. I answered on my way out the door, "At least there won't be any more keeping secrets from your lawyer."

Ted stood rigidly next to me as the jury filed in. My hands shook from the adrenaline of our angry disagreement and the anxiety of knowing that I was about to be fired. The mental picture of me standing blindfolded before a whitewashed stucco wall, cigarette drooping from my mouth, flashed before me. When the judge instructed everyone to be seated, I glanced over at Ted. He wouldn't meet my eye.

Judge Alex brushed the bangs off her forehead and addressed me. "Your next witness, Mr Edwards."

I stood, took a deep breath, and said the words I expected to be my last as Ted's counsel. "The defense calls Mr. Brent Eubanks."

While the bailiff retrieved Brent from the hall, I didn't breathe. I heard Ted stirring as if to rise. Then nothing. I didn't look at Ted, but rather stepped back to hold the swinging gate open for Brent to walk through.

He looked awful. It looked as if he'd shrunk to under five feet in height as he shuffled past me. The immaculate man who kept his wing tips polished to a high gloss and his suits wrinkle-free looked unkempt. There were dark shadows visible under his glasses.

Brent was a zombie on the witness stand. He spoke in a quiet monotone, and the judge had to prompt him repeatedly to speak up. His testimony was all the more effective for being at a whisper. The courtroom, although nearly packed, was as quiet as a tomb. The jurors and spectators craned forward to catch every word. While Brent spoke, Ted remained silent behind me. I made sure not to ever look back. Either he'd fainted or he'd changed his mind about firing me for a second time. My execution had been stayed.

"Mr. Eubanks, please explain for the jury what the Dressler Foundation is."

Tina objected. "Irrelevant." Her calm confidence pre-lunch was disturbed. She'd surprised me with something out of left field with Deidra Avroms and the divorce stuff. She rightly suspected I was about to return the favor.

I replied, "Bear with me, Judge, for a few moments. I'll stake my honor as an attorney that this line of questioning will prove relevant."

"Very well, it had better be. Overruled."

I nodded to Brent and he answered, "Leland H. Dressler, as many people know, was a very successful lumberman and investor who left a sizeable endowment to a foundation in his name after his death. The foundation was to support civic and charitable needs in Lake County. Over the years the money has been used to build the civic center, the community pool, a library, a woman's shelter and to fund scholarships, a literacy program, the food closet, just to name a few."

"How are you associated with the Dressler Foundation?"

"I'm a director and the fund's auditor."

"Was the deceased, Amanda Armbruster, affiliated?'

"Yes. At the time of her death she'd been on the board of directors for three years."

"Shortly before her death, was she chosen to serve on a committee with you?"

"Yes, she was."

"What was the purpose of the committee?"

I didn't think it was possible, but Brent turned more ashen. His answer was barely audible. "To investigate a half-million-dollar loss in the Foundation's portfolio."

Miss Bentley in the back corner of the jury box raised her hand. "Judge, I can hardly hear him. Did he say a million dollars is missing?"

Art Honnecker reached for his notebook and started scribbling. A buzz of whispering and conversation broke out in the gallery. The judge whacked her gavel hard enough to lift Brent Eubanks out of his chair and to make me jump.

"Order! If you cannot hold your tongue, leave the courtroom. Madam Reporter, please read back the witness' last answer." As she did so, Art left his laptop to hold his place and moved for the back door, pulling a cell phone from his pocket.

"Now, Mr. Eubanks, please explain why that sum of money would not be an expected loss for the Foundation."

"The investment by law limits the type of investments the Foundation can make to essentially triple-A rated bonds and government securities, as well as a limited percent of very blue chip mutual funds. The experts who developed the investment formula expected an actuarial return of 5.3%. There were no events in the high grade bond market or stock market to explain the loss."

"Did you chair the three-person committee charged with investigating the lost half million?"

"I did."

"What was Mrs. Armbruster's assignment?"

"She was reviewing all the brokerage and bank statements."

"At some point did she report to you her findings?"

"I object, this is hearsay." Tina was incurring most unpleasant looks from the jury. Now that the lid was off the cookie jar, they wanted a look inside.

"Mr. Edwards?"

"Your Honor, this is offered not to prove the truth of the matter asserted, but rather the state of mind of the declarant, what Mrs. Armbruster believed and what she intended to do about it."

By this time Honnecker was back in his seat. He squeezed over to let an out-of-breath *Leader* sketch artist sit next to him.

"I'll allow it, but this better be going somewhere, Mr. Edwards, and I mean somewhere that has to do with the guilt or innocence of the accused."

"It will, Your Honor, believe me, it will." I turned back to Eubanks. "What did she report?"

"At our second committee meeting she advised that a confirmation slip from S.G. Hayden Securities for two-year treasury bills in the amount of $8,500,000 could not be reconciled with the actual brokerage statement. There was only eight million in the Treasury obligations. To my embarrassment I recognized that this was so. She further said she believed the money had been bundled with money from an entity known as TNPC Investments and placed in an offshore hedge fund."

"What is an offshore hedge fund?"

"An investment company located outside the United States specializing in leveraged investments."

"Are these types of investments risky?"

"They can be."

"Are these types of investments permitted under the terms of the Foundation's investment guidelines?"

"They are not."

"Are you on the Foundation's investment committee?"

"I am."

"Did you approve of this risky investment?"

"I did not know of it at the time it was made. The formal vote of the committee was to buy Treasury bills."

"Do you know what TNPC Investment Company is?"

Brent looked like a man seeing the noose ready for fitting. "I do."

"Tell the court what TNPC stands for."

"Thursday Night Poker Club."

The jurors and the spectators gasped as one. Their jaws dropped.

"What is the Thursday Night Poker Club?"

"It's a group of gentlemen who play cards at the country club the last Thursday of the month. I believe it has been around for some thirty-plus years."

"Are you a member?"

This elicited the first smile Brent had probably experienced in weeks. He shook his head. "Not in my pay or social bracket. Besides, I'm a lousy poker player."

"Surely the money did not go into some giant mega-pot in a high stakes country club poker game. What does TNPC Investments have to do with some big-shot poker players?"

"Object to the reference to 'big-shot.' " Tina didn't rise from the edge of her chair, where she perched like a watchdog about to break a "Stay!" command.

"I'll withdraw the term 'big-shot.' "

"My investigation revealed that the poker club had an investment club into which sizeable contributions were made. That investment club needed an extra $500,000 to match the $4,500,000 the members had raised to fund TNPC Voyager, a private placement hedge fund run out of the Cayman Islands."

"Who is the manager of the Cayman Islands hedge fund?"

Now Brent looked like a deer caught in the headlights.

"Do I have to answer, Judge?" She nodded.

"Xavier Westphal." Almost a whisper.

"Tell the jury about Mr. Westphal."

He spoke as if in a trance. "I think some of them might recognize the name. He was a very successful businessman, politician and benefactor in the county until some years ago, when he moved to the Cayman Islands."

"What connection did he have to the poker club?"

"He was one of its founding members, or so I understand."

The courtroom became a beehive of excited whispers, including jurors animatedly talking to each other. Tina could see her murder case becoming a small scene in a much bigger play about local icons caught with their hands in the poor box. She had to do something.

"Judge, I'm asking you to sanction Mr. Edwards. He has opened a Pandora's box of scandal in the hopes of distracting the jury from the guilt of his client. What's the relevance of all this to the charge against Mr. Armbruster?" Her normally immaculately moussed hair stood in clumps at the sides as she agitatedly ran her hands over her ears.

The judge brought herself back from her musing on the implications of Brent's testimony.

"Counselor, I hope you have something to tie into Amanda Armbruster's death, and I mean something solid, not just speculation, or this court will strike all of the witness's testimony and deal with you in the harshest manner."

I tried not let my shaking hands show as I reached into my briefcase and pulled out a plastic bag with the butterfly sticky note in it that had nearly gotten Max and me killed.

"Yes, Judge, I intend to do just that. Would the clerk please mark this as Exhibit 63?"

I turned and approached Brent. His recoil from the exhibit gave me hope I would get away with this.

"Looking at Exhibit 63, sir, do you recognize this piece of paper inside it?"

I stopped breathing and so did he. He would sink me if he denied it. But his eyes told me he had seen it before.

"I do."

I took a breath. "What is it?"

"It's a note Amanda made at our second meeting of the audit committee."

"Is it her handwriting?"

"I believe so."

"Tell us about it."

"Actually, what happened is that she told me she suspected that instead of the money going into Treasury bonds, they had gone into a foreign currency investment called Chilean Assured Treasury Securities through TNPC. I told her the investment acronym was CATS. She had a *Wall Street Journal* article about the hedge fund going under and another about its guarantor, a company called Dumbarton Oaks Guarantee, collapsing in connection with it. She wanted me to explain. I did the best I could, but I didn't really understand it then. I was confusing her and myself. Then she laughed and said, 'Those Cats sure went to the Dogs.' Then she wrote that note that you have in your hand, that butterfly sticky note, and stuck it back in her file."

"Before I ask to admit the exhibit, let me ask you one more thing. When did this discussion at the investigative committee meeting occur?"

"About two or three weeks before Amanda was killed."

As the exhibit was being marked, I looked for the first time at Ted. He was motioning to me. I turned away, pretending I didn't see him.

"Your Honor, I move the admission of Exhibit 63."

"Miss Botham."

"May I voir dire, Your Honor?"

"You may."

"Mr. Eubanks, whom did you tell about this note before Mrs. Armbruster's death?"

"Tell? I didn't tell anyone."

Tina looked elated. "Just as I thought, Your Honor. A red herring, unless Mr. Edwards is accusing Mr. Eubanks of killing the victim. What possible relevance can this have except to throw the jury off the facts of this case?"

"Mr. Edwards, is it your theory that this witness killed Amanda Armbruster? If not, I'll be denying its admission and we'll be having a rather lengthy session out of the presence of the jury. I hope you have brought your toothbrush." Alex's furrowed brow and narrow-eyed stare were part of what I called her "enough of this nonsense" look. I fancied she practiced it before a mirror whenever I was scheduled to appear before her.

"I don't have my toothbrush, and I don't claim Mr. Eubanks is a murderer. But perhaps another question or two would establish that others knew of the note." My failing voice required I approach the bench.

"Proceed, but this better be good."

"Mr. Eubanks, who besides yourself was at the meeting with Mrs. Armbruster when she wrote the note?"

"The other committee member was Mr. Frederick Hildebrandt."

"Is he a country club member?"

"Yes, but not a member of TNPC, to my knowledge."

"In any event, after the meeting and before Mrs. Armbruster died, did you learn that others knew of the note?"

Again Brent had me by the short hairs. If he lied, I'd be a guest at the county jail for the rest of the trial at least, but Brent was too honest to lie. "Yes," he answered, and I had just drawn two cards to fill an inside straight.

"Who?"

"I heard from Mr. Westphal maybe three or four days after the meeting. I also heard from certain current TNPC members. They told me to keep a lid on this. They were making arrangements to pass the money back into the account, including the interest earned. They asked me to keep Mrs. Armbruster from causing a public scandal while they got the repayment money back in place."

"If you didn't tell them, who did?"

"I don't know."

"Did you mention the problems with Dressler to any of your partners in your firm?"

He looked down and then back up again. He nodded. "I went to them for guidance."

"Do you or any of your partners do accounting work for Mr. Westphal or any other TNPC Investment Club member?"

He looked uncertain and turned to the judge.

"Judge, I don't want to do anything improper. I know accountants are supposed to keep client matters confidential. May I call our firm's attorney before I answer?"

The judge cautioned him and then said, "Mr. Eubanks, you strike me as a man in a difficult situation trying to do as the law requires. We will take a fifteen-minute recess during which you may contact counsel. Bailiff, take the jurors out."

67

By the time the recess had ended, there was uproar in the lobby outside the courtroom. Three TV stations and four radio outlets were on the scene. The sheriff's deputies had to escort Brent through the mob screaming questions and videotaping him. As they pushed a passage for him, poor Brent looked for all the world like the defendant surrounded by deputies shielding him from a mob. I held a courtroom door open for them when they reached it. As he passed me, he gave me a look that told me I'd be needing a new accountant.

While we awaited the judge's entrance, the buzz and excitement rivaled a commodity trading pit. I could barely hear Ted as he spoke directly in my ear.

"Will he name names?"

"I don't know, Ted, he is not speaking to me at the moment," I answered back, well above a stage whisper so as to be heard over the babble.

Brent sat in a chair just inside the bar railing, looking depleted. His left hand kept stroking the balding spot on the top of his head as if searching for hairs to straighten. He had a twitch or tic at the left corner of his mouth. Whatever his attorney had told him must have been a source of little comfort.

Tina marched in, using the files held to her chest as a battering ram to push through the spectators chatting in the aisles. She dropped the files on her desk and bent over to talk animatedly to Brent before leading him off to the attorney conference room.

When the bailiff entered five minutes later from chambers, he strode angrily to the doors at the back of the courtroom to speak to the deputies manning the entrance. He turned to the audience and said, "Anybody not seated in one minute must leave the courtroom."

There was a mad scurry both on the main floor and balcony as people scooted over to make room and people argued about whose spot a given location belonged to.

"I've been here since eight a.m."

"Yeah, but you weren't here when the doors opened after recess."

The game of musical chairs ended exactly sixty seconds later with a number of unlucky dawdlers being escorted out of the courtroom.

The bailiff knocked softly on the door to the chambers, and Judge Alex entered with her reading glasses perched on her nose, a frown on her brow and her law clerk carrying three or four appellate court volumes to leave open on the bench.

"Where is Miss Botham? Where is the witness? I was told we were ready to proceed."

I stood to answer. "Miss Botham took the witness to the conference room a while ago, Your Honor."

She nodded sharply in that direction, and the bailiff scurried through the door. Brent walked back in with a little more bounce in his step, followed by Tina Botham, who smiled smugly while the court reporter adjusted her paper.

"Sorry, Your Honor. Before the jury comes back, I have a motion to make."

"Make it then."

Tina moved to exclude any further evidence of TNPC and the Foundation on the grounds that it was irrelevant to the guilt or innocence of Mr. Armbruster. She further argued that any relevance was greatly outweighed by the prejudicial nature of the testimony in the prosecution's case. She took short steps in front of the bench, a righteous fervor tinged with desperation in her voice.

"My worst fears have been realized. Defense counsel has turned this trial into a circus. My conversations with Mr. Eubanks reveal that Mr. Edwards had been informed that all the money plus interest had been returned to the fund before Amanda Armbruster was killed. Any potential motive the missing money might have provided had vanished. This is nothing more than mudslinging on a grand scale to damage the reputations of prominent citizens in the hope that creating a scandal will distract the jury. I ask that the earlier testimony of Mr. Eubanks be stricken from the record, the witness excused and the jury instructed to disregard."

The judge instructed Brent to return to the stand. "I take it, Mr. Eubanks, that your counsel advised you what my research shows: there is no accountant/client privilege in a court of law."

"Yes, ma'am, but they did advise that this could be very harmful to the clients and the firm. What Miss Botham says is true, all the money had been replaced plus interest four days before Amanda died."

She turned to me. "Where does that leave you, Mr. Edwards? How does Mrs. Armbruster's knowledge of missing Foundation money provide a motive to some poker-playing mystery man, if the loss had been made good?"

I stood, knowing that my argument here would contain the most important words I'd had to say to Judge Alex since I'd walked dejectedly from her apartment years ago, appeal denied.

"Your Honor, Miss Botham has just made my argument for me. It's not that the money found its way back to the poor box that's important. It's that people with great stature and therefore a lot to lose had snuck into church and stolen from it in the first place. Is it a defense to larceny to say I put the silverware back when I saw the police in the front yard, a defense to embezzlement to say it was just a short-term loan? Mrs. Armbruster, had she lived, could've gone to the police and the papers, and in so doing brought the mighty to their knees. It is our theory that she was killed not so the cheats could keep their money, but rather so they could keep something much more valuable: their reputations, their standing, and perhaps even their freedom. Even these days, helping yourself to a half million dollars of charity money is serious business. I know someone such as yourself, a zealous guardian of the public trust, would not look kindly on those who would breach that trust on such a grand scale, no matter how long the miscreant's pedigree, how strong his influence, or expensive his suit."

She waved away my last comment with a dismissive gesture I remembered from my attempts as her suitor years ago to woo her with Irish blarney.

"Mr. Edwards, if you are trying to bolster my backbone to confront the influential, that's hardly necessary. Give me a reason to allow these very distracting matters further before the jury, a reason which has to do with the guilt or innocence of the accused. An accused, I might add, who had his wife's blood on his pajamas, the murder weapon in his hands, and who made confession a short time thereafter."

"Judge, the prosecutor in her opening statement leaned heavily on the theme 'Love or Money.' She repeated it with mantra-like regularity. Motive. Ted killed Amanda because he was jealous, because she was leaving him, because she was rubbing his nose in her approaching freedom with Mr. Firenze. She argued he killed her for the insurance money. She will argue in her closing it was love and money, kill two birds with one stone. Kill her and prevent her divorcing him and cleaning him out, kill her and collect the money needed to save the business. Her motive argument distilled to its essence is, he killed her to avoid losing that which was most precious to him.

"We have perhaps created room for reasonable doubt on the love angle by showing that Mr. Firenze was aroused and angry when his advances were denied. Now, on the money angle we can show there were others who stood to gain if their financial shenanigans never came to light. The captains of our local society were at risk to lose that which was most dear to them, their good names. The jury instructions make clear that, while not an element of the crime, motive is central to deliberations. Surely the court can see how this testimony can be a basis for reasonable doubt, an issue central to deliberations, an issue over which the prosecutor was pounding the table in opening statement. Miss Botham asks the jury to convict, saying only Ted had motive for murder. This evidence shows there were others with equally compelling motives. The evidence meets the prosecutor's evidence and is a basis for reasonable doubt."

Judge Alex looked conflicted. She removed her glasses and rested her forehead in her hands in thought. After a minute Miss Botham spoke up.

"May I respond, Your Honor?"

The judge looked up and nodded.

"Even if all Mr. Edwards says is true, the court must weigh the probative value versus the prejudicial. Smearing the names of prominent citizens all over the courtroom may make great headlines. It will also distract the jury from the evidence of Mr..Armbruster's guilt. Beyond mere speculation, what other evidence does the defense have that anyone in that investment group had the means or opportunity to kill Mrs. Armbruster? What evidence does he have that any of them were at the scene?"

I broke in. "I can prove that at least one of them was at the scene, Your Honor."

There was a gasp. Botham was stunned. The judge, looking intensely interested, asked, "Who might that be, counselor?"

"My predecessor counsel, Mr. M. Stanton Browne. He is a member of TNPC. He is Ted's neighbor. He allowed, in fact encouraged, my client to talk to Detective Bliss against all good judgment."

A mad scramble broke out in the gallery as the reporters broke from their seats, clutching for cell phones on their way to the exit. The gallery was in an uproar of conversation. The judge banged her gavel so hard the stricken block jumped in the air.

"We will have quiet or we will have an empty courtroom, am I clear?"

All went quiet save an elderly gentleman whispering excitedly to the lady next to him. Judge pointed to the man and a deputy removed him.

"Are you claiming, sir, that Mr. Browne killed Amanda Armbruster?"

I held my hands out in supplication. "Judge, I don't know who killed the woman. My client has testified he did not, and I believe him. If I knew who killed her, I would have offered that proof long ago. I'm only saying that Mr. Browne had motive and opportunity. Some other evidence I intend to offer shows he had the means to do it."

"What evidence might that be?"

"I'd rather not say at the moment, Your Honor. Mr. Browne will testify tomorrow, and if I disclose my strategy—how should I say this?—it could affect the impact of the evidence."

"Counselor, I'm losing patience. I'm trying to rule on Miss Botham's motion, which I feel has considerable merit, and you are playing cute with me. If you have nothing further to add, I am prepared to rule."

I held my hand up in a stop signal. "May I have a moment, Your Honor?" Alex nodded. I could see the gauge on her patience tank nearing empty. My mind was racing. If I told her about the golf clubs, perhaps Browne would get to the country club and grab them before Josh could bring them to court. He'd have time to concoct some answer or explanation. I'd purposely never said a word to him about the clubs in the hope that he'd lie on the witness stand and I could catch him at it. I'd been keeping my other arrow in the quiver, and I planned to notch it just as soon as Brent resumed testimony. I wanted both as a surprise, but once the judge has ruled against you, it's almost impossible to get her to un-rule, so I couldn't take that chance.

"Let me express it this way, Judge. Mr. Eubanks has testified that Xavier Westphal was an original founding father of the Thursday Night Poker Club. He has also testified that Mr. Westphal was the principal of the hedge fund in which the Foundation's money was improperly, perhaps illegally invested and lost. I believe he will now testify that the single most important witness in the prosecution's case, Detective Ray Bliss, had a very close relationship to Xavier Westphal, a father-son type relationship. He very definitely would not want to see a father figure he revered tainted by scandal or worse, under criminal investigation."

WJNT reporter Jennifer Caldwell's bottom had just hit the pew when I uttered this. She started to rise, then thought better of it and began madly scribbling in a notebook, waiting for what could possibly come next.

Tina put her hand on counsel table to support herself. Today had contained too may surprises, not all of them good. She rallied to respond.

"What? Now he is saying if it wasn't his fellow member of the bar,

Mr. Browne, who killed her, it was the investigating detective? This is ridiculous. If this keeps up, pretty soon he'll accuse me or the little old gentleman who just got escorted from the courtroom. After all, he seemed to overreact a few minutes ago. Judge, you must stop Mr. Edwards before he accuses again. Where is the evidence that Detective Bliss killed Mrs. Armbruster?" Tina's pert nose remained in its challenging uptilt, but the rest of her body seemed to ebb with the tide of her falling fortunes.

I modulated my failing voice to a calm, reasoned tone. "Judge, I said truthfully that I do not know who killed Mrs. Armbruster, and I am not intending to offer any testimony to prove that Detective Bliss killed her. I am offering it to show he had motive to fabricate the confession in order to bring the matter to a rapid conclusion without any investigation into other suspects and without allowing his father figure to be exposed to scandal and/or prosecution. Should the court have any hesitation on the issue, I mark as Exhibits 64 and 65 some things that came to my attention only as recently as this morning."

I showed the judge the birth certificate and name change document. Her eyebrows lifted in surprise as she grasped their meaning. I rooted around on my desk and found the affidavit from the cottage search I had tried to get admitted while Bliss was on the stand.

"There can be no doubt of Bliss's close ties to Westphal. Evidence that attacks the credibility or motives of the person attesting to the confession must come before the jury. Add that history to this affidavit to search Armbruster's cottage, where he swears to missing 'financial documents providing a motive for murder,' and there can be little doubt he was attempting to cover any tracks leading back to Dressler and Westphal."

Miss Botham sank back in her chair. The judge looked exasperated, the way she used to look when I told her no more than I thought she ought to know when discussing one of our cases over breakfast. Back when she was still in the prosecutor's office and in my bed.

"Why didn't you say so to start? Why all this time and argument?"

"Forgive me, Judge, but if I had not been forced to reveal it now, I'd have just let it come in through the witness. I've found telegraphing your punches to be a very poor trial strategy."

She waved her hand in familiar dismissal of me. "Miss Botham, your objection is overruled. Bailiff, please bring in the jury."

So when the jury came back, Brent named names. Each name brought an audible gasp from the jurors as well as the audience. By the time he'd listed the TNPC investors who had taken a loss in the hedge fund investment, three doctors, a banker, a stockbroker, two car dealers, a lawyer, and a plant manager had been assured of front page mention.

When Brent testified that Westphal had rescued the teenaged Ray Bliss from a group home and supported him until adulthood, the courtroom was completely silent. The jurors stared in wonder at the name change document. "Thanks, R.T.," I offered silently. They pointed out to each other the "financial documents as a motive for murder" in the affidavit. If cross exam had tarnished Ted, these revelations, coupled with the drunk driver extortion racket, destroyed Bliss as a credible witness.

I could see a number of jurors looking at both Ted and myself in a new light. Tina did the best she could, while I sat next to a client who pretended I wasn't there. Brent made clear that the money had all been replaced with interest by the investors before Amanda's death. He said Amanda had told him of her suspicions but had no plans as far as he knew to go public. In fact, the last time he had talked to her, all she had were suspicions. He had told Mr. Westphal when he called that the money must be paid in full or he would blow the whistle. Tina made her point.

"You threatened to blow the whistle, and you are still alive, are you not, Mr. Eubanks?"

He sighed, as if considering the circumstances, the matter might be debatable. "I am."

On redirect I asked very few questions. "But you did agree if the money was returned to the Foundation to keep quiet, didn't you?"

Tears formed and ran down his face. He could no longer speak, so he just nodded.

"Record please show the witness nodded yes."

"It may."

"Amanda made no such promise, did she?"

After a pause in which the silence hung heavily, I went on, "Record please show the witness shook his head no."

"It may."

Brent stumbled out of the courtroom like a man on a heavy sedative. The stampede by the reporters for the door nearly trampled poor Lizzie, who wasn't quick enough to get out of the way.

I should've felt exalted, but I too felt drained. I shuddered as the vestiges of fear that Ted would fire me for this gambit drained away. I felt callous. To save my client I'd thrown a lot of good people to the wolves. I felt guilty imagining the phone ringing in the bank, doctors' offices and car dealerships with the reporters wanting to talk to the boss. I had *Oliver Twist* images of poor street urchins abandoned by the foundation that had given them succor. I felt a shiver of fear when I thought of Xavier Westphal in the north woods of Canada, or the jungles of the Yucatan, or wherever he had his bolt hole, plotting his revenge on the lawyer who talked too much. I should have felt triumphant. Instead, I just felt sad; sad, frightened, and a little unclean.

The five-minute meeting with my client in the lock-up before the deputies came to transport Ted was restrained. Ted appeared despondent. "So many lives ruined," he said, face in hand, shoulders heaving.

"The only life I have to focus on, Ted, is yours," I answered solemnly. Then I tried to kid. "Hey, I thought you were going to can me."

He put his hands on his knees and looked up earnestly to me. "I did all I could to stop you. If I'd fired you, I would've not only been without a lawyer, I would've lost the only friend I've got left in the world. I couldn't face the loneliness." We embraced, his tears leaving a mark on my shoulder.

Billy was sitting on his porch listening to the Tigers when Max and I arrived home at 7:30. He peeled himself from the rocking chair and trotted over. The empty chair continued back and forth, echoing the scene in the Armbruster living room back in April. Tomorrow the man from that empty rocking chair would be the next victim of my defense. I was feeling serious combat fatigue. The blood lust of battle was fading, to be replaced by guilt over the carnage I was causing.

Billy's denim coveralls covered a light blue t-shirt he'd worn so often I knew it said "Physically Phfft!" even though the bibs covered the logo. He was rubbing grease from his hands from the spark plugs he'd been cleaning.

"You're a star, man! Every channel has the story. I just switched off talk radio for the ball game. The scandal is all anybody's talking about. How come you don't look happier? Everybody's saying the jury has to let Armbruster go."

"I'm tired, Billy. I like Brent Eubanks and I just fed him to the sharks. More of the same tomorrow. I've got to do it, but I don't have to like it."

"C'mon, man. You're not working for the Chamber of Commerce. Your client has got to be thrilled."

"Not really. These are his buddies going down in flames. He didn't really want me to do it. It's almost like he'd rather have taken the fall than cause the scandal. Considering how few of them were willing to stand up for him, I don't understand it. In an age where everybody is looking for somebody else to blame, Ted's an old school stand-up guy who doesn't rat on his friends. So, no, he's not thrilled."

Billy stood around while I fed Max, trying to cheer me up. As evidenced by his late season support for the stumbling Tigers, Billy was a champion of lost causes. Making me feel chipper about the devastation I was causing was equally a lost cause. I changed the subject to ask about his new relationship with Louise.

"Think she's a keeper, man. Now, if I can just get her into the boat."

When the Tigers loaded the bases with nobody out in the third, he wandered back to his rocker and left me alone with my thoughts. Max was barking at a water skier when Karen called, making it hard to hear her at first. She too had caught the scandal buzz.

"All the troops down here at the post say you are a magician. Always got something hidden in the old top hat. Thought I'd let you know the betting in our little pool has gone from ten to one for conviction at the start of the case to even money now. Guess who's got twenty bucks at ten to one? Bet you're feeling great."

"You bet on me?"

"Of course. Nobody else would. So tell me about it."

I gave her a recap and then shared my misgivings. She let me talk with only the occasional question and then concluded our conversation by saying, "You're a good man, Charlie Brown."

Next morning a crowd was waiting for M. Stanton Browne as he approached the courtroom steps. His standard patrician smile was gone, replaced with a tight-lipped scowl. The radio and TV microphones were thrust into his face. He uttered terse "no comments" to one and all. The crowd outside the elevator pointed at him and added questions of their own.

"Did you kill her?"

"You think because you're a big shot lawyer it's okay to treat Dressler money like your own bank?"

One wag offered advice. "If I were you, I'd take both the fifths, on Amanda and then one of scotch."

As we waited for court to start in the judge's ante-chamber, Stanton pretended I didn't exist. He looked out the window. He sat in the legal secretary's chair and straightened the pens and paper clips on her desk. He crossed and uncrossed his legs and gave his manicure a careful review. He paced over to the mirror and straightened what little hair remained at the temples. I had resumed flipping through my legal pad after he ignored my "Morning, M. Stanton." The points I'd earned telling him the night before last that his wife would be excused from testifying had been erased.

Only when the law clerk came from chambers to announce court was resuming did he speak. He waited until I held the courtroom access door open for him to hiss in passing, "You'll regret this."

The crowd filled the galleries upstairs and down. As M. Stanton strode briskly to stand before the bench, he pretended not to hear the murmur of contempt from the spectators. His brown-with-maroon-pinstripe Saville Row suit hung impeccably on him as he raised his right hand to be sworn. His "I do so swear" was articulated with determination. It was obvious he saw a way out of the morass that required his unruffled confidence. That being a lifetime trait, he had a full reservoir. It was my job to blow the dam.

"Are you on the board of directors of the Dressler Foundation?"

"I am proud to say I am. Further, I have served as Foundation counsel for many years."

"For which you have billed the Foundation considerable sums?"

"My good man, I'll have you know that I've donated hundreds of hours of time in charitable work for the Foundation. May I ask how much have you volunteered?" His tone remained assured and level.

"Don't you also have hundreds of hours of time as the Foundation's local attorney, which you've been billing at $200 an hour for years?"

"That's a considerable discount from my standard hourly fee."

A look at the faces of the jury revealed they were unimpressed with his generosity and stunned by what he charged for his time.

"Are you a member of the country club?"

"Yes."

"Are you familiar with a group out there called TNPC?"

"It is a group of gentlemen who enjoy a hand of cards once a month. Before you ask, I'll tell you that I am honored to be a member."

"Testimony yesterday has shown that you and your card playing buddies used Dressler monies in contravention of the Foundation's by-laws. As the Foundation's two-hundred-dollar-an-hour attorney, can you confirm this to be so?"

"I don't believe you have sufficient background and experience to understand the Foundation's investment guidelines, so I'll simply say a reasonable construction of the guidelines allowed the investment as it was guaranteed by the other investors. The guidelines require low-risk investments. Since the other investors went surety for the Foundation's money, it was a no-risk investment." His demeanor was assured, the master of the house addressing staff. I could now see how the TNPC members intended to escape prosecution.

Browne continued, "We didn't embezzle the money; we didn't take unauthorized access to the money. In the charitable spirit, we stood ready to guarantee the investment so the Foundation could win big if things worked out, but not lose in the event of trouble."

"Aha, and you have a written commitment evidencing this guarantee?"

"Such a thing would hardly be necessary considering the caliber of the individuals involved."

I started nodding knowingly, as did a couple of heads on the jury box. Browne stopped that by raising a chiding index finger.

"But, as a lawyer for the Foundation, I insisted that such a document be prepared and signed. It's in the Foundation file, which you'd have discovered if you'd taken the time to thoroughly investigate before making baseless accusations and damaging the reputations of many of this community's finest citizens."

I could feel the tide shifting yet again.

"When was the document signed?"

He opened the briefcase, extracted four pages stapled to blue backing cardboard, and flipped to the back page. "January 19th, 1999, about six weeks before the moneys were invested."

I took the documents. "I see it was prepared by your firm."

"Of course, I'm the Foundation's lawyer."

"Apparently you were also the client on the other end of the deal, as you signed as a guarantor."

That slowed him a little. "In this case, I was."

"Isn't it a bit of a conflict of interest, representing both sides of a transaction?"

"It appears so to you, sir. But since all of us only wanted maximum returns with no risk for the Foundation, the deal was written on the strictest terms possible to benefit the Foundation. Perhaps someone such as yourself wouldn't understand, so let me explain it to you." Amazing aplomb from a man whose name had been all over the media the last sixteen hours tied to words like "embezzler," "crooked attorney," and "possibly involved in murder to silence witness."

"Please do."

"The members of the club's investment group are very prudent, very successful investors. We have known and trusted Mr. Westphal for many years. His prior programs have all made very nice returns. All of us in TNPC have devoted time to Foundation fundraising efforts so that more money is available for community work, but the Foundation is an ongoing endowment. We don't invest the principal for community projects. We use the investment return from the principal to do the Foundation's good works. Are you sophisticated enough to understand that?"

Condescension came naturally to Browne. If it weren't for the pedantic tone with which he was lecturing, the audience would've been completely with him. As it was, the jurors were sitting back more relaxed and giving him their full, but reserved attention.

"Aha, you take good care of the chicken and just eat the eggs, eh?" I asked.

"Nicely put, counselor. In this case the hedge fund investment looked like it could generate a lot more eggs to feed the needy, and our personal guarantee made sure no harm could come to the chicken."

Wow, if this kept up, M. Stanton and his poker playing buddies would be up for a commendation instead of an embezzlement indictment. I had to dim the lights of the halo he was creating.

I leaned against the rail in front of the jury box, feigning a relaxation I didn't feel. From there my vision took in both Browne and his former neighbor, my client, Ted. Ted was looking the worse for wear. The new haircut with which we had started the trial was shaggy. The gray hair at the sides had a tinge of yellow. His once full face was thin. The summer-weight, light blue suit looked big on him and in need of a dry cleaner. This once vigorous, handsome man looked old, tired, and worn. The sudden realization of the toll on Ted reminded me of the contrast in Jimmy Carter at Inauguration and Jimmy Carter at the end of his term. Stress etches with a large stylus.

I took a breath to clear my head and went on. "So, if I understand you, the use of Foundation's money was motivated by the poker club's altruistic urge to help the poor, and not by the need to find one more half-million-dollar investor?"

He paused, checking his manicure. "For the most part that is true. I'd not be being one hundred percent honest if I didn't acknowledge that we had nine half-million-dollar investors and needed a tenth. But you see, counselor, we were putting our money where our mouths were. Eight other club members and I also invested $500,000. Unlike with the Foundation's money, nobody guaranteed our loss. When TNPC's investment model broke down, we not only took a devastating loss, we had to dig down and make good the Foundation's money plus interest. As men of honor, we did."

"The nine signatures were all the same day?"

'Yes, yes, check your calendar. It's a Thursday. We dealt with the business after our normal session."

"When was the document filed with the Foundation?"

He placed his left hand and forefinger under his nose and squeezed his upper lip. "Good question, counselor. Through an oversight of mine, it remained in my office file. I think I missed the next Foundation trustee's meeting after January, as I was out of the country."

"Oh, where?"

He smiled sheepishly for the jury. "Grand Cayman. A little escape from the rigors of winter."

"I see. But isn't Grand Cayman the former investment home of the TNPC hedge fund and its founder, Mr. Westphal?"

"I believe it was at the time."

"Is it no longer?"

"I couldn't say. The loss was quite devastating to Mr. Westphal and his firm. I believe he's closed shop and moved on."

"Is 'closed shop and moved on' your lawyer-like way of saying he's in hiding from federal regulators?" I said, straightening and facing him directly.

"I heard some bureaucrats were hoping to speak with him." He glanced at his Rolex as if other pressing matters required his attention.

I shoveled the gravel from my throat and stepped away from the rail to ask, "So during your little escape from winter, which caused you to forget to file this guarantee of your charitable steadfastness with the charity you were doing unselfish good work for, did you see Mr. Westphal?'

"I believe I did. I always do when I'm there. Wonderful chap, very sharp mind."

"Were you the bagman for the five million on that trip?"

He bristled. "If you mean by that, did I bring him a cashier's check to fund the investment, I did."

"When did you correct your oversight and place the guarantee document in the Foundation investment file?"

He shifted a bit, pulled the cuff of his trousers over his sock and smiled a little nervously. "Now, there's the rub. I'm afraid I'd forgotten all about it on my return, so it just sat in my file cabinet for over a year. My term as a Foundation trustee had ended, so I didn't know about the audit and the attempt to trace the money until well after the fact. It was an oversight on my part and of my secretary, for which I've chastised her, but there it is."

"Just when did the document reach the Foundation file in relation to Mrs. Armbruster's death?"

"Before."

"How much before?"

"At least seven to ten days."

"How did it get there?"

"Strangely, through the efforts of Mrs. Armbruster. She mentioned she was on the audit committee and about the loss. I told her what had happened. I suspect that's where your 'Cats went to the Dogs' note came from. That's how I explained it to her. Well, I was shocked to find out that the file made no difference to the investment or our guarantee. I told her we were in the process of collecting from the other investors and told her I'd deliver the documentation attesting to the return of Foundation funds to Mr. Eubanks, which I did."

"How long before her death did you have this conversation with Amanda.?"

"Not long, a couple of weeks."

"What was her reaction to these events?" My questions were now at a staccato pace. With each he started to flinch like a boxer ducking a jab.

"She was upset at first, rightly so. That document should've been in the investment file from the start." He looked assuredly at the jury. Their return gaze and posture indicated they were reserving judgement.

"Did she say what she planned to do?"

"Objection, hearsay." Tina, who had been pretty happy with Stanton's damage control so far, popped from her chair.

"Statement of declarant's future intention, state of mind exception," I replied.

"Overruled."

"At first she was angry," Browne went on. "She planned to make a public report at the next board meeting. I explained it would be embarrassing to a lot of her friends and acquaintances, not the least of which was me. I told her the Foundation was to be made whole, plus interest, and the damage that going public would bring. She agreed to think about it."

"Where was this conversation held?"

"In the Armbruster living room."

"Did you talk to her again?"

"Yes, two or three times, including after all the money had been gathered and replaced. These conversations were by phone."

"How would you characterize these conversations?"

He thought for a moment.

"I'd say they were full and frank discussions."

I coughed. "When I hear that kind of language out of the State Department, it means we didn't agree on a single thing but war has not been declared yet."

He considered.

"It's fair to say we weren't in full agreement, but I think putting the money back in the account really calmed the waters."

"Does that mean that at no time did Amanda Armbruster even agree to keep the Foundation scandal secret?"

Browne bristled, turning somewhat red. He turned to the judge. "Your Honor, I object to that characterization. I've tried to explain that mistakes were made but they've been remedied. No trust monies were lost."

The judge peered over her glasses. "Mr Browne, you are here as a witness, not as an attorney."

Tina bounced up. "I object to Mr. Edwards' question as argumentative." Tina had now formally allied herself with Browne in front of the jury. When it comes to making strange bedfellows, politics has nothing on trial lawyering. I wondered what it might cost Tina in credibility when it came time to argue the case to the jury.

"Sustained, please rephrase, counsel."

"Yes, Your Honor." I bowed slightly to the judge and rephrased, "Witness, at any time prior to her death, did Amanda ever say to you that she would keep quiet about what she knew?"

"Well, I can say I believe she was leaning..."

I held my hand up… stop. "Please, just answer yes or no."

He curled his upper lip as if he'd been approached by a beggar. "No—I can't recall, not exactly."

"As to the timing of the money getting back in the account, the money arrived back in the account after the deceased had discovered its diversion, or let me rephrase that, its improperly documented placement in TNPC," I said, disdain in my voice.

"That's so. Yet I can assure you that it was in the works well before that."

"Let's see, the money vaporizes with TNPC almost six months before it gets paid back, true?"

I took a step closer to Browne. He leaned back. "True."

"But the money doesn't find its way back into the account until Amanda has discovered 'Cats going to the Dogs.' "

Now I'm closer and he's run out of leaning room. There was a first sweat on his forehead. "As I said, it was in the process."

"Are you prepared to concede at least that her discovery speeded up the process?"

He cleared his throat. "Perhaps."

"Were there many discussions with the poker club investors encouraging them to get their money in so Amanda wouldn't blow the whistle?"

Now I was close enough to smell the fear. He loosened his tie and the beads of perspiration gathered on the slick dome of his head. "I guess it might have motivated them to understand that further delay could not be tolerated."

"That argument proved persuasive?" Saying this, I stepped back a little and glanced at the jury, who were mesmerized by the cat and mouse game.

"It did." With me slightly further away, Browne's grip on the arms of the witness chair loosened. He was very confident in the boundaries of his personal space. Threaten those boundaries and he begins to lose his cool, I noted to myself before stepping in again with the next question.

"But even when you reported to her that the money had been replaced, you've told us she had not committed to letting the whole thing get swept under the rug?"

"Listen, Edwards, I mean counselor—" He took a second to gather himself "—we weren't trying to sweep anything under the rug. Everybody did the honorable thing. I don't mean it was easy. Each one of us had taken a half million dollar bath, and now we had to find another fifty-five thousand each to make the Foundation whole for interest it didn't earn. For many of us, myself included, it was quite a hardship. What good would come out of a circus like you've created here? I'll tell you. None. You've embarrassed a lot of fine people, smeared their reputations built over a lifetime, and maybe caused this town's number one benefactor to pull out. I hope you are proud of yourself." He shook his jaw and glared at me. I felt the hatred wash over me like steam in a sauna.

"No, sir. I'm depressed by the whole thing. How do you feel about taking charitable money for an unauthorized purpose and losing the so-called guarantee in your file drawer until Amanda Armbruster caught all you big shots with your hands in the cash register?" Now I was right next to him on the witness stand, the expensive sandalwood cologne struggling to keep the sour anxiety at bay. His calm resolve was gone. He trembled with anger.

"What do you mean, so-called guarantee?" His face was florid, his fists clenched. "I hope you are well insured for slander."

"Perhaps you missed the day in law school when they taught that what is said in a court of law is exempt from libel and slander suits. So are you done with empty threats?"

Tina rose simultaneously with the judge, who was also turning red-faced and banging her gavel.

"Witness, counsel, I am warning you that if there is any more of this infantile sniping, I'll cite you both for contempt and you will pay dearly. Last warning, knock it off."

"Yes, Your Honor, sorry, Your Honor." I tried to keep my own antipathy for Browne in check. Browne just tightened his lips and nodded.

"Move on, counsel," the judge directed.

I asked her, "May I conclude this area by asking if the other investors were upset that replacement hadn't yielded a promise of silence from the deceased?"

Tina rose again, the color in her face matching the red silk blouse that topped her gray skirt. The judge held out her hand to stay her and spoke to me. "You may not, move on."

So I moved on. "Mr. Browne, were you at the Armbruster house the night of the murder?"

He was still so angry he answered without thinking. "No."

"Gee, I could've sworn I saw…"

He caught himself. "Oh, I thought you meant before or at the time of death. Yes, I came over after the police."

"Why?"

"The Armbrusters are longtime friends. Ted was a client. I saw all the police cars out front. I went over and introduced myself as Ted's attorney and gained admittance."

I wanted to get into how he'd inserted himself in the case, but I didn't want to open the door to any conversation he and Ted had had, thereby waiving attorney-client privilege. So I just walked over and picked up Ted's confession from the exhibit table and showed it to him.

"Were you present when Ted spoke to Detective Bliss?"

"Yes."

"You've seen Exhibit Number 6 before?"

He glanced at it.

"I have, numerous times."

"Is there anything inaccurate in that confession?"

He relaxed, apparently knowing how he wanted to handle it.

"You know, I don't know how to answer that. I initialed it that night. I looked at it before I signed it, right after the interview by Detective Bliss."

The rat was jumping ship. He told me I'd be sorry. He was seeing to it.

"Witness, didn't you state in open court before Judge Benson at the preliminary hearing, when you were still Ted's lawyer, that the confession was inaccurate in one major particular…"

"Yes, but—"

"What was that particular?"

"Well, I told Judge Benson, let me see that statement here, where it says 'I grabbed the golf club. I hit her with it.' I said I had heard Ted to say 'I never hit her with it.' "

"Did you tell Judge Benson it was an oversight on your part to initial that confession with that kind of error in it?"

"Well, you see, Detective Bliss's handwriting is a little messy. I'm saying I don't know, as I testify under oath, exactly what Ted said to Bliss. As you've told me at every opportunity, it was a mistake to let Ted talk to the investigation officer. But I had good reason, I thought, to do so."

Then I put my foot in it.

"What reason could that be?"

"He told me in private conversation, before I would even permit the detective to talk to him, that he had not killed her."

Botham stood, a look of triumph lighting her face. "Judge, please note counsel has opened the door to defendant's communication to Mr. Browne."

"So noted."

My question was like making a bad lead at bridge, giving the opponents a slough and a rough. You know it's a mistake as soon as your play hits the table. In this case my mouth had engaged a split second before my brain. I tried not to let my chagrin show, but the little exchange of eye contact between Browne and Botham told me he was going to do it anyway. I still felt like a schmuck for making it so easy. No choice but to press on.

"So to you, his longtime friend and counselor, he said he had not hit her?"

"He did."

"I assume, based on what you told Judge Benson, he said the same to Detective Bliss?"

Tina objected. "Hearsay. What Mr. Browne, then acting as Mr. Armbruster's attorney, may or may not have said to Judge Benson is hearsay. He was not a witness. He was not under oath. It cannot be used substantively by the jury to prove what the defendant said to the detective."

The judge nodded. "I must agree, Mr. Edwards. Find out what he says now."

I nodded. "Did Ted tell the detective he did not hit his wife?"

Browne shrugged his pinstriped shoulders. The sweat was gone. Now was his chance to inflict pain on me. "I don't honestly know. I signed the confession that it was accurate. Why would I do that if it weren't? Then I stated in open court that he said he didn't. Was I remembering our private conversation? Was I just embarrassed that I'd let him talk and hang himself, trying to undo my miserable mistake? I don't know. I've gone over the statement in my mind hundreds of times. I just don't honestly know. I was upset. Amanda was a dear friend. I'd seen her lying there; not a pretty sight at all. It was the middle of the night. Ted was a basket case, I was a basket case. I know I didn't protest too much when the detective said he had to take him in. Was that because I was in shock that my client, after telling me he was innocent, had just confessed his guilt? Did I think he was being arrested because of all the other evidence—the blood on him, the golf club, him the only one there? I don't know. I can say for certain he told me he did not hurt her. To testify under oath whether the statement that Bliss wrote is accurate or inaccurate, I cannot."

The weasel. He'd played all sides now, including the middle, yes, no and maybe. I went back to his statement at the preliminary exam.

"As an officer of the court, you told Judge Benson the statement did not match your memory of what Ted told Bliss?"

Tina was up in a heartbeat. "Judge, you ruled, he's ignoring that, it's hearsay."

"So I did, Mr. Edwards. You want a different flavor from the contempt shop?"

"Certainly not, Judge. It is prior recollection recorded as exception to the hearsay rule. He is testifying now, months later, that he can't remember what he heard. So I am confronting him now with what he said he heard much closer in time to the event. It was made under circumstances that one would hope would cause him to speak truthfully, an officer of the court addressing the court. It was recorded. I have the certified court reporter's record. I should be allowed to proceed."

The judge looked a little non-plussed beneath her robes, reminding me of legal debates in dressing gowns over scrambled eggs years ago on the rare occasion I'd score a small legal point. Alex was first and foremost a student of the law. She flipped open the rules of evidence to MRE 805 and studied it. She shrugged her shoulders. "Proceed. Objection overruled."

I read his statement to Judge Benson. "Did you say that to Judge Benson?"

He shrugged. "I did, but as I sit here now I cannot honestly say which is accurate, Bliss's statement or mine to Judge Benson."

69

The jury had listened to enough of Browne's "on the one hand this and on the other hand that" to know he was the type of fancy pants lawyer they neither liked nor could afford. The best I could do was to have before the jury that at one time, before a court of law, this arrogant man had said my client didn't confess. Time to move on.

"Mr. Browne, in addition to playing poker for money at the country club, you play golf there, too?"

"Mr. Edwards, you of all people should know I do. Haven't forgotten your recent setback, have you?" His demeanor brightened at the memory.

"No, sir. I want to be a sport and give the devil his due. Would you tell the jury to what you refer?"

He smiled and relaxed, his pinstriped suit slackening at the shoulders. Not only had he bent every ear in the locker room, his office, and his social milieu to the point of breaking with his victory, but now he had a whole courtroom full of a new audience. He smiled with relish at the prospect and turned to share his victory with the jurors.

"Well, since you asked. Our club's biggest tournament was last week. The Member-Member. My partner, Dr Richmond, and I teed off with Mr. Edwards and Judge Schneider for the championship match in our flight. I must say our opponents played surprisingly well. Even looked for a while like they might win. But on number 18, I struck a perfect wedge to within a couple feet of the pin, made the putt, and we beat them. Isn't that so, counselor?"

"Yes, it certainly is. And you'll recall I didn't get the opportunity to fully congratulate you then. So as a man of honor, let me congratulate you now." All very gentlemanly. Even Ted stopped fiddling with his soup-stained tie to look up inquisitively about where I was going.

Browne tried to look like what he isn't, a good sport. "Thank you. Well-played. Tooth and nail. Good match."

"And who was your caddy?"

"Young Joshua Reynolds. Fine lad. I'm sponsoring him for the Evans Scholarship, you know. What a golfer that boy is! Hits the ball a country mile."

Tina rose. "Judge, I've been patient, but this jury has more important things to do than listen to a golf recap."

Before the judge could ask me what I was doing, I answered, "Quite right. Just a little scene setting. I'll get to the point, Judge."

I walked to the evidence table and picked up the super wedge. I approached the witness stand, and all the bonhomie disappeared from Browne. He recoiled like he was afraid some blood could seep through the plastic bag onto his Saville Row suit.

"Mr. Browne. Do you know what this is?"

"Of course I do. It's Ted's sand wedge. The murder weapon."

"What brand is it?"

"It's called a Solarz Super Wedge, or Sunny."

"Do you have one like it?"

The rustle in the jury box and courtroom was audible. Browne looked uncertain. He paused. "Gosh, I don't know."

"How can you not know if you have such a club?"

"Well, I mean, I had one. Ted and I each bought one at the Golf King store in Flint. Great little club. Ball flies high and stops on a dime. But then there was this controversy with the PGA standards committee. Something about the grooves. They were rated non-compliant toward the end of last season. So I couldn't use it anymore. I put it someplace. Or did I give it away? Gosh, I can't remember where it is."

"Uh-huh. Golf's very strict about its rules, isn't it, Mr. Browne?"

"Oh, yes. Very honorable game. I'm very strict about the rules myself, even keep a copy in my bag."

"So when the club was banned, you never used yours again?"

"I don't know if I'd say never. I really liked that club. So if I was just out with my wife or hitting a few balls, I might have used it. I'm sure I did, but that was a while back."

"Anyway, since it was illegal, you wouldn't have used it during this golf season in a tournament or match?"

He narrowed his eyes. He knew I knew he had cheated to win the tournament. But having just graciously accepted congratulations and vaunted himself as a stickler for the rules, he wasn't going to say so. "Of course not."

"And you are saying you have lost track of the club over the last few months?"

"Been a while since I've seen it."

I had Joshua and his mother stashed in the attorney conference room and had prearranged with the bailiff to fetch them on my signal. I pointed to Larry now, and he slipped out the back of the courtroom. "Mr. Browne, you and my client are neighbors, are you not?"

"Yes, I live on Bonnie Brae just one door down from Ted. Mrs. Chambers' house is between ours. Ted's been my neighbor for more than ten years. He's been my friend. I've been his attorney."

"The 15th fairway runs behind your house, Mrs. Chambers', and Ted's, does it not?"

"Yes, it does."

"In addition to being a friend, neighbor, and counselor to Ted, are you his golf buddy?"

"Used to be."

"Uh-huh. On the night Ted's wife was killed, you and Ted were preparing for some golf weekend up north, were you not?"

"Ha—yes we were. It's kind of a tradition. About twelve or sixteen members go up to Boyne for a spring golf weekend. Have for many years. 'Course, we couldn't go this year, what with Amanda and everything."

Just as he finished, I heard the back door of the courtroom swing open. I also saw Browne's jaw drop and his face turn red. Stanton blurted, "Joshua, what are you doing here? Why have you taken my clubs? Young man, if this is your idea of a joke, you won't be laughing at Evans Scholarship time… what's the meaning of this?"

The jury was gaping as Josh walked up to the gate granting admittance to the bar, the bag slung over his shoulder.

"Thank you, Joshua," I said. "Please leave the bag with me." I hefted it over the bar, tassels swaying on the hated maize-and-blue Wolverine head covers, and let it come to rest on the bag's legs. "Mr. Browne, this is your golf bag?"

He was boiling mad. "I'll have you arrested! That's my private possession. What is it doing here?"

"It came, sir, as the result of a subpoena I issued for Josh Reynolds to appear in court and produce your golf bag. So before you start threatening the lad's college prospects, was he supposed to ignore a subpoena?"

"So I have you to blame?"

"You most certainly do. Now, can you identify the bag as yours?"

"It's mine," he spat out.

"And the caddy, for the record, was the one you were bragging about when we were discussing the recent tournament?"

"He's my regular caddy."

"Is it part of the caddy's job to hand the golfer the club you ask for?"

"Of course."

"And after you have made your swing, what do you do with the club?"

"We train the caddies to take it back from us, clean the face, and put it back in the bag."

"So your regular caddy would need to be familiar with your clubs so as to hand you the proper club when you ask for it?"

"Yes."

"Mr. Browne, would you please walk over here to the bag and pull out your sand wedge?"

"I don't see the point, Mr. Edwards. We are in a courtroom, not on the golf course." He didn't budge. It was obvious after seeing Josh and his golf bag that he realized what club must be in the bag.

"Okay. Let me caddy for you." I reached in the bag and pulled out the wedge. "Your honor, I ask that this Solarz Super Wedge be marked as exhibit number 65."

The judge nodded. The reporter marked it. I approached the witness stand and Browne shrank back as if he were Dracula and I was Van Helsing with cross in hand.

"Recognize this, Mr. Browne?"

"It's a golf club."

"Yours?"

"I don't know. A lot of those wedges were around before they banned them. I have no idea what it's doing in my bag."

"If you look on the shaft, you can see the little country club sticker with your name on it."

"Okay. I see that. I still don't know what it's doing in my bag. I told you I wasn't using it."

"Weren't you using it to make that wonderful match-winning shot you just bragged to the jury about?"

If he were any redder he'd blow a gasket. "Are you calling me a cheater?"

Ted was nodding in the affirmative, perhaps more shocked at the golf rules breach than he was at looting the Foundation. A couple of the male jurors had that "If the shoe fits—" expression on their faces. I held the club up to the witness and continued, "I'll let the jury decide that. Would you look at the face of the club and tell the jury how the v-shaped nick got on it?"

"A rock in the rough about a year ago."

I picked up Ted's wedge in the plastic bag and held it in my right hand while holding M. Stanton's in my left. "Mr. Browne. Look at the face of your club and that of Mr. Armbruster's. Which is more worn?"

He made a show of looking carefully. "Oh, perhaps mine is. Ted quit playing his when the rules required. I told you I would still use mine occasionally."

"Was one of those occasions the night Amanda died?"

Browne was now drumming his well-tended nails on the arms of the chair at a furious pace, losing the grip on his composure. The sound of his nervous nails was all that was heard for fifteen seconds, until he exploded, "What are you saying? You've called me a crook on the Foundation money. You've called me an idiot for my handling of Ted's case. You've accused me of cheating on the golf course. Now are you accusing me of murder?" He turned to the bench. "Judge, what kind of courtroom is this? I came here with serious professional reservations about client confidences. I came here in the trial of a longtime client and friend. And now I am accused of killing a woman I respected and cherished as a friend. Do I have to put up with this? I object."

The judge looked sternly over her glasses at Browne. "Counselor, perhaps your practice doesn't give you much courtroom exposure. So, I'll remind you that if there is an objection it must come from the prosecutor, not from the witness. I've heard none from Miss Botham. Miss Botham, do you have an objection?'

I looked over at the prosecutor's table. In all the excitement I'd forgotten about her. Tina looked like she wanted to be somewhere else. The arrival of the nicked wedge was the last straw. She looked like the only girl without a partner at a sixth grade dance. She didn't even rise. "No objections, Your Honor."

The judge turned to Browne. "Witness. You will answer the question."

"Aren't I entitled to take the 5th Amendment?"

"If you feel your answer may incriminate you."

Stanton looked about like a rat trapped in a corner by multiple cats. Nowhere to run. He screwed his face up in concentration. The beads of sweat returned to his bald pate. Finally he came to a decision. "I didn't kill her."

"Your golf bag was in the foyer at the Armbrusters' house on the night Amanda died, wasn't it, Mr. Browne?" I asked. He again was conflicted, searching for the best escape.

Finally he chose his poison. "For a time, yes."

"Meaning, the bag was there next to Mr. Armbruster's in the foyer before Amanda died?"

He sighed. "Yes. I got back from Chicago late. My bag was in the back of my Navigator. I was just going to leave it there, but I was having a sandwich in the kitchen when Ted pulled in after midnight. So I carried it over. He didn't answer when I knocked. So I just let myself in. He called to me from upstairs. I just left my bag with the others in the hall. He was already in his pajamas when he came downstairs, so I headed for the front door. He followed me onto the front porch, very upset over an argument he'd had with Amanda at Heather Hollows. I tried to calm him and told him to take a sleeping pill. Then I went home to bed."

"And your Solarz wedge was in the bag?"

"All the guys agreed they'd be legal for our weekend outing. Most of the guys had really seen their short game improve before they were banned. My wedge had been in the garage, and since my bag was in its travel case, I just carried the wedge over and leaned it against the bag. Ted's was resting on the wall next to his bag."

"Where was your golf bag when the police came?"

"Back in the Navigator."

"Tell the jury how that came about."

Browne's posture had changed. His shoulders were slumped. His rigid, nose-in-the-air neck was bowed. He had the look of a condemned prisoner being marched to final punishment. "I moved them."

An audible gasp from the jury and spectators seemed to suck the air out of the courtroom. "Tell the court what happened."

"Ted called, all frantic. Amanda was hurt. I must come right away. I rushed over. There was Amanda, all blood. Ted was pacing about. He too was covered in blood. I asked him what happened." He paused to consider his words. "He was babbling 'Amanda, Amanda. Oh, my God, Amanda!' He begged me to help him, but I felt her carotid artery. She was warm, but she was gone."

I glanced over my shoulder at Ted. His hand tightly covered his mouth, stifling the sobs. The cuff of his white shirt was frayed as he used it to sop the tears. Browne's eyes followed mine. But there was no compassion in them. He looked away and resumed his testimony.

"When I touched her neck, I could see she was lying on top of my club. Without thinking I pulled it out from under her, and I left fingerprints in some of the blood on the shaft. I panicked. I unzipped the bag cover, grabbed my golf towel, and wiped the club and my hands. Then I thought, oh my God. I'm altering evidence. I threw the club in my bag and zipped it up. I asked Ted if he'd called the police. He said right after he called me. I had to get my clubs out of there before the police came. So I grabbed my bag and went out the back door. Before I left I made a big mistake."

"What was that, Mr. Browne?"

"I told Ted to call you."

"That was a mistake, huh?"

"Yes. As I was carrying my bag along number 15 fairway to my house, I realized you'd be a loose cannon. You'd root around and stop at nothing to get him off. You might dig up something on Dressler, and then you'd do just what you've done. Throw a lot of good people to the wolves. Stop at nothing to win. So I washed up and went back to Ted's."

"Were the police there?"

"Yes. Ted was sitting on the bottom steps, moaning and crying. I'd told him to say nothing until you got there. But you were none too quick in arriving. Bliss was getting impatient, threatening to arrest Ted. Ted was beside himself with grief." The pain of the memory was evident in Ted's heaving shoulders and the muffled noises coming from under his hand.

"Did Bliss let you talk to Ted?"

"Only after I told him that you'd be a bull in a china shop and could cause Xavier Westphal real embarrassment."

"Why would you tell Bliss that?"

"I've known Mr. Westphal many years. I know how much Mr. Westphal meant to the detective as a boy. He was like a father to him."

"So Bliss agreed to let you talk to Ted."

"Yes. We were in the living room. I got Ted calmed down some. He told me he didn't know what happened. I convinced him it would be best if I were his lawyer."

"And you told him to keep quiet about your late-night stint as a caddy."

"What…? Oh, no. When I got there he was so shook up I'm not sure he noticed me put the club in the bag. I just told him not to mention I'd been there earlier."

I saw Ted, lost as to what to do with the tears and mucous covering his hand, and I walked over to the stenographer's table and pulled some Kleenex to carry over to him. His eyes were thankful as he took them from me.

I walked back to confront Browne, who now shied on my every approach. "So, let's review. You took a bloody weapon from the scene." With what voice I had left, I summoned my old prosecutor-closing-in-for-the-kill tone.

Browne wasn't used to being spoken to in that way. His answer was huffy. "I wouldn't say that. I took my clubs from the house."

I stepped a little closer and fired, "One of those clubs had blood on it?"

"Some."

"It also had your fingerprints in blood, according to you, from when you put it in your bag?"

Now he had his hands up as if to keep me from coming any nearer. "I suppose."

"And you snuck out the back way on the golf course?"

"I wouldn't call it sneaking."

"Your neighbor says she saw a prowler on the course a half hour earlier. Was that you?"

He tensed. "I'm no prowler."

"You withheld evidence from the police. In fact, you removed bloody evidence from the scene." This with my index finger almost touching his nose.

Tina rose from her seat, her voice now pro forma instead of zealous. "He's badgering the witness."

Alex, who had let herself get lost in the palpable antagonism between Browne and me, stirred herself from being a spectator and became a referee again. "Step back, counsel. Give the man room to breathe." I nodded and took two short steps before turning to await Browne's haughty reply.

"They didn't ask; I didn't say."

"You told Ted to keep your earlier visit out of it. Then you let him give a statement to the police, which purports to be him admitting guilt, and signed your initials to it?"

"I've already given the best explanation I can for that." Not so snooty.

"Let me suggest another. By signing to authenticate a phony confession, you'd be making sure that your golf club, a bloody weapon, which you couldn't wait to get away from the scene, would never point the finger of guilt at you."

That was the straw that broke it. He came out of his seat, nostrils flaring, and shouted, "Accuse me all you want! I didn't kill her!" He realized he was losing it and looked around in confusion before sitting again.

"Then, you take over the defense of your friend, neighbor, and long-term client to make sure that I or some other lawyer doesn't dig up the sordid details of TNPC and the Dressler Foundation."

He roused himself some. "I told you there was nothing sordid. I was, I am, embarrassed that the documentation wasn't in the file at Dressler in a timely fashion."

"So you told Ted it was best for you to be the lawyer. Not because it was best for Ted, but rather, it would avoid your being embarrassed by the Foundation's being short a half million?"

"The money was back in place when Amanda died. I've told you that. Don't you listen?" Lecturing a child.

"Oh, I'm listening." I smiled. "Correct me if I'm wrong. The money was missing and unaccounted for over a period of six months. Then Amanda Armbruster starts digging around and finds out about…" I paused and found the exhibit. "…the cats going to the dogs. TNPC. And suddenly the money is back in place?"

"Ha... well... umm. It's fair to say her investigation allowed us to round up the slowpokes for their share of reimbursement." His eyes shifted and his lips turned down.

"I'll bet it did. And at the same time, her investigation causes a certain lawyer, who is so concerned about his impeccable reputation that he takes bloody evidence from a murder scene, to look in his drawer at the office. Oh, my. Look what I forgot. I forgot to put this guarantee that protected Dressler into the Foundation file. The same guarantee that would protect a bunch of poker-playing bigwigs from criminal embezzlement charges. In fact, it makes them look like saints who wanted, for purely unselfish reasons, to allow the Foundation to make big money along with them, but guarantees the Foundation would suffer no loss. That's the agreement you were telling the jury about." Disbelief colored every word.

"That's correct."

"With that noble charitable agreement and rounding up the slowpokes, you got Brent Eubanks to agree to keep quiet, right? No harm, no foul?"

"Let's say he understood much better than you the devastation public disclosure would cause."

"How about Freddie Hildebrandt, the other member of the audit committee?"

Browne looked surprised. "How did you know about—?" He stopped himself in mid-question, composed himself and answered. "Once Mr. Eubanks was satisfied, Mr. Hildebrandt was willing to act in the best interest of the community."

I took a shot. "Hadn't Mr. Hildebrandt been seeking TNPC membership?"

The way his head jerked was a tell. I speculated M. Stanton wasn't all that hard to read at the poker table.

"Er... We said we'd give him due consideration should our group have an opening."

"Uh-huh. So you'd nicely put a lid on the volcano. The money was back. The guarantee, which you say sat in your drawer forgotten for over a year, was in place. Mr. Eubanks and Mr. Hildebrandt both agreed to keep quiet. You were set. Set except for Mrs. Armbruster. She hadn't quite signed on, had she? And next thing you know, she's dead. And a certain lawyer's illegal golf club had been used to wound her. That about the size of it?"

Like a hunted animal who had run out of avenues of escape, he bolted from his seat and started for me. The bailiffs leaped from their seats and ran for him. I braced for the onslaught. But Browne caught himself a couple of steps from me. He was rigid with anger, his facial muscles taut as string. His hands formed fists at his side. His voice was a tense tremolo.

"Listen, you. You can twist and turn everything however you want. You can throw accusations at the best members of our society. You can smash the biggest charitable benefactor this town ever had or will have, to get your name in lights. But if you think I am going to confess to killing Amanda Armbruster, you're crazy!" All these words he spat into my face, saliva included. Then much more quietly, "Because I didn't."

With that he turned and went back to the witness stand and slumped back down into it. "I am sorry, Your Honor. I am under stress."

I returned to stand behind counsel table and let the quiet after the storm settle over the courtroom. I had what I needed, but I couldn't resist one last question.

"Just like you didn't use that illegal wedge to hit the fabulous shot to win the tournament, right?"

He just glared at me. He saw Joshua still in the courtroom. I think all the confession was out of him. He wasn't prepared to admit he was a cheat at golf.

I gave him twenty seconds and then said, "Forget it. I withdraw the question. Nothing further." I sat down.

The judge looked at the clock on the wall. "We'll take recess. The jury will remember my instructions. Do not discuss the case." Once they were gone, she looked at Browne and me and spoke sternly. "You two are ordered to avoid each other during recess."

Browne shook his head in disgust. I manufactured my best-behavior smile. "No problem here, Judge."

But once she left the bench, Browne, on his way from the stand to the rail door, brushed into me as I bent to straighten my papers at counsel table. "Asshole" was the best the cream of society could manage.

I turned to shove back but noticed the bailiff watching intently. So instead I just held my hands open and shrugged "what's a guy to do?"

The hallway was Babel.

"Way to go, counselor."

"Are they going to charge that crook?"

"Is the case over?"

"Holy catfish! I missed a hair appointment for this. Wait till I tell the girls at the parlor about this!"

When I came back into the courtroom, the bailiff said the break might be a little longer. "Miss Botham is upstairs with the prosecutor. When she comes back the judge wants to meet with you both."

A few minutes later the door to judge's chambers opened and the bailiff waved me over. The judge was behind her desk. She had a "You never cease to amaze me" look on her face, which I hadn't seen since the early days of our romance. Tina sat on the couch dabbing at smeared eye makeup.

Her boss, Alvin Corliss, the man who'd given me my first job, sat in the easy chair in the corner. With a full mane of gray hair swept back over a noble brow and a nicely tailored gray herringbone suit, he looked like he belonged more in the corporate boardroom than judge's chambers. Alvin had been prosecutor so long that he was more politician than lawyer. He'd let his assistants seek the votes of juries while he schmoozed the voters. He leaned over to shake my hand. "Damn it, Edwards. I've got an election coming up, and you're not winning me any votes."

I took one of the straightbacks in front of the judge's desk. "Sorry about that, Alvin. How about I endorse you?" Whatever failings Alvin might have, he'd given me my first job as a lawyer. I'd always appreciate him for that.

He laughed, displaying a gleaming set of pearly whites. "No thanks. Anything but that."

The judge broke in, "Enough chit-chat. In view of recent developments, I suggested Miss Botham meet with her boss to consider best how to proceed from here. What have you decided, Miss Botham?"

"We can't dismiss."

Alvin broke in, "I haven't been in court for the trial. But Tina and I talk every day. I know the file top to bottom. There was… There is substantial evidence of Mr. Armbruster's guilt. Even if Mr. Browne had something to do with Amanda Armbruster's death, and I'm not saying at the moment that he did, it doesn't mean the defendant is innocent. If he is going to go free, let the jury set him loose. They've been sitting there for three weeks. Better them than me. If I dismiss and some jurors tell the papers they were ready to convict, I couldn't get elected if I ran unopposed." I wondered if the prospect of one more term fully vesting a generous pension had jaundiced Alvin more than I realized.

I started to answer, but the judge broke in. "Mr. Prosecutor. I take offense at using my courtroom for damage control for your reelection campaign. Doesn't the job you seem so eager to keep require that you prosecute only the truly guilty?"

Alvin's tan paled a little. "That didn't come out right. What I meant was, from all the evidence, I believe Mr. Armbruster was involved in his wife's death. Whether he acted alone, as we originally thought, or Browne chipped in—sorry for the pun—may be in doubt. But considering his confession, motives, and the other evidence, I myself have no doubt of his guilt. That being so, I cannot approve of dismissal. Let the jury decide."

Alex narrowed her eyes and shook her head at both Alvin and Tina. Nice to see the other side getting a taste from the cup I'd been drinking from all trial long.

So we went back into court. Tina did the best she could with Browne on cross exam. But her heart wasn't in it. The bloodlust for conviction that had coursed through her veins at the start of the case had become an anemia of despondency. Oh, Browne gave her the conversation he'd had with Ted in Browne's trophy room about having a last-ditch plan to raise money. He waffled as best he could on the confession, trying to make it sound like Ted had confessed. He said that he'd felt like a fool for letting it happen, so perhaps he wanted to believe he hadn't. No matter. The jury had heard all they needed to from Mr. Browne. They glared at him with open hostility or looked away with disinterest.

When Tina was done I didn't bother with redirect. After the judge excused him with, "You may go, Mr. Browne," instead of her usual "Witness, you are excused, and thank you for your time," Browne pasted back on his time-honored "noblesse oblige" manner. He stood his full six feet two inches, squared his tie, and made a bow of the head to the judge and the jury. Neither nodded back. The jurors could hardly miss the baleful stare he gave me as he marched past the defense table.

I had been planning on calling a couple of character witnesses, including Ted's mother. I called Mom just long enough for her to remind the jury of Ted's upbringing, his dedication to his family business, and the love he had for his wife.

"I know my son. He loved Amanda too much to ever hurt her. He cried like a baby on the day of her funeral. His last chance to say goodbye, and he couldn't. All he could say was, 'Mama, who could do a thing like that?' " Marjorie cried. A couple of the jurors cried. And Ted sobbed. I rested my case.

The judge asked Tina if she had rebuttal witnesses. She declined. The jury was excused and told to be ready for closing arguments and deliberations first thing in the morning. I slipped out a side door to avoid any temptation to count my chickens before they hatched, and walked back to the office.

I should've felt great. The tide was cresting in our favor at the crucial time. The jury was about to get the case. But I felt uneasy. As much as I detested Browne, I could take no pleasure in his professional destruction. Among the flotsam and jetsam from the shipwreck of Amanda's death and subsequent murder trial, I could see Brent Eubanks' reputation and career floating away. The community standing and prestige of my fellow country club members who were part of TNPC bobbed among the wreckage. Maybe the Foundation would close shop as a result of the scandal. That would be on my conscience. Gianfranco was probably sleeping on the couch and planning his revenge. Xavier Westphal had intimated dire consequences for my muck-raking.

But more than these things, I was wrestling with the doubts that prosecutor Corliss had raised in chambers. Just because Browne might have had something to do with killing her, it didn't mean Ted didn't. For a case I'd been living with twenty-four hours a day for months, there was a lot I didn't know. Now, at the end of trial, I had more questions than when I'd started.

I sat in my office and ruminated while the secretaries shut off their word processors and went home. When the light faded from the sky, I flipped on the desk lamp but couldn't make myself do the job I had to do before I went home… prepare closing argument. I was seized with an ennui, two parts guilt for the harm I was causing, three parts exhaustion, and four parts doubt about the righteousness of the cause.

Finally, around ten p.m., I pulled out the legal pad upon which I had been making notes for closing through the course of the trial. I had enough there for a two-hour summation. By the time I left at one a.m. after sifting, considering, adding, subtracting, and coalescing, I had the shortest closing argument I'd ever given. In the biggest case I'd ever had.

71

For closing, my old white linen suit looked as good as the dry cleaner could make it. I fingered Pop's pocket watch for luck. My voice was back, but I kept it in check, speaking softly and mournfully about what we'd witnessed during the trial. The jurors, whom I called by name to start my closing, looked attentive and thoughtful. But they had looked that way through Tina's closer too.

"Reasonable Doubt. Remember your oath as jurors many weeks ago. If there is a shred of reasonable doubt, you will vote to acquit. The presumption of innocence must be foremost in your minds as you begin, during, and when you conclude your deliberations. The judge will tell you that in her instructions. It is the foundation of our system of criminal justice. It is the mighty fortress which protects us all. And that fortress of justice is built upon the principle that Ted Armbruster is presumed innocent. That presumption requires you to say Not Guilty unless each and every doubt about his innocence has been destroyed by evidence so clear, convincing, and overwhelming that no possible doubt remains. Can you say that, my fellow citizens, when the prosecutor's case is built on lies, and then when those lies failed, on improved lies?

"In golf, to improve your lie is to cheat. It is to ignore the truth about where your ball has come to rest and to create a false reality by cheating to gain advantage. Here in this case, which originated with a bunch of country club poker players improving their lies, it's best not to lose sight of the tangled web that lying creates. First, the lie; then the cover-up, or improved lie; then, when that fails, murder.

"First the lie. Taking charity money for a prohibited purpose so they could make a sure-thing, fast buck. Then improving the lie by pretending it was in the brokerage account. Then lying again by drawing up what I think was obviously an after-the-fact guarantee. Then improving the lie by claiming it was inadvertently left in a law office file drawer. Then getting others to agree to look the other way so nobody gets hurt. But what to do when Amanda won't go along? We have seen that people were willing to commit serious crimes to cover up the first lie, embezzling charitable funds to the tune of a half million dollars. Fraud, to make it look like they hadn't. Bribery, to get Freddie Hildebrandt to look the other way. Perjury, at least I call it that, to have Stanton Browne concoct the so-called guarantee after the fact and claim it sat forgotten in his file drawer. Perhaps extortion to try and persuade Amanda to keep quiet. And when she wouldn't, murder.

"Felonies, all of them. Fraud, embezzlement, extortion, perjury. Serious felonies. When you've been lying and cheating to cover up your felonies, then the next step, murder, is just the last in a spiral of lawless behavior. When Miss Botham started this case, she said 'love or money,' suggesting that Ted had motives for murder. Well, now I say 'love of money' to show you how a bunch of respectable people got themselves into a cycle of lies and improved lies leading to death. Their motivation led to all the crimes I just mentioned. Can you say beyond a reasonable doubt it did not lead to murder? If not, you must acquit."

I turned away from the jurors and walked away for a dramatic pause. It almost completely threw me. Out of the right side of my eyes, Judge Alex gazed with an intensity of interest I'd thought was gone forever. On my left, I was surprised to see Karen, in uniform, squeezed into the front row of the balcony seats. Her strawberry hair caught the highlights from the courtroom chandelier. She, too, was hanging on my every word. The dual image caused a short circuit. I forgot what I'd meant to say next. So I walked over to counsel table, poured myself a cup of water, stepped behind Ted and put my hands on his shoulders, and collected myself. I felt the last spasm of adrenaline my exhausted glands had to give and went on.

"Ask yourself, can I base a conviction on the testimony of Stanton Browne? Remember the smug lie at the start of his testimony, when he claimed he put his club away after it was banned? Then, after the club has been used to strike Amanda not once, but twice, he improves his lie when he, like a shadow Santa Claus, throws his golf bag over his back and gets his club out of the murder scene before the police arrive. Lies when he attests to an inaccurate confession. Backtracks under oath. Then improves his lie by saying he doesn't know which is which. Can you believe him when, caught up in his lies, he says, 'Okay, okay, I lied. But I didn't kill her.'

"What kind of man would use a murder weapon to win a sporting contest? Would he confess to murder when confronted with his lies and deceit leading up to murder? Heck, he couldn't even bring himself to confess to you that he cheated by using the club in a golf tournament, when confronted with the caddy who saw him do it. Unless you can say beyond a reasonable doubt it was not Browne, then you must find Ted not guilty."

My energy wouldn't let me stand still, so I squeezed Ted's shoulders and moved to walking about a ten-foot oval in front of the jury box. The jurors' eyes followed each step of the way.

"What about Bliss? Why did he go to the scene on a murder investigation that belonged to his junior partner? The lie. 'My deputies called for my guidance on what to do with a drunk driver,' says Bliss. The truth? Bartender Hackett calls him in furtherance of an extortion racket. Remember Hackett's testimony that Bliss was more interested in the whereabouts and condition of Mrs. Armbruster than in her husband? You are smart enough to know why now. He is tied to Xavier Westphal and TNPC Investment by bonds that stretch from his childhood. And Amanda Armbruster is a real threat to his father figure.

"When Browne returns from taking evidence from the murder scene, Detective Bliss has a little chat with him about their mutual friend, Westphal. Next thing you know, Ted, whom the paramedics say is so close to collapse he needs to be in the hospital, is having a friendly little chat with

Bliss, with Browne's okay. Why? Bliss and Browne travel in different circles. Oh, but they have Westphal in common. Browne admitted that was part of his conversation the night of the murder. Remember him saying, 'Ken Edwards must not have this case, lest all the lies surrounding TNPC come to light'? Next thing you know, it's all taken care of. Ted's confessed. Browne's initialed it. Only, Ted swears under oath 'I didn't kill her.' Can you believe Browne, who testified yes—no—maybe on the confession? Can you believe Bliss, who through his drunk driving sting knows of Amanda's location at Heather Hollows?"

I stopped to look directly at the jury. A few bit their lips in concentration. I turned away and started again.

"How do we know Bliss didn't follow her until she went home, and then to protect his surrogate father, silenced her? Can you say beyond a reasonable doubt that didn't happen? He had motive, opportunity, and means. Ask yourselves why, when I get to the scene, I am allowed nowhere near Ted; but after Browne and Bliss confer, Browne is ordered right in. And how did Bliss know to ask Ted about insurance if a little birdie hadn't told him?" I fingered my father's watch and felt an energy flow. I took a couple of steps away, then turned back to face the jurors with a renewed passion.

"What about Gianfranco Firenze? Lies about what sounds like attempted rape of Amanda. Finally admits he was reluctant to take no for an answer. Then says, 'Okay, I lied. But I didn't kill her.' Sound like any silk-stocking lawyers you know? Remember Mr. Firenze, at first smooth, polished, handsome, debonair? A knight in shining armor who was just giving the poor lady a ride home? But all of that was a lie. Beneath the smooth exterior lies a man of feral appetites, a man of violence, a man used to getting his own way by force. You saw in the courtroom he was prepared to lie and do violence to me to prevent embarrassment to his wife and whomever his bosses might be. Can you say beyond a reasonable doubt that, after he forced himself on Amanda, she didn't threaten to file a complaint to the police? Can you say beyond a reasonable doubt he wouldn't use violence to avoid rape charges? Think about the man you saw here in court with a rap sheet as long as your arm. Can you believe him beyond a reasonable doubt? If not, you must acquit." With each invocation added to the litany of reasonable doubts, I convinced myself I could see the congregation of jurors nodding closer to the not guilty response.

"Now contrast with Ted. Everyone agrees he loved his wife to a fault. Would hear nothing bad about her. He doesn't, like Mr. Browne, flee the scene with incriminating evidence. In fact, the first thing he does is call 911, begging for help. When the police come, there he is on the floor with his wife's head in his lap. He wants to talk to the police. He is shaking, shocky, and grief-stricken. But he has nothing to hide. He tells Bliss about his love for his wife. He would never hurt her. He won't tolerate others speaking ill of her. He answers truthfully about the insurance and his business problems. He admits the argument with Amanda at the bar. He blames himself for her death. 'If only I hadn't behaved so badly,' he tells us. And he tells you he didn't kill her.

"Imagine the last few months for Ted. The woman he loves taken from him in a most gruesome fashion. Sold down the river by his friend, his neighbor, his trusted lawyer. Accused of a horrible crime he didn't commit. Abandoned by his friends. His business, his life's work shuttered and closed. His life ruined. Why? Because of a series of lies. What you've seen here in the courtroom is only the tip of the iceberg. Lies, improved lies, more lies, and damned lies."

I paused and took two backward steps, making eye contact with each of the jurors. None averted my gaze. Finish line in sight, I let my passion swell and spoke in full voice.

"But now it's time for the lies to stop. If you convict Ted, you are doing so using the testimony of liars, cheats, frauds, mobsters, and miscellaneous crooks. If you do that, you'll have forgotten your oath as jurors. An oath I know you weren't lying about when you took it. Let's review that solemn oath: 'I will presume Ted innocent. If there is a reasonable doubt, I will vote to acquit.' About the witnesses' credibility, I've spoken at length. Now it's time to show that you, the jury, are as good as your word. Speak the truth. On this evidence, that truth is contained in two words. Not Guilty."

I sat down. The relief of finality after closing argument is something every trial lawyer knows. I have done everything I can. I'm done.

I'll give her credit. Tina, as in her closing argument, did rebuttal like her heart was in it. Dressed in a black suit over a crisp white blouse, she moved a wooden step and stood upon it behind the lectern, speaking with a voice full of emotion and conviction. She argued that nobody else had Ted's motives, opportunity and the means at hand. She castigated the defense for creating a circus, a sideshow to distract jurors' attention from the crime charged: murder. Yes, there would be an investigation into TNPC and Mr. Browne's obstructing justice by removing evidence. But, she added, "Even if lawyer Browne's wedge inflicted injury, it was the defendant's club that killed her." She pointed out that Ted hadn't been too truthful about the status of the divorce filings. "Mr. Edwards neglected to mention the biggest liar of them all." She repeated that Ted was prepared to kill to save his business, and it might have been an improved lie on his part to say he meant suicide. She apologized for Bliss, but still held the confession as the genuine article. She asked for a guilty verdict and sat down with a serious, determined look on her face.

In the hall, prior to jury instructions, Karen pushed through the crowd of spectators as Lizzie was shaking my hand. "Excuse me, young lady. Aren't you the bright student Mr. Edwards was telling me about?" Lizzie blushed and Karen continued, "You could do worse than learning from 'Old Silver Tongue' here. Gotta run, Ken. Had to beg the sarge to let me take an early lunch for your closing. You were great!" She leaned forward and pecked me on the cheek, then turned to push her way to the elevator.

Lizzie raised her eyebrows in surprise. "Friend of my dog's," I explained.

72

I'm always nervous when a jury is out, and never more so than now. But I was very optimistic. The case ended on as high a note as it could have. The jury was looking intently at me during my close. Some seemed hesitant to make eye contact with Tina during hers. If they didn't come back with a verdict, the judge would send them home at 4:30 to come back the next day. I was sure they wouldn't want to do that. They had missed a sizeable slice of their own lives. Only a major division of opinion could cause them to go past 4:30.

But when the jury was out an hour, two, three, then four, I was getting pretty jumpy. At the three-hour mark I found myself right back where I'd started. I was so nerved up that I had run across the street to the convenience store. The Marlboro pack lay open on my desk. It was like I'd never quit. If I weren't superstitious enough to believe in divine retribution for backsliding, I'd have lit one and then another. As it was, I'd had an unlit cigarette in my mouth as a pacifier for twenty minutes when Janice knocked on my door.

"You didn't?" I shook my head and threw the unlit cigarette with a very wet filter in the trash. "Oh, by the way. Judge's office called. They have a verdict."

I felt my heart race. It was what I'd wanted. Or was it? I didn't want to wait anymore. But if we lost, I knew what that chasm of despair was like. I tried to look calm as I walked over to the courthouse. I definitely didn't feel it.

Ted was seated at counsel table. He rose to greet me. "What do you think?" he asked hesitantly.

I could see all the angst of the last few months right beneath the surface. "We'll soon know. Hope for the best."

The jury filed in. Sometimes you can tell by who they look at or if somebody smiles at you. They were stonefaced. Nobody was smiling. A hung jury, I thought. They looked tired, but determined. The judge directed them to sit. She looked over to me to see how I was handling the tension. I kept my trembling hands beneath the counsel table. Then she addressed the panel. "I understand the jury has reached a verdict. If so, who speaks for you?"

"I do, Your Honor." Mrs. Tomlinson, the librarian, stood. A ray of hope. She was one of my favorites.

"Please hand the bailiff the verdict form."

It was folded so the bailiff couldn't see, even though he was trying to peek as he approached the bench. The judge opened the form and glanced over her glasses at it. Nothing. No clue. She was as inscrutable to me now as she had been since the break-up. Back to the foreperson went the bailiff. I had long since stopped breathing. Even though the courtroom was packed, there was not a sound. All quiet in anticipation.

When the foreperson had the form back in hand, the judge spoke. "Madam Foreperson, on the charge of murder in the first degree, how do you find?"

Mrs. Tomlinson started to speak. "We the jury..." and then lost her voice, cleared her throat and went on, "We the jury find the defendant NOT GUILTY."

I caught my breath. My God! We'd won this thing! Ted was smiling through his tears and nodding at the jury.

"So say you all?" asked the judge. Everyone nodded, some more enthusiastically than others.

Tina stood to ask that the jury be polled. The clerk pulled the jury sheet and read their names, asking each by name, "Was that and is that your verdict?" They all stood by it.

The back of the courtroom was pandemonium, with media types

rushing for the exit and the spectators talking. Many clapped.

After the judge thanked and dismissed the jurors, Tina behaved like a professional. She walked over to counsel table and extended her hand. As I rose to accept the handshake, she even managed a hint of a smile. "Congratulations. You did one hell of a job."

"Thanks, Tina. You too." Behind her glasses I could see the tension at the edges of her eyes. I had plumbed the abyss of defeat often enough to know her pain. She grabbed her file and exited through the judge's office to avoid the mob. When I looked at Ted, he had his head bowed on his arms on the table. His shoulders were heaving with sobs. I touched his back.

"Hey, partner. Maybe you missed it. They said 'not guilty.' You're a free man."

When he looked up at me, his face was red and streaked with tears. He took a minute to collect himself. A couple of reporters pushed through the bar and were starting to fire questions. I held up my hands to them. "Later, fellas. Give us a minute or two, please." They nodded and moved back.

"Ken, I know I should feel good, but how can I? Nothing will bring Amanda back. While I've been in jail I could sort of pretend she was out there waiting for me. But now when I go home, nobody, just me, all alone." I remembered my last few years, when the only reason for going home was to hang out with my dog. Ted didn't even have a pooch. He looked up at me, lost. "I don't know if I can manage. Amanda's gone. The company is gone. What will I do?" For the first time, I realized that Ted had never contemplated being acquitted.

As I tried to temper my joy at victory to respond, Ted's mother, Marjorie, approached. Ted went to meet her and they embraced, both sobbing. Then, she noticed me standing there, not knowing quite what to do. "C'mon. If anyone ever deserved a hug, it's you."

The picture that graced the front page of the *Leader* the next day was the three of us embracing. They were trying to smile through their tears, while I was trying not to look so darned happy. The headline read "INNOCENT."

Marjorie put her arm around Ted and tried to figure how to get through the mob in the courtroom and in the hallway outside. "C'mon, son. You come home with me for a while. I need to get some meat back on those bones."

I motioned the bailiff over, and he located a couple of deputies. They formed a wedge and pushed easily through the sea of people, took an elevator for themselves, and Ted was gone.

Before they'd left, Ted had grabbed my hand and tried to speak. But words failed him. All he could manage was to mouth the words, "Thank you."

I accepted congratulations from the court clerks and then noticed R.T. seated in the front row. He pushed the swinging doors of the rail open and smiled broadly. "You rascal. Best case of misdirection since Houdini. Way to go. But did Ted do it?"

I laughed. "Not according to the jury."

"Let me buy you a drink," he offered.

"I think a wee bit of celebration is in order. I'll meet you at the Dew Drop."

As I walked down the aisle in the spectator section, I shook hands with the folks who had been there throughout the trial.

"Way to go, counselor."

"Great job."

"Lake Pointe's Clarence Darrow."

Lizzie stood at the end of the last row, beaming. She grabbed my hand, tears of relief on her cheeks.

"Remember! You told me when I graduate from law school I'm coming for an interview."

"I'll remember. But you remember they don't all work out this well."

Then, as we pushed open the doors at the back of the courtroom, there was Karen, still in uniform, just getting off the elevator with her sergeant. She pushed through the crowd and threw her arms around me with such gusto her hat flew off, and I staggered a little. "Happiest I've ever been at a not guilty verdict. I'm so happy for you," she breathed into my ear.

The cameras were flashing and the sarge looked embarrassed. The picture of Karen hugging me appeared on page three over the caption "Cops happy, too."

As she released me, bent down and retrieved her hat and stood back up, I thought, "There is something about a woman in a uniform." I told her of my plans to go celebrate. She said she'd be off at eight and ordered me not to drive.

"It wouldn't do for the man of the hour to get arrested for DUI. Believe me, there are some cops who'd like nothing better. I'll pick you up at 8:15 and we'll do a little celebrating of our own. That is, if you've still got time for me now that you're a star." She smiled and turned her sparkling green eyes up at me. "You do, don't you?"

I laughed from the breadth of my happiness. "Officer, you are the most arresting woman I've ever met. I can think of no one I'd rather share this moment with than you."

She smiled and hugged me again, hard enough for me to feel the curves under the uniform, and kissed me fully. She was still smiling at me as she headed through the dispersing crowd to the elevator, when I heard the courtroom door squeak. Judge Alex, without her robes, looked girlish in a simple white top over a coral skirt. The strange look on her face made me wonder if she'd just gotten bad news. She motioned me over.

"Everything okay?" I asked.

"Think I just saw Marley's ghost." She stopped me before I could ask what she meant. "Ken, I wanted to tell you—" She seemed at a loss for a minute before continuing. We were close enough that I smelled her subtle perfume for the first time in years. "To tell you, well done."

I barely had time to say thanks before she let the door close behind her. Through the small pane of glass in the door I watched her walk away between the rows of now-empty seats. Shafts of sunlight from the balcony windows created an aura of light around her statuesque form. When she reached the rail, she turned to look back. I made a small wave through the window. She raised her hand in response.

I borrowed a cell phone and kept my promise to call the Moondrake sisters.

"Let me guess: the foreperson was Mrs. Tomlinson?" laughed Lydia.

Graciella grabbed the phone from her sister. "Tell you what, Ken. That was some bunny you pulled out of the hat. Sure you don't have a little gypsy magic in the blood?"

"Must have. Thanks for all your help. Couldn't have done it without you."

Judge Ernie had heard the news and made his way over to shake my hand, his cherubic face radiant. "You sum'bitch. I don't believe it. Way to go. Plus, I heard M. Stanton cheated us. Guess he's got more to worry about now. Where's the celebration?"

I went back into the courtroom after talking to the reporters, being sure to give all the credit to the jurors, to pick up my file. Detective Phillip Weston was collecting all the exhibits in a box. He walked over and congratulated me, then added, "If Bliss keeps his nose out of my case, I'm not sure it turns out the same."

"Phil, I'm not so sure either."

73

By the time 8:30 rolled around, I was intoxicated. Jubilation, exhaustion, and alcohol are a heady brew. The Dew Drop Inn is located equidistant from and easy walking distance to the courthouse, the law enforcement center, aka jail, and the newspaper. From early days lawyers, cops, and ink-stained wretches had their own tables and corners of the bar. The downtown secretarial pool could always find somebody who was buying drinks. The jukebox, a classic old Wurlitzer, contained no songs older than 1965 or newer than 1990. At my request, Fleetwood Mac's "Rhiannon" was being replayed about every ten minutes. I was wedged into a crowded booth flanked by Ernie and R.T. The table was littered with empties. When Art Honnecker sprung for a round, I knew I'd done something special.

"Stop the presses. Take the verdict off the front page. Art opened his wallet," the metro editor jibed. He and his fourth estate buddies laughed with the crowd.

Art held up his beer."Money well spent. Thanks to you, we've got a story that won't quit."

My office building tenant, Teutonic Tom, had recently added a lapel carnation to his daily sartorial splendor. He looked more like a young Jackie Gleason every day. However, when he jostled his way through the crowd to our table, he didn't look to be in a joking mood. With an unlit panatela clenched on one side of his mouth, he jerked his head a couple of times to get my attention. As I rose, we almost knocked heads reaching for the last full beer on the table. I let him have it.

We walked over to the idle pinball machine and he stuck out his hand. "Congratulations and all that good shit. I'd be happier if your success wasn't going to cost me a trip before the grievance committee," he muttered, the cigar bobbing with each syllable. My mind was pretty addled, so I just gaped at him. He replaced the cigar with the beer bottle and guzzled almost half in a few swallows before continuing. "Just got off the phone with my divorce client, Cal Salomon, Suzie's husband. He's filing a grievance for disclosing attorney-client privileged matters."

"Why? I didn't use any of that stuff about Suzie and Amanda. Plus, he okayed your telling me."

Tom took another deep swallow, belched, and wiped his lips. "Not that. He wasn't too thrilled with having his name in the front page story about the poker club and the Dressler money."

I was stunned. "You knew about that ripoff and you didn't tell me?"

"If I had, he'd have a real grievance. In the divorce he had to explain where $55,000 of marital moneys went. At first he told me it was a charitable donation. When I questioned him, he coughed it up after swearing me to secrecy. Now he's sure I tipped you."

I leaned against the pinball machine as another ripple from the stone I'd cast into the water revealed itself. I shook my head and touched Tom's arm. "Sorry, pal. Since you didn't tell me, you're in the clear. And I doubt the grievance committee is going to be all that impressed with a philandering embezzler. I'll testify you told me nothing."

Tom finished the last swallow, put the bottle down on the glass pinball top, and stuck the stogie between his lips. "Figured I could count on you. Just grinds me. Sent the bastard my final bill last week for five grand. He told me to stick it up my ass."

"Sorry about that, Tom."

He reached over and pulled me into a bear hug and steered me back to the table. "Sorry to rain on your parade. I needed to tell somebody. Now, let's go get smashed." When we reached the crowd he held my arm aloft. "All hail the conquering hero!"

The mix of alcohol and elation was a heady brew. I was flying. The taste of victory in a big case is an elixir like no other. All the exhaustion, cares, and fears of failure are flushed away. The publicity and éclat couldn't be matched with an unlimited advertising budget, even if you are craven enough to advertise. The strangers who approach you to say, "Boy, if I ever need a lawyer…" are being echoed on barstools throughout town. Their refrain will be repeated over evening papers and around water coolers for days. Defense lawyers and insurance adjusters in civil cases are thinking, "Man, if he can pull that off, what can he do to us?" And all the time, while you remind yourself to answer demurely, "Just lucky," "Smart jury," "My client was innocent," you are thinking to yourself, "Hey, I'm good. Really good."

Oh man, the feeling from the top of the mountain is wonderful. Just when I thought it couldn't get any better, Karen sashayed along the bar in a slinky red dress that left little to the imagination. Every eye in the place followed her over to the crowded booth. "Okay, big shot. Had enough partying? Ready for a private consultation?"

The goofy smile on my face was stretching facial muscles I hadn't used in the longest time. I took a last swallow of beer and replied, "Think you can handle the retainer, Miss?"

Karen smiled and leaned toward me, hands on the table. The décolletage was awe-inspiring. "I have some assets."

I pushed myself up from the booth and in so doing knocked over a couple of dead soldiers. "Oops. Ha ha. Yes, I can see you do. Excuse me, folks, duty calls."

This was a dream. Me and a mysterious, shapely strawberry blonde walking out of the bar arm in arm in front of admiring and envious colleagues. If I'd ever felt more elated, I couldn't remember it. Karen went into the Meijer's to buy a couple of thick T-bones, a bottle of Beaujolais, and a big ham soup bone for Max.

She drove us back to my place and kept me company out by the barbeque while the coals heated. Max achieved nirvana beside us gnawing away on his treat. Billy roared into the drive dressed preppy again. When he walked over to the passenger side and helped a little bitty elf with short dark hair to manage the long step down, I could see why. He escorted her over and introduced her.

"This is Miss Louise. Ain't she the prettiest thing you ever did see? Oops, sorry, Trooper. No offense." Then he grabbed me in a bear hug and whirled me around, which caused what little equilibrium I had left to vanish and Max to drop his bone and growl. Billy set me back down to wobble and laughed.

"Boo ya! Way to go, neighbor. I'm so proud of you." They hung around for a quick one and dashed off for a polka fest at the PLAV hall.

Karen suggested I'd be wise to ease up on the beer if I knew what was good for me. But she didn't stop me when I staggered into the fridge to grab us a couple more Labatts. As the steaks hit the grill, I looked out on the bay and followed the silver path from the shore to the nearly full moon. I stepped back from the Weber and admired her in profile as she gazed at the glimmering ripples on the bay. I had seen some women of equal beauty, but few of them had ever given me the time of day. Now here I was, standing in my own backyard with her, daring to think what we might do after dinner.

"What are you staring at?" She pulled me from my daydream.

"Uh, you, actually. I was just really feeling happy to be here with you. Hope you don't mind."

The corners of her mouth rose in a smile. "Sure you wouldn't rather be back at the bar with your admiring fans?"

"Certain. However, there is one place I'd rather be than where I am right now, though," I said, trying to sound serious.

The smile was replaced by a frown. "Where might that be?"

This was my lucky day, so I went for it. "With you in my arms, kissing you, whispering sweet nothings, holding you."

The smile returned. "Well, what's keeping you?"

As it turned out, nothing. I'm not sure whether it was the beer, the exhaustion, the excitement, or just the sheer pleasure of a really passionate kiss, but I almost fainted. If I were female, you'd say I swooned. About the time my hands dropped from her back to her derriere to pull her ever closer, my legs wobbled and we nearly fell over. She steadied us.

"Are you all right?"

"Sorry. I think I just went on sensory overload. Would telling you I love you count as a sweet nothing?"

I had said the magic words. She told me that maybe I'd better lie down for a minute to make sure I wasn't delirious. So we went back into the living room, and as I was about to sit on the couch she steered me into the dimly-lit bedroom. She had me lie down while she pretended to be a nurse taking my pulse.

"A little fast there, my friend. And you were babbling a minute ago outside."

"You mean the part when I said I love you?"

She nodded.

"Actually bubbling, not babbling. I think those words have been bubbling around inside me for a while, but I don't think I knew it until they popped out."

"Aha, delirious, just like I thought. But I have just the treatment for that."

With that she reached behind herself and unzipped her dress. As she reached to pull the dress over her head, I watched the hem rise over her thighs to lacy white panties, over her flat stomach, and then the matching frilly bra restraining her perfect breasts. For a second the sensuous vision before me was replaced by thoughts of Amanda lying with her skirt hiked on the vestibule floor. But Karen chased the ghosts away. She reached over to the bedside lamp and switched it off. "Now relax. This isn't going to hurt a bit."

And it didn't. Not the first time. Nor the second, after we'd run outside naked to pull the charred remains off the grill. Nor the third, waking near dawn, and me saying, "I still must be delirious. I still love you."

She smiled. "It must be contagious, because I love you, too."

Sometime between passion, afterglow and dreams, I told Karen about how it felt like the scars on my psyche from my failed relationship with Alexandra had finally stopped itching. "Yesterday, watching her walk back through the courtroom, I realized something for the first time. She has scars too."

74

The next few weeks were a whirlwind. The verdict made the first page of the *Free Press* as well as a number of other papers in the state. The *Lake Pointe Leader* did a Sunday feature on the case and the Foundation scandal. The Dressler sisters insisted on meeting with me, and after the meeting, agreed to leave the Foundation intact and in town, provided certain board members were removed and I was among the replacements. So I got to be a hero for keeping the city's biggest charity in town. The office phone rang off the hook. My appointment calendar filled to overflowing.

M. Stanton Browne decided to take early retirement. His house went up for sale, and the state bar initiated disciplinary proceedings. I saw his intern, Lori, on the street one afternoon and she congratulated me warmly, but warned me, too. "Watch out for M. Stanton. He hates you and swears it's not over."

"It's over. He just doesn't know it yet."

I got a postcard from Belize. "Thinking of you." There was no signature, but I had a pretty good hunch that a certain former hedge fund manager was my likely pen pal. And one evening as I went to haul my empty trash barrel from the curb, I was shocked at how heavy it was. Opening the lid, I jumped a mile to see a pig's head staring back at me. The lily in its mouth made me quite certain that Gianfranco was on the other end of the swine-o-gram. But I was so used to being scared and under pressure during the trial that these things didn't bother me quite so much.

I was saddened to see Brent Eubanks take retirement from his firm and resign from Dressler. A bank vice president, Zack Melrose, was transferred out of state as fallout from being a TNPC member, even though he hadn't been part of the investment group.

But the best thing was Karen. Our appetite for each other's company was boundless. If we didn't see each other, we talked on the phone. She'd spend weekends at the cottage. And we started to dance around the subject of marriage. We both agreed time was needed to see if this was just an infatuation or something bigger. Whatever it was, I liked it.

Even Judge Alex and I started to clean old skeletons out of the closet. A week after trial she saw me as I dropped off a brief with her law clerk and invited me into chambers. She'd come out from behind her desk and we sat in the attorney's chairs, facing each other. She wore the string of pearls I'd given her in Jamaica years ago above a lavender sundress. With her blonde hair and summer tan, she looked a model for resort wear.

"Ken, that was the best job of lawyering I expect I'll ever see. I thought you didn't have a snowball's chance. But, by the end of the case I was so convinced that if the jury convicted, I'd have granted judgement non obstante verdicto. Amazing!"

"Thanks. It was pretty touch and go for a while."

She shook her head, causing her tresses to sway in a way that still haunted my sleep. I remembered my dream the night the phone had rung to announce Amanda's death. "And the pressure you were under. That gangster guy. Calls in the middle of the night. The country club set leaning on you. Someone trying to poison Max. You getting run off the road and then almost getting arrested for drunk driving. Bliss behind that, you think?"

We were close enough that the subtle hint of lilac I remembered from perfume at the base of her neck called out to me. I shrugged off the distraction. "Don't know. Bliss still worries me. Firenze has got nothing on him when it comes to rough stuff. He's still suspended. The disciplinary hearings will keep him in check for a while. Losing his job, his power, his pension; I don't think he's the forgive and forget kind. We'll see."

A look of concern crossed her face. "I thought you looked pretty stressed as the case went on, but I had no idea. How did you manage?"

"Barely, Judge. Just barely." I told her a little of my agonizing over revealing the Dressler scandal.

She leaned over and touched my arm, her blue eyes limpid with concern. "And I wasn't making things any easier on you, was I?" I looked down where her hand rested on my arm and noted that her nail polish matched her dress. When I looked back up her eyes lingered on mine, hypnotizing me for an instant. I'd been lost in those eyes before. It wasn't always easy to find my way back out.

She laughed and removed her hand and sat back in her chair. I think she'd reassured herself that she still had a hold on me. I didn't need reminding. I straightened myself and answered, "You were just doing your job. No hard feelings."

Her face took on a composed look. "Speaking of feelings. I need to say this." She paused to consider her words. "I'm sorrier than you'll ever know about what happened to us. I made a big mistake. I was so full of myself at being a judge so young. I let my mom and my sister influence me. They thought you were a loose cannon, a distraction I didn't need." I held up my hands to say stop. She ignored me. "I don't know what would've happened to us. I often wonder. Watching you fight for your client, I was reminded why I fell for you in the first place." She put the back of her thumb against her full lips, the way she did when thinking, and then finished wistfully, "I'd heard you'd found a new lady friend. I saw her congratulating you in the hall after the verdict. I'm happy for you."

Now I understood her Marley's ghost comment and the look on her face at the courtroom door. Only lately had it occurred to me that our breakup had caused her any pain. I touched her arm in rising and said softly, "She's really special. But so are you."

She rose too, her dress caressing her tall, full form. "Right! At the rate I'm going, I'll end up a spinster career woman."

As I reached for the door I laughed and answered, "I doubt that. I'm really glad we talked, though. I'd like us to be friends. Can we do that?"

She took both of my hands in hers and smiled. "Motion granted."

Employer's Life was among those not so happy with the verdict. I filed Armbruster's suit on Amanda's life policy a week after the verdict. We'd agreed to await the verdict before pursuing the claim. Their adjuster, David Huckaby, was a grizzled veteran of disputed life claims. He asked if we could meet before he hired a lawyer to defend the case. I considered that a good sign. We met in my office, and I liked him right away. He was a big bear of a man at six foot three inches and at least 250 pounds. His full head of hair was streaked with gray. His glasses were a prop he put on and took off to gesticulate and make points. His southern Georgia boy drawl came off and on just as easily. When I told him my client was "Jury certified innocent," off came the glasses and on went the drawl.

"No, son. They found him not guilty. There's a mighty big gap between not guilty and innocent."

When I asked him if the prosecution, with all its resources, couldn't prove Ted guilty, why did he think Employer's could, the glasses went back on and the drawl disappeared.

"Because they had to prove him guilty beyond a reasonable doubt. We only need to make it seem more likely than not he was involved. We talked to some of the jurors. They were out four hours because many of them thought he was probably guilty but just not certain enough to convict."

"How many jurors was that exactly?"

He smiled. "I'd rather not say."

After a couple of cups of coffee and a half hour of sparring, we got down to brass tacks. He offered $750,000 of the $2 million policy. I countered at $1.75 million. He closed his file and got up to leave. "If you are thinking like that, I believe the gap is too wide to build a bridge."

"Well, sorry you feel that way. I tell you what. I've got a few more trestle pieces on the flat car. If you've got some on yours, maybe that bridge could still get built. Why don't you write down absolutely the highest number you'd pay and I'll write down the lowest number we'd take and we'll see how far apart we really are."

He sat back down and looked me over again. "I'm still sizing you up, Edwards. I am a fair man, but I don't like to be fooled with."

"I'm not talking about fooling. I'm talking about a full exploration of settlement before we spend a lot of time and money litigating."

"All right, then." He pulled a piece of stationery from his file and handed me one. We each wrote down a number and then exchanged sheets. He was at $1,000,000. I was at $1,400,000. We just looked at each other for thirty seconds. Then he spoke. "Halfway get it done?"

I smiled. "A million two it is."

We shook hands. After he left I called Ted and told him I'd gotten $200,000 more than he'd told me he'd be happy with. "Thank God, Ken. I would've taken nothing just to never see the inside of a courtroom again."

A week or two later we had the settlement papers and the check. When Ted had signed my usual one-third contingent fee retainer on the life insurance claim way back at the start of the case, I'd filed a notice of claim and forgotten it. Now I was sitting on the biggest fee I'd ever earned. When you're hot, you're hot. We worked out a deal with the bank for them to take five hundred thousand against overdue indebtedness and leave the other three hundred in the Armbruster Manufacturing account for Ted to try and resurrect the business.

I went back to being a sole practitioner, albeit one whose phone rang much more often. I pulled out all the files that had been gathering moss for the last few months and tried to get caught up. I ordered extensive remodeling of the cottage after Pastor Munson agreed to sell the place for twice what it was worth. I spent the largest chunk of the remodeling budget on the master bathroom, installing a top of the line, multi-jet walk-in shower. Karen helped me christen it.

I shopped the auto dealers looking to spend the last of my insurance fee, but couldn't bring myself to part with my antique convertible. So I took it downstate for a full course face lift inside and out.

Life was good. Strangely, even as the trial receded from my conscious thoughts, the vision of Amanda reaching out to me in a misty meadow, gleaming talisman in hand, still would visit me from time to time in dreams.

Things would have been so much better if we hadn't had that last perfect October day. For weeks the weather had been cold, gray and damp. All the leaves had turned from brilliant fall tree ornaments to a huge, brown raking chore. Then on Saturday, October 27th, the sun made an encore appearance before fleeing Michigan for the winter. By nine a.m. when the cottage phone rang, it was already sixty-four degrees and the radio DJ was predicting a high near 80. It was Ted on the line.

"Okay, counselor. You've been promising me a round of golf since you took my case back. Can't find a better day than this. What do you say?"

I said yes. We met at eleven at the club for lunch in the men's locker room. The parking lot was nearly empty. Everybody was watching football. Many golfers are like boaters. They put their toys away on Labor Day until next Memorial Day. Late October golf is for the junkies. I walked by the wall of presidents and noticed with a smile that the portraits had been reshuffled to put Ted back in proper chronological order.

As we were chatting over locker room burgers and fries, I noticed Ted was looking better. His skin had color. Some of the tightness around his eyes was gone. His gaunt look was gone too with the ten pounds his mom's cooking had put back on him since the trial. His smile came easily. But occasionally a sad, wistful look would cross his face. He'd come back, but he was nowhere near the confident, hearty man whose picture hung in the hall.

The other club members who passed our table seemed to be divided into two groups: the "great to see you, welcome back" crowd and the "pretend you don't exist, ignore them" group. I asked Ted how it had been going after Dr. Bill Crabtree, a former member of Ted's regular foursome, passed without even a nod.

"About what you'd expect, I guess. Some of the guys who were nowhere to be found when you were looking for character witnesses are my best buddies again. Dr. Crabtree was always closer to Stanton than he was to me. Still, I thought he was my friend. I saw him on the driving range a month ago and tried to set up a match. Here's what he said. 'After what you and your slimeball lawyer did to Stanton Browne and lots of other good people, I wouldn't want to be on the same course with you, let alone the same hole.' Nice, huh?"

"I'm not exactly in line for election as club president either," I said. "The club's lost at least ten members. The state police had a detective out here investigating 'unlawful gaming.' Maybe you've noticed no cash on the table during gin games anymore. Everybody's jumpy. But they're blaming me, not you. In fact, I had a call a couple weeks ago from our illustrious club president suggesting maybe I should move my membership to a different club, as some of the guys were planning to blackball me at the December membership meeting. I told him I'd looked up the club by-laws and I hadn't committed any serious infractions, like failing to pay my dues or bar charges. So if they kicked me out, maybe we could have a nice public lawsuit over retaliatory discharge. I waved the "whistle-blower act" and some other legal hocus-pocus at him. None of which would apply, but it was enough for him to become pretty conciliatory by the end of the call. 'Just a suggestion. Just guys talking. Nothing official.' That sort of thing. In fact, I was thinking of resigning until I got that call. On the other hand, I've picked up three new cases from our golfing brothers since your case."

By 12:30 tee-off I had my wind vest off and was playing in shirt sleeves. I stuffed the vest on top of Ted's maniacal Fighting Irish Leprechaun head cover in the basket between the cart's seats and our clubs. The memory of where last I'd seen it was distractingly vivid. Ted asked if we could use the cart, as his legs were still weak from months of confinement. We played well, and with him giving me two strokes a side, I was holding my own. We laughed, chatted and were relaxed and comfortable in each other's company until the 14th tee. Ted was setting up to hit his drive while I fished around in my bag trying to find a tee.

"Hey, I've got plenty. Top zippered pouch. Take a handful."

As I reached into the pouch, I felt a heavy metal marker mixed in with the tees. I pulled my hand out and there, amongst the tees, was a TNPC marker.

"You find what you need? Hey, what's the matter? Something bite you?"

I picked the marker out of my left hand and held it up with the right. I was speechless. I had never even considered Ted might be in the poker club. Just for an instant Ted's face had a look of panic. Then he regained his composure. "Oh, that. Didn't I tell you I was a member back in the old days when money wasn't so tight?"

I turned the marker in my hand. Solid gold. "No, Ted. I don't believe you mentioned that. In fact, when I asked you what you knew about TNPC your answer was, and I quote, 'not much.' How long ago was it that you were a member?"

He looked around the course. "Gosh, I don't know. A while back. Hey, we'd better get moving. We don't want to slow down the course."

I looked. The only golfers in sight were two holes behind, walking and playing two balls. I put the marker back in the pouch and zipped it up. We both lost focus after that. My triple-bogey lost to his double and so forth the rest of the way in. The conversation, what little we had, was forced and artificial. Neither of us suggested a drink at the clubhouse. I paid him the twenty dollars I had lost, shook hands, and drove off feeling a lot worse than when I drove in. I was so lost in thought I drove right by my freeway exit and had to go twenty miles out of my way to make it home.

Karen had saved her police post-verdict pool winnings to treat me to a first class steak dinner that night. I was a lousy date. My mind wouldn't leave that fancy gold geegaw. Hadn't I heard that the poker club was patting themselves on the back for having twenty of them made when gold bottomed at $255 an ounce? That was only a few years ago. Why hadn't Ted given me more about the club when I was digging into it to defend him?

Karen watched me move my steak around on the plate, barely tasting it, and then reached out and touched my hand. "What is it, Ken? Somebody die?"

"Huh? No, why? Oh, something came up. I'm trying to figure it out."

"Maybe I can help."

"I wish you could." And I did really want to talk to her about it. But she was still a cop and I was still a lawyer with a client. So I tried to shake off the funk and get with the program. But I did such a lousy job of it she had me drop her at home and didn't invite me in.

"Call me when you want to talk about what's on your mind. 'Cause it's certainly not me."

The next few weeks I kept turning that ball marker over in my mind. It didn't matter whether I was in court, in deposition, or watching football on TV. There it was, shining amongst the white golf tees in my hand, forcing my mind in a direction I didn't want to go. Ted hadn't been up front on TNPC. Hell, he'd lied. What else had he kept from me or lied to me about? How much had I ignored or overlooked so as to make the lawyer's leap of faith? Did Amanda know her husband was in the club? She must have. Did he have money in the hedge fund? Did she know it? Was she prepared to expose him along with the rest? If the TNPC cover-up was a motive for others, as I had argued to the jury, why wasn't it a motive for Ted? But if Ted was involved in the Dressler deal, why hadn't M. Stanton or Brent ratted him out?

I didn't have all the answers, but the ones I did have I didn't like. The joy I had felt over the case was evaporating. Instead of freeing an innocent man, had I set a murderer free?

Well, hell. That was my job, wasn't it? Make them prove him guilty.

And they hadn't. So what's to feel bad about? Even when I was sure Ted was innocent, I felt bad about all the lives and careers that went down with the TNPC scandal. Would I have done the same thing if Ted had told me he was in on the rip-off, too?

What about the million two we'd collected from Employer's Life? Man, I'd felt good when I cashed what amounted to the only type of legit contingent fee on a criminal case: beat the rap so convincingly that the insurance company coughed it up. Would I even have filed the civil suit to collect had I known Ted was guilty? Nope. But now I'd spent most of my fee. Paid off all of my mortgage on the office building. Paid the taxes on the money. Bought and fixed up the cottage. Spiffed up my car. Bonused my secretaries. Was it all dirty money? Everything that had glittered like gold since the trial was now tainted or tarnished green since I'd seen that marker in Ted's bag.

I kept telling myself nothing had changed. I had just won the biggest high-profile case of my career. I'd done my job the best way I could. My debts were paid. Business was great. Just leave it alone, I told myself. You don't know he's guilty. It's just a golf ball marker. No biggie. And besides, what are you going to do about it even if the marker means something sinister? Nothing. Even if you wanted to do something, the rules of professional conduct swear you to silence. Can't very well hold a press conference to say I'm feeling guilty 'cause my client just got away with murder. Hell, I don't even know if he did. But after my October golf match with Ted, the dream in which Amanda reached out to me, shiny object in hand, troubled my sleep no longer.

Epilogue

The snow came just after Thanksgiving and it stayed. I learned to push my guilty doubts deep under the frozen ground, and I stayed busy. When the grand jury indicted Xavier Westphal in absentia and ten members of the TNPC for embezzling charitable funds just before Christmas, it came as a surprise to me. Amongst the indicted were M. Stanton and Dr. Richmond, as well as Thad Granger and Cal Salomon. Ted's was the last name on the indictment.

I hadn't heard a thing beforehand. I wasn't too surprised that Ted didn't come to see me. I think we both knew we had nothing much to say to each other since the 14th hole back in October. Nobody else in TNPC much liked me. So lots of out-of-town lawyers could bill for travel expenses.

Poor old Brent Eubanks, the disgraced accountant, proved to be the prosecution's star witness. In return for his testimony he'd been given a free pass. As Tina Botham explained it to me while we were pre-trialing a different case, it was Ted who'd caused the embezzlement in the first place.

It was a casual Friday and she was definitely casual in jeans and a plaid shirt. We sat in the hallway office that had once been mine, and Tina laid it all out for me, keeping any smug righteousness from her voice. Ted had committed to the hedge fund along with the other nine poker players. But with his business in a tailspin, he had come up short at the last minute. The others didn't want to miss out on a sure thing, and Westphal had already set up the leveraged financing. He had to have the money yesterday. So everybody in emergency session over the poker table in the men's locker, with Westphal on a speaker phone, had just decided on a short-term loan from Dressler funds. Ted was certain the valve deal would close in a few weeks and he'd be flush. Thad Granger over at S.G. Hayden said he'd fiddle the amount on the Treasury bill confirm, and Ted would have to pay the missing interest when the financing came through. It being December, they called it playing Winter Rules. Ted had landed in a rough spot. So they'd improve his lie, and everything would be fine.

Only it wasn't. Ted's business got worse. The bank financing was always just over the horizon. Amanda went out and paid cash for a new BMW with money Ted was setting aside. Not to worry. The hedge fund was going to make everybody rich. Things just needed a little more time. Then the cats went to the dogs.

Tina finished by saying, "I see Mr. Armbruster's got a lawyer from Detroit. Did you two have a parting of the ways?"

I was still trying to figure out how I had missed the clues as I rose from my chair. "Seems so."

I had reached the office door and started for the elevator when I felt compelled to turn back. Tina looked up as I stepped back in and pushed the door shut.

"Without revealing any deep, dark grand jury secrets, can you answer one question for me?"

She cocked her head. "Depends."

"If Ted was in it, why wouldn't Stanton have ratted him out when he was on the stand? Why wouldn't Xavier Westphal or Granger or Eubanks have told me when I interviewed them about TNPC? Makes no sense."

"It does if Armbruster had something on them."

"Like what?"

"Like implicating them for inciting him to commit murder. It's common knowledge that Eubanks is our primary grand jury witness. Let's just suppose that two days before the murder there was a meeting in Brent's conference room with Browne, Granger, and the mysterious Westphal, where they leaned very heavily on your former client to keep his wife quiet. The Dressler audit committee meeting was ten days away, and neither Browne nor Armbruster could promise Amanda's silence. Ted was reminded that it was his coming up short that had gotten them in the mess in the first place, that they'd all gone to great effort and expense to put the money back and cover the whole thing up. Now it was his job to see that it stayed buried. When Ted told them about the divorce papers and that he'd lost control of her, Westphal told Ted, quote: 'Do whatever you have to do. But get that woman under control.' And Browne said, 'You owe it to us to keep her quiet. She'll use this against you in a divorce to clean you out. The woman must be stopped.' "

I sunk into the chair, trying to digest all of this. "If Brent can testify to that, then why not charge Browne and Westphal with inciting to murder instead of just embezzlement?"

"Thought about it. Those words fall a little short of 'kill her.' And you got Armbruster off. Pretty hard to convict those two of inciting Armbruster to commit a crime the jury said he didn't commit. Even tried to get Armbruster to testify if we dropped the embezzlement. No interest."

"Still doesn't explain why none of them would tell me of Ted's involvement in TNPC to make sure it never sees the light of day."

She shrugged. "I think it was a Mexican standoff. They rat him out and he is convicted; he rats them out for putting him up to it. Eubanks says both he and Westphal were convinced their proof that the money was replaced pre-death and their civic duty arguments had you off the trail. Plus, I gather Armbruster had your word that you wouldn't bring it out in court without his okay. Did you know Browne went to see Ted at the jail during trial?" I nodded. "M. Stanton reported back that Ted had you in hand. Apparently, Ted wasn't any better at controlling you than he was at controlling his wife. The only person more shocked than me when you started getting into Dressler was your client. If looks could kill, you'd be dead."

"Maybe, but Brent had a chance when I went over to tell him I was making him testify. Why not tell me then?"

" 'Cause during their little tete-a-tete at the jail, your client repeated his threat to Browne to take them down with him. I gather they all decided it was better to face embezzlement charges, which they think they can beat on the so-called guarantee, than have Ted convicted and testifying that they put him up to murder."

I sat there dumbfounded. Tina looked at me inquisitively and finally asked, "Cat got your tongue?"

I nodded and finally pulled myself from the chair, managing only a small wave of acknowledgement as I opened the door.

It was only on Christmas Eve, after all the sordid details had been in the papers, that I was able to tell Karen what had been on my mind since October. We were sitting on my new faux fur rug in front of the fireplace. Max lay on his side, snoring like a trooper. The brontosaurus-femur-sized rawhide that Karen had put a bow on for him had been reduced to a few slobbery fragments. Snow fell in large, soft flakes. I was on my third Jack Daniels, and she had what was left of a bottle of Orvieto in her glass. I'd teared up telling how this holiday with her compared to the last few, alone, watching *Miracle on 42nd Street* and *A Christmas Carol.* The aroma of the Norwegian fir Christmas tree mixed with the red oak in the fire to fill the room. Karen looked great in the black ski pants and sweater I'd left under the tree for her. The diamond earrings I'd put in her stocking caught the colors from the crackling blaze in sparkling prisms. She heard me out and asked, "Can they bring back the murder charge somehow?"

"Nope, double jeopardy. Hell, I still don't know that he did it. I don't understand the two clubs or what injuries, if any, Browne inflicted. But if Ted lied to me about his role in the ripoff—" I let my voice trail away.

After she listened to me talk about how a little bending of the rules had led from one thing to another, she beckoned me to her.

"Come on over here, big guy, and let me improve your lie."

I went willingly.